Doreen Dean   550

"Once again John Katzenbach has written a masterful novel— this time with a thrilling World War II backdrop. In *Hart's War*, Katzenbach blends courtroom drama and wartime intrigue into a riveting page-turner that readers will not soon forget."

—DANIEL SILVA

"Illuminating . . . Scott's fierce determination is a bracing contrast to Hart's resignation, and the scorching indignation of his opening speech to the tribunal rang in my ears for days."

—*The Washington Post Book World*

"A fast-paced murder mystery, adventure novel, and . . . taut courtroom drama . . . It's an unbeatable combination. . . . Katzenbach's storytelling keeps the novel rolling along as quickly as the train in *Von Ryan's Express*."

—*Fort Worth Star-Telegram*

"Scenes of considerable power . . . Katzenbach's best."

—*Philadelphia Inquirer*

**Selected by The Literary Guild®
and the Military Book Club**

*Please turn the page
for more reviews. . . .*

"A COMPELLING MURDER MYSTERY THAT PACKS A WALLOP . . .

[Katzenbach] blends an unerring eye for detail, ear for dialogue, and firm feel for creating memorable characters. . . . There is a refreshing quality to this mystery court drama. . . . At the end of the novel, when you think you've taken the measure of the writer and the drama he has created, Katzenbach delivers a literary punch to the solar plexus that catches the reader unaware and, ultimately, leaves you pondering whether one life is worth more than another."
—*The Denver Post*

"Katzenbach, who has never written less than a superb book, has outdone himself with this war-based legal thriller. . . . Rich in detail with complex and intriguing characters, and exciting courtroom action, this book made me break my own 'lights out time' to stay up and finish it. Don't miss this one."
—*Times Record News* (TX)

"Vivid and unpredictable characters and diabolically imagined suspense . . . This deeply affecting, artfully paced war epic will hold readers enthralled to the nail-biting end."
—*Publishers Weekly* (starred review)

"POWERFUL AND EMOTIONAL ... IT'S ONE OF THE BEST P.O.W. NOVELS SINCE *KING RAT*."
—*New Mystery Magazine*

"An entertaining, intelligent page-turner . . . Katzenbach avoids clichés and stereotypes by creating absorbing, human characters whose psychology doesn't change to fit the slot. The POWs and Germans are varied and multifaceted. . . . The author's treatment of racism is forceful and uncomplicated. Instead of being a passive character trait possessed by only despicable men, racism is portrayed a s a shifting, insubstantial creature that dwells in the hearts of men—black or white, allied or enemy. . . . In this way, Katzenbach explores the issue in a human way, without demonizing racists or making a saint of Scott. That depth works well in promoting tense and interesting interaction among all the characters. This book is also a solid mystery. The plot turns are not outrageous and they take full advantage of the book's skillfully drawn setting. The climax features more action than is expected, providing an unconventional and intelligent conclusion instead of yet another dry courtroom drama."

— *Post-Tribune* (Gary, IN)

"[Katzenbach] does an excellent job of making us feel what it must have been like to live every moment at the mercy of people who'd just as soon kill you as look at you. . . . A fine addition to the literature about World War II."

— *Mystery News*

By John Katzenbach:

Fiction
IN THE HEAT OF THE SUMMER*
THE TRAVELER*
DAY OF RECKONING*
JUST CAUSE*
THE SHADOW MAN*
STATE OF MIND*
HART'S WAR*

Nonfiction
FIRST BORN: The Death of Arnold Zeleznik, Age Nine:
  Murder, Madness, and What Came After

*Published by Ballantine Books

HART'S WAR

John Katzenbach

BALLANTINE BOOKS • NEW YORK

A Ballantine Book
Published by The Ballantine Publishing Group
Copyright © 1999 by John Katzenbach

All rights reserved under International and Pan-American Copyright Conventions. Published in the United States by The Ballantine Publishing Group, a division of Random House, Inc., New York, and simultaneously in Canada by Random House of Canada Limited, Toronto.

This is a work of fiction. Names, characters, places, and incidents are either the product of the author's imagination or are used fictitiously.

Ballantine and colophon are registered trademarks of Random House, Inc.

www.randomhouse.com/BB/

Library of Congress Catalog Card Number: 99-068462

ISBN 0-345-42625-8

Manufactured in the United States of America

First Hardcover Edition: April 1999
First Mass Market Edition: August 2000

10 9 8 7 6 5 4 3 2 1

This book is for Nick, Justine, Cotty, Phoebe, Hugh, and Avery.

Prologue

THE NIGHT SKY

Now he was an old man who liked to take chances.

In the distance, he counted three separate waterspouts bridging the space between the slick blue water surface at the edge of the Gulf Stream and the gray-black phalanx of clouds belonging to the approaching late-afternoon thunderstorms moving steadily out of the west. The waterspouts were narrow cones of darkness, swirling with all the force their landed cousins, tornadoes, had. They were less subtle, though; they did not possess the terrifying suddenness that belonged to storms on the land. They grew instead out of the inexorable buildup of heat and wind and water, finally arcing between the clouds and the ocean. They seemed to the old man to be stately, moving heavily across the waves. They were visible from miles away, and thus easier to avoid—which is what every other boat working the edge of the great river of water that flows north from deep in the warmth of the Caribbean had already done. The old man was left alone on the sea, bobbing up and down on the slow rhythms of the waves, his boat's engine quiet, the twin baits he'd set out earlier lying flat and motionless on the water's inky surface.

He stared at the three spirals and thought to himself that the spouts were perhaps five miles distant, but the winds racing within each funnel at more than two hundred miles per hour could leap those miles easily. As he watched, it occurred to him that the waterspouts had gradually picked up their pace, as if they'd grown lighter, and suddenly more nimble. They seemed to be dancing together as they moved toward

him, like two eager men who kept cutting in on each other on
the dance floor as they jockeyed for the attentions of an attractive young lady. One would stop and wait patiently while
the other two moved in a slow circle, then suddenly swing
closer, while the other bounced aside. A minuet, he thought,
danced by courtiers at a Renaissance court. He shook his
head. That wasn't quite right. Again he watched the dark fun-
nels. Perhaps a square dance in some rural barn, the air filled
with fiddle music? A wayward breeze suddenly caused a pen-
nant on one of the outriggers to flap hard, making a slapping
sound, before it, too, fled, as if it were frightened by the
stronger winds moving relentlessly in his direction.

The old man took in a sharp breath of hot air.

Less than five miles, he told himself. More like three.

The waterspouts could cover that distance in minutes
if that was their desire. Even with the big two-hundred-horse
engine in back, which would shoot the open fisherman across
the waves at thirty-five knots, he knew he was already too
late. If the storms wanted to catch him, they could.

He thought their dance in a way elegant, in a way stylized.
But it had energy. Enthusiasm. It had rhythm and syncopation. He strained and imagined for an instant that the winds
carried sounds of music. Strains of blaring horns, beating
drums, and wild soaring strings. A quick, decisive riff from
a guitar. He looked up at the darkening sky, huge black
thunderheads that muscled their way across the blue Florida
air toward him. Big-band music, he told himself abruptly.
That's what it is. Jimmy Dorsey and Glenn Miller. The music
of his youth. Music that burst with jazzy excitement and
force, bugles driven with abandon.

A thunderclap riveted the distance and he saw a streak of
lightning flash toward the ocean's surface. The wind picked
up around him, steadily, whispering a warning in the snapping of the lines to the riggers and the pennants. He looked
again at the waterspouts. Two miles, he said.

Leave and live. Stay and die.

He smiled to himself. Not time for me yet.

In a single, quick motion, he twisted the ignition key on the
console, firing up the big Johnson motor, which growled at

him, as if it had been impatient, waiting for his command, reproaching him for trusting his life to the vagaries of an electronic switch and a gas-powered engine. He idled the boat in a half-circle, putting the storm at his back. A spatter of raindrops spotted his blue denim work shirt, and he could abruptly taste the fresh rainwater on his lips. He moved swiftly to the stern and reeled in the two baits. He hesitated one moment longer, staring at the waterspouts. Now they were a mile away, looming large and terrifying, looking down at him as if astonished at the temerity of the insignificant human at their feet, nature's giants stopped in their charge by his insolence, hesitating, shocked by his challenge. The ocean had changed color, the blue deepening to a dense dark gray, as if trying to reach up and blend with the approaching storm.

He laughed as another thunderclap, closer, like a cannon, exploded in the air.

"Can't catch me," he shouted into the wind. "Not yet."

And with that he thrust the throttle forward. The open boat surged through the gathering waves, engine pitch high like a mocking laugh, the bow rising up, then settling into a plane, skimming across the ocean, heading for clear skies and the last, quickly fading sunshine of the long summer day, a few miles ahead, and closer to the shoreline.

As was his habit, he stayed out on the water until long after the sun had set. The storm had wandered far out to sea, maybe causing some problems for the large container ships beating their steady paths up and down the Florida Straits. Around him, the air had cleared, the sweep of heavens blinking with the first stars of the night-deep sky. It was still hot, even out on the water, the air surrounding him with a slippery humid grip. He was no longer fishing, in fact had not really done so in hours. Instead, he sat on a cooler in the stern, holding a half-finished bottle of cold beer in his hand. He took the opportunity to remind himself that the day was coming when the engine would stall, or his hand wouldn't be quick enough on the ignition switch, and a storm such as that evening's would teach him one last lesson. This thought made him shrug inwardly. He thought to himself that he'd had a luxurious life, filled with success and replete with the trappings of happiness—all of it delivered by the most astonishing accident of luck.

Life is easy, he reminded himself, when you should have died.

The old man turned and glanced off to the north. He could see a distant glow from Miami, fifty miles away. But the immediate darkness around him seemed complete, although oddly liquid. There was a looseness to the atmosphere in Florida that he suspected was created by the ever-present heat and humidity. Sometimes, as he looked up into the sky, he longed for the tight clarity of the night in his home state of Vermont. The darkness there had always seemed to him to be pulled taut, stretched to its limits across the heavens.

It was the moment for which he waited out on the water, a chance to stare up into the great expanse above him without the irritation of light and city noise. The mighty North Star, the constellations, as familiar to him as the breathing of his wife as she slept. He picked them out, comforting in their constancy. Orion and Cassiopeia, Aries and Diana, the hunter. Hercules, the hero, and Pegasus, the winged horse. The two dippers, the easiest of all, Ursa Major and Ursa Minor, the first he'd learned as a child more than seventy years earlier.

He took a deep breath of steamy air, then he spoke out loud, adopting a deep, drawling southern accent that wasn't his own but had belonged once, years before, to someone he knew—not for long, but knew well—and said:

"Find us the way home, Tommy, willya?"

There was a lilt to the words, almost a singsong quality. After more than fifty years, they still rang in his ear with the same easygoing grinning tones, just as they had once, coming across the tinny intercom of the bomber, the drawl defeating even the most deafening noise from the engines and the bursts of flak exploding outside.

And he answered out loud, just as he had back then dozens of times:

"Nobody worry about a damn thing. I could find the base blindfolded."

He shook his head. Except for the last time. Then all his skills, reading radio beacons, dead reckoning, and marking the stars with an octant, none had done them any good.

He heard the voice again: "Find us the way home, Tommy, willya?"

I'm sorry, he said to the ghosts. Instead of finding the way home I found death.

He took another swig of beer, then held the cool glass of the bottle to his forehead. With his free hand he started to reach into his shirt pocket, where he had placed a page torn from that morning's *New York Times*. He stopped his fingers, just as they reached the paper. He told himself that he didn't need to read it again. He could remember the headline: FAMED EDUCATOR DIES AT 77; WAS INFLUENTIAL WITH DEMOCRATIC PRESIDENTS.

Now, he said, I must be the last who was there that knows what truly happened.

He took a deep breath. He remembered suddenly a conversation he'd had with his eldest grandchild, when the boy was only eleven and had come to him holding a picture. It was one of the few photos the old man had of that time when he himself was young, not that much older than his grandson. It showed him sitting by an iron stove, reading intently. His wooden bunk was in the background. Some rough woolen clothes were hanging from a makeshift line. There was an unlit candle on the table beside him. He was very thin, almost cadaverously so, and his hair was cropped short. In the picture, he had a small smile on his face, as if what he was reading was humorous. His grandson had asked:

"When was this taken, grandfather?"

"During the war. When I was a soldier."

"What did you do?"

"I was a navigator on a bomber. At least, that's what I was for a while. Then I was merely a prisoner, waiting for the war to end."

"If you were a soldier, did you kill anyone, grandfather?"

"Well, I helped to drop the bombs. And they probably killed people."

"But you don't know?"

"That's right. I don't know for sure."

But that, of course, was a lie.

He thought to himself: Did you kill anyone, grandfather?

And then the honest answer: Yes, I did. I killed a man. And not with a bomb dropped from the air. But it's a long story.

He felt the obituary in his pocket, tapping the fabric of his shirt with his hand.

And now I can tell it, he thought.

The old man stared up into the sky once again, and sighed deeply. Then he turned to the task of discovering the narrow inlet into Whale Harbor. He knew all the navigation buoys by heart, knew each light that dotted the Florida shoreline. He knew the local currents and the daily tides, could feel the slip of the boat through the water, and knew if it was being pulled even slightly off its course. Steering through the darkness, he traveled slowly, but steadily, with the utter confidence of a man walking late at night through his own house.

Chapter One

THE NAVIGATOR'S
RECURRING DREAM

He had just awakened from the dream when the tunnel coming out beneath Hut 109 collapsed. It was just before dawn, and it had been raining hard off and on since midnight. It was the same dream as always, a dream about what had happened to him two years earlier, as close to being as real in the dream as real was until the very end.

In the dream, he didn't see the convoy.

In the dream, he didn't suggest turning and attacking.

In the dream, they didn't get shot down.

And in the dream, no one died.

Raymund Thomas Hart, a skinny, quiet young man of unprepossessing appearance, the third in his family after both his father and grandfather to carry the saint's name with its unusual spelling, lay cramped in his bunk in the darkness. He could feel damp sweat gathered around his neck, though the spring night air was still chilled with the leftover cold of winter. In the short moments before the wooden supporting beams eight feet underground snapped under the weight of the rain-soaked earth and the air filled with the whistles and shouts of the guards, he listened to the thick breathing and snores of the men occupying the bunk beds around him. There were seven other men in the room, and he could recognize each by the distinctive sounds they made at night. One man often spoke, giving orders to his long dead crew, another whimpered and sometimes cried. A third had asthma, and when the weather turned damp wheezed through the night.

Tommy Hart shivered once and pulled the thin gray blanket up to his neck.

He went over all the familiar details of the dream as if it were being played out like a motion picture in the darkness surrounding him. In the dream, they were flying in utter quiet, no engine sound, no wind noise, just slipping through the air as if it were some clear, sweet liquid, until he heard the deep Texas drawl of the captain over the intercom: "Ahh, hell boys, there ain't nothin' out here worth shootin' at. Tommy, find us the way home, willya?"

In the dream, he would look down at his maps and charts, octant and calipers, read the wind drift indicator and see, just as if it were a great streak of red ink painted across the surface of the blue Mediterranean waves, the route home. And safety.

Tommy Hart shivered again.

His eyes were open to the nighttime, but he saw instead the sun reflecting off the whitecaps below them. For an instant, he wished there was some way he could make the dream real, then make the real a dream, just nice and easy, reverse the two. It didn't seem like such an unreasonable request. Put it through proper channels, he thought. Fill out all the standard military forms in triplicate. Navigate through the army bureaucracy. Snap a salute and get the commanding officer to sign the request. Transfer, sir: One dream into reality. One reality into dream.

Instead, what had truly happened was that after he had heard the captain's command, he'd crawled forward into the Plexiglas nose cone of the B-25 to take one last look around, just to see if he could read a landmark off the Sicilian coastline, just to be completely certain of their positioning. They were flying down on the deck, less than two hundred feet above the ocean, beneath any probing German radar, and they were blistering along at more than two hundred fifty miles per hour. It should have been wild and exhilarating, six young men in a hot rod on a winding country road, inhibitions left behind like a patch of rubber from tires squealed in acceleration. But it wasn't that way. Instead, it was risky, like skating gingerly across a frozen pond, unsure of the thickness of the ice creaking beneath each stride.

He had squeezed himself into the cone, next to the bombsight and up to where the twin fifty-caliber machine guns were mounted. It was, for a moment, as if he were flying alone, suspended above the vibrant blue of the waves, hurtling along, separated from the rest of the world. He stared out at the horizon, searching for something familiar, something that would serve as a point on the chart that he could use as their anchor for finding the route back to the base. Most of their navigation was done by dead reckoning.

But instead of spotting some telltale mountain ridge, what he'd seen just on the periphery of his field of vision was the unmistakable shape of the line of merchant ships, and the pair of destroyers zigzagging back and forth like alert sheepdogs guarding their flock.

He'd hesitated, just an instant, making swift calculations in his head. They'd been flying for more than four hours and were at the end of their designated sweep. The crew was tired, eager to return to their base. The two destroyers were formidable defenses, even for the three bombers flying wing to wing in the midday sun. He had told himself at that moment: Just turn away and say nothing, and the line of ships will be out of sight in seconds and no one will know.

But instead, he did as he'd been taught. He had listened to his own voice as if it were somehow unfamiliar.

"Captain, targets off the starboard wing. Distance maybe five miles."

Again, there'd been a small silence, before he'd heard the reply: "Well, I'll be a damn horned frog. Tommy, ain't you the peach. You remind me to take you back with me to West Texas and we'll go hunting. You got some pair of eyes, Tommy. Eyes sharp like yours, boy, ain't no jackrabbit for miles gonna get away from us. We'll have ourselves some fine fresh jackrabbit stew. Ain't nothin' in this world taste any better, boys. . . ."

Whatever else the captain had said, Tommy Hart had lost in the shuffle, as he quickly crawled back through the narrow tunnel toward the midships, making way for the bombardier to assume his position in the nose. He was aware that the *Lovely Lydia* was making a slow bank to the right, and knew that their movement was being mimicked by *The Randy Duck* on their left and *Green Eyes* off their starboard wing. He returned to the small steel chair he occupied just behind the pilot and copilot and looked down at his charts again. He had thought: This is the worst moment. He wished he had the bombardier's duty, but they were the flight leaders, and that had given them an extra crewman for the sortie. By standing up, he could peer out between the two men flying the plane, but he knew he would wait until the last few seconds before doing that. Some fliers liked to see the target come up. He'd always thought of it as staring at death.

"Bombardier? You ready?" The captain's voice had increased in pitch, but still seemed unhurried. "Ain't gonna take but one little ol' bite at these boys, so let's make it worth our whiles to be here." He laughed, which echoed over the intercom. The captain was a popular man, the sort of person who could find some dry, tumbleweed humor in even the direst of situations; who defeated almost all their obvious fears with the steady Texas drawl that never seemed ruffled, or even mildly irritated, even when flak was exploding around the plane and small pieces of deadly red-hot metal were ringing against the Mitchell's steel frame like the insistent knocking of some boorish and angry neighbor. The less obvious fears, Tommy knew, could never be completely destroyed.

Tommy Hart closed his eyes to the night, trying to squeeze away memory. This didn't work. It never worked.

He heard the captain's voice again: "All right, boys, here we go. What is it our friends the limeys say? 'Tally ho!' Now, anyone here got any idea what the hell they mean by that?"

The twin fourteen-cylinder Wright Cyclone engines started screaming as the captain pushed them far past their redline. The maximum speed of the Mitchell was supposed to be two hundred and eighty-four miles per hour, but Tommy Hart knew they had pressed past that point. They were coming in out of the sun as best they could, low against the horizon, and he thought showing up nice and dark in the sights of every gun in the convoy.

Lovely Lydia shuddered slightly as the bomb bay doors opened, and then again, buffeted in the sky by the sudden wind of fire, as the guns awaiting them opened up. Black puffs filled the air, and the motors screamed in defiance. The copilot was shouting something incomprehensible as the plane ripped through the air toward the line of ships. Tommy had risen from his seat, finally staring through the cockpit window, his hands gripping a steel support bar. For the smallest of moments, he caught sight of the first of the German destroyers, its wake streaming out in a white tail behind it, as it spun about in the water, almost like a ballet dancer's pirouette, smoke from all its weapons rising into the air.

Lovely Lydia was slammed once, then again, skewing through the sky. Tommy Hart had felt his throat dry up, and some sound was welling up from deep within himself, half a shout, half a groan, as he stared out ahead at the line of ships desperately trying to maneuver out of the path of the bombing run.

"Let 'em go!" he'd shouted, but his voice had been lost in the scream of the engines and the thudding of the flak bursting all around them. The plane carried six five-hundred-pound bombs, and the technique used in skip-bombing a convoy was not unlike shooting a twenty-two at a line of metal ducks in a state fair sideshow, except the ducks couldn't fire back. The bombardier would ignore the Norden bombsight, which didn't really work all that well anyway, and line up each target by eye, release a bomb, then twitch the plane and line up the next. It was fast and frightening, speed and terror all mixed together.

When done properly, the bombs would rebound off the surface of the water and careen into the target like a bowling ball bounced down an alleyway toward the pins. The bombardier was only twenty-two, fresh-faced, and from a farm in Pennsylvania, but he had grown up shooting deer in the thick woods of the countryside of his home state, and he was very good at what he did, very cool, very composed, unaware that every microsecond took them closer to their own deaths, just as it took them closer to the deaths they were trying to achieve.

"One away!" the voice from the nose of the plane crackled over the intercom, distant, as if shouted from some field far away. "Two gone! Three!" *Lovely Lydia* was shuddering bow to stern, torn by the force of the bullets flying toward her, the release of the bombs and the speed of its own wind ripping at her wings. "All away! Get us out of here, captain!"

The engines surged again, as the captain pulled back on the stick, lifting the bomber into the air. "Rear turret! What y'all see?"

"Jesus, Mary, and Joseph, captain! One hit! No three! No, damn it, five hits! Jesus Christ! Omigod, Omigod! They got the *Duck*! Oh, no, *Green Eyes,* too!"

"Hang on, boys," the captain had said. "We'll be home for dinner. Tommy, check it out! Tell me what y'all see back there!"

Lovely Lydia had a small Plexiglas bubble in the roof, designed for the navigator to use for observation, although Tommy preferred to climb into the nose. There was a small metal step that he used to push himself up into the bubble, and he took a quick glance behind them and saw huge black spirals of smoke rising from a half-dozen ships in the convoy and a massive red explosion from an oil tanker. But his attention to the success of their work was short-lived, for what he'd immediately seen had frightened him far more in that moment than anything in the bombing run—not the speed, not the scream of the engines, not the wall of bullets they'd passed through. What he saw was the unmistakable red-orange of flames shooting from the port engine, licking across the surface of the wing.

He had screamed into the intercom: "Port side! Port side! Fire!"

Only to hear the captain reply nonchalantly, "I know, they're on fire, helluva job, bombardier. . . ."

"No, damn it, captain, it's us!"

The flames were shooting out of the cowling, streaking the blue air, and black smoke was smudging the wind. We're dead, Tommy had thought right then. In a second or two, or maybe five or ten, the flames will hit the fuel line and race back into the wing tank and we'll explode.

He had stopped being afraid at that moment. It was the rarest of sensations, to look out at something taking place just beyond his reach and recognize it for what it was—his own death. He felt a slight twinge of irritation, as if frustrated that there was nothing he could do, but resigned. And, in the same second, felt an odd, distant sort of loneliness and worried about his mother, and his brother, who was somewhere in the Pacific, and his sister and his sister's best friend, who lived down the block from them back in Manchester and whom he loved with a painful, dogged intensity, and how they would all be hurt far worse and for far longer than he was about to be, because he knew the explosion that was about to overtake them would be quick and decisive. And into this reverie he'd heard the captain drawl one last time, "Hang on tight, boys, we're gonna try for the water!" and *Lovely Lydia* started to dive down, reaching for the waves that were their only real chance, to dump themselves into the water and extinguish the fire before the plane exploded.

It seemed to him that the world around him was screaming not words from memory, not sounds that belonged to the earth, but the crackling noise of some hellish circle of tormenting flame. He had always told himself that if they went into the drink, he would jam himself up behind the reinforced steel sled of the copilot's seat, but he didn't have time to get there. Instead, he hung desperately onto a ceiling pipe, riding into the blue of the Mediterranean ocean at nearly three hundred miles per hour, and looking for all the world in that terrifying moment like some nonchalant Manhattan commuter hanging from a subway train strap patiently waiting for his stop.

In his bunk, he shivered again.

He remembered: The sergeant in the turret screaming. Tommy had staggered a step toward the gunner because he'd known that the man was locked into his seat, and the safety catch wouldn't release because the impact must have jammed it shut, and he was crying for help. But in that second, he had heard the captain yell to him, "Tommy, get out! Just get out! I'll help the gunner!" There were no sounds from the others. The captain's order was the last sound he'd heard from any of the crew of the *Lovely Lydia*. He'd been surprised that the side hatch had opened, and surprised again when his Mae West had actually worked, helping him to bob on the surface like a child's cork toy. He'd paddled away from the plane, then turned back, waiting for the others to exit, but none had.

He'd called out once: "Get out! Get out! Please get out!"

And then he'd floated, waiting.

After a few seconds, *Lovely Lydia* had abruptly pitched forward, nose down, and silently slid beneath the water's surface, leaving him alone in the ocean.

This had always disturbed him. The captain, the copilot, the bombardier, and both gunners, they had always seemed to him to be so much quicker and sharper than he was. They were all young and athletic, coordinated, and skilled. They were quick and efficient, good shots with a machine gun or a basketball, fast around the bases legging out an extra base rap, and he had always known they were the real warriors on the *Lovely Lydia*, while he'd always thought of himself as this silly bookworm student, a little thin, a little clumsy, but good with calculations and a slide rule, who had grown up staring at the stars in the sky above his Vermont home, and thus, more by accident than patriotic design, had become a navigator and was more or less along for the ride. He had thought of himself as merely a piece of equipment, an appendage on the flight, while they were the fliers and the killers and the real men of the battle.

He did not understand why he had lived and all the men who'd seemed so much stronger than he had died.

And so he'd floated alone on the sea for nearly twenty-four hours, salt water mingling with his tears, on the edge of delirium, swimming in despair, until an Italian fishing boat had plucked him from the waves. They were rough men who'd handled him with surprising gentleness. The fishermen had wrapped him in a blanket and given him a glass of red wine. He could still remember how it burned his throat as he drank. And when they came to shore, they had dutifully handed him over to the Germans.

That was what had really happened. But in his dream the truth always evaporated, replaced instead by a much happier reality, where they were all alive, and gathered beneath the wing of the *Lovely Lydia*, trading jokes about the Arab merchants outside their dusty North African base, and boasting about what they would do with their lives and their girlfriends and wives when they got back to the States. He had sometimes thought, when they were still alive, that the men on the *Lovely Lydia* were the best friends he would ever have, and then sometimes thought that they would never see each other again, once the war was over. It had never really occurred to him that he would never see them again because they were all dead, and he was still alive, because this had never really seemed a possibility.

In his bunk, he thought: They will be with me always.

One of the prisoners in another bed shifted, the wooden slats creaking and obscuring the man's words as he talked in his sleep, the noise dissolving into an almost girlish moaning sound.

I lived and they died.

He cursed often at his eyes, and how they'd betrayed them all by spotting that convoy. He thought incongruously that if only he'd been born stone blind, instead of blessed with especially acute eyesight, then they'd all still be alive. It did no good, he knew, to think like that. Instead, he vowed that if he survived the war, one day he would travel all the way across the country to West Texas, and after he arrived there, he would drive deep into the scrubland and arroyos of that harsh land and take up a rifle and begin to kill jackrabbits. Every jackrabbit he could spot. Every jackrabbit for miles around. He envisioned himself shooting dozens, hundreds, thousands, a great slaughter of rabbits. Killing jackrabbits until he fell to the earth exhausted, ammunition expended, the barrel of the rifle seared red hot. Surrounded by enough dead jackrabbits to last his captain an eternity.

He knew he would not be able to fall back to sleep.

So, he lay back, listening to the rain striking the metal roof and resounding like gunshots. And mixed in that sound came a low and distant thud. And moments later, shrill whistles and frantic shouts, all in the unmistakable angry German of the prison camp guards. He swung his feet out of the bunk and was pulling on his boots when he heard a pounding on the barracks door and *"Raus! Raus! Schnell!"* It would be cold on the parade ground, and Tommy Hart reached for his old leather flight jacket. The men around him were hurrying to dress, pulling on their woolen underwear and cracked and worn flight boots as the first insinuations of dawn light came filtering through the grimy barracks windows. In his hurry to get dressed, he lost sight of the *Lovely Lydia* and its crew, letting them fade into the near part of his memory as he quickly joined the flow of men heading out into the damp early morning chill of Stalag Luft Thirteen.

Second Lieutenant Tommy Hart shuffled his feet in the light brown mud of the parade compound. The grumbling had started within a few minutes of the assembly—an *Appell* in German—and now, whenever a guard walked by, the men would begin to catcall, and complain.

The Germans, for the most part, ignored them. Occasionally a *Hundführer*, with his snarling shepherd at his side, would turn at the groups of men, and make motions as if he were ready to let the dog loose, which had the intended effect of quieting the airmen, if only for a few minutes. Luftwaffe Oberst Edward Von Reiter, the camp commandant, had quickmarched past the formations hours earlier, pausing only when accosted by the Senior American Officer, Colonel Lewis MacNamara, who immediately launched into a series of rapid-fire complaints. Von Reiter listened to MacNamara for perhaps thirty seconds, then casually saluted, raising a riding crop to the brim of his cap, and gestured for the SAO to return to his position at the head of the blocks of men. Without another glance at the row of airmen, Von Reiter had disappeared in the direction of Hut 109.

The kriegies mumbled and stamped their feet, as the day grew around them. Kriegies was what they called themselves, a shortening of the German *Kriegsgefangene*, which loosely translated into "war captured." Standing, waiting, was both boring and exhausting. It was something they were familiar with, but hated.

There were nearly ten thousand Allied prisoners of war held in the camp, split almost equally between two compounds, North and South. The U.S. fliers—all officers—were in the southern compound, while British and other Allies were situated to the North, a quarter mile away. Passage between the camps, while not unusual, was mildly difficult. An escort and an armed guard and a compelling reason were necessary. Of course, a compelling reason could be manufactured by the quick exchange of a couple of cigarettes passed to one of the ferrets, which was what the kriegies called the guards who roamed the camps, armed only with the sword-like steel probes they used to poke into the ground. The guards with the dogs were called by their official names, because the dogs scared everyone. There were no walls at the camp, but each of the compounds was surrounded by a twenty-foot-high fence. Two rows of barbed concertina wire on either side of a metal chain link. Every fifty yards along the fence was a stolid, squat wooden tower. These were manned around the clock by humorless and unbribable machine-gun crews, goons, with Schmeisser machine pistols hung around their necks.

Ten feet inside the main fence the Germans had strung a thin strand of wire from wooden stakes. This was the deadline. Anyone crossing that line was assumed to be trying to escape, and would be shot. At least, that was what the Luftwaffe commandant told each prisoner upon arrival at Stalag Luft Thirteen. The reality was that the guards would let a prisoner, who donned a white smock with a red cross prominently centered on it, pursue a baseball or football if it rolled to the exterior fence, although sometimes, for amusement, they would wave a prisoner after the item, then fire a short burst into the air above his head or into the dirt at his feet. Walking the deadline was a favorite kriegie activity; the airmen would pace endless laps at the limit of their confinement.

The May sun rose rapidly, warming the faces of the men gathered on the parade ground. Tommy Hart guessed they had been standing in formation for nearly four hours, while steady processions of German officers and enlisted men had passed by, heading toward the collapsed tunnel. The enlisted men carried shovels and pickaxes. The officers wore frowns.

"It's the damn wood," a voice from the formation spoke. "It gets wet, it gets rotten, won't hold up a damn thing."

Tommy Hart turned and saw that the man speaking was a wiry West Virginian, copilot on a B-17, and a man whose father had grown up working in the coal mines. He'd presumed the West Virginian, whose flat voice twanged with disgust, was prominent in escape planning. Men with knowledge of the earth—farmers, miners, excavators, even a funeral home director shot down over France who lived in the next hut over—were enlisted in the efforts within hours of their arrival at Stalag Luft Thirteen.

He had made no efforts to escape the camp. Nor did he have any great desire to try, unlike many of the other men. It was not that he didn't want to be free, which he did, but that he silently knew that in order to escape he would have to descend into a tunnel.

And this he could not do.

He supposed his fear of enclosed spaces came from the time he accidentally locked himself inside a basement closet when he was no more than four or five. A dozen terrifying hours spent enclosed in darkness, in heat and tears, hearing his mother's distant voice calling to him yet unable to raise his own, he was so panicked. He probably would not have characterized the fear that remained with him from that day as claustrophobia, but that, in effect, was what it was. He'd joined the air corps at least in part because even in the tight confines of the bomber, he was still out in the open. The idea of being inside a tank or a submarine had been far more frightening to him than the fear of enemy bullets.

So, in the oddly uncertain prison world of Stalag Luft Thirteen, Tommy Hart knew one thing: If he ever did get out, it would have to be through the front gate. Because he would never voluntarily descend into a tunnel.

This made him think of himself as content—although that was probably not the right word, more willing or resigned—to wait for the end of the war despite the rigors of Stalag Luft Thirteen. He was occasionally enlisted as a stooge—to take up a position where he could keep an eye on one of the ferrets, an early warning system designed by the camp security officers. Any German walking within the camp was constantly followed and observed by a system of overlapping watchers, with redundant signaling methods. Of course, the ferrets knew they were being watched, and consequently tried their best to evade the security, constantly altering their routes, and their paths.

"Hey! Fritz Number One! How long you gonna keep us standing here?"

This voice bellowed with unmistakable authority. The man behind it was a fighter pilot from New York, a captain. The outburst was directed at a solitary German, dressed in the gray coveralls, with a soft campaign hat pulled down on his forehead, that was the standard ferret uniform. There were three ferrets with the first name of Fritz and they were always addressed by their name and number, which irritated them immensely.

The ferret turned, eyeing the captain. Then he stepped up to the man, who stood at parade rest in the front row. The Germans had each block of the formation gather in rows of five, easier for counting.

"If you did not dig, captain, then there would be no need for standing here," he said in excellent English.

"Hell, Fritz Number One," the captain replied. "We didn't do no digging. This was probably some more of your lousy sewage system that went and fell in. You guys ought to get some of us to show you how it's done."

The German shook his head.

"No, *Kapitän,* this was a tunnel. To escape is foolhardy. Now it has cost two men their lives."

This news silenced the airmen.

"Two men?" the captain asked. "But how?"

The ferret shrugged. "They were digging. The earth falls in. They are trapped. Buried. A loss. Most foolish."

He raised his voice slightly, staring at the formation of his enemies.

"It is stupid. *Dummkopf.*" He bent down, and scraped up a handful of muddy ground, which he squeezed between long, almost feminine fingers. "This earth. Good for planting. Growing food. This is good. Good for your games. These are good, too . . ." he gestured toward the compound athletic field. "But not strong enough for tunnels."

The ferret turned back to the captain.

"You will not fly again, *Kapitän,* until after the war. If you live."

The captain from New York simply stared at the ferret hard, finally replying, "Well, we'll see about that, won't we?"

The ferret made a lazy salute, and started to move off, pausing only as he reached the end of the formation. There he had a quick exchange with another officer. Tommy Hart leaned forward and saw that Fritz Number One had reached out his hand, and that a quick pair of cigarettes had been slipped to him. The man who had passed the smokes was a wiry, short, smiling bomber captain from Greenville, Mississippi, named Vincent Bedford, but he was the formation's expert negotiator and trader, and because of his skills had been nicknamed Trader Vic after the famous restaurateur.

Bedford had a thick, southern drawl, with an excitable quality to it. He was an excellent poker player, a more than passable shortstop who'd done some time in the minor leagues. Before the war, he'd been a car salesman, which seemed appropriate. But what he truly excelled at was the commerce of Stalag Luft Thirteen, turning cigarettes and chocolates and tins of real coffee that arrived either in Red Cross parcels or packages from the States into clothing and other goods. Or he would take extra clothing and turn that into foodstuffs. No trade was beyond Vincent Bedford, and rarely did he come out on the wrong end of an exchange. And, in the unusual event that he had, then his gambler's instincts repaired his losses. A poker game could replenish his stock as effectively as a parcel from home. He seemed to trade in other items as well; always knowing the latest rumor, always getting the latest war news just slightly ahead of everyone else. Tommy Hart assumed that in his trades he'd somehow acquired a radio, but didn't know this for certain. What he did know was that Vincent Bedford was the man in Hut 101 to see. In a world where men had little, Vincent Bedford had amassed a prisoner-of-war-camp fortune, stockpiling coffee and foodstuffs and woolen socks and long underwear and anything else that might make life in the bag slightly more livable.

The few times that Trader Vic wasn't making some trade, Bedford would launch into grandiose and idyllic descriptions of the little town he hailed from, always delivered in the soft drawl of the Deep South, slowly, lovingly. More often than not, the other airmen would tell him they were all moving to Greenville after the war, simply to get him to shut up, because talk of home, no matter how elegiac, prompted a homesickness that was dangerous. All the men in the camp lived on the edge of one despair or another, and thinking of the States did no one any good, though it was almost the only thing they did think about.

Bedford watched the ferret move away, then turned and whispered something to the next airman in formation. It only took a few seconds for the news to pass through the group, and on to the next formation.

The trapped men were named Wilson and O'Hara. They were both prominent tunnel rats. Tommy Hart knew O'Hara slightly; the dead man had occupied a bunk in their hut, but in another room, so he was merely one of the two hundred faces crammed into the barracks. According to the information being whispered down the rows of kriegies, the two men had descended into the tunnel late that past night, and were busily trying to shore up the support beams when the soft ground had given way around them. They'd been buried alive.

And, according to the information Bedford had acquired, the Germans had decided to leave the bodies of the two men where the ground had collapsed in on them.

The whispered talk quickly gave way to voices starting to be raised in anger. The formations of men seemed to take on a sinuous sort of life, as lines straightened, shoulders were thrust back. Without command, men snapped to attention.

Tommy Hart did the same, but not without a last glance down the lines of men to where Trader Vic was standing. He was struck by what he'd seen, and unsettled slightly by something elusive, that he could not put a word to.

Then, before he had time to assess what it was that had disturbed him, the captain from New York shouted out: "Killers! Goddamn murderers! Savages!" Other voices from other formations picked up the same message, and the air of the compound filled rapidly with bellows of outrage.

The SAO stepped to the front of the formations, and turned and stared at the men with a glare that seemed to demand discipline, although his own anger was evident in the cold gray look in his eyes and the rigid jut to his jaw. Lewis MacNamara was old-time army, a full bird colonel with over twenty years in uniform, who rarely needed to raise his voice and was accustomed to being obeyed. A stiff man, who seemingly saw his imprisonment as just another in a long line of military assignments. As MacNamara assumed a parade rest facing the kriegies, his legs slightly apart, his arms held tightly behind his waist, a pair of goons snapped back the bolts on their weapons, an act of mostly menace, but with just enough determination that the men in formation hesitated, and slowly quieted.

No one truly thought the goons would open fire on the massed airmen. But no one was ever completely certain of this.

The camp commandant, trailed by a pair of aides who walked gingerly through the mud in their polished riding boots, hove into view, which prompted some whistles and catcalls, studiously ignored by Von Reiter. Without a word to the SAO, the commandant addressed the formations loudly.

"We will count now. Then you are dismissed."

He paused, then added.

"The count, it will be two men short! Idiocy!"

The airmen remained silent, standing at attention.

"This is the third tunnel in the past year!" Von Reiter continued. "But it is the first tunnel to cost men their lives!" The commandant was shouting, his voice infected with frustration. "Further escape attempts will not be tolerated!"

He paused, then stared across at the men. He lifted a bony finger and pointed like a wizened schoolteacher at an unruly class.

"There has never been a successful escape from my camp! Never! And there will be none!"

He paused, his eyes sweeping over the assembled kriegies.

"You have been warned," he concluded.

In the momentary silence that swept across the formations of men, Colonel MacNamara stepped forward. His own voice carried the same weight of command as Von Reiter's. His spine was rigid, his posture a portrait of military perfection. That his uniform was frayed and ragged seemed oddly to underscore his taut bearing.

"I would like to take this opportunity to remind the *Oberst* that it is the sworn duty of every officer to attempt to escape from the enemy."

Von Reiter held up his hand, cutting off the colonel.

"Do not speak to me of duty," he said. "Escape is *verboten*!"

"This duty, this *requirement*, is no different for the Luftwaffe airmen being held by our side," MacNamara loudly added. "And if a Luftwaffe flier died in *his* attempt, he would be buried by his own comrades, with full military honors!"

Von Reiter frowned, started to reply, then stopped. He nodded his head, just slightly. The two men stared hard at each other, as if struggling over something between them. A tug-of-war of wills.

Then the commandant gestured for the SAO to accompany him, and he turned his back on the gathered men. The two senior officers disappeared from the kriegies' sight, marching stride for stride in the direction of the main gate, which led to the camp offices. Instantly, ferrets appeared at the head of each block formation, and the airmen began the familiar and laborious process of being counted. Midway through the roll call the kriegies heard the first deep, thudding explosion, as German sappers placed charges along the length of the collapsed tunnel, filling it with more of the sandy yellow dirt that had choked the life from the two tunnel men. Tommy Hart thought there was something wrong, or perhaps unfair, in enlisting to fly in the clean, clear air, no matter how deadly it could be, only to die alone and suffocating, trapped eight feet beneath the earth. He did not say this out loud.

The tunnel coming out from 109 had been concealed underneath a washroom sink, and after going straight down, had taken a sharp right turn, heading for the wire. Of the forty huts in the compound, 109 was second closest to the perimeter. To reach the safety of the dark line of tall fir trees that signaled the edge of a deep Bavarian forest, the tunnel diggers were required to burrow more than a hundred yards through the dirt. The tunnel had made it less than a third of the way. Of the three tunnels dug during the past year, it had traveled the farthest, and had the highest of hopes attached to it.

Like virtually every other kriegie in the camp, by midday Tommy Hart had walked over to the deadline and stared out at the remains of the tunnel, trying to imagine what it must have been like for the two men trapped beneath the surface. The sapper's charges had left the earth churned up, grass streaked with muddy brown dirt, cratered with depressions where the explosions had caused the tunnel ceiling to collapse. A guard crew had poured wet concrete into the tunnel's entranceway in Hut 109.

He sighed loudly. There were two other pilots, B-17 men wearing heavy sheepskin coats despite the mild temperatures, standing nearby, taking in the same elusive vista.

"It doesn't seem all that far," one man said, with a sigh.

"Close," his companion agreed, muttering.

"Real close," the first pilot said. "Into the forest, through the trees, find the road to town and you're in business. Just gotta make it to the station and a rail line heading south. Jump some old freight train destination Switzerland and you're on your way. Damn. Real close."

"Not close at all," Tommy Hart disagreed. "And too damn obvious from the North tower."

Both men hesitated, then nodded, as if they, too, knew their eyes were betraying them. War has a way of shrinking and expanding distances, depending on the threat involved in traveling through the contested space. It's always hard to see clearly, Tommy thought, especially when one's life might be at stake.

"I'd still like just one little old chance," one of the men said. He was perhaps a little older than Tommy, and much stockier. He hadn't shaved, and he wore his campaign hat pulled down hard to his eyebrows. "Just one chance. I think if I could just get to the other side where there ain't no wire, well, hell, ain't nothing on this earth gonna stop me then—"

"Except maybe a couple of million Krauts," his friend interrupted. "And you don't speak any German and where you gonna go to, anyways?"

"Switzerland. Beautiful country. All cows and mountains and those fancy little houses . . ."

"Chalets," the other man said. "They call 'em chalets."

"Right. I figure maybe a couple of weeks getting nice and fat eating chocolate. Nice big, fat milk chocolate bars served up by some pretty blond farm girl in pigtails whose mommy and daddy ain't nowhere around. Then maybe right back home to the States, where I got a girl maybe give me some damn special hero's-type welcome, you better believe."

The other pilot slapped him on the arm. The leather jacket muffled the sound.

"Dreamer," he said. He turned toward Tommy Hart. "Been in the bag long?" he asked.

"Since November, forty-two," Tommy replied.

Both men whistled.

"Whoa! Old-timer. Ever made it out?"

"Not once," Tommy replied. "Not for a minute. Not even for a second."

"Man," the B-17 pilot continued, "I only been here five weeks and I'm already so crazy, don't know what the hell I'm gonna do. Kinda like having an itch, you know, right in the middle of your back. Right where you can't reach it."

"Better get used to it," Tommy replied. "Guys try to blitz out. Get dead fast."

"Never get used to it," the man said.

Tommy nodded in agreement. Never get used to it, he thought. He closed his eyes and bit down on his lip, breathing in hard.

"Sometimes," Tommy said softly, "you've got to find your freedom up here. . . ." He tapped his forehead.

One of the pilots nodded, but the other airman had turned back toward the main camp.

"Hey," he said, "look what's coming."

Tommy pivoted quickly and saw a dozen men marching in tight formation across the wide expanse of the compound's exercise ground. The men had obviously decked themselves out in Stalag Luft Thirteen finery; they wore ties, their shirts and jackets were pressed, there were sharp creases in their pants. Prisoner-of-war-camp dress uniforms.

Each man in the group was carrying a musical instrument. The May sun suddenly reflected off the brass of a trombone, glinting sharply. A drummer had slung a single snare around his waist so that it hung in front of him, and as the men approached, he began to snap out a rolling, fast metallic beat.

The squad leader was set slightly ahead. His eyes were locked forward, staring through the wire to the forest beyond. He had two instruments in his hands, a clarinet, held in his right, and a trumpet, which glistened, polished to a rich golden brown sheen. All the men maintained formation, quick-marching in unison, the leader calling out an occasional cadence above the steady rat-a-tat of the snare drum.

It took no more than seconds for the odd constellation to attract the attention of the other kriegies. Men began to stream from the huts, jostling shoulder to shoulder to see what was going on. In front of some of the side barracks there were officers tending to small gardens, and they dropped their makeshift tools to the dirt and fell in behind the marching squad. A baseball game, just getting under way in the exercise yard, stopped. Gloves, bats, and balls were left behind as the players joined the throng that had collected behind the marching men.

The squad leader was a short man, balding slightly, thin and muscular like a bantamweight wrestler. He seemed oblivious to the hundreds of airmen who had materialized behind him, continuing to march, eyes straight ahead. He repeatedly blared the cadence—"Right, your right, right . . ."—as the squad did a sharp left wheel that would have done justice to a West Point drill team, and approached the deadline. On the leader's barked command—"Squad . . . Halt!"—they came to a rest a few feet from the wire, their feet stamping in unison against the muffled dust.

The German machine gunners in the nearest tower swung their weapon in the direction of the men. They seemed both curious and intent. Their eyes were just visible beneath the dull gray steel helmets they wore, peering above the barrel of the gun.

Tommy Hart watched, but then overheard one of the B-17 pilots still standing by his side whisper in a deep voice of quiet despair: "O'Hara. The little Irish mick who died in the tunnel last night. He was a New Orleans boy, just like the bandleader. They enlisted together. Flew together. Played music together. I think he was the clarinet. . . ."

The bandleader turned to the men, and called out: "Stalag Luft Thirteen Prisoner's Jazz Band . . . attention!"

The squad clicked their heels together.

"Take positions!" he ordered.

The squad stepped smartly into a semicircle, facing the barbed wire and the scar on the earth that marked the tunnel's final progress and where the two diggers lay buried. The men lifted their instruments to their lips, waiting for the signal from the bandleader. Saxophones, trombones, French horns, and cornets stood at attention. The drummer's sticks paused over the skin of the snare. A guitarist fingered the fretboard, a pick in his right hand.

The bandleader's eyes swept over each of the men, assessing their readiness. Then he did an abrupt about-face, turning his back to the band. He strode three steps forward, right to the edge of the deadline, and in a swift motion, set the clarinet down against the wire. He raised up, snapped off a sharp salute to the instrument, and again performed an about-face. The bandleader seemed to quiver, for an instant, as he returned to his position in front of the assembled musicians. Tommy Hart saw a small tremble in the bandleader's lips as the man slowly lifted his trumpet to his mouth. He could see that tears were streaking down the cheeks of both the tenor sax man and one of the trombone players. The men all seemed to hesitate, and silence filled the air. The bandleader nodded, licked his lips as if to steady them, raised his left hand, and began to mark time.

"On the downbeat," he said. " 'Chattanooga Choo-choo.' Make it hot! Make it *real* hot! One, two, three, and four . . ."

The music burst forth, exploding like a star shell in the air around them. It soared into the sky, lifted above the barbed wire and the guard tower, flying birdlike into the clear blue, and disappearing, fading in the distance beyond the tree line and its promise of elusive freedom.

The musicians played with ferocity, unbridled intensity. Within seconds beads of sweat emerged on their foreheads. Their instruments bent and swayed with the rhythms of the music. Every few moments one of the band members would step forward into the center of the semicircle, soloing, dominating the syncopation, cutting loose with a saxophone's plaintive wail or a guitar's edgy energy. The men did this without a sign or a signal from the bandleader, reacting more to the surge of music that they had created, an old-time revivalists' intensity, responding as if some heavenly hand reached down and nudged them gently on the shoulder. "Chattanooga Choo-choo" flowed like a river directly into "That Old Black Magic" and then into "Boogie Woogie Bugle Boy of Company B"—where the bandleader stepped to the forefront, blasting out trumpet calls in time with the other instruments. The music continued, unrestrained, unfettered, uninterrupted, dipping, swaying, inexorable in its force, each tune smoothly blending with neighborly friendliness into the next.

The huge crowd of kriegies stood stock-still, quiet, listening.

The band played nonstop for close to thirty minutes, until the members seemed red-faced, like sprinters exhausted by the effort, gasping for air. The leader, sweat dripping from his forehead, lifted his left hand from the trumpet as they swept into the final searing bars of "Take the A Train," raising it high above his head, and then abruptly sliced it down through the air, and the band, on cue, stopped.

There was no applause. Not a sound emerged from the massive crowd of men.

The bandleader looked across at the members of the group and nodded his head slowly. Sweat and tears mingled freely on his face, glistening on his cheeks, but his lips had creased into a half-smile of sorts, one that appreciated what they'd done, but still twisted with the sadness of the reason. Tommy Hart did not see or hear the command, but the band abruptly stepped into parade rest positions, instruments held like weapons at their chests. The bandleader walked over to a trombonist, handed the man his own trumpet, then did a sharp about-face, quick-marching to the wire and picking up the lone clarinet. Still facing out to the woods and the great world beyond the wire, the bandleader lifted the instrument to his lips and trilled out a single, long slow scale. Tommy did not know if the man was improvising or not, but he listened carefully as the clear, smooth notes of the clarinet danced through the air. Tommy thought the music not unlike the birds he was used to seeing in the rolling fields of his Vermont home in the fall, just before the great migrations south. When alarmed, they would rise up into the air in unison, milling about for a moment or two, then suddenly taking wing and, gathering together, flying en masse off into the sun. That was what the clarinet's tunes were doing. Rising up, searching to find shape and organization, then soaring off into the distance.

The last note seemed especially high, especially lonesome.
The bandleader stopped, slowly lowering the instrument

from his lips. For an instant he held the clarinet against his chest. Then he pivoted sharply and called out a command: "Stalag Luft Thirteen Prisoner Jazz Band . . . attention!"

The band snapped together, like the carefully fitted pieces of a machine.

"By column of twos . . . about-face! Drummer please . . . forward march!"

The jazz band began to move away from the wire. But where before they had been quick-marching, now they moved slowly, deliberately. A funeral cadence, each right foot hesitating slightly before falling to the earth. The drummer's beat was slow and doleful.

The mass of kriegies parted, letting the band march through, moving at just more than a crawl, then closed ranks behind them, as the prisoners slowly returned to whatever activity they could find to get them through the next minute, the next hour, the next day of confinement.

Tommy Hart glanced up. The two German guards in the tower continued to train their machine gun on the gathering of men. They were grinning. They don't know, he thought to himself, but for just a few minutes there right in front of their eyes and their weapons we all became free men once again.

He had some time before the afternoon count, so Tommy returned to his bunk room to get a book. Each hut at Stalag Luft Thirteen was constructed from a combination of prefabricated wood and beaverboard, drafty and cold in the winter, stifling hot in the summer. When it rained, and the men were forced indoors, the rooms gained a musty, green odor, a smell of sweat and confinement. There were fourteen rooms in each hut, each holding eight men in bunks. The kriegies had learned that by moving one of the beaverboard walls just a few inches, they could create hollow spaces between the walls, which were used for concealing escape items ranging from uniforms recut to resemble ordinary suits to picks and axes used by tunnelers.

Each hut contained a small washroom with a sink, but showers were located in a building between the North and South camps, and men needed an escort to use them. They were not used regularly. Each hut also included a single working toilet, but it was operated only at night, after lights out. During the day, the kriegies utilized outside privies. These were known as *Aborts*, and accommodated a half-dozen men at a time. They afforded a slight degree of privacy— wooden partitions separated the polished wooden seats. The Germans provided adequate supplies of lime, and *Abort* details liberally scrubbed the area with strong disinfecting GI soap. Each pair of huts shared an *Abort*, which was located between the buildings.

The men cooked for themselves, each hut maintaining a rudimentary kitchen with wooden stove. The Germans provided some minimal rations, mostly potatoes, terrible-tasting blood sausage, turnips, and *kriegsbrot*—the hard, dark war bread upon which the entire nation seemed to exist. Kriegies were inventive cooks, coaxing varied and different tastes from the same foodstuffs by mixing and matching. The food parcels either shipped by relatives or issued by the Red Cross were the foundations for their meals. The men were always hungry, but rarely starving, although to many the distinction seemed narrow.

Stalag Luft Thirteen was a world within a world.

There were daily classes in art and philosophy, musical performances almost nightly in Hut 112, which had been dubbed The Luftclub, and a theater with its own regular troupe. It was currently performing *The Man Who Came to Dinner* to rave reviews in the camp newspaper. There were spirited athletic competitions, including a storied softball rivalry between the top team in the South compound and a squad from the British North camp. The British did not totally understand many of the subtleties of baseball, but two of the pilots in their camp had been bowlers for the national cricket team before the war, and they had adapted quickly to the concept of throwing strikes. There was a lending library, which kept an eclectic combination of mysteries and classics.

Tommy Hart, though, had his own collection of books.

He had been midway through his third year at Harvard Law School when Pearl Harbor had been bombed. While some of his classmates had deferred enlisting until the end of the academic year and graduation, he had quietly joined a line outside the recruiting station near Faneuil Hall in down-

town Boston. He had put down the air corps on his recruit-
ment papers on a whim, and several weeks later had carried
his suitcase across Harvard Yard in the midst of a January
snowstorm, heading toward the T, a ride to South Station, and
a train to Dothan, Alabama, and flight training.

Shortly after his capture, he'd filled out a form for the
International Red Cross that was supposed to notify his
family that he still lived. He'd left much of the form blank, not
fully trusting the Germans who would process the document.
But near the bottom had been a space that requested SPECIAL
ITEMS NEEDED. On this line he'd written, mostly as a lark: *Edmund's Principles of Common Law, Third Edition,* 1938,
University of Chicago Press. To his surprise, the book was
waiting for him when he arrived at Stalag Luft Thirteen, although it had been mailed by the YMCA organization.
Tommy had clutched the thick volume of legal precedents to
his chest throughout his first night at the camp, like a child
would hold a favorite and reassuring teddy bear, and for the
first moment since he'd seen the flames streaking across the
Lovely Lydia's right wing, actually dared to think he might
survive.

Edmund's Principles had been followed in quick order by
Burke's Elements of Criminal Procedure and by texts on
torts, wills, and civil actions. Tommy had acquired works on
legal history and a secondhand but valuable copy of the
life and opinions of Oliver Wendell Holmes. He had also
requested a biography and selected writings of Clarence
Darrow. He was particularly interested in the man's famous
jury summations.

So while others sketched or learned lines and hammed it
up on stage, Tommy Hart had studied. He'd envisioned every
course in his final year, and had replicated each. He wrote
mock papers, submitted mock arguments and legal documents, debated both sides of every point and issue that he
could find, creating persuasive claims to buttress either side's
position on every fake dispute he could imagine.

And while others planned escape and dreamed of freedom,
Tommy learned the law.

Once a week, on Friday mornings, he would bribe one of
the Fritzes with a couple of cigarettes to take him to the

British compound, where he would be greeted by Wing Commander Phillip Pryce and Flying Officer Hugh Renaday. Pryce was beyond middle age, one of the oldest men in both camps, white-haired, sallow-chested, and thin, with a reedy voice and flaccid skin that seemed to hang from his arms. He always seemed to be struggling, red-nosed and sniffling, with a cold or a virus that threatened to turn into pneumonia, regardless of what the weather was.

Before the war Pryce had been a prominent London barrister, a member of an ancient and venerated set of chambers. His Stalag Luft Thirteen roommate, Hugh Renaday, was half his age, only a year or so older than Tommy, and sported a large, bushy mustache. The two men had been captured together when their Blenheim bomber had been shot down over Holland. Pryce often would point out, in his aristocratic, high-pitched tones, that it was all a terrible mistake that he was at Stalag Luft Thirteen at all. It was, he would say, a place for the younger men. He'd only been on that bomber on that particular flight because he'd grown increasingly frustrated with nightly sending men out on dangerous missions that cost them their lives, and so, one night, against express orders, he'd taken the place of a sick turret gunner on the Blenheim.

"Bad choice, that," Pryce would mutter.

Renaday, a thickset tree-stump of a man even though the camp diet melted pounds from his rugger's frame, would counter, "Ah, but who wants to die in bed at home?"

And Pryce would reply: "But, my dear lad, we all do. You young men simply need the perspective of age."

Renaday was a rough-edged Canadian. Before the war he had been a criminal investigator for the provincial police in Manitoba. A week after he enlisted in the RCAF, he'd received word of his acceptance into the Royal Canadian Mounted Police. Faced with the choice of following the career he'd always dreamed of or sticking with the air corps, he'd reluctantly put off his appointment to the Mounties. He would always conclude the conversation with Pryce by saying, "Spoken like an old man."

On Fridays, the three men would regularly meet and discuss the law. Renaday had a policeman's attitudes, all straightforward, fact-driven, and direct, constantly seeking the narrowest line through any case and argument. Pryce was the precise opposite, a master of subtlety. The older man liked to soliloquize on the aristocracy of conflict, the princeliness of distinctions between the facts and the law. More often than not, Tommy Hart served as the bridge between the two men, charting his course between the older man's flights of intellectualism and the younger man's dogged pragmatism. It was, he thought, a part of his schooling.

He hoped the tunnel collapse would not prevent him from attending their regular weekly session. Sometimes, after discovering a concealed radio or other contraband, the Germans would lock down the camps as punishment, and the men would be forced to spend days indoors. Travel between the two compounds would be curtailed. Once a soccer game between North and South squads was canceled, to the fury of the British, and relief of the Americans, who'd known they were destined to be slaughtered, and much preferred to play their British counterparts in basketball or baseball.

This week, the three men were scheduled to discuss the Lindbergh kidnapping. Tommy was to argue the carpenter's defense, Renaday taking the part of the state, with Pryce acting as arbiter. He felt unprepared, constricted not merely by the facts but by his position. He had felt much more comfortable the previous month, when they'd argued the details of the Wright-Mills murder case. And he'd been much more confident in the dead of winter, when they'd dissected the legal aspects of Jack the Ripper's Victorian killing spree. To his immense delight, his British friends had been constantly on the defensive during that debate.

Tommy took his copy of *Burke's Criminal Procedure* from a shelf next to his bunk and exited Hut 101. Early in his stay at Stalag Luft Thirteen he had designed and built himself a chair using the leftover wooden crates in which Red Cross parcels were shipped to the camp. The chair resembled an Adirondack-style chair, and for POW camp furniture was widely admired and immediately and frequently copied. The chair had several important details: It only required a half-dozen nails to hold it together and it was actually fairly comfortable. He sometimes thought it had been his only real contribution to camp life.

He moved the chair into the midday sun and opened the text. He was, however, hardly a paragraph into his reading before a figure hovered into view, and he looked up at the same moment he heard the familiar Mississippi drawl.

"Hey, Hart, how y'all doin' this fine day?"

"I don't think I'd call it a fine day, Vic. Another day. That's all."

"Well, another day for you and me, maybe. But the last day for a couple of good old boys."

"That's true enough . . ."

Tommy had to hold his hand up, blocking the sun, in order to clearly see Vincent Bedford.

"Some men, they got the need, you know, Hart? They got the big desire. It pains 'em so much, they got to try anything to get out. What it amounts to, why, now I got an empty bunk in my room and somebody's writing that big hurt letter to some poor folks back home. Other men, well, they look at that barbed wire and they figure the best way to get past it is to wait. Be patient. Other men, well, they see something else."

"What is it you see, Vic? When you look at the wire?" Tommy asked.

The southerner grinned.

"Same thing I always see, wherever I be."

"Which is?"

"Why, lawyer man, I see an opportunity."

Tommy hesitated, then replied, "And what opportunity brings you to me?"

Vincent Bedford knelt down, so that he was on eye level with Tommy. He was carrying two cartons of brand-new American cigarettes. He poked them at Tommy.

"Why, Hart, you know what I'm looking for. I want to make a trade. Same as always. You got something I want. I got lots that you need. We're simply trying to reach an accommodation. A mutual opportunity, I'd say. An arrangement promising satisfaction to all parties."

Tommy shook his head.

"I've told you before, I won't trade it."

Bedford smiled with mock astonishment.

"Everyone and everything has a price, Hart. You know that. I know that. Hell, when you think about it, that's pretty much what those law books of your'n say on each and every page, don't they? And anyways, what y'all think is so important about knowing what time it is? There ain't no special time, here in this place. Wake up the same every day. Bed at night, jus' the same. Eat. Sleep. Roll call. Every day, jes' the same. So, tell me, Hart, why y'all need that watch so damn much?"

Tommy glanced down at the Longines watch on his left wrist. For an instant the steel casing reflected a burst of sunlight. It was an excellent watch, with a sweep hand and jeweled mechanism. It kept precise time and seemed oblivious to the shocks and batterings of war. But, more important, etched into the back were the words *I'll be waiting* and the initial *L*. Tommy merely had to listen to the muffled ticking to be reminded of the young woman who'd given it to him on his last leave home before shipping out. Bedford, of course, knew none of this.

"It's not the time it keeps," Tommy said in reply. "It's the time it promises."

Bedford laughed out loud.

"Man, what you mean by that?"

The southerner smiled again. "Suppose I fix it so you gets to see those limey friends of yours whenever you want? I can do that. Suppose you start getting an extra parcel each week? I can make that happen, too. What you need, Hart? Food? Some warm clothes? Maybe books? Even a radio. I can get you one. A good one, too. Then you be able to listen to the truth and not have to rely on all the scuttlebutt and rumor that floats around this place. You jes' got to name your price."

"Not for sale."

"Damn." Bedford stood up, finally irritated. "Y'all ain't got no idea what I can get with a watch like that."

"Sorry," Tommy replied briskly.

Bedford seemed to snarl for a moment, then replaced the look of angry frustration with another grin.

"Time will come, lawyer man. And you'll end up needing to take less than you're offered here today. Ought to know when a trade is ripe. Don't want to be making no trades when you truly need somethin'. Always get the short end, then."

"No deals. Not today. Not tomorrow. Be seeing you, Vic."

Bedford shrugged, with an exaggerated motion. He seemed about to say something else, when both men heard the shrill whistle of the afternoon *Appell*. Ferrets materialized by each block of huts, shouting *"Raus! Raus!"* and men began to emerge from the buildings, slowly making their way to the parade ground.

Tommy Hart ducked back inside Hut 101 and replaced the legal text on the shelf. Then he joined the flow of men shuffling through the afternoon sun toward the assembly.

As always, they gathered in rows five deep.

The ferrets counted, walking up and down the rows, trying to make certain no one was missing. It was a tedious process, one the Germans seemed to accept with dedication. Tommy could never understand how it was that they weren't bored senseless by the twice-daily exercise in simple mathematics. Of course, he conceded inwardly that on a day that two men died in a tunnel, the ferret who missed a count would very likely find himself on a troop train bound for the eastern front. So the guards were being cautious and precise, even more so than their usual cautious and precise natures ordinarily allowed for.

When the count was satisfactorily accomplished, the ferrets returned to the front of the formations, reporting to the *Unteroffizier* assigned to that day's task. He would, in turn, report to the commandant. Von Reiter did not attend every *Appell*. But in order for the men to be dismissed, he had to give the order. The kriegies found this extra wait wildly irritating, as the *Unteroffizier* disappeared through the front gate, heading toward Von Reiter's office.

The delay this afternoon seemed lengthy.

Tommy stole a glance down the formation. He noticed that Vincent Bedford was at attention two spaces away. He looked back to the front, and saw that the *Unteroffizier* had returned and was speaking with SAO MacNamara. Tommy could just make out a look of concern on the face of the colonel, then MacNamara did an abrupt turn and marched out the gate with the German, disappearing into the commandant's office.

It was ten minutes before MacNamara reappeared. He

strode swiftly back to the head of the formations of airmen. But then he seemed to hesitate for an instant before speaking out, in a large, parade ground voice:

"New prisoner coming in!"

MacNamara paused again, as if he wished to add something.

But the kriegies' attention swung quickly in that momentary delay, to where a single U.S. flier, flanked on either side by goons with rifles, was emerging from the commandant's office. The flier was tall, a half foot taller than either of the guards accompanying him, trim, wearing the sheepskin jacket and soft helmet of a fighter pilot. He marched forward rapidly, his leather flight boots kicking up small puffs of dust from the earth, coming to attention in front of Colonel MacNamara, where the flier snapped off a salute that seemed creased, it was so sharp.

The kriegies were silent, staring ahead.

The only sound Tommy Hart heard, in those seconds, was the unmistakable drawl of the Mississippian, whose every word was filled with undeniable astonishment:

"I'll be goddamned . . ." Vincent Bedford said loudly. "It's a damn nigger!"

Chapter Two

THE BALL TO
THE FENCE

The arrival of First Lieutenant Lincoln Scott at Stalag
Luft Thirteen galvanized the kriegies. For nearly a week,
he replaced Freedom and the War as the primary topic of
conversation.

Few of the men had had any inkling that black pilots were
being trained by the U.S. Army Air Force at Tuskegee, Alabama, and fewer still were aware that they'd begun fighting
over Europe late in 1943. Some of the later camp arrivals,
B-17 pilots and crew mainly, told of flights of shining,
metallic P-51 fighters diving through their formations in pursuit of desperate Messerschmidts, and how the 332nd fighter
wing wore distinctive red and black chevrons painted on their
tail rudders. The men from these bombers had had the luxury
of some experience in their acceptance of the men from the
332nd; as they pointed out in debate after debate, it really
didn't make much difference to them who it was or what
color they were, as long as the fighters drove off the attacking
109s, because being chopped apart by the twin twenty-
millimeter cannons mounted in the stubby Messerschmidt's
wings and dying in a flaming B-17 was an ugly, frightening
business. But there weren't many of these crewmen in the
camp, and there was still widespread disagreement among
the kriegies as to whether any black man had the required
intelligence, physical ability, and the necessary heart to fly
warplanes.

Scott himself seemed unaware that his presence stirred
loud and sometimes contentious arguments. On the evening

he arrived in the camp, he had been assigned to the bunk in Hut 101 that had been occupied by the dead clarinet-playing tunneler. He had greeted the other men in the room in a perfunctory manner, stowed what few belongings he had with him beneath the bed, then crawled into his space and remained quiet for the remainder of the night.

He told no warrior's tales.

Nor did he volunteer information about himself. How he'd been shot down remained unknown, as did his hometown, his background, and his life. Over his first few days in the bag, a few kriegies made efforts to engage him in conversation, but Scott politely and firmly rebuffed each attempt. At mealtimes, he fashioned simple spreads from his allotted Red Cross parcels. He did not invite anyone to share with him, nor did he ask anyone to share from their parcels. What he received he used, alone. He did not join in camp conversations, nor did he sign up for classes, courses, or activities. On his second day at Stalag Luft Thirteen he obtained from the camp library a ripped and worn copy of Gibbons's *The Decline and Fall of the Roman Empire*, and from the YMCA he accepted a Bible, both of which he read silently, sitting outdoors in the sunshine, back against the hut, or on his bed, bent toward one of the windows, searching for the weak light that filtered past the grime-streaked glass and wooden shutters into the room.

He seemed, to the other kriegies, mysterious. They were surprised by Scott's standoffishness. Some found arrogance in his aloofness, which translated into a number of thinly veiled cracks. Others merely found his solitude unsettling. All the men, even those like Tommy Hart who might have been seen as loners, relied on and needed each other, if only to reassure themselves that they weren't alone in the world of confinement that was Stalag Luft Thirteen. The camp created the oddest of psychological states: They were not criminals, but they were in prison. Without each other's support and constant reminders that they belonged to a different life, they would be adrift.

But outwardly, Lincoln Scott seemed immune to this.

By the end of his first week inside Stalag Luft Thirteen, when not wrapped up with Gibbons's history or with the Bible, he had taken to spending his days walking the perimeter of the compound. One circuit after another, for hours. He would stride rapidly along the dusty trail, a foot inside the deadline, eyes riveted to the ground except for occasional pauses, where he would stop, turn, and stare out at the distant line of pine trees.

Tommy had watched him, and was reminded of a dog on a chain, always moving at the very limit of its territory.

He had been one of the men who made an effort in the first few days to enter into a conversation with Lieutenant Scott, but had had no more success than any other. In the midst of a mild afternoon, shortly before the order to start the evening count was to be given, he had approached the lieutenant as the black man made one of his tours of the edge of the camp.

"Hey, how you doing?" Hart had said. "My name's Tommy Hart."

"Hello," Scott had replied. He did not offer his hand, nor did he identify himself.

"You settled in okay?"

Scott had shrugged. "Seen worse," he muttered.

"When new guys come in it's sort of like having the daily paper delivered to the house, only a couple of days late. You've got all the latest, and even if it's out of date, it's still better than what we've got, which is rumor and official crap over the illegal radios. What's really happening? How's the war going? Any word on the invasion?"

"We're winning," Scott had answered. "And no. Lots of men sitting in England. Waiting, same as you."

"Well, not exactly the same as us," Tommy said, grinning, and gesturing toward a machine-gun crew in the guard tower.

"No, that's true," Scott said. The lieutenant had kept walking, not looking up.

"Well, you must know something," Hart asked.

"No," Scott had replied. "I don't."

"Well," Tommy had persisted, "suppose I walk along with you and you tell me everything you don't know."

This request brought the smallest of smiles to the black man's lips, just the slightest turn upward, and he blew out some wind, as if concealing a laugh. Then, almost as quickly as that moment was there between them, it dissipated.

"I really prefer to walk alone," Scott had said briskly. "Thanks for asking, though."

Then he'd continued his trek, as Tommy stopped and watched him stride on.

The following morning was Friday, and after the morning *Appell* Tommy went back to his bunk. From a small wooden box beneath the bed, he took several fresh packages of Lucky Strikes from a carton that had been delivered in his latest Red Cross parcel. He also grabbed a small metal container marked EARL GREY TEA, and the uneaten majority of a large chocolate bar. In his jacket pocket, he secreted a small can of condensed milk. Then he collected several sheets of brown scrap paper, which he'd used to scrawl notes upon in cramped, tight handwriting. These he stuffed between the pages of a worn text on forensic evidence.

He walked outside Hut 101, searching for one of the three Fritzes. The morning was warm, and sunlight gave the yellow-gray dirt of the compound a glow.

Instead he spotted Vincent Bedford pacing along, with a determined look on his face. The southerner paused, his face turning rapidly into a look of anticipation, and quickly approached Tommy.

"I'll sweeten the deal, Hart," he said. "You're just a hard nut to crack. What'll it take to get that watch?"

"You haven't got what it will take. Sentimental value."

The Mississippian snorted. "Sentiment? Girl back home? What makes you think you'll get back there in one piece? And what makes y'all think she'll be waiting for you once you do?"

"I don't know. Hope? Trust?" Tommy replied, with a small laugh.

"Those things don't amount to much in this world of ours, Yankee. What counts is what you got right now. In your hand. That y'all can use right away. Maybe ain't gonna be no tomorrow. Not for you, maybe not for me, maybe not for any of us."

"You're a cynic, Vic."

The southerner grinned

"Well, maybe so, maybe so. Nobody never called me that before. But I won't deny it."

They were walking slowly between two of the huts, and they emerged onto the edge of the exercise area. A softball game was just starting up, but beyond the outfield, both men caught sight of the solitary figure of Lincoln Scott, marching along the edge of the perimeter.

"Sumbitch," Bedford muttered. "Today I got to do something about this situation."

"What situation?" Tommy asked.

"The nigger situation," Bedford replied, turning and staring at Hart as if he were unbelievably stupid for not seeing the obvious. "The boy's using up a bunk in my room and that ain't right."

"What's not right about it?"

Bedford didn't answer directly. "I suppose I got to go tell old man MacNamara, and then he'll switch the nigger into another room. Boy ought to be housed in some place by himself, so's to keep him separate from the rest of us."

Tommy shook his head. "Seems he's doing that pretty effectively by himself without any help from you," he said.

Trader Vic shrugged. "Ain't right. And anyway, what's a Yankee like you know about niggers? Nothing. Absolutely goddamn nothing." Bedford drew out each vowel sound, giving each word an elongated importance. "Why, I'll bet, Hart, that you ain't hardly ever even seen one before, much less lived with 'em, the way we do down South. . . ."

Tommy didn't reply to this, because there was some truth in what Bedford said.

"And what we come to know about 'em ain't good," Trader Vic continued. "They lie. Why, they lie and cheat all the damn time. They're thieves, every one of 'em, as well. Good many of 'em are rapists and criminals, too. Not all, mind you. But a good many. Now, I'm not saying that they maybe might not make good soldiers. Why, that's a possibility, because they don't see things exactly the way white folks do, and they can probably be educated properly in how to kill, and do a right good job at it, I suspect, same as like chopping wood or fixing a machine, though flying a Mustang, I can't see that.

They just ain't the same as you and me, Hart. Hell, you can see that just by watching that boy walk his way around the deadline. And I think it'd be a whole lot better if old man MacNamara figured that out before some trouble happens, because I know niggers, and there's always trouble wherever they are. Believe it."

"What sort of trouble, Vic? Hell, we're all stuck here, just the same."

Vincent Bedford burst out into a small laugh, shaking his head vigorously back and forth.

"The one thing may be true, Hart, that we're all stuck here, though that remains to be seen, don't it? And the other, why, it absolutely ain't the same. No sir. Not the same at all."

Vincent Bedford pointed at the wire.

"The wire be the same. But everybody here sees it different. You see it one way, I see it another, and the old man sees it a third. Likely even our boy walking along out there, why he's probably started seeing it in his own way, too. That's the wonder of life, Hart, which I'd even expect an over-educated and tight-ass Yankee like yourself to figure out. Ain't nothing ever the same for two men in this world. Not ever. Except maybe death."

Tommy thought that of all the things he'd heard Bedford say, this last observation was probably as close to the truth as he ever came.

Before he could reply, Bedford clapped him on the shoulder. "Why hell, Hart, you're probably thinking that I'm prejudiced, but it ain't so. I ain't no stars and bars–waving, tobacco-chewing, white-hooded, night-riding Klansman. No sir. In fact, I have always treated every nigger good. Treat 'em like men. That's my way. But I know niggers, and I know they cause trouble, and that's what we'll have here."

The southerner turned and eyed Tommy.

"Trust me," Trader Vic continued with a small laugh. "Trouble'll be coming. I can tell. Best to keep folks separated." He smiled again.

Tommy kept silent.

Bedford brayed. "Hell, Hart, you know, I'll bet even money that maybe my great-granddaddy took a shot at one of your ancestors once or twice, back in the great war of independence, except that ain't what your damn fool Yankee textbooks call it now, is it? Good thing for you that the Bedfords never were much in the way of marksmen."

Tommy smiled. "The Hart family traditionally was always good at ducking," he said.

Bedford burst out laughing. "Well," he said, "that's a valuable ability, Tommy. Keep that family tree alive for centuries to come."

Still smiling, he stepped away. "Well, I'm gonna go do my talking with the colonel. You change your mind, come to your senses and wanna make that trade, you know I am definitely open for business twenty-four hours a day, and Sundays, too, because right now I think the good Lord is paying more attention elsewhere, and not watching out for this particular flock of sheep too damn much."

From the playing field, several kriegies started yelling in their direction and waving at Vincent Bedford. One of them waved a bat and ball above his head.

"Well," the Mississippian said, "I guess I'll have to put off talking with the big boss man until this afternoon, 'cause these boys need someone to show them how the great game of baseball is properly played. Be seein' ya, Hart. You work on changing your mind . . ."

Tommy watched as Trader Vic trotted toward the field.

From the opposite direction, he heard a distinctly American voice shout out, *"Keindrinkwasser!"* in half-fractured German. Then he heard the same call answered from a hut a few yards away. The German phrase stood for "not drinking water" and was what the Krauts printed on the steel barrels used for hauling sewage. It was also the standard kriegie early warning for the men in the huts to know that a ferret was walking through the camp in their direction and gave any men involved in escape activities time to hide their work, whether it was digging or forging documents. The ferrets were rarely pleased to be called sewage.

Tommy Hart hurried toward the sound of the voices. He hoped it was Fritz Number One who'd been spotted lurking around the compound, because he was generally the easiest ferret to bribe. He did not dwell long on what Bedford had said.

It took a half-dozen cigarettes to persuade Fritz Number One to accompany him to the northern compound. The two men marched through the camp gate into the space that separated the two compounds. On one side there was a barracks for guards, and then the commandant's offices. Behind that was a brick-and-mortar coldwater shower block. Two guards with slung rifles were standing outside, smoking.

From inside the showers, Tommy Hart could hear voices raised in song. The British were great chorale lovers. Their songs were invariably wildly ribald, dramatically obscene, or fantastically offensive.

He slowed his pace and listened. The men were singing "Cats on the Roof" and he swiftly recognized the refrain.

"Oh, cats on the roof, cats on the tiles . . .
"Cats with the syphilis and cats with the piles . . ."

Fritz Number One had also slowed.

"Do the British know any normal songs?" he asked quietly.

"I don't think so," Tommy replied.

The voices bursting from the shower room launched into a song called "Fuck All of It."

"The commandant," Fritz Number One said softly, "I do not think he enjoys the British singing. He no longer permits his wife and their little daughters to come visit him in his office when the British officers are going to the showers."

"War is hell," Tommy said.

Fritz Number One quickly raised his hand to cover his mouth, as if blocking a cough, but in reality to stifle a laugh.

"We must all do our duty," he said with a hidden cackle, "however we see it."

The two men walked past a gray cinder-block building. This was the cooler—the punishment barracks—with a dozen windowless and bare cement cells hidden inside. "Empty now," Fritz Number One said.

They approached the gate to the British compound. "Three hours, Lieutenant Hart. This is adequate?"

"Three hours. Meet you in the front."

The ferret swung his arm toward a guard, gesturing for the man to push the gate open. Tommy could see Flying Officer Hugh Renaday waiting just beyond the gate and he hurried forward to meet his friend.

"How's the wing commander?" Tommy asked, as the two men walked swiftly through the British compound.

"Phillip? Well, physically, he seems more run down than ever. He can't seem to shake this cold or whatever the bloody hell it is, and the last few nights he's been coughing, a wet, nasty cough, all night long. But in the morning he shrugs it all off and he won't let me take him to the surgeon's. Stubborn old bastard. If he dies here, it'll serve him right."

Renaday spoke with a brusque, flat Canadian accent, words that were as dry and windswept as the vast prairie regions that he called home, but contradictorily tinged with the frequent Anglicism that reflected his years in the RAF. The flying officer walked with a lengthy, impatient stride, as if he found the travel between locations to be inconvenient, that what was important to him was where one came from and where one ended up and the distance between really just an irritation. He was wide-shouldered and thickset, muscled even though the camp had stripped pounds from his frame. He wore his hair longer than most of the men in the camp, as if daring lice and fleas to infest him. None had been so foolhardy as of yet.

"Anyway," Renaday continued, as they turned a corner, passing two British officers diligently raking soil in a small garden, "he's damn glad today's Friday, and that you're visiting. Can't tell you how much he looks forward to these sessions. As if by using his brain he defeats how lousy the rest of him feels."

Renaday shook his head and added: "Other men like to talk of home, but Phillip likes to analyze these cases. I think it reminds him of what he was once and what he's likely to be when he gets back to jolly old England. He ought to be sitting in front of a warm fireplace, lecturing a few acolytes in the intricacies of some obscure legal point, wearing silk slippers and a green velvet smoking jacket, sipping from a cup of the

finest. Every time I look at the old bastard, I can't imagine
what the hell he was thinking when he climbed on board that
damnable Blenheim."

Tommy smiled. "Probably thinking the same thing we all
thought."

"And what, my learned American friend, might that have
been?"

"That despite the large and near constant volume of in-
credibly persuasive evidence to the contrary, nothing much
bad was going to happen to us."

Renaday burst into a deep, resonant laugh that made some
of the gardening officers pick up their heads and pay a brief
spot of attention before returning to their well-raked plots of
yellow-brown earth.

"God's bitter truth there, Yank."

He shook his head, still smiling, then gestured. "There's
Phillip now."

Wing Commander Phillip Pryce was sitting on the steps to
a hut, a book in one hand. He wore a threadbare olive blanket
draped across his shoulders despite the warmth, and had his
cap pushed back on his head. His eyeglasses were dropped
down on his nose, like a caricature of a teacher, and he
chewed on the end of a pencil. He waved like a child at a parade when he spotted the two men striding in his direction.

"Ah, Thomas, Thomas, delighted as always. Have you
come prepared?"

"Always prepared, Your Honor," Tommy Hart replied.

"Still smarting you know," Pryce continued, "from that
hiding you gave Hugh and me over the elusive Jack and his
unfortunate crimes. But now we're ready to do battle with
one of your more sensational cases, what. I would think it was
our turn, what do you say, with the bats?"

"At bat," Renaday said, as Hart and Pryce warmly shook
hands. Tommy thought the wing commander's firm handshake was perhaps a little less so than usual. "You say *at* bat,
Phillip. Not *with* the bats. The umpire says 'Batter up!' and so
on and that's what gets it all started."

"Incomprehensible sport, Hugh. Not unlike your foolish
but beloved hockey in that regard. Racing hell-bent around

on the ice in the freezing cold, trying to whack some defense-less rubber disk into a net and at the same time avoid being clubbed nearly to death by your opponents."

"Grace and beauty, Phillip. Strength and perseverance."

"Ahh, British qualities."

The men laughed together.

"Let's sit outside," Pryce said. He had a soft, generous voice, filled with reflection and enthusiasm. "The sun feels fine. And, after all, it's not something we English are all that accustomed to seeing, so, even here, amid all the horrors of war, we should take advantage of Mother Nature's temporary beneficence, no?"

Again the men smiled.

"Gifts from the ex-colonies, Phillip," Tommy said. "A little of our bounty, just a small repayment for your managing to send every bungling idiot general across the seas in seventy-six, to be taken advantage of by our New World brilliance."

"I shall ignore that most unfortunate, childish, and mistaken interpretation of a decidedly minor moment in the illustrious history of our great empire. What have you brought us?"

"Cigarettes. American, minus the half-dozen it took to bribe Fritz Number One . . ."

"His price, I think, has oddly gone up," Pryce muttered. "Ah, American tobacco! Virginia's best, I'll warrant. Excellent."

"Some chocolate . . ."

"Delightful. From the famous Hershey's of Pennsylvania . . ."

"And this . . ." Tommy Hart handed the older man the tin of Earl Grey tea. He had had to trade with a fighter pilot, who chain-smoked two packs of cigarettes a day, to get it, but he thought the price cheap when he saw the older man's face crease into a wide grin. Pryce immediately burst into song.

"Hallelujah! In excelsis gloria! And us doomed to reusing over and over that poor tired tin of foul alleged darjeeling. Hugh, Hugh, treasures from the colonies! Riches beyond our wildest imagination. The makings of a proper brew up! A sweet to cut the appetite, a real, honest-to-goodness cup of tea to be followed by a leisurely smoke! Thomas, we are in your debt!"

"It's the parcels," Tommy replied. "Ours are so much better than yours."

"True, alas. Not that we prisoners don't appreciate the sacrifices being made by our beleaguered countrymen, but—"

"The damn U.S. parcels are far better," Hugh Renaday interrupted. "The British parcels arc simply pathetic. Foul tins of kippers and ersatz jams. Something they call coffee, but which clearly isn't. Awful. Canadian parcels aren't all that bad, they're just a little shy of the sorts of stuff Phillip is looking for."

"Too much tinned meat. Not enough tea," Pryce said with mock sadness. "Tinned meat that looks like it was carved from the backside of Hugh's old horse."

"Probably was."

The men laughed again, and Hugh Renaday took the chocolate and tin of tea inside the hut to brew up cups for the three men. In the interim, Pryce lit a cigarette, leaned back, and, closing his eyes, let the smoke slowly slide from his nostrils.

"Phillip, how are you feeling?" Tommy asked.

"Nasty as always, dear boy," Pryce replied without opening his eyes. "I take some satisfaction in the consistency of my physical state. Always bugger-all bad."

He blinked his eyes open, and leaned forward. "But at least this still works fine." He tapped his forehead. "Have you prepared a defense for your accused carpenter?"

Tommy nodded. "I have indeed."

The older man smiled again. "You have some ideas? Fresh ideas, eh?"

"Argue for a change of venue. Vociferously. Then plan on bringing in some fancy-Dan wood experts or scientists to tear away at Hugh's man, the so-called forensic timber expert. Why, I suspect there's really no such thing, and I damn well ought to be able to find some Harvard or Yale type to testify that way! Because it's the ladder testimony that kills us. I can explain away the gold notes, explain away the other stuff. But the man testifying that the ladder could only have been made from the wood in Hauptmann's garage—so much of the case rests on that testimony."

Pryce moved his head slowly up and down. "Continue. There is much truth to what you say."

"You see, the wooden ladder—that's what forces me to put Hauptmann on the stand in his own defense. And when he gets up there, in front of all the cameras and newsmen in the midst of that circus . . ."

"Deplorable, I agree . . ."

"And he talks in that accent . . . and everyone hates him. From the moment he opens his mouth. I believe they hated him when he was accused, of course. But when that foreign accent tumbles out . . ."

"The case turns so much on that hatred, does it not, Thomas?"

"Yes. An immigrant. A rigid, brutish man. Much to instantly dislike. Put him in front of that jury and it's like taunting them to convict him."

"A solitary rodent of a man. A difficult client."

"Yes. But I must find a way to turn his weaknesses into strengths."

"Not quite so easy."

"But crucial."

"Ah, you are astute. And what of the famed aviator's odd identification? When he claims to recognize Hauptmann's voice as the voice he heard in the darkened cemetery?"

"Well, his testimony is preposterous on its face, Phillip. That he could recognize a man's half-dozen, no more, words years later . . . I think I would have prepared a surprise for Colonel Lindbergh on cross-examination."

"A surprise? How so?"

"I would plant three or four men with heavy accents in different locations in the courtroom. And in quick succession have each rise, and say 'Leave the money and go!' just as he claimed Hauptmann did. The state will object, of course, and the judge will find it contemptuous. . . ."

Pryce was grinning. "Ahh, but a little theater, no? Playing a bit to that huge crowd of horrid reporters. Underscoring a lie. I can see it quite clearly. Courtroom packed, all eyes on Thomas Hart, hypnotized as he wheels and produces these other men, and turns to the famous aviator and says, 'Are you sure it was not him? Or him? Or him?' and the judge's gavel ringing, and men of the press racing for the telephones. Creating a little circus of your own to counteract the circus arrayed against you, correct?"

"Precisely."

"Ahh, Thomas, you have the makings of a fine lawyer. Or perhaps the devil's own assistant if we all die here and end up in Hell. But remember caution. To many of the folk in that audience, in that jury, and the judge, as well, Lindbergh was a saint. A hero. A perfect knight. One must use great caution when showing a man with the glow of public perfection about him to be a liar. Keep that in mind! Here comes Hugh with the tea. Speaking of perfection!"

The older man reached for the cup of steaming liquid, and held it close to his nose, drinking in the vapors. "Now," he said, slowly, "if only we had . . ."

Tommy reached into his jacket pocket for the can of condensed milk, simultaneously finishing the older man's sentence. ". . . some fresh milk?"

Phillip Pryce laughed. "Thomas, my son, you will go far in life."

He poured a generous dollop into his white ceramic cup, then took a long pull at the lip, his pleasure obvious. Then he looked across the cup at Renaday. "Now that I've been properly bribed by the Yank, Hugh, I hope you've prepared as well?"

Renaday poured a more conservative touch of milk into his own tea and nodded vigorously.

"Of course, Phillip. Although I have been placed at a significant disadvantage by the unseemly bribery by our friend from the States, I have. The evidence I have at hand is overwhelming. The ransom money—those distinctive gold certificates—found hidden in Hauptmann's home. The ladder—which I can prove was carved from the boards of his own garage. His lack of a credible alibi—"

"And lack of confession," Tommy Hart briskly interrupted. "Even after he's been subjected to hours and hours of your harshest questioning."

"That confession. Or lack thereof," Pryce interjected, "that is most troubling, Hugh, is it not? It is most surprising, also, that it could not be obtained. You would think the man would crumble under the efforts of the state police. You would think, too, that he would be filled with remorse at taking the poor child's life. You would imagine that these pressures, from within and without, would be well-nigh insurmountable, especially to a rough man of limited education. And that, in due time, this confession, which would answer so much and free us from so many dogged questions, would arrive. But instead, this dull workingman steadfastly maintains his innocence. . . ."

The Canadian nodded. "It surprises me that they could not break him. I damn well could have, and without resorting to what you folks in the lower forty-eight call the third degree. Now, I do concede a confession would be helpful, perhaps even important, but . . ."

Hugh Renaday paused, then smiled at Tommy. "But I don't need it. Not really. The man comes to the courtroom draped in guilt. Cloaked in guilt. Fully dressed out and equipped with guilt. Pregnant with guilt . . ." Renaday puffed out his stomach and patted it with a thump. The three men laughed at the image. "There's little for me to do, save help the hangman tie his noose."

"Actually, Hugh," Tommy said quietly, "in New Jersey they favored the electric chair."

"Well," the flying officer said, as he broke off a square of chocolate and popped it into his mouth before handing the bar to Pryce, "then they damn well ought to have it warmed up and ready to fly."

"Probably have difficulty finding volunteers for that job, Hugh," Pryce burst out. "Even with a war on."

The wing commander's laugh disintegrated into a series of wracking coughs, which settled when he took a long sip of tea, once again bringing a wide grin to his wrinkled face.

The argument went well, Tommy thought, as he and Fritz Number One retraced their steps through the zone between the two compounds. He had made some points, conceded some, battled hard on every procedural question, losing most, but not without a fight. On the whole, he was pleased. Phillip Pryce had decided to put off on issuing any ruling and allow further discussion the following week, much to Hugh

Renaday's theatrical dismay and mock-bitter claims that Tommy's unfair bribery was clouding their friend's usually perceptive vision. This was a complaint none of the three men took particularly seriously.

After walking side by side for a moment or two, Tommy noticed that the ferret seemed oddly quiet. Fritz Number One enjoyed using his language skills, often privately suggesting that after the war he would be able to turn them to good use and financial reward. Of course, it was difficult to tell whether Fritz Number One meant after they had won the war, or lost it. It was always difficult, Tommy thought, to tell precisely how fanatic most of the ordinary Germans were. The occasional Gestapo man who visited the camp—especially in the wake of failed escape attempts—wore his politics openly. A ferret such as Fritz Number One—or the commandant, for that matter—was a much harder read.

He turned to the German. Fritz Number One was tall, as he was, and thin, like a kriegie. The main difference was that his skin had a healthier glow to it, not like the sallow, pasty appearance all the prisoners gained within their first few weeks inside Stalag Luft Thirteen.

"What's the matter, Fritz? Cat got your tongue?"

The ferret looked up quizzically. "Cat? What does this mean?"

"It means: Why are you so silent?"

Fritz Number One nodded. "Cat holding your tongue. This is clever. I will remember."

"So? What's the problem?"

The ferret frowned and shrugged. "Russians. Today," he said softly. "They are clearing space for another camp for more Allied prisoners. We take the Russians and use them for the labor. They live in tents barely a mile away. Other side of the woods."

"And?"

Fritz Number One lowered his voice, swiveling his head around quickly to make certain no one could overhear him.

"We work the Russians to their deaths, lieutenant. There are no Red Cross parcels with tinned beef and cigarettes for them. Just work. Very hard. They die by the dozens. By the hundreds. I worry that if the Red Army ever finds out how we have treated these prisoners, their revenge will be harsh."

"You're worried that when the Russians show up . . ."

"They will not show charity."

Tommy nodded, thinking: Serves you right.

But before he could say anything, Fritz Number One held out his hand, stopping him. They were perhaps thirty yards from the gate to the southern compound, but Fritz Number One was unwilling to cross the short distance. To his left, Tommy suddenly saw why: A long, sinewy column of men was marching toward them, and he could see that they would pass directly in front of the entrance to the American compound. He paused, watching with a mingling of curiosity and despair, thinking: These men are no different. They have lives and homes and families and hopes. But they are dead men, marching past.

The German soldiers guarding the column wore battle dress. Their machine pistols swept over the shuffling line of men. Occasionally one would shout *"Schnell! Schnell!"* urging them to hurry, but the Russians moved at their own deliberate and painstaking pace. Marching with utter exhaustion. Tommy could see sickness and hurt behind their thick beards, in their recessed, haunted eyes. Their heads were bent, each step forward seemingly agonizing. Occasionally he could see one man, or two, gazing at the German guards, muttering in their own tongue, and then he could spot anger and defiance, mingled with resignation. What he saw was the most unusual of conflicts: Men covered with the tattered clothing of harshness and deprivation, yet undefeated by their condition, even knowing they had no hope. The Russians slowly shuffled forward, marching to the next minute, which was nothing but sixty seconds closer to their inevitable deaths.

Tommy found himself choking, unable to speak.

But in that moment, he saw a remarkable thing:

Inside the American compound, just beyond the wire, Vincent Bedford had been at the plate, in the midst of a softball game. Like all the players, and the rest of the kriegies, he had seen the Russian prisoners' painful approach. Most of the

Americans stood riveted in place, fascinated by the skeletons shuffling past.

But not Bedford. With a bellow, he'd dropped the bat to the dust; waving his arms and shouting furiously, Trader Vic had turned and raced back into the nearest hut, the thick wooden door slamming with a resounding shot behind him.

For an instant, Tommy was confused, not understanding what Bedford was yelling. But it became clear within seconds, because the Mississippian emerged from the hut almost as quickly as he had first disappeared, but now his arms were filled with loaves of dark German-issued bread. He was shouting: *"Kriegsbrot! Kriegsbrot!"* at the other POWs in his distinctive southern drawl. Then, without hesitating to see if his message was understood, Vincent Bedford ran forward, sprinting quickly to the camp gate. Tommy saw the German guards suddenly swing their weapons in his direction.

A German *Feldwebel*, wearing a soft campaign hat, broke away from the squad guarding the gate, dashing toward Bedford and waving his arms. The *Feldwebel* was shouting, *"Nein! Nein! Ist verboten!"* As he raced toward the U.S. airman, the *Feldwebel* was struggling to remove his Mauser pistol from his holster. He stood in front of Bedford, just as Trader Vic reached the gate.

The column of Russians slowed even further, their heads pivoting toward the shouting. Now they were barely moving despite the sudden insistent commands from the guards, *"Schnell! Schnell!"*

The *Feldwebel* stared angrily at Bedford, eyes narrowed with hatred, as if, in that second, the American and the German were no longer prisoner and guard, but merely deadly enemies. The *Feldwebel* managed finally to get his weapon out, and with frightening, serpentlike speed, brought it to bear directly on the southerner's chest. *"Ist verboten!"* he repeated harshly.

Tommy saw a wild look in Bedford's eyes.

"Verboten?" He spoke in a high-pitched drawl, his lip pulled back in a sneer. "Well, guess what, fella? Fuck you."

Bedford stepped briskly to the side of the German, ignoring the weapon. In a single, graceful, and smooth motion, he cocked back his arm, and like a shortstop fielding a grounder deep in the hole, he threw a loaf of bread over the top of the barbed-wire fence. The loaf spun in the air, cart-wheeling through the sky, arcing like a tracer round until it landed directly in the midst of the Russian prisoners.

The column of Russians seemed to explode. Without leaving their formation, they all pivoted, facing the American camp. Their arms were raised instantly in entreaty, and their deep voices pierced through the May afternoon. *"Brot! Brot!"* they shouted over and over again.

The German *Feldwebel* thumbed back the hammer of his pistol, making a clicking sound that Tommy heard above the entreaties of the Russians. The other guards chambered rounds as well. But they all stood in place, none making a move either toward Bedford or the column of Russians.

Bedford turned to the *Feldwebel* and said, "Why don't y'all just relax, buddy. You can kill 'em all tomorrow. But today, at least, they're gonna get to eat." He grinned wildly, and tossed another loaf over the fence, then a third. The *Feldwebel* stared hard at Bedford for a moment, as if internally debating whether he should fire, then shrugged in an exaggerated fashion. He slowly returned his pistol to its holster.

By this time dozens of other kriegies had emerged from the huts, their arms laden with the hard loaves of German bread. Men started to line the fence, and within minutes a rain of bread cascaded down upon the Russian prisoners, who without breaking formation gathered up each morsel. Tommy saw Bedford launch his final loaf, then stand back, arms folded, smiling widely.

The Germans allowed the scene to continue.

After a few moments, Tommy noticed a single loaf of bread that didn't quite have the distance. Short-armed was the baseball term for a throw that was destined to land shy of its target. This loaf fell to the earth a dozen feet away from the column of men. In the same instant, he saw a small, rabbitlike Russian soldier on the edge of the lines of men spot the loaf. The man seemed to hesitate, taking note that no other prisoner had broken formation to retrieve the precious bread. At that second, Tommy could suddenly imagine the man's mind, calculating, assessing his chances. Bread was life. Leaving formation could be death. A danger. A risk. But a great prize.

He wanted to shout out to the man: "No! It's not worth it!" but he could not remember the Russian, *"Nyet!"*

And in that hesitation, the soldier abruptly darted from the column of men, bent over, his outstretched arms reaching for the short loaf.

He did not make it.

A single, ragged burst from a machine pistol pierced the air, shattering the cries of the prisoners. The Russian soldier pitched forward, sprawling a few feet away from the precious loaf. He twitched once, his back arcing in agony, a dark bloodstain spreading into the dust around him, then lay still.

The column of prisoners seemed to shudder along its length. But instead of shouts of outrage, the Russians grew instantly silent. It was a quiet laced with hatred and fury.

The German guard who'd fired slowly walked up to the body and nudged it with his boot. He worked the bolt on his weapon, ejecting the spent clip, replacing it with a new load. Then he gestured sharply at two men from the column, who slowly stepped out, crossed the short distance, and bent down to pick up the body. Both men slowly made the sign of the cross over their hearts, but one of the men, his eyes lifted toward the German guard, reached out and seized the deadly loaf of bread. The Russian soldier had a snarl plastered across his face, like some cornered animal turned at bay, a wolverine or a badger, ready to defend itself with whatever tooth and claw it had left in its tattered arsenal. Then the prisoners grasped the body, lifting it to their shoulders like some gory prize. They returned to the line of men, but only after staring harshly at the murderous guard for several long instants. Tommy Hart was afraid the Germans might open up on the entire column, and he quickly looked around for someplace to take cover.

"Raus!" the German commanded. There was a touch of nervousness in his voice. The lines of men reluctantly struggled back into rough formation and slowly started forward again.

But from deep within the column, a single anonymous voice surged upward in a slow, sad song. Deep, resonant, the strange foreign words drifted into the air above the line of prisoners, rising above the muffled, shuffling sound of their feet. None of the Germans made any immediate effort to halt the song and it continued, its words perhaps incomprehensible to Tommy but its meaning apparent. The singing finally faded away, as the column disappeared into the distant line of fir trees.

"Hey, Fritz," he whispered, though he knew the answer. "What was he singing?"

"It was a song of thanks," Fritz Number One quietly responded. "And a song of freedom."

The ferret shook his head.

"It will likely be his last song," he said. "The singer will not come alive from the forest."

Then he pointed Tommy toward the gate, where Vincent Bedford remained standing. The Mississippian was also watching the Russians until they passed from sight. His smile had slid from his face, and Bedford lifted his right hand and touched the brim of his cap. A small salute.

"I did not think," Fritz Number One muttered, as he hurriedly motioned for the gate guard to open up, "that our friend Trader Vic was a man of such bravery. It was foolhardy to risk his life for some Russian that is going to die maybe today, maybe tomorrow. But soon. But it was very brave."

Tommy nodded. He thought much the same. But he was even more surprised to learn that Fritz Number One knew Vincent Bedford's camp nickname.

As the gate to the South Compound swung shut behind him, Tommy caught a glimpse of Lincoln Scott. The black flier was standing in the distance, on the edge of the deadline, staring out to where the Russians had entered the thick dark line of trees. As always, Lincoln Scott stood alone.

Shortly before the Germans turned off the electricity for the night, Tommy slid into his bunk in Hut 101. He perched a work on civil procedure on his upraised knees, but found himself unable to absorb the dry prose of the textbook. The case synopsis seemed dull and unimaginative, and he found his mind wandering to the courtroom in Flemington and the trial that had been held there. He recalled what Phillip Pryce had said about hatred forming the undercurrent to the legal proceedings, and thought there had to be a way to turn that rage around. He thought the best lawyer finds a way to harness whatever external force is directed at his client and take advantage of it.

He kept a few stubs of pencil in a tin by his bed, and he twisted beneath his blanket, grabbing for one, and reaching at the same time for a sheet of scrap paper. He wrote this last thought down, and decided he would reexamine the carpenter's case once again. He smiled to himself, thinking this was a small act of legal desperation, because the facts that Hugh Renaday was stolidly relying upon were arrayed like a phalanx of hoplites against him. Still, he acknowledged, Phillip was a man of subtlety, and an intriguing argument might serve to shift him away from the evidence. That would be a major coup, he thought. He wondered what sort of reputation the attorney who freed Bruno Richard Hauptmann would gain. Even in this fictional re-creation of the case.

He looked down at his watch. The Germans were oddly erratic in when they shut the lights off. For people who did most everything with utter predictability, this was unusual, and almost inexplicable. He guessed not more than thirty more minutes of light remained in the hut.

He took the watch off his wrist, and turned it over, reading the inscription as he slid his finger across it. He closed his eyes and found that he could shut away the camp sounds and smells, and taking a deep breath could find himself back in Vermont. There was a tendency to fantasize about the special moments back home—the first time Lydia and he kissed, the first time he felt the soft curve of her breast beneath his palm, the moment he knew he would love her no matter what happened to him. But he fought off these memories, favoring daydreams about the ordinary, the routine days of growing up. He would remember pulling a glistening rainbow trout that rose to his dry fly from a small curve in the Mettawee River, where the flow of water had carved out a little pool that held big fish, and only he seemed to know about it. Or the early September day he'd helped his mother as she packed his bags for the academy, folding each shirt two or three times before placing it gently in the big leather suitcase. He'd been an excited fourteen that day, and hadn't really understood why she kept dabbing away tears.

He squeezed his eyes shut. The ordinary days were the special ones, he thought. The special days were spectacular. Events to be memorialized.

He took a deep breath and slowly opened his eyes.

Tommy let out a long, slow sigh. It takes a place like this, he realized, to make you understand.

He shook his head slightly, reaching for the textbook, his attention driven like a herder's cattle team into focus, with mental whip and imagined sharp words.

He was lying like that, in his berth, concentrating on the case law governing a dispute between a paper corporation and its employees from more than a dozen years earlier, when he heard the first angry shout coming from one of the other bunk rooms in Hut 101.

The sound made him sit up sharply. He pivoted his head, like a dog that catches a scent on an odd breath of wind, turning toward the noise. He heard a second, then a third shout, and the thudding noise of furniture slammed against the thin walls.

He swung himself out of the bunk, as did the other men in his room. He heard a voice say, "What the hell's going on?" But by the time the question was out, he'd already headed to the central corridor running the length of Hut 101 and toward the noise of the fight in progress. He barely had time to think how unusual this was, but in all his months at Stalag Luft Thirteen he'd never, not once, seen or heard of two men coming to blows. Not over a poker game loss, or a hard slide into second base. Not a dispute on the hard dirt basketball court, or over a theatrical interpretation of *The Merchant of Venice*.

Kriegies did not fight. They negotiated. They debated. They took the minor defeats of camp in complete stride, not because they were soldiers trained to military discipline, but because they understood implicitly that they were all in the bag together. Personalities that clashed invariably found ways of working out their differences, or studiously avoided each other. If men held rage, it was rage at the wire and at the Germans and at the bad luck that had put them there, although most realized that in its own way the bad luck that had caused them to be shot down was the greatest good luck of all.

Tommy ran toward the voices, hearing intense fury and uncontrolled rage. It was hard for him to understand what the fight was about. Behind him, the corridor was filling with the curious, but he'd managed to move quickly, and so he was among the first men to arrive at Trader Vic's bunk room.

What Tommy saw astonished him.

A bunk bed had been partially overturned, and was leaning up against another. A hand-hewn wooden locker filled with cartons of cigarettes and tins of foodstuffs lay scattered in one corner. Some clothes were strewn about and several books were dashed to the floor.

Lincoln Scott stood alone, back against one wall. He was breathing hard and his fists were clenched.

The other bunkmates were arrayed in front of Vincent Bedford.

The Mississippian had a trickle of red blood streaking down from beneath his nose, across the corner of his mouth, and onto his chin. He was struggling against four men, who pinned his arms back, holding him. Bedford's face was flushed, his eyes wild.

"You're a dead man, nigger!" he shouted. "Hear me, boy? Dead!"

Lincoln Scott said nothing, but stared at Bedford.

"I'm gonna see you die, boy," Bedford screamed.

Tommy felt himself abruptly shoved aside, and as he pivoted, he heard one of the other kriegies abruptly cry: "Attention!" In the same instant, he saw the unmistakable figure of Colonel MacNamara, accompanied by Major David Clark, his executive officer and the camp's second in command. As all the men in the room clicked their heels together and saluted, the two men pushed themselves into the center of the bunk room, rapidly surveying the detritus from the fight. MacNamara's face reddened swiftly, but his voice remained even and harshly calm. He turned to a first lieutenant Tommy knew only vaguely but who was one of Trader Vic's roommates.

"Lieutenant, what happened here?"

The man stepped forward. "A fight, sir."

"A fight? Please continue."

"Captain Bedford and Lieutenant Scott, sir. A dispute over

some items Captain Bedford claimed were missing from his private locker."

"Yes. Continue."

"Blows were exchanged."

MacNamara nodded, his face still filled with restrained anger. "Thank you, lieutenant. Bedford, what have you to say in this matter?"

Trader Vic, shoulders pushed back, stepped forward with precision despite his disheveled appearance.

"Items of personal importance were missing, sir. Stolen."

"What items?"

"A radio, sir. A carton of smokes. Three bars of chocolate."

"Are you certain they are missing?"

"Yes sir! I keep very careful count of my inventory at all times, sir."

MacNamara nodded. "I believe you do," he said stiffly. "And you believe Lieutenant Scott to have committed this robbery?"

"Yes sir."

"And you accused him of this?"

"Yes sir."

"Did you see him take the items?"

"No sir." Bedford hesitated slightly. "I returned to the bunk room. He was the only kriegie here. I made my usual evening count of the stock—"

MacNamara held up his hand, shutting him off. He turned to Scott. "Lieutenant, have you taken any items from Bedford's locker?"

Scott's voice was husky, rough-edged, and Tommy thought he was trying to withhold emotion. His eyes were straight ahead, as if fixed not on any person, but the opposite wall, and his shoulders remained thrust back.

"No sir."

MacNamara narrowed his own eyes, staring hard at the black flyer.

"No?"

"No sir!"

"You maintain you've taken nothing from Captain Bedford?"

Asking the same question three times got Lincoln Scott to turn slightly, so that his eyes locked with Colonel MacNamara's.

"Correct, sir."

"So, you believe Captain Bedford is mistaken with his accusation?"

Scott hesitated, assessing the question before replying.

"I would not characterize what Captain Bedford is, or is not, sir. I merely state that I have not taken any possessions that rightfully belong to him."

MacNamara scowled at the response. He pointed a finger at the flier's chest.

"Scott, I will see you tomorrow morning after *Appell* in my room. Bedford, you I will see . . ." for a moment, the briefest of seconds, the commanding officer hesitated. Then he spoke sharply: "No, Bedford, I'll see you first. Right after morning roll call. Scott, you be waiting outside, and when I've finished with him, I'll see you. In the meantime, I want this place cleaned up. I want it completely shipshape in five minutes. And as for tonight, there will be no further outbursts. Absolutely none! Do you men understand that?"

Both Bedford and Scott slowly nodded, and replied in unison: "Yes sir."

MacNamara half-turned to exit, then thought better of it. He abruptly swung toward the lieutenant he'd first questioned. "Lieutenant," he said sharply, bringing the officer to attention. "I want you to gather a blanket and anything else you might need for this night. Tonight, you will occupy Major Clark's bunk." MacNamara swiveled toward his second in command. "Clark, tonight I think it might be advisable—"

But the major cut him off. "Absolutely, sir." He saluted crisply. "No problem. I'll get my blanket." The second in command turned to the young lieutenant. "Follow me," he said briskly. Then he turned toward Tommy and the other kriegies crowding the hallway. "End of show!" he said loudly. "Back to your bunks. Now!"

This the kriegies, including Tommy Hart, did rapidly, scattering and scooting down the hallway like so many cockroaches when a light has been shined on them. For a few minutes, from his own space, he could hear footsteps resounding off the wooden flooring in the central corridor.

Then a suffocating silence, followed by the sudden arrival of darkness when the Germans cut the electricity. This thrust all the huts into night's black and spilled inky calm over the small, compacted world of Stalag Luft Thirteen. The only light was the erratic sweep of a searchlight over the wire, across the rooftops of the huts, probing the shadows of the camp. The only noise was the distant and familiar crunching noise of a nighttime bombing raid on factories in some nearby city, reminding the men, as they struggled to drift off to whatever nightmares awaited them, that much of great significance and importance was happening elsewhere.

Rumors flew around the compound the following morning. There was talk that both men were going to be sent to the cooler, others suggested that an officers' court was to be convened to hear the dispute over the alleged stealing. One man said he'd heard it from a top source that Lincoln Scott was going to be shifted to a room by himself, another said that Bedford had organized support from the entire southern contingent of kriegies, and that regardless of what Colonel Mac-Namara did, Lincoln Scott's days were numbered.

As was usually the case, none of the more exotic rumors were true.

Colonel MacNamara met with each man privately. Scott was told he would be moved to a different hut when a bunk became available, but that MacNamara was not willing to order a man to shift locations to accommodate the black flier. Bedford was told that without credible, eyewitness evidence that something had been stolen, his accusations were groundless. He was ordered to leave Scott alone until a switch could be accomplished. MacNamara commanded both men to get along until other arrangements could be made. He pointedly reminded them that they were both officers in an army at war, and subject to military discipline at all times. He told them he expected them both to behave as gentlemen and that there would be nothing more to the matter. This last suggestion carried the complete weight of the colonel's temper, and it was clear, the kriegies universally agreed when they heard of this, that no matter how much the two men might now actually hate each other, being at the very top of Colonel MacNamara's shit list was far worse.

There was an uneasiness in the camp for the next days.

Outwardly, Trader Vic went back to wheeling and dealing, and Lincoln Scott returned to his reading and to his solitary turns around the camp perimeter. Inwardly, Tommy Hart suspected much more was happening with both men. He found it all very curious, and actually intriguing. There was a distinct fragility to life in a prisoner-of-war camp; any cracks in the carefully constructed veneer of civilization that they'd created was dangerous to them all. The awful routine of confinement, the stress of their near-death when they were shot from the sky, the fear that they'd been forgotten, or worse, were being ignored, lurked just beneath all their moments, every waking minute. They fought constantly against isolation and despair, because they all knew these were enemies that equaled the Germans in threat to them all.

It was the middle of a fine afternoon, sunlight pouring over the dull, drab colors of the camp, glinting off the wire. Tommy, a law book under his arm, had just exited from one of the *Aborts*, and was going to find a warm spot in which to read. A furious softball game was going on in the exercise field, men's voices raised in all the usual catcalls and taunts that accompany the game of baseball, intermixed with the occasional thump of bat against ball, and ball into mitt. Just beyond the game, Tommy saw Lincoln Scott walking the deadline.

The black man was perhaps thirty yards behind the right fielder, his head down, as usual, his pace steady, yet somehow tortured. Tommy thought Scott was beginning to resemble the Russians that had marched past and disappeared into the woods.

He hesitated, then decided he would make another effort to speak with the black flier. He guessed that since the fight in the barracks no one had spoken, other than in a perfunctory manner, to Lincoln Scott. He doubted that Scott, no matter how strong he thought he might be, could keep up the combination of self-imposed isolation and ostracism without going crazy.

So, Tommy stepped deliberately across the compound, not

really thinking about what he would say, but thinking that someone ought to say something. As he approached, he noticed that the right fielder, who had turned and stared briefly at the passing flier, was Vincent Bedford.

As he walked in their direction, Tommy heard a distant whomping sound, instantly accompanied by a cascade of hoots and cries. He twisted and saw the white shape of a softball curving in a graceful parabola against the blue Bavarian sky.

In the same instant, Vincent Bedford turned, and raced back a half-dozen strides. But the arc of the ball was too quick, even for an expert like Bedford. The softball landed behind him with a thump in the dust, raising a small puffy cloud, and, filled with momentum, immediately rolled past the deadline, up against the wire.

Bedford stopped short, as did Tommy.

Behind them, the batter who'd launched the shot was circling the bases, shouting out, while his teammates cheered, and the other fielders yelled across the dirt diamond toward Bedford.

Tommy Hart saw Bedford grin.

"Hey, nigger!" the southerner called out.

Lincoln Scott stopped. He raised his head slowly, pivoting toward Vincent Bedford. His eyes narrowed. He said nothing in reply.

"Hey, little help, how 'bout it, boy?" Bedford said, gesturing to the softball resting up against the barbed wire.

Lincoln Scott turned and saw the ball.

"C'mon, boy, get the damn ball!" Bedford shouted.

Scott nodded, and took a step toward the deadline.

In that second, Tommy realized what was about to happen. The black flier was about to step over the deadline to retrieve the baseball without first donning the white smock with the red cross that the Germans provided for exactly that purpose. Scott seemed unaware that the machine-gun crew in the nearest tower had swiveled their weapon, and that it was trained on him.

"Stop!" Tommy shouted. "Don't!"

The black flier's foot seemed to hesitate in midair, poised

over the thin wire of the deadline. Scott turned toward the frantic noise.

Tommy found himself running forward, waving his arms. "No! No! Don't!" he cried.

He slowed as he passed Bedford. He heard Trader Vic mutter, "Hart, you damn Yankee fool . . ." beneath his breath.

Scott remained stock-still, waiting for Tommy to approach him.

"What is it?" the black man asked sullenly, but with just a tinge of anxiety in his voice.

"You have to wear the damn jacket to cross the deadline without being shot," Tommy said breathlessly. He pointed back toward the baseball game, and they saw one of the kriegies who'd been playing half-running across the field, carrying the smock, which fluttered in the breeze he made by hurrying. "If you don't have the red cross on, the Germans can shoot. Without warning. It's the rule. Didn't anyone tell you?"

Scott shook his head, but only slightly.

"No," he said slowly, staring past Tommy at Bedford. "No one told me about the jacket."

By this time the kriegie carrying the smock had arrived at the deadline. "Got to wear this, lieutenant," the man said, "unless you're looking to commit suicide."

Lincoln Scott continued to stare past the man, directly at Vincent Bedford, who stood a few feet away. Bedford pulled off his leather baseball mitt and started massaging it, working the leather slowly and deliberately.

"So," Trader Vic called out again, "you gonna get us the ball, boy, or what? Game's wasting away here."

Tommy squared around toward Bedford. "What the hell are you trying to pull, Bedford? They would have shot him before he'd gone two feet!"

The southerner shrugged, and didn't reply. He continued to grin widely.

"That would have been murder, Vic," Tommy shouted. "And you damn well know it!"

Bedford shook his head. "What'cha saying, Tommy? All I asked was for that boy there to get us the ball, 'cause he was closer. Why, of course I thought he'd wait for the smock. Any damn fool knows that you gotta be wearing those colors if you want to cross the deadline. Ain't that right?"

Lincoln Scott slowly pivoted, and turned his glance up toward the machine-gun crew leaning out over the tower, watching the gathering of kriegies closely. He reached out and took the pullover with the red cross and held it in his hand for a moment. Then he held it up, so the machine gunners could see it.

Then he deliberately dropped it to the dirt.

"Hey," the kriegie said. "Don't do that!"

In the same instant, Lincoln Scott stepped over the deadline. He kept his gaze on the machine-gun crew in the tower. They stepped back, crouching behind their weapon. One of the crew worked the bolt on the side of the gun, which made a sharp, metallic clicking sound that resounded through the suddenly still camp air, while the other grasped the belt of bullets, ready to feed it into the gun's maw.

His eyes still locked on the gunners, Scott strode across the short space to the wire. He reached down and seized the softball, then walked slowly back to the deadline. He stepped over the line stiffly, gave the Germans in the tower a final, contemptuous glance, and then turned from the machine gunners to Vincent Bedford.

Bedford was still grinning, but the smile was fading and seemed false. He slipped the mitt back onto his left hand and pounded the leather palm two or three times.

"Thanks, boy," he said. "Now fire that pill right on over here so's we can get back to the game."

Scott looked at Bedford, then glanced down at the ball. He picked up his eyes slowly, and stared past Bedford, toward the center of the baseball diamond, and beyond, to where the catcher, a kriegie umpire, and the next batter were standing. Scott hefted the softball in his right hand, then, abruptly stepping past Tommy, took a half-jumping stride forward and unleashed the ball in a single, savage throw.

Scott's toss carried on a direct line, like a shot from a fighter's cannon, across the dusty field, toward home plate. It bounced one time in the infield before slapping into the surprised glove of the catcher. Even Bedford's mouth dropped open slightly at the speed and distance of the throw.

"Damn, boy," Bedford said, surprise tinging his words. "Y'all got some kinda arm there."

"That's right," Scott said. "I do." Then he turned, and without saying another word resumed his lonely walk around the deadline.

Chapter Three

THE *ABORT*

Shortly after dawn on the third day following the incident at the wire, Tommy Hart was slowly awakening from another sleep rich in dreams when the high-pitched and shrill sounds of whistles once again catapulted him into alertness. The noise erased a strange dream-vision in which his girlfriend Lydia and the dead captain from West Texas were sitting on the small front porch of his parents' white clapboard house in Manchester in side-by-side rocking chairs, each beckoning to him to join them.

He heard one of the other men in the room mutter: "Christ, what is it this time? Another tunnel?"

A second voice replied as the slapping sound of feet hitting the wooden floors filled the air: "Maybe it's an air raid."

A third voice chimed in: "Can't be. No sirens. Gotta be another tunnel, goddamn it! I didn't know they were digging another tunnel."

Tommy pulled on his pants and blurted out, "We're not supposed to know. We're never supposed to know. Only the tunnel kings and the escape planners are supposed to know. Is it raining?"

One of the other men pulled back the shutters over the window. "Drizzling. Shit. Cold and wet."

The man at the window turned back to the rest of the crew in the bunk room and added with a small lilt to his voice, "They can't expect us to fly in this soup!"

This statement was immediately greeted by the usual mixture of laughter, groans, and catcalls.

From the bunk above him, Tommy heard a fighter pilot wonder out loud, "Maybe somebody tried to blitz out through the wire. Maybe that's what's going on."

One of the first voices replied with a sarcastic snort: "That's all you fighter jocks ever think: That somebody's gonna blitz out on their own."

"We're just independent thinkers," the fighter pilot replied, giving the other man a halfhearted, playful wave. Several of the other fliers laughed.

"You still need permission from the escape committee," Tommy said, shrugging. "And after the last tunnel failure, I doubt they'd give anybody permission to attempt suicide. Even some crazy Mustang jockey."

There were a few grunts of assent to this comment.

Outside, the whistles continued, and there was the rumbling and thudding noise of booted men running in formation. The kriegies in Hut 101 started to reach for woolen sweaters and leather flight jackets hanging from makeshift lines stretched between the bunks, while shouts from the guards urged them to hurry. Tommy laced his boots tightly, grabbed his weatherbeaten cap, and quickly made his way into the push of Allied prisoners emerging from their bunks. As he passed through the barracks door, he turned his face upward to a deadening gray sky, feeling a misty rain on his face and a deep foglike chill penetrate past the barrier of underwear and sweater and jacket. He instantly raised his collar, hunched his shoulders forward, and started for the assembly ground.

But what he saw almost made him stop.

Two dozen German soldiers, in long, winter-issue greatcoats, their steel helmets glistening with moisture, ringed the *Abort* located between Hut 101 and Hut 102. Hard-eyed and wary, the soldiers faced the Allied airmen, rifles at the ready. They seemed poised, as if awaiting a command.

There was only one entrance to the *Abort*, at the near end of the small wooden frame building. Von Reiter, the camp commander, a gray overcoat tinged with a red satin lining more suitable for a night at the opera draped haphazardly across his shoulders, stood outside the single *Abort* doorway.

As usual, he had his riding crop in his hand, but now he repeatedly smacked it against the polished black leather of his boots. Fritz Number One, at rigid attention, stood a few paces away. Von Reiter ignored the ferret as he watched the kriegies hurry past him. Other than the nervousness with the riding crop, Von Reiter stood like one of the sentinel fir trees that lined the distant forest, oblivious to the hour and the cold. The commandant's eyes darted over the rows of men forming on the assembly ground, almost as if he were intent on counting them all himself, or as if he recognized each face as it passed by.

The men gathered into blocks and came to attention with their backs to the *Abort* and the squad of soldiers surrounding it. A few kriegies tried to twist about and see what was happening behind them, but the "eyes front!" command came barked from the center of the formation. This made them all nervous; no one likes having armed men standing behind them. Tommy listened carefully, but could not make out what was happening in the *Abort*. He shook his head slightly, and whispered to no one and everyone at the same time:

"That's a helluva place to dig a tunnel. Who thought that baby up?"

A man behind him answered, "The usual geniuses, I guess. Situation normal . . ."

"All fucked up . . ." a couple of voices spoke in unison.

Then yet another man in the formation added, "Yeah, but how the hell did the Krauts ever find it? Man, it's the best, worst place to be digging. If you could stand the smell . . ."

"Yeah, if . . ."

"Some guys would be willing to crawl through the shits to get out of here," Tommy said.

"Not me," he heard in reply. But another voice just as quickly disagreed.

"Man, if I could get outta here, I'd crawl through a lot worse stuff. Hell, I'd do it just for a twenty-four-hour pass. Just for a day, Christ, even a half day on the other side of that damn wire."

"You're crazy," the first man said.

"Yeah, maybe. But stayin' in this dump ain't doing much for my overall state of sanity, neither."

A number of voices murmured in agreement.

"There goes the old man," one of the airmen whispered. "And Clarkie, too. Looks like they got fire in their eyes."

Tommy Hart saw the Senior American Officer and his second in command pace across the front of the formations, then swing past the men, heading toward the *Abort*. MacNamara marched with the intensity of a West Point parade ground drill instructor. Major Clark, whose legs seemed half the size of the senior officer's, struggled to keep pace. It might have been slightly comic were it not for the hard look on each man's face.

"Maybe they can figure out what this is all about," the same voice muttered. "I hope so. Man, my feet are already soaked. I can hardly feel my toes."

But an immediate answer was not forthcoming. The men remained at attention for another thirty minutes, occasionally shuffling their feet against the cold, shivering. Thankfully, the drizzle stopped, but the skies above them lightened only dully as the sun rose, revealing a wide gray world.

After nearly an hour, the kriegies saw Colonel MacNamara and Major Clark accompany Oberst Von Reiter through the front gate, and disappear into the camp office building. They had still not been counted, which Tommy found surprising. He did not know what was going on, and his curiosity was energized. Anything out of the routine of camp life, he thought, was to be welcomed in its own way. Anything that was different, anything that reminded them that they were not isolated. In a way, he hoped the Germans had discovered another tunnel. He liked acts of defiance, even if he wasn't altogether comfortable issuing them himself. He liked it when Bedford threw the bread to the Russians. He was pleased, although surprised, at Lincoln Scott's rashness at the wire. He liked anything that reminded him that he wasn't merely a kriegie, but an actual person. But these things were few and far between.

After another lengthy wait, Fritz Number One came to the head of the formations. In a loud voice, he announced, "At ease. The morning count will be delayed for a few moments more. You may smoke. Do not leave your position."

The captain from New York called out, "Hey, Fritz! Whadda

'bout letting us go take a leak. Some of the guys gotta go real bad."

Fritz Number One shook his head sharply.

"Not allowed. Not yet. *Verboten*," he said.

The kriegies grumbled, but relaxed. The smell of cigarette smoke wafted about him. Tommy, however, noticed that Fritz Number One, who by all rights should have immediately cadged a smoke off some prisoner, remained standing, his eyes searching over the columns of men. After a few seconds, Tommy saw that Fritz Number One had spotted the man he was looking for, and the ferret strode forward toward the men from Hut 101.

Fritz Number One approached Lincoln Scott.

"Lieutenant Scott," the ferret said in a normal, but low voice, "you will please to accompany me to the commandant's office."

Tommy saw the black airman hesitate for an instant, then step forward. "If you wish," Scott said.

The pilot and the ferret then quick-marched across the assembly ground and through the front gate. Two guards swung it open for them, closing it just as swiftly behind them.

For a second or two, the formations of men were quiet. Then abruptly voices picked up, like the wind right before a storm.

"What the hell?"

"What do the Krauts want with him?"

"Hey, anybody know what fer Christ's sake is going on?"

Tommy kept quiet. Now his curiosity was racing, fueled by the voices around him. It's all very strange, he thought. Strange because it is out of the ordinary. Strange because nothing like this has ever happened before.

The men continued grumbling and muttering for nearly another hour. By now, whatever morning was going to penetrate the gloomy skies had managed its weak efforts and whatever warmth the day could promise had arrived. Not much, Tommy thought. The men were hungry. Many had to go to the toilets. All were wet and cold.

And all were curious.

A few moments later, Fritz Number One again appeared at the gate. The guards opened it and he half-ran through, heading straight for the men from Hut 101. Fritz Number One was slightly red-faced, but there was nothing in his approach that indicated anything about what was going on.

"Lieutenant Hart," he said, coughing back short gasps of breath, "would you please come with me now to the commandant's office?"

From directly behind him, Tommy heard a man whisper, "Tommy, get the lowdown on what's going on, will ya?"

"Please, Lieutenant Hart, right away, please," Fritz Number One pleaded. "I do not like to keep Herr Oberst Von Reiter waiting."

Tommy stepped forward to the ferret's side.

"What's going on, Fritz?" he asked quietly.

"Just to hurry please, lieutenant. The *Oberst* will explain."

Fritz Number One was quick-marching through the gate.

Tommy stole a rapid glance around him. The gate creaked as it swung shut behind his back, and he had the distinctly eerie sensation that he was walking directly through a door that he'd never known existed. He wondered for a moment whether the sensation he felt at that second was the same as what the men who bailed out of their stricken planes experienced, as they tumbled free into the cold, clear air, everything they'd known before as familiar and safe abruptly cut away from them in that instant of panic, leaving only the single passionate desire to live. He decided it was.

He took a deep breath, and hurried up the wooden steps to the commandant's office, his boots resounding off the floor like a volley of rifle shots.

On the wall directly behind the commandant's desk was the obligatory full-color portrait of Adolf Hitler. The artist had captured the *Führer* with a distant, exulting look in his eyes, as if he were searching Germany's idealized future and saw it to be perfect and prosperous. Tommy Hart thought it was a look few Germans had anymore. B-17s in the daytime and Lancasters at night in repeated waves make the future look less rosy. To the right of the portrait of Hitler was a smaller picture of a group of German officers standing beside the charred and twisted wreckage of a Russian Topolev fighter. A smiling Von Reiter was in the center of the group in the photograph.

The commandant, however, wore no smile as Tommy walked to the center of the small room. Von Reiter was seated behind his oaken desk, a telephone at his right hand, some loose papers on the blotter in front of him, next to the ubiquitous riding crop. Colonel MacNamara and Major Clark stood to his left. There was no sign of Lieutenant Scott.

Von Reiter stared across at Tommy and took a sip from a delicate china cup of steaming ersatz coffee.

"Good morning, lieutenant," he said.

Tommy clicked his heels together and saluted. He stole a single glance at the two American officers, but they were standing aside, their posture alert, but at ease. They, too, wore stern, rigid expressions.

"Herr Oberst," Tommy answered.

"Your superiors have some questions for you, lieutenant," Von Reiter said. His English was accented but excellent, every bit as good as Fritz Number One's, although the ferret could probably have passed for American with the slang he'd acquired slinking around the American compound. Tommy doubted the aristocratic Von Reiter was interested in learning the words to "Cats on the Roof." Tommy half-turned to face the two Americans.

"Lieutenant Hart," Colonel MacNamara began slowly. "How well do you know Captain Vincent Bedford?"

"Vic?" Tommy replied. "Well, we're in the same hut. I've made trades with him. He always gets the better of the bargain. I've spoken with him a few times about home, and complained about the weather or the food—"

"Is he a friend of yours, lieutenant?" Major Clark abruptly demanded.

"No more, no less than anyone in the camp, sir," Tommy answered sharply. Major Clark nodded.

"And," Colonel MacNamara steadily continued, "how would you characterize your relationship with Lieutenant Scott?"

"I have no relationship, sir. No one does. I made an effort to be friendly, but that was it."

MacNamara paused, then asked: "You witnessed the altercation between the two men in their bunk room?"

"No sir. I arrived after the men had been separated, only seconds before yourself and Major Clark entered the room."

"But you heard threats made?"

"Yes sir."

The SAO nodded. "And then, I'm told, there was a subsequent incident at the wire. . . ."

"I would not characterize it as an incident, sir. Perhaps a misunderstanding of the rules that might have had fatal results."

"Which, I'm told, you prevented by shouting a warning."

"Perhaps. It happened swiftly."

"Would you say that this incident served to increase or further exacerbate already tense feelings between the two officers?"

Tommy paused. He had no idea what the men were driving at, but told himself to keep his answers short. He could see that both Americans and the German were paying close attention to everything he said. He warned himself inwardly to be cautious.

"Sir, what's going on?" he asked.

"Just answer the question, lieutenant."

"There was tension between the men, sir. I believe it was racial in nature, although Captain Bedford denied that to me in one conversation. Whether it was increased or not, I wouldn't know."

"They hated each other, correct?"

"I could not say that."

"Captain Bedford hates the Negro race and made no effort to hide that fact from Lieutenant Scott, is that not true?"

"Captain Bedford is outspoken, sir. On any number of topics."

"Would you think it safe," Colonel MacNamara asked slowly, "to say that Lieutenant Scott would likely have felt threatened by Captain Bedford?"

"It would probably be hard for him not to. But—"

Major Clark snorted an interruption. "The Negro is here for less than two weeks and already we have a fight where he takes a cheap shot at a brother officer, and higher-ranking to boot, we have probably well-founded accusations of theft, and then an alleged incident at the wire . . ." He stopped abruptly, then asked, "You're from Vermont—correct, Hart? There are no Negro problems in Vermont that I know of, correct?"

"Yes sir. Manchester, Vermont. And we don't have any problems that I'm aware of, sir. But we're not currently in Manchester, Vermont."

"That is obvious, lieutenant," Clark said sharply, his voice rising slightly with anger.

Von Reiter, who had been sitting quietly, spoke out briskly. "I would think the lieutenant would be an appropriate choice for your task, colonel, judging from the careful way he answers your inquiries. You are a lawyer, not a soldier, lieutenant, this is true?"

"I was in my final year at Harvard Law School when I enlisted. Right after Pearl Harbor."

"Ah." Von Reiter smiled, but humorlessly. "Harvard. A justly famed institution for learning. I attended the University of Heidelberg, myself. I intended to become a physician, until my country summoned me."

Colonel MacNamara coughed, clearing his voice. "Were you aware of Captain Bedford's combat record, lieutenant?"

"No sir."

"A Distinguished Flying Cross with oak clusters. A Purple Heart. A Silver Star for action above Germany. He did his tour of twenty-five, then volunteered for a second tour. More than thirty-two missions before being shot down—"

Von Reiter interrupted. "A most decorated and impressive flier, lieutenant. A war hero." The commandant wore a shining black iron cross on a ribbon around his own neck, and he fingered it as he spoke. "An adversary that any fighter of the air would respect."

"Yes sir," Tommy said. "But I don't understand . . ."

Colonel MacNamara took a deep breath and then spoke sullenly, in a voice of barely restrained rage.

"Captain Vincent Bedford of the United States Army Air Corps was murdered sometime after lights out last night here within the confines of Stalag Luft Thirteen."

Tommy's jaw dropped open slightly.

"Murdered, but how . . ."

"Murdered by Lieutenant Lincoln Scott," MacNamara said briskly.

"I don't believe—"

"There is ample evidence, lieutenant," Major Clark interrupted sharply. "Enough to court-martial him today."

"But . . ."

"Of course, we won't do that. Not today, at least. But soon. We expect to form a military court of justice shortly to hear the charges against Lieutenant Scott. The Germans" and here MacNamara made a small gesture toward Commandant Von Reiter—"have consented to allow us to do this. In addition, they will comply with the court's sentence. Whatever it might be."

Von Reiter nodded. "We request only that I be allowed to assign an officer to observe all details of the case, so that he may report the outcome to my superiors in Berlin. And, of course, should a firing squad be necessitated, we would provide the men. You Americans, surely, would be present at any execution, though—"

"A what?" Tommy blurted. "You're joking, sir."

No one, of course, was joking, a fact he understood instantly. He took a deep breath. His head seemed to spin dizzily, and he struggled to keep control. He detected that his voice had risen when he asked, "But what do you want from me, sir?" He directed the question to Colonel MacNamara.

"We would like you to represent the accused, lieutenant."

"Me, sir? But I'm not—"

"You have the legal knowledge. Your bunk is filled with texts on the law, surely there's something there about military justice. And your task is relatively simple. You need merely to make certain that Lieutenant Scott's military and constitutional rights are protected while justice is done."

"But, sir—"

Major Clark snapped his interruption sharply: "Look, Hart. It's an open-and-shut case. We have evidence. We have witnesses. We have motive. We have opportunity. We have well-documented hatred. And we damn well don't want a riot on our hands when the rest of the camp finds out that a damn nig . . ." he started, then stopped, paused, and rephrased his sentence ". . . when the camp finds out Lieutenant Scott killed an extremely popular, well-known, and highly respected, decorated, and dedicated officer. And killed him in a brutal, savage fashion. We will not have a lynching, lieutenant. Not while we are in command. The Germans want to avoid this, as well. Hence, due process. Of which you are to be an important part. Someone needs to make a show of defending Scott. And that, lieutenant, is an order. From me, from Colonel MacNamara, and from Oberst Von Reiter, as well."

Tommy Hart inhaled deeply. "Yes sir," he said. "I understand."

"Good." Major Clark nodded. "I will personally handle the prosecution of the case. I would think a week, ten days from now, we can schedule our tribunal. Best to get this over with quickly, commandant."

Von Reiter nodded. "Yes," the German said, "we should move with diligence. To hurry might be unseemly. But lengthy delay would create as many problems. Let us move with all due speed."

Colonel MacNamara turned to the commandant. "I will have the names of the officers selected for the court-martial tribunal in your hands by this afternoon."

"Excellent."

"And," the colonel continued, "I think we can safely conclude business by the end of the month. Early June at the latest."

"That, too, would be acceptable. I have already summoned a man whom I will designate as the liaison officer between your proceedings and the Luftwaffe. Hauptmann Visser is en route. He will be here within the hour. . . ."

"Excuse me, colonel," Tommy said quietly.

MacNamara pivoted in his direction. "Yes, lieutenant? What is it?"

"Well, sir," Tommy spoke with some hesitation, "I understand the need for tying this up rapidly, but I have a few requests, sir. If that's okay. . . ."

"What is it, Hart?" Clark spoke briskly.

"Well, I need to know precisely what this 'evidence' you have consists of, sir. And the names of any witnesses. I don't mean any disrespect, major, but I also need to personally inspect the murder scene. I may also need someone to help me prepare a defense. Even for an open-and-shut case."

"Someone to help? Whatever for?"

"Someone to share the burden. This would be traditional, sir, in any capital case."

Clark frowned. "Perhaps back in the States. I'm not sure that's totally necessary given our circumstances here at Stalag Luft Thirteen. Who do you have in mind, lieutenant?"

Tommy took another deep breath. "That would be Flying Officer Hugh Renaday of the RAF. He's in the North Compound."

Clark instantly shook his head. "I don't think involving the British is a good idea. This is our dirty laundry and it's best we wash it by ourselves. Out of the question . . ."

But Von Reiter let a small grin slip across his face.

"*Herr* major," the commandant said, "I think it wise that Lieutenant Hart be given every possible accommodation in the difficult and delicate task that he has been assigned. This way any impropriety will be avoided clearly. His request for assistance is not unreasonable, no? Flying Officer Renaday, lieutenant, he has some experience in matters of this sort?"

Tommy nodded. "Yes sir."

Von Reiter nodded in return. "Then I think perhaps he is an excellent suggestion. And, Colonel MacNamara, his assistance will not mean that another of your officers will have to be compromised by this unfortunate incident and its inevitable outcome."

Tommy thought this an interesting statement, but kept quiet.

The SAO narrowed his gaze at the German, taking his time to assess what the commandant had said. "You are correct, *Herr Oberst*. This makes perfectly good sense. And having a Brit involved, instead of another American—"

"He's a Canadian, sir."

"Canadian? All the better. Request approved, then, lieutenant."

"The crime scene, sir. I need to—"

"Yes, of course. As soon as the body is removed. . . ."

Tommy was surprised. "The body hasn't been removed?"

"No, Hart. The Germans will detail a squad as soon as the commandant orders it."

"Then I want to see it. Right now. Before anything has been disturbed. Has the scene been secured?"

Von Reiter, still with the faintest of smiles on his lips, nodded. "It has not been disturbed since the unfortunate discovery of Captain Bedford's remains, lieutenant. I can assure you of that. Other than myself, and your two superior officers, no one has examined the location. Except, perhaps, the accused."

He continued to smile. "I must hasten to inform you, that your request is precisely the same as that made by Hauptmann Visser when I spoke with him early this morning."

"And the evidence, Major Clark?" Tommy asked.

The major snarled, staring at Hart with distaste.

"I will compile it and make it available to you at the earliest appropriate moment."

"Thank you, sir. And I have another request, as well, sir."

"Another request? Hart, your task here is simple. Protect the accused's rights with honor. No more, no less."

"Of course, sir. But I think I need to speak with Lieutenant Scott to do that. Where is he?"

Von Reiter continued to smile, obviously taking some pleasure in the discomfort of the American officers.

"He has been escorted to the cooler, lieutenant. You may see him after you have inspected the crime scene."

"With Flying Officer Renaday, please, sir."

"As you requested."

There was a boxlike intercom on the desk in front of Von Reiter, and he reached out to it, pressing a switch. A buzzer went off in the adjoining office, a door immediately swung open, and Fritz Number One entered the room.

"Corporal, you will accompany Lieutenant Hart to the North Compound, where the two of you will find Flying Officer Hugh Renaday. Then you will escort these two men to the *Abort* please, where you discovered the remains of Captain Bedford, and provide whatever assistance they might need. When they have completed their inspection of the body and the area surrounding it, please take Lieutenant Hart to see the prisoner."

Fritz Number One saluted sharply. *"Ja wohl, Herr Oberst!"* he blurted in German.

Tommy turned toward the two American officers. But before he could say anything else, MacNamara raised his hand to his cap brim in a slow salute.

"You are dismissed, lieutenant," he said slowly.

Phillip Pryce and Hugh Renaday were in their bunk room inside the British compound when Tommy Hart, accompanied by Fritz Number One, appeared at the door. Pryce was balancing in a stiff-backed, rough-hewn wooden chair, with his feet perched up on the top of the black steel potbellied stove in a corner of the bunk room. He had a stub of a pencil in one hand and a book of crossword puzzles in the other. Renaday was sitting a few feet away, a dog-eared Penguin paperback of Agatha Christie's *The ABC Murders* in his hands. They both looked up when Tommy hovered in the doorway and immediately burst into smiles.

"Thomas!" Pryce almost shouted. "Unexpected! But always welcome, even unannounced! Come in, come in! Hugh, to the cupboard quickly, let us entertain our guest with some appropriate foodstuff! Have we any chocolate left?"

"Hello, Phillip," Tommy said quickly. "Hugh. Actually, I'm not making a social call."

Pryce dropped his feet to the floor with a thud.

"Not social? Ah, most intriguing. And by the distinctively harried look on your young face, something of significance, I'll wager."

"What's the problem, Tommy?" Hugh Renaday asked, standing. "You look like, well, you look like something's up. Hey, Fritz! Take a couple of smokes and wait outside, how about it?"

"I cannot leave, Mr. Renaday," Fritz Number One said.

Hugh Renaday stepped forward, while Phillip Pryce also stood.

"Is there a problem at home, Tommy? With your folks or the famous Lydia that we've heard so much about? Surely no . . ."

Tommy shook his head vigorously. "No, no. Not at home."

"Then what is the matter, lad?"

Tommy spun about. The other occupants of the hut were out, which he thought was fortunate. He did not expect the news of the murder to be secret long, but he recognized that it might be wise to conceal it as long as possible.

"There's been an incident over in the American camp," Tommy said. "I have been ordered by the SAO to help with what for lack of another word I'll call the 'investigation.' "

"What sort of incident, Tommy?" Pryce asked.

"A death, Phillip."

"Holy mother, this sounds like trouble," Hugh Renaday burst out. "How can we help you, Tommy?"

Tommy smiled at the hulking Canadian. "Well, actually, Hugh, they've authorized me to enlist you. You're supposed to accompany me, right now. Kind of like an aide-de-camp."

Renaday looked surprised.

"Why me?"

Tommy grinned. "Because idleness is the devil's playground, Hugh. And you've been far too idle for far too long."

Renaday snorted. "That's cute," he said. "But not an answer."

"In other words, my brusque Canadian compatriot," Pryce interrupted briskly, "Tommy will fill you in shortly."

"Thank you, Phillip. Exactly."

"Is there something I can do in the interim?" Pryce asked. "Eager does not describe my enthusiasm."

Tommy smiled. "Yes. But we'll have to talk later."

"Very secretive, Tommy. Hush, hush and all that. You have definitely pricked my not insubstantial curiosity. Don't know if this old heart could actually stand to wait too long."

"Bear with me, Phillip. But things are just happening. I got authorization for Hugh to help. It was just a guess, but I didn't think they would allow me anyone else. At least not officially. Especially a high-ranking British officer. And especially one who was a famous barrister before the war. But Hugh will fill you in on everything we learn, and then we can talk."

The older man nodded. "Rather have a direct hand in whatever it is," he said. "But without details, I can still see your point. This death, then, I take it, has some importance? A political importance, perhaps?"

Tommy nodded.

Fritz Number One shuffled his feet. "Please, Lieutenant Hart. Mr. Renaday is ready. We should make our way now to the *Abort*."

Both the Canadian and the British officer looked surprised again.

"An *Abort*?" Pryce asked.

Tommy stepped into the room and reached out and grasped the older man's hand. "Phillip," he said quietly, "you have already been a better friend than I could have ever asked for. I will need all your expertise and all your capabilities over the next few days. But Hugh will have to provide the details. I hate to make you wait, but I can't see any other way. At least, not yet."

Pryce smiled. "But, my dear boy, I understand. Military foolishness. I will wait here like the perfect soldier that I am, awaiting your pleasure. Exciting, what? Something truly different. Ah, delightful. Hugh, seize your coat and return fairly well stuffed with information. Until then, I will stay warm by the fire, allowing myself to fantasize with anticipation."

"Thanks, Phillip," Tommy said.

Then he quietly leaned forward, and whispered into Pryce's ear the words: "Lincoln Scott, the Negro fighter pilot. And do you remember the Scottsboro boys?"

Pryce inhaled sharply. The quick intake of wind degenerated into a hacking cough. He nodded with comprehension.

"Damn damp weather. I recall that case. Infamous. Go swiftly," he said.

Renaday was swinging his thick arms into his coat. He also grabbed a pencil and a thin and precious pad of drawing paper.

"All set, Tommy," he said. "Let's go."

The two airmen, with Fritz Number One urging them to hurry, marched toward the American compound. Tommy Hart filled in Renaday on what he'd learned in the commandant's office, and briefed him on both the fight and the incident at the wire. Renaday listened carefully, asking an occasional question, but mostly simply absorbing the details.

As the gate to the South Compound swung open for them, Renaday whispered: "Tommy, it's been six years since I was at a real crime scene. And what we had for murders out in Manitoba were drunken cowboys knifing each other in bars. Usually there wasn't much to process, because the culprit would be sitting there covered with blood, beer, and Scotch."

"That's okay, Hugh," Tommy said quietly. "I've *never* been to a crime scene."

The morning count had obviously been accomplished while he'd been at the commandant's office. The men had been dismissed, but still dozens of kriegies milled about the assembly yard, smoking, waiting, aware that something unusual was going on. The German guards maintained their tight ring around the *Abort*. The kriegies watched the Germans; the Germans watched them.

The clumps of airmen stepped aside carefully as Tommy, Hugh, and Fritz Number One approached the latrine. The guard squadron allowed them to pass. But Tommy hesitated at the door.

"Fritz," he asked, "you found the captain?"

The ferret nodded. "Shortly after five this morning."

"And what did you do, then?"

"I immediately ordered two *Hundführers* who were patrolling the perimeter of the camp to come to the *Abort* and make certain no one entered. Then I went to inform the commandant."

"How was it you found the body?"

"I heard a noise. I was just outside Hut 103. I did not move quickly, lieutenant. I was uncertain what I'd heard."

"What sort of noise?"

"A cry. Then nothing."

"Why did you go into the *Abort*?"

"It seemed that the noise had come from there."

Tommy nodded. "Hugh?"

"Did you see anyone else?" the Canadian asked.

"No. I heard some doors closing. That is all."

Renaday started to ask a second question, then stopped. He thought for an instant, then demanded: "After you found the body, the *Abort* was left for a time. How long was it before you returned with the two *Hundführers*?"

The ferret looked up into the gray sky, trying to add up the time. "A few minutes, certainly, flying officer. I did not want to blow my whistle and raise an alarm until I had informed the commandant. The men were located at the wire just outside Hut 116. A few seconds, maybe a minute to explain to them the urgency of the situation. Five minutes, perhaps. So, in total, perhaps as many as ten minutes."

"Are you certain that there was no one else about when you discovered the body?"

"I did not see anyone, Mr. Renaday. After I spotted the body, and after I made certain Captain Bedford was dead, I used my torch to quickly sweep the building. But the night was still upon us, and there are many shadowy places a man could hide. So I cannot be completely certain."

"Thank you, Fritz. One last thing . . ."

The ferret stepped forward.

"I want you to go find us a camera. Thirty-five millimeter, loaded with film. With a flash attachment and at least a half-dozen flashbulbs. Right now."

"Impossible, flying officer! I know of no—"

Renaday instantly stepped forward, pushing his face up toward the lanky ferret's nose.

"I know you know who's got one. Now, go get it, and bring it here without letting anyone know what the hell you're doing. Got that? Or would you prefer it if we marched over to the commandant's office and demanded it?"

Fritz Number One looked panicked for a moment, trapped between duty and the desire to be correct. Finally, he nodded.

"One of the tower guards is an amateur photographer. . . ."

"Ten minutes. We'll be inside."

Fritz Number One saluted, turned on his heel, and hurried away.

"That was smart, Hugh," Tommy Hart said.

"Figured we might need some pictures." Then Hugh turned to Tommy and seized him by the arm. "But look, Tommy. What's our job here, after all?"

Tommy shook his head.

"I'm not sure. All I can tell you is that Lincoln Scott is going to be accused of doing what's inside the *Abort*. And the major says they've got all the evidence they need to convict him. I suppose we should try to help him as much as we can."

And with that, the two men stepped up to the door to the latrine.

"Ready?" Tommy asked.

"Forward the light brigade," Hugh replied. "Theirs not to reason why . . ."

"Theirs but to do and die," Tommy finished the refrain. He thought this might have been a poor verse to select at that moment, but he did not say this out loud.

The *Abort* was a narrow building, with a single door located at one end. The wood-plank floor of the building was raised up several feet, so that one had to walk up a short flight of rough steps to enter. This was to allow space beneath the privies for huge green metal drums that collected the waste. There were six stalls, each with a door and partitions to provide privacy. The seats were hewn from hardwood and polished to a shine by use and near-constant scrubbing. Ventilation was provided by slatted windows up just beneath the roof line. Twice each day *Abort* details carted off the barrels of waste to an area in a corner of the camp where it was burned. What wouldn't burn was dumped in trenches and covered with lime. About the only thing the Germans provided the kriegies in abundance was lime.

A stranger walking into an *Abort* for the first time might have been overcome by the fetid thickness of the smell, but the kriegies were used to it, and within a few days of their arrival at Stalag Luft Thirteen, the airmen learned that it was one of the few places in the camp where one could go and have a few minutes of relative solitude. What most of the men hated was the lack of toilet paper. The Germans didn't provide any, and the Red Cross parcels were skimpy, preferring to send foodstuffs. Men used any possible scrap of paper.

Tommy and Hugh paused in the doorway.

The familiar stench filled their nostrils. There was no electricity in the *Abort*, so it was dim and dark, lit only by the gray overcast sky that filtered through the high slatted windows.

Renaday hummed briefly, a nameless snatch of music, before stepping forward.

"Tommy," he said, "think for a second. It was five in the morning, right? That's what Fritz said?"

"Correct," Tommy answered, keeping his voice low. "What the hell was Vic doing here? The inside toilets were still operating. The Krauts don't shut off the plumbing until midmorning. And this place would have been pitch black. Except for the searchlight that sweeps over it . . . what? . . . every minute, maybe ninety seconds. You wouldn't be able to see a thing."

"So, you wouldn't come out here unless you had some good reason. . . ."

"And going to the bathroom isn't the reason."

Both men nodded.

"What're we looking for, Hugh?"

Hugh sighed. "Well, they teach you in cop school that the crime scene can tell you everything that happened if you look closely enough. Let's see what we can see."

In unison, the two men stepped into the *Abort*. Tommy swung his eyes right and left, trying to absorb what had taken place, but uncertain in that second precisely what he was looking for. He moved ahead of Renaday, and pushed forward. He paused just before reaching the final stall in the row, pointing down at the floor. "Look there, Hugh," he said quietly. "Doesn't that look like a footprint? Or at least part of one?"

Renaday knelt down. On the wooden floor of the latrine was the clear outline of the front of a boot heading toward the *Abort* stall. The Canadian touched the outline gingerly. "Blood," he said. He looked up slowly, his eyes on the door to the last stall. "In there, I guess," he spoke out with a small, quick inhale of breath. "Check the door first, see if there's anything else."

"Like what?"

"Like a bloody fingerprint."

"No. Not that I can see."

Hugh got out his sketch pad and pencil. He quickly started to draw the interior layout of the *Abort*. He also noted the shape and direction of the footprint.

Tommy pushed the stall door open slowly, like a child peeking into his parents' room in the morning.

"Jesus," he whispered sharply.

Vincent Bedford was sitting on the privy seat, his pants

pulled down to his ankles, half-naked. But his upper torso was thrust back against the wall, and his head lolled slightly to the right. His eyes were open wide in shock. His chest and shirt were coated with deep maroon streaks of blood.

His throat had been cut. On the left side of his neck the skin was laid open in a gory flap.

One of Trader Vic's fingers was partially severed and hung limply at his side. There was also a slashing cut in his right cheek, and his shirt was partially ripped.

"Poor Vic," Tommy said quietly.

The two airmen stared at the dead body. Both had seen a great deal of death, and seen it in horrific form, and they were not sickened by what they witnessed in the *Abort*. The sensation both men felt in that second was different, it was a shock of context. They had both seen men ripped asunder by bullets, explosions, and shrapnel; eviscerated, decapitated, and burned alive by the vagaries of battle. Both men had seen the viscera and other bloody remains of turret gunners actually hosed out of the Plexiglas cocoons where they'd died. But all those deaths came within the context of battle, where they both expected to see death at its most brutal. In the *Abort* it was different; here a man who should have been alive was dead. To die violently on the toilet was something altogether shocking and genuinely frightening.

"Jesus is right," Hugh said.

Tommy noticed that the flap over the chest pocket of Bedford's blouse was lifted at the corner. He thought that would have been where Trader Vic kept his pack of smokes. He leaned across toward the body and lightly tapped the pocket. It was empty.

Both men continued to examine the body. Tommy kept reminding himself inwardly to measure, to assess, to read the portrait in front of him as he would the page of a textbook, carefully, critically. He reminded himself of all the criminal cases he'd read in so many casebooks, and how often a small detail resulted in the crucial observation. Guilt or innocence hanging on the tiniest of elements. The glasses that fell from Leopold's jacket. Or was it Loeb's? He couldn't remember. Staring across at Vincent Bedford's body, he felt completely inadequate. He tried to recollect his last conversation with the

Mississippian, but this, too, seemed lost. He realized that the body tucked into the privy in front of him was quickly becoming the same as so many other bodies. Something simply shunted away and relegated to nightmare, joining the throngs of other dead and mutilated men inhabiting the dreams of the living. Yesterday it was Vincent Bedford, captain. Decorated bomber pilot and hotshot trader of campwide renown. Now he was dead, and no longer a part of Tommy Hart's waking life.

Tommy let out a long, slow draft of breath.

He searched the landscape of murder in front of him.

And then he saw what was wrong.

"Hugh," he said very quietly, "I think I see a problem."

Renaday quickly looked up from his sketch pad. "Me, too," he replied. "Clearly . . ." But he did not finish his statement.

Both men heard a noise from outside the *Abort*. There were German voices raised, sharp-edged and insistent. Tommy reached across and seized the Canadian by the arm.

"Not a word," he said. "Not until we can talk later."

"Bloody right. You got it," replied Renaday.

The two men then turned and walked from the latrine, stepping out into the chilled misty air, feeling the closeness of the smell and of what they'd seen drop away from them like so many droplets of moisture. Fritz Number One was standing by the front door, strapped in strict attention. In his hand at his side was a camera with a flash attachment.

A foot or two away, a German officer stood.

He was of modest height and build and seemed slightly older than Tommy, perhaps closing on thirty, although it was difficult to tell for certain because war aged men differently. His close-cropped thick hair was jet black, but tinged with premature gray around the temples, the same color as the leather trenchcoat he wore above a sharply pressed but slightly ill-fitted Luftwaffe uniform. He had very pale skin, and on one cheek he sported a jagged red scar just beneath the left eye. He wore a thin, well-groomed beard, which surprised Tommy. He knew that naval officers in the German military often wore beards, but he'd never seen a flier with one, even a sparse one such as this officer maintained. He had eyes that seemed knifelike, slicing their gaze forward.

The officer turned slowly toward the two kriegies, and Tommy saw that he was also missing his left arm.

The German paused, then asked: "Lieutenant Hart? Flying Officer Renaday?"

Both men came to attention. The German returned their salutes.

"I am Hauptmann Heinrich Visser," he said. His English was smooth, accented only slightly, but tinged with a slight hissing sound. He looked at Renaday sharply.

"Did you fly a Spitfire, flying officer?" he asked abruptly.

Hugh shook his head.

"Blenheim," he replied. "Second seat."

Visser nodded. "Good," he muttered.

"Does it make a difference?" Renaday demanded.

The German slid a small cruel smile across his face. When he did this, the scar seemed to change color slightly. And the smile was crooked. He made a small gesture with his right hand toward his missing arm.

"A Spitfire took this," he said. "He managed to come around behind me after I killed his wing man." He kept his voice even and controlled. "Forgive me," he added, still pacing each word carefully. "We are all imprisoned by our misfortunes, are we not?"

Tommy thought this a philosophical question better suited for a dinner table and a fine bottle of wine, or a rich liqueur, than standing outside a latrine and in the gory presence of a murdered body. He did not say this out loud. Instead, he asked:

"You are, I believe, *Hauptmann,* to be some sort of a liaison? Exactly what duties does this include?"

Hauptmann Visser relaxed, shuffling his feet momentarily in the muddy earth. He did not sport the riding boots that the commandant and his assistants preferred. Instead, he wore more utilitarian, but highly polished, black boots. "I am to witness all aspects of the situation, then make a report back to my superiors. We are bound by the Geneva Convention to account for the well-being of every Allied prisoner of war in our possession. But here, now, I am merely in charge of having the remains removed. Then perhaps it will be possible for us to, how do you say? Compare our findings? At a later juncture."

Hauptmann Visser turned toward Fritz Number One.

"This soldier was providing you with a camera?"

Hugh stepped forward. "It is customary in a murder investigation to take photographs of the body and of the crime scene location. That is why we demanded Fritz obtain the camera for us."

Visser nodded. "Yes, this is true. . . ."

He smiled. Tommy's first impression was that the *Hauptmann* seemed a dangerous man. His tone of voice seemed gentle and accommodating, but his eyes told a different tale.

"But only in a routine situation. This situation, alas, is decidedly not routine. Photographs could be smuggled out of the camp. Used for propaganda purposes. I cannot permit this."

He reached out his hand for the camera.

Tommy thought Fritz Number One was ready to pass out. His chest was drawn up, his spine rigid, his face pale. If he had dared to even take a breath of air in the *Hauptmann*'s presence, Tommy Hart had been unaware. The ferret immediately thrust the camera forward to the officer.

"I did not think, *Herr Hauptmann,*" Fritz Number One started. "I was told to assist the officers . . ."

Visser cut him off with a laconic wave.

"Of course, corporal. You would not see the danger in the same way that I might."

He turned back to the two Allied airmen. "That, precisely, is why I'm here."

Visser coughed, a dry, gentle sound. He turned, gesturing to one of the armed soldiers still ringing the *Abort*. He handed this man the camera. "See that it is returned to its owner," he said. The guard saluted, draped the camera's strap over his shoulder, and returned to his sentry position. Then Visser removed a package of cigarettes from his breast pocket. With surprising dexterity, he extricated one from the pack, returned the remainder to his pocket, and produced a steel lighter, which immediately flickered with flame.

He took a long drag on the cigarette, then looked up,

one eyebrow slightly raised: "You have completed your inspection?"

Tommy nodded.

"Good," the German said. "Then the corporal will accompany you to see your . . ." he hesitated, then, still smiling, said, "your charge. I will complete matters here."

Tommy Hart thought for a second, then whispered to the Canadian: "Hugh, stay here. Keep as close a watch on the *Hauptmann* as you can. And find out what he does with Bedford's body."

He looked over at the German. "I think it would be critical to have a physician examine Captain Bedford's remains. So that at least we can be certain of the medical aspects of this case."

"Damn right," Hugh said in an almost whisper. "No photos. No doctor. That's bloody-all fucked."

Hauptmann Visser shrugged, not acknowledging the Canadian's obscenity, though he surely heard it. "I do not think this would be practical, given the difficulties of our current situation. Still, I will examine the body carefully myself, and if I think your request is warranted, I will send for a German physician."

"An American would be better. Except we don't have one."

"Doctors make poor bombardiers."

"Tell me, *Hauptmann,* do you have knowledge in criminal investigations? Are you a policeman, *Hauptmann?* What do you call it? *Kriminalpolizei?*" Tommy threw the questions across the dirt ground.

Visser coughed again. He raised his face, still smiling crookedly.

"I look forward to our next meeting, lieutenant. Perhaps we will be able to speak at greater length at that point. Now, if you will excuse me, there appears much to do and not much time to accomplish it."

"Very good, *Herr Hauptmann,*" Tommy Hart said briskly. "But I have ordered Flying Officer Renaday to remain behind and personally witness your removal of Captain Bedford's remains."

Visser's eyes darted at Tommy Hart. But his face wore the same accommodating smile. He hesitated, then said:

"As you wish, lieutenant."

With that, the German stepped up, passed Tommy, and headed into the *Abort*. Renaday hurried after him. Fritz Number One waved wildly, now that the officer was out of sight, for Tommy to follow him, and the two men set off across the camp again. The milling knots of kriegies still gathered on the parade ground let them pass. Behind him, Tommy Hart could hear the men murmur with questions and speculation, and perhaps the first few tones of anger.

There was a single guard clutching a Schmeisser machine pistol standing outside the door to cooler cell number six. Tommy thought the man young, probably no more than eighteen or nineteen. And although he stood at attention, the guard seemed nervous, almost scared to be in such close proximity to the kriegies. This was not all that uncommon, Tommy thought. Some of the newer and younger, less experienced guards arrived at Stalag Luft Thirteen so propagandized about the *Terrorfliegers*—terror-fliers, according to the constant harangue of Nazi broadcasters—in the Allied armies that they believed the kriegies all to be bloodthirsty savages and cannibals. Of course, Tommy knew that the Allied air war was admittedly one that was predicated upon the twin concepts of savagery and terror. Night and day incendiary raids on the populated centers of the cities could hardly be considered something different. So he guessed that the unsettling thought of coming into close contact with a black *Terrorflieger* kept the teenager's finger dancing around the trigger of the Schmeisser.

The young guard wordlessly stepped aside, pausing only to unbolt the door, and Tommy stepped past him into the cell.

The walls and floor were a dull gray concrete. There was a single overhead bare lightbulb and a solitary window up in the corner of the six by nine room. It was dank, and seemed a good ten degrees colder inside the cell than outdoors, even on the overcast, rainy day.

Lincoln Scott had been sitting in a corner, his knees drawn up to his chest, across from the sole piece of furniture in the cell, a crusted metal pail for waste. He stood up rapidly as

Tommy entered the room, not exactly coming to attention, but certainly close to it, rigid and stiff.

"Hello, lieutenant," Tommy said briskly, almost officiously. "I tried to introduce myself to you the other day. . . ."

"I know who you are. What the hell is going on?" Lincoln Scott demanded sharply. His feet were bare and he wore only pants and blouse. There was no sign in the cell of either his sheepskin flight jacket or boots, and he must have had to fight to prevent himself from shivering.

Tommy hesitated.

"Haven't you been told—"

Scott interrupted. "I haven't been told a damn thing! I'm pulled out of formation and hustled into the commandant's office sometime this morning. Major Clark and Colonel MacNamara demand I hand over my jacket and boots. Then they question me for a half-hour about how much I hate that cracker bastard Bedford. After that, they asked me a couple of questions about last night, and then the next thing I know, I'm being escorted into this delightful place by a couple of Kraut goons. You're the first American I've seen since this morning's session with the colonel and the major. So, Lieutenant Hart, please tell me what in the hell is going on!"

Scott's voice was a mingling of restrained fury and confusion. Tommy was taken aback.

"Let me get this straight," he said slowly. "You haven't been informed by the major. . . ."

"I told you, Hart. I haven't been told a thing about anything! And what the hell am I doing in here? Under guard—"

"Vincent Bedford was murdered last night."

Scott's mouth opened and his eyes widened for an instant, before narrowing and fixing Tommy Hart with an unwavering gaze.

"Murdered? Here?"

"Major Clark informs me that you will be charged with this crime."

"Me?"

"Correct."

Scott leaned back against the cement wall, almost as if he'd been struck by a steady, surprise blow. The black flier took a deep breath, steadied himself, and once again stood ramrod straight.

"I've been assigned to help you prepare a defense to the charge." Tommy hesitated, then added, "And I must warn you that they consider this to be a capital offense."

Lincoln Scott nodded slowly before he replied. His shoulders were thrust back. His eyes fixed on Tommy Hart. He spoke slowly, deliberately, his voice slightly raised, as if he could weight each word with a passion that reached beyond the cement walls of the cooler cell, avoided the guard and his automatic weapon, and traveled past the rows of huts, over the wire, beyond the woods, and all the way across Europe to freedom.

"Mr. Hart . . ." he said, each word echoing in the small room, "if you believe nothing else, believe this: I did not kill Vincent Bedford. I may have wanted to. But I did not."

Lincoln Scott took another deep breath.

"I am innocent," he said.

Chapter Four

ENOUGH EVIDENCE

Tommy was momentarily taken aback by the forcefulness of Lincoln Scott's denial. He realized he must have looked astonished because the black flier immediately burst out:

"What's the matter, Hart?"

Tommy shook his head.

"Nothing."

"Liar," Scott snorted. "What was it that you expected me to say, lieutenant? That I killed the racist bastard?"

"No . . ."

"Then what?"

Tommy took a slow breath, organizing his thoughts. "I didn't know what you would say, Lieutenant Scott. I hadn't really considered the overall question of your guilt or innocence yet. Only that you are about to be charged with a crime."

Scott exhaled sharply, and took a few steps around the tiny cooler cell, shrugging his shoulders against the damp cold. "Can they do that?" he demanded suddenly.

"Do what?"

"Charge me with a crime. Here . . ." He swung his arm around as if encompassing the entirety of the prisoner-of-war camp.

"Yes, I believe so. We are technically still under the command of our own officers and members of the army and therefore subject to military discipline. I suppose, technically, you would argue that we are in a combat situation, and consequently controlled by the special regulations that imply. . . ."

98

Scott shook his head.

"It doesn't make sense," he said briskly. "Unless you're black. And then it makes perfectly reasonable sense. God-damn it! What the hell did I ever do to them? What conceivable evidence could they have?"

"I don't know. All I know is that Major Clark said there was ample evidence to convict you."

Scott snorted again. "Crap," he said. "How can there be any evidence when I had nothing to do with the cracker s.o.b.'s death? And how did it happen, anyway?"

Tommy started to answer, then stopped himself.

"Why don't we talk about you first," he said slowly. "Why don't you tell me what happened last night."

Scott pushed his back up against the gray cement cooler wall, staring up toward the tiny window for a moment, collecting his thoughts. Then he blew out slowly, turned his gaze on Tommy, and shrugged.

"There's not much to tell," he said. "After the afternoon count, I walked a bit. Then I ate alone. I read in my bunk until the Krauts turned off the lights. I rolled over and went to sleep. I woke up once in the middle of the night. Needed to take a leak, so I got up, lit a candle, and went down to the toilet. I did my business, returned to the bunk room, climbed back into the sack, and didn't wake up until the Germans started whistling and shouting. Next thing I knew, I was in here. Like I told you."

Tommy tried to imprint every word on his memory. He wished he'd at least brought a notepad and pencil with him, and cursed himself for his forgetfulness. He promised himself he would not make that mistake again.

"Did anyone see you? When you awoke?"

"How would I know?"

"Well, was anyone else in the toilet?"

"No."

"What were you doing there, that late?"

"I told you . . ."

"Nobody wakes up and starts walking around in the middle of the night, not here, not now, unless they're sick or they can't sleep because they're afraid of having nightmares.

Maybe back at home you might, but not here. So, which was it?"

Scott smiled briefly, but not at something he found amusing.

"Not exactly a nightmare," he replied. "Unless you consider my situation a nightmare, which, of course, is a distinct possibility. More an accommodation."

"What do you mean?"

"Well, Hart," Scott began slowly, making each word clear and distinct. "We aren't supposed to be outside after dark. *Verboten,* right? Krauts might use you for target practice. Of course, guys still do it. Sneak out, dodge the ferrets and the searchlights, slip into the other huts. The tunnel guys and the escape committee, they like to work at night. Clandestine, hush-hush meetings and secret work crews. But no one's supposed to know who they are and where they're working. Well, in a way, I'm sort of a highly specialized tunnel rat, myself."

"I don't get it."

"Of course you don't get it. I wouldn't expect you to," Scott said with barely restrained anger. Then he continued, speaking slowly, as if explaining something to a recalcitrant child. "White guys don't like sharing a toilet with a black man. Not everybody, of course. But enough. And those that don't like it, well, they take this very personally. For example, Captain Vincent Bedford. He took it extremely personally."

"What did he say?"

"He said to find another place. Of course, there *isn't* another place, but that small detail didn't seem to bother him much."

"How did you reply?"

Lincoln Scott laughed sharply.

"I didn't. Other than to tell him to go screw himself." Scott took a deep breath, watching Tommy's face. "Maybe this comes as a surprise to you, Hart? Have you ever been down South? They like things separate down there. White toilets and colored toilets. Anyway, if I go outside, try to use the *Abort,* I could get shot by some trigger-happy Kraut. So, what do I do? Wait until everyone's asleep, especially that redneck bastard, and I can't hear anybody moving in the corridor, and that's when I go. Quiet as can be. A secret piss, I suppose. At least a piss that doesn't draw too much attention. A piss that *avoids* all the Vincent Bedfords in this camp. That's why I was up in the middle of the night and sneaking around."

Tommy nodded. "I see," he said.

Scott turned to him angrily, thrusting his face directly in front of Tommy's. His eyes were narrowed, each word he spoke freighted with rage. "You don't see a thing!" he hissed. "You have no idea who I am! You don't have any idea what I've been through to get here! You are ignorant and unaware, Hart, just like everybody else! And I don't imagine that you have any real inclination to learn."

Tommy took a single step backward, then stopped. He could feel an anger of a different sort rising within him, and he returned Lincoln Scott's words with a thrust of his own.

"Maybe I don't," he said coldly. "But right now I'm the only thing standing between you and a firing squad. You might be smart to keep that in mind."

Scott turned away, suddenly facing the cement wall. He lowered his forehead to the damp surface, then raised his hands to the smooth cement, so that he seemed to be balancing there, as if his feet weren't on solid ground, but instead gripping the narrowest of tightropes.

"I don't need any help," he said quietly.

Still reverberating inwardly with an ill-defined rage, Tommy's first inclination was to tell the black flier that was fine with him, and walk out. He was perfectly happy returning to his books, his friends, and the routine of camp life he'd created for himself, simply letting each minute collect inexorably into an hour, and then add up into another day. Waiting for someone else to bring his imprisonment to a conclusion. A conclusion that held out the possibility of life, when so much that had happened to him had promised him death. He thought sometimes that he'd somehow managed to bluff his way to a pot in some uniquely deadly poker game, and having swept his winnings, even as meager as they were, into his arms, that he was unwilling to gamble again. Not even willing to look at a new hand of cards dealt to him. He had reached a most curious and unexpected position in life. He lived surrounded by a world where there was danger and threat in almost any action, no matter how simple or inconsequential. But by doing nothing, by remaining perfectly still and unnoticed on the small island of Stalag Luft Thirteen, he could survive. Like whistling past a graveyard. He started to open his mouth to tell Scott this, then stopped himself.

He took a deep breath, holding the air in his lungs.

Tommy thought in that second that it was the most curious of things: Two men could be standing next to each other, breathing the same air, but one could taste the future and freedom in each whiff, while the other could sense nothing but bitterness and hatred. And fear, as well, he considered, because fear is the cowardly brother of hatred.

And so, instead of telling Lincoln Scott to screw himself, Tommy replied, in as quiet a voice as the black flier had just used: "You are mistaken."

Scott did not move, but asked, "Mistaken, how?"

"Because everyone here in this camp needs help to some degree or another, and at the moment, you need it far more than anyone else."

Scott remained silent, listening.

"You don't have to like me," Tommy said. "You don't even have to respect me. You can hate me, for all it matters. But right now, you need me. And we will get along much better if you understand that."

Scott remained pensive for several long seconds, before finally speaking. He still kept his head to the wall, but his words were distinct. "I'm cold, Mr. Hart. I'm very cold. This place is freezing, and it's all I can do to keep my teeth from chattering. How about that for starters: Can you help me get something warm to put on?"

Tommy nodded. "Do you have any spare clothing, other than what they took from you this morning?"

"No. Just what I was shot down with."

"No extra socks or a sweater from home?"

Lincoln Scott laughed sharply, as if this was ridiculous. "No."

"Then I'll get some from somewhere else."

"I would appreciate it."

"What size shoes?"

"Twelve. But I'd prefer my flight boots back."

"I'll work on that. And the jacket, too. Have you eaten?"

"The Krauts gave me a hunk of stale bread and a cup of water this morning."

"All right. Food, too. And blankets."

"Can you get me out of here, Mr. Hart?"

"I will try. No promises."

The black flier turned from the wall and eyed Tommy with an unwavering gaze. Tommy thought that it was probably the same narrowing of focus that Lincoln Scott used when he fixed a German fighter in the sight of his Mustang's machine guns. "Make a promise, Hart," Scott said. "It won't hurt you. Show me what you can do."

"All I can tell you is that I'll do my best. I'll go talk to Mac-Namara after I leave here. But they're worried. . . ."

"Worried? About what?"

Tommy hesitated, then shrugged. "They used the words *riot* and *lynching*, lieutenant. They were afraid that friends of Vincent Bedford might want to avenge his death before they've convened their court and heard evidence and rendered a verdict."

Scott nodded slowly. He smiled wryly. "In other words, they would prefer to have their own lynching, but in their own time, and to make it all look as official as possible."

"It would seem that way. My job is to prevent it from happening quite the way they want."

"I shouldn't expect this will make you too popular," Scott said.

"Let's not worry about that. Let's stick to the case."

"What is their case?"

"That's my next task. To find out."

Scott paused, breathing hard, almost like a man who'd just sprinted a race.

"Do what you can, Mr. Hart," he said slowly. "I don't want to die here. Don't get me wrong about that. But if you ask me, whatever you do won't make a damn bit of difference, because my guess is that minds are already made up, and a verdict already rendered. Verdict. What a stupid word, Hart. What a truly stupid word. Do you know it comes from the Latin: to speak the truth. What a crock. What a lie. What a goddamn lie."

Tommy did not respond to this.

Scott suddenly looked down at his hands, turning them over, as if searching them, or inspecting the color.

"It has never made a difference, Hart, do you understand? Never!" Scott's voice rose sharply. "Goddamn never! Black is guilty, no matter what. It's always been like that. Maybe it will always be that way."

Scott ran his hand over the brown wool of his service blouse.

"We all thought this might make it different. This uniform. Every last goddamn one of us. Guys die, Hart; they die hard and some die horribly, but their last thoughts are of home and making a difference for everyone they're leaving behind. What a lie."

"I'm going to do my best," Tommy said again, but then stopped, realizing that whatever he said would sound pathetic.

Scott hesitated again, then he slowly turned his back.

"I appreciate your help," he said. "Whatever you can manage." The resignation in the black flier's voice implied that not only did he have no expectations of help, but that he doubted that any, if delivered, would have any impact.

Both men were quiet for a moment, before Scott said bitterly: "You know what's funny, Hart? I got shot down on April first. April first, nineteen forty-four. April Fool's Day. I got one of the Nazi bastards and my wingman got another and we had run out of ammo before the bastards jumped us. The two guys we shot down never managed to bail out. Two confirmed kills. I thought the joke was on them, but it would appear I am mistaken. Joke's on me. Maybe they did get me, after all."

Tommy Hart was about to ask a question, anything to keep the black flier talking, when he heard footsteps and voices entering the cooler corridor, beyond the thick wooden door of the cell. Both men turned at the sound of the door being unlocked and swinging open.

Four men entered the cell, crowding along the wall. Colonel MacNamara and Major Clark stood to the front, while Hauptmann Heinrich Visser and a corporal with a stenographer's pad hung to the rear. The two American officers returned salutes, then Clark took a single step forward.

"Lieutenant Scott," he said, briskly, "it is my unfortunate

duty to inform you that you are officially being charged with the premeditated murder of Captain Vincent Bedford of the United States Army Air Corps on this day, the twenty-second of May, nineteen forty-four. . . ."

Visser quietly translated for the stenographer, who scribbled furiously.

". . . As you have been made aware, I'm certain, by your counsel, this is a capital offense. If you are convicted, the court will either sentence you to be held in isolation until such time as U.S. military authorities can take charge of your person, or it may order your immediate execution, which our captors will perform. A preliminary session with the court has been scheduled for two days from today. You may enter a plea at that time."

Clark saluted and stepped back.

"I have done nothing!" Lincoln Scott burst out.

Tommy came to attention and spoke out sharply: "Sir, Lieutenant Scott denies totally having any connection whatsoever with the killing of Captain Bedford! He unequivocally states his innocence, sir! He also requests the return of his personal items and his immediate release into camp population."

"Out of the question," Clark replied.

Tommy Hart turned toward Colonel MacNamara. "Sir! How is Lieutenant Scott expected to prepare his defense to these erroneous charges from a cooler cell? This is completely unfair. Lieutenant Scott remains innocent until he is proven to be guilty, sir. Back home, even with the seriousness of the charges, he would still only be confined to barracks pending the trial. I'm asking nothing more."

Clark turned to MacNamara, who seemed to be considering the request. "Colonel, you can't . . . Who knows what trouble we would have? I think it best for all concerned if Lieutenant Scott remains here, where he is safe."

"Safe until you arrange a firing squad, major," Scott muttered.

MacNamara glared at the two lieutenants. He held up his hand. "That's enough," he said. "Lieutenant Hart, you are fundamentally correct. It is important that we maintain all available military rules. However, this is a special situation."

"Special, my ass," Scott said, glaring at the commanding officer. "Just typical Jim Crow justice."

"Watch your tongue when speaking to a superior officer!" Clark shouted. He and Scott snarled at each other.

Tommy stepped forward. "Sir! Where can he go? What can he do? We're all still prisoners here."

MacNamara paused, clearly pondering his alternatives. His face was flushed red and his jaw set, as if he was struggling with the legitimacy of the request weighed against the insubordination of the black flier. MacNamara took a deep breath and finally spoke in a low, controlled voice. "All right, Lieutenant Hart. Lieutenant Scott will be released into your custody after tomorrow morning's count. One night in the cooler, Scott. I will need to make an announcement to the camp, and we will need to clear a room for him. Alone. I won't have him in routine contact with any other men. During this time, he will be confined to the immediate area of his barracks unless he is in your presence and engaged in legitimate defense inquiries. I have your word on this?"

"Absolutely." It was not lost on Tommy that this arrangement was more or less exactly what Vincent Bedford had wanted. Before he'd been murdered.

"Scott, I need your word, as well," MacNamara hissed, then added, "As an officer and a gentleman, of course."

Lincoln Scott continued to glare at the colonel and the major.

"Of course . . ." he said. "As an officer, and a gentleman. You have my word." He snapped off his reply.

"Very good, then we will—"

"Sir," Tommy interrupted. "Lieutenant Scott's personal items, sir! When will they be returned to him?"

Major Clark shook his head. "They won't be. Find something new for him to wear, lieutenant, because the next time you see his shoes and his jacket will be at trial."

"Why is that, sir?" Hart asked.

"Because both items are covered with Vincent Bedford's blood," Major Clark replied with a sneer.

Neither Lincoln Scott nor Tommy Hart replied to this announcement. In the corner of the cooler cell the German stenographer's scratching pen finally paused after Heinrich Visser translated the final few words.

The late afternoon sky had darkened, and a light, cold rain was falling when Tommy exited the cooler block. The sky above his head promised nothing but more of the same. He hunched his shoulders and turned up his jacket collar and hurried toward the gate to the American compound. He spotted Hugh Renaday waiting for him, his back up against the exterior wall of Hut 111. Hugh was smoking furiously—Tommy saw him finish one cigarette and light a new one off the butt of the old—and staring up into the sky.

"At home, the spring is always late, just like this," Hugh said quietly. "Just when you think it will finally get warm and summer will come racing in, it will snow. Or rain. Or something."

"Vermont's the same," Tommy said. "No one calls it spring. We call it mud season. The time between winter and summer. A slimy, slippery, useless, messy pain in the ass interlude."

"More or less what we have here," Hugh said.

"More or less." Both men smiled.

"What did you learn from our infamous client?"

"He denies having anything to do with the murder. But—"

"Ah, Tommy, *but* is a terrible word," Hugh interrupted. "Why is it that I doubt I'm going to like what I'm about to hear?"

"Because when MacNamara and Clark waltzed in to announce that formal charges were being prepared, Clark blurted out that Vincent Bedford's blood is on both Scott's boots and his jacket. I presume that's what he meant earlier when he said they had enough evidence to convict him."

Hugh released his breath slowly. "That's a problem," he said. "Blood on the boots and a bloody boot mark in the *Abort*. Bloody hell . . ."

"It gets a little worse." Tommy spoke softly.

Hugh snorted, slightly wide-eyed. "Worse?"

"Yes. Lincoln Scott was in the habit of leaving his bunk in the middle of the night to use the toilet. Sneaking out of the bunk room to the latrine so that he wouldn't offend the sensibilities of whatever white officers didn't want to share a toilet with a black man. He did this last night, conveniently lighting a candle to find his way."

Hugh slumped back against the building. "And the problem is . . ." he started.

"The problem is," Tommy continued, "someone probably did see him. So at some point during the night, he's absent from the bunk room and there's a witness somewhere in the camp who will testify to that. Clark will argue that was when the opportunity for murder arose."

"That could have been the most dangerous piss he's ever taken."

"I was thinking the same."

"Have you explained this to Scott?"

"No. I would not say our first meeting went particularly smoothly."

Hugh looked quizzically at his friend. "No?"

"No. Lieutenant Scott has, shall we say, little confidence in his chances for justice."

"What did he—"

"He believes that minds are already made up. He may be correct."

"Bloody right about that, I'd say," Renaday muttered.

Tommy shrugged. "We'll see. So, what did you find out? Especially about Visser. He seems . . ."

"A little different from other Luftwaffe officers?"

"Yes."

"My impression as well, Tommy. Especially after watching him in that *Abort*. The man has been to more than one crime scene, I'll wager. He went through the place like some sort of damnable archaeologist. There wasn't a square inch of that place that he didn't eyeball. He didn't say a word. Didn't even acknowledge my presence, except for one time, and that took me by surprise."

"What did he say?"

"He pointed down at the bootprint, stared at it for a good sixty seconds, like it was some speech he was trying to memorize, then he lifts up his head, looks over at me standing there, and he says, 'Flying officer, I might suggest you take a piece of paper and trace this as best you can.' I bloody well took his suggestion. In fact, I made a couple of sketches. Made some maps of the location of the body and the layout of the *Abort*. I did a quick drawing of Bedford's body, showing the wounds. Tried to put in as much detail as possible. Actually, ran out of paper, and Visser ordered one of the goons to go get me a brand-new pad from the commandant's office. It might come in handy in the days to come."

"Curious," Tommy said. "It was like he was trying to help."

"Seemed that way. Which I wouldn't trust for one damn second."

Tommy thrust his back up against the hut. The small roof overhang kept the misting rain off their faces.

"Did you see what I saw in the *Abort*?" Tommy asked.

"Think so."

"Vic wasn't killed in the *Abort*. I don't know where he was killed, but it wasn't there. That's where he was put by somebody or somebodies. But not killed."

"That's what I thought," Hugh said briskly, smiling. "Sharp eyes, Tommy. What I saw was some blood on Trader Vic's blouse but not on those naked thighs. And none on the *Abort* seat or on the floor around him. So where's all the blood? Man gets his throat cut, ought to be blood jolly well everywhere. I took a closer look at the wound in the neck, too. Right after Visser did. Visser reached down with that single hand and like he was some sort of scientist, wipes away some of the blood, and measured with his fingers the slice in Trader Vic's throat. The jugular is cut, all right. But the slice sort of stops after no more than a couple of inches. Two inches, maximum. Maybe even a little less. Visser doesn't say a word, but he turns to me holding his thumb and index finger apart like so." Renaday held up his hand, demonstrating. "And then there's the little matter of Vic's nearly severed finger and cut marks on the hands. . . ."

"As if he was fighting back against someone with a knife."

"Right-o, Tommy. Defensive wounds."

Tommy nodded. "A crime scene that isn't a crime scene. A Kraut who seems to be helping the wrong side. I'd say we have a few questions."

"True enough, Tommy. Questions are good. Answers are

bloody well better. You saw MacNamara and Clark. Do you think it will be sufficient merely to throw doubts all over their case?"

"No."

"Neither do I." Hugh lit another cigarette, staring at the smoke that curled from his lips, and then looking at the glowing tip. "Before we got shot down, Phillip liked to say that these things will kill us, sooner or later. Maybe so. But it seems to me that they're about fifth or sixth on the current list of deadly threats. Far behind the Germans, or maybe getting deathly sick. Or I don't know what else. And right now, I'm wondering if maybe there aren't a few other items we could add to the list of deadly possibilities. Like ourselves."

Tommy nodded, as he reached into his own pocket and pulled out a package of smokes. "Tell Phillip everything," he said. "Don't leave out a detail."

Hugh smiled. "He'd line *me* up at dawn and shoot me himself if I did. Poor old sod's probably pacing back and forth in the bunk room now, behaving for all the world like some overeager child on Christmas eve." He finished his cigarette and flicked it out onto the ground. "Well, I'd better get going before he swoons from unchecked anticipation and curiosity. Tomorrow?"

"Tomorrow you meet Lieutenant Scott. Bring that famous policeman's eye to bear, will you?"

"Of course. Although it might be a damn sight easier for me if he was a lumberjack. And a drunken one, at that."

When he walked into the bunk room where Trader Vic had lived, Tommy was greeted with a dank silence and glares. The six remaining kriegies were packing their meager possessions together, readying themselves to move. Blankets; thin, scratchy German-issue sheets; whatever extra clothing the men had acquired; cooking utensils; and Red Cross foodstuffs were being gathered in piles on the floor. Men were also taking the hay-stuffed pallets off the bunks and folding them over for transport.

Tommy walked over to Lincoln Scott's space. He saw the Bible and Gibbons's *Fall* on a makeshift wooden table constructed from a trio of parcel boxes. Inside the top box was

Scott's stash of foodstuffs—all the tinned meats and vegetables, condensed milk, coffee, sugar, and cigarettes that the
black flier had accumulated. He also had a small metal
church key for opening the tins, and he'd fashioned himself a
metal frying pan, using the steel lid from a German waste
barrel, attaching a flattened handle that was also steel to the
lid by jamming the handle into a small slice on the lid surface.
Scott had wrapped an old, tattered cloth around the handle to
serve as a grip. Tommy admired the construction of the frying
pan. In it, Lincoln Scott displayed typical kriegie ingenuity.
The energy to make something out of nothing was the one
thing all the prisoners held in common.

For a moment, Tommy stood by the bunk, staring at the
meager collection of possessions. He was struck in that
second by the limits to what all the kriegies had. The clothes
on their backs, some food, some tattered books. They were
all poor.

Then he turned away from Scott's items. Across the room
two men were sorting through a wooden chest. The chest itself was an unusual sight. It had clearly been constructed by a
carpenter who'd spent time on making the edges fit securely,
and sanding the surfaces to a polished sheen. Vincent Bedford's name, rank, and dog tag number were carved in the
blond wood in an ornate script. The two men were busily separating foodstuffs from clothing. And, to Tommy's surprise, he
saw one of the men remove a thirty-five-millimeter Leica
camera from amid the clothing.

"Is that Vic's stuff?" he asked. A foolish question, because
the answer was obvious.

There was silence for a couple of seconds, before one of
the men replied: "Who else?"

Tommy approached closely. One of the men was folding a
dark blue sweater. It was a thick, closely knit wool. German
naval issue, Tommy thought. He had seen a sweater like that
only once before, and that was on the body of a U-boat
crewman that had washed ashore in North Africa not far from
their base. The Arabs who had discovered the sailor's body
and transported it to the Americans in hope of payment had
fought hard over the sweater. It was extremely warm, and the
natural oils of the wool repelled moisture. At Stalag Luft

Thirteen, in the midst of the harsh Bavarian winter, the sweater would have been a valuable commodity to shivering kriegies.

Tommy continued to gaze over the assembled riches. He had to stop himself from whistling in appreciation of Trader Vic's hoard. He counted over twenty cartons of cigarettes alone. In a camp where cigarettes were often the preferred currency of trade and barter, Bedford was a millionaire many times over.

"There has to be a radio," he said after a moment. "And probably a good one, too. Where's that?"

One of the men nodded, but made no immediate reply.

"Where's the radio?" he asked again.

"None of your fucking business, Hart," the man sorting through the items muttered. "It's hidden."

"What's going to happen to Vic's stuff?" Tommy wondered.

"What's it to you, lieutenant?" The other man working through the collection turned abruptly. "I mean, why is it any of your business, Hart? Ain't you got enough to do with defending that murdering nigger?"

Tommy didn't reply.

"Asshole," one of the men blurted out. "We ought to just shoot the bastard tomorrow."

"He says he didn't do it," Tommy said. This statement was greeted with hisses and a few snorts of near-rage.

The American flier kneeling in front of the chest held up his hand, as if to quiet the other men in the barracks room. "Sure. Of course. That's what he says. What did you expect? The boy had no friends and Vincent was popular with everybody. And they sure as hell didn't like each other none too much right from the first minute, and after they had that fight, the boy probably figured he'd better get Vic before Vic got him. Just like a goddamn dogfight, lieutenant. I mean, what are fighter pilots trained to do? There's only one absolute, essential, can't be broken goddamn rule for fighter pilots: Shoot first!"

There was a murmur of assent from the other airmen in the room.

The flier looked over at Tommy. He continued speaking in

a level, taut voice, filled with anger: "Have you ever seen a Lufberry circle, Hart?"

"A what?"

"A Lufberry circle. It's something you learn about on Day One of fighter training. Probably the Luftwaffe learns about it on their first day of training in 109s, too."

"I was always in bombers."

"Well," the pilot continued, still speaking bitterly, "a Lufberry circle is named after Raoul Lufberry, the First World War ace. Basically it's this: Two fighters start following each other in an ever-tightening circle. Sort of round and round the mulberry bush, the monkey chases the weasel. Only, who's chasing whom, huh? Maybe the damn weasel's chasing the monkey. Anyway, you get into a Lufberry circle and the fighter that manages to turn faster, inside the other, without either stalling out or losing consciousness, wins. The other dies. Simple. Nasty. That's a Lufberry circle and that's what Vincent and the nigger were in. Only problem: The wrong guy won."

The man turned away.

"What's happening to Vic's stuff?" Tommy asked again.

Without turning, the pilot shrugged as he answered.

"The food? Well, Colonel MacNamara told us all to share it. Spread it about all over Hut 101. Maybe have one little feast, courtesy of Vic. That'd be a good way of remembering him, wouldn't it? One night where no one in the whole damn hut goes to bed hungry. Anyway, the cigarettes are going to the escape committee, whoever the hell they are, who will use them for bribing the Fritzes or any other ferret that needs bribing. Same for the camera and the radio and most of the clothes. It's all being turned over to MacNamara and Clark."

"Is this everything?"

"This? Hell, no. Vic has a couple of secret stash spots around the camp. Probably two, maybe three times what you see here. Damn, Hart. Vic was easygoing, too. Didn't mind sharing all his shit, you know what I mean? I mean, guys in this bunk ate better, weren't so fucking cold in the winter, and always had plenty of smokes. Hell, he took care of us, all right. Vic was gonna get us all through the war alive and in one piece, and the nigger you're gonna help took all that away from us."

The man rose, pivoting sharply, staring at Tommy Hart.

"MacNamara and Clark themselves come on in here, tell us to pack up, we're moving out. Gonna leave the nigger in here alone, 'cept maybe for you. Good thing, Hart. I don't think the black bastard would have made it to his fucking trial. Vic was one of us. Maybe even the best of us. At least the man knew who his friends were, and he watched out for them."

The flier paused, narrowing his gaze.

"Tell me, Hart. You know who your friends are?"

It was nearly dark by the time Tommy Hart managed to return to Scott's cooler cell. He'd talked one of his reluctant bunk-mates out of a spare olive-colored turtleneck sweater the man had been sent from home. He'd also obtained a pair of size thirteen army-issue shoes from a modest stockpile kept by the kriegies in charge of distributing Red Cross parcels. The collection of clothes was supposed to go to men who arrived at the prisoner-of-war camp with their uniforms in tatters after having bailed out of stricken warplanes. He'd also taken two thin blankets from Scott's bunk, along with a tin of processed meat, some canned peaches, and half a loaf of nearly stale *kriegsbrot*. The guard outside the cooler cell seemed hesitant to allow the items inside until Tommy offered him a pair of cigarettes, and then he was waved ahead.

Shadows already filled the cell, creeping in through the solitary window vent near the ceiling, making the cooler's air cold and gray. The stark overhead bulb was weak and dim and seemed defeated by the onset of night.

As before, Scott was hunched down in a corner. He rose stiffly as Tommy entered the cell.

"I did what I could," Tommy said, handing over the clothes.

Scott grabbed for them eagerly.

"Jesus," he said, tugging on the sweater and then the shoes, throwing a blanket across his shoulders and, almost in the same motion, grabbing for the can of peaches. He ripped open the lid and drained the sweet and sticky contents in a single gulp. Then he started to work on the tinned meat.

"Take your time, make it last," Tommy said quietly. "It will fill you up better that way."

Scott paused, his fingers filled with a morsel of meat halfway to his mouth. The black flier considered what Hart had said and then nodded.

"That's right. But damn, Hart, I'm starved."

"Everyone's always hungry, lieutenant. You know that. The question is: To what degree? You say 'I'm starved' back home, and all it means is that it's been maybe six hours since you ate last and you're ready to sit down and tuck in. Pot roast, maybe. With steamed vegetables and spring potatoes and lots of gravy. Or a pan-fried steak with french fries. And lots of gravy. Here, of course, 'I'm starved' means something much closer to the truth, doesn't it? And if you were one of those poor Russian bastards that went marching by the other day, then, well, 'I'm starved' to them would be even closer to reality, wouldn't it? It wouldn't just be a couple of words. A throwaway phrase. Not at all."

Scott paused again, this time chewing his bite of food slowly, deliberately.

"You are correct, Hart. And a philosopher as well."

"Stalag Luft Thirteen brings out the contemplative side of my nature."

"That's because the one thing we all have in abundance is time."

"That's true."

"Except, perhaps, for me," Scott said. Then he shrugged and managed a small smile. "Fried chicken," he said quietly. Then he laughed outward, a single burst. "Fried chicken with greens and mashed potatoes. The typical black folks' Sunday afternoon at home after church with the preacher coming to dinner meal. But damn, cooked just right, with a little garlic in the potatoes and some pepper on the chicken to give it a little bite. Cornbread on the side and with a cold beer or a glass of fresh lemonade to wash it all down. . . ."

"And gravy," Tommy said. He closed his eyes for an instant. "Lots of thick, dark gravy . . ."

"Yes. Lots of gravy. The type that's so thick, you can hardly pour it out of the container. . . ."

"That you can stick a spoon in, and it'll stand upright."

Scott laughed a second time. Tommy offered him a cigarette, which the black flier took. "These things are supposed to cut the appetite," he said, inhaling. "I wonder if that's true."

Scott looked down at the empty tins.

"You think they'll give me a fried chicken dinner for my last meal?" he asked. "I mean, isn't that traditional? Condemned man gets his choice before facing the firing squad."

"That's a ways off," Tommy said sharply. "We aren't there yet."

Scott shook his head fatalistically. "Anyway, Hart, thanks for the food and the clothes. I'll try to pay you back."

Tommy took a deep breath:

"Tell me, Lieutenant Scott. If you didn't kill Vincent Bedford, who did? And why?"

Scott turned away. He blew a smoke ring up toward the ceiling, watching it waft back and forth and then dissipate in the gloom and growing darkness.

"I haven't the slightest idea," he answered sharply. He tugged the blanket draped around his shoulders tight to his body, then slowly lowered himself into the corner of the cooler, almost as if he were descending into a pool of still, dark waters.

Fritz Number One was waiting outside the cooler entrance to escort Tommy back into the American compound. The ferret was smoking, and shuffling his feet nervously. He tossed the half-smoked cigarette away when Tommy emerged from the cooler, which surprised him, because Fritz Number One was a true addict to tobacco, just like Hugh, usually burning the cigarettes down to their stubs before reluctantly discarding them.

"It is late, lieutenant," the ferret said. "Lights out will be soon. You must be in your quarters."

"Let's go, then," Tommy said.

The two men marched deliberately toward the gate under the gaze of a pair of machine gunners in the nearest tower, and a *Hundführer* and his dog that were readying themselves to check the perimeter. The dog barked once at Tommy before being hushed by its handler with a jerk on the glistening metal chain around its neck.

The gate creaked shut behind them and the two men continued wordlessly across the assembly ground, heading toward Hut 101. Tommy thought he would probably have more questions for Fritz Number One at some later point. But at this moment, he was mostly intrigued by the ferret's fast pace. "We should hurry," the German said.

"What's the rush?" Tommy asked.

"No rush," Fritz replied, and then contradicting himself again, added, "You must be in your bunk room. Quick."

The two men reached the alleyway between huts. The fastest route to Hut 101 led down that way. But Fritz Number One grabbed Tommy by the arm, tugging him toward the outside of Hut 103.

"We should go this way," the ferret insisted.

Tommy stopped in his tracks. He pointed ahead. "That's the right way," he said.

Fritz Number One pulled at his arm a second time. "This way will be fast, too," he said.

Tommy looked oddly at the ferret, then down the near-black alleyway. The searchlights had been turned on, and one swept over the top of the nearest hut. In the passing light, Tommy could see the misty rain and fog. Then he realized what was located at the end of the alleyway, just around the corner of the two huts and just beyond his sight line. The *Abort* where Bedford's body was found.

"No," Tommy said abruptly. "This is the way we're going."

He pulled his arm from Fritz Number One's grip with a jerk, and took off through the gloomy shadows and lurking darkness of the alleyway. The ferret hesitated only a second before joining him.

"Please, Lieutenant Hart." He spoke quietly. "I was told to take you the longer way."

"Told by whom?" Hart asked, continuing to march forward. Both men were walking from darkness to darkness, their path illuminated only by weak light that crept from the interior of the huts, where the modest electricity was still functioning, and the occasional sweeping searchlight beam.

Fritz Number One did not answer, but he did not have

to. Tommy Hart strode determinedly around the corner, and immediately saw three men standing outside the *Abort*. Hauptmann Heinrich Visser, Colonel MacNamara, and Major Clark.

The three officers turned when Tommy appeared. MacNamara and Clark instantly looked angry, while Visser seemed to grin slightly.

"You're not authorized to be here," Clark blurted out.

Tommy came to attention, saluting stiffly. "Sir! If this has something to do with the current case . . ."

"You are dismissed, lieutenant!" Clark said.

But as he said this, three German soldiers struggling to carry a long, dark rubberized sheet between them, emerged from the interior of the *Abort*. Tommy realized that Vincent Bedford's body was wrapped inside the sheet, shrouded from view. The three soldiers gingerly walked down the stairs and set the body down. Then they came to attention in front of Hauptmann Visser. He quietly gave an order in German, and the men lifted the body again. They carried it around the building corner and out of sight. At that moment, another German soldier appeared in the doorway to the *Abort*. This man was wearing a black butcher's-style apron and carried a soapy, dripping scrub brush in his hand. Visser barked another order to this soldier, who saluted, and then returned inside the *Abort*.

Clark then took a step forward, toward Tommy. His voice was narrow, pinched, and angry.

"I repeat: Lieutenant, you are dismissed!"

Tommy saluted again, and rapidly headed toward Hut 101. He thought he'd seen several interesting things, not the least of which was the curious idea that it had taken over twelve hours to remove the murdered man's body from the location where it had been discovered. But more curious was that the Germans were cleaning the *Abort*. This was a task the kriegies routinely performed for themselves.

He stopped just outside the entrance to his hut, breathing hard. If there was any evidence remaining inside the *Abort*, it was gone now, he told himself. For a moment, he wondered whether Clark and MacNamara had seen what he and Hugh Renaday had: That Trader Vic's killing took place somewhere else. He wasn't certain about their abilities to read a scene like the one he'd investigated that morning.

But he was certain of one thing: Heinrich Visser had.

The question, he thought, was whether the German had shared his observations with the American officers.

By all rights, he should have been exhausted by the day, but the questions and confusions he had gathered in his consciousness kept him lying rigidly in his bunk long after the lights went out, and past when each of the other members of the room had slipped into their own fitful night's sleep. More than once he'd closed his eyes to the snores, the breathing sounds, and the darkness, only to see Vincent Bedford's body stuffed into the *Abort* stall, or Lincoln Scott huddled in the corner of the cooler cell. In an odd way, all the troublesome images from that day that kept him awake were refreshing, almost exhilarating. They were different, unique. There was an excitement attached to them that quickened his heart and his head. When he finally did drop away, it was with the pleasurable thought of the meeting in the morning that he expected to have with Phillip Pryce.

But it was not morning light that awakened him.

It was a rough hand, closing over his mouth.

He pitched directly from sleep into fear. He half-jerked up in the bunk, only to feel the pressure of the hand shoving him back down. He twitched, trying to rise, but then stopped, as he heard a voice hissing in his ear: "Don't move, Hart. Just don't move at all. . . ."

The voice was soft, slithery. It seemed to sidle past the abrupt thudding of blood in his ears, the immediate racket of his heartbeat.

He lay back on the bed. The hand still covered his mouth.

"Listen to me, Yankee," the voice continued in a tone barely above a whisper. "Don't look up. Don't turn around, just listen to me. And y'all won't get hurt. Can you do that? Just nod your head."

Tommy nodded.

"Good," the voice said. Tommy realized that the man was kneeling by the side of the bunk, just behind his head, enveloped in darkness. Not even the occasional sliver of light from a passing searchlight sweep striking the exterior of the hut and penetrating past the window's wooden shutters helped him to see who was gripping him so tightly. He realized it was the man's left hand over his mouth. He did not know where the man's right hand was. And he did not know whether it held some sort of weapon.

Abruptly, he heard a second voice, whispering from the other side of the bunk. He was startled, and his body must have shaken slightly, because the grip across his mouth tightened even more.

"Ask him," the second voice demanded. "Just ask him the question."

The man at his side grunted quietly.

"Tell me, Hart. Are you a good soldier? Can you follow orders?"

Tommy nodded again.

"Good," the voice whispered, hissing still. "I knew it. Because, you see, that's all that we want you to do. All that's required of you. Just follow your orders. Now, do you remember what your orders are?"

He continued to nod.

"Your orders, Hart, are to help justice be done. No more. No less. You'll do that, won't you, Hart? See that justice is done?"

He tried to speak, but the hand clamped across his mouth prevented him.

"Just nod your head again, lieutenant."

He nodded, as before.

"We're just making sure of that, Hart. Because no one wants to see justice avoided. You'll be absolutely certain that justice is done, won't you?"

Tommy did not move.

"I know you will," the voice hissed a final time. "We all know you will. Everyone in this place . . ." Tommy could sense the man on his left moving away from the bunk over toward the bunk-room door. "Don't turn. Don't speak. Don't light a candle. Just lie there, Hart. And remember you only have one job ahead of you: just follow orders. . . ." the man said. He squeezed painfully hard one time, then released his grip, before slinking away into the darkness. Tommy could hear the door creak open and then close. Gasping for breath like a fish suddenly plucked from the ocean, Tommy remained rigidly on his bed as he'd been told, the normal night sounds of the other men in the room slowly returning to his ears. But it was some time before his heart rate slowed from the deep drumming that pounded in his chest.

Chapter Five

THREATS

Tommy kept his mouth shut as the kriegies flooded from the huts for the morning *Appell*. The early sky had lightened slightly, turning from dull, metallic gray to a horizon of tarnished silver that held out the hope of clearing. It was not as cold as it had been the day before, but there was still an unpleasant dampness in the air. Around him, as always, men complained, men grumbled, men muttered obscenities, as they formed the usual five-deep rows and began the laborious process of being counted. Ferrets moved up and down the rows, calling out numbers in German, starting over and repeating themselves when they lost track or were distracted by some kriegie asking a question. Tommy listened carefully to every voice, straining hard to recognize in the snatches of words that flowed at him from the collected airmen the sounds of the two men who'd visited him in the night.

He stood at parade rest, pretending to be outwardly relaxed, trying to appear bored as he had for hundreds of similar mornings, but inwardly stretched taut with an unruly turmoil and an unfamiliar anxiety that, had he been slightly older and more worldly, he might have recognized as fear. But it was a far different fear from the fear he and all the other kriegies were accustomed to, which was the universal fear of flying straight into a squall of tracer rounds and flak. He wanted to pivot around, to search the eyes of the men surrounding him in the formation, thinking suddenly that the two voices who'd arrived at his bunkside in the midnight of the camp would be watching him carefully now. He surreptitiously shifted his eyes about, darting glances to the right and left, trying to pick out and identify the men who had told him that his job was simply to follow orders. He was surrounded, as always, by the men who flew in all the ships of war. In Mitchells and Liberators, Forts and Thunderbolts, Mustangs, Warhawks, and Lightnings.

Someone was watching him, but he did not know who.

The catcalls and complaints of that morning were the same as every morning. The ragged lines of U.S. airmen were no different from what they were any day—except for the two men absent. One dead. One in the cooler and accused of murder.

Tommy exhaled slowly and had to control himself to keep from twitching. He could feel his heart accelerate, almost as fast as it did during the night when he'd been awakened by the hand closing over his mouth. He felt almost light-headed and his skin burned, especially his back, as if the eyes of the men he sought were scorching him.

The morning air he gasped at was cool, suddenly tasting to him like a smooth pebble plucked from the bottom of one of the trout streams of his home state, placed under his tongue on a hot day. He closed his eyes for a moment, envisioning fast, dark waters bubbling with white froth as they coursed through some narrow rapids on the Battenkill or the White River, waters that had fallen out of the crags of the Green Mountains, made by late-melting snow and racing toward the larger watersheds of the Connecticut or Hudson. The image calmed him.

He heard a ferret close by, grunting out numbers.

He opened his eyes and saw that they had nearly completed, the count. He looked across the yard and, almost as if on cue, saw Oberst Von Reiter, accompanied by Hauptmann Heinrich Visser, emerging from the office building and making their way past the cordon of saluting camp guards through the front gate toward the assembled fliers. As always, Von Reiter was dressed with rigid precision, each crease of his immaculately tailored uniform slicing the air, and Tommy imagined that as he strode forward they made the same whistling sound as a sabre slashing the wind did. Visser, on the other hand, appeared slightly less neat, a little crumpled, almost as if he'd slept in his uniform the night before. The empty sleeve of his greatcoat was pinned together but still flapped as he kept pace with the taller camp commandant.

Tommy watched the *Hauptmann*'s eyes, and saw that as he approached, they were sweeping across the rows of kriegies, taking in and measuring the men as they came to attention. He had the sensation that Visser looked on them with some anger that he concealed carefully but not totally. Von Reiter, Tommy thought, even with all his military bearing and Prussian appearance, like a caricature from a propaganda poster, remained nothing more than a glorified jailer. But Visser, he was the enemy.

Colonel MacNamara and Major Clark stepped from the formations to confront the two German officers. There was a quick exchange of salutes and whispered conversation, then MacNamara turned, took a step forward, and loudly addressed the assembly.

"Gentlemen!" MacNamara shouted. Any residual noise among the kriegies ended instantly. The men craned forward to hear the commanding officer speak. "You are by now all aware of the despicable murder of one of our number. It is now time to end all the rumors, scuttlebutt, and loose talk that has surrounded this unfortunate event!"

MacNamara paused, waiting until his eyes rested on Tommy Hart.

"Captain Vincent Bedford will be interred with military honors at noon today in the burial ground behind Hut 119. Shortly after that point, the man accused of his murder, Lieutenant Lincoln Scott, will be released from the cooler into the custody of his counsel, Lieutenant Thomas Hart of Hut 101. Lieutenant Scott will be confined to his quarters in that hut at all times, unless engaged in legitimate inquiries in preparation of his defense."

MacNamara swung his eyes away from Tommy and back to the rows of men.

"No one is to threaten Lieutenant Scott! No one is to speak with Lieutenant Scott unless they have pertinent information to impart! He is under arrest and is to be treated that way! Do I make myself clear?"

This question was answered without a sound.

"Good," MacNamara continued. "Lieutenant Scott will appear before a military court-martial tribunal for a preliminary hearing within twenty-four hours. His trial on the accusations is scheduled for next week."

MacNamara hesitated, then added: "Until that tribunal reaches a conclusion, Lieutenant Scott is to be treated with courtesy, respect, and total silence! Despite your feelings and the evidence already collected, he shall be presumed to be not guilty until a military court determines otherwise! Any violation of this order will be dealt with harshly!"

The colonel had drawn himself up, shoulders back, legs spread, his hands clasped behind his back. The force of his command was like an ocean wave flooding over the kriegies. There wasn't even a grumble from the back of the ranks of men.

Tommy exhaled slowly. He thought it would have been hard for the Senior American Officer to make a statement to the camp that was more prejudicial. Even the words *not guilty* were spoken in a tone designed to imply the precise opposite. He wanted to step forward out of the lines and say something in defense of Lincoln Scott, but bit his lip, reined in an urge he knew would help no one and might actually harm his case, and remained silent.

MacNamara waited for an instant, then swung toward the German officers. They saluted, Von Reiter as always lifting his leather riding crop to the brim of his cap, then snapping it down to his polished boots with a cracking sound.

Major Clark marched to the front of the formation, moving like a middleweight closing in on an injured opponent hanging from the ropes. He faced the airmen, and bellowed: "Dismissed!"

In silence, the kriegies dispersed across the compound.

Fritz Number One was nowhere to be found, which surprised Tommy, but one of the other ferrets was aware of the order allowing him to travel to the British portion of the camp, and after Tommy had plied him with a pair of cigarettes in order to tear him away from what the ferret considered the absolutely essential duty of crawling around and poking through the muddy dirt under Hut 121, escorted him through the gate, past the offices and the shower block and the cooler, and up to the North Compound.

Hugh Renaday was waiting just inside the barbed wire, pacing aggressively as was his style, circling around within a small space, smoking continuously. He stopped and waved as Tommy hurried toward him.

"Eager to get to it, counselor. Come on, Phillip's as excited as a hound in heat. He's got some ideas . . ."

Hugh stopped, in the midst of the rush of words, staring at his friend. "Tommy, you look terrible. What's wrong?"

"Does it show all that much?" Tommy replied.

"Pale and drawn, my friend. Couldn't you sleep?"

Tommy managed a smile. "More like someone didn't want me to sleep. Come on, I'll fill you and Phillip in at the same time."

Hugh clamped his mouth shut, nodded, and the two men quick-marched through the compound. Tommy smiled inwardly as he recognized one of his friend's better qualities. Not too many men, when their curiosity is pricked, are able to instantly silence themselves and start scrutinizing details. It is a quality that borders on the taciturn, perhaps an angle off the reflective. Tommy wondered whether Hugh was as quietly efficient with both his observations and his emotions in the cockpit of a bomber. Probably, he thought.

Phillip Pryce was in the bunk room he shared with Renaday, monkishly hunched over a rough-hewn wooden desk, scribbling notes on a sheet of writing paper, gripping a small needle of pencil tightly in his long patrician fingers. He looked up and coughed once hard, as the two men entered the room. A cigarette stub was perched on the end of the table, burning, ashes littering the planks of the floor below. Pryce smiled, looked around himself for the smoke, picked it up, and waved it in the air like a philharmonic conductor directing the crescendo of a symphony.

"Many ideas, my dear boys, many ideas . . ." Then he looked at Tommy more closely, and said, "Ah, but I see that more has happened in the space of a few short hours. And what new information do you have for us, counselor?"

"A little middle-of-the-night visit from what I took to be the Stalag Luft Thirteen vigilante committee, Phillip. Or perhaps the local chapter of the Ku Klux Klan."

"You were threatened?" Renaday asked.

"No. More like I was reminded . . ." Tommy launched into a brief description of being awakened by the hand on his mouth. He discovered that merely by telling his two friends what had happened, some of the echoes of anxiety within him fled. But he was also smart enough to understand that the sensation of wellbeing was as false as perhaps his fear was. He more or less decided to maintain a certain degree of wariness, some position between the two extremes of fear and safety. " 'Just follow orders' . . . that's what they told me," he said.

"Bastards," Hugh blurted. "Cowards. We should take this directly to the SAO and—"

Phillip Pryce held up his hand, shutting his roommate off mid-complaint. "First off, Hugh, my boy, we're not going to impart *any* information—even of threats and intimidation—to the opposition. Weakens us. Stengthens them. Right?" He reached for another cigarette, replacing the one that he'd neglected. He lit this, then blew out a long, narrow stream of smoke, which he watched as it hung in the air.

"Please, Tommy, if you will. A complete description of everything that you saw and did after Hugh left your side. And, if you can, re-create every conversation word for word. To the best of your memory . . ."

Tommy nodded. Taking his time, using every bit of recollection he had, he painstakingly retraced all his steps of the previous night. Hugh leaned up against a wall, arms crossed, concentrating, as if he were absorbing everything Tommy said. Pryce kept his eyes raised to the ceiling, and he leaned back on his chair, the wooden slats creaking as he rocked slightly.

When Tommy finished, he looked over at the older Englishman, who stopped rocking and leaned forward. For just an instant, the weak light filtering through the grimy window gave him a dark and shadowy appearance, like a man rising from bed after an intimacy with death. Then, as abruptly, this cadaverous look dissipated, and the angular, almost academic appearance returned, accompanied by a wry and engaged smile.

"*Yankee* these nocturnal visitors called you, you say?"

"Yes."

"How intriguing. What an interesting choice of words. Did you detect any other obvious southernisms about their language? A slow, sibilant drawl, perhaps, or some other, colorful contraction, like a *y'all* or an *ain't* that would support the geographical impression?"

"There was a *y'all*," Tommy replied. "But they whispered. A whisper can sometimes hide inflection and accent."

Pryce nodded. "Most true. But the word *Yankee* does not, correct? It immediately leads one in a most obvious direction, true?"

"Yes. Another northerner would never use that word. Nor would someone from the Midwest or West."

"The word prompts assumptions. Draws one inevitably to conclusions. Makes one think clearly in a certain manner, does it not?"

Tommy smiled at his friend. "It does, indeed, Phillip. It does indeed. And what you're suggesting is?"

Pryce sneezed loudly, but looked up with a grin. "Well," he said slowly, relishing each word as he launched himself forward. "My experience is much the same as Hugh's. Ninety-nine times out of a hundred it will be the unfortunate lumberjack who has committed the apparently clear-cut brutality. Usually what is obvious is also true. . . ."

He paused, still letting his smile wander around his face, curling up the corners of his mouth, lifting his eyebrows, crinkling his chin.

". . . But there is always that one in a hundred situation. And I distrust words and language that prompt one to conclusions instead of the more solid world of facts."

Pryce rose from his seat and moved across the room, as if abruptly driven by ideas. He opened a small chest made from an empty parcel box and removed tea and cups.

"Phillip," Tommy said, feeling a sense of relief for the first time that morning, "you sly dog. You're driving at something. What is it?"

"No. No. Not quite yet," Pryce replied, almost cackling. "I think I shall not speculate further until I know more. Tommy, my dear boy, throw another fagot on the stove, let us have tea. I have prepared some notes for you that should help you with procedural matters to come. I have also suggested some avenues of inquiry. . . ."

Pryce hesitated, then added, instantly dropping the humor from the edges of his words, adopting a seriousness that weighted them in Tommy's mind: "The next few hours will be critical, I suspect. More will happen that influences this case. Watch your client carefully when he is released. Hugh, rely on your own instincts. I think it would be wise for all of us if we could fix in our own minds a settled belief in Lieutenant Scott's denial."

Both men nodded. Pryce took a deep breath.

"Belief is an odd thing for a defense counsel, Tommy. It is not necessary to believe in your client to defend him. Some would say that it is easier to not truly have an opinion, that the maneuverings of the law are only clouded by the emotions of trust and honesty. But this situation is not one that lends itself, I think, to the usual interpretations. In our case, to defend Lieutenant Scott, I think you must subscribe wholeheartedly to his innocence, no matter how difficult he makes that achievement. Of course, with this belief goes greater responsibility. His life will truly be in your hands."

Tommy nodded. "I will search for the truth when I see him," he said, rather portentously, which caused Phillip Pryce to smile again, like a headmaster at a boys' school slightly bemused by the overeagerness but undeniable sincerity of his charges.

"I think we're some ways from discovering truths, Tommy-lad. But it would be wise to start hunting for them. Lies are always easier to find than truths. Perhaps we can exhume a few of those."

"Will do," Tommy replied.

"Ah, that's the Red, White, and Blue, All-American attitude. Thank God for that."

Pryce coughed and laughed, then he turned to the younger men.

"And Tommy, Hugh, one further thing. A critical thing, I think."

"What is it?"

"Find the spot where Trader Vic was murdered. The location will speak loudly."

"I'm not sure how."

"You will find it by doing what a true advocate must do to truly understand his case."

"What is that?"

"Put yourself into the hearts and minds of everyone involved. The murdered man. The accused. And do not neglect the men who stand in judgment. For there may be many reasons that buttress the prosecution of a case, and many reasons a verdict is delivered, and it is critical that before that event takes place, you understand completely and utterly all the forces at work so diligently."

Tommy nodded.

Pryce reached for a teapot and grandly swished it in the air to determine if it was filled with water, then plopped it on top of the old cast-iron stove.

"Hugh's famous lumberjack may be sitting on the floor with a discharged gun in his lap and reeking from alcohol. But who gave him the gun? And who poured him the drink? And who called him a name, prompting the fight? And, more important, who truly stands to lose or gain by the death of the poor sod lying on the barroom floor?"

Pryce smiled again, grinning at both Renaday and Hart. "All the forces, Tommy. All the forces."

He paused, then added, "My goodness, I haven't had this much fun since that damnable Messerschmidt got us in his sights. Tea ready, Hugh?" For a moment, the older man's smile flickered, as he added, "Of course, probably young Mr. Scott fails to find all this quite so intriguing as I do."

"Probably not," Tommy said. "Because I still think they mean to kill him."

"That's the bloody problem with war," Hugh Renaday muttered as he tended to the teapot and the chipped, white ceramic mugs. "There's always some right nasty bastard out there trying to kill you. Who wants a spot of milk?"

* * *

The guard outside Lieutenant Lincoln Scott's cooler cell let the two fliers in without a word. It was closing in on noon, though the interior of the cell made it seem more like the gray of the hour just after dawn. Tommy assumed that Scott's pseudo-release order would be processed soon, but he thought it would be more interesting to question Scott when he was still in the unsettled state that the isolation and starkness of the cooler created. He said as much to Hugh, who'd nodded and replied: "Let's let me take a whack at him. The old provincial policeman's dull but sturdy approach, perhaps?"

This Tommy agreed to.

The Tuskegee airman was in a corner of the cooler doing push-ups when Tommy and Hugh entered. Scott was snapping off the exercises, his body rising and falling like a metronome, counting out the numbers, the words echoing in the small, damp space. He raised his head as they came through the door, but did not stop until he reached one hundred. Then he pushed himself to his feet, staring at Hugh, who met his gaze with a singularly intense response of his own.

"And this is?" Scott asked.

"Flying Officer Hugh Renaday. He's my friend, and he's here to help."

Scott extended his hand, and the two men shook. But the black man did not release Hugh's grip immediately. Instead, they remained linked for a second or two in silence, while the black flier stared hard into every angle of the Canadian's face. Hugh returned the look with as withering a glare of his own.

Then Scott said: "A policeman, right? Before the war."

Hugh nodded.

Scott suddenly dropped his hand. "All right, Mr. Policeman. Ask your questions."

Hugh smiled briefly. "Why do you think I have any questions for you, Lieutenant Scott?"

"Why else would you be here?"

"Well, clearly Tommy needs help. And if Tommy needs assistance, then so do you. And we are speaking of a crime, which means evidence and witnesses and procedures. Do you not think a former policeman can help with these matters? Even here, in Stalag Luft Thirteen?"

"I suppose so."

Hugh nodded. "Good," he said. "Glad to get that straight, right off the top. A few other things you can clear up, as well, lieutenant. Now, it would be safe to say that the victim, Captain Bedford, hated you, correct?"

"Yes. Well, actually, Mr. Renaday, he hated who I am, and what I stood for. He didn't know *me*. He just hated the concept of *me*."

Hugh nodded. "An interesting distinction. He hated the idea that a black man could be a fighter pilot, is that what you're saying?"

"Yes. But it was probably a little deeper even than that. He hated that a black man would aspire and excel at a province ordinarily reserved for whites. He hated progress. He hated achievement. He hated the idea that we might actually be equal."

"So, on the afternoon that he tried to lure you into stepping over the deadline, that would have been not really directed at you personally, but more at what you represent?"

Scott hesitated, then answered: "Yes. I believe so."

Hugh smiled. "Then those Kraut machine gunners wouldn't really have been cutting you in half, it merely would have been some ideal?"

Scott did not reply.

Hugh smiled wryly. "Tell me, lieutenant, dying for some ideal, is it less painful? Is your blood somehow a different color when you die for a concept?"

Again, Scott remained silent.

"And, might I ask, lieutenant, did you hate in return in a similar fashion? Did you not really hate Captain Bedford, but hate instead what you consider to be the antique and prejudiced views he embodied?"

Scott's eyes had narrowed and he paused before replying, almost as if suddenly wary.

"I hated what he represented."

"And you would do anything to defeat those odious views, correct?"

"No. Yes."

"Well, which is it?"

"I would do anything."

"Including die yourself?"

"Yes, if I thought it was for the cause."

"That would be the cause of equality?"

"Yes."

"Understandable. But would you kill, as well?"

"Yes. No. It's not that damn simple, and you know it, Mr. Renaday."

"Ah, call me Hugh, lieutenant."

"Okay, Hugh. It's not that damn simple."

"Really? Why not?"

"Are we having a conversation about my case, or in general?"

"Are the two that separate, Lieutenant Scott?"

"Yes, Hugh."

"Then tell me how?"

"Because I hated Bedford and I wanted to kill every racist ideal that he represented, but I didn't kill him."

Hugh leaned back against the cooler wall.

"I see. Bedford represents everything you want to destroy. But you didn't seize that opportunity?"

"That's correct. I didn't kill the bastard!"

"But you would have liked to?"

"Yes. But I didn't!"

"I see. Well, sure is convenient for you that he's dead, isn't it?"

"Yes!"

"Lucky for you, as well?"

"Yes!"

"But you didn't do it?"

"Yes! No! Damn it! I may have wanted to see him dead, but I didn't kill him! How many times must I tell you that?"

"I suspect many more. And it's a distinction that Tommy's going to have some little difficulty arguing in front of a military tribunal. They are notoriously obtuse when it comes to these sorts of subtleties, lieutenant," Hugh said sarcastically.

Lincoln Scott was rigid now with anger, the muscles on his neck standing out like lines forged at some hellishly hot foundry. His eyes were wide, but his jaw was thrust forward; rage seemed to stream from his body like the sweat that ringed his forehead. Hugh Renaday stood a few feet away, leaning against the cooler wall. His body seemed languid, relaxed. Occasionally he punctuated a point with an offhand wave of his arm, or by rolling his eyes, looking upward, as if mocking the black flier's denials.

"It's the truth! How hard is it to argue the truth?" Scott fairly shouted, the words bouncing off the walls of the cell.

"And what relevance does the truth really have?" Hugh replied softly.

This question seemed to stop the black man abruptly. Scott was bent forward at the waist, but rendered slightly open-mouthed, as if the force of words gathered in reply had jammed his throat like commuters hurrying toward a rush-hour train. He turned to Tommy for a moment, almost as if he wanted him to come to his assistance, but he still said nothing. Tommy kept his own mouth clamped shut. He thought they were all being measured, in that small room, heights, weights, eyesight, blood pressure, and pulse. But more important, whether they were on the right side or the wrong side of a violent and unexplained death.

Into this small silence, Hugh Renaday eagerly stepped.

"So," he said briskly, like a mathematician reaching the end of a long equation, "you had motive. Plenty of motive. A goddamn abundance of motive, correct, lieutenant? And we already know you had the opportunity, for you have also rather blissfully admitted to everyone arrayed against you about leaving your bunk in the middle of the night in question. All that's lacking, really, is the means. The means to perform the murder. And I suspect our counterparts are examining that question as we speak."

Hugh eyed Scott narrowly. He continued to speak in irritating, frank terms:

"Don't you think, Lieutenant Scott, that it makes much more sense to admit it? Own up to the killing. Really, in many respects, no one will blame you. I mean, certainly Bedford's friends will be outraged, but I think we could argue fairly successfully that you were provoked. Provoked. Yes, Tommy, I truly think that's the way to go. Lieutenant Scott should openly admit what happened . . . it was a fair fight, after all, wasn't it, lieutenant? I mean, him against you. In the *Abort*. In the dark. It very well could have been you lying there. . . ."

"I did not kill Captain Bedford!"

"We can argue a lack of premeditation, Tommy. Some bad blood between men that leads inevitably to a rather typical fight. The army deals with these all the time. Manslaughter, really . . . probably do a dozen years, hard labor, nothing more—"

"You're not listening! I didn't kill anyone!"

"Except Germans, of course . . ."

"Yes!"

"The enemy?"

"Yes."

"Ah, but wasn't Bedford just as great an enemy?"

"Yes, but . . ."

"I see. It's all right to kill the one, but jolly well wrong to kill the other?"

"Yes."

"You don't make any sense, lieutenant!"

"I didn't kill him!"

"I think you did!"

Again Scott opened his mouth to reply, then stopped. He stared across the small space at Hugh Renaday, breathing hard, like a man fighting ocean waves and currents, struggling to make the safety of the shore. He seemed to make some sort of inward decision, and then he spoke, in a cold, harsh fashion, evenly and direct, a voice of restrained passion, the voice of a man trained to fight and kill.

"If I had decided to kill Vincent Bedford," Lincoln Scott said, "I would not have done so in secret. I would have done it in front of everyone in the camp. And I would have done it with this . . ."

With those words, Scott suddenly stepped across the space separating himself from Renaday, throwing a roundhouse right fist through the air, but abruptly stopping short of the Canadian's face. The punch was savage and lightning-fast, delivered with accuracy and brutality. The black man's clenched hand hovered inches away from Renaday's chin, remaining there.

"This is what I would have used," Scott said, almost whispering. "And I wouldn't have made any damn secret out of it."

Hugh stared at the fist for a second, then looked at the black man's flashing eyes.

"Very quick," he said in his quiet voice. "You've had training?"

"Golden Gloves. Light heavyweight champion for the Midwest. Three years running. Undefeated in the ring. More one-punch knockouts than I can count."

Scott turned toward Tommy. "I quit boxing," he said stiffly, "because it got in the way of my studies."

"And those were?" Hugh demanded.

"After obtaining my undergraduate degree magna cum laude from Northwestern, I received a Ph.D. in educational psychology from the University of Chicago," Lincoln Scott replied. "I have also done some graduate work in the unrelated field of aeronautical engineering. I took those courses in order to become an airman."

He dropped his fist to his side and took a step back, almost turning his back on the two white men, but then stopping and looking at them, in turn, in the eyes.

"And I have killed no one, except Germans. As I was ordered to do by my country."

The two men left Lincoln Scott in the cooler cell and walked into the South Compound. Tommy breathed in hard; as always, the tight confines of the cooler cells triggered a slight unsettled sensation within him, like a reminder to be afraid. The cooler was as close as he wanted to get to confinement and his lurking claustrophobia. It was not a cave, a closet, or a tunnel, but it had some of the dreary, dark aspects of each, and this made him nervous, stirring his childhood fear within him.

An odd quiet seemed to have settled across the American section of the camp; the usual numbers of men weren't out in the exercise yard, nor were men walking the perimeter with the same steady, frustrated march. The weather had improved again, breaks of sunshine and blue sky interrupting the overcast Bavarian heavens, making the faraway lines of pine trees in the surrounding forest glisten and gleam in the distance.

Hugh strode forward, as if the quickness in his feet mirrored the calculations in his head. Tommy Hart kept pace beside him, so that the two men were shoulder to shoulder, like a pair of medium bombers flying in tight protective formation.

For a moment, Tommy looked up. He imagined rows of planes lining runways throughout England, Sicily, and North Africa. In his mind's ear, he could hear the drone of the massed engines, a steady, great roar of energy, increasing in pitch and thrust, as phalanxes of planes raced down the tarmac and lumbered up, laden with their heavy bomb loads, into the clearing skies. He saw above him a shaft of daylight streaking through the thinning clouds and thought that there were officers and flight commanders sitting at desks in safe offices throughout the world seeing the same sunlight and thinking that it was a fine day to send young men off to kill or to die. A pretty simple question, that, he thought to himself. Not much of a selection. Not much of a choice.

He lowered his eyes and thought about what he'd seen and heard in the cooler. He took a deep breath, and whispered to his companion: "He didn't do it."

Hugh didn't answer until a few more strides across the muddy compound had passed beneath his feet. Then he said, also quietly, as if the two men were sharing some secret, "No. I don't think so, either. Not after he put that fist in my face. Now *that* made sense, I guess, if anything around here can be said to make sense. But that's not the problem, is it?"

Tommy shook his head as he answered.

"The problem is that right now everything seemingly points to him. Even his denials are more suggestive of his being the killer than not. It wasn't hard for you to turn him inside out, either. Makes me wonder what sort of a witness on his own behalf Lieutenant Scott can be." Tommy was struck by a thought: When the truth seems to support a lie, wouldn't the reverse be accurate as well? He did not say this out loud.

"We still haven't considered the blood on his shoes and jacket. Now, Tommy, how the hell did that get there?"

Tommy walked a few more paces, himself, considering this. Then he answered swiftly, "Well, Hugh, Scott told us that he sneaks out to use the toilet at night. No one sneaks anywhere wearing a pair of clomping flight boots on old creaking wooden flooring, do they? Wake up the world that way.

And no one wears their flight jacket to bed, even if it is cold. I'll bet he hung his from a nail on the wall, just the same as everyone else in that room. Same as you and same as I. How hard would it have been to borrow these items?"

Hugh grunted. Then he said, "I'll jolly well wager my next chocolate bar that this is precisely what Phillip was driving at earlier. A frame-up."

"Fine, but why?"

Hugh shrugged. "That one eludes me, Tommy. I haven't the slightest idea."

The two men continued walking quickly, until Hugh asked, "I say, Tommy, we seem to be in a hurry, but where are we heading?"

"To the funeral, Hugh. And then I want you to go find someone and interview him."

"Who would that be?"

"The doctor who examined Trader Vic's body."

"I didn't know a doctor had examined the body."

Tommy nodded his head. "Someone has. In addition to Hauptmann Visser. We just need to find that person. And in this camp there are only two or three logical candidates. They're all over in Hut 111, where the medical services are located. That's where you're heading. I'll do the escort job for Lieutenant Scott. Not going to make him walk across the camp alone . . ."

"I'll join you for that. It's not likely to be pleasant."

"No," Tommy replied with more bravado than he thought necessary. "I'll do it alone. I want your participation to be concealed, at least until we get our first hearing. And even more critically, let's make certain that no one knows how Phillip is guiding our hands. If there is some sort of frame-up and conspiracy and whatever, it's better that whoever it is doesn't know that one of the Old Bailey's best is aligned against him."

Hugh nodded.

"Tommy," he said, grinning slightly, "there is some slyness to you, as well." He laughed sharply, but not with a great deal of amusement. "Which is probably a right good thing," he muttered, as they walked faster, "given what we're up against. Whatever the bloody hell that is."

The hulking Canadian took another few strides forward, and then asked, "Of course, Tommy, one question does leap fairly swiftly to mind: What the hell sort of conspiracy could we be talking about?" Hugh came to an abrupt stop. He looked up, across the exercise yard, past the deadline, past the towers, the machine-gun crews, the wire, and the long cleared space beyond. "Here? I wonder, whatever could we be talking about?"

Tommy followed his friend's eyes, staring out past the wire. He wondered for an instant whether the air would taste sweeter on the day he was freed. That was what poets always wrote, he thought: The sweet taste of freedom. He fought off the urge to think of home. Images of Manchester and his mother and father sitting down to a summertime dinner, or Lydia standing beside an old bicycle on the dusty sidewalk outside his house on an early fall afternoon, when only the smallest insistence of winter is in the early evening breezes. She had blond hair that dropped in burnished sheets to her shoulders and he found himself reaching up, almost as if he could touch it. These pictures rushed at him, and for a single instant the harsh, grimy world of the camp started to fade from his eyes. But then, just as swiftly as they came, they fled. He looked back at Hugh, who seemed to be waiting for an answer to his question, and so he replied, with only the smallest hesitation and doubt in his voice:

"I don't know. Not yet. I don't know."

Kriegies did not die, they merely suffered.

Inadequate diet, the obsessive-compulsive manner in which they threw themselves into sports, or the makeshift theater or whatever activity with which they decided to while away time, the oddity of their anxieties about whether they would ever return home coupled with the ill-adjustment to the routines of prison life, the seemingly constant cold and damp and dirt, poor hygiene, susceptibility to disease, boredom contradicted by hope, which was in turn contradicted by the ubiquitous wire—all these things made for a curious tenuousness and fragility to life. Like Phillip Pryce's lingering cough, they were constantly being intimidated by death, but rarely did it come knocking with its harsh demands and fear-some requirements.

In his two years in confinement, Tommy had only seen a dozen deaths, and half of these were men who went wire-crazy and tried to blitz out in the middle of the night, dying in the fences with homemade metal cutters in their hands, chopped apart by a sudden burst from a *Hundführer*'s ma-chine pistol or a tower machine-gun crew. And over the years, there were a few men who had arrived at Stalag Luft Thirteen after suffering terrible injuries falling from the air and then inadequate care in German hospitals. The day and night con-stancy of the Allied bombing raids had limited the precious medicines and antibiotics available to the Germans, and many of their better surgeons had already died in forward hospitals treating men on the Russian front. But Luftwaffe policy toward the occasional Allied airmen seemingly at risk from wounds or disease was to arrange repatriation through the Swiss Red Cross. This was usually accomplished before the unlucky flier succumbed. The Luftwaffe preferred termi-nally sick or injured kriegies to die in the care of the Swiss; then they appeared less culpable.

He could not recall an instance where a kriegie was buried with military honors. Usually deaths were handled quietly, or with some sort of informal moment, like the jazz band's hon-oring one of their own. He thought it surprising that Von Rei-ter would permit a military funeral; the Germans wanted kriegies to think like kriegies, not like soldiers. It is far easier to guard a man who thinks of himself as a prisoner than it is to guard a man who thinks of himself as a warrior.

At the dusty juncture formed by two huts and converging alleys, Tommy pointed Hugh in the direction of the medical services hut, and hurried down the narrow walkway between 119 and 120, which would take him to the burial ground. He could hear a voice coming from around the corner, but could not make out the words being spoken.

He slowed as he rounded the corner of Hut 119.

Some three hundred kriegies stood in formation beside the hastily prepared gravesite. Tommy immediately recognized almost all the men from Hut 101, and a smattering of other fliers, probably someone representing each of the remaining buildings. Six German soldiers carrying bolt-action rifles stood at parade rest just slightly to the side of the squares of men.

Trader Vic's coffin had been predictably nailed together from the light-colored wooden crates that delivered the Red Cross parcels. The flimsy balsa wood was the preferred building material for virtually every bit of furniture in the American camp, but Tommy thought with some irony that no one expected it to form the walls of their own casket. Three officers stood at the head of the coffin: MacNamara, Clark, and a priest, who was reading the twenty-third psalm. The priest had been shot down over Italy the previous summer, when he'd taken his charge of administering to the flock of airmen in a light bomber group perhaps a bit too seriously, and had elected to fly on one of their runs over Salerno at a time when German antiaircraft troops on the ground were still active, and German fighters still plied their deadly trade in the air.

He had a flat, reedy voice that managed to dull even the famous words of the psalm. When he said, "The Lord is my shepherd . . ." he made it sound like God was actually tending sheep, not watching over those at risk.

Tommy hesitated, not knowing whether he should join the formations or merely keep watch from the periphery. In that momentary pause, he heard a voice from his side, which took him by surprise.

"And what is it, Lieutenant Hart, that you expect to see?"

He turned sharply toward the questioner.

Hauptmann Heinrich Visser was standing a few feet away, smoking a dark brown cigarette, leaning back against Hut 119. The German held the smoke like a dart; lifting it languidly to his lips, but relishing each long pull.

Tommy took a deep breath.

"I expect to see nothing," he replied slowly. "People who go somewhere with expectations are generally rewarded by seeing what they anticipated. I'm merely here to observe, and whatever I do see will be what I need to see."

Visser smiled. "Ah," he said, "a clever man's response. But not very military."

Tommy shrugged. "Well, then I guess I'm not a perfect soldier."

Visser shook his head. "We shall see about that, I suppose. In the days to come."

"And you, *Hauptmann*? Are you a perfect soldier?"

The German shook his head. "Alas, no, Lieutenant Hart. But I have been an efficient soldier. Remarkably efficient. But not perfect. These things, I think, are not precisely the same."

"Your English is quite good."

"Thank you. I lived for many years in Milwaukee, growing up with my aunt and uncle. Perhaps had I stayed another year or two, I would have considered myself to be more American than German. Can you imagine, lieutenant, that I was actually quite accomplished at the game of baseball?" The German glanced down at his missing arm. "No longer, I suppose. Regardless. I could have stayed. But I did not. I elected to return to the fatherland for my education. And thus did I get caught up in the great things that took place in my country."

Visser swung his eyes toward the funeral. "Your Colonel MacNamara," the German said slowly, his eyes measuring the SAO carefully. "My first impression is that he is a man who believes his imprisonment at Stalag Luft Thirteen is a black mark on his career. A failure of command. I cannot tell, sometimes, when he looks at me, whether he hates me and all Germans because that is what he has been taught, or whether he hates me because I am preventing him from killing more of my countrymen. And I think, in all these hatreds, he perhaps hates himself, as well. What do you think, Lieutenant Hart? Is he a commanding officer you respect? Is he the sort of leader who gives a command and men follow instantly, without question, without regard to their own lives and safety?"

"He is the Senior American Officer, and he is respected."

The German did not look at Tommy, but he laughed.

"Ah, lieutenant, already you have the makings of a diplomat."

He took a single, long puff on the cigarette, then dropped it to the dirt, grinding it under the toe of his boot.

"Have you the makings of an advocate? I wonder."

Visser smiled, then continued, "And is that what is truly required of you? I wonder about this, too."

The *Hauptmann* turned to Tommy. "A funeral is so rarely about finality, isn't this true, lieutenant? Are they not really much more the beginning of something?"

Visser's smile bent around the corner of his mouth, twisting with the scars. Then he turned away, once again watching the proceedings. The pastor's voice had moved on to a reading from the New Testament, the story of the loaves and fishes, a poor choice because it would probably make all the assembled kriegies hungry. Tommy saw that there was no flag draping the coffin, but that Vic's leather flight jacket, with the American flag sewn onto the sleeve, had been carefully folded and placed in the center of the box.

The pastor finished reading and the formations came to attention. A trumpeter stepped from the ranks and blew the soulful notes of taps. As these faded into the midday air, the squad of German soldiers stepped to the front, lifted their weapons to their shoulders, and fired a single volley into the clearing sky, almost as if they were blasting away the remaining gray clouds and carving a hole of blue.

The noise of the shots echoed briefly. It was not lost on Tommy that the sound was the same as it would be if the same six soldiers were gathered into a firing squad.

Four men stepped from the formation and, using ropes, lowered Trader Vic's coffin into the ground. Then Major Clark gave the order to dismiss, and the men turned away, walking in groups back into the middle of the compound. More than a few stared at Tommy Hart as they moved past him. But no one said a word.

He, in turn, met many pairs of eyes, his own gaze narrowed and hard. He guessed that the men who'd threatened him were in the knots of passing airmen. But who they might be he had no idea. No single pair of eyes spoke to him with a threat.

Visser lit another cigarette and started humming the French tune "Aupres de ma Blonde," which had a lilt to it that seemed to insult the ragged solemnity of the funeral.

Tommy abruptly saw Major Clark striding toward him. Clark's face was rigid, his jaw thrust forward.

"Hart," he said briskly. "You are not welcome here."

Tommy came to attention. "Captain Bedford was my friend, as well, major," he replied, although he wasn't sure this was completely true.

Clark did not reply to this, but turned instead to the *Hauptmann*, saluting. "Hauptmann Visser, will you please see to the release of Lieutenant Scott, the accused, into Lieutenant Hart's custody. Now is certainly a reasonable time."

Visser saluted in return, smiling.

"As you wish, major. I will see to it immediately."

Clark nodded. He glanced again at Tommy. "Not welcome," he said again, as he turned and strode away. Behind him, Tommy could hear the first thudding sound of a clod of dirt being shoveled onto the lid of Trader Vic's coffin.

Hauptmann Visser escorted Tommy Hart back to the cooler to release Lincoln Scott. Along the way, the German officer signaled to a pair of helmeted guards and to Fritz Number One to accompany them. He continued to hum brisk, lively cabaret tunes. The sky above them had finally completely cleared, the last wisps of gray clouds fleeing toward the east. Tommy looked up and spotted the white contrails of a flight of B-17s crossing the plate of watery blue. It would not be long before they were attacked, he thought. But they were still high, maybe five miles up, and still relatively safe. When they dropped through the sky toward the lower altitudes for the bombing run, then they were in the greatest danger.

He looked across at the squat, ugly cooler and thought the same was true for Lincoln Scott. For a moment he thought that it might be safer to leave him in confinement, but then, almost as quickly, the thought fled. He squared his shoulders and realized that what he faced was no different from the airmen in the sky above him. A mission, an objective, their passage threatened the entire route. He stole one more glance skyward, and thought that he could do no less than those men above him.

Scott was on his feet instantly as Tommy entered the cell.

"Damn, Hart, I am ready to get out of here," he said. "What a hellhole."

"I'm not sure what to expect," Tommy replied. "We'll just have to take it as it comes."

"I'm ready," Scott insisted. "I just want out of here. Whatever happens, happens." The black man seemed knotted, coiled, and ready to burst.

Tommy nodded. "All right. We will walk across the compound directly to Hut 101. You will go straight to your bunk room. When we get there, we'll consider our next step."

Scott nodded.

The black flier blinked hard when they emerged into the daylight. For a moment, he rubbed his eyes, as if to clear the darkness of the cooler cell away from them. He was clutching his clothing and his blanket beneath his left arm, leaving the right free. His fist was clenched tight, as if he was ready to throw the same roundhouse that he'd sent whistling at Hugh Renaday earlier that morning. As his eyes adjusted, Scott seemed to stand more upright, regaining his athleticism, so that by the time the group reached the gate, he was striding with a military purposefulness, almost as if he were marching on the edge of a West Point parade ground, readying himself to pass in review of a group of dignitaries. Tommy stayed at his side, in turn flanked by the two guards, a step behind Fritz Number One and Hauptmann Visser.

At the barbed-wire and wood-framed gate to the southern camp, the German officer stopped. He spoke a quick few words to Fritz Number One, who saluted, then another few words to the guards.

"Do you wish for an escort back to your hut?" he asked Lincoln Scott.

"No," Scott replied.

Visser smiled. "Perhaps Lieutenant Hart will see the value in an escort?"

Tommy took a quick look through the wire at the compound. A few groups of men were out; things looked normal. There was a baseball being tossed about, other men were walking the perimeter track. He could see men lying back up against the buildings, some reading, some talking. A few men were sunbathing, their shirts off in the warming air. There was nothing that indicated that a funeral had taken place less than an hour earlier. Nothing that suggested anger, or rage. Stalag Luft Thirteen looked as it had every day for years.

And this troubled Tommy. He took a deep, slow breath.

"No," he said. "We'll be fine by ourselves."

Visser sighed deeply, an almost mocking sound.

"As you wish," he said. He half-snorted, looking over at Tommy. "This is ironic, no? Me offering you protection from your own comrades. Most unusual, do you not think, Lieutenant Hart?" Visser didn't really seem to expect a reply to his questions, and Tommy wasn't willing to give him one, anyway. Visser then spoke a few words in German and the armed guards stepped aside. Fritz Number One also moved out of their path. He was frowning, and seemed nervous. "Until later, then," Visser said. He hummed a few short bars of some unrecognizable tune, his now-familiar small, cruel smile sliding around his face. The officer then stopped, turned to the soldiers manning the gate, and with a wide swing of his only arm, gestured for the gate to open.

"All right, lieutenant, let's go. Steady march," Tommy said.

Shoulder to shoulder, the two men stepped forward.

The gate had only begun to swing shut behind them when Tommy heard the first whistle. It was joined by another, and then a third and fourth, the high-pitched sounds blending together, traveling the length and breadth of the camp within seconds. The men throwing the softball back and forth stopped, and turned toward them. Before they had traveled twenty yards, the false normalcy of the camp was replaced by the noises of hurrying feet, and the rattling and thudding of wooden doors swinging open and slamming shut.

"Keep your eyes front," Tommy whispered, but this was unnecessary, as Lincoln Scott had straightened up even more, and was stepping across the compound with the renewed determination of a distance runner who finally spies the finish line.

In front of them, crowds of men streamed from the huts, moving as quickly as if the ferrets' whistles were calling them to an *Appell* or as if the air-raid sirens had sounded an alarm. Within seconds, hundreds of men had gathered in a huge, seething block, not a formation as much as a barricade. The crowd—Tommy wasn't yet sure whether it was closer to a mob—gathered directly in their path.

Neither Lincoln Scott nor Tommy Hart slowed their stride as they approached the congregation.

"Don't stop," he whispered to Lincoln Scott. "But don't fight, either."

Out of the corner of his eye, he caught a barely perceptible nod from the Tuskegee airman's head, and he heard a slight grunt of acknowledgment.

"Killer!" He could not tell precisely where the word came from, but somewhere within the bubbling tide of men.

"Murderer!" Another voice chimed in.

A deep, rumbling noise started to come from the men who blocked their path. Words of anger and hatred mingled freely with epithets and catcalls. Whistles and booing supported the noises of rage, growing in frequency and intensity as the two fliers continued forward.

Tommy kept his eyes straight ahead, hoping that he would spot one of the senior officers, but did not. He noticed that Scott, jaw set with determination, had increased the pace slightly. For a moment, Tommy thought the two of them not unlike a ship racing headlong toward a rocky shoreline, oblivious to the wreck that awaited them.

"Goddamn murdering nigger!"

They were perhaps ten yards from the mass of men. He did not know whether the wall would open or not. At that second, he spotted several of the men who shared his own bunk room. They were men he thought of as friends; not close ones, but friends nonetheless. They were men with whom he'd shared foodstuffs and books and the occasional reverie about life at home, shared moments of longing and desires and dreams and nightmares. He did not, in that instant, think they would harm him. He wasn't certain of this, of course, because he no longer was sure how they looked upon him. But he thought they might have some hesitation in their emotions, and so, with just the smallest bump shoulder to shoulder, against Scott, he shifted direction to head directly toward them.

He could hear Lincoln Scott's breathing. It was quick and short, small gasps of air snatched from the effort their pace demanded.

Other voices and insults reverberated around him, the

words crossing the space between the fliers faster than his feet could carry him.

He heard: "We should settle this now!"

And worse, a chorus of assent.

He ignored the threats. In that second he suddenly recalled the wonderfully calm voice of his dead captain from Texas, steering the *Lovely Lydia* into yet another hailstorm of flak and death, and without raising his voice, speaking steadily over the bomber's intercom, saying, "Hell, boys, we ain't gonna let a little bit of trouble bother us none, are we?" And he thought that this was a storm that he was going to have to fly directly into the center of, keeping his eyes straight ahead, just as his old captain had done, even though the last storm had cost him his life and the lives of all the others in that plane, save one.

And so, without breaking stride, Tommy launched himself at the gathering of fliers. Linked invisibly but just as strongly as if they were roped together, he and Lincoln Scott tossed themselves at the men blocking their path.

The crowd seemed to waver. Tommy saw his roommates step back and to the side, creating a small *V*-like opening. Into that breach, he and Scott sailed. They were enveloped immediately, the crowd sliding in behind them. But the men to their front made way, even if only slightly, just enough for them to continue forward.

The closeness of the men seemed to buffet them like winds. The voices around them quieted, the catcalls and epithets suddenly fading away, so that they struggled forward through the mass of men in an abrupt, eerie silence, one that was perhaps worse than the noise of the insults had been a few moments earlier. It seemed to Tommy that no one touched them, yet it was still difficult to step forward, like wading through fast-running water, where the current and power of the river pushed and tugged hard at his legs and chest.

And then, suddenly, they were through.

The last few men cleared from their path, and Tommy saw the route to the huts open wide, empty of men. It was like bursting in their plane from a dark and angry thunderhead into clear skies and safety.

Still in lockstep, marching in tandem, Tommy and Scott headed fast for Hut 101. Behind them, the crowd remained silent.

Scott sounded like a man who'd just boxed fifteen rounds. Tommy realized his own short and wheezy breathing duplicated that of the black flier.

He did not know why he turned his head slightly, at that moment, but he did. Just a slight shift of the neck, and a gaze off to his right. And in that small glance, he caught a brief glimpse of Colonel MacNamara and Major Clark, standing just behind one of the grime-streaked windows of an adjacent hut, partially concealed and watching their progress across the compound grounds. Tommy was riveted with a sudden, almost uncontrollable outrage, directed at the two senior officers, for allowing their own express order to be contradicted. "No threats . . . treat with courtesy . . ." that was what MacNamara had demanded in no uncertain terms. And then he'd witnessed the violation of that order. Tommy almost, in that second, turned and headed toward the two commanders, filled with instant indignation and a desire for confrontation. But into the midst of that abrupt anger he heard another voice speaking to him, suggesting that perhaps he had just learned something important, something he should keep to himself.

And it was this voice that he decided to follow.

Tommy turned away, although he made absolutely certain that MacNamara and Clark had seen that he'd seen them spying on their progress from behind the window. With the black flier at his side, he climbed the wooden planks into Hut 101.

Lincoln Scott spoke first.

"Well," he said quietly, "it seems bleak."

At first Tommy wasn't certain whether the fighter pilot was speaking about the case or the room, because the same could have been said of both. Everything accumulated by the other kriegies who'd once shared the space had been removed. All that remained was a single wooden bunk with a dirty blue ticking pallet stuffed with straw. A solitary thin gray blanket had been left behind on the top. Lincoln Scott tossed his remaining blankets and clothing down on the bed. The over-head electric bulb burned, although the room was filled with the remaining diffuse light of afternoon. His makeshift table and storage area were at the head of the bed. The flier looked inside and saw that his two books and store of foodstuffs were all intact. The only thing missing was the handmade frying pan, which had inexplicably disappeared.

"It could be worse," Tommy said. This time it was Scott's turn to look at him, trying to guess whether it was the accommodations or the case that he was speaking of.

Both men were quiet for an instant, before Tommy asked: "So, when you went to bed at night, after sneaking around to the toilet, where did you put your flight jacket?"

Scott gestured to the side of the door. "Right there," he said. "Everybody had a nail. Everybody hung their jackets there. They were easy to grab when the sirens or the whistles went off." Scott sat down heavily on the bed, picking up the Bible.

Tommy went over to the wall.

The nails were missing. There were eight small holes in the wooden wallboard arranged in groups of two, and spaced a couple of feet apart, but that was all.

"Where did Vic hang his coat?"

"Next to mine, actually. We were the last two in line. Everybody always used the same nail, because we wanted to be able to grab the right jacket in a hurry. That was why they were spaced out, in pairs."

"Where do you suppose the nails are now?"

"I haven't any idea. Why would someone take them away?"

Tommy didn't answer, although he knew the reason. It wasn't only the nails that were missing. It was an argument. He turned back to Scott, who was starting to leaf through the pages of the Bible.

"My father is a Baptist minister," Scott said. "Mount Zion Baptist Church on the South Side of Chicago. And he always says that the Good Book will provide guidance in times of turmoil. Myself, I am perhaps more skeptical than he, but not totally willing to refuse the Word."

The black flier's finger had crept inside the pages of the book, and with a flick, he opened the Bible. He looked down and read the first words he saw.

"Matthew, chapter six, verse twenty-four: 'No man can serve two masters; for either he will hate the one, and love the other; or else he will hold to the one and despise the other.' "

Scott burst out with a laugh. "Well, I guess that makes some sense. What do you think, Hart? Two masters?" He snapped the Bible shut, then slowly exhaled. "All right, what's the next step? Now that I've gone from one prison cell to the next, what's in store for me?"

"Procedurally? A hearing tomorrow. A formal reading of the charges. You declare your innocence. We get to examine the evidence against you. Then, next week, a trial."

"A trial. A nice word to describe it. And counselor, your approach?"

"Delay. Question authority. Challenge the legality of the proceedings. Request time to interview all the witnesses. Claim a lack of proper jurisdiction over the matter. In other words, fight each technicality as hard as possible."

Scott nodded, but in the motion of his head there was some resignation. He looked over at Tommy. "Those men just now, in the compound. All lined up and shouting. And then, when we passed through, the silence. I thought they wanted to kill me."

"I did, too."

He shook his head, his eyes downcast.

"They don't know me. They don't know anything about me." Tommy didn't reply.

Scott leaned back, his eyes looking up to the ceiling. For the first time, Tommy seemed to sense a mingling of nervousness and doubt behind the flier's pugnacity. For several seconds, Scott stared at the whitewashed boards of the roof, then at the bare bulb burning in the center of the room.

"I could have run, you know. I could have got away. And then I wouldn't be here."

"What do you mean?"

Scott's voice was slow, deliberate. "We had already flown our escort mission, you see. We'd fought off a couple of attacks on the formation, and then delivered them to their field.

We were heading home, Nathaniel Winslow and myself, thinking about a hot meal, maybe a poker game, and then hitting the hay, when we heard the distress call. Right in the clear, just like a drowning man calling out to anyone on the shore to please throw him a rope. It was a B-17 flying down on the deck, two engines out and half its tail shot away. It wasn't even from the group we were supposed to be guarding, you see, it was some other fighter wing's responsibility. Not the 332nd. Not ours, you see. So we didn't really have to do anything. And we were low on fuel and ammo, but there the poor bastard was, with six Focke-Wulfs making run after run at him. And Nathaniel, you know, he didn't hesitate, not even for a second. He turned his Mustang over on its wing and shouted at me to follow him, and he dove on them. He had less than three seconds of ammunition left, Hart. Three seconds. Count them: one, two, three. That's how long he could shoot. Hell, I didn't have much more. But if we didn't go in there, then all those guys were going to die. Two against six. We'd faced worse odds. And both Nathaniel and I got a kill in our first pass, a nice side deflection shot, which broke up their attack, and the B-17, it lumbered out of there and the FWs came after us. One swung around onto Nathaniel, but I came up before he could line him up and blew him out of the air. But that was it. No more ammo. Got to turn and run, you know, and with that big turbocharged Merlin engine, weren't none of those Kraut bastards gonna catch us. But just as we get ready to hightail it home, Nathaniel, he sees that two of the fighters have peeled off after the B-17, and again, he shouts at me to follow him after them. I mean, what were we going to do? Spit at them? Call them names? You see, with Nathaniel, with all of us, it was a matter of pride. No bomber we were protecting was going down. Got that? None. Zero. Never. Not when the 332nd was there. Not when the boys from Tuskegee were watching over you. Then, goddamn it, you were gonna get home safe, no matter how many damn planes the Luftwaffe sent up against us. That we promised. No black flier was going to lose any white boys to the Krauts. So Nathaniel, he screams up behind the first FW, just letting the bastard know he's there, trying to make the Nazi think he's dead if he doesn't get out of there. Nathaniel, you know, he was a helluva poker player. Helped put himself through college taking rich boys' allowances. Seven card stud was his game. Bluff you right out of your shorts nine times out of ten. Had that look, you know the one, the 'I've got a full house and don't you mess with me' look, when really he's only holding a lousy pair of sevens. . . ."

Lincoln Scott took another deep breath.

"They got him, of course. The wing man came around behind and stitched him good. I could hear Nathaniel screaming over the radio as he went down. Then they came after me. Blew a hole in the fuel tank. I don't know why it didn't explode. I was smoking, heading down, and I guess they used up all their ammunition getting me, because they broke off and disappeared. I bailed out at maybe five thousand feet. And now I'm here. We could have run, you know, but we didn't. And the damn bomber made it home. They always made it home. Maybe we didn't. But they did."

Scott shook his head slowly.

"Those men out there in that mob. They wouldn't be here today if it'd been the 332nd flying escort duty over them. No sir."

Scott lifted himself from the bed, still clutching the Bible in his hand. He used the black-jacketed book to gesture toward Tommy, punctuating his words.

"It is not in my nature, Mr. Hart, to be accepting. Nor is it in my nature to just let things happen to me. I'm not some sort of carry your bags, tip my hat, yessuh, nosuh, house nigger, Hart. All this procedural crap you mentioned, well, that's fine. We need to argue that stuff, well, you're the lawyer here, Hart, let's argue it. But when it comes right down to it, then I want to fight. I did not kill Captain Bedford and I think it's about damn time we let everyone know it!"

Tommy listened closely, absorbing what the black man had said and how he'd said it.

"Then I think we have a difficult task ahead of us," he said softly.

"Hart, nothing in my life up to this point has been easy. Nothing truly worthwhile ever is. My preacher daddy used to say that every morning, every evening. And he was right then, and it's right now."

"Good. Because if *you* didn't kill Captain Bedford, I think we're going to have to find out who did. And why. And I don't think that will be an easy task, because I haven't got even the slightest idea how to get started."

Scott nodded, and opened his mouth to speak, but before any of the words came out, he was distracted by the sound of marching boots coming from the exterior corridor. The steady resonant noise stopped outside the doorway and seconds later the single thick wooden door to the bunk room flew open. Tommy turned swiftly toward the sound, and saw that MacNamara and Clark, along with a half-dozen other officers, were gathered in the hallway. Tommy recognized at least two of the men as former occupants of Trader Vic and Lincoln Scott's bunk room.

MacNamara stepped into the room first, but then stood just to the side. He didn't say anything, but crossed his arms, watching. Clark, as always, was directly behind him, passing rapidly into the center of the room. The major stared angrily at Tommy, then fixed Lincoln Scott with a harsh, angry stare.

"Lieutenant Scott," Clark hissed, "do you still deny the charges against you?"

"I do," Scott replied, equally forcefully.

"Then you will not object to a search of your belongings?"

Tommy Hart stepped forward. "We do indeed object! Under what rule of law do you think you can come in here and search Lieutenant Scott's personal property? You need a warrant. You need to show cause at a hearing, with testimony and with supporting evidence! We absolutely object! Colonel . . ."

MacNamara said nothing.

Clark turned first to Tommy, then back to Lincoln Scott. "I fail to see what the problem is. If you are indeed innocent, as you claim, then what would you have to hide?"

"I have nothing to hide!" Scott answered sharply.

"Whether he does, or does not, is irrelevant!" Tommy's voice was raised, insistent. "Colonel! A search is unreasonable and clearly unconstitutional!"

Colonel MacNamara finally answered in a cold, slow voice. "If Lieutenant Scott objects, then we will bring this matter up at tomorrow's hearing. The tribunal can decide. . . ."

"Go ahead," Scott said briskly. "I did not do anything, so I have nothing to hide!"

Tommy glared at Scott.

The black flier ignored Tommy's look and sneered at Major Clark.

"Have at it, major," he said.

Major Clark, with two other officers at his side, approached the bed. They quickly felt through the stuffed mattress and rifled the few clothes and blankets. Lincoln Scott stepped a few feet away, standing alone, back up against one of the wooden walls. The three officers then flipped through the pages of the Bible and *The Decline and Fall of the Roman Empire*, and examined the makeshift storage table. Tommy thought, in that second, that the men were making the most perfunctory of searches. None of the items they inspected was really being closely scrutinized. Nor did they seem particularly interested in what they were doing. A sense of nervousness flooded over him, and he once again burst out, "Colonel, I repeat my objection to this intrusion! Lieutenant Scott is not in a position to intelligently waive his constitutional protections against unlawful search and seizure!"

Major Clark seemed to smile at Tommy.

"We're almost finished," he said.

MacNamara did not reply to Tommy's plea.

"Colonel! This is wrong!"

Suddenly the two officers accompanying Major Clark reached down and lifted the corners of the wooden bunk. With a scraping noise, they shifted it perhaps ten inches to the right, dropping it back to the wooden flooring with a resounding clunk. In almost the same motion, Major Clark bent down to one knee, and started examining the floorboards that were now exposed.

"What are you doing?" Lincoln Scott demanded.

No one answered.

Instead, Clark abruptly worked one of the boards loose, and with a single, sharp motion, lifted it up. The board had been cut and then replaced in the floor. Tommy instantly recognized it for what it was: a hiding place. The space between the cement foundation and the wooden flooring was perhaps three or four inches deep. When he'd first arrived at Stalag

Luft Thirteen, this had been a favorite kriegie concealment location. Dirt from the many failed tunnels, contraband, radios, uniforms recut into civilian clothing for escapes planned but never acted upon, stockpiles of useless emergency escape rations—all were hoarded in the small vacant space beneath the floor in each room. But what had seemed so convenient to the kriegies had not failed to gain the attention of the ferrets.

Tommy remembered that Fritz Number One had been inordinately proud of himself the day he'd uncovered one of the hiding places, because the discovery of one led him immediately to the uncovering of more than two dozen similar locations in different bunk rooms in other huts. Consequently, the kriegies had abandoned stashing items beneath the flooring over a year earlier, which frustrated Fritz Number One, because he kept searching the same spots over and over again.

"Colonel!" Tommy heard himself shouting. "This is unfair!"

"Unfair, is it?" Major Clark replied.

The stocky senior officer reached down into the empty space and came up, smiling, clutching a long, flat homemade blade in his hand. The blade was perhaps a foot long, and one end had been wrapped with some sort of material. The piece of metal had been flattened and sharpened and caught a malevolent glint of light, as it was removed from beneath the flooring.

"Recognize this?" Clark said to Lincoln Scott.

"No."

Clark grinned. "Sure," he said. He turned to one of the officers who had been hanging at the rear of the group. "Let me see that frying pan." The officer suddenly held out Lincoln Scott's handmade cooking utensil. "How about this? This yours, lieutenant?"

"Yes," Scott answered. "Where did you get it?"

Clark clearly wasn't answering the question. Instead, he turned, holding both the homemade frying pan and the homemade knife. He glanced at Tommy but directed his words to Colonel MacNamara. "Watch carefully," he said.

Slowly, the major unwrapped the odd olive drab cloth that Scott had used to make the handle of the frying pan. Then, just as slowly and deliberately, he unwrapped the blade's grip.

Then he held up both strips of cloth. They were of the same material and of nearly identical length.

"They look to be the same," Colonel MacNamara said sharply.

"One difference, sir," Clark replied. "This one"—he held up the one that had wrapped the knife handle—"this one here appears to have Captain Bedford's blood staining it."

Scott straightened rigidly, his mouth opened slightly. He seemed about to say something, but instead turned and looked at Tommy. For the first time, Tommy saw something that he took to be fear in the black flier's eyes. And, in that second, he remembered what Hugh Renaday and Phillip Pryce had spoken of earlier that day. Motive. Opportunity. Means. Three legs of a triangle. But when they had talked, the means had been missing from the equation.

That was no longer true.

Chapter Six

THE FIRST HEARING

At the following morning's roll call, the kriegies assembled in their usual ragged formations, except for Lincoln Scott. He stood apart, at parade rest, arms clasped behind his back, legs spread slightly, ten yards away from the nearest block of men, waiting to be counted like every other prisoner. He wore a blank, hard expression on his face and kept his eyes straight ahead, looking neither right nor left until the count was completed and Major Clark bellowed the dismissal. Then he immediately turned on his heel and quick-marched back to Hut 101, disappearing through the wooden door without a word to any other kriegie.

Tommy thought for a moment of pursuing him, then turned away. The two men had not discussed the discovery of the knife—other than for Scott to deny any knowledge about it. Tommy had spent the night in his own bunk fitfully, night-marishly, waking more than once in the dark feeling a sullen, helpless cold surrounding him. Now he quickly headed for the front gate, at the same time waving at Fritz Number One to provide an escort. He saw the ferret spot him and seem to hesitate, as if eager to avoid him, then seemingly think twice of that desire, stop and wait. Before he reached the ferret, however, Tommy was intercepted by Major Clark. The major wore a slight, mocking grin that did little to mask his feelings.

"Ten A.M., Hart. You and Scott and the Canadian who's helping out and anyone else you damn well need. We're going to be set up in the camp theater. My guess is that we're going to play to overflow crowds. Standing room only, huh, Hart? What sort of performer are you, lieutenant? Think you can put on a good show?"

"Anything to keep the men occupied, major," Tommy replied sarcastically.

"That's right," Clark answered.

"Will you provide me with lists of evidence and witnesses at that time, major? As you are required by military law."

Clark nodded. "If you want . . ."

"I do. I'm also going to need to inspect the alleged evidence. Physically."

"As you wish. But I fail to see—"

"That's precisely the point, major," Tommy interrupted. "What you fail to see."

He saluted and, without waiting for a command, turned sharply and headed toward Fritz Number One. Before he'd taken three steps, he heard the major's voice bursting like a shell behind him.

"Hart!"

He stopped and pivoted.

"Sir?"

"You were not dismissed, lieutenant!"

Tommy came to attention. "Sorry, sir," he said. "I was under the distinct impression we'd finished our conversation."

Clark waited a good thirty seconds, then returned the salute. "That's all, lieutenant," he said briskly. "Until ten A.M. Be on time," he added.

Once again, Tommy turned, heading rapidly toward the waiting ferret. He thought he'd taken a risk, but a calculated one. Far better to have Major Clark furious with him, because that would only serve to draw his focus away from Scott. Tommy sighed deeply. He thought things could not seem much worse for the black airman, and not for the first time since the discovery of the homemade knife the prior evening, Tommy felt a deepening sense of discouragement travel through him. He felt as if he only had the flimsiest idea what he was doing—in fact, it seemed to him he hadn't *done* anything—and realized that Lincoln Scott would be standing in front of a German firing squad if he didn't come up quickly with some sort of genuine scheme.

As he walked, he shook his head, thinking it was all well and good to suggest that they find the real killer, but he was unsure what the first step would be in that search. In that second, he longed for the simple navigational tasks aboard the *Lovely Lydia*. Find a marker, use a chart, note a landmark, make some simple calculations with a slide rule, bring out the sextant and take a sighting, and then chart a course to safety. Read the stars glittering above in the heavens and find the way home. Tommy thought it had been easy. And now, in Stalag Luft Thirteen, he had the same task in front of him, yet was unsure what tools to use to navigate. He walked along quickly, feeling the early morning damp loosen in the air around him. It would be another good day for flying, he thought to himself. This was incongruous. Far better to wake up to fog, sleet, and wildly tossing storms. Because if it were a clear, bright, warm day, this meant men would die. It seemed to him that death was better delivered on gray, cold days, the chilling, wet times of the soul.

Fritz Number One was shuffling his feet as he waited. He made a smoking gesture, making a *V* with two fingers and then lifting them to his lips. Tommy handed him a pair of cigarettes.

The ferret lit one, and placed the other carefully in his breast pocket. "Not so many good American smokes now, with Captain Bedford dead," he said, eyes sadly following the thin trail of smoke rising from the end of the burning cigarette. The ferret smiled wanly. "Maybe I should be quitting. Better maybe to quit than smoke the ersatz tobacco we are being issued."

Fritz Number One strode along with his head declined, giving him the appearance of a lanky, gangly dog that has been disciplined by its master. "Captain Bedford always had plenty of smokes," he said. "And he was most generous. He took good care of his friends."

Tommy nodded, but was suddenly alert to what the ferret was saying. "That's what the men in his bunk room said, too."

Almost exactly, Tommy thought to himself. Word for word.

Fritz Number One continued. "Captain Bedford, he was liked by many men?"

"It seemed that way."

The ferret sighed, still walking along rapidly. "I am not so sure of this, Lieutenant Hart. Captain Bedford, he was very clever. Trader Vic was a good name for him. Sometimes men are too clever. I do not think clever men are always so well liked as they maybe believe. Also, in war, to be so clever, this is not a good thing, I also think."

"Why is that, Fritz?"

The ferret was speaking softly, his head still bent.

"Because war, it is filled with mistakes. So often the wrong die, is this not true, Lieutenant Hart? The good man dies, the bad man lives. The innocent are killed. Not the guilty. Little children die, like my two little cousins, but not generals." Fritz Number One had deposited an unmistakable harshness in the soft words he spoke. "There are so many mistakes, sometimes I wonder if God is really watching. It is not possible, I think, to outwit war's mistakes, no matter how clever you may be."

"Do you think Trader Vic's death was a mistake?" Tommy asked.

The ferret shook his head.

"No. That is not what I mean."

"What are you saying?" Tommy demanded sharply, but beneath his breath.

Fritz Number One stopped. He looked up quickly, and stared at Tommy. He seemed about to answer, but then, in the same moment, looked past Tommy's shoulder, his eyes directed at the office building where the commandant administered the camp. His mouth was partly open, as if words were gathering within his throat. Then, abruptly, he clamped shut, and shook his head.

"We will be late," he said between tightly pursed lips. This statement, of course, meant nothing, because there was nothing to be late for—save the mid-morning hearing still several hours distant. The ferret made a quick, dismissive gesture, pointing toward the British compound, and hurried Tommy in that direction. But not fast enough to prevent Tommy from tossing a single glance over his shoulder at the administration building, where he caught sight of Commandant Edward Von Reiter and Hauptmann Heinrich Visser standing on the front steps, busily engaged in a rapid-fire conversation, both men seemingly on the verge of raising their voices angrily.

Phillip Pryce and Hugh Renaday were waiting for Tommy just inside the entrance to the British compound. Hugh, as always, was pacing about, almost making circles around their older friend, who wore his anticipation more subtly—in the lift of his eyebrows, the small upward turn at the corners of his mouth. Despite the fine morning that was rising around them, bright sunshine and advancing temperatures, he still draped a blanket across his shoulders, again giving him an antique, almost Victorian look. His cough seemed immune to the advantages of the spring weather, still punctuating much of what he said with dry, hacking sounds.

"Tommy," Pryce said, as the American quickly approached. "Let us walk a bit on this excellent morning. Walk and talk. I've always found that sometimes movement can stimulate one's imagination."

"More bad news, Phillip," Tommy replied.

"Well I have interesting news," Hugh replied. "But you first, Tommy."

As the three men traveled around the perimeter, just inside the British camp's similar barbed-wire deadline and looming guard towers, Tommy filled them in on the discovery of the knife.

"Had to be planted there," he concluded. "I mean, the whole show was orchestrated like some carnival magic act. Poof! The murder weapon. The *alleged* murder weapon. It made me furious, too, the way Clark baited Lincoln Scott into agreeing to the search. I would bet my GI insurance that they already knew the knife was there. Then they make this little scene of searching his stuff, not that he has much, and then wham! Bang! They pull back the bed and find a loose board. Scott probably didn't even know there was a hiding place underneath the flooring. Only the old boys in the camp know about those spaces. Totally transparent, the whole performance . . ."

"Yes," Pryce said, nodding, "but nastily effective. No one, of course, will see the transparency, but the word that the murder weapon has been discovered will likely further poison the atmosphere. And giving it all the veneer of legality, as well. The issue, Tommy, of course, is less *how* it was planted than *why*. Now, perhaps the *how* will provide us the *why*, but the reverse is often true, as well."

Tommy shook his head. He was a little embarrassed, but spoke quickly, so as not to display it. He had not yet made that particular leap of logic.

"I don't have an answer to that, Phillip. Other than the obvious: to close all the loopholes through which Lincoln Scott might manage to extricate himself."

"Correct," Pryce said, with a small flourish of his hand in the air. "What I find most interesting is that we seem, once again, to be thrust into an unusual situation. Do you not see what has taken place, so far, with each aspect of this case, Tommy?"

"What?"

"The distinctions between truth and falsehood are very fine and narrow. Almost imperceptible . . ."

"Go on, Phillip."

"Well, in every situation, with every piece of evidence that has surfaced so far, Lincoln Scott is pushed into the awkward position of providing an alternate explanation to the arrival of a fact. It is as if our young black flier must counter everything by saying, 'Now see here, let me give you another reasonable explanation for this and for that and for this, too.' But is this something that young Mr. Scott seems capable of?"

"Not very bloody likely," Hugh muttered. "It wasn't hard for me to trip him up, and I'm on his bloody side. And it seems Clark only had to say, 'If you have nothing to hide . . .' and Scott eagerly jumped into his trap."

"No," Tommy agreed rapidly. "He is very intelligent and always at least a little bit angry and obviously goddamn headstrong. He is a fighter, a boxer, and I think he's used to direct confrontation. Even violent ones. This is, I think, a poor combination of traits to have in an accused man."

"Quite so, quite so," Pryce said, nodding. "Does this not make you think of a question, or two?"

Tommy Hart hesitated, then replied forcefully.

"Well, a man is murdered and the accused is black and a loner and unpopular, which makes him terribly convenient for most everyone involved, and there is a stack of decidedly obvious evidence against him that is difficult to counter."

"A perfect case, perhaps?"

"Very perfect, so far."

"Which should make one wonder. In my experience, perfect cases are rare."

"We need to create a less perfect scenario."

"Precisely. So, where does that leave us?"

"In trouble, I think," Tommy said, smiling wryly.

The older man grinned, as well. "Yes, yes, that would seem so. But I am not completely sure of that. Regardless, do you not think it is time to turn some of these disadvantages to our benefit? Especially Mr. Scott's aggressive behavior?"

"Sure. Okay. But how?"

Pryce laughed out loud. "Well, isn't that the eternal question? Same for a lawyer, Tommy, as it is for a troop commander. Now, listen to Hugh for a moment."

Tommy turned toward the Canadian, who was on the verge of laughing. "Little bit of the old but unfamiliar and hardly common in Stalag Luft Thirteen sort of good news, Tommy, of which we've had so precious little. I found the man who examined Captain Bedford right where you said he'd be, in the medical services hut."

"Good. And he said?"

Hugh continued to smile. "Most curious, what he had to say. He said he was ordered by Clark and MacNamara to prepare Bedford's body for burial. He was told *not* to perform any sort of even half-baked autopsy. But the fellow couldn't really help himself. You know why? He's a young guy, what you folks in the States call a real go-getter, a hotshot first lieutenant decorated in combat who doesn't particularly like taking damn fool orders and who has coincidentally spent the past three years working in his uncle's mortuary in Cleveland, Ohio, while putting money away to attend medical school. He got drafted after finishing a single semester. Gross anatomy, you know, right off the bat in medical school. So, there was this body and the lad was shall we say 'academically' curious. About such delightful things as rigor mortis and lividity."

"Sounds good, so far."

"Well, he had the most intriguing observation."

"Which is?"

"It wasn't slicing his throat that killed Captain Bedford. No great outpouring of blood from a slashed jugular."

"But the wound . . ."

"Oh, that was the wound that killed him. But it wasn't delivered like this . . ."

Hugh stopped, lifted his fist to his throat as if holding a blade, and then drew it across the front rapidly with a cutting motion. "Or like this . . ." This time, Hugh stood facing Tommy and slashed the air between them, like a child playacting at a sword fight.

"But that's—"

"That's what we thought. More or less. But no, our erstwhile doctor thinks the killing blow was, well, let me show you . . ."

Hugh moved behind Tommy and suddenly reached around him with his right arm, grasping the American underneath the chin with his thickly muscled forearm and partially lifting him into the air in the same second, using his hip for leverage, so that Tommy's toes abruptly reached for the earth. In the same movement, Hugh brought his left hand up firmly, again in a fist, as if grasping a knife, and jabbed it against the side of Tommy's neck, just beneath the jawbone. A single, sharp blow, not a slash as much as a punch with the fictional point of the blade.

The Canadian dropped Tommy back to the ground.

"Jesus," Tommy said. "Just like that?"

"Correct. And did you notice which hand held the knife?"

"Left." Tommy smiled. "And Lincoln Scott is right-handed. At least, that was the hand he threw the punch at Hugh with. Intriguing, gentlemen. In-fucking-triguing." Tommy snorted the obscenity, which made the others grin. "And our young doctor-in-training? He based this helpful conclusion on what precisely?"

"The size of the wound for the first part, and then the lack of obvious fraying around the edges of the wound. You see, a slash produces a different appearance to even the semitrained and partially educated eye than a stab."

"And a first-year medical student saw this?"

Hugh grinned again, punctuating his reply with a quick

laugh. "A most interesting medical student. With a most unique background."

Pryce was also smiling. "Tell him, Hugh. This is delicious, Tommy. Simply delicious. A fact that tastes nearly as good as a large slice of rare roast beef and a generous dollop of Yorkshire pudding."

"Okay. Sounds good. Shoot."

"Our mortuary man did all the gangster funerals in Cleveland. Everyone killed by the local mobs. Every last one. And they apparently had a bit of prewar trouble between competing, ah, interests in that fine city. Our soon-to-be doctor laid out the bodies of at least three men with their necks cut in the precise same way, and curious lad that he is, he asked his uncle about it. And his uncle conveniently explained that no professional killer would ever just slash a man's throat. No sir. Far too bloody. Far too messy. And difficult. And oftentimes the poor bastard with the neck laid open has just enough energy remaining to pull out one of those quite large thirty-eight-caliber pistols that the gangsters seem to favor and squeeze off a few shots, which, of course, is awkward for the assassin trying to exit, stage left. So they use a different technique. A long-bladed stiletto punched upward, as I demonstrated. Slices the vocal cords on the way to the brain so the only sound you hear perhaps is a little gurgle, twist it around once or twice to mess up the gray matter, and the man drops to the floor dead. Very dead. And it's neat. Hardly any blood at all. Do it just right, and the only risk you have to yourself is fraying your shirt as the blade passes over the arm that lifts the victim off the floor."

"And obviously," Tommy said eagerly, "the wound is delivered . . ."

Hugh finished the sentence for him, ". . . from behind. Not in front. In other words . . ."

Tommy stepped in, ". . . an assassination and not a fight. A sneak-attack, not a confrontation. With a stiletto. Interesting."

"Precisely," Hugh said, with a small laugh. "Good news, as I said. Lincoln Scott may be many things, but he doesn't seem like some sort of lurking back-stabber."

Pryce nodded, listening. "And there's one other rather intriguing aspect of this style of killing."

"What's that?" Tommy asked.

"It is the exact same method of silencing a man that is taught by His Majesty's Commando Brigades. Neat. Quiet. Effective. Fast. And, by extrapolation, perhaps taught by your American counterparts in the Rangers. Or elsewhere in your more clandestine services."

"How do you know that, Phillip?"

The older man hesitated before replying.

"I'm afraid I have some education in commando techniques."

Tommy stopped, staring at the frail barrister.

"Phillip, I can't really see you as a commando." He laughed as he spoke, but when Pryce turned toward him, the laugh faded, for he saw his friend's face had fallen, graying even in the sunlight, stricken with a hurt that seemed to reverberate from deep within.

"Not me," Pryce said, choking slightly. "My son."

"You have a son?" Tommy asked.

"Phillip," Hugh chimed in, "you never said anything—"

Pryce raised his hand to stop the other men's questions. For an instant the older man seemed so pale that he was almost translucent. His skin had turned a pasty, fishlike color. At the same time, he took a step toward them, but he staggered as he came forward, and both Tommy and Hugh reached out, as if to grasp him. Again he held up his hand, and then, abruptly, Pryce simply sat down in the dust of the perimeter path. He looked up sorrowfully at the two fliers, and said slowly, painfully, "My dear boys. Dear Tommy and Hugh. I'm sorry. I had a son. Phillip Junior."

Tears were pushing at the crinkled edges of the wing commander's eyes. His voice seemed like leather cracking under tension. Between the tears that started to slide down his cheeks, Pryce smiled, as if this great sadness within him was also, oddly, amusing.

"I suppose, Hugh, he's the reason I'm here, now."

Hugh bent over toward his friend. "Phillip, please . . ."

Pryce shook his head. "No, no. Jolly well should have told you lads the truth months ago. But kept it all bottled up, you know. Stiff upper lip. Carry on and all that. Didn't want to be more of a burden than I already am . . ."

"You're not a burden," Tommy said. He and Hugh dropped

to the ground and sat next to their friend, who started to speak as his eyes traveled beyond the wire, out toward the world beyond.

"Well, my Elizabeth died at the start of the Blitz. I'd asked her to go to the country, but she was stubborn. Delightfully so, you know, truly that was why I loved her. She was fearless and she wasn't for a moment going to allow some little Austrian corporal to run her out of *her* home, no matter how many damn bombers he sent over. So I told her when the sirens sounded, to make her way to the underground, but she sometimes preferred to sit out the raids in the basement. The house took a five-hundred-pounder straight on. At least she didn't suffer. . . ."

"Phillip, you don't have to . . ." Hugh said, but the older man simply smiled and shook his head.

"So then there was just Phillip Junior and myself. And he'd already enlisted, you see. Nineteen years old, and a commissioned officer in the Black Watch. All kilts and pipes swirling with that screeching noise that the Scots call music, claymores, and tradition. His mother, you see, she was a Scot, and I think he thought he owed it to her. The Black Watch, Clan Fergus, and Clan McDiarmid. Hard men all. They were trained as commandos, fought at Dieppe and St. Nazaire, and Phillip Junior would come home on leave and show me some of the more exotic techniques he'd been educated with, including how to silence a sentry—which was precisely what we've run into here. He used to say that their instructor, this wiry little red-haired Scot you could hardly understand his brogue was so thick, would always end his lectures on killing with the phrase: 'Gentlemen, remember: Always be neat.' Phillip Junior loved that. 'Be neat,' he'd say, as I cut us some beef for dinner. And then he'd laugh. Great laughter, boys. He had a huge, unrestricted bellow of a laugh. It would simply stir up like a volcano and burst forth. He loved to laugh. Playing rugger during his public school days, he'd be grinning and laughing even with blood dripping from his nose. I thought when his mother was killed that he would no longer take such joy in life, but even with that sadness weighing on him, he was still irrepressible. He loved every breath he took. Delighted in it. And he, in turn, was loved. Not just by me, his dull and doting dad, of course, but by his chums at school, and all the young ladies at socials, and then by the men he commanded, because all of them knew him to be guileless and brilliant and dependable. A child becoming a man. He seemed to grow larger with every minute, and I was in awe of what the world held out for him."

Pryce took a deep breath

"They had a rule, you know, in the commandos. Behind Kraut lines, if you were wounded, you were left behind. A nasty rule, that. But essential, I suppose. The group is always more important than the individual. The target and the assignment are more important than any one man. Any one life."

Pryce choked on the words.

"But you know," he continued, "that simply wasn't my boy's style. No. Not Phillip Junior. Too loyal, I suppose. A friend would never abandon a friend, no matter how awful things appeared, and that's what he was. A friend to all."

Hugh was gazing through the wire. He had a faraway look in his eyes, almost as if he could just make out the prairies of his home, just beyond the sentinel trees at the edge of the Bavarian forest. "What happened, Phillip?" he asked quietly.

"His captain took three rounds in the leg, just tore it all to hell, you know, and Phillip wouldn't leave him. North Africa, you see. Not terribly far from Tobruk, in that great mess of things Rommel and Montgomery made. So my Phillip carried his commander ten miles through that damnably hot desert with the Afrika Korps everywhere around them, right up on his back, the captain threatening to shoot himself every mile of the way, ordering Phillip to leave him behind, but of course Phillip wouldn't. They walked all day and most of the night and they were only two hundred yards from British lines, and he finally handed over the captain to a couple of the other men. There were German patrols working everywhere in the night, the lines were so fluid, you didn't really know who was friend and who was foe. Very dangerous. Possible to get shot by either side, you see. So, he sent the team ahead, carrying the captain, and he stayed behind to cover their retreat, last man with the Bren gun and some grenades. Told them all he'd be right along in a shake or two. The others made it home. Phillip didn't. Don't know exactly what happened. Missing in action, you understand, not even officially dead, but of course I know the truth. I got a letter from the captain. Nice fellow. An Oxford don, actually, read the classics and taught some Latin and Greek before the war. He told me that there had been explosions and machine-gun fire from the spot where Phillip had set up his rearguard. He told me that Phillip must have fought desperately hard against all the odds, because the firing went on for some time, furiously, more than enough time for the rest of his team to reach safety. That was Phillip, wouldn't you know. He would gladly have traded his life for those of the others, but he wouldn't trade it cheaply. No, not Phillip. It would take more than a few of those Kraut bastards to kill him. The captain, he lost his leg. But he lived because my boy carried him to safety. Phillip, they put him up for a VC. And he lost his life."

Pryce shook his head again.

"He was beautiful, my boy. Perfect and lovely and beautiful. He could run, you know. Run forever. I could see him on the playing fields when he was younger at the end of a match when everyone else was wheezing and dragging and he would still be loping along, laughing, effortless. Just for the joy of it. And I suppose that was the way he felt, right up to the end, even with the bastards closing in on him and his ammunition expended. And on the day I got that letter from the captain, Hugh, any hope I had left within me died, and all I wanted to do was to kill Germans. Kill Germans and die myself. Kill them for killing everything I loved. And that's why I climbed into that Blenheim alongside you, Hugh. And the gunner I replaced? He wasn't really ill. No. I ordered him out, because I wanted to man that gun. It was the only way I knew to kill the bastards."

Pryce sighed hard, raising his hand to his cheeks, gently touching with his fingertips the moisture flowing down. He looked over at Tommy and Hugh.

"You boys, you both remind me of Phillip in different ways. He was tall and studious, like you, Tommy. And he was strong and athletic, like you, Hugh. Now, damn it, don't either of you die. I couldn't stand it, you see."

Phillip Pryce took a deep breath. He wiped the tears away from his eyes with the sleeve of his tunic.

"I think," he said slowly, inhaling deeply with seemingly every third word, "that it would do my poor torn and broken heart good to see our young and innocent Mr. Scott live, as well. Now, let us turn our attention to this morning's hearing."

Lincoln Scott was seated on the edge of his lone bunk in the empty room when Tommy, accompanied by both Hugh and Pryce, entered. It was shortly before ten A.M. and the black flier was holding the unopened Bible in his lap, almost as if the words within could emanate directly through the worn dark leather binding and be absorbed into his heart through the palms of his hands. He rose as the three men entered. He nodded toward Tommy and Hugh, and then looked at Phillip Pryce with some curiosity.

"More help from the British Isles?" he asked.

Pryce stepped forward, his hand extended.

"Precisely, my boy. Precisely. My name is Phillip Pryce."

Scott shook his hand firmly. But at the same moment, he smiled, as if he'd just heard a joke.

"Something amusing?" Pryce asked.

The black flier dipped his head. "In a way, yes."

"And what would that be?"

"I'm not your boy," Scott said.

"I beg your pardon?"

"You said, 'precisely, my boy. . . .' Well, I'm not your boy. I'm not anyone's *boy*. I am a man."

Pryce cocked his head to the side.

"I don't think I totally follow . . ." he started.

"It's the word: *boy*. When you call a Negro *boy*, it is derogatory. Slave talk. Out of the past. That's what Captain Bedford called me, over and over, trying to get beneath my skin," Scott said, his voice level, but marked with a cold, edgy restraint that Tommy recognized from their prior conversations. "He, of course, wasn't the first cracker bastard to insult me that way since I enlisted, and probably won't be the last. But I am not your, nor anyone else's, boy. The word is offensive. Didn't you know this?"

Pryce smiled. "How intriguing," he said with unmistakable enthusiasm. "What is a modest term of friendliness in the speech of my country takes on an utterly different connotation to Mr. Scott, with his background. Fascinating. Tell me, Lieutenant Scott, are there other words in common English use that are impregnated with such different meanings that I should be aware of?"

Scott seemed slightly taken aback by Pryce's response.

"I'm not certain," he said.

"Well, if there are, please let me know. I sometimes think when talking to young Tommy here, that we made a great error a couple of centuries back when we allowed you Americans to appropriate our wonderful native tongue. We should never have shared it with you adventurers and ne'er-do-wells." Pryce spoke rapidly, almost merrily.

"And why are you here?" Scott interrupted sharply.

"But, my dear . . ." Pryce stopped himself. "My dear lad? Is that acceptable, lieutenant?"

Scott shrugged an agreement.

"Well, I am here to lend a little behind the scenes assistance and expertise. And before you enter into this morning's little hearing, I wanted to meet you for myself."

"You are an attorney, as well?"

"Indeed, I am, lieutenant."

Scott looked askance, as if not believing the wisp of a man standing in front of him. "And you wanted to inspect me? Like some side of beef? Or a carnival sideshow freak? What was it that you came over here to see?" He threw out the questions with a harsh near-rage, so that they blistered the air of the room.

Pryce, still breezy, hesitated briefly, like a comedian's pause before dropping the punch line. Then he fixed the black flier with a single, penetrating look.

"I expected to see only one thing, lieutenant," he said quietly.

"And what was that?" Scott replied, his voice slightly high-pitched. Tommy could see that the knuckles of the hand holding the Bible had turned a lighter color, he was squeezing them so tightly.

"Innocence," Pryce responded.

Scott took a deep breath, filling his barrel chest with air.

"And how is it that you can see this, Mr. Pryce? Is innocence like a flight jacket that I can put on in the morning, or when it's cold? Is it in the eyes, or the face, or in the way I stand at attention? Is it a mannerism? A smile, perhaps? Tell me, how does one wear a quality such as innocence? Because I'd like to know. It might help in my situation."

Pryce seemed delighted by the questions thrust in his direction like so many rifle shots.

"You wear innocence by not pretending to be something other than what you are."

"Then you should have no problem," Scott answered, "because that's the way I am."

Pryce nodded. "Perhaps. Are you always this angry, lieutenant? Do you always bristle at the people trying to help?"

"No. Yes." The black flier snorted. "I am who I am. Take it or leave it."

"Ah, an American attitude, to be sure."

"I am an American. I may be black, but I am an American."

"Then perhaps it would be wise," Phillip Pryce gestured toward Tommy, "to trust your fellow American trying to help you."

Scott's eyes narrowed, focused sharply on the older British flier. "While all my other fellow Americans are trying to kill me?" he asked with a noticeable sneer. "Trust, I've learned, is something best left to those who earn it, not those who ask for it. You earn it under pressure. In the air, flying wing to wing in a gusty crosswind. You earn it when you dive through a flight of Messerschmidts. It's something that's not easy to get, and once achieved not easy to lose."

Pryce burst out in laughter.

"Absolutely!" he said. "You are absolutely correct!"

He turned toward Tommy and Hugh. "The lieutenant is a philosopher, as well, Tommy. You did not tell me this."

Scott still didn't seem to know what to make of the wiry, partially emaciated British gentleman laughing, wheezing, coughing, and obviously taking complete delight in the turns and twists of their conversation.

"You're a lawyer?" he asked again, slightly incredulous.

Pryce turned back briskly. He stared directly at Lincoln Scott for several long seconds. And when he did answer this question, he did so in a deadly serious, low-pitched, and intense voice.

"I am. And the bloody well best you will ever encounter. And this is what I suggest you do this morning. Tommy, pay close attention."

For a moment, Scott seemed hesitant. But as the wing commander continued to speak, he started to nod his head in agreement. Tommy and Hugh joined in, so that as Pryce spoke softly, the other men were gathered in a tight knot around him.

The theater at Stalag Luft Thirteen was located in the center of the camp, next to the hut where the Red Cross parcels and mail were delivered, adjacent to the makeshift medical services building. It was slightly wider than the housing huts, low-slung and hot when the temperatures rose, freezing in the winter. But any performance was jam-packed, from the camp jazz band to *The Front Page*, performed on the slightly raised stage with dripping candles in footlights fashioned from processed meat tins. Occasionally a German propaganda newsreel was shown, or a feature film of happy, singing Bavarian maidens—all projected by an ancient, cranky machine that frequently broke the film strips—to the wild applause of the prisoners. The best seats in the front of the room were constructed from leftover crates. Others were rough boards nailed together to make uncomfortable pews. Some men would bring blankets to sit on, cramming their backs against the thin processed-wood walls.

At precisely ten A.M. on the wristwatch that had been so coveted by Vincent Bedford, Tommy strode through the wide double doors that opened into the theater, flanked on one side by Hugh Renaday and on the other by Lincoln Scott. The men marched in step, shoulders drawn back tightly, their uniforms as pressed and as clean as they could make them. Their boots resounded off the flooring planks with determined precision. In unison, the three men wheeled directly up the center aisle, eyes to the front, quick-paced, maintaining formation, like a color guard on parade.

The auditorium was filled to capacity and beyond. Men were jammed into every corner and cranny of the space, shoulder to shoulder, straining to see. Others hung outside, groups of fliers listening through the open windows. Kriegie heads pivoted like falling dominoes as the accused man and his two defenders paced by. A makeshift bar had been created at the foot of the stage, two two-board tables set next to each other, facing three chairs set behind a longer table propped in the middle of the platform. Each chair was occupied by a senior camp officer, with Lewis MacNamara in the center seat. He was fingering a wooden mallet that hovered over a hunk of two-by-four. A homemade gavel. Major Clark, accompanied by another officer whom Tommy recognized from the search the prior evening, was already seated at the prosecution's table. In a far corner at the front of the stage, Hauptmann Heinrich Visser, accompanied again by a stenographer, was seated. He was pushing back on his wooden, stiff-backed chair, so that he was balancing against the wall, a slightly bemused look on his face. The kriegies had afforded him some space, so Visser and the stenographer were isolated, their steel-gray uniforms standing out amid the sea of woolen olive drab and tanned brown leather that the American fliers wore.

The room, which had been noisily buzzing with anticipatory conversation, fell into a complete silence as the three men marched past, maintaining their lockstep and rhythm. Wordlessly, Lincoln Scott and Hugh took seats at the defense table. Tommy, standing between the two, remained on his feet, staring up at Colonel MacNamara. He held several legal texts in one hand and a notepad in the other. These he abruptly dropped to the tabletop with a solid thud, like the report of a distant mortar round.

Colonel MacNamara stared down at the three men, fixing each in turn, then said briskly: "Are you ready to proceed, lieutenant?"

Tommy nodded. "Yes. Are you planning on presiding, colonel?"

"I am. As Senior American Officer, it is my duty—"

"I would object!" Tommy said loudly.

MacNamara stared at him. "Objection?"

"Indeed. The potential exists for you to be called as a witness in this matter. That would preclude your being able to preside."

"Witness?" MacNamara looked both puzzled and slightly angry. "How so?"

But before Tommy could reply, Major Clark leapt up. "This is unreasonable! Colonel, you are required by your position as commander of the American sector to preside over these proceedings. I don't see what testimony you could possibly give—"

Tommy interrupted. "A defense in a capital case should have the widest possible leeway in bringing forth evidence—any evidence—they believe will help their case. Anything less would be unfair, unconstitutional, and more fitting for the jackbooted thugs we are fighting than freeborn Americans!"

With these final words, Tommy swung around waving his arm at Heinrich Visser and the stenographer, who scratched away at his pad, although his forehead seemed to have reddened. Visser dropped his chair legs forward, like twin shots, and seemed about to stand, but he did not. Instead he merely stared straight ahead and continued to smoke his cigarette.

MacNamara held up his hand.

"I will not limit the defense, you are correct. As for my own potential testimony, well, that remains to be seen. We will cross that particular bridge if and when we arrive at it."

He made a slight nod toward Visser, as he spoke.

Tommy nodded, as well. Behind him, amid the packed crowd of kriegies, he could hear a few mumbled words, but these were followed by numerous hushings. The men wanted to hear.

MacNamara continued. "Today we are here merely for a plea. And lieutenant, as you have requested, Major Clark has compiled a list of witnesses and evidence. Let's get on with the business, please."

Major Clark turned to Tommy. He gestured toward the man seated beside him. "Lieutenant Hart, this is Captain Walker Townsend. He will be assisting me in these matters."

Captain Townsend, a lean, athletic man with thinning,

sandy-colored hair and a pencil-styled mustache on his upper lip, half-rose from his seat, nodding toward the three men at the defense table. Tommy guessed that he was probably in his early thirties.

"He will be in charge of the witnesses and evidence. You may make necessary arrangements through him," Major Clark continued in his snappy, military voice. "I believe that is all we have, for this moment, colonel. We can proceed with the recording of the plea."

MacNamara hesitated, then said in a loud, penetrating voice:

"First Lieutenant Lincoln Scott, you are accused of the premeditated murder of Captain Vincent Bedford. For the record, how do you plead?"

Scott fairly leapt to his feet to answer, but held his tongue for several seconds. When he did speak, it was loud, decisive, and with unbridled intensity. "Sir!" His voice filled the entire auditorium. "Not guilty, Your Honor!"

MacNamara seemed about to reply, but Scott beat him to the silence that had filled the room, half-pivoting where he stood, so that he partially faced the kriegie audience. His voice soared like his preacher father's, filling the air above the crowd of men.

"It is true that I despised Vincent Bedford! From the first minute that I arrived in this camp, he treated me like a dog. Worse than a dog! He insulted me. He baited me. He taunted me with obscene and hate-filled names. He was an utter racist and he hated me every bit as much as I came to hate him. He wanted me dead from the moment I arrived here! Every man here has heard how he tried to kill me, by trying to get me to cross the deadline. But to this, I did nothing! Any other man here would have been justified in fighting Vincent Bedford and maybe even killing him for what he tried to do! But I did nothing of the sort!"

Major Clark had leapt to his feet, waving his arms, trying to get the court's attention. He began to yell, "Objection! Objection!" but Scott's voice was the greater, and the black flier prevailed.

"I came here to kill Germans!" Scott shouted, suddenly

swinging about and pointing an accusing finger directly at Visser. "Germans like him!"

Visser's face instantly paled, and he abruptly dropped the cigarette from his solitary hand to the floor, grinding it beneath his boot. He half-rose in his seat, then slumped back. He fixed the black flier with an unbridled look of hatred. Scott met the gaze with a similarly hard look of his own.

"Maybe some people in the camp have forgotten that's why we're here," he said loudly, swinging his eyes to MacNamara and then Clark and finally back to the assembled kriegies. "But not me!"

He paused, letting the sudden silence grip the theater.

"I have been goddamn successful at killing the enemy! There were nine swastikas painted on the side of my bird before I got shot down." Scott stared across the rows of men. "And I'm not alone. That is why we're here!"

And then he paused again, just snatching a quick burst of air, so that his next words resonated throughout the auditorium. "But someone at Stalag Luft Thirteen has something else in mind! And that someone killed Vincent Bedford. . . ."

Scott drew himself up, his voice barreling through the still air of the theater. He jabbed the air with his finger. "It could be you, or you, or the man next to you. . . ." As he spoke, he pointed randomly into the audience, fixing each kriegie that he selected with a steady, unwavering gaze. "I don't know why Vincent Bedford was killed. . . ." He took a deep breath, and then shouted: "But I'm going to find out!"

Then Scott swung back, facing MacNamara, whose face had reddened, but who at the same time seemed to be listening intently to every word the black flier said, and who seemed to have collected his own anger and stored it someplace deep within himself.

"Not guilty, colonel. Not guilty. Not guilty. Not damn guilty! Not in the slightest!"

And then he abruptly sat down.

The room immediately burst into a tangled Babel of voices, explosions of hurried, excited speech as the collected kriegies reacted to Lincoln Scott's words. Colonel MacNamara oddly allowed the cacophony to continue for a minute before he started to hammer the hunk of wood, bellowing for order and silence.

"Good job," Tommy whispered directly into the black flier's ear.

"That'll give them something to think about," Scott responded. Hugh was fighting to keep from grinning.

"Order!" MacNamara shouted.

As swiftly as it had burst forth, the noise started to dissipate, suddenly leaving only the sound of the mallet striking the wood. Into this vacuum, Tommy leaped. He shoved his chair back and rose to his feet. He made a small gesture toward Scott and Hugh, and they, too, pushed up. The three men snapped their heels together, coming to attention.

"Sir!" Tommy bellowed, drawing every bit of stentorian presence from deep within his chest. "The defense will be ready to proceed at zero eight hundred hours on Monday, directly after the morning *Appell*!"

The three men saluted in unison. MacNamara wordlessly nodded just slightly, and lifted two fingers to his own forehead, returning the salute. Then the accused and his two defenders pivoted, and assuming the same winged formation they used when entering the room, the three men exited the bar, and marched down the center aisle again. Silence followed their heavy tread on the wooden flooring. Tommy could see surprise, confusion, and doubts on the faces of the men jammed into the theater. This was what he had expected their performance would engender. He had anticipated, as well, Major Clark's tight-faced anger and Colonel MacNamara's more calculated reaction. However, the look that had taken him aback had been the wry, almost delighted smile on the face of Clark's assistant, Walker Townsend. The captain had seemed oddly energized, as if he'd just heard some great and glorious piece of good news, which was, Tommy Hart thought to himself, the precise opposite response that he'd expected from the challenge they had thrown down.

And as he marched forward, he felt a quiver within him, almost a cold shaft that went through his heart like the first icy breath on a winter morning back home in Vermont. But this lacked the clarity of those times, replacing it with a darkness and a murkiness that seemed almost fog-ridden. Somewhere

in that audience, facing him, he knew, was the real reason
Vincent Bedford had died. And that man was likely to be
less enthusiastic about the threat Lincoln Scott had publicly
issued.

And that man might do something about it.

Tommy reached out, shoulders still locked squarely, head
back, and pushed open the doors, rapidly exiting the packed
theater and rushing out into the midday sunshine of late
spring at Stalag Luft Thirteen. He stopped and gasped
sharply, breathing in deeply from the rusty, tainted, impure,
and barbed-wire enclosed air of imprisonment.

Chapter Seven

MOUSE ROULETTE

After the hearing, they left Lincoln Scott alone in his bunk room. The black flier had been electric, excited, by the morning's action. He had shaken hands with both Tommy Hart and Hugh Renaday, and then suddenly dropped to the floor and started in on rapid-fire push-ups. They made plans to meet later in the day to map out their next step, and Tommy left Scott behind, the Tuskegee airman dancing lightly in a corner of the room, shadowboxing imaginary opponents, snapping hard left jabs and swooping right haymakers, using the bright midday light that filtered through the bunk-room windows and threw just enough darkness into the corners to create the shadows necessary for the mock-fight.

Hugh spotted a ferret snooping around Hut 105, probing the dirt in a small garden by the side of the barracks. The ferret demanded three cigarettes to accompany the two men back to the British camp, where they intended to inform Phillip Pryce about the morning's session. Tommy negotiated him down to two smokes, and the three men rapidly crossed the exercise area, heading to the front gate. A baseball game had started up, and there were some men doing calisthenics on the side, calling out numbers in unison. Both groups paused slightly as they passed by—not stopping what they were doing, but slowing, taking note. Tommy braced for a verbal onslaught, but nothing was said in their direction, no catcalls, no obscenities, no epithets.

He took this as a positive sign. If they'd managed to sow

some doubt amid the kriegies with the forcefulness of Lincoln Scott's words of denial, then that was good. Perhaps the same questions were rooting in the minds of the three judges.

He wished he knew more about the two officers who sat by MacNamara's side on the tribunal. He made a mental note to find out who they were and where they came from, and how they'd arrived at Stalag Luft Thirteen. He wondered whether the circumstances of each kriegie's capture wasn't some sort of window on who they were, or who they might become, and thought to ask Phillip Pryce about this. He thought, too, that he needed to understand the SAO better, as when all was said and done, he doubted whether the two men flanking him on the tribunal would vote against him. He recalled what Phillip Pryce had said on the first day—"all the forces at work"—and reminded himself to take better care of answering that question.

He found himself walking swiftly, almost a half-trot, as if the weight of the things he needed to do was prodding him in the back. He guessed that some of the same thoughts were powering Hugh as well, because the Canadian was keeping pace without complaint or question. The German ferret, however, dragged behind lazily, and more than once the two airmen gestured for him to hurry.

"Tommy," Hugh said quietly, "we need to find the murder location. Every hour that passes it gets colder. The man we're looking for has had more than enough opportunity to cover it up. In fact, I have my doubts we'll ever find it."

Tommy nodded his reply, but said, "I have an idea, but I need to wait just a little longer."

Hugh snorted once and shook his head. "We'll never find it," he repeated.

The gate swung open for them—Tommy took note that the regular gate goons were becoming accustomed to their back and forth travels, which he thought might be a valuable thing, although he didn't know precisely how. They continued through the area between the camps. There was singing coming from the shower house, and Renaday started to hum along as they both recognized the words to "Mademoiselle from Armentières," bellowed at the usual high volume:

". . . Mademoiselle from Armentières, parlez-vous? Ma-

demoiselle from Armentières, parlez-vous? Mademoiselle
from Armentières, hasn't been fucked in forty years, hinky-
stinky parlez-vous . . ."

Like many of the British songs, this one dated back to the
First World War, and grew increasingly ribald.

Tommy had his attention on the shower house when he
suddenly heard the brusque, harsh German command from
behind, overcoming the echoes of the song: "Halt!"

The ferret instantly snapped his cigarette from his lips and
came to attention. Hugh and Tommy swung toward the sound
of the voice. As they pivoted they saw an adjutant in shirtsleeves half-running down the steps from the administration
building and crossing the dusty road toward them. This was
unusual. German officers did not like to be seen by the kriegies in anything less than full uniform, nor did they ever like
to appear rushed, unless someone higher up on the chain of
command had issued an order.

The adjutant hurried up to them. His English was fractured, but he was able to make himself clear: "Hart, pliss vit
me. You, Renaday, back to home . . ."

He pointed at the British compound ahead.

"What's this about?" Tommy demanded.

"Vit me, pliss," the adjutant said. He waved his arms to add
some urgency to his words. "Not to want to keep waiting,
pliss. . . ."

"I still want to know what this is all about," Tommy
replied. The German officer's face seemed to contract, and he
stamped his foot once, raising a dusty puff of dirt.

"Is ordered. See Commandant Von Reiter."

Renaday's right eyebrow shot up.

"Now, isn't that interesting," he said quietly. He turned to
the ferret, who had not moved a muscle. "Okay, Adolf, let's
go. Tommy, I'll be waiting with Phillip. Very curious sum-
mons, this," he added.

The German officer seemed immensely relieved that
Tommy was willing to accompany him, and he held the
door open for the American as they stepped inside the administration building. Several of the clerks sitting behind
desks looked up curiously as he entered, but then when the

officer followed, they dutifully returned their eyes to whatever documents they had in front of them. German military bureaucracy was steady and thorough; more than anything, it sometimes seemed, they hated the ingenuity and creativity of their prisoners. Tommy was pushed once in the direction of the commandant's office, which made him stop, pivot, stare at the adjutant with a narrow gaze. When the officer stepped back, dropping his hands, Tommy turned again and walked sharply across the floor and pulled open the door to Von Reiter's room.

The commandant was behind his desk, waiting. A single, uncomfortable chair was arranged in front of the desk, for Hart to sit in, which he did, as Von Reiter gestured toward it. But as soon as he sat, the German immediately rose to his feet so that he towered above Tommy. Von Reiter, too, was in shirtsleeves, his tailored white shirt glistening in the light pouring through a wide window that overlooked the two compounds. The starched collar pushed at the officer's ruddy throat. The jet black Iron Cross he wore around his neck gleamed against the immaculate shirtfront. His dress jacket hung from a hook on the wall, a polished black leather gun belt with a Luger in a holster hanging next to it. The commandant walked over to his jacket and brushed a piece of imaginary lint from the lapel. Then he turned to Tommy.

"Lieutenant Hart," he said slowly, "your work goes well?"

"We are only in the beginning stages, *Herr* commandant," Tommy answered carefully. "And certainly Hauptmann Visser can fill you in with whatever details you require."

Von Reiter nodded, and returned to his seat.

"Hauptmann Visser is, how do you put it? Staying in touch?"

"He takes his job seriously. He seems most attentive."

Von Reiter moved his head in a half-nod.

"You are here many months, lieutenant. An old-timer, as Americans say. Tell me, Mr. Hart, you find life at Stalag Luft Thirteen to be . . . acceptable?"

This question surprised Tommy, but he tried to withhold any sign of this sensation. He shrugged, in an exaggerated fashion.

"I'd rather be home, *Herr* commandant. But I am also glad to be alive."

Von Reiter nodded and smiled. "This is the one quality all soldiers share, true, Hart? No matter how harsh life is, it is still better to enjoy it, because death is so easy to acquire in war, do you not think?"

"Yes, *Herr* commandant."

"Do you believe you will live through the war, Hart?"

Tommy inhaled sharply. This was the one question, bluntly put, no kriegie ever asked or answered, never gave voice to, not even in a joke, because it immediately opened the door to all their deep and uncontrollable fears. The wake-up-choking-in-the-middle-of-the-night fears. The staring-at-the-barbed-wire-in-the-middle-of-the-day fears. It invoked the names and faces of all the men who had died in the air around them and all the men still breathing, but destined to die in the seconds, minutes, hours, and days to come. He slowly released his breath and answered obliquely, forcing himself not to truly dwell on this, the worst of all questions.

"I am alive today, *Herr* commandant. I hope to be alive tomorrow."

Von Reiter's eyes seemed piercing. His stiffness, Tommy thought, masked a man of considerable intellectual intensity and rigid formality. This was always a dangerous combination.

"Captain Bedford, he undoubtedly felt the same on the final day of his life."

"I wouldn't know what he felt," Tommy replied, but of course, this was a lie, for he did know.

Von Reiter continued to fix Tommy with an unwavering gaze. After a momentary silence, he continued his queries:

"Tell me, Hart, why do Americans hate the blacks?"

"Not all Americans do."

"But many, yes?"

Tommy nodded. "Yes. It seems so."

"And why is that?"

Tommy shook his head.

"Complicated. I'm not sure I really could say."

"You do not hate Lieutenant Scott?"

"No."

"He is inferior to you, no?"

"Doesn't seem that way."

"And also you believe in his innocence?"

"I do."

"If he has been falsely accused, as you say, then we have many problems. Many problems. Both for your commander, and myself."

"I haven't really considered that question, *Herr* commandant. Perhaps."

"Yes, this will be true. It might be wise for you to examine this question, lieutenant. But perhaps, on the other hand, he is truly guilty and you are merely doing what you have been ordered. Americans are fond of showing the world how just and fair they are. They speak of rights and laws and their beloved founding fathers and their documents. Thomas Jefferson and George Washington and the Bill of Rights. But I think they forget about order and discipline, too. Here, in Germany, we have order. . . ."

"Yes. I've seen it."

"And here in Stalag Luft Thirteen, we have order, as well."

"I suppose."

Von Reiter paused again. Tommy shifted about in his seat, eager to leave. He did not know what the commandant was searching for, and in the absence of this knowledge, he was uncomfortable about what information he might impart unwittingly.

The German laughed briefly. "And sometimes, I think this is correct, lieutenant, justice for Americans, the show is more important than the truth. Do you not agree?"

"I haven't thought of it."

"Truly?" Von Reiter looked at him quizzically. "And you a student of your own laws?"

Tommy did not reply. Von Reiter smiled again.

"Tell me, Lieutenant Hart, for I am eager to know: Which is more dangerous, if Scott is guilty or if he is innocent?"

Tommy remained silent, not answering the question. He could feel sweat trickling down beneath his armpits, and the room seemed to increase in heat. He wanted to leave, yet was rooted to his seat. Von Reiter's voice was rough-edged, but penetrating. He thought in that second the commandant was a man who saw secrets within secrets, and he told himself that the commandant's creased uniform and stiff-backed bearing were every bit as deceptive as Hauptmann Visser's cryptic, questioning glances.

"Dangerous for whom?" Tommy answered cautiously.

"Which result will cost men their lives. Guilt or innocence, lieutenant?"

"I don't know. It is not my job to know."

Von Reiter allowed himself a small, unfriendly laugh, nodded, and idly picked up a sheet of paper from his desk, staring at it for a moment before continuing.

"Vermont is your home, no?"

"It is."

"It is a state not unlike here. Thick woods and harsh winters, I believe?"

"It has many quite beautiful forests and a long, hard winter season, yes," he said slowly. "But it is not like here."

Von Reiter sighed. "I myself have only been to New York. And just once. But London and Paris many times. Before the war, of course."

"I never traveled all that much."

The commandant took a long look out the window.

"If Lieutenant Scott is declared to be guilty, will your colonel truly demand I provide a firing squad?"

"You should ask him."

The commandant frowned.

"No one has escaped from Stalag Luft Thirteen," he said slowly. "Only the dead, like the unfortunate men in the tunnel. And now, such as Captain Bedford. It will remain that way, do you not think, lieutenant?"

"I never try to guess what the future holds," Tommy replied.

"It will remain that way!" Von Reiter said forcefully. Then he swung away from the window.

"Do you have a family, Lieutenant Hart?"

"Yes. Of course."

"A wife? Children?"

"No. Not yet." He hesitated as he spoke.

"But there is a woman, no?"

"Yes. Waiting back home."

"I hope that you will live to see her again," Von Reiter said briskly. He waved his hand at Tommy, signaling the end of the meeting. Tommy rose, and started toward the door, but Von Reiter added one other question, almost as an afterthought. "Do you sing, Lieutenant Hart?"

"Sing?"

"Like the British."

"No, *Herr* commandant."

Von Reiter shrugged again, grinning. "You should perhaps learn. As I have. Perhaps after the war I will write a book containing all the music and words to the filthy British songs and thus I will make some money to welcome my old age." The commandant laughed out loud. "Sometimes we must learn to accommodate that which we also hate," he said. Then he turned his back on Tommy and stared out of his window at the two compounds. Tommy moved swiftly through the office door, unsure whether he had just been threatened or warned, and thinking that there was probably much the same menace contained within each.

Tommy passed a game of mouse roulette going on in one of the bunk rooms as he hurried to Renaday and Pryce's quarters. A half-dozen British officers were seated around a table, each with a modest stack of cigarettes, chocolate, or some other foodstuffs in front of them. Betting materials. In the center was a small carton, with airholes punched in the sides. The men were shouting, joking, mercilessly insulting and teasing each other, back and forth. American pilots' obscenities tended toward the short and brutal. The British, however, seemed to take some delight in the exaggerations and florid language of their verbal assaults. The air was filled with these.

But at a sudden signal from the croupier, a lanky, thickly bearded pilot wearing an old gray blanket tied around his waist as a sort of half-kilt, half-dress, the men grew instantly silent. Then, once the quiet was complete, the croupier lifted the lid of the box and a captured mouse timidly peeked out over the edge.

Mouse roulette was simple. With a little prodding and encouragement from the croupier, the mouse would tumble onto the tabletop, and look about himself at the waiting but absolutely stock-still, hardly breathing, rigid and perfectly silent men. The only rule was that no one could do anything to attract the mouse in the slightest; the terrified kriegie mouse would eventually break out in one direction, scurrying toward what it so fervently believed was the least threatening presence and safety. Whichever man was closest to the breakout was declared the winner. The problem with mouse roulette, of course, was that more often than not, the fleeing mouse would try to escape into the space between two of the men, which led to great mock disputes trying to assess what the mouse's true intentions had been, other than freedom, which was always its single-minded and greatest hope and desire.

Tommy watched the game for a moment, up until the point the mouse made its futile break, then he hurried on as the game dissolved into loud laughter and counterfeit arguments.

When he arrived at the door to the bunk room, he saw there was a third man sitting in the room alongside Pryce and Renaday, who looked up quickly as Tommy entered. The stranger was a dark-haired but fair-complected young man, very thin, like Pryce, with narrow wrists and a sunken chest, which gave him an oddly birdlike appearance behind a pair of wire-rimmed spectacles. His smile was cocked slightly to the left, almost as if his entire body were leaning in that direction. All three men rose, as Tommy stepped forward.

"Tommy, this is a friend of mine," Hugh said briskly. "Colin Sullivan. From the Emerald Isle."

Tommy shook hands. "Irish?" he asked.

"I am, indeed," Sullivan replied. "Irish and Spitfires," he added. Tommy had difficulty imagining the slight young man wrestling with the controls of a fighter plane, but did not say this out loud.

"Colin most generously has offered to help out," Phillip Pryce said. "Show him, my boy."

The Irishman reached down and Tommy saw that he had a large sketch pad half-stuck under the bed. "Actually," Sullivan said to Tommy, "Irish, Spitfires, and three boring years at the London School of Design before getting involved in all the patriotic foolishness that seems to have landed me here."

Sullivan opened the sketch pad, and handed Tommy the

first drawing. It was a dark vision of Trader Vic's body, stuffed into the *Abort* stall, rendered mainly in the gradations of gray created by a charcoal pencil. "I had to work with Hugh's recollections," Sullivan said, smiling. "And surely you know that the Canadians, being a hairy and rough-hewn people as wild as Indians and with the imaginations of buffalo, have no natural gifts for the poetry of description, like my countrymen and myself," he said, tossing a quick smile at a grimacing, but obviously pleased, Hugh Renaday. "So it's the very best I could do, allowing for my limited resources. . . ."

Tommy thought the sketch caught the murdered man's figure perfectly. It was both nightmarish and brutal, in the same space. Sullivan had used some precious paints to display the modest blood streaks on the American's body. They stood out sharply, in dramatic contrast to the darker, somber tones of the pencil's shadings. "This is fantastic," Tommy said. "That's exactly what Vic looked like. Are there more?"

"Aye, absolutely," Sullivan said, with a quick grin. "Not precisely what my old life-drawing professor probably had in mind back in my school days, but he did always rather tediously lecture us to employ that which is at hand, and though I might prefer some naked *fraulein* posing provocatively with a thank-you-very-much smile . . ."

He handed a second drawing to Tommy. This showed the critical neck wound on Trader Vic's body.

"I worked with him on that one," Hugh said. "Now what we'll need to do is take it and show it to the Yank who examined the body, just to make certain it's accurate."

Tommy flipped to another sketch, this a drawing of the interior of the *Abort* displaying distances and locations. An ornate, feathered arrow pointed toward the bloody footprint on the floor. A final sketch was a redoing of the tracing of the bootprint that Hugh had done on the scene.

"A damn sight better than my clumsy efforts," Renaday said, grinning. "Like usual, all this was Phillip's idea. He knew Colin was my friend, but of course, I hadn't thought of putting him on the case."

"It was fun," Colin Sullivan said. "Far more intriguing than yet another bloody drawing of the northeast guard tower. That's the one that gets the best afternoon light, you know, and the one we in the camp art classes all dutifully troop out and draw every day that it's not raining."

"I'm impressed," Tommy said. "These will help. I can't thank you enough."

Sullivan shrugged.

"Back home in Belfast," he said, now speaking slowly, "well, let me put it to you this way, Mr. Hart: I'm Irish and I'm a Catholic, and that fact alone should tell you that I've been treated like a nigger probably every bit as often as your Lincoln Scott has been in the States. So, there you have it. I'm more than pleased to help out."

Tommy was slightly taken aback by the forcefulness of the slight Irishman's sudden vehemence. "These are excellent," he said again. He was about to continue with praise, when he was interrupted by a cold and quiet voice from behind him.

"But there is an error," the voice said.

The Allied fliers pivoted, and saw Hauptmann Heinrich Visser standing in the doorway, staring across the room directly at the drawing in Tommy's hands.

None of the three men responded, letting silence swirl through the small space, filling the room like a bad scent on a weak wind. Visser stepped forward, still regarding the drawing with a studious and intent look. In his only hand, he carried a small, brown leather portfolio, which he set down on the floor at his feet, as he leaned forward and jabbed an index finger at the drawing that mapped the scene.

"Right here," he said, turning to Renaday and Sullivan. "This is mistaken. The bootprint was another few feet over, closer to the *Abort* stall. I measured this distance myself."

Sullivan nodded. "I can make that change," he said in an even voice.

"Yes, make that change, flying officer," Visser said, lifting his eyes from the drawing, and staring narrow and hard at Sullivan. "A Spitfire pilot, you said."

"Yes."

Visser coughed once. "A Spitfire is an excellent machine. Quite a match even for a 109."

"That is true," Sullivan said. "The *Hauptmann* has personal experience with Spitfires, I would imagine." The Irishman then pointed directly at the German officer's missing arm. "Not the best of experiences, too, I'll wager," Sullivan added coldly.

Visser nodded. He did not reply, but his face had paled slightly and Tommy saw his upper lip quiver.

Sullivan took a deep breath, which did nothing to change his own slight and sallow appearance. "I am sorry for your wound, *Hauptmann*," he said, his voice taking on even thicker inflections and accents from his native country. "But I think that you are among the truly fortunate. None of the men piloting 109s that I shot down ever managed to bail out. They are all up in Valhalla, or wherever it is that you Nazis think you go when you pull a cropper for the fatherland."

The words from the Irishman were like blows in the small room. The German straightened his shoulders as he stared at the young artist with unbridled anger. But his voice did not betray the rage that the *Hauptmann* must have felt, for his words remained even, icy, and flat.

"This is perhaps true, Mr. Sullivan." Visser spoke slowly. "But still, you are here in Stalag Luft Thirteen. And no one knows for certain whether you will ever see the streets of Belfast again, do they?"

Sullivan did not answer. The two men eyed each other hard, without compromise, and then Visser turned back to the drawing and said, "And there is another detail that you have gotten wrong in the drawing, Mr. Sullivan. . . ."

The German pivoted slightly, looking at Tommy Hart.

"The bootprint. It was facing the other direction."

Visser took his finger and pointed down at the sketch. "It was heading in this direction."

He motioned toward the back of the *Abort* to where the body was discovered.

"This," Visser continued, coldly, "I think you will find, is an important fact."

Again, none of the Allied fliers spoke. And in this second silence, Visser turned again, so that now he was facing Phillip Pryce.

"But you, Wing Commander Pryce, you will already have seen this, and you will, I have no doubt whatsoever, understand its true significance."

Pryce simply stared at the German, who smiled nastily,

handed the sketches back to Tommy Hart, and reached down to his leather portfolio. With some dexterity, using his only hand, he managed to extract a small, tan, dossier folder from within the portfolio.

"It took me no small amount of time to obtain this, wing commander. But when I did finally acquire it, ah, the intrigue that it held. Quite interesting reading."

The other men in the room remained quiet. Tommy thought Pryce's breath was filled with the wheeziness of tension.

Heinrich Visser looked down at the dossier. His smile faded, as he read:

"Phillip Pryce. Wing Commander, 56th Heavy Bomber Group, stationed in Avon-on-Trent. Commissioned in the RAF, 1939. Born, London, September 1893. Educated at Harrow and Oxford. Graduated in the top five in his class at both institutions. Served as an air adjutant to the general staff during the first war. Returned home, decorated. Admitted to the bar, July 1921. Primary partner in the London firm of Pryce, Stokes, Martyn and Masters. At least a dozen murder trials argued, all of the most sensational, with great headlines and all due attention, without a single loss . . ."

Heinrich Visser stopped, looked up, fixing the older man.

"Not a single loss," the German repeated. "An exemplary record, wing commander. Outstanding record. Quite remarkable. And probably quite remunerative, as well, no? And at your age, it would have seemed that you had no need of enlisting, but you could have remained throughout the war enjoying the comforts of your position and resting amid your quite noteworthy successes."

"How did you obtain that information?" Pryce demanded sharply.

Visser shook his head.

"You do not truly expect me to answer that particular question, do you, wing commander?"

Pryce took a deep breath, which caused him to cough harshly, and shook his head.

"Of course not, *Hauptmann*."

The German closed the dossier, returned it to his portfolio, and glanced across at each of the men, in their turn.

"Not a single loss in a capital case. Quite a phenomenal accomplishment, even for a barrister as prominent as yourself. And this case, where you have been so ably, yet so discreetly, assisting young Lieutenant Hart? You do not predict that it might become your very first failure?"

"No," Pryce said abruptly.

"Your confidence in your American friend is admirable," Visser said. "I do not know that it is widely shared beyond these walls." Visser smiled. "Although, after this morning's performance, perhaps there are some who are reevaluating their opinions."

Visser worked the portfolio up beneath his remaining arm.

"Your cough, wing commander. It seems quite severe. I think you should see to its treatment before it worsens further," the German said briskly. Then, with a single, farewell nod, he turned sharply on his heel and strode from the room, the metal tips of his boots making a machine-gun–like sound against the worn wooden boards.

The four Allied fliers remained silent for a moment, until Pryce broke the quiet: "The uniform is Luftwaffe," he said thinly, "but the man is Gestapo."

It was later in the day when Tommy hurried across to the South Compound, heading toward the medical services tent to interview the Cleveland mortuary assistant. He was troubled by Visser's appearance. On the one hand, the German seemed to be trying to help—as evidenced by his pointing out the flaws in the crime scene sketches. But then there was so much unmistakable threat in everything he said. Pryce, in particular, had been unsettled by the *Hauptmann*'s unstated intentions.

As he paced quickly through the darkening shadows that littered the alleys between the housing huts, Tommy Hart found himself thinking about the game of mouse roulette he'd seen earlier. He decided that he would no longer feel anything but sympathy for the mouse.

There were a couple of airmen standing outside the medical services hut, smoking. They parted as he approached, and one of the fliers said, "Hey, Hart, how's it going?" as he passed.

He found Lieutenant Nicholas Fenelli inside one of the small examination rooms. There was a small table, a few hard-backed chairs, and a tabletop covered with a rough white sheet. Light from a single overhead electric bulb filled the room. On a pair of wooden shelves that had been nailed to one wall there was an array of medicines—sulfa drugs, aspirin, disinfectants—and creams, bandages, and compresses. The selection was modest; all the kriegies knew that getting sick or injured was dangerous in Stalag Luft Thirteen. A routine illness could easily become complicated by the lack of proper medical materials, despite the efforts of the Red Cross to keep the dispensary stocked. The Allied prisoners believed that the Germans regularly pilfered the precious medicines for their own hard-pressed hospitals, but this was denied by the Luftwaffe commanders, who scoffed at the allegations. The more they scoffed, the more the kriegies were convinced they were being robbed.

Fenelli looked up from behind the table as Tommy entered.

"The man of the hour," he said, extending his hand. "Hell, that was some show you put on this morning. You got an encore planned for Monday?"

"I'm working on it," Tommy replied. He glanced around. "You know, I've never been in here before. . . ."

"You're lucky, Hart," Fenelli said brusquely. "I know it ain't much. Hell, best I can do is lance a boil, maybe clean out some blisters, or set a broken wrist. Other than that, well, you got trouble." Fenelli leaned back, glanced out the window, and lit a cigarette. He gestured at the medicines. "Don't get sick, Hart. At least not until you think Ike or Patton and a column of tanks is just down the road." Fenelli was short, but wide-shouldered, with long, powerful arms. His curly black hair hung over his ears, and he was in need of a shave. He had an open grin, and a cocky, self-assured manner.

"I'm not planning on it," Tommy said. "So, you're going to be a doctor?"

"That's right. Back to med school as soon as I get my sorry butt outta here. Shouldn't have too much trouble with gross anatomy class after all the stuff I've seen since I got my greetings from Uncle Sam. I figure I've seen just about every body part from toes to guts to brains all laid out nice and special thanks to the fucking Krauts."

"You worked in the mortuary back home. . . ."

"I told all that stuff to your buddy, Renaday. All true. And not nearly as bad a place to work as folks'll think. One thing you can always count on: Working in a mortuary is a nice, steady job. Never a shortage of stiffs heading your way. Anyway, as I told your Canadian buddy—shit, I wouldn't want to get in a fight with him, you see the shoulders on him? Anyway, I told him, soon as I saw that knife wound in Trader Vic's neck, I knew what the hell had happened. Didn't have to look at it for more than one second, although I did. Took a nice long look. I seen it before and I know how it got put there, and I haven't got no trouble telling anyone who's interested."

Tommy handed Fenelli the sketch of the neck wound that Colin Sullivan had made. The American swiftly nodded.

"Hey, Hart. This fella can draw, all right. Yeah. That's exactly what it looked like. Even the edges, man, he's got them just right. Not sliced, like you'd think, but just frayed a bit where the knife went in, bang! and then got worked around. . . ."

As he spoke, Fenelli mimicked the blade entering the throat. Tommy took a deep breath, imagining the last second of panic that Trader Vic must have felt as he was grasped from behind.

"So, if I call you to the stand . . ."

As he spoke, Fenelli handed Tommy back the sketch of the neck wound.

"Sure. No problem. Maybe piss off Clark a bit. But that man's in genuine need of pissing off. Tight-ass career army type. Screw him."

Fenelli laughed out loud.

"Hey," he said, grinning, "you gonna spring this on Monday? Not bad, Hart. Not bad at all. That old fart Clark don't have nothing going for him like this."

"Not Monday," Tommy replied. "But soon enough. Think you can keep your opinions to yourself?" he asked. "No matter what happens when Clark starts to trot out his witnesses and evidence . . ."

"You mean you want me not to go around shooting my mouth off and telling everybody that Vic bought it just like some low-level capo did on some real dark street corner back home? Sure. You may not learn a lot working in a funeral home in Cleveland, but you do learn how to keep your mouth shut."

Tommy reached out and shook Fenelli's hand. "I'll be in touch," he said. "Just don't go anywhere."

The would-be doctor laughed hard. "You're a card, Hart."

Tommy was about to exit the door to the dispensary when Fenelli said, "Hey, Hart, one thing. You know this guy that's sitting next to Clark?"

"Townsend, I think his name is?"

"That's the guy. You know anything about him?"

"No. I was going to head over to his hut now."

"I know him," Fenelli said. "We came into this shithole same time, same transport. He was a Liberator pilot, shot down over Italy."

"Did he have a story?"

Fenelli grinned. "Hey, Hart, everybody's got a story, don't you know? But that ain't what I think you're gonna find interesting about Captain Walker Townsend, no sir." Fenelli mimicked a slight southern accent as he spoke. "You know what Captain Townsend was back in the States before landing his ass over here?"

Tommy did not say anything. Fenelli continued to smile.

"How about chief assistant district attorney in Richmond, Virginia? That's what he was, and you can bet every damn carton of smokes you've got that's the reason Clark has him sitting in the next seat."

Tommy breathed out slowly. This made sense to him.

"And one other cute little detail, Hart, which I remember from the two days Townsend and I spent in the same stinking cattle car while we was being shipped here. Man tells me he did *all* the murder prosecutions in Richmond. And the man likes to tell me that hell, he's got more men on death row in ole Virginny than he did bombing missions before he got shot down. Like that was some sort of funny kinda ironic thing and all."

Fenelli reached into his shirt pocket, removing another cigarette, which he lit, blowing rings of smoke into the air.

"Just thought you might like to know who you're really up against, Hart. And it for sure ain't that hot-headed idiot Major Clark. Good luck."

Tommy found Captain Walker Townsend in his bunk room in Hut 113 working on a crossword puzzle contained in a dog-eared paperback booklet filled with various games. The captain had nearly completed the puzzle, writing each entry in faint pencil strokes, so that it could be erased upon completion and traded for a can of processed meat or a chocolate bar to some other bored kriegie.

Townsend looked up as Tommy entered the room, smiled, and immediately asked: "Hey, lieutenant. What's a six-letter word for failure?"

"How about *fucked*?" Tommy responded.

Townsend roared with laughter, a voice much greater than his slight build would seem to have accommodated. "Not bad, Hart," he said. His accent was definitely southern, but only in the mildest way. It lacked the Deep South contractions and distinctions that marked Vincent Bedford's speech as well as many others'. His was almost gentle, rhythmic, closer to a lullaby's tones. "Y'all are sharp. But somehow, I don't think that's what the editors of the *New York Times* had in mind when they put this together. . . ."

"Then how about *defeat*?" Tommy suggested.

Townsend looked down at the puzzle for an instant, then smiled. "That works," he said. He put his pencil and the paperback down on the bunk. "Damn, I hate those things. Always make me feel dumb. You just got to have one of those minds that works the right way, I guess. Anyways, when I get back home, I won't never do another."

"Where's home?" Tommy asked, already knowing the answer.

"Why, the great state of Virginia. The capital city of Richmond."

"What did you do before the war?" Tommy asked.

Townsend shrugged, still smiling. "Why, a little bit of this and a little bit of that. And then I got my law degree and went to work for the state. Good work, working for the state. Steady hours and a nice paycheck at the end of the week and a pension waiting down the road some time."

"State attorney? What's that? Land acquisitions and zoning regulations?"

"More or less," Townsend replied, still smiling. "Of course, I didn't have the same advantages as you. No sir. No Harvard University for me, I'm afraid. Just night classes at the local college. Worked all day in my daddy's store—he sold farm equipment just outside the city. Went to school at night."

Tommy nodded. He wore a smile of his own, one that he hoped would make Townsend believe that he'd swallowed the lies without chewing.

"Harvard's overrated," he said. "I think you learn as much about the law in a lot of less fancy places. Most of my classmates were only interested in getting their degrees and getting out and making a fast buck, anyway."

"Well," Townsend said, lifting his shoulders, "still seems to me to be a mighty fine place to be studying the law."

"Well," Tommy said, "at least you're a graduate. So you've got more practical experience than I do."

Townsend held his hands out in a what-do-you-know gesture. "Probably not all that much more, what with your moot courts and such up there in Boston. And hell, Hart, this military tribunal ain't much like what we got back home in all those county courthouses."

No, Tommy thought. I bet it isn't, but the outcome is designed to be the same. He did not say this out loud. Instead, he said, "Well, you've got a list of witnesses for me. And I'd like to inspect the evidence. . . ."

"Why, I've been waiting for you all day, since this morning's hearing—fine job you did on that, too, I must admit. Why, Lieutenant Scott, he seemed filled to the very brim with the righteous indignation of the truly innocent. Yes sir. He did. Why, I must say that all I've heard from the other kriegies all this long day has been doubt and questions and wonderment, which is, I'd wager, more or less what y'all had in mind. But, of course, they haven't seen the evidence in this matter, as I have. Evidence doesn't lie. Evidence doesn't make nice speeches. All it does is point the finger of guilt. Still, my hat's off to you, Lieutenant Hart. You had a fine start."

"Call me Tommy. Everybody else does. Except for Major Clark and Colonel MacNamara."

"Well then, Tommy, I must congratulate you on this first day."

"Thank you."

"But as you'd expect, I'll be doing my best to make it a mite harder from here on in."

"That's exactly what I'd expect. Starting Monday morning."

"Right. Monday morning, zero eight hundred, like y'all said. Just so's we understand, there's nothing personal. Just following orders."

Tommy breathed in sharply. He'd heard that phrase before. As he exhaled, he thought to himself that the one thing he was absolutely sure of was that before the end of Lincoln Scott's trial, things were going to get very personal. Especially toward Captain Walker Townsend, who seemed to have so little trouble lying to him.

"Of course. I understand perfectly," he replied. "Now, the list? The evidence?"

"Why, I have those items for you here, right now," Townsend said. He reached beneath his bunk and removed a small wooden locker made from balsa wood. He removed a leather flight jacket, a pair of sheepskin-lined flying boots, and the homemade knife. The two strips of cloth, one from the frying pan handle and the other from the knife, were wrapped up. Townsend also removed these and spread them out on the bunk.

Tommy looked at those first. The Virginian sat back in his seat, saying nothing, watching Tommy's face for reactions. Tommy was reminded of the players in the game of mouse roulette right at the moment the croupier released the frightened mouse. The players remained still, expressionless, mentally urging the terrified animal in their direction. Tommy adopted much the same visage.

There was no doubt in his mind that the two cloth strips were the same, and that the one from the blade seemed to have small but noticeable flecks of blood on one edge. He noted this, then set the cloth back down. He picked up the knife and carefully measured its dimensions. It was constructed from a flattened piece of iron, almost two inches wide and nearly fourteen inches long. Its point was triangulated, but only one edge had been sharpened into a razor.

"Almost like a small sword," Townsend said. He mock-shuddered. "Nasty item to kill someone with, I say."

Tommy nodded, replacing the knife on the table and picking up the flight boots. He turned them over in his hands, inspecting the flat leather soles that had been stitched onto the softer fur-lined tops. He noted that the bloodstains were predominantly on the toes of the boots.

"Good thing it's nearly summer," Townsend said. "It would be a shame to not be wearing those things in the winter, now, wouldn't it? 'Course, this damn German weather is as unpredictable as I've ever seen. One day we're all out of doors, sunning ourselves like on some trip down to Roanoke or Virginia Beach. Next, well, standing around the morning *Appell* freezing our tails off. It's like it can't make up its mind to get on with the summer. Ain't like that back home. No sir. Virginia we get that nice easy winter and early spring. Long about now there's honeysuckle in bloom. Honeysuckle and lilacs. Like to fill the air with sweetness . . ."

Tommy set the boots back on the bed, and gingerly lifted the leather flight jacket. He saw why Lincoln Scott had not noticed the bloodstains when he reached for the coat after awakening in the near-dark to the sound of German whistles and cries. There was blood on the left knit wrist cuff, and another small streak near the collar on the same side. A larger stain was located on the back. He turned the jacket around once or twice more, then shook his head slowly, sighing.

"Well," Tommy said. "Back home I'd probably claim these items were all seized illegally, without due process."

"Now, I'm not thinking that's an argument likely to work here and now, Tommy," Townsend said. "Maybe back home, but—"

Tommy interrupted him. "But not here. You're right about that. Now about that list?"

Townsend reached into his shirt breast pocket and removed a piece of paper containing ten names and their hut locations.

He handed it over to Tommy, who accepted it, without looking at the names, sliding it into his own shirt pocket.

"I suppose it is premature to start talking about sentencing," he said slowly. "I mean, I think I managed today to prevent a lynching from taking place. But we should discuss the possibilities given the likely outcome, don't you think, captain?" With a defeated look in his eyes, Tommy swung his hand over the array of evidence.

"Why, Tommy, please call me Walker. And yes, I do believe that is premature, as you say. But I am most willing to have these discussions at a later point. Maybe on Monday afternoon, what do you think?"

"Thanks, Walker. I'll get back to you on that. And thanks for being so reasonable about all this. I think Major Clark is—"

Townsend interrupted. "A mite difficult? Temperamental, perhaps?"

He laughed and Tommy, smiling falsely, joined him. "That's for sure," he said.

"The major has been in the bag too damn long. As have we all, I suppose, because maybe one minute's a minute too long. But he and the colonel mostly. Far, far too long, I'd say. And too long for you, too, Tommy, from what I've been told."

Tommy patted his chest where the list was now located. "Well," he said, stepping back. "Thanks again. I'm back to work."

Walker Townsend gave a small nod and reached for his crossword puzzle. "Well, then, you need anything from the prosecution, Tommy, you just feel welcome to come see me anytime, day or night, at your convenience."

"I appreciate that," Tommy said. *Liar,* he thought to himself. He made a small, false-friendly wave, and turned quickly. He took in a razored, long breath of cool air, thinking that for the first time since the moment he'd viewed Trader Vic's body stuffed into the filthy *Abort,* he'd just seen hard evidence instead of mere words, no matter how forcefully spoken, that persuaded him that Lincoln Scott was absolutely innocent of the airman's murder.

The luminous dial on the watch Lydia had given him read ten minutes past midnight when Tommy gingerly slipped from the relative warmth of his bunk and felt the cold floor penetrate through his thin, oft-darned wool socks. He perched on the edge of the bed for an instant, like a diver waiting for the right moment to launch himself toward the water. The night sounds of the bunk room surrounded him with a steady familiarity, the same snores, coughs, whimperings, and wheezes coming from men he'd known for months and yet thought he hardly knew at all. The darkness seemed to envelop him, and he fought off a momentary, unsettled panicky sense, some of the leftover residue of his claustrophobia. The nights always seemed to be as close as the closet he'd shut himself into as a child. It took a conscious force of will to remind himself that the bunk-room darkness wasn't the same.

One of the guard tower searchlights swept across the outside window, boarded to the night, the strong light penetrating the cracks in the wooden shutters for a few seconds, traveling across the far wall. He welcomed the light; it helped to orient him to where he was and push away the childhood nightmare memories that dogged him in all tight, dark spaces.

Reaching down beneath the bunk, he found his boots. Then, with his left hand, he located his leather flight jacket and the stub of a candle fixed into an empty processed-meat tin can. He did not light the candle, preferring to wait for the next searchlight sweep, which would provide him with just enough light to slip from the bunk through the door and out into the hut's central corridor.

Tommy did not have to wait long for the light to sweep past. As it threw its filmy yellow brightness across the room, he rose, boots, jacket, and candle in hand, took three quick strides to the door, and slipped through. He stopped in the corridor for an instant, listening behind him, making certain that he had arisen without waking any of the other men in his room. Silence, save for the routine noises of sleep, surrounded him. He reached into his pants pocket and removed a single match, which he scraped on the wall and which burst into flame. He lit the candle, and moving like some ghostly apparition, he tiptoed down the corridor, heading steadily toward Lincoln Scott's room.

The black flier was asleep in a heap in the solitary bunk,

but the pressure of Tommy's hand on his shoulder made him lurch upright, and for a moment Tommy thought Lincoln Scott was going to throw one of his lethal-looking right crosses in his direction, as Scott twisted in the bed, groaning obscenities.

"Quiet!" Tommy whispered. "It's me, Hart."

He held the candle up to his face.

"Jesus, Hart," Lincoln Scott muttered. "I thought . . ."

"What?"

"I don't know. Trouble."

"Maybe I am," Tommy continued, speaking softly.

Scott swung his feet out of the bunk. "What're you doing here, anyway?"

"An experiment," Tommy replied. He grinned. "A little reenactment."

"What do you mean?"

"Simple," Tommy said, still speaking softly. "Let's pretend this is the night Vic died. First you show me exactly how you got up and moved around on that night. Then we're going to try to figure out where Vic went before he landed nice and dead in the *Abort*."

Scott's dark head nodded. "Makes sense," he said briskly, shaking sleep from his eyes. "What time is it?"

"A little after midnight."

Scott rubbed a hand across his face, moving his head up and down. "That would be about right," he said. "I don't have a clock, so there was no way for me to tell for certain what the time was. But it was pitch black and the place was quiet and it seems to me that would be about right. Maybe a little earlier or an hour or so later, but not much more. Certainly not close to dawn."

"Just before dawn was when his body was discovered."

"Well, I was up earlier. I'm sure of it."

"Okay," Tommy said. "So, you got up . . ."

"This is more or less where my bunk was," Scott continued. "Four double-decker bunks, two on each side. I was closest to the door, so the only person I was worried about disturbing was the guy on top of me. . . ."

"Bedford?"

"Directly across the room. Bottom bunk."

"Did you see him?"

Scott shook his head. "I didn't look," he replied.

Tommy was about to stop the black flier, because this answer didn't make any sense to him, but he hesitated, then asked, instead, "Did you light the candle at your bed?"

"Yes. I lit it, then shielded it with my hand. Like I said, I didn't want to wake the others. I left my boots and jacket . . ."

"Where exactly?"

"Boots at the end of the bunk. Jacket on the wall."

"Did you see either of them?"

"No. I didn't look. And I had no reason to suspect someone might take them. I was meaning to do my business and get back into the rack as quickly as possible. The toilet's not far and I wanted to be real quiet. I went barefoot. Even though it was goddamn cold. . . ."

Tommy nodded, still troubled, then he shook this off and said, "All right, let's go. Show me exactly what you did that night—except this time, bring your boots and jacket. Move the same way, at the same speed." He checked the dial of his watch, timing the black flier.

Without a word, Scott rose. Like Tommy, he seized his boots in his hand. Slightly bent at the waist, he stepped away from the bunk. He gestured toward where the other men would have been sleeping, pointed at the wall where his jacket now hung from a single nail. Still moving quietly, but being trailed by Tommy, Scott walked across the room in perhaps two long strides, and swung the door open. Tommy took note that unlike many of the doors in the hut, this one seemed to have had its hinges oiled. It made a single creaking sound that he did not think in and of itself was enough to awaken even the lightest sleeper. And it only clicked once, as it closed behind them and they were in the corridor.

Scott gestured toward the single toilet. It was placed in a makeshift stall, hardly bigger than a wardrobe, only twenty feet from Scott's bunk room. Tommy held his candle up above his head to light their route. Their feet padded silently against the wooden floor.

Outside the toilet, Scott finally spoke. "Inside. Used the toilet, then returned to the room. That's it."

Tommy looked down at the green light of his watch face.

No more than three minutes had passed since Scott had stepped from his bunk. He turned and looked all the way back down the corridor. For a single instant, his stomach contracted and he swallowed hard. The darkness of his fear of enclosure scratched at his heart. But he fought off the clammy sensation and concentrated on the problem at hand. The only exit to the hut was at the far end, past all the remaining bunk rooms. He thought that to travel from the toilet to the outside, anyone would have to walk past close to one hundred sleeping men, behind a dozen closed doors. But there was no telling who might hear footsteps. Who might be awake. Who might be alert.

"And you saw no one?" he asked again.

Scott turned away, staring back into the darkness.

"No. I told you. No one."

Tommy ignored the hesitation in the Tuskegee airman's voice and pointed forward. "All right," he said quietly. "So much for what you did. Now for what Trader Vic might have done."

Still with their boots in their hands, the two men quietly maneuvered down the hut's central corridor, using the weak candle light to illuminate their path. At the entrance door to Hut 101, Tommy paused, thinking. A searchlight swept past, throwing its light onto the steps for an instant as it traveled forward. Tommy looked back down the corridor, toward the bunk rooms. The searchlight was outside and to the left, which meant that it covered every room on that side of the building, which was the side that he and Lincoln Scott and Trader Vic had all lived on. He realized that it was conceivable that someone could exit from one of the windows on the right side of the hut; they would only catch a portion of the searchlight's path as it swept across the walls and roof. But it would have been impossible for anyone to move through the sleeping kriegies in the tight spaces of the bunk rooms on that side unless something had been prearranged. He was certain that the men who left in the night to tunnel, especially the ones who had died beneath the ground so recently, had been from that side of the hut. Anyone else—escape committee types, forgers, spies, for whatever reason—would need to alert the entire membership of the room of whatever window they intended to use. This, he thought, violated every principle of military secrecy. Even though the men could be trusted, it was a foolish chance to take. Also, it identified the men who were working late into the night, which was another security violation.

So, Tommy thought, measuring, assessing, adding factors together as swiftly as possible, feeling slightly like he did in the moment before some white-haired law school professor chalked an essay question on a blackboard, anyone needing to exit Hut 101 in the middle of the night, and needing to do it without attracting attention either from his fellow prisoners or the Germans, would probably risk going out the front door.

The searchlight swept past again, light quickly filtering through the cracks in the door and then, just as swiftly, fading back into darkness.

The Germans did not like to use the searchlights, especially on nights when there were British bombing raids on nearby installations. Even the most uneducated German soldier could guess that from the air the sight of probing searchlights would make the camp appear to be an ammunition dump or a manufacturing plant, and some hard-pressed Lancaster pilot, having fought off frightening raids by Luftwaffe night fighters, might make an error and drop his stick of bombs right on top of them.

So the searchlight use was erratic, which only made them more terrifying to anyone who wanted to maneuver from one hut to another at night. It was difficult to time their sweeps because they were so haphazard.

Tommy took a deep breath. Getting caught in a searchlight's beam probably meant death.

At a minimum, it would prompt whistles and alerts, and if one got his hands up fast enough, before a *Hundführer* or one of the tower goons pulled his Schmeisser machine pistol into a firing position, probably only a fortnight in the cooler. And getting caught outside would also compromise the tunnel or the meeting or whatever purpose the kriegie had for being out. So, Tommy considered, there never was a routine motivation for exiting the hut after lights out.

He slowly released his pent-up wind, making a whistling sound between his teeth.

Nothing routine about this excursion, either, he thought.

Tommy zipped up his flight jacket, and bent down to tie on his shoes, gesturing for Scott to do the same.

Scott started to smile. The easygoing, devil-may-care grin of a warrior accustomed to danger. "This is dicey, huh, Hart?" he whispered. "Don't want to get caught."

Tommy nodded. "Getting caught isn't quite the problem. Getting dead is. Don't really want to get shot," he said. His throat had parched suddenly, the dryness reaching his tongue. "Not now . . ."

"Not ever," Scott said, still grinning. Tommy thought Scott probably felt closer to being a fighter pilot then than he had in any second since he'd first leapt free of his burning plane over occupied territory. As he knotted his boots, the black flier asked, "So, where we heading first?"

"The *Abort*. And then we'll backtrack a bit."

"What're we looking for, exactly?" Scott asked.

"Exactly? I don't know. But possibly? We're looking for a spot where someone might feel comfortable committing a murder."

With that, Tommy turned to the door. He blew out the candle. He was breathing in a shallow, steady fashion, poised like a sprinter getting ready to start a race. As soon as the searchlight swept over the front of the hut, he grabbed at the door handle, jerked it open, and with Scott inches behind him, dove out into the inky darkness creeping right behind the searchlight's beam.

Chapter Eight

A PLACE THAT
ACCOMMODATED MURDER

Tommy took two dozen fast strides forward, sprinting furiously, then threw himself up against the wall of Hut 102, breathing hard, pushing his back stiffly to the wooden frame of the building, trying to meld together with the hard boards. He watched as the searchlight's beam danced away from him, erratically poking and probing the corners and edges of the huts, like a dog sniffing for some prey at the fringe of some tangled briars. The searchlight seemed to him to be alive, tinged with evil. He inhaled sharply as the beam hesitated at the roofline of an adjacent hut, then, instead of proceeding toward more distant barracks, inexplicably began to sweep back toward him, abruptly retracing its steps. He shrank back in sudden fear, frozen in position, unable to move, as the light crept steadily toward him, closing in on him inexorably. The beam was perhaps three feet away, malevolent, searching as if it somehow knew he was there, but unsure of precisely where, in some deadly version of the children's game of hide-and-seek, when he felt Scott's hand suddenly seize his shoulder and savagely drag him down.

Tommy dropped to the cold earth, and felt himself being pulled back into a small depression next to the hut. He scrambled backward, crablike.

"Head down," Scott whispered urgently.

As he buried his face in the dirt, the searchlight passed across the building above them. Tommy squeezed his eyes shut, waiting for the whistles and shouts from the goons in the tower manning the light. For an instant, he thought he could hear the unmistakable sound of a round being chambered in a rifle—then there was silence.

Gingerly he raised his face from the dust, the dry, musty taste lingering on his lips. He saw the beam of light had swept away, across a nearby roof, probing the distance, as if hunting for some new quarry. He let his wind out slowly, making a sighing sound. Then he heard Scott beside him, speaking softly in a voice that clearly made its way past a grin: "Well, that was goddamn close."

He pivoted, just able to make out the black airman's shape prone in the dirt beside him.

"Gotta move a little faster when trouble starts coming in your direction," Scott whispered. "Good thing you weren't in a fighter, Hart. Stick to bombers, nice and steady and solid bombers. Don't need to react quite so quickly in bombers. And maybe when you get back to the States you better stick to noncontact sports, too. No football, no boxing for you. Golf would be good. Or fishing. Or maybe just read a lot of books."

Tommy frowned. He felt a sudden surge of competitiveness within him. In prep school and then as an undergraduate, he'd been an excellent tennis player. And growing up in Vermont, he'd learned to be an expert skier. He wanted to say something about the capacity to stand on the lip of some snow-covered ridge, cold wind cutting through woolen clothing, staring down the side of some steep trail, and the abandon that he would call up from deep within to launch himself over the edge and down. He thought it took a different sort of recklessness and bravery. But he knew it wasn't the same as climbing into the ring to face down another man bent on harm and hurt, the way Lincoln Scott had. That was something more primal, and he wasn't sure he could do that.

He thought suddenly that there were many questions about himself that needed answering, and that he had postponed asking almost every one of them of himself.

"You gonna be okay, Hart?" Scott asked sharply.

"I'm fine," Tommy replied, shaking the questions from his imagination. "A little spooked. That's all."

Scott hesitated, still slightly amused, then added: "All right, counselor. Lead the way. Tight formation. Wing to wing."

Tommy scrambled to his feet, regaining his bearings. He

took a long, slow breath of the nighttime air, like inhaling black vapors, and realized that it had been almost two years since he'd been outside of the hut in the dead of midnight. Prisoner-of-war camp demanded the most simplistic of routines: Lights out shortly after dark. Go to bed. Go to sleep. Fight off nightmares and sleep terrors. Wake up at dawn. Rise. Be counted. Do it all again.

In his months inside Stalag Luft Thirteen there had been perhaps a dozen nighttime air raids close enough for the camp sirens to be sounded, but the Germans hadn't provided any bomb shelters inside the wire, nor had they allowed the men to construct any, so prisoners weren't scrambled out into the dark to seek protection from their own high in the air above them. Instead, at the first alarm, the Germans merely sent ferrets through the camp rapidly padlocking the doors to each hut. Their fear was that kriegies would try to use a raid as a diversion to escape, and in this they were probably correct. There were always some prisoners willing to risk everything on a whim. Escape was a powerful narcotic. The men addicted might use any advantage available—even when they understood that no one had as yet been successful at escaping from Stalag Luft Thirteen. The Germans knew this, and locked the doors as the sirens sounded. So the airmen waited out the approaching deep whomp-whomp-whomp of bombs in silence and near-panic inside their huts, knowing that any one bomb in the arsenals that they themselves had once carried through the sky could level any of the flimsy wooden huts with ease, killing everyone inside almost as an afterthought.

Tommy did not know why the Germans didn't lock them into the huts every night. But they didn't. Probably because they would have had to lock down every window as well, which would have taken hours to accomplish. And then the kriegies would have constructed false doors and escape hatches to give themselves access to the night. So during a raid the doors were locked and the windows left open, which made no real sense. Tommy always supposed that had bombs actually started to fall on the camp, there was no way of telling what the kriegies would do, so he believed the exercise of locking the doors was actually useless. Still, the Germans did this, without explanation. Tommy presumed there was some stiff and inviolable Luftwaffe regulation they were following, even if it made utterly no sense.

His eyes slowly adjusted to the night surrounding him. Shapes and distances that were so familiar in the daytime sluggishly took on form and substance. Black silence enveloped him and he became aware of Scott's steady breathing at his side.

"Let's move," the Tuskegee airman urged softly, but insistently.

Tommy nodded, but took one long look up into the sky above them. The moon was nearly full, shedding helpful sheets of wan light over their course, but what he looked for were the stars. He counted the constellations, recognizing forms in the familiar arrangements above, warmed to the great swath of filmy white that was the Milky Way. It was, he thought, like seeing an old friend approaching in the distance, and he half-raised a hand as if he were about to wave a greeting. He realized that it had been months since he'd stood outside in night's quiet and read the heavens above. He reminded himself that he was the navigator, and with a long, last glance at the blinking dots of light above, he darted forward, heading toward the *Abort*.

The two men zigzagged from shadow to shadow, moving swiftly toward the distinct joined odors of lime and waste emanating from the *Abort*. The familiar, musty smell that to the men in their prior lives might have been overwhelming and disgusting was, to the kriegies, as routine as bacon frying on a Sunday morning back home.

Their feet made padding sounds against the damp earth. They did not talk until they reached the entrance to the *Abort*, where Tommy hesitated, kneeling down in a spot of greater darkness, letting his eyes penetrate the night around them, searching for the next move.

"Where to, counselor?" Scott said under his breath. "What are you looking for?"

Tommy narrowed his eyes, thinking hard. After a moment, he turned and whispered to Scott. "You're the strong man. All right. Imagine you've got to carry Vincent Bedford. Fireman's carry, over your left shoulder. He weighs what? One fifty-five? One sixty?"

"One sixty, maybe one seventy, max. He was a skinny little bastard. But he ate better than the rest of us. A middleweight."

"Okay. One seventy. But deadweight. How far can you carry that body, Scott? Left shoulder."

"I wouldn't use my left shoulder . . ."

"I know that."

In the darkness, he could see the fighter pilot's head nod in comprehension. "Not too far. Probably farther than you might think, because the killer's adrenaline would be pumping something furious. But still, not too far. It's not like carrying some buddy whose life you want to save. So, maybe a hundred yards. A little more or maybe a little less, depending on how nervous you are."

Tommy measured to himself. He started to calculate an equation, using distance, factoring in the sweep of the searchlights and proximity to the huts. There was a spot, he thought, close enough so that it would be this *Abort* that the killer chose, and not one of the others. And a route to the *Abort* that provided some safety.

He nodded his head, but thought the *why* of the murder still eluded him.

"He needs to avoid the searchlight and the goons by the wire and not make a sound that might wake up some kriegie, and this is where he ends up. So where do we go, lieutenant?" Tommy said. "Give me your best guess."

Scott hesitated for a second, his head pivoting, surveying the darkness ahead of them, then he whispered, "Follow me." Without waiting for an acknowledgment from Tommy, the black airman darted across the alleyway between the two huts, past the entrance to the *Abort*. Working his way slowly, staying close to the wall of Hut 102, he maneuvered to the end of the building. Tommy jogged to keep pace.

From where they were standing in the shadows, both men could see the wire, thirty yards ahead, sweeping away from them, angled out to enclose the exercise and assembly areas. A guard tower rose up in the pitch black, another fifty yards distant. In the moonlight they could see the profiles of a pair of goons, on the platform. Tommy knew the tower contained both a searchlight, now shut off, and a thirty-caliber machine gun. He shuddered. He was about to speak when Lincoln Scott filled in his very words, spoken in a whisper.

"Not this way. Not with those Krauts up there. Too risky."

From somewhere in the darkness, a *Hundführer*'s dog barked once, only to be shushed by his handler. The two Americans shrank back against the wall.

"The other way, then," Tommy said. "Longer, but . . ."

". . . safer," Scott finished.

He immediately began working his way back to where they had started. Moving quietly, it took the two men almost a minute to reach the front of Hut 102. To their left, across the open space of the yard, were the stairs to Hut 101, which they'd exited earlier.

Lincoln Scott took a single step out toward the stairs to Hut 102, then immediately shrank back. His movement caused Tommy Hart to hug the wall, and within seconds, he saw why: The searchlight that had dogged them at the start of their excursion was playing about, erratically lighting up the corner of another hut a short distance away.

The same damn problem as at the other end, Tommy thought abruptly. He could feel his breathing coming in short, wheezy gasps. The searchlight was death. Maybe not certain death, but possible death, and he hated it with a sudden and total anger.

He knelt down, watching it sweep across the distance, cutting through the darkness like a sabre.

Scott lowered himself beside Tommy. "I doubt he came this way, either," he said. "Not weighed down and carrying a body."

Tommy half-turned, staring down the black corridor toward the *Abort*. "I don't think he was killed anywhere here. Too much noise. Too close to all the windows. If Vic shouted, even just once, someone would hear him. They could hear a fight, too. But the problem is, I don't see how you could carry a body around either end of the building. So, how the hell does it get here?"

"Maybe he didn't carry it around," Scott said quietly. "You know, the same problem exists for any of the escape committeemen or the tunnelers—anyone in Hut 101 who needs to be out and somewhere else at night, right?"

"Right," Tommy said, starting to think.

"Well, that means there's another route. One that only a few folks know about," Scott said. "Only the men who need it."

Scott craned his head past Tommy. He lifted his hand and pointed back down the length of Hut 102. "There's a crawl space," he said, still keeping his voice soft. "There's got to be. A way to pass completely under this hut, come out on the other side . . ."

Scott didn't continue. Instead he started to creep back the length of the hut, peering under the edge of the building. At the fourth window, shuttered above their heads, he suddenly ducked down and whispered sharply, "Follow me, Hart."

With those words, the black airman abruptly wiggled beneath the lip of the hut, his legs and feet disappearing as if they'd been swallowed up by the earth.

Tommy dropped to the hard ground, bending over, staring underneath Hut 102. For an instant he could detect just the slightest sensation of movement in the utter darkness beneath the barracks and he realized that it was Scott worming his way beneath the floorboards. The narrow blackness of the space under Hut 102 was enveloping. He inhaled sharply, reeling back a step, almost as if the emptiness of the space had reached out and grabbed at him. His heart started to race and he felt a sudden heat on his forehead. He gasped again, almost as if it were hard to breathe, and he told himself: You can't go in there.

He would not give a word to the terror that swept over him. It was deep, rooted hard within his heart and reaching down into the pit of his stomach, where it twisted and clenched at his guts. He shook his head. Not a chance, he said. Not under there.

He forced himself to look again into the crawl space and saw that Scott had traversed the breadth of the barracks and emerged on the far side. There was just enough moonlight for Tommy Hart to make out the distant exit. A skinny passageway that unless you were looking for it wouldn't be noticed. The hut was probably not more than thirty feet from side to side, but to Tommy this seemed an impossibly long road. He shook his head again, but penetrating past the voice within him that refused to follow was Scott's urgent whisper: "Come on, Hart! Damn it! Hurry up!"

He told himself: It's not a tunnel. It's not a box. It's not even underground. It's just a tight fit with a low ceiling. In the day-light, it wouldn't be a problem. Just like crawling under a car to work on a transmission.

He heard again, more insistent: "Come on, Hart! Let's go!"

Tommy realized it was his idea to be out of the bunk rooms at midnight. He realized that searching for the murder location at night was his idea. Everything was his idea. He realized that this was something he had to do, and so, trying feverishly to clear his mind of all fears and tremors, locking his eyes on the distant exit, he thrust himself under the building, crawling rapidly with a desperate man's urgency.

He scrambled forward, pawing at the loose dirt beneath the hut. His head bumped against the flooring above him, but he pushed ahead, feeling the first awful taste of panic rise in his throat, threatening to freeze all his muscles. For an in-stant, he thought he was lost, that the exit had disappeared. He imagined he was drowning and he struggled against the wave of fear. He lost track of time, unable to tell whether he'd been in the passageway for seconds or hours, and he started to cough and choke as he scrambled ahead. He could feel the panic taking him over, thought that he was going to pass out and then he burst through, rolling forward, only to be grabbed by Scott, and pulled to his feet.

"Jesus, Hart!" the black airman whispered. "What the hell's the matter?"

Tommy gasped for breath, like a man rescued from wildly tossed seas.

"Can't do it," he said slowly. "Not in enclosed spaces. Claustrophobia. Just can't do it."

His hands were shaking and sweat streaked down his face. He shivered, as if the night had suddenly turned cold.

Scott draped an arm around Tommy's shoulder. "You're okay," he said. "You made it. It wasn't that bad, huh?"

Tommy shook his head. "Never again," he said.

Breathing in harshly, he picked up his head and surveyed

the darkness around them. It was like being in another world, to suddenly arrive in the alleyway between two unfamiliar huts. Though there was little difference in reality, it seemed to be odd, unique. He swept his eyes down the corridor.

And then he saw what he thought he needed to see.

The huts had been laid out in typical German regimentation, row upon row. But Hut 103 had been angled slightly nearer the end of Hut 102. The stump of a large tree that had been cut when the campsite had been cleared had not been removed, and the building had been pushed closer to the adjacent hut. The narrowing V shape caused by the odd convergence of the two huts created a darker, shadowy spot. He pointed in that direction.

"Down there," he said. "Let's go."

The two men maneuvered down the length of the barracks once again until they reached the end. He saw that there was some cultivated earth, and he just made out the shapes of some garden plants. But the area was far blacker, protected from the night better than the ends of the other huts. The roofline cut off the moonlight. The narrowing space seemed to defy the searchlight, which lingered on an opposite hut's roof, spreading some light in the alleyway, but creating many deep shadows as well. And the wire, with its perimeter guards and goon tower, was pushed out to accommodate another series of tree stumps. This made him pause, for he realized that in the day, the same spot would receive less sunlight. And this made it an odd location for any kriegie to place a garden.

Tommy considered. An easy place to wait hidden. A quiet place. Very dark. He walked forward, then turned, realizing that he was concealed by the darkness, while anyone making their way down the alleyway would be outlined against distant searchlights. He nodded slowly to himself, and spoke directly to his own imagination. A spot, he told himself, that provided much of what a killer needed.

Tommy felt a rush of excited satisfaction, though one lingering question plagued him, and dampened his enthusiasm: Why would Trader Vic have stepped into that particular darkness? What had drawn him to that spot, where a man with a stiletto was waiting for him to turn his back?

Something had beckoned Vincent Bedford to the juncture

of the two huts. Something he thought was safe. Or profitable. Either was a possibility with Trader Vic. But it was death that had waited there for him.

Tommy slowly turned, staring at the huts around him. He dropped to one knee, feeling the clumps of dirt of the garden.

And why would he have to be moved after he was killed? It would be far less of a risk for the killer to simply leave Bedford's body where the killing took place. Unless there was something nearby that he did not want to draw attention to.

"What do you think?" Scott whispered. "This the place? Sure seems like about the best place to do someone real quietlike."

"I think I'll make a point to come back in the daylight," Tommy replied, as he nodded his head. "See what I can see. But I'd say this spot's a good candidate for the murder location."

"Then let's get the hell out of here."

Tommy rose. "All right," he said. But as he took a step forward, Scott suddenly grabbed his arm.

Both men froze.

"What?" Tommy whispered.

"I heard something. Quiet."

"What?"

"I said 'Quiet!' "

Both men slipped back to the wall of the hut, squeezing hard against it. Tommy held his breath, trying to erase from the night even the noise of his own wind. And into this silence, he heard a thudding sound. Unmistakable but quick, and he couldn't make out where it came from. He slowly exhaled, and heard a second noise, almost a scraping or rustling sound. He bit down hard on his lip.

Scott tugged at Tommy's sleeve. He held a finger over Tommy's mouth to signal silence, then gestured for Tommy to stay close. The black airman then started to move, catlike, graceful, but with an undeniable urgency, through the darkness of the alleyway. Tommy thought Scott seemed to be well educated in the ability to move silently. He tried to keep pace, stepping forward as softly as he could manage, hoping his footsteps would be muffled against the surrounding night.

But every motion he made seemed to him to be a racket.

He could feel his pulse racing, and he pivoted his head, searching the darkness for the source of the sounds that trailed them. Every shadow seemed to move, every slice of nighttime held some form that eluded distinction. Each drop of blackness seemed to mask a gesture that threatened them.

Tommy thought he could hear breathing, then he thought he could hear boots tramping in the nearby exercise yard, then he realized he could hear nothing for real, save the nasty fear-noise of his own heart pounding away within his chest.

They reached the crawl space and Tommy's hands started to shake. Acid bile filled his dry throat and he wasn't certain that he could speak.

Scott paused, bending toward Tommy, cupping his hand around his ear and whispering. "I'm pretty damn sure someone's back there following us. If it's a Kraut, we can't show him the passageway beneath the hut. They figure out that kriegies are using the crawl space and they'll dump concrete in there tomorrow. Can't do that. We're gonna have to try to make it around the front. Dodge the searchlight."

Tommy nodded, an odd wave of relief coursing through him as he recognized he wouldn't have to traverse the passageway again. And with that relief came the understanding that Scott's observation was correct. Tommy thought that at least Scott was still thinking like a soldier. But at that moment, he didn't know what frightened him more: being forced to crawl beneath Hut 102 or trying to elude the searchlight or waiting for whoever was following them through the darkness to emerge. They all seemed equally evil.

"But maybe it's one of our guys," Scott whispered. "And maybe that's worse. . . ." He let his words trail off into the slippery cool air.

With a single glance backward into the void behind them, Scott crept forward to the front edge of Hut 102. Tommy followed on his heels, tossing his own gaze backward once or twice, imagining forms darting through the black night behind them. At the front of the hut, Scott bent down and peered around the edge.

Almost immediately, the black flier pivoted toward Tommy.

"The light's pointing away!" he said, his voice still barely above a whisper but with the demands of a shout. "We go, now!"

Without hesitating, Scott burst around the corner, dodging the stairs to Hut 102, arms pumping, flat out sprinting for the door to Hut 101, like a halfback who spots a hole in the line. Tommy had launched himself directly behind Scott, moving rapidly, although not quite able to keep pace with the black flier. He saw the searchlight's beam cutting through the night away from them, blessing them with the same darkness that had seemed a moment earlier to be filled with terrors. Then he saw Scott take the steps up to their barracks in a single leap, grabbing at the door handle and jerking the door open. As the searchlight abruptly changed direction, and began to race across the dirt ground and wooden huts toward him, Tommy pushed himself forward, flying the last few feet through the air a step ahead of the light, tumbling through the open door. Scott dragged the door closed as he fell to the floor inside the hut, next to Tommy. There was an instant halo of light that passed over the exterior of Hut 101, then proceeded on, oblivious to their presence inside the door.

Both men were quiet, their breath coming in rapid, spasmodic bursts. After close to a minute, Scott lifted himself up on one elbow. At the same time, Tommy felt around for the candle he'd left behind, then found a match in his shirt pocket. The match flickered as he struck it against the wall and the candle threw weak light on the black airman's grin.

"Any more adventures planned for this evening, Hart?"

Tommy shook his head. "Enough for tonight."

Scott nodded, still grinning. "Well, then, I'll see you in the morning, counselor."

He laughed. His teeth flashed as they reflected the candlelight.

"I wonder who it was that was out there with us? A Kraut? Or maybe someone else?" Scott snorted. "Kinda makes one wonder, don't it?" Then he shrugged, rose to his feet so that he loomed up over Tommy and, slipping out of his flight boots, padded off down the corridor without speaking another word.

Tommy reached down to pull his own boots off, wondering the same thing. Friend or foe? And which was which? As he tried to unlace the shoes, he discovered his hands were still quivering, and he had to take a minute to get them under control.

It was a fine morning, warm, filled with springtime promises, with only a few billowy white clouds scudding across the distant horizon like sailboats on a faraway sea—the sort of morning that made the war seem distant and illusory. It seemed to affect the Germans, as well; they completed the morning count rapidly, dismissing the men with more than the usual quick efficiency. The kriegies dispersed throughout the camp lazily, some men gathering into knots and just idly standing about smoking in the assembly yard discussing the latest war rumors, gossiping, and telling the same jokes they had already told day in and day out for months and sometimes years. Others picked up and formed the ubiquitous baseball game. A number of men stripped off their shirts and moved chairs out into the sunshine to bathe in the warmth, and others started walking the wire, like strolling through a park, although the sun glistened off the barbed wire to remind them where they were.

As he expected, Tommy Hart saw Lincoln Scott quick-marching from the assembly ground and entering Hut 101 alone, looking neither to right nor left, to return to his room, his Bible, and his solitude. Then Tommy started to retrace their steps from the midnight before.

He tried not to attract any attention to himself, though he realized, ruefully, that by behaving in such an obviously nonchalant manner he was undoubtedly more noticeable rather than less. But there was nothing he could do about this. He moved slowly, almost as if absentmindedly. He ignored the crawl space under the fourth window of Hut 102, fighting off the urge to inspect it during the daytime. He had a lingering question or two about that passageway, but he had not fully formulated the questions in his mind. Only that, like so many things, something struck him as oddly out of place. There was some connection, some linkage that he didn't fully comprehend, he thought. In addition, he did not want anyone to know that he and Scott had located this route beneath the huts.

So he made his way slowly around the front of Hut 102, scuffling his feet in the dirt, occasionally pausing to lean up against the building and smoke, turning his head toward the sunshine. In the daytime, the distance seemed benign. He swallowed hard against a chill that passed through him as he remembered the race against the searchlight from the previous night.

It took a few lazy minutes before he turned and started to travel quickly down the alleyway formed by the juncture of the two barracks. In the daytime, the V caused by the tree stump was even more pronounced, and he was surprised that he'd never noticed it before.

Tommy paused before approaching the spot at the end of the two huts. He turned around sharply, trying to see if he was being watched, but it was impossible to tell: There was a kriegie on a stoop, darning socks, the needle reflecting the sunlight as he pulled it through the wool; another was leaning in a spot of sunshine, reading a tattered paperback book with seeming intensity. Two men near the front of Hut 103 were idly tossing a softball back and forth, and three other men a few feet distant were engaged in some debate that seemed to require much gesturing and laughter. Other men wandered past, some moving slowly, others rapidly, as if they had some pressing engagement; it was impossible to tell if any one of them was inspecting him. Leaning back against the wall of the hut, he lit another cigarette, trying to blend in with the camp routine as unobtrusively as possible. He smoked slowly, his eyes darting about, surveying the other men, and when he finished, he flicked the butt away. Then he abruptly turned and headed to the juncture of the two huts.

The small garden that he had just been able to make out in the dark seemed desultory and almost abandoned. There were some potatoes and some greens struggling to take root. This was unusual: Most prisoner-of-war gardens were tended with extraordinary care and single-minded dedication; the men who tilled them were devoted to their tiny patches of dirt, not merely for the food they created, which helped supplement the meager rations culled from Red Cross parcels, but because of the great morsels of time they occupied.

This garden was different. It had a shadowy, neglected air

to it. The earth was turned, but clumps of dirt hadn't been broken up. Some of the plants needed trimming. Tommy bent down, kneeling, and felt the ground. It was damp and moist, which was what he would have expected, given the lack of sunshine that filtered into the spot. There was a slight musty and rotten smell to the ground.

He stared at the brown dirt. If there had been any blood spilled here, he thought, it would have been a simple matter for the killer to return the following day and simply cultivate it into the earth. Still, he let his eyes move slowly across the plain, right to the edge of Hut 103.

Then he stopped, his heart quickening.

His eyes fixed upon a faded gray, worn wooden board, just above the ground. There was a small but substantial streak of dark brown clearly marring the wall. Almost maroon colored. Dry, flaky.

Tommy stood up sharply. He had the presence of mind to spin about, once again checking to see if he was being observed. His eyes inspected each of the men lingering within his sight line. It was possible, he realized, that none of them, or all of them, were keeping watch over what he was doing. He calculated in his head rapidly, as he turned back to the small stain he'd noticed. He took a deep breath. If it was what he thought it was, and if he approached it, he knew he would be signaling something to the man who had killed Vincent Bedford, and it was not a signal, he was certain, he wanted anyone to read. There is a fine line, he thought, between defending a man by denial—by attacking the evidence against him and offering different explanations for actions—and the moment that the defense takes a different tack. Shifts its sails and sets off on the more dangerous course, where the finger of accusation is pointed at someone new. Tommy knew there were risks in stepping forward.

He glanced about, once again.

Then, shrugging inwardly, he picked his way amid the ill-tended rows of vegetables to the side of Hut 103. He knelt down, reaching for the wooden wallboard, touching the smear of dark with his fingertips.

His first touch persuaded him that it was dried blood.

Looking down, he ran his fingers through the dirt. Any

other signs of death would have been absorbed, but this board had captured some. Not much, but some, nonetheless. He tried to picture the sequence at night. The man with the blade. Vic's back turned. The swift jab, delivered assassination-style.

He thought: Vic must have jerked about and fallen, slumping in the arms of the man who killed him, bending just slightly, dripping his life away for a moment, unconscious, death hurrying to take possession of his heart.

Shuddering, Tommy turned once again to the wallboard. He realized that the same angles that had created the darkness in the spot had also prevented the recent rain from washing away the bloodstain. This was, he thought, nastily ironic, and it filled him with a cold, harsh amusement.

For an instant, he was unsure what to do. If he'd had the Irish artist with him, he would tell him to sketch the spot. But he realized that the likelihood of him going and finding Colin Sullivan in the North Compound and then returning through the gate and finding the bloodstain untouched were slim. It was smarter to presume that someone was watching him.

So, instead, he reached down and seized hold of the board, and tugged hard. There was a cracking sound as the flimsy wood gave way.

He rose up, with the broken hunk of wood. The bloodstain was captured in the center of the board. He looked down and saw that the damage done to the wall of Hut 103 was minimal, but noticeable. He turned away, and realized that at least a dozen kriegies had stopped whatever they were doing and were regarding him intently. He hoped the curiosity in their faces was typical kriegie curiosity, driven by a fascination with anything that was even the slightest bit unusual or different, anything that might break the tedious routines of Stalag Luft Thirteen.

He shouldered the board, like a rifle, and wondered whether he had just done something terribly foolhardy and eminently dangerous. Of course, he thought to himself, that was what the war was all about: putting oneself at risk. That was what was easy. The tricky part was surviving all the chances one took.

He marched to the end of the hut and saw that one of the men playing catch with the softball was Captain Walker Townsend. The Virginian nodded at Tommy, took in the section of board slung over Tommy's shoulder, but did not interrupt his game. Instead, he reached up and plucked the softball from the air with a graceful, practiced motion. The ball made a sharp, slapping sound as it stuck in the pocket of the captain's faded leather baseball glove.

He delivered the blood-marked board to Lincoln Scott, who had looked up from his bunk with surprise and some enjoyment when Tommy entered the room.

"Hello, counselor," he said. "More excursions?"

"I retraced our steps from last night and I found this," Tommy replied. "Can you keep it safe?" he asked. Scott reached out and took the board out of his hands and turned it over, inspecting it.

"I guess so. But what the hell is it?"

"Proof that Trader Vic was killed between Huts 102 and 103, right where we thought. I believe that's dried blood."

Scott smiled, but shook his head negatively. "It might be. It might also be mud. Or paint. Or lord knows what. I don't suppose we have any way of testing it?"

"No. But neither does the opposition."

Scott still regarded the board with skepticism, but at least nodded his head slightly in agreement. "Even if it is blood, how do we prove it belonged to Bedford?"

Tommy smiled. "Thinking like a lawyer, lieutenant," he said. "Well, I don't know that we have to. We merely suggest it. The idea is to create enough doubt about each aspect of the case against you that the whole of their picture crumbles. This is an important piece."

Scott still looked askance. "I wonder whose garden that is?" Scott asked, as he gingerly fingered the ripped piece of wood, turning it over and over in his hands. "Might say something."

"It might," Tommy acknowledged. "Though my guess is that I probably should have found that out before drawing attention to the spot. Not a helluva big chance anyone will volunteer that information now, I would think."

Scott nodded, turned, and placed the board beneath his bunk.

"Yeah," he said slowly. "Why should anyone help me?"

The black flier straightened up, and without warning, his

jocularity fled. It was as if he'd suddenly been ripped from the abstract of his situation, back to its reality. He quickly spun his eyes around the bunk room, past Tommy, examining each of the stolid wooden walls, his prison within a prison. Tommy could sense that Scott had traveled somewhere within his head, and when he'd returned, he'd also returned to his sullen, angry, the-world-against-him attitude. Tommy did not point out that it seemed that a number of people were already helping the black flier. Instead, he turned toward the door to exit the room, but before he could step in that direction, Scott stopped him with a fierce glance and a bitter question: "So what's next, counselor?"

Tommy paused before replying. "Well, drudge-work mostly. I'm going to interview some of the prosecution witnesses and find out what the hell they're going to say and then go and talk strategy with Phillip Pryce and Hugh Renaday. Thank God for Phillip. He's the one putting us ahead, I think. Anyway, once I've done that, then you and I will start preparing hard for Monday morning because I'm sure Phillip is already outlining a scenario he'll want us to follow precisely."

Scott nodded, snorting slightly. "Somehow," he said quietly, "I don't think that it's going to work out quite as theatrically as all that."

Tommy had turned and was halfway through the door, but there was so much frustration in Scott's words that he turned and asked, "What's the problem?"

"You don't see the problem? What, are you blind, Hart?"

Tommy hesitated, stepping back into the small bunk room. "I see that we're accumulating evidence and information that should show the prosecution's efforts to be so many lies. . . ."

Scott shook his head.

"You'd think the truth would be enough."

"We've gone over that," Tommy said with brisk finality. "It rarely is. Not merely in a court, but in life."

Scott sighed, and drummed his fingers against the leather jacket of the Bible.

"So, we can show that Bedford wasn't killed in the *Abort*. We can suggest that he was killed in a fashion resembling an assassination. We can argue the actual murder weapon wasn't the knife that was so damn conveniently planted here—

although we can't really explain why Bedford's or somebody else's blood was all over it. We can claim that my boots and my jacket were stolen on the night in question by the real murderer—but that particular truth is going to be a hard one for any judge to swallow, huh? We can attack every aspect of the prosecution's case, I suppose. And what good does it do us? They still have the strongest piece of evidence available to them. The evidence that's going to put me in front of that firing squad."

Scott shook his head sharply from side to side.

Tommy stared at the mercurial fighter pilot and for the first time since meeting him in the cooler cell thought him to be a truly complicated man. Scott had returned to his bed, hunkered down, shoulders slumped forward. It was like the portrait of an athlete who knows that the game is lost although there is still time remaining on the clock. The score insurmountable no matter what occurs. He lifted his massive right fist and rubbed it hard against his temples. The confident adventurer of the night before, the man who rose to the hunt in the darkness and danger of the camp at night, had disappeared. The fighter pilot who had led the mission of the midnight past seemed to evaporate, replaced by a resigned, discouraged man; a man filled with strength and speed but shackled by his situation. Tommy was struck by the thought that it seemed at least in part that history was as much a part of the case against him as was any morsel of evidence.

"What's that?" he asked.

Scott sighed slowly, then broke into a rueful smile. "Hatred," he said.

Tommy did not reply, and so the black flier continued after a momentary hesitation.

"Do you have any idea how exhausting it is to be hated by so many men?" he asked.

Tommy shook his head.

"I didn't think so," Scott said, bitterness crawling over his words. He thrust back his shoulders, as if gaining a second wind. "Anyway, here is what is true and what they can prove, beyond any damn reasonable doubt: I hated Bedford and he hated me and now he's dead. That hatred is all they need. Every witness they call, every bit of evidence—no matter how faked or false or phony, Hart—will have that hatred supporting it. And every decision being made in this 'trial' we're starting on Monday, well, it has the same hatred coloring it. They all hate me, Hart. Every one of them. Oh, I suppose there are men in the camp who maybe don't care all that much, one way or the other, and some who know that my fighter group saved their asses aloft maybe more than once, and those men are willing to tolerate me. Might even be inclined to give me the benefit of the doubt. But when you get right down to it, they're all white and I'm black, and what that means is hatred. Why do you think it will be any different on Monday, no matter what we prove? It has never been different. Never. Not since the first slave was taken off the first slave ship in irons and put on sale in the open marketplace."

Tommy started to speak. There was something in the grandiosity of Scott's words that irritated the hell out of him, and he was eager to say it. But Scott held up his hand like a policeman on a street corner directing traffic, cutting him off.

"I'm not blaming you, Hart. And I don't think you're necessarily one of the worst, you know. And I do think you're trying your damnedest. And I'm appreciating that. I really am. I just sometimes sit here, like this morning, and realize it ain't going to do me any damn good at all."

He smiled, shaking his head.

"So," he continued, "I want you to know, Hart, that I'm not blaming you for what happens, no matter what. I just blame all that hatred. And you know what's almost funny? You've got it, too. You and Renaday and Pryce. Maybe not as much as MacNamara and Clark and that sorry-ass dead man, Bedford, but you've got it, somewhere inside of you, probably where you can't see it or hear it or feel it. But it's there, the exact same hatred. And I'm thinking that when it comes right down to the end of all this, that last little bit of hatred for me and the folks like me, well, it'll cause you to do something. Or not do something, it amounts to the same. Maybe not something terribly big, or seemingly important or crucial, but something nonetheless. Like not ask a key question. Not want to rock the boat. Who knows? But in the end, well, saving my sorry life and ass won't quite be worth the price you'll be asked to pay."

Tommy must have appeared surprised, because Scott laughed again, still tossing his head back and forth.

"You just have to understand, Mr. White Harvard from Vermont. It's inside you and there ain't nothing you can do about it," Scott continued, his words momentarily lapsing into a singsong yessuh-nosuh tone that mocked his situation. ". . . And when the end comes, there it will be. That ol' devil, hatred. And so, you jes' won't take a step that you might have, like if I was another white man. You jes' won't have no part of doin' that, no suh. . . ."

Scott exhaled slowly, and let his voice return to the educated flat Chicago tones with which Tommy was familiar. "But you understand, Hart, I'm not holding this against you. You're doing your best, and I appreciate that. At least, you think you're doing your best. It's just I understand the nature of the world. We may be locked up behind barbed wire here in Stalag Luft Thirteen, but human nature doesn't change. That's the problem with education, you know. Shouldn't take the boy off the farm. It opens his eyes and what he sees isn't always what he might want to see. Like blacks and whites. And what happens? What always happens. Because there isn't any piece of evidence in this entire world strong enough to overcome the evidence of hatred and prejudice."

Scott gestured toward the blood-marked board beneath the bunk.

"Especially some hunk of wood," he said.

Tommy thought for a moment about the black flier's speech, then shrugged. "I can think of one thing," he replied.

Scott smiled. "You can? You must be a damn sight smarter than I thought, Hart. What might that be?"

"Someone else hated Trader Vic more than you did. All we have to do is find that particular hatred. Someone hated Vic enough to kill him, even here."

Scott leaned back on his bed, bursting into laughter. "Well, Hart," he said, his chest expanding and his voice loud. "You're right, I guess. But it seems to me, in this war, murdering one another's about the easiest damn thing we do. And I'm not all that sure it all the time has a whole lot to do with hatred. More often than not, it seems to have more to do with *convenience*."

Scott spoke this last word with sarcastic emphasis, before continuing. "But what you say has possibilities. Even if they are unlikely ones."

Lincoln Scott stretched again, like a tired man. Then he slowly rose to his feet and walked over to Tommy Hart. "Stick out your hand, Hart," Scott said abruptly.

Tommy held out his arm, thinking that it was an odd moment for Lincoln Scott to want to shake hands. But this wasn't what Scott did. Instead, he simply poised his own hand next to Tommy's. Black and white.

"See the difference?" Scott asked. "I don't know what we can say that's going to make anyone in that courtroom forget it. Not for one second. Not one lousy second."

Scott turned away, but stopped and twisted back toward Tommy. "But trying should be fun. And I'm not the type that likes to go down without a fight, you know, Hart? You learn that in the ring. You learn it in a college classroom when you're the only Negro there and you damn well better work harder than all your white classmates if you expect not to flunk out. I learned it at Tuskegee when the white instructors washed guys out of the program—guys who could fly circles around any white pilot—for failing to salute them on the parade ground fast enough. And when on the night before we were to ship out to go to battle and die for our country, the good old boys in the local chapter of the Klan took it upon themselves to give us a proper southern send-off by burning a cross right outside the camp perimeter. Fairly well lit up the night, that did, because the white M.P.s guarding the camp didn't think it necessary to call in the fire brigade to put out the flames, which also tells you something. You learn it in a prisoner-of-war camp, too, when *nigger* is the first word you hear as you march through the gate, and it doesn't come out of some Kraut's mouth, either. Losing may be inevitable. Hell, Hart, we all die sometime, and if this is going to be my time, well, so be it. But not without taking a swing or two. Maybe throwing a punch. You see, how you retain your dignity is by fighting hard and moving forward. That's what my daddy the preacher used to say on Sunday mornings. No matter how little the step might be, keep moving forward. Even when you know the outcome already."

"I don't presume that—" Tommy started, but Scott again cut him off.

"That's the luxury of a decidedly white attitude. My own attitude has a different color," Scott said. This time, as he turned away from Tommy, he reached back down to the bunk for his Bible. But instead of sitting, he went over to the bunk-room window, leaning up against the wall at its side and staring out into the camp, though precisely what Scott was suddenly looking for Tommy could not tell.

There were a half-dozen kriegies waiting in the corridor outside Lincoln Scott's solitary bunk room. They straightened up as Tommy closed the door behind him, suddenly standing together, blocking his path to the outside. Tommy stopped in his tracks, eyeing the men in front of him.

"Someone got a problem?" he asked slowly.

There was a momentary silence, then one man stepped forward. Tommy recognized him. He had been one of Trader Vic's roommates and his name was on the witness list that Tommy carried in his breast pocket.

"That would depend," the kriegie answered.

"Depend on what?"

"Depend on what you're up to, Hart."

The man stood squarely in the center of the corridor. He folded his arms across his chest. But the others gathered in a phalanx behind him. There was little doubt about the menace in their eyes, and none in the way they stood. Tommy breathed in sharply, lowering his own hands, and clenching them into fists. He told himself to keep his wits about him.

"I'm simply doing my job," he said slowly. "What is it you're doing?"

The roommate was barrel-chested, shorter than Tommy, but with a thicker neck and arms. He was in need of a shave, and he'd pushed his slouched hat back on his head.

"What I'm doing is checking on you, Hart."

Tommy stepped forward. "No one checks on me," he said briskly. "Now, out of the fucking way."

The group of men tightened formation, blocking his progress. The roommate stepped directly into Tommy's path, chest pushed out, so that now the men were only inches apart.

"What was with the board, Hart? The one you ripped from Hut 103?"

"My business. Not yours."

"You're goddamn wrong about that," the roommate replied. This time he punctuated his words by stabbing a finger three times in Tommy's chest, making him step back a single stride. "What was with the board? It got something to do with that murdering bastard that killed Vic?"

"You'll find out same time as everybody else."

"No. I think I'll find out now."

The roommate stepped forward, as did the men behind him. Tommy searched their faces. He recognized most; they were men who'd played baseball with Vic, or who'd assisted him in his trades. One of the men, hanging near the back, to Tommy's surprise, was the bandleader who'd led the jazz concert at the wire for the man who'd died in the tunnel. He hadn't known that Vic was friends with any of the musicians, and this made him pause for a moment.

The roommate jabbed his finger into Tommy's chest a second time, grabbing for Tommy's attention. "I don't hear you, Hart."

He didn't reply, but behind him, he suddenly heard the door to Scott's door swinging open. He did not turn, but he was suddenly aware of another presence behind him, and he guessed, judging from the faces of the kriegies, that Scott was approaching.

The men fell into a silence, and Tommy could hear sharp breaths of air, as men waited for something to happen. After a moment, the roommate spoke. "Fuck off, Scott. We're talking to your mouthpiece here. Not you."

Scott was now at Tommy's shoulder. Tommy was surprised to hear both harshness and amusement in the black flier's response.

"Is there going to be a fight?" he asked almost lightly. "Because if there is, well, I'd like that. I'd really like that, because I know who I'm taking a piece of first."

There was no immediate reply, and Lincoln Scott laughed.

"Yes, indeed," Scott said. "I definitely think I'd like a real good fight. Even with bad odds, you know. I've been cooped up here without enough proper exercise all these weeks, and I think a fight is precisely what I need. Maybe help get some of the tension out of my system before we head to court on Monday. I could use that. I genuinely could. So what do you say, gentlemen? Who's ready to get started?"

Again there was a momentary silence, then the roommate stepped back.

"No fight," he said. "Not yet. Against orders."

Scott laughed again. A low, hard, even, humorless laugh. "Too damn bad," he said. "I was really looking forward to one."

Tommy saw some confusion mingle with anger in the face of the roommate. What he didn't see was fear, and he thought that the man might be thinking that he was a match for the black flier.

"You'll get your chance," the man said to Scott. "Unless they shoot your black ass first."

Before Scott could answer this, Tommy suddenly pointed at the roommate. "You're on the damn list," he said sharply. The man pivoted toward him.

"What list?"

"Witness list." Tommy again looked at the faces of the men in front of him. Two of the other men standing there were also among the men the prosecution was going to call. One was another roommate of the murdered captain, the other was an occupant of another bunk room in Hut 101, from down the corridor. "You, and you, too," Tommy said briskly. "Actually, glad you're here. You can save me some time finding you. What are you going to testify to on Monday? I want to know, and I want to know right goddamn now."

"Screw you, Hart. We don't have to say anything," the man from down the hallway said. He was a lieutenant and had been in the bag for close to a year. Second seat on a B-26 Marauder that had been shot down near Trieste.

"That's where you're wrong, lieutenant," Tommy said coldly, endowing the word *lieutenant* with the same intonation that he would have attached to an obscenity. "You are required to tell me precisely what you will testify about on Monday. If you don't believe this, then we can go and find Colonel Mac-Namara and he will so inform you. Of course, I would also be obligated to inform him about this little gathering here. He might conceivably also interpret it as a violation of his direct order. I don't know—"

"Screw you, Hart," the man repeated, but with less conviction.

"No, screw you. Now answer the damn question. What are you going to testify to, lieutenant . . ."

"Murphy."

"That's right. Lieutenant Tim Murphy. I believe you come from western Massachusetts. Springfield, if I remember correctly. Not far from my home state."

Murphy looked away angrily. "You have a good memory," he said. "All right, Hart. I will be called to testify about the fight and the other confrontations between Scott, there, and the deceased. Threats and other menacing statements made in my presence. That's what these other men will be speaking to, as well. Got it?"

"Yeah, I got it." Tommy turned to the roommate. "That correct?"

The man nodded. A third also shrugged in agreement.

"You got a voice?" Tommy asked the third flier.

"Yeah," the man said in an unmistakable flat, midwestern tone. "I got a voice. And I'm gonna use it on Monday to see his sorry ass get convicted."

Lieutenant Murphy stared past Tommy, hard at Scott.

"Isn't that right, Scott?" the man asked. The black airman remained silent, and Lieutenant Murphy snorted a mocking laugh.

"That remains to be seen," Tommy said. "I wouldn't bet my last pack of smokes on it." This, of course, was false bravado, but it still felt good, tumbling from his mouth. He turned to the other men standing in the corridor. "I'd like to hear all of your voices, one by one."

"What the hell for?" one of the men who'd been silent asked.

Tommy smiled nastily. "Funny thing about voices. Once you hear one, especially a cowardly one that threatens you in the middle of the damn night, well, you're not likely to forget that, are you? I mean, that voice, those words, the sounds they make, why, they damn well are gonna stick right in the front of your head for a long time to come. And you sure as hell aren't gonna forget that voice, are you? Even if there's no clear face to assign to it, you're still not going to forget the voice."

He looked at the remaining men, including the bandleader.

"You have a voice?" Tommy demanded.

"No," the bandleader replied. Then he and two of the other men abruptly turned and rapidly marched away down the corridor. None of them were big men, but they still walked with distinct size and anger. And if they had an inadvertent *y'all* or *Yankee* in their language, as did the two men who'd paid him the threatening visit in the middle of the night several days past, they had not shared it with Tommy.

Trader Vic's roommate looked over at Scott. "You'll get your fight someday," he said. "I can promise that . . ."

Tommy could sense Scott coiling beside him.

". . . nigger," the man concluded.

Tommy stepped forward, blocking the path of the explosion he believed was coming from Scott. He pushed his face up against the roommate's, so that they were almost nose to nose.

"There's an old saying." Tommy spoke quietly, almost whispering. "It goes something like this: 'God punishes those whose prayers He answers.' You might think about that."

The roommate narrowed his eyes for just an instant. Then, instead of answering, he grinned, stepped back a single stride, spit sharply at the wooden floor, right at Tommy's boots, and then executed a precise, military about-face and marched away down the corridor, followed by the remaining men.

Tommy watched until the door to the assembly yard opened and clattered shut as they slammed it behind them.

Scott exhaled slowly. "I think we will fight," he said. "Before they shoot me."

He paused, then added. "The rest? Well, Hart, that was what I was talking about. Hatred. Ain't nice in person, is it?"

Scott didn't wait for a reply, but disappeared back into his room, leaving Tommy alone in the corridor. Tommy leaned up against the wall, catching his breath. He felt an odd exhilaration, and was curiously flooded with a long-forgotten memory of a time right before he and his bomber group had headed overseas. They'd been flying in formation over the coast of New Jersey, on a spring day not unlike this one, steadily making their way northeast toward Boston's Hanscom Field and their jump-off place to cross the Atlantic.

They were in the lead plane, and the captain from West Texas was looking out over New York City, talking in a rapid-fire monologue, excited about seeing the skyscrapers of Manhattan for the very first time. "Hey, Tommy," he'd called out over the intercom, "where the hell's that big ol' bridge?" And Tommy had replied with a small laugh, "Captain, they've got lots of bridges here in New York and they're all big. But the George Washington? Just take a look to the north, captain. About ten miles right up the river." There had been a momentary pause, while the captain looked, and then he'd abruptly put the Mitchell into a short dive. "Come on, boys," he said, "let's have some fun!"

The formation had followed the *Lovely Lydia* down to the deck, and the next thing Tommy knew, they were flying right up the Hudson, the easygoing whitecaps of spring water glistening beneath their wings. The captain steered the entire group under the bridge, their engines echoing and roaring as they passed beneath some astonished motorists, who'd stopped in mid-span as the flight passed below them, close enough so that Tommy could see the wide eyes of one small boy who waved frantically and joyously at the bombers. The intercom was filled with the whoops and hollers of excited crewmen. The radio crackled with the shouts from the pilots of the other planes in the formation.

Everyone knew what they'd done was dangerous, illegal, and foolhardy, and they were likely to get their butts chewed out at the next checkpoint, but they were all young men who thought it still a delightfully fine and outrageous idea on a beautiful, breezy afternoon. The only thing that might have made the daredeviltry better would have been some young women to admire it. Of course, Tommy thought, this was months before any of them knew anything about the lonely and ugly deaths that awaited so many of them.

He looked down the empty corridor of Hut 101 in Stalag Luft Thirteen and remembered that moment and wished he could feel that sort of excitement once again. Risk and joy, instead of risk and fear. He thought that was what the reality of war stole from him. The innocent chanciness of youth.

Tommy sighed deeply, shook the memory from his head, and walked down the corridor. His boots echoed in the empty space. He flung open the door, and stepped down into the dirt of the camp ground, the sunlight blinding him for an instant. As he raised his hand to shield his eyes from the glare, he saw two men standing just a few feet apart from each other, both watching him. One was Captain Walker Townsend, who had abandoned his baseball glove. The other was Hauptmann Heinrich Visser. The two men had obviously been speaking together. But their conversation stopped when he hovered near.

Chapter Nine

THINGS THAT WEREN'T
WHAT THEY SEEMED

By midday, Tommy had finished interviewing the remaining witnesses arrayed against Lincoln Scott and all had told him obvious bits and pieces of the same story—tales of anger and enmity between two men that transcended the prisoner-of-war camp, and spoke more about the situation back home in the States.

All the kriegies on Captain Townsend's witness list had seen the hatred displayed by the two men. One man told how he'd watched Trader Vic pick up Scott's Bible and taunt him, picking out random passages and applying racist interpretations to the Good Book's words, insults that seemed to make the black flier seethe with anger. Another declared he'd seen Scott tearing in half the scrap cloth that later became the handles to both the pan and the knife. A third described how the two men had fought when Bedford accused Scott of the theft, and how quick the Tuskegee airman had been with his fierce right cross, catching Vic in the upper lip. If Scott had hit him in the jaw, the kriegie said, Bedford would have dropped in his spot.

As he wandered through the camp, alone with his thoughts despite the presence of five thousand other American airmen, Tommy added each small piece of testimony from each witness together, and recognized that the confidence displayed by Captain Townsend and Major Clark was well founded. Portraying Scott as a killer was not going to be an overly difficult task. Indeed, by failing to conform, by remaining aloof and independent, the black flier had consistently behaved in a manner that was likely to make most of the kriegies believe him capable of this different type of killing. It was the simplest leap of imagination: from loner to murderer.

Tommy kicked at the dirt and thought: If Scott had made friends, if he'd been outgoing, communicative—then the vast majority of the kriegies would have ignored the color of his skin. Tommy was sure of this. But, by setting himself alone and apart from his first minute at Stalag Luft Thirteen—no matter how justified he might have been in taking that route—Scott had created the makings of his own tragedy. In a world where everyone was struggling with the same fears, illness and death and loneliness, and the same hungers, food and freedom, he had behaved differently, and that behavior, as much as distrust over the color of his skin, was the cause of the hatred arrayed against him.

Tommy was persuaded that the murder charge was buttressed by that antagonism, which, from the prosecution's viewpoint, was probably ninety percent of their case. The bloodstains, being absent from the bunk room on the night of the murder, the discovery of the knife—all these things when taken together painted a compelling portrait. It was only upon examining each separately that the supposition unraveled somewhat.

Somewhat, he thought. Not completely.

A troubling doubt crept into his empty stomach and he bit down on his lower lip, pensive.

Tommy stopped, taking a moment to look up into the sky above, the typical penitent's search for guidance from the heavens. The normal sounds of the camp surrounded him, but they faded away, as he considered the situation. He thought to himself at that moment that for much of his young life, he'd waited for events to happen to him. He blindly believed— even if incorrectly—that he'd been a passive participant in so much. His home. His school. His service. That he'd managed to stay alive to this point was more by the accidents of good fortune than by anything he'd deliberately seized for himself.

He understood that this waiting for life to happen to him might not work much longer. Certainly, it wasn't going to work for Lincoln Scott.

As he walked, he shook his head, sighing deeply. He felt no

closer to understanding why Trader Vic was killed than he had on the morning of the murder. And, absent the ability to get up before the tribunal and offer an alternative, he realized Scott's chances were slight.

There was a spot of sunshine striking against the exterior wall of Hut 105, making it glisten and seem almost new, and Tommy walked over to it. He slumped against the hut and slowly sank to the hard ground, where he stayed, seated, turning his face toward the warmth. For a moment the sun burned his eyes, and he raised a hand to his forehead. From where he was sitting, he could see through to the wire, and beyond to the woods. There was sound coming from the distance, and he bent toward it, straining to determine what it was. After a moment, he recognized the occasional noisy thud and crash of a tree being felled, and he guessed that just beyond the line of dark trees that marked the start of the forest was where the Russian slave-prisoners were clearing space. It wouldn't be long, he guessed, before the sounds of hammers and saws would be heard as construction began on another camp to hold more Allied airmen. This was what Fritz Number One had told him was under way, and he had no doubt that the ever-present sight of B-17 contrails high in the sky during the day and the deep nighttime rumblings of British raids on nearby installations and rail lines meant that the Germans were acquiring new Allied crews with depressing frequency.

For a long moment he listened to the faded sounds coming from the forest and he supposed that it was back-breaking work being performed by men close to starvation, sick, and near death. He shuddered briefly, imagining what life was like for the Russian prisoners. Unlike the Allied fliers, they had no building compound. Instead, they camped in all weather under makeshift lean-tos and leaky tarpaulins stretched as tents, behind temporary barbed-wire rolls. No toilets. No kitchens. No shelter. Snarling dogs and trigger-happy guards watching over them. There were no Geneva Convention rules governing their imprisonment. It was not unusual to hear the occasional sharp report of a rifle, or burst of machine-gun fire from the woods, which all the kriegies understood to mean that some Russian had realized the inevitability of his death, and had done something to hasten it.

Tommy shook his head briefly, and thought: Death must seem like freedom to those men.

Then he looked at the tall fences of barbed wire enclosing Stalag Luft Thirteen and realized: Imprisonment must seem like death to some men right here.

He felt an odd quickening in his stomach, as if he'd seen something that was surprising. He stared at the wire again. Not a bad spot, he thought abruptly. The guard tower to the north is a good fifty yards away and the one to the south another seventy-five. Their searchlights wouldn't quite overlap, either. Nor did the fields of fire belonging to the machine guns mounted on either side of the tower. At least, that was what he guessed because he knew himself not to be expert in these sorts of details, although others inside the camp were.

He suddenly thought to himself: If I were a member of the escape committee, this would be a spot I would give serious consideration to. He narrowed his eyes, trying to guess the distance to the forest. One hundred yards, minimum, he thought. A football field. Even if you managed to blitz through the wire with a pair of homemade shears, it was still too far for anyone not willing to risk everything on a single dash for freedom.

Or was it?

Tommy scraped up a handful of loose, sandy earth, and let it stream through his fingers. It was the wrong dirt. This he knew from talking with men who'd worked on the unsuccessful tunnels. Too hard and dry, too unstable. Forever caving in. Vulnerable to the probes from the ferrets. He shuddered at the idea of digging beneath the surface. It would be stifling, hot, filthy, and dangerous. The ferrets also occasionally commandeered a heavy truck, loaded it with men and material, and drove it, bouncing along, around the outside perimeter of the camp. They believed the weight would cause any underground tunnel to collapse. Once, more than a year earlier, they'd been right. He remembered the fury on Colonel MacNamara's face when the long days and nights of hard work were so summarily crushed.

It was the same look of frustration and despair that the

colonel wore a few weeks back, when the two men digging had been buried alive. Tommy looked over at the barbed wire. No way out, he told himself. Except the worst way.

And then, in that second, he wondered whether this was true.

To his left, he suddenly spotted an officer with a metal hoe working a small patch of garden, dutifully cultivating the rows of turned earth over and over again. There were similar gardens all along the length of Hut 106. All were well-tended.

Dirt, he thought, fresh dirt. Fresh dirt being blended with old.

He wanted to stand, look closer, but with a great internal tug at his emotions and a lassoing of the ideas that began to spring to his mind, he remained where he sat.

Tommy took a long, slow breath, releasing the air like a man ascending through the water. He lowered his head, trying to make it seem as if he were lost in thought, when in reality his eyes were darting back and forth, searching the area around him. He knew someone was watching him. From a window. From the exercise yard. From the perimeter path. He did not know precisely who, but he knew he was being watched.

Abruptly, from the front of the hut, he heard a sharp wolf whistle, the double-pitched sound that in happier places meant a pretty woman was sashaying past. Almost immediately afterward, there was the sound of a metal waste container being slammed shut twice, another double report. Then he heard a single kriegie voice call out: *"Keindrinkwasser!"* in a distinctly flat, twangy American accent. Someone from the Midwest, Tommy thought.

He stretched out his arms, like a man who'd been dozing, and lifted himself to his feet, dusting off his pants. He noticed that the officer who'd been tending the garden across from where he was seated had disappeared, and this made him very curious, though he took pains to hide this observation. A few moments later, Fritz Number One came sauntering around the front of the hut. The ferret was making no attempt to move through the camp with any concealment; he knew that his own presence had already been noticed by the fliers assigned to stooge duty that day. He was merely reminding the kriegies that he was there, as always, and alert. When Fritz Number One saw Tommy, he walked over to him.

"Lieutenant Hart," he said, grinning, "perhaps you have a smoke for me?"

"Hello, Fritz," Tommy replied. "Yes, if you'll escort me to the British compound."

"Two smokes then," Fritz answered. "One for each direction."

"Agreed."

The German took a cigarette, lit it, took a deep drag, and slowly blew out smoke. "Do you think the war will end soon, lieutenant?"

"No. I think it will go on forever."

The German smiled, gesturing with his hand for the two of them to start moving across the compound toward the gate. "In Berlin," the ferret said slowly, "they talk of nothing except the invasion. How it must be thrown back into the sea."

"Sounds like they're worried," Tommy said.

"They have much to worry about," Fritz answered carefully. He looked up into the sky. "A day like this one would be right, don't you think, lieutenant? For launching an attack. That is what Eisenhower and Montgomery and Churchill must be imagining back in London."

"I wouldn't know. All I did was navigate a plane. Those gentlemen rarely consulted me with their plans. And anyway, Fritz, planning invasions wasn't my particular cup of tea."

Fritz Number One looked momentarily confused. "I do not understand these words," he said. "What has drinking tea to do with military maneuvers?"

"It's another saying, Fritz. What it means is that I don't have any sort of education or interest in that thing."

"Cup of tea?"

"That's right."

"I will remember." The two men continued toward the sentries at the gate, who looked up as they approached. "Again you have helped me, lieutenant. Someday I will speak truly like an American."

"It's not the same thing, Fritz."

"Same thing?"

"Not the same as being one."

The ferret shook his head. "We are what we are, Lieutenant Hart. Only a fool apologizes. And only a fool refuses to take advantages from what is in front of him."

"True enough," Tommy answered.

"I am not a fool, lieutenant."

Tommy took a sharp breath and measured quickly what the German was saying, listening hard to the soft tones, trying to see into the suggestions beyond the words.

The two men marched in unison toward the British compound. Right before they reached the gate, Tommy asked in an idle voice that masked his sudden intensity, "The Russians building the new camp . . . how close to completion are they?"

Fritz shook his head. He continued to speak in a quiet, concealed voice. "A few months, perhaps. Maybe a little time longer. But perhaps never. They die too fast. Every few days the trains arrive at the station in town bringing a new detachment. They are marched into the woods and take over for the men who have died. It seems that there is no end to Russian prisoners. The work goes slowly. Day after day, the same." The ferret shuddered slightly. "I am glad to be here, instead," he said.

"You don't go over there?"

"Once or twice. It is dangerous. The Russians hate us very much. In their eyes, you can see they wish us all dead. Once a *Hundführer* released his dog into the camp. A big Doberman. A vicious beast, Lieutenant Hart, more a wolf than a dog. The fool thought it would teach the Ivans a lesson. Idiot." Fritz Number One smiled briefly, shaking his head. "He had no respect. This is stupid, don't you think, Lieutenant Hart? One must always respect one's enemy. Even if one hates, one must still have respect, no? Anyway, the dog disappeared. The fool stood at the wire, whistling and calling, 'Here, boy! Here, boy!' Idiot. In the morning, the Ivans threw out the skin. That was all that was left. They ate the rest. The Russians, I think, are animals."

"So you don't go over there?"

"Not often. Sometimes. But not often. But see this, Lieutenant Hart . . ."

Fritz Number One quickly glanced around to see if there

were any German officers in the vicinity. Spying none, he slowly removed a shiny brass object from the breast pocket of his tunic.

". . . Perhaps you would like to make a trade? This would make an excellent souvenir, when you finally return home to America. Six packs of cigarettes and some chocolate, maybe two bars, what do you say?"

Tommy reached out and took the object from Fritz's hand. It was a large, heavy, rectangular belt buckle. It had been polished carefully, so that the red hammer and sickle embossed on the buckle glistened in the sunlight. Tommy hefted it in his hand and wondered for a moment whether Fritz had traded bread for it, or whether he'd simply removed it from the waist of a dead Russian soldier. The thought made him shudder.

He handed it back. "Not bad," he said. "But not what I'm looking for."

The ferret nodded. "Trader Vic," he said, with a wry smile, "he would have seen the value, and he would have met my price. Or come very close. And then he would have turned around and made a profit."

"You did much business with Vic?" Tommy asked idly, although he listened carefully for the answer.

Fritz Number One hesitated. "It is not permitted," he said.

"Many things that happen aren't permitted," Tommy replied.

The ferret nodded. "Captain Bedford was always seeking souvenirs of war, lieutenant. Many different items. He was willing to trade for anything."

Tommy slowed his pace as they approached the entrance to the British compound, nodding, realizing that the ferret was trying to tell him something, and Fritz Number One put out his hand and just touched Tommy's forearm. "Anything," the German repeated.

Abruptly, Tommy stopped. He turned and eyed Fritz Number One carefully. "You found the body? Right, Fritz? Just before morning *Appell*, right? Fritz, what the hell were you doing in the compound then? It was still dark, and no Germans are wandering around inside the wire after lights out, because the tower guards have orders allowing them to shoot anyone seen moving around the camp. So why were

you there, when you could have been shot by one of your own
men?"

Fritz Number One smiled. "Anything," he whispered. Then
he shook his head. "I have helped you now, lieutenant, but to
say more might be extremely dangerous. For the both of us."
The ferret gestured toward the gate to the British compound,
swinging open to allow him to enter.

Tommy held a number of questions in check, passed the
German another cigarette as he had promised, and then, after
a momentary hesitation, pressed the remainder of the
package into the ferret's hand. Fritz Number One grunted a
surprised thanks and broke into a grin. Then he waved
Tommy forward, and watched as the American walked into
the British camp, looking for Renaday and Pryce, Tommy's
head starting to swim with ideas. Neither man paid much attention to a squad of British officers, all carrying towels,
soap, and meager assortments of spare clothing, heading in
the opposite direction toward the shower block. A pair of
desultory, bored, and unarmed German guards, their heads
drooping as if they were fatigued, escorted the men, who
cheerily marched through the dust of the front gate, breaking
into the usual wildly ribald song as they strolled past.

"Most curious," Phillip Pryce said, leaning his head back momentarily to scan the skies for a stray thought, then pitching
forward and fixing Tommy with his most unwavering gaze.
"Truly, most intriguing. There's no doubt, my lad, that he was
trying to say something?"

"No doubt whatsoever," Tommy replied, kicking at the
ground, raising a puff of dirt with his boot. The three men
were collected by the side of one of the huts.

"I don't trust Fritz, not any of the Fritzes, not Number One,
Two, or Three, and I don't trust any other bloody fucking
Kraut," Hugh muttered. "No matter what he says. Why would
he help us? Answer me that one, counselor."

Pryce coughed hard once or twice. He was sitting with his
pants rolled up in a spot of warm sunshine, both feet lowered
into a rough dented steel basin that he periodically replen-
ished with near-boiling water. He held one foot up, eyeing it.
"Blisters, boils, and athlete's foot, which, of course, in my

case is an immense contradiction in terms," he said with a mock-rueful grin. He coughed dryly once again. "My God, I'm bloody well falling apart at the seams, boys. Nothing seems to work too well." He smiled again, turning toward the Canadian. "You're right, of course, Hugh. But on the other hand, what incentive would Fritz have to lie?"

"I don't know. He's a right devious bastard. And always angling for promotions and medals or whatever it is the Krauts like to reward their bloody hard workers with."

"A man out for himself?"

"Absolutely, goddamn right," Hugh snorted.

Pryce nodded, turning back to Tommy, who anticipated what the older man was about to say and beat him to it.

"But, Hugh," he said swiftly, "that suggests that he would be telling me the truth. Or at least trying to point me in some correct direction. Even if he is a German, we all agree that Fritz is mainly out for himself. And he sees everything in the camp as an opportunity. More or less the same way Trader Vic did."

"So," Hugh asked, "what do you suppose he's talking about?"

"Well, what are we missing? What do we need to know?"

Hugh smiled. "Two things: the truth—and the means of finding it."

Pryce nodded. He turned back to Tommy and spoke with sudden intensity: "I think this could be important, Tommy. Very much so. Why *was* Fritz inside the wire in the predawn dark? He could very well have paid for that little trip with his life if he'd been spotted by one of these teenagers that the Krauts are enlisting and putting up in the guard towers. And it doesn't seem to me that Fritz is the type of gentleman to risk an accidental death unless the reward is great."

"Personal reward," Hugh added. "I don't think Fritz does much for the fatherland unless it helps him out, as well."

Pryce clapped his hands together once, as if the ideas flooding through his head were as warm as the water he was pouring over his ravaged feet. But when he spoke, it was slowly, with a deliberateness that surprised Tommy. "Suppose Fritz's presence implies *both*?" Pryce then made his hand into a fist and waved it with a sense of triumph in the air in front of him. "I think, gentlemen, that we have been slightly foolish. We have spent our time considering the murder of Trader Vic and the accusation against Lincoln Scott in precisely the manner that the opposition desires. Perhaps it is time to consider these things differently."

Tommy Hart sighed. "Phillip, once again, you're being cryptic and slightly obtuse."

"But that's my manner, my dear boy."

"After the war," Tommy said, "I think I shall require you to come visit the States. A lengthy visit. And I will force you to sit around an old woodstove inside the Manchester General Store one day in the dead of winter when the snow is piled up about six feet high outside the window and listen to some old Vermonters talk about the weather, the crops, the upcoming fishing season in the spring, and whether or not this kid Williams the Red Sox have playing for them will ever amount to anything in the majors. And you will discover that we Yankees speak concisely and always directly to the point. Whatever the hell that point might be."

Pryce burst into a laugh tinged with coughing.

"A lesson in forthrightness, is that what you have in mind?"

"Yes. Precisely. Straight-shooting."

"Ah, a distinctly American phrase, that."

"And a quality that will be needed on Monday morning at zero eight hundred, when Scott's trial commences."

Hugh grinned. "He's right about that, Phillip. Take it from me: our southern neighbors are nothing if not straightforward. Especially MacNamara, the SAO. He's right out of West Point and probably has the uniform code of military conduct tattooed on his chest. It won't do a lick of good to *suggest* anything in trial. The man has little imagination. We're going to have to be exact."

Pryce seemed abruptly to be lost in thought.

"Yes, yes, that is so," he said slowly, "but I wonder . . ."

The emaciated, wheezing Englishman held up his hand, cutting off both Tommy and Hugh from speaking. Both men could see his mind working hard behind his eyes, which darted about.

"I think," Pryce started slowly, after a long pause, "that we should reassess the entirety of the crime. What do we know?"

"We know that Vic was killed in a hidden spot an entire alleyway away from the location where his body was actually found. We know that his corpse was discovered by a German ferret who shouldn't have been inside the camp at that hour. We know that the murder weapon and the very method of death are different from that which the prosecution will contend. . . ."

Tommy paused, then added, "Arrayed against these elements, we have Lincoln Scott's bloody shoes, bloodstained flight jacket, a weapon that also has blood on it, though it is doubtful that it was used in the killing. . . ."

Tommy sighed, continuing, "And we have well-documented animosity and threats."

Pryce nodded his head slowly. "Perhaps we would be wise to examine all the factors separately. Hugh, tell me: What does moving the body tell you?"

"That the murder location would compromise the killer."

"Would Lincoln Scott have moved the body closer to his own hut?"

"No. That would make no sense."

"But putting Vic in the *Abort* made sense to someone."

"Someone who needed to make certain that the actual crime scene vicinity wasn't searched. And, if you consider it, who would do more than a perfunctory examination of the body inside the *Abort*? The place smells. . . ."

"Visser did," Hugh grunted. "It didn't seem to bother him in the slightest."

"Ah," Pryce grinned. "An interesting observation. Yes. Tommy, I think it is safe to assume that despite his Luftwaffe uniform, Herr Visser is Gestapo. And a policeman with expertise. And it is doubtful that whoever moved Vic's body would have anticipated his arrival on the scene. They would probably have assumed that the somewhat prissy and stiff Von Reiter would be in charge of the crime scene. Now, would Commandant Von Reiter have carefully searched the *Abort*? Not bloody likely. But all this prompts a second question: If the killer wanted to avoid a search of a specific location . . . well, who was he afraid of? Germans or Americans?"

Tommy raised an eyebrow. "The trouble is, Phillip, every time I think we're making some sort of progress, new questions arise."

Hugh snorted. "Damn right. Why can't things be simple?"

Pryce reached out and touched the hulking Canadian on the arm. "But you see, accusing Scott of the crime *is* simple. And therein lies the lie, if you will."

Pryce wheezed a laugh, which translated into a cough, but still smiling, still enjoying himself, still delighting in each intricacy they unfolded, he turned back to Tommy.

"And the unexplained and somewhat surprising appearance of Fritz Number One on the scene? This tells us what?"

"That he had a deeply compelling reason to be there."

"Do you think that the illicit trade of some item of contraband could bring Fritz and Trader Vic out in the dead of night at considerable risk to the both of them?"

"No." Tommy spoke before Hugh could reply. "Not for a minute. Because Vic had already managed to trade for all sorts of illegal items. Cameras. Radios. Souvenirs. *'Anything . . .'* Fritz said. But even the most special of acquisitions can still be managed in regular daytime hours. Vic was an expert at that."

"So, whatever it was that put both Vic and Fritz Number One out and abroad in the midst of considerable danger had to be something extremely valuable to the both of them. . . ." Pryce mused. "And something that was best hidden from everyone else in the camp."

"You're assuming that it was the same thing that brought them out. We don't know that," Tommy said sharply.

"But, I suspect, it is the avenue we are obligated to travel," Pryce said with determination. He turned to Tommy. "Do you see something in all this, Thomas?"

And Tommy did. *"Something best hidden . . ."* An electric idea raced through his imagination. He was about to speak, when the thoughts of all three men were sharply interrupted by a sudden burst of shouts and alarm coming from outside the wire, past the main gate. In unison, all three turned toward the noise, and as they did, they stiffened as they heard the staccato sound of a weapon being fired, the crack of the rifle riveting the afternoon air.

"What the bloody hell . . ." Hugh started to ask.

Almost instantly, a detachment of guards, their uniforms hastily thrown on, but bearing weapons at port arms, emerged from a building in the administration compound. The soldiers were jamming steel helmets onto their heads, trying to button their tunics. The squad took off sharply, running down the road past the commandant's office, a *Feldwebel* shouting hurried instructions. No sooner had the air filled with the heavy tread of their boots slapping into the hard dirt road, than at least a half-dozen ferrets blasting away at their whistles came racing through the front gate, screaming obscenities and urgent commands between shrill shrieks from their whistles. The siren that was ordinarily used only for air raids started up, wailing loudly. Tommy, Hugh, and Pryce all saw Fritz Number One in the midst of the group. The German spotted them and, waving his arms wildly, roared angrily: "In formation! Line up! Line up! *Raus! Schnell!* Immediately! We must count!"

None of the ferret's usual wheedling jocularity was contained in any of the words. His voice was high-pitched, insistent, and frantically demanding. He pointed a finger at Tommy. "You! Lieutenant Hart! You are to stand to the side and be counted with the British!"

Another nearby volley of rifle shots creased the air.

Without any further explanation, Fritz Number One raced into the center of the camp, continuing to shout commands. As he passed, the parade ground began to fill with British airmen, all struggling into their jackets, pulling on boots, jamming caps on their heads, hurrying toward the unexpected *Appell.* Tommy turned to his two companions, only to hear Phillip Pryce feverishly whisper a single wonderful, yet terrible, altogether heart-stopping word:

"Escape!"

The British airmen stood at attention in their assembly yard for nearly an hour, as ferrets moved up and down the rows of men, counting and recounting, swearing in German, refusing to answer any questions, especially the most important. Tommy lingered perhaps a half-dozen yards to the side of the last block of men, flanked on either side by two other

American officers who'd also been caught inside the British compound when the escape attempt took place. Tommy only barely recognized the two other Americans; one was a chess champion from Hut 120 who frequently bribed goons to let him pass over to where the competition was better. The other was a slender actor from New York who'd been enlisted by the British for one of their theatrical performances. The onetime fighter pilot made a more than convincing blond bombshell, when decked out in homemade wig, cheap makeup, and a slinky black evening gown refashioned by the camp's tailors from scraps of worn and tattered uniforms, and was therefore in demand in both compounds' theatrical productions.

"Still can't figure what fer Christ's sakes is going on," the chess master whispered, "but the Krauts sure look angry as hell."

"Lotsa talk. And a couple of those formations look to be shy more than a couple of men," the actor replied. "Think they'll keep us here much longer?"

"You know the damn Germans," Tommy replied softly. "If there's only nine guys standing where yesterday there were ten, well, hell, they've got to count maybe a hundred times over and over, just to make sure they're right. . . ."

Both the other Americans grunted in assent.

"Hey," the chess champion muttered, "look who's coming. The Big Cheese, himself. And ain't that the new little cheese, right at his side? The guy who's supposed to be watching over your show, right, Hart?"

Tommy looked across the compound and saw that a red-faced Oberst Von Reiter, in full dress uniform, as if he'd been interrupted on the way to an important meeting, was striding down the steps of the main office building. Trailing behind him, in his usual slightly rumpled, much less spit-and-polished appearance, was Hauptmann Heinrich Visser. In contrast to Von Reiter's hard-edged eyes and ramrod bearing, Visser seemed to have a faint look of amusement on his face. But Visser's half-smile could just as easily have been a look of cruelty, Tommy thought, which probably spoke a great deal about the sort of man he was.

The two officers were trailed by a substantial squad of goons, all bearing machine pistols or rifles. In the midst of this group, close to two dozen British officers, all in various forms of undress—including two totally naked men—emerged from the camp offices. One man was limping slightly. The two naked men wore immense grins on their faces. All seemed cheery, and more than slightly pleased with themselves, despite the fact that they were marched forward with their hands clasped behind their heads.

The actor and the chess champion saw the same contrast between the Germans and the English at the same moment Tommy did. But the chess champion whispered, "The limeys might think this is something of a joke, but I'll bet the house that Von Reiter doesn't find it all so damn funny."

The officers and the captured men marched past the gate and came to a rest at the front of the formations of British airmen. The Senior British Officer, a mustachioed, ruddy-faced bomber pilot with a shock of reddish hair streaked with gray, stepped to the front, calling the men in their ranks to attention, and several thousand sets of heels clicked together smartly. Von Reiter glared at the SBO, then turned to the rows of airmen.

"You British, you think war is some game? Some sort of sport, like your cricket or rugby?" he demanded in a loud, angry voice that carried over the heads of the assembled men. "You think we play at this?"

Von Reiter's fury fell like a thunderstorm on their heads. No one replied. The captured men behind him slowly grew silent.

"It is all a joke to you?"

From within the ranks a single voice called out in a heavy mock-Cockney accent: "Anything to break the bleedin' monotony, guv'nah!"

There was laughter, which faded quickly under Von Reiter's glare. His eyes flashed with rage.

"I can assure you that the Luftwaffe High Command does not consider escape to be a laughing matter."

From another section, a different voice, this time with an Irish lilt, answered, "Well then, boyo, the joke's on you this time!"

Another smattering of laughs, which again ceased almost instantly.

"Is it now?" Von Reiter asked coldly.

The Senior British Officer stepped forward. Tommy could hear him quietly reply, somewhat contradictorily, "But my dear Commandant Von Reiter, I assure you, no one is making jokes—"

Von Reiter sliced his riding crop through the air, cutting off the British officer's response.

"Escape is forbidden!"

"But, commandant—"

"Verboten!"

"Yes, but—"

Von Reiter turned to the assembly. "I have this day received new directives from my superiors in Berlin. They are simple: Allied airmen attempting to escape from prisoner-of-war camps within the Reich will now be treated as terrorists and spies! Upon your capture, you will not be returned to Stalag Luft Thirteen! You will be shot on sight!"

Silence seized the assembly. It took several seconds for the Senior British Officer to reply, and when he did, it was in a flat, cold voice.

"I would warn *Herr Oberst* that what you suggest is a direct violation of the Geneva Convention, of which Germany is a signatory. Such treatment of escaping Allied personnel would constitute a war crime, and anyone engaging in such behavior will eventually find *himself* facing a firing squad. Or a hangman's noose, *Herr Oberst*. That, I can promise!"

Von Reiter turned to the British officer. "I have my orders!" he answered briskly. "Legal orders! And do not speak to me, wing commander, of war crimes! For it is not the Luftwaffe that nightly drops incendiaries and delayed-fuse bombs upon cities filled with noncombatants! Cities filled with women, children, and the elderly! Expressly against your beloved Geneva Convention rules!"

As he spoke, Von Reiter glanced over at Hauptmann Visser, who nodded, and instantly barked out a command to the men guarding the British fliers who'd been involved in the escape attempt. The Germans immediately chambered rounds in their rifles, or manipulated the firing bolt on the Schmeisser machine pistols they carried. These made a distinctively evil clicking sound. The squad encircling the British officers raised their weapons into firing positions.

For several long seconds there was utter quiet on the parade ground.

His face suddenly pale, drawn tight, the Senior British Officer stepped forward sharply into the silence.

"Are you threatening a massacre of unarmed men?" he shouted. His voice abruptly turned high-pitched, almost girlish with fear and near-frenzy. There was more than a tinge of panic in each word he spoke.

Von Reiter, still red-faced but with the irritating coolness that superiority of firepower brings, turned to the British officer. "I am well within my rights, wing commander. And I am merely following direct orders. From the highest levels in Berlin. To disobey would result in perhaps my own firing squad."

The SBO stepped closer to the German. "Sir!" he shouted. "We are all here as witnesses! If you murder these men . . ."

Von Reiter glared at the Englishman. "Murder? Murder! You dare talk to me of murder! With your firebomb attacks upon unarmed civilians! *Terrorfliegers!*"

"You will hang, Von Reiter, if you give the order to fire! I'll fashion the bloody noose myself!"

Von Reiter took a deep breath, calming himself. He eyed the SBO with irritation. Then he smiled cruelly. "You, wing commander, are the officer in charge. This foolish escape attempt today is *your* responsibility. Will you offer yourself to the firing squad, in return for the lives of these men?"

The Senior British Officer's jaw dropped in astonishment and he did not immediately reply.

"It would seem a most fair trade, wing commander. One man's life to save the lives of two dozen."

"What you're suggesting is a crime," the officer answered.

Von Reiter shrugged. "War is a crime," he said briskly. "I am merely asking you for a decision officers make frequently. Will you sacrifice one man for the good of many? Yourself? Quickly, wing commander! Your decision!"

The camp commandant lifted his riding crop in the air, as if about to give the command to open fire.

The rows of British airmen seemed to stiffen, then waver,

as if rage like a wind passed down each line. Voices started to rise, angrily. In one of the nearby guard towers a machine gun pivoted on its base, making a creaking sound as it was brought to bear on the assembly.

The two dozen would-be escapees seemed to shrink together. Where they had worn boisterous smiles and wide grins as they emerged from interrogation, now they had paled, staring out at the weapons that covered them.

"Commandant!" the Senior British Officer shouted hoarsely. "Don't do something you might later regret!"

Von Reiter eyed the officer carefully. "Regret? Regret killing the enemy that is doing such a fine job of killing my own people? Where should I find something in that to regret?"

"I'm warning you!" the officer cried out.

"I'm still awaiting your decision, wing commander! Will you take their places?"

Tommy stole a look at Heinrich Visser. The German could do little to hide his pleasure.

"I think they're going to do it," whispered the actor standing next to him. "Damn it, I think they are!"

"No, they're bluffing," said the chess master.

"Are you certain?" Tommy asked, under his breath.

"No," the chess master replied quietly. "Not at all."

"They're going to do it," repeated the actor. "They're really going to do it! I heard they shot men that escaped from one of the other camps. Fifty Brits, I heard. Went out through a tunnel, were on the lam for weeks. Executed as spies. I didn't believe it, but now . . ."

Von Reiter paused, letting the tension build in the air around him. The goons with their fingers on the triggers of their weapons waited for a command, while the assembled British airmen stood rock-still, in terror at what seemed about to unfold.

"All right, commandant!" the Senior British Officer said loudly. "I'll take their place!"

The camp commandant turned slowly, lowering his riding crop languorously. He placed one hand upon a black-sheathed ceremonial dagger that he wore in the belt of his dress uniform. Tommy caught sight of this gesture, and looked intently at the ceremonial weapon. Then he saw that Von Reiter's other hand had begun to swish the riding crop around his polished, glistening black leather boots.

"Ah," he said slowly. "A brave but foolish decision." Von Reiter paused, as if savoring the moment. "But in this instance, it will not be necessary," he said to the Senior British Officer, but before the man could raise his voice in protest again, Von Reiter pivoted and shouted out to Heinrich Visser: "*Hauptmann!* Each man who tried to escape from the shower building, fifteen days in the cooler! Bread and water only!"

Fear like a sudden wind seemed to ooze from the huddled men. One man sobbed out loud. Another gripped the arm of his neighbor, his knees wobbly, supporting himself. A third swore angrily, shaking a fist at the German officer, challenging him to fight.

Then the commandant turned back to the SBO. "Now you have been warned!" he said angrily. "We will not let anyone else who tries to escape off so lightly!" He raised his voice again, addressing the entire gathering of Allied airmen. "The next man who is caught outside the wire will be shot! On that you have my promise! Let there be no confusion on this account. There has never been a successful escape from this camp, and there will not be! This is your home for the duration of the war. The Reich will not expend valuable military resources hunting down escaping Allied airmen! This is the limit of the resources we will spend."

As he spoke, Von Reiter unbuttoned the breast pocket flap of his steel-gray dress uniform jacket, and reached inside. He removed a single thin rifle cartridge, which he held up for the entire assembly to see. After a moment, he turned and flipped the cartridge to the Senior British Officer.

"As a reminder," he said sharply. "And, of course, there will be no more shower privileges for the British compound for the next fortnight, either."

With that, the camp commandant made a gesture of dismissal at the gathered men, turned on his heel, and, accompanied by the other German officers and guards, exited the camp. Tommy Hart caught sight of the grin Heinrich Visser wore. He also saw that the *Hauptmann* had seen him, standing to the side.

"I thought they were gonna do it, for sure," whispered the actor from New York. "Jesus, that was damn close."

"No shit," said the chess master. "Absolutely no shit." Then the chess player added another question. "Hey, you guys think MacNamara and Clark over on our side know about that directive? The shoot-to-kill order? You think maybe that was some kinda elaborate Kraut bluff? Maybe trying to scare us?"

"Well, it sure worked," said the actor, blowing out a long breath of pent-up air. "I don't think it was any bluff. But I'll tell you this: MacNamara and Clark, they know about those orders. For sure. The thing is, they don't care—not one little bit."

"It's a war, remember?" Tommy said.

The two other men grunted in assent.

Phillip Pryce was tending to a battered steel kettle, boiling water for tea, and Hugh Renaday had gone off to try to discover what had happened in the escape attempt. Pryce fussed about the stove, not unlike some elderly crone. Tommy could just make out the muffled sounds of a quartet of voices, singing popular songs a cappella in another bunk room. The whistle of the kettle seemed to blend with the ghostly voices, and for an instant, Tommy looked around and thought the world had returned to some sort of reasoned normalcy.

"We were making some progress, I think," he said to Pryce. The older man nodded.

"Tommy, lad, it seems to me that there is much to be suspicious about and little time remaining in which to investigate the truth. At zero eight hundred on Monday you will be expected to begin fighting on Mr. Scott's behalf. Have you considered what will be your opening gambit?"

"Not yet."

"It might be wise to start."

"There's still so much we don't know."

Pryce paused, hovering over the tea cups. "Do you know what bothers me, Tommy, about this case?"

"I'm listening."

The older man seemed to take his time with every action. He examined the worn tea leaves in the bottom of each ceramic cup carefully. He lifted the water kettle gingerly from the stove. He breathed in some of the steamy vapors that smoked from the opening.

"It is the sense that there is something here that is different from what it appears."

"Phillip, please explain."

He shook his head. "I am getting too old and too frail for all this," he said, grinning. "I think it is a medically proven fact that the older one gets, the more quick one is to spot conspiracies. Skulduggery. Cloak and dagger stuff. Sherlock Holmes wasn't a young man, now, was he?"

"Well, he wasn't an old guy. Dr. Watson was. Holmes was in his thirties, maybe?"

"Quite so, quite so. And he would be suspicious, would he not? I mean, this is all so straightforward, from the prosecution's point of view. Two men hate each other. Race is the reason. One man dies. The survivor must be guilty of the murder. *Quod erat demonstrandum.* Or ipso facto. Some fancy latinate construction to define the situation. But none of it seems in the slightest bit clear to me."

"I would agree, but it seems there isn't much time left for exploring."

"I wonder," Pryce said with a lifted eyebrow, "whether or not that is part of the design."

Tommy was about to respond when he heard the heavy tread of Hugh's flight boots coming down the hut's central corridor. Seconds later the door burst open, and the Canadian rushed into the room. He was grinning widely.

"Do you know what those clever bastards tried to pull off?" he almost shouted. There was a schoolboy's delight creeping into his every word.

"What was it?" Tommy asked.

"Well, get this: The same group had been heading off to the shower building every day, same hour, same minute, for nearly two weeks, rain or shine, bellowing all those songs out, the ones that get that old sod Von Reiter so upset. . . ."

"Yes. I passed them on the way in," Tommy said.

"Well, you did indeed, Tommy, my friend, but today they were ten minutes earlier than usual. And the two goons escorting them? They were two of our guys in overcoats cut and dyed to look like the Krauts! They marched into the shower and half the gang undresses and starts singing away, just as usual. The other half leap into their clothes and come waltzing straight out, where the two phony guards put them into formation and start walking them toward the woods. . . ."

"Hoping no one notices a damn thing!" Pryce burst out with a laugh.

"Precisely," Hugh continued. "And they might have made it, too, if some damn ferret isn't coming down the road on a bicycle. He notices that the 'goons' aren't carrying weapons, and he stops, the men break for the woods, and the game is up!"

Hugh shook his head. "Damn clever. Almost pulled it off, as well."

The men all laughed together. It seemed marvelously preposterous for an escape attempt, yet fabulously creative.

"I don't think they'd have gotten far," Pryce said, between coughs. "After all, their uniforms would have given them away."

"Well, not precisely, Phillip," Hugh said. "Three of the men—the true authors of the scheme, so I gather—had civilian clothing underneath their uniforms, which they planned to shed in the forest. They also had excellent forged papers. Or so I'm told. They were the ones who were supposed to make it out. The others were mainly to cause some trouble and consternation for the Krauts."

"I wonder," Tommy asked slowly, "if anyone had known of this new order that allegedly allows for the shooting of prisoners, whether they would have volunteered for a diversion so readily."

"You're dead on, there, Tommy," Hugh answered. "It's one thing to muck around with the Krauts if all it's going to cost you is a fortnight in the cooler singing 'roll out the barrel . . .' and shivering through the night. A whole different thing if the bastards are going to put you in front of a firing squad. You think it was some sort of bluff? I can't believe . . ."

"Yeah, you're right," Tommy said with a brisk confidence that was perhaps ill-placed. "They can't go around shooting prisoners of war. Why, there would be hell to pay."

Pryce shook his head and held up his hand, cutting off the conversation. "A prisoner of war is supposed to be in uniform, and he's supposed to provide his name, rank, and serial number, when demanded. A man in a suit of clothes carrying phony identity cards and forged work permits? That man could easily be taken for a spy. When do you stop being the one and start being the other?"

Pryce took a deep breath.

"We shoot spies. Without any due process. And so do the Germans."

He looked closely at the two airmen and nodded his head slowly. "I have no doubt that Von Reiter will do precisely that, in the future," he said. "I believe our lads, clever as they might have been, were in serious jeopardy there for several minutes. Jeopardy they might not have foreseen. Von Reiter may not be some brown-shirted fanatic Nazi, but he surely is a German officer, through and through. There's probably generations of stiffly Teutonic service to the fatherland running in his quite cold veins. Give Von Reiter a direct and unambiguous order, and he'll follow it to the letter. Without question."

"That is," Tommy interrupted, "if he actually *did* receive such an order. He could have just been blowing smoke."

Hugh nodded. "Tommy's got a point, Phillip."

Pryce smiled. "Tommy, it seems to me that you're learning subtlety rapidly. Of course, it makes little difference to us whether he received that order or not—as long as we stay put, right here in our delightful accommodations. But the threat of shooting . . . well, that's real enough, isn't it? And so Von Reiter achieves much of what he desires merely by raising the ugly possibility of firing squads. The only way to test the truth is to escape . . ."

"And be caught," Tommy finished the sentence.

Pryce sighed. "Von Reiter is a clever man. Do not underestimate him just because he looks like some Saturday morning puppet show character in those clothes of his." The onetime barrister coughed again, and added, "A cruel man, I think. Cruel and ambitious. Traits he shares, I suppose, with that slimy weasel Visser. A dangerous concoction, that . . ."

As he spoke, all three men became aware of the sound of footsteps coming down the corridor. Boots hitting the wooden planks with precision.

"Goons!" Hugh muttered.

Before the two others had time to respond, the door to the small bunk room flew open, revealing Heinrich Visser. Behind him stood a dwarfish man, paunchy and barely over five feet in height, wearing a poorly cut black business suit, holding in his hands a black homburg hat that he nervously fondled. The man peered out into the room from behind thick glasses. Standing just to the rear were four heavyset German soldiers, each with a weapon held at the ready. Within seconds of their arrival, the corridor behind them filled with curious British airmen torn from the casino of mouse roulette by the appearance of the armed men.

Visser stepped into the narrow bunk room, eyeing the three men.

"Ah, perhaps we are engaged in a strategy session? A critical discussion of the facts and the law, wing commander?"

Visser addressed his question to Pryce.

"Tommy has much work to do, and little time remaining. We were lending him what expertise our experience allows. This should not come as much of a surprise to you, *Hauptmann*," Pryce replied.

Visser shook his head slowly. He fingered his chin with his sole hand, as if thinking.

"And do you make progress, wing commander? Does the defense of Lieutenant Scott begin to take shape?"

"We have little time, and so we raise questions. We are still seeking answers," Pryce responded.

"Ah, such is the lot of any true philosopher," Visser said, musing. "And you, Mr. Renaday, with your policeman's heart, have you found any hard facts that assist you in this search?"

Hugh scowled at the German. He gestured around the room. "These walls are facts," he said contemptuously. "The wire is a fact. The machine-gun towers are facts. Beyond that, I haven't much to say to you, *Hauptmann*."

Visser smiled, ignoring the insult contained in the words and tones of the Canadian's response. Tommy did not like the fact that Visser seemed oblivious to insult. There was a dangerousness in the officer's mocking smile.

"And you, Mr. Hart, have you come to rely greatly on Mr. Pryce?"

Tommy hesitated, unable to see where the German was heading with his questions. "I welcome his analysis," he responded carefully.

"It is comforting to have such an expert at your side, no? A famous barrister, when your own expertise in these type of matters is so unfortunately limited?" Visser persisted.

"Yes, it is."

The German grinned. Pryce coughed twice, holding his hand over his mouth. Visser pivoted toward the old man, as if drawn to the sound.

"Your health, wing commander, it improves?"

"Not bloody likely in this rathole," Hugh muttered ferociously.

Pryce shot a quick glance at his blustering Canadian companion, then replied, "My health is fine, *Hauptmann*. My cough lingers, as you can readily see. But my strength is fine, and I eagerly look forward to the remaining time I have here, before my countrymen arrive one fine day at the front gates and then proceed to shoot the bloody lot of you."

Visser laughed as if what Pryce had said was somehow a joke. "Spoken like a warrior," he said, continuing to grin. "But I fear, wing commander, that your bravery masks your illness. Your stoicism in the face of such sickness is admirable."

He stared at Pryce, the smile fading into a chilling, deep look that spoke of great hatred whirling around within him, not so much hidden as encapsulated.

"Yes," Visser continued slowly, nastily, "I fear you are more sick than you are willing to let on to your comrades. Far more sick."

"I'm fine," Pryce repeated.

Visser shook his head. "I think not, wing commander. I think not. Regardless, allow me to introduce my companion to you: This gentleman is Herr Blucher of the Swiss Red Cross. . . ."

Visser turned to the diminutive man, who nodded toward the prisoners and clicked his heels together, simultaneously making a small bow.

"Herr Blucher . . ." Visser continued, smugness creeping

into his voice, "has arrived this very day directly from Berlin, where he is a member of the Swiss legation there."

"What the bloody hell . . ." Pryce started, but then he stopped, fixing the German with a cold look of his own.

"It is against the interests of the Luftwaffe High Command to have a distinguished and justly famed barrister such as yourself perish here amid the rough and deprived life of prisoners of war. We are concerned with your persistent illnesses, wing commander, and alas, because we lack the proper medical facilities for treatment, it has been decided by the highest authorities that you are to be repatriated. Good news, Mr. Pryce. You are going home."

The word *home* seemed to echo in sudden silence.

Pryce stood stock-still in the center of the small room. He drew himself to attention, trying to gather some military bearing. "I don't believe you," he said abruptly.

Visser shook his head. "Ah, but it is true. At this very instant at a camp in Scotland, a captured German naval officer suffering from similar maladies is being informed by the Swiss representative there that he is to be returned to his homeland. It is the simplest of trades, wing commander. Our sick prisoner for their sick prisoner."

"I don't believe you," Pryce repeated.

The man identified as Herr Blucher took a single step forward. He spoke in fractured, Germanicized English: "Is true, Mr. Pryce. I will be escorting you by train to Switzerland. . . ."

Pryce turned sharply, staring at Herr Blucher. "You're no bloody Swiss," he said, spitting. Then he swung about and fixed Visser with a harrowing glance. "Lies!" he said instantly. "Bloody lies, Visser! There's no trade! There's no exchange!"

"Ah," Visser replied, sickeningly sweetly, "but I assure you, wing commander, this is so. Even as we speak. A naval officer who will be allowed to return to the loving arms of his wife and children—"

"Lies! Black lies!" Pryce interrupted, shouting.

"But Mr. Pryce, you are mistaken," Visser said unctuously. "I thought you would be pleased at the thought of returning home."

"You lying dog!" Pryce cried. He turned to Tommy Hart and Hugh Renaday, his face a portrait of instant and complete despair.

"Phillip!" Tommy blurted out.

Pryce took an unsteady step toward Tommy, reaching out and seizing the younger man by the sleeve of his jacket, as if he was suddenly weakened.

"They mean to kill me," Pryce said softly.

Tommy shook his head, and Hugh pushed past the two of them, thrusting himself directly in Visser's face. He jabbed a blunt finger sharply into the *Hauptmann*'s chest.

"I know you, Visser!" the Canadian hissed. "I know your face! If you are lying to us, I will spend every second of every day of every month for the remainder of my years on this earth hunting you to the ground! You will not be able to hide, you Nazi scum, because I will be like a nightmare on your ass until I find you, and I will kill you with my own bare hands!"

The one-armed German did not shrink back. Instead, he merely stared directly into Hugh's eyes, and said slowly, "The wing commander is to gather his possessions immediately and accompany me. Herr Blucher will see to his care, while in transit."

Visser's mocking grin slid past the Canadian, back to Phillip Pryce. "Alas, wing commander, we have no time for elaborate farewells. You are to embark immediately. *Schnell!*"

Pryce started to reply, then stopped, turning again to Tommy Hart. "I'm sorry, Tommy. I had hoped we three would walk out the gate together as free men. That would have been ever so nice, would it not?"

"Phillip!" Tommy choked, unable to speak the words that flooded him.

"You will be fine, lads," Pryce continued. "Stick together. Promise me this: You will survive! No matter what happens, you boys are to live! I expect much from the both of you, and even if I'm not there to see it, as I'd hoped, that doesn't mean you shan't accomplish what you are capable of!"

Pryce's hands quivered, and there was a warble in his voice. The older man's fear filled the room.

Tommy shook his head. "No, Phillip, no. We'll still be

together and you can show me Piccadilly, and what was that restaurant? Just like you've promised. It will be okay, I know it."

"Ah, Simpson's on the Strand. I can taste it now. So, Tommy, you and Hugh will have to go there now without me, and raise a glass on my behalf. Nothing cheap, mind you! Hugh, no bottle of beer! A nice red wine. Something prewar and expensive, the color of deep burgundy. Something that plays a waltz across your taste buds, and cascades down your throat. That sounds wonderful. . . ."

"Phillip!" Tommy could barely control himself.

Pryce smiled at him, and then at Hugh, whose arm he also reached out and seized. "Boys, promise me you'll not let them leave my carcass in the woods somewhere where the animals will gnaw on my old bones. Force them to return my ashes, and then spread them somewhere nice. Maybe over the Channel after all this is over. I think I would like that, so that the tides can wash them up on our beloved island's shore. But anywhere where it is free, boys. I don't mind dying alone, lads, but I'd like to think my remains went somewhere where they can enjoy a tiny breath of freedom—"

Visser interrupted sharply. "There is no time! Wing commander, please ready yourself!"

Pryce turned and scowled at the German. "That's what I *am* doing!" he answered. He returned his eyes to his two younger companions. "They'll shoot me in the forest," he said softly. His voice had regained some strength, and he spoke with an almost matter-of-fact sense of resignation. It was as if Pryce wasn't afraid so much as he was irritated by the thought of his imminent death. "Tommy, lad, here's what they will tell you," he whispered. "They'll say I attempted to flee. That I made some sort of break for freedom. There was a struggle, and they were forced to fire their weapons. It will all be a lie, of course, and you boys will know it—"

Visser interrupted again, smiling with the same upturned scowl that he wore earlier when Von Reiter was threatening to shoot the British airmen who'd tried to escape. "A prisoner exchange," Visser said. "Nothing more. So that the wing commander's health is not our responsibility."

"Stop lying," Pryce said arrogantly. "No one believes you, and it makes you appear foolish."

Visser's smile faded.

"I am a German officer," he said bitterly. "I do not lie!"

"The hell you don't," Pryce snorted. "Your lies fill this room with a disgusting stench."

Visser took an angry step forward, then halted himself. He stared at Phillip Pryce with unbridled hatred. "We are leaving," he said with barely restrained ferocity. "We are leaving now! This minute, wing commander!"

Pryce grabbed at Tommy once again. "Tommy," he whispered, "this is not a coincidence! Nothing is what it seems! Dig deeper! Save him, lad, save him! For more than ever, now, I believe Scott is innocent!"

Two German soldiers stepped into the room, reaching out for Pryce, ready to drag him from the bunk room. The wiry, frail Englishman faced them down, and shrugged his shoulders at them. Then he turned to Hugh and Tommy, and said, "You're on your own now, boys. And remember, I'm counting on you to live through all this! Survive! Whatever happens!"

He turned back to the Germans. "All right, *Hauptmann*," he said with a sudden, exceedingly calm determination. "I'm ready now. Do with me what you will."

Visser nodded, signaled the squad to surround him, and without another word, Pryce was marched down the corridor and through the front door. Tommy, Hugh, and the other British airmen of the hut raced after them, trailing after the old barrister, who marched with his shoulders stiffly back, his spine erect. He did not turn once as the odd procession crossed the assembly area. Nor did he hesitate as they passed through the gate, where steel-helmeted goons kept their weapons at the ready. Just beyond, adjacent to the commandant's barracks, there was a large, black Mercedes motorcar waiting, its engine running, a small plume of exhaust trailing from its rear pipes.

Visser grasped a door and held it open for the Englishman. The Swiss Blucher quickly waddled around to the other side, and flung himself into the vehicle.

But Pryce paused for a single instant at the door to the motorcar, twisting around, and for a single, slow moment, stared back toward the camp, looking through the ubiquitous

wire to where Tommy and Hugh stood helplessly watching his
disappearance. Tommy saw him smile sadly, and raise his hand
and make a small farewell wave, as if he were gesturing toward
the waiting heavens, and then he gave a quick thumbs-up, and
in the same motion, reached up and doffed his cap to all the
British airmen gathered by the wire, with all the bravado of a
man unafraid of any death, no matter how rough or lonely. Several of the airmen raised their voices to cheer, but this noise
was cut short when one of the guards pushed Pryce roughly
down into the backseat, and he disappeared from view.

With a roar, the car's engine accelerated. The tires spun in
the dirt. Raising a dust cloud behind and bouncing slightly on
the rough roadway, it headed off in the direction of the line of
tall trees and the forest.

Visser, too, watched the car depart. Then, the one-armed
German turned slowly, victoriously, his face wearing a laugh
that spoke of success. He stared across toward Tommy and
Hugh for several seconds, before he sharply turned on his
heel and marched into the office building. The wooden door
clacked shut behind him.

Tommy waited. A sudden, abrupt silence enclosed him and
inwardly he filled with resignation and rage, unsure which
emotion would gain prominence. He half-expected to hear a
single cracking pistol report rising from the woods.

"Bloody hell," Hugh said softly after a few moments had
passed. Tommy half-pivoted and saw there were tears streaming down the hulking Canadian's cheeks, and then realized
that the same was true of his own. "We're on our own, now,
Yank," Hugh added. "Bloody fucking war. Bloody fucking
goddamn fucking bloody fucking war. Why does everyone
who's worth more than half a damn on this sodden earth have
to die?" Hugh's voice cracked hard once, filled with an unrelenting sadness.

Tommy, who did not trust his own voice at that moment in
the slightest, did not reply. He recognized, too, that he had absolutely no answer to this question.

Tommy trudged through the lengthening afternoon shadows,
feeling the first intimations of the evening's chill fight past
the remaining sunlight. He tried to force himself to think of

home instead of Phillip Pryce, tried to imagine Vermont in the early spring. He thought it was such a time of promise and expectation, after the harshness of winter. Each crocus that pushed itself through the damp and muddy soil, each bud that struggled to burst on the tip of its tree branch, held out hope. In the spring, the rivers choked with the runoff from melting winter snows, and he remembered that Lydia especially had liked to bicycle to the edge of the Battenkill, or to a narrow slot on the Mettawee, both places that he would later work hard for rising trout in the summer evenings, and watch as white frothy water burst and burbled and battled its way over the rocks. There was something invigorating in watching the sinuous muscularity of the water then; it had a life to it that spoke of better days to come.

He shook his head, sighing, the images of his home state distant and elusive. Almost every kriegie had some vision of home that they could rely upon, to conjure up in moments of despair and loneliness, a fantasy of the way things could be, if only they survived. But these familiar daydreams seemed suddenly unreachable to Tommy.

He stopped once, in the center of the assembly yard, and said out loud: "He's dead by now." He could envision Pryce's body lying prone in the woods, the false Swiss Blucher standing above him with his Luger pistol still smoking. Not since the moment he'd seen the *Lovely Lydia* slide beneath the Mediterranean waves, leaving him bobbing in his life vest alone on the surface of the sea, had he felt so utterly abandoned. What he wanted to imagine was his home, his girl, and his future, but all that he could see were the dreary barracks of Stalag Luft Thirteen, the ever-present wire encircling him, and the recognition that his nightmares would now include a new ghost.

He smiled, for a moment, at the irony. In his imagination, he introduced his old captain from West Texas to Phillip Pryce. It was the only way, he thought right then, that he could prevent himself from breaking down and crying. He thought that Phillip would be stiff and formal, at first, while the captain from West Texas would be gregarious, a little overblown, but engaging all the same with his boyishness and enthusiasm. He envisioned the two shaking hands and thought that it would probably take them both a short time to come to understand each other—Phillip, of course, would complain that they spoke utterly different languages—but that they would find much in each other to like, and it would not be long before they would be telling jokes and slapping one another on the back, instantly the best of friends.

As he rounded the corner, heading toward Hut 101, Tommy imagined the initial conversation between the two ghosts. It would have some hilarity to it, he thought, before the two dead men realized how much they had in common on this earth. He smiled briefly, bittersweet, not a smile that spoke of any lessening of the troubled sensation dogging him, but a smile that had at least a small amount of release within it.

It was right at that moment that he heard the first raised angry voice. The anger was deep, impatient, and insistent, a cascade of fury and obscenities. And it took him no more than another second or two to recognize whose voice it was that was shouting—although he couldn't quite make out all the words that were being bellowed.

He broke into a run, sprinting around the front of the barracks, and as the entranceway to Hut 101 came into view, he saw Lincoln Scott standing on the top step to the hut. In front of him were seventy-five to a hundred milling kriegies, all staring up at the black flier in a jostling, unsteady silence.

Scott's face was contorted with anger. He jabbed a finger into the air above the other airmen.

"You are cowards!" he shouted. "Every last one of you! Cowards and cheats!"

Tommy didn't hesitate. He raced forward.

Scott's hand melded into a fist, which he waved in the air. "I will fight any one of you. Any five of you! Hell, I'll fight you all, you cowards! Come on! Who's gonna be first!"

Scott squared his shoulders, assuming a fighting stance. Tommy could see his eyes racheting from man to man, ready.

"Cowards!" the black flier cried out again. "Come on, who wants a piece of me?"

The mass of men seemed to seethe, shifting back and forth, like the water in a pot right before it begins to boil up.

"Fucking nigger!" a voice called out, indistinguishable

from the packed mass of men. Scott pivoted to the sound of the words.

"This nigger's ready. Are you? Come on, goddamn it! Who's gonna be first?"

"Screw you, killer! You're gonna get yours from a Kraut firing squad!"

"Is that so?" Scott replied, his fists still clenched in front of him, his body twisting toward the sound of each catcall. "What, you aren't man enough to try me on? Gonna let the Krauts do your dirty work for you? Chickens!" He squawked out mockingly, a rooster sound. "Come on," he challenged the crowd again. "Why wait? Why not try and take a piece of me now! Or aren't you men enough?"

The crowd surged forward, and Scott once again bent over slightly, like a boxer preparing for the inevitable jab to come flying his way, but readying the right cross counterpunch as a reply. A deadly reply. A boxing axiom: You must take one to give one, and Scott seemed utterly prepared for that trade-off.

Tommy reached down and summoned the deepest, most authoritative voice he could manage, and from the back of the mob, suddenly shouted out: "What the hell is going on!"

Scott stiffened slightly when he recognized Tommy's presence. He didn't answer, but remained in a fighting stance, facing the crowd.

"What's going on?" Tommy demanded again. Like a swimmer working through a heavy surf, he pushed his way through the center of the crowd of white airmen. There were several faces he recognized; men who were scheduled to testify at the trial, men who had been Trader Vic's roommates and friends, the leader of the jazz band and a few of his companions, who had threatened him in the corridor the previous day. These were the faces of the angriest men, and he suspected that the men who'd threatened him in his bed were there in that crowd. Only he recognized that he didn't have time to scrutinize every face.

The crowd parted reluctantly to let him pass, and he paused at the first step to Hut 101, turning and facing the men. Lincoln Scott hovered just behind him.

"What is going on?" he asked again.

"Ask the nigger," a voice from the mob answered. "He's the one that wants to fight."

Tommy did not turn to Scott, but instead slid his body between the front row of the crowd and where the black airman was perched. He pointed directly at the man who'd spoken. "I'm asking you," he said briskly.

There was a momentary hesitation, then the man answered, "Well, I guess your boy there doesn't cotton to some of the local artwork. . . ."

Several men started to laugh.

"And because he ain't much of an art critic, well, he comes storming out of the hut there, challenging each and every one out here just minding their own business to a fight. Damn, he looks right ready to have it out, one by one, with just about everyone in this damn camp, excepting maybe you, Hart. But the rest of us, well, he looks like he wants a piece of every flier here."

Before Tommy could respond, another voice came bellowing from perhaps fifty yards away. "Attention!"

The kriegies pivoted and saw Colonel Lewis MacNamara and Major Clark rapidly striding toward the gathering. Captain Walker Townsend hovered just behind them, pausing at the periphery to watch. At almost the same moment, a squad of German guards, perhaps a half-dozen men, trotted into view, coming around the same corner from the assembly yard that Tommy had passed seconds earlier. They carried rifles and were marching double-time, their boots slapping the dry camp dirt. They were being led by Hauptmann Visser.

The Germans and the two senior American officers arrived at the front of Hut 101 at almost the same moment. The Germans assumed guarded positions, rifles at the half-ready, while Visser stood forward of the squad. The kriegies all snapped to attention, standing ramrod straight in their positions.

MacNamara moved through the crowd slowly, as quiet grew around him, examining the face of each airman. It was as if the SAO were imprinting the name and identity of each man in the mob on his memory. Visser remained halted a few feet back, waiting to see what MacNamara would do. The SAO moved with an angry deliberateness, like an officer conducting an inspection of a particularly slovenly unit. His face was red, his temper clearly ready to burst forth, but the angrier he looked, the more calculated his every motion became. It took him several minutes to reach the steps to Hut 101, where he looked first at Tommy, fixing him with a long, rigid glance, then at Scott, then finally back to Tommy.

"All right," he said quietly, in a voice that belied his rage, "Hart, please explain. What the hell is going on here?"

Tommy saluted sharply, and replied: "I only just arrived moments ago, sir. I was seeking to ascertain the same answer."

MacNamara nodded.

"I see," he said slowly, although he clearly did not see. "Then perhaps Lieutenant Scott can take this opportunity to enlighten me."

Scott, too, saluted sharply. He hesitated, as if gathering his words, then replied: "Sir. I was challenging these men to a fight, sir."

"A fight?" MacNamara asked. "All of them?"

"Yes sir. As many as was necessary. Some of them. All of them. It did not make a difference to me. Sir."

MacNamara shook his head. "Why would you do this, lieutenant?"

"My door, sir."

"Your door? What about your door, lieutenant?"

Scott paused. He took a deep breath.

"See for yourself, colonel," he replied.

MacNamara started to respond, then stopped. "Very well," he said. He took a step forward, only to hear Heinrich Visser's voice. "I think, colonel, that I shall accompany you."

The German was making his way through the crowd of men, which parted swiftly to allow him to pass. Visser mounted the steps, nodding toward MacNamara. "Please," he gestured to Scott, "show us what it is that would prompt a man to attempt to battle such uneven odds."

Scott eyed the German with disdain. "A fight is a fight, *Hauptmann*. Sometimes the odds are completely irrelevant to the cause of the fight."

Visser smiled. "A brave man's concept, lieutenant. Not a pragmatic man's."

MacNamara interrupted sharply. "Scott, lead the way. Now, if you please!"

Tommy was the last through the double doors into Hut 101. The uneven tread of the men echoed in the barracks as they traveled down to the last door, which marked Scott's quarters. There they paused, staring at the wooden exterior.

In large, deep knife strokes, someone had carved: DIE NIGGER KKK.

"Not even very grammatical," Lincoln Scott said sourly.

Visser stepped forward, removed a black leather glove from his sole hand, and then slowly ran the tip of his finger over the words, outlining each. He did not speak, and carefully, using his teeth, tugged the glove back into place.

MacNamara's face was marred by a scowl. He turned to Scott. "Do you have any idea, lieutenant, specifically, who placed these words on your door?"

Scott shook his head. "I left my room only to go and use the *Abort*. I was not gone for more than a few minutes. When I returned, the message was there."

"And you thought to take on everyone in sight?" MacNamara asked, still harnessing the fury that leeched onto the edge of each word. "Although you had no *real* idea who carved the words here when your back was turned."

Scott hesitated, then nodded. "Yes sir," he said. "Precisely."

Behind them, they all suddenly heard the sound of the doors to Hut 101 swinging open, and heavy footsteps in the corridor. All the men gathered in front of Scott's room pivoted, and saw that Commandant Von Reiter was marching directly toward them. He was accompanied by two junior-grade officers, both of whom kept their hands nervously on the holsters of their pistols. Behind them, trying to remain inconspicuous, but still eager to see, was Fritz Number One. As he had been only a few hours before, Von Reiter was in his dress uniform.

The camp commandant pushed forward and halted a few feet away from the door. For a long, silent moment, he stared at the words, then he turned to MacNamara, as if seeking an explanation.

MacNamara didn't hesitate.

Pointing a finger directly at the commandant, he spoke briskly and harshly. "This, *Herr Oberst,* is precisely what I warned you about! Had it not been for the arrival of Lieutenant Hart and myself, we might have had a riot on our hands!"

MacNamara pivoted toward Scott. "Lieutenant, while I can understand your rage—"

"Begging the colonel's pardon, but I don't think you can, sir—" Scott started to reply. MacNamara raised a hand, shutting him off.

"We have due process. We have a procedure! We must adhere to regulations! I will not have a riot! I will not allow a lynching! And I will not allow you to be goaded into a fight!"

He switched back instantly to Von Reiter. "I warned you, commandant, that this situation is dangerous. I'm warning you again!"

Von Reiter hissed his reply, equally furious: "You must control your own men, Colonel MacNamara! Or else I will be forced to extreme measures!"

The two men glared at each other. Then, abruptly, MacNamara turned to Tommy. "We will proceed at zero eight hundred on Monday! And this"—he pivoted back to Von Reiter—"I want a new door on this room within the hour! Understand?"

Von Reiter started to reply, then paused, and nodded. He rapidly spoke a few words in German to one of the adjutants, who clicked his heels together, saluted, and hurried down the corridor.

The German commandant said, "Yes. This will be seen to. You, colonel, will take steps to remove the mob outside. Correct?"

MacNamara nodded. "It will be taken care of."

The Senior American Officer paused, then added ominously, "But the *Oberst* can see for himself the threats we are all under. Trouble is likely."

"You will control your men!" Von Reiter said sharply.

"I will do that which is within my power," MacNamara answered stiffly.

Tommy had a sudden thought, and he stepped quickly forward. "Sir!" he said sharply. "I think it would be appropriate if Lieutenant Scott had the benefit of his counsel around the clock. I am willing to move into his room with him." Then he turned to the German officer, and added, "And I can think of no better bodyguard than Flying Officer Renaday. I would like permission for him to move from the British compound into this bunk room for the duration of the trial."

Von Reiter thought momentarily, then shrugged. "If you so desire, and there are no objections from your commanding officer . . ."

MacNamara shook his head. "Probably a good idea," he said.

"Hauptmann Visser will see to the transfer," Von Reiter ordered.

"Yes," Tommy said, staring, with unbridled animosity, at the one-armed German. "He's good at transfers." He thought, right at that second, that if there were a way to kill Visser, he would gladly have done it, because all he could see in his mind's eye was the forlorn face of Phillip Pryce as he was forced into the backseat of the car that took him to what Tommy believed was a swift and lonely death.

Von Reiter took a long measurement of the anger he saw between Tommy and Visser, nodding his head. "All right," he said to MacNamara. "Dismiss the men. It is nearly time for the evening *Appell* regardless."

The Germans then all turned and marched down the corridor. MacNamara took a second to turn to Tommy Hart and Lincoln Scott. "Lieutenant Scott, you have my apologies," MacNamara said stiffly. "There's nothing more I can say."

Scott nodded, and then saluted. "Thank you, sir," he said, endowing the words with as few thanks as possible.

Then the Senior American Officer turned and followed the Germans down the corridor. For a moment, Tommy and Lincoln Scott remained in the hallway.

"Would you have fought them?" Tommy asked.

"Yes," Scott replied brusquely. "Of course."

"And don't you think that's precisely what they wanted?" Tommy continued.

"Yes, you're probably right about that, too," Scott conceded. "But what choice did I have?"

Tommy didn't answer this, because he didn't see any alternative. What he said instead was: "I think it would be a good idea if we stopped doing precisely what everyone who hates you expects you to do."

Scott opened his mouth to answer, then hesitated, pausing over his words. Then he nodded. "You make a salient point, Hart. I agree."

Scott stood beside the door to the bunk room, and ushered Tommy inside. "I appreciate your offer," he said. "But I can—"

Tommy cut him off. "I can put a bunk over against the wall, and Hugh should stay closest to the door. In case there are any others who might want to try something in the night. There aren't too many who would be willing to fight their way through him to get to you."

Scott again started to speak, stopped, and then nodded. "Thank you," he said. Tommy smiled. He guessed that this was the first time he'd heard the black airman use those words with any significant degree of sincerity. He pointed at the wall where he intended to move his bunk. "I'll just get my stuff," he said, and then he paused.

A sudden, nasty fear slid through him.

Tommy's eyes raced around the room, searching the spare and sparse area.

"What is it?" Scott asked, suddenly alarmed by the look on Tommy's face.

"The board. The board with Vic's blood on it. That proves he was killed outside the *Abort*, then moved there. That I left here with you earlier . . ."

Tommy spun about, searching.

"Where the hell is it?"

Scott turned to the farthest corner. "I set it right there," he said slowly. "It was there when I left to go to the *Abort*."

But both men could see that the board had disappeared.

Chapter Ten

FIREWOOD

Immediately after the regular evening *Appell*, Tommy Hart and Lincoln Scott headed directly for Colonel MacNamara's quarters. The two men walked swiftly yet silently across the assembly yard and directly into Hut 114, not speaking to anyone else, not speaking between themselves, passing small groups of kriegies getting ready to prepare their dinners. For the most part, the men were carefully assembling various items gleaned from Red Cross parcels, combining foodstuffs— tinned beef or sausage, dried vegetables and fruits, and the ever-present processed milk called Klim that was the basis for virtually every sauce they could concoct. That afternoon, the Germans had provided some *kriegsbrot* and a meager issue of hard turnips and musty potatoes.

An enterprising kriegie cook could create an incredible range of meals from the materials in a Red Cross parcel, taking chances with ingredients (processed pork roll fried with strawberry jam garnished with tinned fruits). The more successful chefs often posted new recipes on the Stalag Luft Thirteen bulletin boards, and these recipes were attempted and revamped in dozens of different ways throughout the camp. The airmen replaced bulk with invention, and every new kriegie learned to both cook and eat slowly, trying to make each small, inadequate bite both evoke some memory of some fine meal eaten under far better circumstances, and at the same time last far longer than it deserved. No one wolfed down their food in Stalag Luft Thirteen.

As they passed down the central corridor of the hut,

Tommy snuck a sideways glance over at Scott. As always, Scott was marching erect, with a tautness to his face that spoke of both anger and aggressiveness. Tommy thought there was some sort of enigmatic toughness to Scott that he did not even begin to understand, which sprang from some well within the man that Tommy doubted he would ever see. In the same instant, he wondered what the black flier thought when he looked over at him. Scott had the rare capacity to make whoever was walking at his side appear smaller. Tommy thought this quality came from what one had seen of life, and how it had been absorbed deep within, and Lincoln Scott had seen much. As for himself, he did not think Vermont and Harvard equaled the journey that Lincoln Scott had traveled, even though both men had arrived in the same place at the same time. There was one thing Tommy knew for sure: Scott still did not look like a prisoner of war. Perhaps he had lost weight—this was inevitable given the stark and bare diet—but there was no look of sullen resignation, nor one of cowed patience, which is its own type of defeat, in his quick dark eyes.

Tommy wondered about himself. Did Stalag Luft Thirteen melt the fighter out of him as surely as it did pounds? Had he lost desire? Assertiveness? Pugnacity? The qualities that made a young man look forward to life. He sometimes dogged himself with questions, wondering whether he would be able to invoke these traits when he needed them most.

Especially now, he thought, when Phillip Pryce is gone, and there is only his memory to remind me when to call on them. Tommy bit down on his lip, wrestling with emotions. It was as hard to imagine Phillip dead as it was to believe him still alive. It was as if the Englishman had been plucked from Tommy's existence with the finality of death but none of the reality. He'd waved, and then he'd vanished. No explosion. No fire. No shrieks for help. No blood. The portrait in his mind's eye of the wry, unafraid smile that Phillip wore in that last moment was like a hard blow to his stomach.

Tommy walked quickly and steadily at Lincoln Scott's side, but inwardly he felt alone.

"You gonna do the talking, Hart? Or should I?"

Scott's barely constrained ferocity ripped Tommy from his

thoughts. He answered instantly. "I'll start off, but make sure MacNamara knows your feelings. You understand what I'm saying?"

Scott nodded. "Yeah," he said, lowering his voice. "Be a gentleman, a very pissed-off gentleman, but don't say anything that insults the bastard, because he's the judge and he might choose tomorrow's proceedings as get-even time."

"That's close enough," Tommy said. He reached out and rapped sharply three times on the Senior American Officer's door. In the second they paused, waiting, Scott muttered, "I'll be a gentleman, Hart. But you know, I'm getting tired of being reasonable all the time. I sometimes think I'm gonna be reasonable right up to the moment I hear them give the command to fire."

"I'm not sure you have been," Tommy replied weakly, and Scott snorted, amused.

They heard a voice call for them to enter, and Scott swung open the door. Lewis MacNamara was seated in a distant corner of the room, his stockinged feet up on his bunk, a pair of scratched and bent reading glasses slid down on his nose. He had a tin plate of half-eaten ubiquitous kriegie stew on the blanket beside him, and a dog-eared copy of Dickens's *Great Expectations* open in his hand. Tommy recognized this combination instantly. Standard kriegie approach to eating: take a bite, chew slowly, read a paragraph or two, take another bite. Sometimes it seemed that Time was as much their enemy as the Germans.

MacNamara slowly lowered the novel, eyeing the two visitors with interest, as they took several quick steps into the center of the small room, and fixed themselves at attention. The Senior American Officer had, by virtue of rank, acquired one of the rare two-person bunk rooms. But Major Clark, his roommate, was oddly absent. Tommy had the presence of mind to glance around, thinking maybe there would be some picture on the wall or souvenir propped in the corner that might tell him something about the SAO's personality that he could later use. But there was nothing that revealed anything.

"Lieutenants . . ." MacNamara said as he touched his forehead with a return salute. "Please, stand at ease. Why are you here?"

"Sir. We wish to report a theft, sir," Tommy answered sharply.

"A theft?"

"Correct."

"Please continue."

"A key piece of evidence acquired by myself, which I planned to introduce at trial tomorrow, was removed from Mr. Scott's quarters. We suspect this theft took place during the time he was confronting the men in front of Hut 101. Sir, we protest this action in the most vigorous way!"

"Evidence, you say. What sort of evidence?"

Tommy hesitated, and the SAO quickly added, "There's no one from the other side here, Mr. Hart. And I will keep whatever information you provide me in strictest confidence."

"I'm certain you will, sir," Tommy said, but did not believe it for an instant. He didn't dare to throw a glance at Lincoln Scott.

"Good." MacNamara's voice had a firmness to it that could have concealed irritation, but Tommy was unsure. "I ask again: What sort of evidence?"

"It was a wooden board, sir. Ripped from the side of a building. There were clear traces of Trader Vic's blood marking it. Spatter traces, I believe they're called by professionals."

MacNamara started to open his mouth, then stopped. He swung his feet off the bed, staring down for a second at his wriggling toes concealed by threadbare socks. Then he sat up more sharply, as if paying closer attention.

"A wooden board, you say? A bloodstained wooden board?"

"Correct, sir."

"How can you be certain it was Captain Bedford's blood?"

"I can arrive at no other reasonable conclusion, sir. Nobody else has bled that substantially."

"True enough. And this board proved what? In your own estimation?"

Tommy hesitated, before replying: "A key element of the defense, sir. It relates to where Trader Vic was actually murdered and attacks the prosecution's perception of the crime."

"It came from the *Abort*?"

"I didn't say that, sir."

"It came from some other location?"

"Yes sir."

"And you believe this shows what?"

"Sir, if we can show that the crime took place in some different spot, then it calls into serious question the entirety of the prosecution's case. They claim that Mr. Scott followed Captain Bedford out of Hut 101 and that the subsequent confrontation and fight took place between the buildings, by the *Abort*. Evidence that suggests a different scenario supports Lieutenant Scott's denials, sir."

MacNamara again paused, measuring his words carefully. "What you contend is accurate, lieutenant. And now this item is gone?"

Before Tommy could reply, Scott burst out: "Yes sir! Stolen from my room. Lifted, robbed, filched, pilfered, poached, or purloined! Whatever word you want, sir. Right when my back was ever so goddamn conveniently turned!"

"Watch your language, lieutenant."

Scott stared hard at the Senior American Officer. Then he slowly spat out his next words. "All right, colonel. I'll watch my language. I would certainly hate to go to a firing squad with an excess *goddamn* on my lips. It might offend someone's delicate sensibilities."

MacNamara did not so much glare at Scott as he did shrug with a sort of acceptance of the black flier's fury, as if Scott's outrage was oddly unimportant. Tommy took note of this silently, and then stepped slightly forward, emphasizing his words with sharp hand gestures.

"Sir, you will recall that in some regards it was Trader Vic's accusation that Lieutenant Scott stole something from him that triggered all this. Certainly much of the animosity stemmed from that incident. And now, it is Lieutenant Scott who has been victimized, and what has disappeared is far more critical than any wartime souvenir, pack of smokes, or chocolate bar!"

MacNamara held up his hand. He nodded his head slowly.

"I am aware. What is it you want me to do?"

Tommy smiled. "At a minimum, sir, I would think we should question every member of the prosecution under oath.

They are, after all, the ones who benefit from this illegal action. I would think that we should further question every witness for the prosecution, because many of those men seem to carry the same animosity toward Lieutenant Scott that Captain Bedford did. We should also question some of the men who have been most overt in their threats toward Lieutenant Scott. And I would think that we should delay tomorrow's proceedings substantially. Furthermore, I would think that this theft of key evidence would underscore Scott's presumption of innocence. In many regards, the theft is de facto evidence of his total innocence! It is certainly equally likely that the board was stolen by the actual murderer! I would argue that you should immediately dismiss the accusation against Lieutenant Scott."

"Absolutely not!"

"Sir! The defense has been crippled by the illegal and immoral actions of others, right here inside the camp! That suggests—"

"I can see what it suggests, lieutenant! But it proves nothing. And there is no proof that this evidence actually existed or would have achieved the dramatic results you claim."

"Sir! You have the word of honor of two officers!"

"Yes, but beyond that—"

"What?" Scott interrupted. "Is our word less substantial? Less important? Less truthful? It somehow doesn't count for the same? Maybe you think *mine* is less valuable. But Hart's word of honor is the same color as yours or Major Clark's or anyone else's in Stalag Luft Thirteen!"

"I didn't say that, lieutenant. It is none of those things. But it does lack corroboration." MacNamara spoke softly. Almost as if he were trying to be conciliatory.

"Other officers saw me obtain the board," Tommy interjected.

"Who? Why are they not with you, now?"

Tommy instantly envisioned Trader Vic's roommates and the members of the jazz band that had confronted him in the corridor of Hut 101. He thought they were probably the men who had stolen the board. And he knew they would lie about the theft. But he knew who couldn't lie.

"I am unsure who they were."

"Do you think you can find them?"

"No. Except for one."

"And who might that be?"

"Captain Walker Townsend, sir. The chief prosecutor. He saw me with the item in question."

This name made the SAO stiffen, and rise to his feet. For several seconds, he seemed to be thinking deeply. He turned away from the two men, walked to one side of the small room, then turned, and took several strides back, so that he was once again facing the two lieutenants. Tommy could see the SAO calculating, almost as if he were inspecting the damage done by combat to an aircraft, trying to determine whether it would fly. Again, Tommy took note of MacNamara's reaction as much as he did anything the SAO had said. He hoped that Lincoln Scott was equally alert.

Abruptly, MacNamara waved his hand in the air, as if he'd finished the equation in his mind, and written a result. "All right, gentlemen. We will deal with this matter before the tribunal in court tomorrow. You can raise your questions then, and perhaps Captain Townsend and the prosecution will have some answers for you at that point."

MacNamara looked over toward the two younger men. He both frowned and smiled and in the same gesture, shook his head slightly.

"You may have struck a blow, Lieutenant Hart. A well-placed and accurate blow. Whether it does great injury to the prosecution remains to be seen. But I will keep an open mind on the issue."

Tommy nodded, although he wasn't sure he believed this and doubted that Scott would consider it anything but a blatant lie. He saluted. He started to pivot toward the exit, but Scott, at his side, hesitated. Tommy had a sudden surge of nervousness over what Scott was about to say, but he saw the black flier point down at the novel that had been left open on MacNamara's bunk.

"Do you enjoy Dickens, sir?" he suddenly asked.

Colonel MacNamara let a small look of surprise cross his face before he replied, "Actually, this is the first I've had time to read. I never was one for fiction, when I was younger. History and mathematics, mainly. That was the stuff that helped you into West Point and the reading that kept you there. I don't even believe they offered a class at the Point that read Dickens. Of course, I never had all the free time growing up and going to school that I've now got right here, thanks to the damn Krauts. But so far, this seems quite interesting."

Scott nodded. "My own schoolwork was dominated by technical literature and textbooks, too," he said, a small smile filtering across his face. "But I still made time for the classics, sir. Dickens, Dostoyevsky, Tolstoy, Proust, Shakespeare. Need to read Homer and some of the Greek tragedies, as well. Hard to consider oneself properly educated without a fundamental grounding in the classics, sir. My mother taught me that. She's a teacher."

"That may very well be true, lieutenant," MacNamara responded. "I hadn't considered it in precisely those terms."

"Really? I'm surprised. Well, regardless, Dickens was an interesting writer, sir," Scott continued. "There's one important thing to remember, when reading any of his best works."

"What's that, lieutenant?" MacNamara asked.

"Nothing is exactly as it seems at first," Scott answered. "That was Dickens's genius." Then he added, "Good night, sir. Enjoy your reading."

The two young airmen then exited the SAO's bunk room.

By the time they walked out of Hut 114, darkness had crept into the air around them, turning the world into the weak and faded, indistinct gray of dusk. The barbed-wire walls around the camp perimeter seemed like so many twisting lines of black penciled against the leftover daylight. Most of the kriegies were already in their bunk rooms, preparing for the night, anticipating the evening chill that slipped inexorably over the camp. The two men could see an occasional airman hurrying through the start of the evening, his pace dictated less by the encroaching cold than by the night that threatened him. Darkness could always mean death, especially at the hands of some nervous, poorly trained teenage guard carrying a machine pistol. Tommy looked up, through the first moments of gloom, toward a nearby guard tower, and saw that there were two goons resting there, their arms on the edge, like men at a bar. But both goons were watching them closely, expecting them to hurry their stride.

"Not bad, Hart," Scott said. His own eyes had followed Tommy's, up to the guard tower and the two German soldiers watching them. "I especially liked that part about tossing the charges. Won't work, of course, but it made him a bit nervous, and gave him something nasty to think about tonight when the Krauts shut off the lights, and I liked that."

"Worth a try."

"Anything's worth a try at this point. And you know who would have liked it? The old limey, the one they shipped out. Pryce would have admired the maneuver, even if it didn't work."

"Probably right about that," Tommy replied.

"But there aren't a lot of tricks lurking at the bottom of this barrel, are there, Hart?"

"No. We still have Fenelli, the medic. His testimony should shed some doubt on things. And when he shoots his mouth off it will mess up Captain Townsend's neat little package. But I wish we had something else. Something concrete. The real murder weapon, maybe. Some other witness. Something. Something convincing. That's why that damn board was so critical."

Scott nodded. "It would be nice."

They took a few steps through the start of the evening, and then Tommy asked the black flier, "Tell me, Scott, what's your take on MacNamara?"

Scott hesitated, then asked his own question. "How so? Do you mean as an officer? Or as a judge? Or, maybe, as a human being? Which?"

"All. Or whichever you want to answer. Come on, Scott, what's your impression?"

Tommy could see a small grin creep across the black airman's lips. "As an officer, he's a by-the-book professional military man. A career officer looking for advancement and probably being eaten alive every second he has to sit here, completely forgotten, while his classmates from West Point go and do what West Pointers do, which is generally to send men out to get killed and then get to pin medals on their own chests and enjoy their promotions up the military ladder. As a judge, well, I suspect he'll be more or less the same, though he will bend over backwards at odd moments to appear that he's being fair."

"I agree," Tommy said. "But there's a difference between actually being fair and appearing to be fair."

"Bingo," Scott said quietly. "Now, as a person, well . . . Do you have any idea, Hart, just how many Lewis MacNamaras I've met in my life?"

"No."

"Dozens. Hundreds. Too many to count."

"I don't follow."

Scott sighed and nodded. "MacNamara is the difficult type that vociferously and publicly denies being even a tiny bit prejudiced, then automatically raises the bar just a little farther whenever a Negro threatens to reach up and leap over. He'll talk about fairness and equality and meeting established standards, but the truth is that the standard I have to surpass is far different from the one that you do, Hart. And mine always gets a little tougher the closer I get to success. I've seen MacNamara in the schools I've attended, from elementary school on the South Side of Chicago right through the university. MacNamara was the Irish policeman who walked my block taking payoffs and keeping everyone in line, and the grade school principal who made us share every book three ways in each class and prevented anyone from taking the book home at night and really studying what was in it. MacNamara was there when I enlisted and went through basic training. He was the officer who looked down at my academic record, including a Ph.D., and then suggested I become a cook. Or maybe a hospital orderly. But something menial and unimportant. And then, when I scored the highest grade on the entrance exam for flight school, it was a MacNamara who demanded I retake the test. Because of some irregularity. The only irregularity was that I outperformed all the white boys. And when I finally qualified, MacNamara was down there in Alabama, waiting for me. I told you before: cross-burnings outside the camp and almost impossible standards inside. The MacNamaras down there would flunk you out of the program for a single mistake on a written exam. You'd wash out for any error, no matter how minor, in the air. You want to know why the boys from Tuskegee are the best damn fighter pilots in the army air corps? Because we *had* to be! Like I say, one set of rules for you, Hart, a different set of rules for me. You want to know the funny thing?"

"The funny thing?"

"Well," Scott said, smiling, "it's not precisely funny. But ironic, okay?"

"Well, what's that?"

"That when all is said and done, it's a whole lot easier for me to deal with the Vincent Bedfords of the world than it is the Lewis MacNamaras. At least Trader Vic never tried to hide who he was and how he felt. And he never claimed to be fair when he wasn't."

Tommy nodded. The two men were walking through the brisk air. There was a freshness to the evening breeze, one that evoked memories of Vermont in him.

"It must be difficult for you, Scott. Difficult and frustrating," Tommy said quietly.

"What?"

"To always immediately see hatred in everyone you meet and to always be so damn suspicious about everything that happens."

Scott started to reply, his right hand raised in a small dismissive wave that stopped midway in the air in front of them. Then he smiled again. "It is," he said. He coughed briefly. "It is indeed a difficult chore." He shook his head, still grinning. "One that, as you can tell, seems to occupy my every waking minute." He tossed his head back, a quick burst of laughter escaping from his lips. "You caught me on that, Hart. I seem to keep underestimating you."

Tommy shrugged. "You wouldn't be the first," he said.

"But don't you underestimate me," Scott said.

Tommy shook his head. "That would be the one thing I doubt I would ever do, Scott. I might not understand you, and I might not like you. I might not even completely believe you. But I'll be damned if I'll ever underestimate you."

Scott smiled and laughed again. "You know something, Hart?" he said briskly. "I must admit you keep surprising me."

"The world is filled with surprises. It's never quite the way it seems. Isn't that precisely what you told MacNamara about Dickens's world?"

Scott kept smiling and nodded.

"Vermont, huh? You know, I've never been there. Visited Boston once, but that was as close as I got. Do you miss it?" He paused, shook his head, then added, "That's a stupid question, because the answer is so obvious. But I'll ask it anyway."

"I miss everything," Tommy replied. "I miss my home. My girl. My folks. My little sister. The damn dog. I miss Harvard, for Christ's sake, which is something I never thought I'd say out loud. Do you know what I miss? The smells. I never thought being free had a distinct odor to it, but it does. You could taste it in the air, every time the wind picked up. Fresh. It was in my girl's perfume when I took her out on our first date. In my mother's cooking on Sunday morning. Sometimes I walk out of the huts and all I see is the wire, and I think I'll never get beyond it and never smell any of those things ever again. Not for even a minute. Not ever again."

The two men took a few more steps forward, right to the entrance to Hut 101. There Scott stopped. He turned his head about for a moment, checking to see if anyone was watching them. It seemed as if they were alone right there in the final moments of day's light, before the crush of darkness fell over the camp. Scott reached down into his breast pocket and removed a frayed and cracked photograph. He took a slow, lingering look at the picture, then handed it over to Tommy.

"I was lucky," Scott said quietly. "The morning of my last mission, I just grabbed their picture and stuck it in my flight suit, right next to my heart. I don't know why. Never did it on any other mission excepting that last one. But I'm real glad I have it."

There was a little light coming from the edge of the doorway, and he twisted so that it fell across the photograph. It was a simple snapshot of a young, delicate, cocoa-colored woman sitting in a rocking chair in the living room of a trim, well-furnished house, cradling a small baby in her arms. Tommy stared at the picture. He saw the woman's eyes were alert and filled with a soft joy. The baby's right hand was outstretched, reaching up toward its mother's cheek.

There was a small crack in Lincoln Scott's voice when he added, "I don't know if they've been told I'm alive. It's a very hard thing, Hart, to imagine someone you love thinks you dead. . . ." He stopped.

Tommy returned the picture to Scott. "Beautiful," he said. This was the obligatory response, but a truthful one, nonetheless. "I'm sure the army has informed them you're a prisoner."

Scott nodded. "Yes, I suppose so. But then, you might suspect I would have received a letter or a package or something from home, and I haven't. Not a word." He took another long look at the photograph before returning it slowly to his pocket. "I've never seen the baby. He was born after I was shipped overseas. Makes it hard to imagine he's real. But he is. Probably cries a lot. I did when I was little, or so my mother likes to tell me. I suppose I'd like to live to see him, if only just one time. And I'd like to see my wife again, too." He hesitated, then added, "Of course, that's no different for you, or MacNamara or Clark or Captain Townsend or the Krauts or anyone else in this damn place. Even Trader Vic. He probably wanted to go back to Mississippi as bad as anyone. I wonder who he had waiting for him back home?"

"His boss at the used-car dealership," Tommy said.

There was a bridge game going on in one bunk room, with as many kibitzers following the play as there were players. Unlike poker, or Hearts, both of which lent themselves to more rowdy levels of participation and overflow crowds of observers, the bridge game flowed quietly until the last few tricks of the hand, which prompted intense and raucous discussion about the precise manner in which the cards were played. Kriegies loved the arguments as much as they loved the games; it was another way that something modest was exaggerated, stretched out to consume more of the frustrating minutes of imprisonment.

The door to Scott's room, with its offensive carving, had been replaced, just as the Germans had promised. But as the two men approached, they saw that it was ajar. Tommy might have been surprised, but he immediately heard loud humming and snatches of song coming from the bunk room, and he recognized Hugh Renaday's rough voice amid the mingled off-key tunes and lavishly obscene lyrics.

They stepped in, and saw the Canadian in the process of making up his sleeping area. Tommy's modest accommodations were pushed to the wall, his law books stacked beneath the bunk, some spare clothes hung from a string between two nails. It wasn't much, but some of the starkness and painful isolation of the room had been diminished. Hugh was tacking an out-of-date calendar to the wall. The year-old date was less significant than the portrait of the scantily clad and significantly endowed, doe-eyed young woman that graced the month of February 1942.

"Can't be without February," Hugh said, as he stepped back, admiring the picture. "She cost me two packs of smokes. I fully intend to find her after the war and propose to her perhaps ten seconds after we've been introduced. And I won't be taking no for an answer."

"Funny," Tommy said, staring attentively and admiringly at the pin-up. "She doesn't look very Canadian. I doubt she's ever chewed on a piece of blubber or even harpooned a seal. And her outfit, well, it doesn't look like it would be terribly effective in the northern wintertime. . . ."

"Tommy, my friend, I do believe you're missing the point here entirely." He laughed, and so did Tommy. Then Hugh reached out and grasped the black flier's hand, shaking it hard. "Glad to be here, mate," he said.

Scott replied, "Welcome to the *Titanic*." He turned and started toward his bunk, but then stopped abruptly. For an instant, he remained rigid, then he pivoted back toward Hugh.

"How long have you been here?" Scott abruptly demanded.

The Canadian looked surprised, then shrugged. "Half hour, maybe. Didn't take too long to unpack and stow my things. Fritz Number One brought me over, after the South Compound's *Appell*. We had to stop and check something with Visser, and then with one of Von Reiter's adjutants. Numbers stuff mainly. Paperwork. I guess they want to make sure they get the count straight in both camps. Don't want to go chasing about, sounding off all their whistles and alarms, looking for someone who's merely switched compounds."

"Did you see anyone when you arrived?" Scott questioned sharply.

"See anyone? Sure, there were kriegies all over the place."

"No, I mean in here."

"In here? Not a soul," Hugh replied. "Door was shut tight. New door, too, I noticed. But what's eating you, mate?"

"That," Scott said, suddenly pointing to a corner of the room.

Tommy pushed to Scott's side. He saw what the black airman was pointing toward instantly. Resting upright in the far corner of the bunk room was the missing wooden board that had been marked with Trader Vic's blood.

He covered the distance in a single stride, grabbing at the hunk of wood, quickly turning it over, back and forth, in his hands, examining it. Then Tommy looked up at Lincoln Scott, who remained in the center of the small space.

"See for yourself," he said bitterly.

Tommy pitched the board to Scott, who seized it from the air. He turned it over once or twice, just as Tommy had.

But Hugh was the first to speak. "Tommy, lad, what the hell's the matter? Scott, what's with the hunk of wood?"

Scott shook his head and muttered an obscenity. Tommy answered the question. "That's all it is, now," he said. "Might as well toss it in the stove. This morning, it was a critical piece of evidence. Now, it's nothing. Just firewood."

"I don't get it," Hugh said. He took the board from Scott.

It was Scott who explained, as he handed it over. "A little while ago, it was a board that Tommy discovered right outside Hut 105, covered with Trader Vic's blood. Proof in our hands that he was killed someplace other than where his body was found. But someone has gone to considerable trouble in the last few hours to steal the board from this room and then clean it of any traces of Vic's blood. Probably poured boiling water all over it, right into every little crack and splinter, and then scrubbed it with disinfectant."

Hugh lifted the board to his nose, sniffing. "You're right about that. Smells of lye and suds . . ."

"Just as if it came from the *Abort*," Tommy said. "And I'll wager you a carton of smokes that we could go over to Hut 105 and find that someone has cut in a different piece of wood at the spot where I ripped this out."

Scott nodded. "No bet," he said. "Damn."

He smiled wryly. "They're not stupid," he added cautiously, sadness filling every sound he spoke. "Stupid would have been just to steal the damn board. But stealing it, cleaning it of all traces, and then returning it to this room, now, that's clever, isn't it, Mr. Policeman?"

He looked over at Hugh, who nodded and continued to inspect the board. "If I had a microscope," he said slowly, "maybe even just a magnifying glass, I could probably find traces that the cleaning job left behind."

Tommy gestured widely. "A microscope? Here?" he asked cynically.

Hugh shrugged. "I'm sorry," he said. "Might as well ask for a winged chariot to carry us home."

"They're very damn clever," Scott continued, pivoting toward Tommy. "This morning we had a piece of hard evidence. Now we have nothing. Less than nothing. And poof! There goes tomorrow morning's arguments, counselor. And right alongside any hope of delaying the trial."

Tommy didn't at first reply. No sense in adding words to the simple truth.

"Actually," Hugh was quick to interject, "now you've got a problem. You told MacNamara about this theft?"

Tommy instantly saw where the onetime policeman was heading. "Yes. Damn. And now we've got a board that doesn't show what we claimed it did. That hunk of useless wood is as dangerous now as any of the evidence the prosecution does have. We damn well can't hold it up and say it *used* to have Vic's blood on it. Nobody would believe that for a second."

Tommy turned to Scott. "Now we've got the board, and its presence in our possession turns us into a pair of liars."

Hugh smiled. "But they just still might believe you if you continue to say it was stolen."

As he spoke, Hugh took the board and carefully propped it up against the edge of his bunk. Then, as his words dwindled into the air of the bunk room, he suddenly lifted his right leg and slammed it against the board. The savage kick splintered the board into two pieces. A second, equally hard kick turned it into kindling.

Tommy grimaced, shrugged, and said, "The cooking stove is down the corridor."

"Then I need to cook something," Renaday replied. He gathered the chunks of wood in his arms and exited the room.

"I guess that board is still stolen," Scott said. "I wonder if the bastards who stole it in the first place thought ahead far enough."

"I doubt they'd anticipate us destroying it," Tommy replied. He felt slightly uneasy at what they'd done. My first real case, he thought, and I destroy evidence. But before he had the chance to temporize about the morality of what they'd accomplished with two well-placed kicks, Lincoln Scott was speaking.

"Yeah. They were probably counting on us being honest and playing by the rules, because that's what we've been doing, right up to now. The problem is, Hart, no one else seems to be. Think about it: the carving on the door. Somebody knew that would bring me out of the room. Somebody knew I'd react the damn fool way I did, challenging everybody to a fight. *KKK* and *nigger*. Like waving a red flag in front of a bull. And I fell for it, went dashing out front, ready to fight the whole damn camp if necessary. And, right as I'm making a fool out of myself, someone sneaks in here and lifts the only solid piece of evidence we've got. And then, as soon as my back was turned again, zip, they brought it back. But ruined as evidence. And worse, because with that board sitting in the corner, we're going to appear to MacNamara and the entire camp to be a pair of liars."

Something frightening occurred to Tommy at that moment. He slowly inhaled, staring across at Lincoln Scott, who was continuing to speak.

The black flier sighed deeply. "Our expert barrister is suddenly removed. Our pathetic evidence is destroyed. All the lies make sense. All the truths seem nonsense."

What Tommy saw, in that moment, was that slowly but surely they were being squeezed into a location where all that remained of their defense was Scott's denials. He suddenly saw that no matter how forceful they were, they were still exceedingly fragile. And any discrepancy, any inconsistency, might turn the strength of those denials into ammunition against him.

He started to say this, but stopped when he saw the stricken look on Lincoln Scott's face. It seemed to him, in that second, that much of Scott's rage and frustration slid away from him, leaving behind nothing except a great, ineffable sadness. Scott's shoulders slumped forward. He put a hand to his eyes, rubbing hard. Tommy looked across the small room at Scott and realized, in that precise second, why the black flier had greeted everyone with distance and standoffishness from his first minute in the captivity of Stalag Luft Thirteen. What he saw was that there is nothing more hurtful and lonely in the world than to be different and isolated, and that Scott's only defense against the jealousy and racism he knew would be waiting for him had been to fire his own anger first, like the fighter pilot he was.

Tommy realized that everything in the case was a trap. But the worst of the traps was the one Scott had inadvertently created for himself. By not allowing anyone to know who he really was, he had made it easy for them to kill him. Because they would not care. No one knew about the wife, the child, waiting at home, nor did they know about the preacher father who urged him forward to advanced degrees or the mother who made him read the classics. Lincoln Scott had made it seem to all the other kriegies that he wasn't like them, when, in truth, he was no different, not in the slightest.

It must be a terrible thing, Tommy guessed, to believe that the nails and wood that you purchased yourself to build walls were now being used to fashion your own coffin.

"So, counselor, what's left? Not much, is there?"

Tommy didn't reply. He watched Scott put a hand to his forehead, as if in pain. When he pulled it away, he looked over at Tommy. There was anguish in his words, and Tommy abruptly realized how hard it must be for those who are accustomed to staring across the ring or through the sky and seeing their enemy clearly arrayed before them to be suddenly trying to fight against something as elusive and vaporous as the hatred Scott was now up against. "Some people seem to be going to a whole lot of trouble just to make absolutely damn for certain sure that this poor old nigger gets shot. And they sure as hell seem to have some damn fast timetable, too."

Then without another word, Lincoln Scott threw himself down on his bunk, tossing his thick forearm over his eyes, blocking out the unrelenting light from the single overhead bulb. He remained in that position, motionless, not even looking up, when Hugh reentered the bunk room. He stayed that way, not moving, like a man on a slab, right to the moment that the Germans cut the electric power to the huts, plunging all three men into the usual complete darkness of prisoner-of-war camp.

It was nearly midnight by the luminous dial on the watch that Lydia had given him and Tommy found himself unable to sleep, filled with an unruly nervousness that was not dissimilar to the anxiety he felt on the eve of his first combat mission. Within himself, he could sense some doubt, some fear, some frustration at the capriciousness of the world that had put him in this situation. He sometimes thought that true bravery was merely acquiring the ability to act, to do what needed to be done, in the face of all these emotions that urged him to find someplace safer and hide. He listened to the light sounds of sleep coming from the two other men in the room, wondering for a moment why they were not equally energized and didn't find sleep equally elusive. He supposed there was resignation in Lincoln Scott's breathing, and acceptance in Hugh Renaday's.

He felt neither of these emotions.

What he thought was that nothing had gone right in the camp from the moment Fritz Number One found Trader Vic's body. The steady routine of camp life—critical to both captors and captured—had been disturbed profoundly, and promised to be further disrupted when the black airman's trial started in the morning.

He mentally chewed on this idea for a moment, but it only led him to more confusion. There seemed to him to be so many layers of hatred at work, and for an instant he felt despair at ever sorting all of them out. Who was hated the most? Scott? The Germans? The camp? The war? And who was doing the hating?

Tommy slowly exhaled, and thought that questions made for poor armor, but they were all he had. His eyes open to the night, he stared up toward the ceiling of the bunk room, wishing that he could look up into the stars at home, and find the same comforting trail through the blinking celestial canopy that he'd always sought out when he was younger. It was an odd thing, he realized, to go through life believing that if a person could find one familiar route through the distant heavens, then they would believe that a similar course could be charted through the nearby swamps and shoals of earth.

This thought made him smile bitterly to himself, because in it he recognized Phillip Pryce's handiwork. What made Phillip such a fine barrister, Tommy thought, was that he was psychologically always a step or two ahead. Where others saw mere facts stiffly arrayed, Phillip saw huge canvases, drawn to the edge in nuance and subtlety. He did not know that he could ever fully achieve Pryce's capabilities, but he thought achieving some would be far better than none.

Tommy asked himself: What would Phillip have said about the disappearance and sudden reappearance of the crucial wooden board? Tommy breathed slowly. Phillip would say to look to who gains what. The prosecution gains, Tommy considered. But then Phillip would ask: Who else? The men who hate Scott for his skin, they too gained. The real killer of Vincent Bedford, he gained as well. The people who didn't gain were the defense, and the Germans.

He continued to breathe in and out, slowly.

That was an odd combination, Tommy thought. Then he asked himself: How are these others aligned?

He did not know the answer to that question.

Like a sudden storm surge ripping across a cold mountain lake, driving whitecaps onto still waters, Tommy danced amid all the conflicting ideas within him. Some men wanted Scott executed because he was black. Some men wanted Scott executed because he was a murderer. Some men wanted Scott executed for revenge.

He inhaled sharply, holding his breath.

Phillip was right, he thought suddenly. I'm looking at it all backward. The real question is: Who wanted Vincent Bedford dead?

He did not know. But someone did, and he still hadn't any idea who.

Questions made a racket in his head, so that when the soft sound of feet outside the closed bunk room door finally penetrated to his ear, he was startled. It was a padding sound, men in their stockings, moving carefully to conceal their travel.

He felt his throat abruptly constrict, his heart begin to race.

For an instant, he thought they were about to be attacked, and he pushed himself up onto an elbow, about to whisper an alarm to Scott and Renaday. His hand reached out in the darkness, seeking some kind of weapon. But in that momentary hesitation, the footsteps seemed to fade. He bent forward, listening hard, and heard them rapidly disappear down the central corridor. He took another deep breath, trying to calm himself. He insisted in that second that it had just been an ordinary kriegie, forced to use the solitary indoor toilet late at night. The same toilet that had caused so much trouble.

Then he stopped, and told himself that was wrong. There were two, and more probably three, sets of footsteps outside the door. Three men trying to move silently with a single purpose. Not a lonesome flier feeling ill. And then he realized there was no accompanying sound of rushing water coming from the toilet.

Tommy swung his feet out of the bunk, rising silently and tiptoeing across the room, making absolutely certain he didn't disturb his sleeping companions. He pressed his ear up against the solid wood of the door, but could hear nothing else. The blackness seemed complete, save for the occasional wan light from an errant searchlight, as it swept the outside walls and rooftops and penetrated through the cracks in the wooden window shutters.

He slowly, gingerly, swung open the door just the smallest fracture, so that he could slip through noiselessly. Out in the corridor, he crouched down, trying to make himself hidden. He pitched forward slightly, at the waist, craning to make out noises in the darkness. But instead of sound, a flicker of light caught his eye.

At the far end of the hut, at the distant entrance that he and Scott had used on their own midnight excursion, Tommy could see a lone candle's flame. The light was like a single, faraway star.

He held himself still, watching the candle. At first he could not make out how many men were waiting by the door, but more than one. There was a momentary silence, and he could make out the sweep of the searchlight as it crept past the entrance. The searchlight was like a bully, swaggering about the camp. In almost the same instant, the candle was extinguished.

He heard the creak of the front door to Hut 101 opening, and the small thud of it being closed seconds later.

Two men, he thought. Then he instantly corrected himself. Three men.

Three men went through the front door a few minutes after midnight.

They used a candle's light just as he and Scott had, to put on their flight boots while they waited for the searchlight to creep past. And then, just as he and Lincoln Scott had a few nights earlier, they'd immediately jumped into the darkness traveling behind it.

He took another slow, long breath. Three was very dangerous, he thought. A large and clumsy group to slip outside. One was the easiest, moving alone, patiently and cautiously. Two, as he'd found out with Scott, was tricky. Two men had to work in a coordinated fashion, like a pair of fighters diving to an attack, one plane in the lead, the other covering the wing. Two men were likely to talk, even though in whispers. Two men raised the chance of detection considerably. But three men exiting, one after the other, like diving from a stricken bomber into a sky filled with flak and pirouetting planes and falling through the air before opening a parachute, three was very dangerous and almost foolhardy. Three men would invariably make too much noise. Three men would find fewer accommodating dark spots to hide in. The exaggerated movement of three men was likely to catch the eyes of the tower goons, no matter how sleepy and inattentive they might be. Three was taking a huge risk.

And so the reward for those three men had to be great.

He slumped up against the wall, composing himself before he slid back into Scott's bunk room.

Three men in the corridor, sneaking out into the midnight.

Three men chancing their lives on the eve of the trial.

Tommy did not know how these things were connected. But he thought it might be a good idea to find out. He just did not know how.

Chapter Eleven

ZERO EIGHT HUNDRED

One of the camp's least efficient ferrets had already counted the formation of airmen three times, and when he started in again, going down the five-deep rows with his monotonous *eins, zwei, drei,* he was met with the usual catcalls, insults, and general groaning from the assembled kriegies. Men stomped their feet against the damp, chilly morning air, made nastier by a stiff breeze slicing in from the north. The sky overhead was a slate gray marred with a pair of pinkish-red streaks on the eastern horizon, more of the indecisiveness of the German weather that seemed to be forever trapped between winter and spring. Tommy hunched his shoulders against the wind, shivering slightly in the weak light in the hour just past dawn, wondering where the prior day's warmth had fled to and still filled with doubt about the gathering set for eight A.M. Just to his right, Hugh shuffled to get his circulation going and swore at the ferret, "Get it right this time, yah bloody idiot!" while to his left, Lincoln Scott stood motionless, as if unaffected by the cold and wet. Some moisture glistened on the black flier's cheeks, making it appear almost as if he'd been crying.

The ferret hesitated, staring down at a notepad, on which he was listing numbers. This act of doubt, signaling that he might start over for a fifth time, brought a cascade of obscenities and useless threats from the Allied prisoners. Even Tommy, who usually kept quiet during all these small insults of assembly, muttered to himself a quick, "Come on, Jesus, get on with it. . . ." as a sharp sword of wind sliced through his battered old leather flight jacket.

But he stopped when he heard the voice directly behind him speaking softly, yet insistently: "Hart? Maybe I got something for you."

He steeled himself, not turning, half expecting an insult. The voice seemed familiar, and after a moment, he recognized that it came from a captain from New York who lived in one of the bunk rooms across the hall from him. The captain was a fighter pilot, like Scott, who'd been shot down while escorting B-17s in a raid over Big B, which was Allied airmen's slang for Berlin.

"You still looking for information, Hart? Or you got everything under control?"

Tommy shook his head, but didn't turn back toward the man in formation behind him. Both Lincoln Scott and Hugh Renaday remained still, as well. "I'm listening," Tommy said. "What is it you want to say?"

"Kinda pissed me off, you know," the pilot continued, "the way Bedford always had whatever anyone needed. More food. More clothes. More of everything. Need this, he had it. Need that? He had that, too. And always got more for whatever it was than you wanted to give up. Didn't seem hardly fair. Everybody in the bag supposed to have it more or less the same, but it sure weren't the same for Trader Vic."

"I'm aware. Sometimes seemed like he was the only kriegie in this place never losing weight," Tommy responded. The man muttered a grunt in agreement.

"Hey," the captain said, "of course, on the other hand, he sure didn't end up the same neither."

Tommy nodded. This was true, but, of course, there was no guarantee that they all wouldn't end up just as dead as Vincent Bedford. He didn't say this out loud, though he knew it was never far from any airman's waking thoughts, and certainly featured in many kriegies' dreams. It was one of the prisoner-of-war camp credos: Don't speak of what truly frightens you, for that will surely come to pass.

"No kidding," Tommy said. "But you've got something you want to tell me?"

From the adjacent formation on Tommy's right, there was a scattering of angry shouts and complaints. Tommy figured the ferret counting that group had messed up again, as well. The New Yorker hesitated again, as if reconsidering what he was about to say. Then he grunted an obscenity or two, indicating that whatever internal argument he'd had, had been resolved, and he said, "Vic made a couple of trades, right before his death, that got my attention. Not just my attention, hell, a couple of other guys, too, noticed that Vic was being real busy. I mean, more busy than normal, and normal he was busy all the time, if you follow my drift."

"Keep talking," Tommy said quietly.

The fighter pilot snorted, as if finding the memory distasteful. "One of the things he got, man, I only saw it just the one time, but I remember thinking who the hell wanted that? I figured had to be some heavy-duty souvenir, yah know, but it sure was an unusual one, 'cause if the Krauts ever found it during one of their goddamn hut searches, well, anyone would know there'd be hell to pay, so I couldn't see getting it, myself, but . . ."

"What are you talking about?" Tommy asked, probably more sharply than necessary, but still speaking under his breath.

The captain from New York paused again, then replied: "It was a knife. Like, a special knife. Like the type that Von Reiter wears when he's got his fanciest gotta go meet the bosses uniform on."

"Like a dagger? Real thin and long?"

"That's the type. This was SS super special, too. I saw it had one of those death's head skulls on the handle. Very Nazi. The real deal. Probably only get that for doing something real wonderful for the fatherland, yah know. Like burning books or maybe beating up on women and kids, or shooting unarmed Russians. Anyway, I couldn't see it as a souvenir. No sir. Get caught with that in your kit, and the Krauts were likely to slam your butt into the cooler for a fortnight. They take that ceremonial stuff pretty seriously. Krauts got no sense of humor whatsoever."

"Where did you see it?"

"Vic had it. I saw it just once. I was in his room, playing some cards with his roommates when he came in with it. Said it was a special order. Wouldn't say who it was going to, but Vic sure made it seem like somebody had paid him something extra special for it. A big deal trade, I'd guess. Somebody wanted that knife something fierce. He squirreled it away with the rest of his loot, wouldn't say who it was going to. I didn't think much about it, until Vic got killed and they said it was with a knife, and I was wondering whether it mighta been that very same knife. Then I heard that it was some homemade job that Scott made up. Then I heard some scuttlebutt that maybe it wasn't, and I started thinking about that knife again. Anyway, don't know if it's helpful, or not, Hart, but thought you might be interested. Wish I knew who got it. That would help a whole lot more. But still, there it is. Someplace in this lousy camp's an SS dagger. And I'd be wondering about that, if I was you. Would be kinda unusual, too, if it turned out that Trader Vic got murdered with a weapon that he made a deal for."

"Where do you think he got it?"

The captain from New York snorted a small laugh.

"Only one ferret's got that sort of juice, Hart. You and I both know."

Tommy nodded. Fritz Number One.

He heard, in that second, a catch in the captain's voice, as the man continued.

"One other thing's been bothering me. Don't know if it's important, or not . . ."

"Go on," Tommy said.

"It could be nothin'. I mean, who knows about this shit, right?"

"What was it?"

"You remember back a coupla weeks when the tunnel out of 109 collapsed? The one where the two guys got caught and died?"

"Sure. Who doesn't?"

"Yeah. Right. Sure as hell that MacNamara and Clark remember. I think they were counting on that sucker. Anyways, right around that time Vic was real busy. I mean, real busy. I saw him ducking out more than once, middle of the night."

"How would you know that?"

The captain laughed briefly. "C'mon, Hart. There's some questions you shouldn't wanna be asking, unless you got some special reason. Look at me, man. I ain't more than five feet six. Just barely qualified for fighters wid' my height. And I usta be a motorman in a subway. Now, that should tell you that maybe because I ain't some big, tall college guy like yourself and Scott, there, that maybe somebody's got some other type job for me every so often. You know, the type of job where tall ain't no special advantage, yah don't mind much getting your hands dirty, and it sure as hell helps to be usta being underground."

Tommy nodded. "I got you."

The pilot continued. "You know, the night those guys died, I was supposed to be with 'em. Hadn't been for my sinuses actin' up, I'da been buried in that sand, too. Right alongside 'em. I been thinking about that a lot."

"Lucky."

The fighter pilot caught his words, then continued: "Yeah. Guess so. Luck's a funny thing. Sometimes real hard to tell exactly who's got it and who ain't, you follow what I'm saying? Scott, there. You can ask him about luck, Hart. All fighter jockeys know about luck. Good luck. Bad luck. Whatever the fates got in store for you kinda luck. Goes with the job description."

"So, what are you saying?"

"What I'm saying is this: I heard, real reliable, that Trader Vic came into some pretty unusual stuff right about that same time. Stuff that some folks in here would find mighty valuable. Like Kraut identity cards, travel vouchers, and some currency. You know, Reichsmarks and that sort of stuff. He also came up with something very interesting: a train schedule. The honest-to-God real deal, that bit of info. Now ain't that the sort of information that can only come from one place and costs a helluva lot and that some people around here would do anything to get their hands on. And I do mean anything."

"When I saw them divvying up Vic's stuff after he was killed I didn't see anything like that," Tommy said.

"No. And you wouldn't. Because stuff like what we're talking about would go direct to the right folks. No matter how good he's got his stuff stashed, why, those documents and papers and shit would be very dangerous. And you could never be completely sure that the Kraut who traded for the stuff wouldn't come right back at you, searching for your stash with a buncha other goons. And if they found any of that stuff, they'd likely seize just about everything you had before tossing you in the cooler for the next hundred years, so it was stuff you'd be turning over to the right folks real goddamn fast, you see what I'm saying? The folks that have some use for that stuff would know what to do with it, and they would be doing whatever it was real quick, you know?"

"I think I'm getting the picture—" Tommy started, only to have his words sliced off by the captain directly behind him.

"But yah can't, not really, 'cause even I don't get it. Those guys get killed in the tunnel, and then, just afterward, Bedford gets all these valuable papers, schedules and crap that the escape committee needs, whoever the hell they are, bunch of anonymous bastards, if you ask me. Even when I was digging, I never knew who the hell was planning the show. All they care about is how many yards we done, and how many yards we got left to do. But I did know this: They would give their right arms for those papers. . . ."

The pilot snorted another laugh, as if he'd inadvertently made a joke. "Hell," he said briskly, "then they'd all look just like that goddamn Nazi, Visser, that's skulking around here and always keeping his beady little eyes on you, Hart."

Even Tommy smiled at that thought.

The New Yorker coughed, and continued, "But I'm thinking that the stuff has gotta be worthless to anybody planning an escape, 'cause the Krauts are now dropping satchel charges into the goddamn tunnel and filling it in. The timing don't make sense. I mean, they needed that stuff *before* the damn tunnel got caved in. Weeks before, so's the forgers can prepare documents and the tailors making escape clothes can work on their stuff and guys heading out can memorize the schedule and practice speaking Kraut. Not after, and that's when Vic got it. Maybe you can dope it out, Hart. But I can't, and it's been on my mind for weeks. It bothers me."

Tommy nodded, but didn't reply at first, thinking hard. "You still digging?" he asked suddenly.

The captain hesitated, then replied with a shrug in his voice. "Ain't supposed to be answering that question, Hart, and you sure as hell know you ain't supposed to be asking it."

"Sorry," Tommy replied. "You're right."

The man hesitated slightly, then continued, "But hell, Hart, I just want out of here. I want out of here so damn bad some days I think it makes me more hungry than anything. I ain't never been locked up before, and I'm damn certain I ain't never gonna be locked up again. When I get back to Manhattan, let me tell you, I'm gonna be walkin' the straight and narrow, for sure. You get under the ground working, that's what you keep thinkin' about. All that loose sand and dust. Cave-ins all the damn time. Can't hardly breathe. Can't hardly see. Man, it's like digging your own grave. Scare the bejeesus out of you."

At that moment, Hugh, who'd been craning to hear the fighter pilot's words, interjected, "Maybe one of Vic's friends could provide some answers about where that knife and those documents disappeared to, what do you think?"

The captain from New York burst out in a short, nasty half-cough, half-wheezing tone of amusement. "Vic's friends? Friends? Man, have you ever got the wrong impression."

"What do you mean?" Tommy asked.

The pilot hesitated, then said slowly, "You know all those guys, the ones that keep getting into Scott's face? Vic's roommates and the others. The ones causing all the trouble?"

"Yeah, we know 'em," Hugh said, bitterly.

"Well, they like to say they were Vic's friends. That Vic was taking care of 'em and all that. Load of crap, let me tell you. Absolute one hunnert percent bull. Makes for some sort of real convenient explanation for what they've been doing to Scott, which ain't the way a lot of us in the bag would be playing it, no sir. But let me tell you something, Hart. Trader Vic was all about helping out Trader Vic. Nobody else. Vic had no friends. None. None whatsoever."

The man paused, then added, "That's something you might want to think about."

From the front of the assembly, a German adjutant shouted, "*Achtung!* Attention!" Tommy craned his head slightly, and saw Von Reiter had arrived at the head of the formations and was receiving obligatory salutes from the ferrets who had finally satisfactorily completed the count. All kriegies present and accounted for. Another day in the bag ready to begin. MacNamara was summoned forward, where, after the usual momentary exchange between the commanding officers, he turned and dismissed the Allied airmen. As the blocks of men instantly dissolved, Tommy quickly pivoted to try to catch the captain from New York, but the pilot had already melted into the mass of kriegies momentarily milling about before starting another day of captivity. Only this day held out the promise of being far different from all that had gone before.

Tommy had not moved more than ten yards through the dispersing airmen when he heard his name being called and he turned and saw Walker Townsend waving at him. He paused, sensing Hugh Renaday and Lincoln Scott coming to a halt beside him, and the three of them watched the captain from Richmond trot up to them. He wore his usual wry half-smile, and had his cap pushed back on his forehead in a relaxed manner that contradicted the biting wind that pushed sharply at all of them.

"Captain?" Tommy said.

"Morning, boys," Townsend answered cheerily. "Sure as hell will be glad to get home to Virginia. Hell, here it is, nearly time for summer to show up, and it still feels like a damn winter morning. Why's anybody want to live in this country, anyways? So, Tommy, y'all set for the opening act of our little show?"

"I could use more time," Tommy replied.

"Well, seems to me you've been right busy, nonetheless," Townsend replied. "And I don't believe anyone is inclined to postpone matters none. Anyways, I wonder if you might just join me for a moment over yonder near Hut 122, where Colonel MacNamara would like a word or two prior to the start of this morning's activities."

Tommy raised his head, staring down the row of huts. Hut 122 was one of the most isolated barracks.

"Mr. Renaday, you may join us, as well."

"Scott, too, if this is something about the case," Tommy said.

Walker Townsend let a small look of annoyance slip across his face, before restoring the same easygoing grin. "Sure. That makes some sense. Gentlemen, I do believe we're keeping the commanding officer waiting. . . ."

Tommy nodded, and they followed Townsend through the early morning light and cold. After a few yards, Tommy slightly slowed his pace. He made a small head gesture to Hugh Renaday, who read his motion perfectly, accelerated, and stepped up beside the prosecutor, instantly breaking out into a loud, "I've never been to Virginia, captain. You ever been up to Canada? We like to think that when God made the other countries, He was just practicing, but when He made Canada, He'd got it right, finally. . . ." At the same time, Tommy dropped a step or two back, and Lincoln Scott, seeing the shift in positions, hovered closely.

"This little meeting isn't supposed to be happening, Hart," the black airman said. "Right?"

"Precisely. Keep your eyes and ears open . . ."

"And my mouth shut?"

Tommy shrugged as he nodded. "It rarely hurts to play one's cards close to the vest."

"That's a white man's attitude, Hart. In my situation, or circumstances, you might say, well, it rarely helps. But that's a complicated distinction that you and I can discuss sometime under better conditions. Assuming I live through all this."

"Assuming we all live through it."

Scott coughed a laugh. "True enough. No shortage of people getting killed in this war."

They could all see the Senior American Officer pacing near the entrance to the hut, smoking rapidly. Major Clark was standing nearby, also wreathed in cigarette smoke, which blended with the gray, vaporous breaths that came every time any of the men exhaled into the cold air. Clark dashed his butt to the ground as the men approached. MacNamara took a long, final pull at the cigarette, then sharply ground it beneath his boot. There was a quick round of salutes, and the SAO glared briefly at Walker Townsend.

"I thought you were only going to summon Lieutenant Hart," MacNamara said sharply. "That was my order."

Townsend started to reply, then simply remained at attention as MacNamara cut off any words with a quick wave of the hand. He turned to Lincoln Scott and Tommy Hart.

"I have been troubled about your accusations," he said briskly. "The implications of the theft of evidence are substantial and could threaten the entirety of this morning's planned sessions."

"Yes sir," Tommy started. "That is why a delay would be—"

"I haven't finished, lieutenant."

"Sorry, sir."

MacNamara cleared his throat. "The more I thought about this matter, the more I came to believe that bringing it up in open court in front of the entire camp population as well as the representatives from the Germans would only serve to confuse the situation considerably. The tension in the camp surrounding the murder and now with the arrival of the trial, as evidenced by the confrontation following the discovery of the carvings on Scott's door . . . well, gentlemen, I am concerned. Mightily concerned."

Tommy could sense Scott, standing at his side, about to speak, but the black flier instead swallowed his retort and MacNamara continued to talk.

"Consequently, Lieutenant Hart, Lieutenant Scott, I took it upon myself to summon Captain Townsend, and confront him with the charges you have made, and he assures me that no member of the prosecution nor any witness he is planning on calling to the witness stand were in any way whatsoever involved in this alleged theft."

"Why, Tommy, I thought y'all were just collecting some firewood for the cooking stove, that's all. . . ." Townsend said brightly, interrupting the colonel, but not receiving a rebuke. "I had no idea it had something to do with our case."

Tommy pivoted toward Townsend. "The hell you did!" he said. "You followed me over there and observed me prying that board from the wall. You knew exactly what I was doing. And you were equally concerned that Visser saw the same . . ."

"Keep your voice down, lieutenant!" Clark interjected.

Townsend continued to shake his head. "Nothing of the sort," he said.

Tommy turned to Colonel MacNamara. "Sir, I object—"

Again the colonel cut him off. "Your objection is noted, lieutenant. But . . ." he paused, eyeing Scott for a moment, before turning his gaze on Tommy, and then speaking with a solidity that seemed to even stop the cold wind, "it is my decision that the matter of this bloodstained board is now closed. If it did exist, then it was probably understandably mistaken for firewood and innocently burned by some third party genuinely unaware of its significance. That is, *if* it actually did exist, of which there remains absolutely no concrete proof in the slightest. Mr. Hart, you may still argue what you wish at trial. But there will be no mention of this alleged evidence without some independent corroboration. And we will hear any claims you might make about it and what it might show in private, out of the sight of the Germans! Do I make myself clear?"

"Colonel MacNamara, this is wrong and unfair. I protest—"

"Your protest is also noted, lieutenant."

Scott was seething, instantly brought to a boilover by the summary dismissal of their claims. He stepped forward, his fists clenched at his side, jaw stuck outward, about to vent his fury, only to be met with a withering stare from the commanding officer. "Lieutenant Scott," MacNamara whispered coldly, "keep your mouth shut. That's a direct order. Your counselor has spoken on your behalf, and further debate will only worsen your situation."

One of Scott's eyebrows shot upward in angry inquisition.

"Worsen?" he asked softly, controlling his rage with internal ropes and hawsers, padlocks and chains.

The single-word question fell into a silence surrounding the men. No one took up a response.

MacNamara continued to freeze the three members of the defense with his steady glare. He allowed the quiet to continue for a few seconds, then he slowly lifted his hand to the edge of his cap, deliberately, the pace displaying his own knotted angers. "You are all dismissed until zero eight hundred"—he looked down at his watch—"which is fifty-nine minutes from now."

Then MacNamara and Clark turned and headed inside the hut. Townsend, too, started to leave, but Tommy shot out his right arm and seized the captain by the sleeve.

Walker Townsend pivoted like a sailboat coming about under a stiff breeze, and faced Tommy, who had but one word for him, before releasing him: "Liar!" Tommy whispered into the Virginian's face.

The captain half-opened his mouth to respond, then thought better of it. He spun about and marched off swiftly, leaving the three members of the defense alone at the side of the hut.

Scott watched the captain walk away, then he took a deep breath and leaned back against the wall of Hut 122. He reached inside his flight jacket slowly, removing a half-eaten bar of chocolate. He broke off three small chunks, handing one each to Tommy and Hugh, before popping the smallest of the three into his own mouth. For a moment, the trio stepped out of the wind, against the building, letting the richness of the Hershey's bar melt in their mouths, awakening their taste buds.

Tommy allowed the chocolate to turn to mush on his tongue before swallowing. "Thanks," he said.

Scott grinned. "Well, that was such a bitter little meeting, I figured we all needed something to sweeten up our existences, and the chocolate was all I currently had available."

The three men all laughed at the joke.

"I would hazard a guess, lads," Renaday said, "that perhaps we should not be expecting too many rulings heading our direction during the upcoming proceedings."

Scott shook his head. "Nah," he said. "But he'll still throw us some bones, won't he, Hart? Not the important bones. The ones with meat on them. But some of the smaller ones will still come our way. He wants it to look fair. What did I say before? A lynching. But a *fair* one."

Scott sighed. "Hell," he said, "that was funny. Well, maybe not outright funny, but amusing. Except that it's happening to me." He shook his head.

Tommy nodded. "Learned something, though. Something I hadn't really thought of. You didn't see it, Scott?"

The black airman swallowed and looked quizzically at

Tommy for a moment. "Keep talking, counselor," he said. "What was there to see?"

"MacNamara was real concerned about how things play out in front of the Germans, wasn't he? I mean, here we are, stuck over here out of sight of everybody in the camp just about, and he's talking about not letting the Krauts see anything. Especially something that might suggest that Trader Vic was killed someplace other than that *Abort*. Now I find that sort of interesting, because, if you think about it, what they really want to show the damn Nazis is how damn bend-over-backwards fair we are in our trials. Not the exact opposite."

"In other words," Scott said slowly, "you think this railroad is part show?"

"Yeah. But it should be show in the opposite direction. That is to say, a railroad that doesn't *look* like a railroad."

"Well, even if it is, what good does that do me?"

Tommy paused. "That's the twenty-five-cent question, isn't it?"

Scott nodded. For a moment he seemed deep in thought.

"I think we learned something else, too. But of course, there's not enough time to do anything about it," the black flier added.

"What's that?" Renaday asked.

Scott looked up into the sky. "You know what I hate about this damn weather?" he asked rhetorically. He answered his own question immediately. "It's that one minute the sun comes out, you can take off your shirt and feel the warmth and you think that maybe there's some hope, and then you wake up the next day and it seems like winter's back and there's nothing but storms and cold winds on the horizon." He sighed, took out the candy bar, and once again broke off a piece for each of them. "I might not be needing this much longer," he said. Then he twisted toward Hugh. "What I learned from this little get-together," he said slowly, "is what we should have assumed from the start. That the chief prosecutor is willing to lie about what he saw right in front of the commanding officer. What we should be wondering about is what other lie he's got planned."

This observation caught Tommy by surprise, though upon an instant's reflection, he believed that it was absolutely accurate. He warned himself: There's a lie somewhere. He just didn't know where it was. But that didn't mean he shouldn't be ready for it.

Tommy glanced down at his watch. "We'd better get a move on," he said.

"Wouldn't want to be late," Scott said. "Though I'm not sure that showing up is such a really great idea, either."

Hugh smiled and waved at the nearest guard tower. Two cold goons were huddled in the center, trapped by the wind. "You know what we should do, Tommy? Wait until everybody's gathered at the trial and then just walk out the front gate like those Brits tried. Maybe nobody'd notice."

Scott laughed. "We probably wouldn't get too far. I have my doubts that there are a whole lot of Negroes walking around Germany right at this moment. I don't think we're to be included in the great Nazi master plan. Which might make it a little tricky for me to be out and about in the countryside, escaping."

Scott continued to snort with amusement. "Isn't that the damnedest thing, when you think about it? I'm probably the only guy in all of Stalag Luft Thirteen the Krauts *don't* have to guard. I mean, where could I go? How could I hide? A little hard for me to blend in with the local populace and go unnoticed, wouldn't you say? No matter how I was dressed, or what sort of forged documents I had, I still think I just might stand out a little."

He pushed himself off the wall, straightening up, still grinning.

"Time to go, counselor," Scott said.

Tommy nodded. He glanced over at the black flier and thought that Scott would be a fine sort to have at one's side in any fair fight. For an instant he wondered how his old captain from West Texas would have treated the Tuskegee airman. He had no idea what the captain's prejudices were or were not. But one thing he knew for certain, the captain had a way of assessing one's reliability and coolness under tough circumstances, and on that score, he believed, Lincoln Scott would have gained his admiration. Tommy doubted he could appear as calm with all that was happening to Scott were the situations reversed. But then, he thought, Scott was absolutely right about one thing: Their situations could never really be reversed.

Kriegies were shochorncd into cvcry available square inch of the theater building, taking every seat, jamming the aisles. As before, crowds of men encircled each window outside the hut, craning to see and hear the action expected within. There was a slightly increased German presence, as well, with ferrets lingering on the edges of the crowds, and an armed squad of helmeted goons collected by the front door. The Germans seemed as intrigued as their prisoners, though their understanding of what was taking place was surely limited by language and custom. Still, the promise of a break in the dreary camp routine was attractive to all, and none of the guards seemed particularly put off at having received the duty.

Colonel MacNamara, flanked by the two other officer members of the tribunal, sat at the center of the head table. Visser and his accompanying stenographer were shunted to the same side as before. A single stiff-backed wooden chair had been arranged in the center of the bar area where witnesses could sit. As before, there were tables and chairs for the defense and the prosecution, only this time Walker Townsend had taken the more prominent chair, while Major Clark sat at his side.

At precisely zero eight hundred, Tommy Hart, Lincoln Scott, and Hugh Renaday, once again mimicking a flight of fighters, quick-marched through the open doors, down the center aisle, their flight boots striking at the wooden floorboards with machine-gun–like urgency. Airmen seated in their path scrambled to move out of their way, then slid back into position as they swept past.

The accused and his two defenders took their seats at the designated table wordlessly. There was a momentary lull, while Colonel MacNamara waited for the buzzing voices and shuffling bodies to calm down. After a few seconds, there was silence in the makeshift courtroom. Tommy stole a quick glance over at Visser, and saw that the German's stenographer was leaning forward, pen poised above a notepad, while the officer once again balanced on the back two legs of his own chair, appearing almost nonchalant, despite the atmosphere of excited tension in the room.

MacNamara's loud voice caused him to refocus on the SAO.

"We are gathered here, today, under the provisions of the United States Military Code of Justice, to hear the matter of the United States Army versus Lincoln Scott, first lieutenant, who is accused of the premeditated murder of United States Army Air Corps Captain Vincent Bedford while both men were prisoners of war, under the jurisdiction of the German Luftwaffe authorities here at Stalag Luft Thirteen. . . ."

MacNamara paused, letting his eyes sweep over the assembled crowd.

"We will now proceed . . ." he started, only to stop in mid-sentence as Tommy pushed himself sharply to his feet.

"I would object," Tommy said briskly.

MacNamara stared at Tommy, narrowing his gaze.

"I would at this time renew my objections to proceeding. I would renew my request for additional time to prepare the defense. I am at a loss, Your Honor, as to why we are in such a rush to hold these proceedings. Even a small delay will allow for a far more thorough review of the facts and the evidence—"

MacNamara coldly interrupted.

"No delays," he said. "That has been discussed. Sit down, Mr. Hart."

"Very good, sir," Tommy said, taking his seat.

MacNamara coughed and let silence fill the room before continuing. "We will now get under way with opening arguments . . ."

Once again, Tommy pushed to his feet, scraping the chair backward and then clicking his heels together. MacNamara eyed him coldly.

"Objection?" he asked.

"Indeed, yes, Your Honor," Tommy replied. "I would renew my objections to these proceedings taking place at this time because under United States military law, Lieutenant Scott is entitled to representation by a fully accredited member of the bar. As Your Honor is acutely aware, I have not yet reached that position, whereas my worthy opponent"—he gestured toward Walker Townsend—"has indeed. This creates an unfortunately prejudiced environment, where the prosecution has an unfair advantage in expertise. I would request that these proceedings be delayed until such time as Lieutenant Scott has made available to him a fully qualified counselor, who can more fully advise him of his rights and potential tactics in confronting these baseless charges."

Again, MacNamara continued to stare at Tommy, as the young navigator sat back down.

Lincoln Scott whispered to him, then, in a voice that contained a grin that was hidden from his lips and the men who were eyeing them. "I like that one, Hart. I definitely like it. Won't work, of course, but I truly like it. And anyways, what would I want with another lawyer?"

To their right, Walker Townsend arose. MacNamara nodded toward him and the easygoing, slightly accented words of the prosecutor filled the air.

"What my colleague suggests is not unreasonable, Your Honor, although I would argue that Lieutenant Hart has already amply demonstrated his abilities in the courtroom. But I do believe that throughout much of the defense's preparation they were assisted quite ably by a senior British officer, who is also a well-known barrister in that nation, sir, fully versed in all the diverse elements of criminal proceedings—"

Tommy immediately leapt up, slicing off the southerner's words.

"And who was summarily removed from the camp by the German authorities!"

He angled forward, staring at Visser.

"And probably murdered!"

This word pitched the gathering of kriegies into hubbub and turmoil. A tangle of voices cascaded through the room. Visser didn't budge. He did, however, slowly reach for one of his long, brown cigarettes, which he took his time to remove and ignite, carefully manipulating the package and then the lighter with his only arm and hand.

"There is no evidence of that!" Townsend replied, his voice raised slightly.

"Indeed," Colonel MacNamara added. "And the Germans have given their assurances—"

"Assurances, sir?" Tommy interrupted. "What assurances?"

"The German authorities have assured us that Wing Commander Pryce was to be safely repatriated," MacNamara said sternly.

Tommy felt an ice-cold anger within his stomach. For a moment, he was almost blinded by outrage. There was, he realized, absolutely no reason whatsoever for the Senior American Officer at Stalag Luft Thirteen to have any knowledge at all about Phillip Pryce's removal from the camp. Pryce was under British jurisdiction and their own chain of command. That MacNamara had received an *assurance*, no matter what sort, meant only that they were somehow involved in his removal. This recognition battered him, and for a moment he staggered inwardly, trying to assess what it truly meant. But he had no time for reflection, so instead, he blurted out:

"They are our sworn enemy, sir. Whatever assurances they might have given to you must be interpreted in that light."

He paused, then demanded: "Why would you think they would not lie? Especially to cover up a crime?"

Again MacNamara glared at Tommy. He banged a few times on his homemade gavel, although the kriegies in the courtroom had already quieted. The hammering sound echoed slightly.

"I do remember that fact, lieutenant, and there is no need for you to remind me. No delays!" he burst out. "Opening statements!"

The SAO turned to Walker Townsend. "You are ready, captain?"

Townsend nodded.

"Then proceed! Without further interruption, Lieutenant Hart!"

Tommy started to open his mouth, as if to reply, though in reality he had nothing he wanted to say, having already accomplished what he wished, which was to put everyone in the camp on notice that whatever they thought, convicting Scott wasn't going to be a milk run. And so, he sat down, still troubled by what he'd heard so far. He stole a quick glance over at Townsend, who seemed to be slightly flustered by the defense's first salvos. But Townsend was a veteran, Tommy could see, of both the courtroom and combat, and within a few seconds had composed himself. He took several strides to the center of the room, half-turning so that he was addressing the tribunal, the assembled airmen, and, in part, the German observers. He was about to begin when there was a small disturbance from the rear of the theater building. Out of the corner of his eye, Tommy saw Visser slam his chair upright and rise to his feet. So did the stenographer, instantly coming to attention. MacNamara and the other members of the tribunal all rose, and this prompted Tommy to reach out and grasp Lincoln Scott by the sleeve, and the two of them also stood. As they did, they heard the rat-a-tat sound of well-heeled boots coming down the center aisle, and they half-turned and saw Commandant Von Reiter, as usual accompanied by a pair of adjutants, approaching the makeshift courtroom.

It was MacNamara who spoke first.

"Commandant," he said. "I was not aware you planned to attend this session."

Von Reiter threw a single glance over at Visser's instantly scowling face, then replied with an offhand wave, "But Colonel MacNamara, the opportunity to witness the famed American style of justice is rare indeed! Alas, my duties will not permit me to attend the entirety of the trial. But I will be pleased to come when I can manage. Surely, this would not be a problem?"

MacNamara allowed a small smile of his own to slide across his face. "Of course not, commandant. You are welcome at any time. I only wish that I had made arrangements for a seat."

"I will be pleased to stand," Von Reiter said. "And please, keep in mind that Hauptmann Visser is the official observer for the Reich as provided by Luftwaffe High Command. My presence is merely, well, how shall I say it? Merely to satisfy my own curiosity about these matters. Be so kind as to continue."

Von Reiter smiled and moved to the side of the theater building. Several kriegies quickly moved to make a space for him, jamming themselves amid their own countrymen to avoid coming into contact with the austere German commandant, almost as if the sense of ancient aristocracy that he wore was somehow a disease best avoided by the democratic citizen-soldiers of the air corps. Von Reiter seemed aware of the shuffling, and he leaned up against the wall with a bemused look on his face.

The SAO returned to his seat, gesturing for the others to do the same. Then he nodded at Walker Townsend.

"You were about to begin, Captain. . . ."

"Yes sir. I will be brief, Your Honor. The prosecution expects to demonstrate that Lieutenant Lincoln Scott and Captain Vincent Bedford experienced a sense of racial animosity from the former's arrival at the camp. This animosity manifested itself in a number of incidents, including at least one outright fight, when Captain Bedford accused Lieutenant Scott of stealing from him. Numerous witnesses will testify to this. It is the prosecution's contention that Mr. Scott, in fear for his own life because of threats made by Captain Bedford, manufactured a weapon, stalked Bedford, finally confronted him in the *Abort* located between Huts 101 and 102 at a time when all prisoners are required to be in their barracks, that they fought and Captain Bedford was killed. Lieutenant Scott, the evidence will show, had the desire and the means to commit this murder, Your Honor. The evidence that the prosecution will bring is overwhelming. Sadly, there is no other logical conclusion to the events that have unfolded."

Walker Townsend let this last sentence fill the theater. He took a single, quick glance over toward Von Reiter, then back to MacNamara. Then he sat down.

MacNamara nodded, then looked over at Tommy Hart.

"Mr. Hart? Your opening statement, if you please."

Tommy rose, words beginning to form in his imagination, outrage and indignation filling his gorge, and then he took a deep breath. The hesitation allowed him a second, no more, to think, and he roped in his emotions.

"Your Honor," he said with a small smile, "the defense in this matter will reserve the right to make its opening statement until the completion of the prosecution's case."

MacNamara stared at Tommy.

"That is unusual," he said. "I'm not sure—"

"We have the absolute right, under military law, to postpone our opening," Tommy said swiftly, not having any idea at all whether he was right or wrong. "We are under no obligation to display our defense to the prosecution until such time that it becomes our turn to present it."

Again MacNamara hesitated. Then he shrugged.

"As you wish, lieutenant. Then we will proceed with the first witness."

To MacNamara's left, Commandant Von Reiter took a step forward. The SAO turned toward him, and the German, still wearing a small smile that lingered on the corners of his upper lip, spoke out: "Do I understand that Lieutenant Hart is permitted to not offer his defense at this time? That he can wait for perhaps a more advantageous moment?"

MacNamara replied, "Yes. That is correct, *Herr Oberst*."

Von Reiter laughed dryly. "How clever," he said, making a small gesture toward Tommy. "But, alas, that is what I was most interested in hearing. So, colonel, if you will excuse me now, I will return at some later time. For I am greatly familiar with the prosecution's contentions concerning Lieutenant Scott. But it is the replies that have been constructed by Lieutenant Hart that intrigue me far more."

The German commandant raised two fingers to the brim of his cap in a languid salute. "With your leave, colonel . . ." he said.

"Of course, commandant."

"Hauptmann Visser, I leave this in your hands."

Visser, who had once again risen to his feet, clicked his heels together sharply, the sound echoing above the crowd.

Von Reiter, as always trailed by his two doglike adjutants, then stepped from the courtroom, the eyes of the assembled Allied prisoners following him. As his bootsteps faded, MacNamara bellowed, "Call your first witness!"

Tommy watched, as Townsend stepped forward, and thought to himself that what he'd seen had seemed most theatrical. He had the sensation that he was observing a well-acted play being performed by experts, but using some strange and indecipherable language, so that while he could understand many of the actions, the overall thrust of the

words eluded him. This, he considered, was a very strange reaction to have.

Then he slid this sensation into an internal compartment,
for examination later, and he focused on the arrival of the first
witness.

Chapter Twelve

THE FIRST LIE

The prosecution built their case against Scott steadily throughout the day, closely following the progression that Tommy had expected. Bedford's overt racism, needling, taunting, accusations, and Deep South prejudice emerged in tale after tale from witness after witness. Set against that was the near-constant portrayal of Lincoln Scott as a man isolated, alone, enraged, being baited into a deadly action by the constancy of Trader Vic's derision.

The problem, as Tommy saw it, was that calling a man a *nigger* wasn't a crime. Nor was calling a man who had repeatedly put his own life on the line for white aircrews a *nigger* a crime, even if it should have been. What was a crime, was murder, and throughout the day, the tribunal, the German observers, and all the assembled kriegies of Stalag Luft Thirteen heard nothing from the witness stand except what they would all consider to be a perfectly reasonable motive for that desperate act of killing.

It made a sort of crazy deadly sense: Trader Vic was a thoughtless bastard, and Scott wasn't able to ignore it. Or get away from it. And so he killed the southerner before Bedford took the opportunity to turn his own virulent hatred into action and now Scott should die for that preemptive strike. Tommy wondered whether this wasn't some variation on a plot that had already played itself out in dozens of forgotten rural courtrooms from Florida, through Georgia, into the Carolinas, across to Tennessee and Arkansas, Mississippi and Alabama. Anywhere the Stars and Bars continued to fly.

That it was happening in a Bavarian forest seemed to him to be as awful and as inexplicable as anything else.

At the defense table, he listened while another witness walked through the crowded courtroom to take his place at the stand.

The trial had stretched into the late afternoon, and Tommy scratched some notes on one of his precious sheets of paper, trying to prepare a cross-examination, thinking how compelling the prosecution's case was. The vise that Scott was captured within was truly intractable: No matter how outrageous or evil Trader Vic's treatment of the Tuskegee airman had been, it still didn't amount to a justification for his killing. Instead, the situation played directly into the most subtle of fears felt by many of the white members of the air corps: that Lincoln Scott was somehow a threat to all of them, a threat to their futures, and a threat to their lives—all because he unapologetically wore his difference on his skin. Lincoln Scott, with all his intelligence, athleticism, and arrogance, had been turned into more of an enemy than the Germans manning the guard towers. Tommy believed this transformation was the crux of the prosecution, and he remained at a loss as to how to explode it. He knew he had to make Scott seem to be one of them. A simple kriegie. A POW. Suffering the same. Fearful of the same. Lonely and depressed and wondering if he would ever get home again, just the same as every other man in the camp.

The problem was, Tommy realized, that when he put Scott on the stand, the black flier would inevitably be himself: razor-sharp, muscular, and determined, uncompromising and tough. Lincoln Scott would no more be willing to show himself to be as vulnerable as the rest of them than would some spy captured by the Gestapo. And Tommy thought there was little chance that any of the men craning to hear every word coming from the witness stand would understand that at Stalag Luft Thirteen they were all in their own unique ways alike. No better than any other man. No worse.

He had managed, he thought, some inroads. He made a point of bringing out from every witness that it was never Scott who initiated the tension between him and Vic. He also underscored, with every man who took the stand, that Scott got nothing special. No extra food. No extra privileges. Nothing that made his life any better, and much, thanks to Vincent Bedford, that made his life far more miserable.

But while bringing this out might help, it still didn't attack the essence of the case. Sympathy was not doubt, and Tommy knew this. Sympathy was also not a defense, especially for an innocent man. In fact, he understood that in some ways it made matters worse. Every kriegie in the camp had, at one time or another, wondered where his own breaking point might lie. Where all the fear and deprivation they faced daily would overcome whatever control they had. They'd all seen it, when men went wire-crazy and tried to blitz out, only to end up, if they were lucky, in the cooler or, if they were unlucky, in the burial ground behind Hut 113. What the prosecution was building slowly toward was finding Scott's breaking point.

In front of him, Colonel MacNamara was swearing in the witness. The man raised his hand and took an oath to tell the truth, just as he would in a regular courtroom. MacNamara, Tommy thought, was being a stickler for the details and trappings of authenticity. He wanted the proceedings to seem real and not some makeshift jury-rigged prisoner-of-war camp construction.

"State your name for the record," MacNamara boomed, as if there were an official record, as the witness sat stiffly in the chair and Walker Townsend began to hover close by. The witness was one of the roommates. Murphy, the lieutenant from Springfield, Massachusetts, who had confronted Tommy in the corridor. One of the men making the most trouble over the past weeks. He was a slightly built man, in his early twenties, with a few leftover childhood freckles still playing on his cheeks. He had deep red hair, and he was missing a tooth, which he tried to cover up when he smiled, giving his face a lopsided appearance.

Tommy checked his notes. Lieutenant Murphy was in the middle of the list of witnesses Townsend had provided, but he was being called out of order. Threats and animosity between the deceased and the accused. No love lost, whatsoever. That was what Tommy saw in his notes. He knew, as well, that Murphy had been one of the men who'd seen him with the bloodstained board. But he suspected the lieutenant would lie about it, if he tried to ask him.

"This will be our final witness for the day," MacNamara announced. "Correct, captain?"

Walker Townsend nodded. "Yes sir," he replied. He had a small smile flitting across his lips. The prosecutor hesitated, then had Murphy describe how he arrived at Stalag Luft Thirteen. He also had the lieutenant provide a modicum of information about himself, blending the two, so that Murphy's story would seem to every man in the theater to be no different from his own.

As the witness began to speak, Tommy was not paying very close attention. He was still riveted by the idea that he knew that he was closer to the truth about how Trader Vic died, though the why still eluded all of them. The difficulty was how he was to get this alternate version out from the witness stand, and he remained at a loss as to how he could accomplish this. Scott was the one who'd accompanied him on the nocturnal visit to the site where he believed the killing had taken place. But Scott was the last person he wanted to tell that tale from the witness stand. It would appear self-serving and fantastic. It would seem as if Scott was merely lying to protect himself. Without the bloodstained board to back up his story, it would seem nothing more than a not particularly well concocted lie.

He felt almost sick. The truth is transparent. Lies have substance.

Tommy sighed, breathing in deeply, as Walker Townsend patiently continued to ask mundane background questions of Murphy, who answered every one with a quick eagerness.

I'm losing, he thought.

Worse. Every minute, an innocent man takes a stride closer to a firing squad.

He stole a sideways glance at Scott. He knew the black flier understood this. But the iron in his face remained constant. An expression of deeply muted anger.

"Now, lieutenant," Townsend said loudly, gesturing at the man on the witness chair, then pausing, as if trying to impart some added weight to his question, "you hail from the state of Massachusetts, do you not?"

Tommy, still troubled by all the divergent thoughts crashing around within him, was still only half paying attention. Townsend had this languorous, slow-paced style to his queries, a sort of nonchalant, genteel approach that lulled the defense into some state of unobservant quiet. Prosecutors, Tommy understood, liked weight of testimony every bit as much as they liked drama. Ten people steadily saying the same thing over and over was far better than one person delivering it theatrically.

But the next question got Tommy's attention.

"Now, lieutenant, Massachusetts is a state well known throughout the Union for its advanced and altogether enlightened racial atmosphere, is it not?"

"It is, captain."

"Did it not raise one of the first all-black regiments to fight in the great War Between the States, or what some of us consider the Great War of Secession? A most valorous group under a justly famed white commander?"

"It did, yes sir . . ."

Tommy rose. "I object. Why do we need a history lesson, colonel?"

MacNamara waved his hand. "I'll allow some leeway," he said, "as long as the prosecution makes its point rapidly."

"Thank you," Townsend answered. "I will move swiftly. You, Lieutenant Murphy, come from Springfield. A lifelong resident of that fair city in that state, famed as a birthplace to our own revolution, are you not? Bunker Hill, Lexington, and Concord—these important sites are all neighbors, are they not?"

"Yes sir. In the eastern portion of the state."

"And in growing up, it was not unusual for you to come into contact with Negroes, is that correct, sir?"

"Correct. Several attended my high school. And there were others that were employed at my place of business."

"So, you, sir, are not a bigot?"

Again Tommy jumped up. "Objection! The witness cannot conclude this about himself! Why—"

MacNamara cut him off. "Captain Townsend, please make your point."

Townsend nodded again. "Yes sir. My point, sir, is to show

this tribunal that there is no southern conspiracy here operating against Lieutenant Scott. We do not hear solely from men who hail from states that seceded from the Union. The so-called slave states. My point, Your Honor, is that men from states with long traditions of harmonious coexistence of the races are here willing, no, eager, I dare say, to testify against Lieutenant Scott, and who witnessed actions the prosecution feels are crucial to the sequence of events that resulted in this most despicable murder. . . ."

"Objection!" Tommy jumped up, shouting. "The captain makes a speech designed to enflame the court."

MacNamara stared over at Tommy. "You are correct, lieutenant. Objection sustained. Enough with the speech, captain. On with the questions."

"I would further point out that simply because someone comes from a particular section of the United States gives him no greater or lesser claim on the truth, Colonel. . . ."

"Now, Mr. Hart, it is you who makes speeches. The tribunal can judge the integrity of witnesses without your assistance. Sit down!"

Tommy sat down hard, and Lincoln Scott immediately leaned over, whispering. "Racial harmony, my ass. Murphy was just as fast as Vic was with the word *nigger*. Just spoken in a different accent, that's all."

"I remember," Tommy said. "In the corridor. I may remind him on cross-examination."

Townsend had sauntered over to the prosecution's table. Major Clark reached down beneath and removed the dark sheet-metal frying pan that Scott had constructed to fix his meals. The major handed it to Townsend, who pivoted and approached the witness.

"Now, lieutenant, I'm showing you an exhibit that we have introduced as evidence. Do you recognize this, sir?"

"I do, captain," Murphy replied.

"How do you recognize it?"

"I watched as Lieutenant Scott constructed the frying pan, sir. He was in the corner of the barracks room in Hut 101 that we all shared. He fashioned the pan out of a piece of metal liberated from one of the German refuse bins, sir. I have seen other kriegies do the same, but I remember thinking that

Scott seemed to have some expertise with metalwork, because this was the best version of the frying pan that I had seen in my months here."

"And what did you observe next?"

"I saw that he had some leftover metal that he was beginning to form into some other shape. He used a piece of wood to hammer out the bends and wrinkles, sir."

"Please tell the tribunal what you next witnessed."

"I left the room, briefly, sir, but when I returned, I saw Lieutenant Scott wrapping the handle of this leftover piece of metal with an old strip of cloth."

"What was it that he appeared to have constructed?"

"A knife, sir."

Tommy jumped up. "Objection! Calls for a conclusion."

"Overruled!" MacNamara bellowed. "Continue, lieutenant."

"Yes sir," Murphy said. "I remember asking Scott, right then, what the hell did he need that for? Damn thing was near as big as a sword—"

"Objection!"

"On what grounds?"

"This is hearsay, colonel."

"No, it isn't. Please continue."

"I mean," Murphy persisted, "I'd never seen anyone in this camp ever construct something like that. . . ."

Townsend had once again crossed over to the prosecution's table. Major Clark handed him the flattened metal blade. The prosecutor held it up before him, almost like Lady Macbeth, then he slashed it through the air several times.

"Objection!" Tommy shouted again. "These histrionics . . ."

MacNamara nodded. "Captain Townsend . . ."

The southerner smiled. "Of course, Your Honor. Now, Lieutenant Murphy, is this the device you saw Lieutenant Scott manufacture?"

"It is," Murphy replied.

"Did you ever see him use this knife to prepare his food?"

"No sir. Like a lot of us, he had a small, folding penknife that's much more efficient."

"So, Scott never used this blade for any legitimate purpose?"

"Objection!" Once again Tommy was on his feet.

"Sit down. This is why we're here, Lieutenant Hart. Answer the question, Lieutenant Murphy."

"I never saw him use the blade for any legitimate purpose, no sir."

Townsend hesitated slightly, then asked: "And when you saw Lieutenant Scott form this blade, did you ask him why he needed it?"

"Yes sir."

"And his reply, Lieutenant Murphy?"

"Well, sir, I remember his words exactly. They were: 'For protection.' And so I asked him who he needed to be protected from, and Scott said: 'That bastard Bedford.' Those were his words, sir. Just as I remember. And then he told me, clear out, without my asking any question beforehand, 'I ought to kill the son of a bitch before he kills me!' That's what he said, sir. I heard him clear as day!"

Tommy thrust himself up, throwing his own chair backward, so that it clattered loudly on the floor. He stood stiffly, shouting, "Objection! Objection! Colonel, this is outrageous!"

MacNamara bent forward, his own face red, almost as if he'd been interrupted in the midst of some backbreaking job of work.

"What precisely is outrageous, lieutenant? The words your client spoke? Or something else?" The Senior American Officer's words were marred with contempt.

Tommy took a deep breath, fixing MacNamara with as harsh a look as the SAO had for him. "Sir, my objection is twofold. First, this testimony comes as a complete surprise to the defense! When asked what he would testify to, this witness replied, 'Threats and animosity. . . .' There was no mention of this alleged conversation! I believe that it is fantasy! Made-up lies, designed to unfairly influence . . ."

"You may try to bring that out under cross, lieutenant."

Walker Townsend, smiling lightly, one eyebrow slightly raised, interrupted, then. "Why, Your Honor, I fail to see where there has been any deception whatsoever. The man told Lieutenant Hart he would testify about threats. And that is precisely what we have just heard from Lieutenant Murphy. A threat. It is not the prosecution's province to make sure that

Lieutenant Hart adequately prepares by seeking additional information from a witness prior to trial. He asked a question of this witness and he received an answer, and he should have pursued it further, if he considered this testimony to be potentially so harmful—"

"Your Honor, this is unfair attack! I object!"

MacNamara shook his head. "Once again, Lieutenant Hart, I must insist you sit down. You will have an opportunity to cross-examine the witness. Until then, be quiet!"

Tommy did not sit, but remained standing. He surreptitiously gripped the edge of the table for support. He didn't dare look over at Lincoln Scott.

Walker Townsend held up the handmade knife.

" 'I ought to kill the son of a bitch,' " he bellowed out, the thunder in his voice only accentuated by all the soft tones he'd used before. "And when did he say this?"

"One, maybe two days before Captain Bedford was murdered," Murphy replied, smugly.

"Murdered with a knife!" Townsend said.

"Yes sir!" Murphy blurted out.

"A prophecy!" Townsend crowed. "And now this blade, Lieutenant Lincoln Scott's blade, is stained with the blood of Captain Vincent Bedford!"

He walked over to the prosecution's table and slammed the knife down hard, flat against the table planks. The noise resounded through the silent courtroom.

"Your witness," he said, after a suitable pause for effect.

Tommy rose, his head jumbled with outrage, doubt, and confusion. He opened his mouth, only to see Colonel MacNamara raise his hand, slicing off his words.

"I believe we shall have to wait to have the cross-examination in the morning, lieutenant. We are closing in on time for the evening *Appell*, are we not, *Hauptmann?*"

For the first time in what seemed like an hour, Tommy pivoted toward the one-armed German. Visser was nodding his head. He seemed to take some time, however, before answering. Instead, for several long seconds, the German stared at Lieutenant Murphy, as the Liberator copilot shifted uncomfortably in his seat. Then Visser slowly searched around the courtroom, examining Lincoln Scott and Tommy Hart, then swinging over to the prosecutors, and finally back to Colonel MacNamara. "You are correct, colonel," Visser replied. "This would, perhaps, be an appropriate and convenient moment for dismissal."

Visser rose and the stenographer at his side clapped shut his notebook.

MacNamara banged his homemade gavel down. "Until tomorrow, then. We will reconvene without delay directly after the completion of the morning count! Lieutenant Murphy?"

"Yes sir?"

"You are not to discuss your testimony with anyone. Got that? Not anyone, prosecution, defense, friends, or foes. You can talk about the weather. You can talk about the army. You can talk about the lousy food, or the lousy war. But what you can't talk about is this case. Do I make myself clear?"

"Yes sir! Absolutely."

"Fine then," MacNamara briskly said. "You are dismissed." He looked up at the assembled men. "You are all dismissed."

He rose and the kriegies all scrambled to their feet, coming to attention as the members of the tribunal pushed back from their table and stiffly exited the theater. They were followed by Major Clark and Captain Townsend, who had trouble containing his grin as he swept past Tommy, and then, in quick order, Visser and most of the other Germans. One or two of the ferrets who lingered slightly behind urged the kriegies to depart, their hoarse cries of "*Raus! Raus!* You are dismissed!" cutting through the air behind Tommy's head.

Tommy closed his eyes for a moment, searching the black emptiness within. After a second, he opened up, and turned to Lincoln Scott and Hugh Renaday. Scott was staring straight ahead, his eyes fixed upon the empty witness chair. Unblinking. Rigid.

Hugh leaned forward. "Well," he said slowly, "that was a shot across the bow, what? How do we prove that bastard is lying?"

Tommy started to reply, although he was unsure what he was going to say, only to be cut off by Scott.

The black flier's voice was dry, parched. It rasped and echoed slightly in the theater. They were alone now. "It wasn't a lie," Scott said quietly, almost as if each word he spoke were painful. "It was the truth. It's exactly what I said to the slimy son of a bitch. Word for word."

By the time they finished the evening *Appell* and returned to their room in Hut 101, Tommy was seething. He slammed the door shut behind them and pivoted to face Lincoln Scott.

"You could have goddamn told me," he said, his voice rising in pitch like an engine accelerating. "It might have been helpful to know that you threatened the life of the murder victim right before he was killed!"

Scott started to reply, then stopped. He shrugged and sat down heavily on the edge of his bed.

Tommy's hands were balled into fists, and he circled the space in front of the black flier.

"I look like a goddamn idiot!" he raged. "And you look like a killer! You told me you didn't know anything about that damn knife, and now it turns out you built the damn thing! Why didn't you tell me?"

Scott shook his head, as if unwilling to answer that question. "After I shot my mouth off to Murphy, I stuck it next to where I kept my Red Cross box. It disappeared the next morning. The next time I saw it was when Clark pulled it out from the hiding place that I didn't know about, right under the bunk."

"Well that's great," Tommy said furiously. "That's a great story. I'm sure just about everyone will believe that. . . ."

Again Scott looked up, ready to reply, then stopped himself.

"How the hell do you expect someone to defend you when you won't tell him the truth?" Tommy demanded furiously.

Scott opened his mouth, but nothing came out. Instead, he kept his head bent, almost as if in prayer, until he finally sighed deeply and whispered a reply. "I don't," he said.

Tommy's jaw dropped, in surprise. "What?"

Scott's eyes rose slightly, peering at Tommy. "I don't want to be defended," he said slowly. "I don't need to be defended. I have no desire to be defended. I shouldn't be in a position where I have to be defended! I have done nothing! Nothing except tell the truth! And if those truths don't work out right for you, well, I can't do anything about that!"

With each sentence, Lincoln Scott had stiffened, finally rising to his feet, his hands clenched tightly in front of him.

"So I threatened the bastard! What's wrong with that? So I made a show of constructing a knife? That's not against the goddamn rules, because there are no rules! So I told him I would kill him. I had to say something, for Christ's sake! I couldn't just sit around quietly, ignoring everything the bastard was saying and doing! I had to put Bedford on notice, somehow, that I wasn't like every weak-kneed, terrified, ignorant black man that he's been bullying and holding down every minute of every day of his whole damn life! I had to get across to that bigoted bastard that it didn't make any difference to me if I was all alone here. I wasn't going to shuffle off into some corner and yassuh, nosuh, take all his abuse, just like all those others. I'm not a slave! I'm a free man! So I constructed a goddamn sword, and let him know I would use it! Because the only thing the goddamn Bedfords of this world understand is the same violence they want to deliver to you! They're cowards, when you stand up to them, and that's all I was doing!"

Scott, seething himself, stood stock-still in the center of the room. "Do you understand now?" he asked Tommy.

Tommy stood up, directly in front of the black flier. Their faces were only inches apart.

"You're not free," he said starkly, punctuating each word with a short choppy hand motion. "Neither you, nor I, nor anyone else here is free!"

Scott shook his head vigorously, side to side.

"You might be a prisoner, Hart. Renaday might. Townsend and MacNamara and Clark and Murphy and all the others might. But not me! They may have shot me down and locked me up here and now they may march me in front of a firing squad for something I didn't do, but no sir, I will never see myself as a prisoner! Not for a second, understand! I am a free man, temporarily trapped behind barbed wire."

Tommy started to reply, and then stopped. There was the problem, in the proverbial nutshell. The weight that Scott carried went far deeper than a simple murder accusation.

Tommy stepped back and took a few paces in a circle in the small room, thinking.

"Have you ever, in your entire life, trusted a white man?" he suddenly asked.

Scott took a single step backward, as if the question struck him like a hard jab. "What?"

"You heard me," Tommy said. "Answer the question."

"What do you mean, *trust?*"

"You know exactly what I mean. Answer the question!"

Scott's eyes narrowed, and he hesitated before replying. "No black man, in today's world, can get ahead without the help of some well-meaning white folks."

"That's not a goddamn answer!"

Scott started, stopped, then smiled. He nodded. "You're correct." He paused again. "The answer is no. I have never trusted any white man."

"You were willing to use their help, though."

"Yes. In school, generally. And my father's church sometimes benefited from charities."

"But every smile you made, every time you shook hands with a white man, that was a lie, wasn't it?"

Lincoln Scott sighed slightly, almost as if amused. "Yes," he said. "In a way, yes."

"And when we shook hands, that was a lie, too."

"You could see it that way. It is simple, Hart. It's a lesson you learn early on in life. If you're going to rise up and be someone, you can rely only on yourself!"

"Well," Tommy said slowly, "by relying solely on yourself, I would say your future prospects have diminished some in recent days." He made no attempt to hide his sarcasm, and Lincoln Scott seemed to bristle, in return.

"That may be true," Scott answered, "but at least when I hear that firing squad commander give the order, I'll know that no one ever stole from me that which is more important than my life."

"Which would be?"

"Dignity."

"Does a helluva lot of good for you when you're dead."

"That's where you're wrong, Hart. Completely wrong. Which is the difference between you and me. I want to live just as much as you, or any other man here. But I'm not willing to be someone different in order to survive. Because that would be a far greater lie than those being spoken from this witness stand. Or any other location."

Tommy paused, considering what Scott had said. Finally, he shook his head.

"You are a difficult man to understand, Scott. Very difficult."

Scott smiled enigmatically. "You presume I want to be understood."

"All right. Point well taken. But, it seems to me that you are only willing to fight these accusations on your own terms."

"That is the way that I know."

"Well, listen to me when I tell you that we're going to have to do something different, because we're not going to win as it stands now."

"I understand that," Lincoln Scott said, sadly. "But what you fail to understand is that there are different sorts of victories. Winning in this phony kangaroo court may not be as important as refusing to change who I am!"

Tommy was taken aback by this statement, and not quick to respond. But the sudden silence between the two men was filled by Hugh Renaday. He had been standing, shoulder to the wall, watching and listening throughout all the angry words shared between the two men, remaining silent. But now he finally stepped forward, shaking his head. "You're a pair of damn fools," he said sharply. "And both blind as bats."

The two men turned toward the Canadian, who was grinning almost maniacally, as he spoke. "Neither of the two of you fools can see the big picture, here. Can you now?"

Scott lightened up, just a small amount, in that second. "But you're going to tell us, right?"

"I am, indeed," Hugh snorted. "Where's Phillip Pryce when one truly needs him? You know, Tommy, if he is dead and looking down at you from up above somewhere, the old limey bastard is probably choking on your words."

"Maybe so, Hugh. Enlighten me."

Hugh stomped about for a moment, then lit a cigarette.

"You, Lincoln, you want to undo the world! You want change, as long as it isn't you that changes. And you, Tommy, you're so mesmerized by playing by the rules that you can't see how unfair they are! Ah, you're both crazy, and neither of you is acting with any bloody sanity whatsoever."

He pointed at Lincoln Scott. "You made yourself into a perfect man to accuse, didn't you? I mean, someone in this damn camp wanted to kill Trader Vic, and went out and did it, and then you couldn't have made yourself any damn more convenient for him to shift the blame right onto your bloody ass! True enough?"

Scott nodded. "That's not the most elegant way of putting things. But true enough. Seems that way."

"And, I dare say, you couldn't make it any damn easier for Townsend to convict you, either."

Scott nodded. "But . . ." he started.

Hugh shook his head. "Ah, don't speak to me of buts and maybes and hopefullys and all that crap! There is only one solution to this situation, and that is winning, because when all is said and done, that's the only thing that matters! Not how you win, or why you win, or even when you win. But win you must, and the sooner you see that, the better off we shall all be!"

Scott stopped. Then nodded. "Perhaps," he said.

"Bloody right! You think about that! You've been so damn busy proving that you're better than anyone else here, you've forgotten to see how you're exactly the damn same! And you, Tommy, you haven't done what you said we'd do, which is to fight back! Use their own damnable lies against them!"

Hugh coughed hard. "Didn't Phillip teach you a bloody thing?" He looked down at the end of his smoke, then pinched off the burning ember, stomping on it as it tumbled to the floor, and then stuffing the half-smoked butt into his blouse breast pocket. "I'm hungry," he said. "And I think it's damn time we ate, though why I'm sitting about with the two of you posturing fools is beyond me. You both want to win, and you want to win in the goddamn *right* way, or else it's somehow not right? This is a bloody war! People are dying every second of the day and night! It's not a boxing match with Marquess of Queensberry rules! Go to war, damn it, the two of you! Stop playing fair! And until the two of you put your heads together and agree to do that, well, a pox on both of you."

"A plague," Scott said, smiling.

"All right, then," Hugh snorted. "A plague, if you prefer."

"That's what Mercutio says, as he dies," Scott continued. " 'A plague o' both your houses!' Capulets and Montagues."

"Well, bloody Mercutio and bloody Shakespeare got it bloody right!" Hugh went over to his bunk and reached beneath it, removing a Red Cross parcel with foodstuffs.

"Damn it," he said, as if the parcel and its limited contents were somehow surprising. "All I have left is one of those damn awful British Red Cross parcels. Weak tea and tasteless kippers and crap! Tommy, I hope you've got something better. From the States. Land of Plenty and Abundance."

Tommy thought for a moment, then asked, "Hugh, what was the German ration for tonight?"

Hugh looked up, snorting hard. "The usual. *Kriegsbrot* and some of that damn awful blood sausage. Phillip used to take it and bury it in the garden, even when we were starving. Couldn't bring himself to eat it. Neither can I. Neither can anyone I know, in either compound. How the Krauts manage to swallow it is beyond me, as well."

Blood sausage, Tommy thought suddenly. It was a staple of the German issue to the kriegies, and just as routinely refused even when they were starving. The sausage was disgusting stuff, thick tubes of what the prisoners thought was congealed offal liberally mixed with slaughterhouse blood, given a hard enough consistency by mixing it with sawdust. No matter how it was cooked, it still tasted like eating waste matter. Many of the men buried it, as Pryce had done, in the hope that it might serve as fertilizer. The theater troops in both British and American compounds occasionally mashed it up and used it as a prop in some play's scene that called for blood.

He turned suddenly to Scott. "Did you ever eat it?"

The black airman looked surprised, then shook his head. "I collected it once or twice, tried to figure out a way of cooking it, but same as everybody else, it was just too damn disgusting."

"But you got the ration, right?"

"Yes."

Tommy nodded. "Hugh," he said slowly. "Take a couple of cigarettes and go out and see if you can't find someone with some of the sausage. The worst, foulest, most repulsive log of

German blood sausage you can find, and make a trade for it. Bring it back here. I've got an idea."

Hugh looked confused, then shrugged. "Whatever you say," he said. "Although I think you've gone bloody daft." He patted his blouse to make sure he had some smokes and headed out into the corridor.

As soon as the door shut, Tommy turned to Lincoln Scott.

"All right," he said. "Hugh makes good sense. If you have no objection, I think now's the time to stop playing by their rules."

Scott hesitated before nodding.

Colonel MacNamara reminded Lieutenant Murphy that he was still under oath as the flier resumed his seat in the center of the makeshift courtroom and the morning session was set to get under way. Everyone was in the same position as the day before, defense, prosecution, hundreds of kriegies jamming the seats and aisles, Visser and the stenographer in their customary corner, and the stiff-faced tribunal watching over all of it.

Murphy nodded, squirmed once in his seat, trying to get comfortable, then waited for Tommy Hart to approach with a small, anticipatory smile on his face.

"Springfield, Massachusetts, correct?"

"That's right," Murphy replied. "Born and raised."

"And you say you worked alongside Negroes?"

"Right, again."

"On a daily basis?"

"Daily, yes sir."

"And what sort of business was this?"

"My family were part owners of a meat processing plant, Mr. Hart. A small, local plant, but we had contracts for numerous restaurants and schools in the city."

Tommy thought for a moment, then continued slowly. "Meat processing? Like steaks and chops?"

Murphy grinned. "Yes sir. Steaks so thick and tender you didn't need no knife to cut them. Porterhouse and sirloin, even filet mignon"—he pronounced it *feelit migg-non*—"chops that taste sweet almost like candy. Lamb chops. Pork chops. And hamburger, finest in the state, without a doubt.

Man, what I wouldn't give for one of those right about now, cooked on an outdoor fire . . ."

The entire theater both laughed and groaned at the airman's words. A ripple of talk went through the room, all variations on the same, as one man whispered to the next, "What I wouldn't do for a ribeye steak, grilled with onions and mushrooms . . ."

Tommy let the laughter subside. He wore a small, crooked smile of his own.

"Meat processing can be a pretty foul business, can't it, lieutenant? I mean, slaughtered animals, guts, blood, shit, and fur. Got to get rid of all that waste, just leave the good parts behind, correct?"

"That's the game, lieutenant."

"Getting rid of all that foul, disgusting stuff, that's where the Negroes worked, right, lieutenant? They didn't have the well-paying jobs, did they, these Negroes you worked with? They were the people who took care of the mess, right? The mess that the white men didn't want to deal with."

Murphy hesitated, then shrugged. "That's the jobs they seemed to want."

"Sure," Tommy replied. "Why would anyone want something better?"

Lieutenant Murphy didn't answer this question. The courtroom had once again quieted.

Tommy moved about in front of Lieutenant Murphy, pacing in a small circle, first turning his back on the man, then suddenly pivoting to face him. Every motion he made, Tommy thought, was designed to unsettle the man.

"Tell me, Lieutenant Murphy, who is Frederick Douglass?"

Murphy thought hard for a moment, then shook his head. "I'm not sure. Isn't he a general on Ike's staff?"

"No. Actually," Tommy said slowly, "he was a longtime resident of your state."

"Never heard of him."

"That doesn't surprise me."

Walker Townsend rose to his feet. "Your Honor," he said with a tone of exasperated impatience. "I fail to see what is the point of this cross-examination. Lieutenant Hart has yet to ask the witness about the gentleman's trial testimony. He complained of history lessons yesterday offered by the prosecution, and yet returns today with some question about a man who died decades ago—"

"Colonel, it was the prosecution that made the point about Lieutenant Murphy's racial 'enlightenment.' I'm only following up on that."

MacNamara scowled, then said, "I will permit these questions as long as you hurry up and make your point, lieutenant."

Tommy nodded. At the defense table, Lincoln Scott whispered to Hugh Renaday, "There's one of the bones tossed in our direction."

Pausing for just an instant, Tommy turned back toward Murphy, who again shifted in his seat. "Who is Crispus Attucks, lieutenant?"

"Who?"

"Crispus Attucks."

"Never heard the name. Another Massachusetts man?"

Tommy smiled. "Good guess, lieutenant. Now, you say you are not a bigot, sir, but you cannot identify the Negro who died at the infamous Boston Massacre, and whose sacrifice was celebrated by our founding fathers at that pivotal moment in our nation's history? Nor do you recognize the name of Frederick Douglass, the great abolitionist, many of whose writings were committed to print in your fair state."

Murphy stared angrily at Tommy but did not reply. "History wasn't my best subject in school," he said bitterly.

"Obviously. Now, I wonder what else you don't know about Negroes."

"I know what I heard Scott say," Murphy spat out sharply. "And that's a whole damn sight more important than some history lesson."

Tommy hesitated, and nodded. "Indeed. Now, you're not very bright, are you, lieutenant?"

"What?"

"Smart." Tommy fired his questions rapidly, picking up momentum and raising his voice. "I mean, you had to go to work in the family business, weren't bright enough to do something on your own, correct? How'd you qualify for officer's training, anyway? Your daddy know somebody who pulled some strings? And that school where you said Negroes attended beside you. I bet you didn't even get grades as good as theirs, did you? And you were happy keeping those Negroes sweeping up while you made money, correct? Because if you ever gave one of them a chance, you were afraid they'd do a hell of a lot better job than you could, right?"

"Objection! Objection!" Walker Townsend shouted. "He's asking ten questions at once!"

"Lieutenant Hart!" Colonel MacNamara started.

Tommy swung his face down toward Murphy. "You hate them because they make you afraid, don't they?"

Again Murphy didn't reply. He simply seethed.

"Lieutenant Hart, I warn you, sir," MacNamara said, slamming his gavel down sharply.

Tommy stepped back from the witness, staring across the small space at Murphy, looking into his eyes.

"You know, Lieutenant Murphy, I can tell what you're thinking right now."

"What's that?" Murphy asked, between tightly clenched teeth.

Tommy smiled. "Why, you're thinking, 'I ought to kill that son of a bitch . . .' aren't you?"

Murphy scowled. "No," he said. "I'm not."

Tommy nodded, still grinning. "Sure you aren't." He stood up straight and gestured toward the packed audience and the kriegies hanging by the windows, listening to every word. "I'm sure that everyone here believes that denial. Absolutely. I must be one hundred percent wrong. . . ."

Sarcasm swirled around every one of Tommy's words.

"I'm sure you didn't think, 'I ought to kill that son of a bitch . . .' and you received perhaps one tenth of one percent of the abuse that Trader Vic subjected Lincoln Scott to on each and every day since Mr. Scott first arrived at Stalag Luft Thirteen!"

"He said it," Murphy persisted. "I didn't."

"Of course he did," Tommy answered. "But he didn't say: 'I'm *going* to kill that son of a bitch,' or 'I *must* kill that son of a bitch,' or 'I *plan* to kill that son of a bitch *tonight*. . . .' He didn't say any of those things, did he, lieutenant?"

"No."

"He said what anyone else might have said, under the exact same circumstances."

"Objection! Calls for the witness to speculate," Townsend shouted.

"Ah, withdrawn, then," Tommy interjected. "Because we surely wouldn't want Lieutenant Murphy to *speculate* about anything."

MacNamara glared down at Tommy. "You've made your point," he said. "Are you finished with this witness?"

Tommy shook his head. "Not quite."

He walked over to the prosecution's table and picked up the knife.

"Now, Lieutenant Murphy, were you, or anyone else in the barracks room, in the habit of sharing meals with Lieutenant Scott?"

"No."

"In every other room, people share foodstuffs and take turns doing the cooking, correct?"

"It seems that way."

"But Scott was excluded?"

"He didn't seem to want to be a part—"

"Oh, of course. He'd rather starve on his own, all by himself."

Murphy glared again, and Tommy continued.

"So he ate alone. I presume he fixed his own meals, as well."

"Yes."

"So you really wouldn't know for sure what knife he might have used at any given point to prepare his meals, would you?"

"He had a penknife. I saw him use it."

"Did you always watch him fix his meals?"

"No."

"So you really have no idea whether or not he might have used this homemade blade, on any occasion, do you?"

"No."

With the blade still in his hand, Tommy walked over to the defense table. Hugh reached down by his feet and handed Tommy a small parcel. Tommy put the knife down, and then took the parcel over to the witness.

"You are an expert on meats, lieutenant. After all, your

family owns a meat-packing business. Lucky for you, I guess. I would hate to have to have you rely on your own wits to get ahead. . . ."

"Objection," Townsend yelled. "Lieutenant Hart insults the witness!"

"Lieutenant," Colonel MacNamara said coldly, "I'm warning you. Do not persist along this road."

"Right, colonel," Tommy said briskly. "I would surely hate to insult anyone. . . ."

He sneered at Lieutenant Murphy, who eyed him with an ill-disguised fury of his own.

"Now, lieutenant, be so kind as to identify this for us."

Murphy reluctantly reached out and took the parcel from Tommy Hart. He swiftly unwrapped it and grimaced. "German blood sausage," he said. "Everyone's seen this before. Standard issue from the Krauts."

"Would you eat this?"

"No one I know in the entire camp eats it. People'd rather starve."

"Would you, the expert on meats and meat processing, eat this?"

"No."

"What goes into this sausage, lieutenant?"

Murphy scowled again. "Hard to say. The sausage we make back in the States is thick, solid, and carefully prepared. Sanitary. No one gets sick off of what we fix and send to market. This stuff, well, who knows? Lots of pig's blood and other types of waste matter, loosely packed in sheaths of intestines. You wouldn't want to know what could be in there."

The sausage was almost gelatinous. It was a deep brown-black color, tinged with red. It gave off a foul odor.

Tommy took the parcel and removed the sausage, holding it up for the audience to recognize. There was some uncomfortable laughter of recognition in the crowd.

Then Tommy moved back to the defense table. He picked up the homemade blade, then seized one of his precious white sheets of notepaper from the desk. Before the prosecution caught on to what he was doing, Tommy wrapped the paper around the handle of the knife, covering the cloth that was already stained. He held the blade up, theatrically, as

Walker Townsend jumped up and shouted out "Objection!" once again. Tommy ignored the word, and ignored the sudden gaveling from the tribunal's table. Instead, he took the knife and swiftly plunged it down hard across the thick middle of the sausage, cutting it in half. Then he chopped at the sausage twice more, making certain that the paper-wrapped handle creased the mess of false meat. The room seemed to fill with an exaggerated pungent smell of waste, and the kriegies closest to the defense table groaned as the smell struck them.

Tommy ignored the objections flooding from the prosecution, and paced directly in front of Lieutenant Murphy. He raised his own voice above all the other noise, and silenced the room with his question: "What do you see on the paper, lieutenant? The paper around the handle?"

Murphy paused, then shrugged.

"It looks like blood," he said. "Specks of blood."

"About the same amount of blood that mars the cloth and which the prosecution claims with no supporting evidence whatsoever belongs to Trader Vic!"

Stepping back from the witness, Tommy shouted, "No further questions." He took the knife and unwrapped the paper from the handle, holding it above his head so that the entire courtroom could see the splatter marks. Tommy then walked over to Walker Townsend and handed the paper to the prosecutor, who shook his head from side to side. The knife, however, he jabbed by the point into the tabletop, leaving it vibrating like a tuning fork in the once again silent courtroom.

Chapter Thirteen

THE PROSECUTION'S
LAST WITNESS

Tommy spotted Fritz Number One counting the adjacent formation of kriegies at the following morning's *Appell*. He kept the lean ferret locked in his sight throughout the assembly, ignoring the light rain that fell from dark gray skies, staining the brown leather of his flight jacket with streaks of black dampness. When Major Clark saluted Oberst Von Reiter and saw the usual nod from Colonel MacNamara, and then spun sharply and bellowed out the dismissal, Tommy surged through the melee of fliers, pushing his way directly to where Fritz and some of the other ferrets were gathered at the edge of the exercise yard, smoking and divvying up the day's assignments. The German looked up as Tommy approached, frowned, and immediately stepped away from the others.

Tommy stopped, a few feet away, and beckoned to the ferret, cocking a single finger with exaggeration like some impatient and harsh schoolteacher overseeing a laggardly student. Fritz Number One looked about nervously for an instant, then took a few quick strides to Tommy's side.

"What is it, Mr. Hart?" he asked swiftly. "I have many duties to perform this morning."

"Sure you do," Tommy replied. "What, there's some spot that needs to be inspected for the ten millionth time? You need to be sneaking around somewhere urgently? Come on, Fritz. You know the only show in town today is Scott's trial."

"I still have my duties, Mr. Hart. We all do. Even with the trial."

Tommy shrugged in an overstated, disbelieving fashion.

"Okay," he said. "I'll only take a minute or two of your valuable time. Just a couple of questions, then you can get back to whatever is so damn important." Tommy smiled, paused for a second, then demanded in a loud voice that carried to where the other ferrets were gathered: "All right, Fritz. I want to know where you got the knife from, and when exactly you traded it to Vic. You know which one I'm talking about: the murder weapon. . . ."

Fritz Number One paled, and grabbed Tommy by the arm. Shaking his head, he pulled the American flier into the lee of one of the huts, where he responded both angrily and with what Tommy detected was more than a small share of nervousness. "You cannot be asking me this, Lieutenant Hart! I have no idea of what you are speaking—"

Tommy interrupted the instantaneous whining response with a sharp-edged reply of his own. "Don't bullshit me, Fritz. You know precisely what I'm talking about. A German ceremonial dagger. Maybe SS type. Long and thin and with a death's head skull at the tip of the handle. Very similar to what Von Reiter wears when he's all decked out and ready to go to some important function. Trader Vic wanted one, and you got it for him, not long before he was killed. Like a couple of days at the most. I want to know about it. I want to know word for word what Vic said to you when he traded for that knife, and where it was supposed to go and who was supposed to get it. I want to know everything you did. Or maybe you'd prefer if I took my questions to Hauptmann Visser. I betcha he'll be real interested in knowing about that knife."

The German reeled back, almost as if he'd been struck, pressing against the wall of the hut. Fritz Number One looked ill.

Tommy took a deep breath, then added, "Why, I'll wager a pack of Luckies that it's against some Luftwaffe rule to trade an actual weapon to a prisoner of war. And especially some fancy special Nazi-type honor of the fatherland big deal dagger . . ."

Fritz Number One twisted about, looking over Tommy's shoulder, making certain that no one had hovered close enough to hear their conversation. He stiffened visibly when he heard Tommy speak Visser's name.

"No, no, no," he replied, shaking his head back and forth. "Lieutenant, you do not understand how dangerous this is!"

"Well," Tommy answered in tones as blandly matter-of-fact as he could muster, "why don't you tell me?"

Fritz Number One's voice quivered and his hands shook slightly as he gestured. "Hauptmann Visser would have me shot," he whispered. "Or sent to the Russian front, which is the same. Exactly the same, except maybe not as quick and maybe a little worse. To trade a weapon to an Allied airman is *verboten*!"

"But you did it?"

"Trader Vic, he was insistent. At first, I told him no, but it was all he could speak about. A souvenir, he promised me. Nothing more! He had a special customer, he said, willing to pay a large price. He needed it without delay. That day. Immediately! He told me it had great value. More value than anything else he'd ever traded for."

For a moment, Tommy swallowed hard, imagining the cold-bloodedness of the man who performed the ultimate swindle upon Trader Vic, getting the camp's entrepreneur to provide him with the weapon that he would then use to kill him. Tommy felt his mouth dry up, almost parched at the thought.

"Who wanted it? Who was Trader Vic fronting for?"

"I don't understand *fronting* . . ."

"Who was he making the deal for?"

Fritz Number One shook his head. "I asked. I asked more than once, but he would not tell me this name. But he said it was a sweetheart deal. That is what his words were, Lieutenant Hart. Sweetheart. I did not understand this either, until he explained it to me."

Tommy frowned. He was not sure that he totally believed the ferret. Nor was he at all sure he disbelieved him. Something in between. And it certainly hadn't turned into a sweetheart deal for one man.

"Okay, so you didn't get the name. So where did you steal the knife? From Von Reiter?"

Fritz Number One shook his head rapidly. "No, no, I could never do that! Commandant Von Reiter is a great man! I would be dead a long time ago, fighting the Ivans, if he had not brought me here with him when he received his orders. I was only a mechanic on his flight crew, but he knew I had the gift for languages, and so I accompanied him. It was death to remain behind, in Russia! Death. Winter, freezing cold, and death, Lieutenant Hart. That was all there was for us in Russia. Commandant Von Reiter saved me! I shall never be able to fully repay Commandant Von Reiter! If I am able to live through the war, it will be because of him! And here, I serve the commandant as best I can. I would never steal from him!"

"From someone else, then?"

Again Fritz shook his head. He whispered his response frantically, his words almost hissing, like air escaping from a punctured tire. "To steal this item from a German officer, and then trade it to an Allied airman, lieutenant, this would be a death warrant! The Gestapo would come for you! Especially so, if Hauptmann Visser were to discover it!"

"So you didn't steal it?"

Fritz continued to shake his head. "Hauptmann Visser does not know of this dagger, Lieutenant Hart! He suspects, but he does not know for certain. Please, he cannot learn. It would mean great trouble for me. . . ." In the slight hesitation at the end of his voice, Tommy heard distinctly that it would not be Fritz alone who suffered if this particular trade were exposed. And so he asked the obvious question.

"And who else, Fritz? Who else would be in trouble?"

"I will not say."

Tommy stopped. He could see the tremor in Fritz's jaw, and he believed he knew the answer to his question. Fritz had already told him. And, Tommy thought, there was probably only one man in the camp who could have provided that specific dagger without first stealing it. He decided to press the ferret further.

"Tell me about the commandant and Visser," Tommy asked suddenly. "Do they—"

"They despise each other," Fritz interrupted.

"Really?"

"It is a deep and terrible hatred. Two men who have worked closely together for months. But they have nothing together but contempt. Contempt and complete hatred for each other.

Each would be gladdened greatly to see an Allied bomb drop in the lap of the other."

"Why is that?"

The ferret shrugged, sighing, but his voice was shaky, almost like an old woman's. "Visser is a Nazi. He wishes the camp were his to command. The policeman son of a provincial schoolteacher. His father's party number is less than one thousand! He hates all the Allies, but especially the Americans because he once lived among you and the British fighter pilots because one of them took his arm. He hates that Oberst Von Reiter treats all the prisoners with respect! Commandant Von Reiter, he comes from an old, important family, who have served in the Wehrmacht and the Luftwaffe for many generations. There is no love lost between the two. I should not be speaking of these things, Lieutenant Hart! I will say no more."

Tommy nodded. This didn't surprise him terribly. He scratched at his own cheek, feeling the day's stubble growing there, then fired another question, taking the ferret by surprise.

"What did you get, Fritz? When you traded the knife?"

Fritz Number One shuddered, almost as if a sudden fever had slid through his body. Either the damp rain or sweat had broken out on his forehead, and his words continued to quiver.

"I got nothing," he answered, shaking his head back and forth.

Tommy snorted. "That doesn't make any damn sense! You're telling me that this was a big deal, the biggest deal, and that Trader Vic had a buyer already lined up ready to pay through the nose, and now you're saying you got nothing in return? Bullshit! Maybe I should go talk to Visser. I'm sure he has all sorts of extremely clever and decidedly unpleasant methods for extracting information. . . ."

Fritz Number One shot out his hand, grasping Tommy by the arm.

"Please, Lieutenant Hart, I am begging you. Do not speak to the *Hauptmann* of these matters! I fear that even Oberst Von Reiter would not be able to protect me!"

"Then what did you get? What was the trade?"

Fritz Number One lifted his head, eyes skyward, as if

wracked by sudden pain. Then he lowered his eyes, and whispered to Tommy Hart: "The payment was due the night Captain Bedford was murdered!" The ferret's voice was so low, Tommy had to crane forward. "He was to meet me with the payment in the dark that night. But he never arrived at our meeting place."

Tommy inhaled slowly. There was the explanation for the ferret being in the camp after lights out.

"What was the payment?" Tommy insisted.

Fritz Number One straightened up suddenly, leaning back against the wall of the hut as if Tommy had thrust a weapon into his chest. He shook his head. He was breathing hard, as if he'd just sprinted some distance.

"Do not ask me this question, Mr. Hart! I cannot say more. Please, I am begging you now, my life depends on it, other lives, as well as my own, but I cannot say to you more of this matter."

Tommy could see tears in the corner of the ferret's eyes. His face had turned a wan, gray color, like the sky overhead, the sickly, agonizingly fearful appearance of a man who can see his own death lurking close by and beckoning. Tommy was surprised, and he took a small step back, as if the look on Fritz Number One's face scared him as well.

"All right," he said. "All right for now. I'll keep my mouth shut. For now. No promises for later, but for now, we'll keep this between ourselves."

The German quivered again and broke into a grateful smile filled with reprieve. He seized Tommy's hand and shook it hard.

"I shall never forget this kindness, Lieutenant Hart. Never!"

The ferret took a step back, away from Tommy. "I will be in your debt, Lieutenant Hart! I will not forget this."

And with that, he lurched away, hurrying out into the dank morning. Tommy watched Fritz Number One's head twisting about, trying to ascertain whether he'd been observed in this conversation. On the one hand, Tommy knew he had just acquired enough information to blackmail Fritz Number One into doing whatever he wanted, probably for the duration of the war. But on the other, he was left more filled with questions than ever before. And one question that dominated all the others: What was the payment for the weapon that was turned on Vic? He watched as Fritz Number One scurried across the exercise yard, and wondered who else might have the answer to that question. He glanced down at his wristwatch, felt a pang of loneliness crease across his heart. For a single second, he wondered what time it was back home in Vermont, and he had trouble remembering whether it was earlier or later. Then he dismissed this unfair thought when he realized that if he did not hurry, he would be late for the beginning of that morning's proceedings.

The throngs of kriegies were already surrounding the makeshift theater and jamming the aisles as Tommy arrived for the trial's start. As he'd feared, everyone else was in place. The tribunal behind their table at the front, the prosecution seated and waiting impatiently, Lincoln Scott and Hugh Renaday in their chairs, Hugh wearing a concerned look. Off to the side, Hauptmann Visser was smoking one of his thin, brown cigarettes, while the stenographer next to him nervously fiddled with his pencil. Tommy picked his way down the center, stepping over feet and outstretched legs, stumbling once as he tripped over a pair of flight boots, thinking to himself that his solitary entrance was much less dramatic than when he had joined the two others and walked in formation.

"You've kept everyone waiting, lieutenant," Colonel MacNamara said coldly, as he stepped to the front of the room. "Zero eight hundred means precisely that. In the future, Lieutenant Hart—"

Tommy interrupted the Senior American Officer.

"I apologize, sir. But I had business crucial to the defense."

"That may well be, lieutenant, but—"

Tommy interrupted MacNamara again, which he was absolutely certain would infuriate the commanding officer. He didn't really care.

"My first and primary duty is to Lieutenant Scott, sir. If my absence caused a delay, well, then it equally demonstrates vividly, once again, sir, the unfortunate rush that this proceeding takes place within. Based on information that has just been made available to me, I would once again renew my objections to the trial continuing, and would request additional time to investigate."

"What information?" MacNamara demanded.

Tommy sauntered to the front of the prosecution's table, and picked up the homemade blade that Scott had fashioned. He turned it over once or twice in his hand, then set it down again, looking up at MacNamara.

"It has to do with the murder weapon, colonel."

Out of the corner of his eye, Tommy saw Visser stiffen in his seat. The German dropped his cigarette to the floor, and ground it beneath the heel of his boot.

"What about the murder weapon, lieutenant?"

"I'm not really at liberty to speak openly, colonel. Not without considerable further investigation."

Captain Townsend rose from his seat with liquid confidence in his voice. "Your Honor, I believe that the defense seeks delay simply for delay's sake. I believe that absent some real showing on their part of dire necessity, that we should continue—"

MacNamara held up his hand. "You are correct, captain. Lieutenant Hart, take your seat. Call your next witness, Captain Townsend. And Lieutenant Hart, do not be late again."

Tommy shrugged, and took his place. Lincoln Scott and Hugh Renaday both leaned over toward him. "What was that all about?" Scott demanded. "You find out something helpful?"

Tommy whispered his reply. "Maybe. I found out something. But I'm not sure how it helps."

Scott leaned back. "Great," he muttered under his breath. He picked up the stub of a pencil from the rough table and tapped it against the wooden surface. Scott fixed his eyes on the morning's first witness, another officer from Hut 101, who was being sworn in by MacNamara.

Tommy checked his notes. This was one of the witnesses who saw Scott in the hut's central corridor on the night of the murder. He knew what was coming was the worst sort of testimony. An officer with no particular connection to either Scott or Trader Vic, who would tell the court that he saw the black airman outside his bunk room, maneuvering through the darkness with the aid of a single candle. What the witness would describe were all actions that any man might have performed. Taken independently, they were benign. But in the context of that murderous night, they were damning.

Tommy inhaled deeply. He had no idea how to assault this testimony. Mostly, because it was true. He knew that within a few moments, the prosecution would have painted an important brush stroke of their case—that on the night of Trader Vic's death, Lincoln Scott was out and about, not pathetically shivering in his bunk beneath a thin, gray German-issue blanket, dreaming of home, food, and freedom like almost all the captive men in the South Compound.

He bit his lower lip, as Captain Townsend slowly began to question the witness. In that second, he thought the trial a bit like standing in the sand on the beach, just where the froth of the surf plays out, right at the point where the nearly spent force of the wave can still pull and tug at the sand, making everything unstable and unsteady beneath the feet. The prosecution's case was like the undertow, slowly dragging everything solid away, and right at that moment, he had no real idea how to put Lincoln Scott back on firm earth.

Shortly after midday, Walker Townsend called Major Clark to the witness stand. He was the final name on the prosecution's list of witnesses and, Tommy suspected, would be the most dramatic. For all of Clark's blustery anger, Tommy still suspected him of having a streak of composure that would emerge on the stand. It would be the same sort of composure that had allowed the major to steer his crippled, burning B-17, with only a single engine functioning, to a safe landing in a farmer's field in the Alsace, saving the lives of most of his crew.

When his name was called out by the Virginian, Major Clark rose swiftly from his seat at the prosecution's table. Back ramrod straight, he crossed the theater quickly, seizing the Bible that was proffered and swearing loudly to tell the truth. He then sat in the witness chair, eagerly awaiting Townsend's first question.

Tommy watched the major closely. There are some men, he thought, who managed to wear their imprisonment with a rigid, military sense of decorum; Clark's uniform was worn, patched, and tattered in numerous places after eighteen months at Stalag Luft Thirteen, but the way it draped on his bantam-weight frame made it seem as if it were newly cleaned and pressed. Major Clark was a small man, with a hard face, humorless and stiff, and there was little doubt in Tommy's mind that he was a man who had narrowed his course through the world down into the twin requirements of duty and bravery. He would acquire the one and perform the other with a complete singleness of purpose.

"Major Clark," Captain Townsend asked, "tell the court how it was that you came to this prisoner-of-war camp?"

The major bent forward, ready to begin his explanation, just as every other kriegie witness had, when Tommy arose. "Objection!" he said.

Colonel MacNamara eyed him. "And what might that be?" he inquired cynically.

"Major Clark is a member of the prosecution. I would think that fact alone would preclude him from testifying in this matter, colonel."

MacNamara shook his head. "Probably back home, yes. But here, due to the exigencies and uniqueness of our situation, I will allow both sides some latitude in who they call to the stand. Major Clark's role in the case was more akin to investigating officer. Objection is overruled."

"Then I have a second objection, colonel."

MacNamara looked slightly exasperated. "And that would be what, lieutenant?"

"I would object to Major Clark describing the history of his arrival here. Major Clark's courage on the battlefield is not at issue. The only point it serves is to create an exaggerated sense of credibility for the major. But, as the colonel is well aware, brave men are capable of lying, just as easily as cowards are, sir."

MacNamara glared at Tommy. Major Clark's face was set and hard. Tommy knew the major would take what he had just said as an insult, which was precisely what he had intended.

The colonel took a deep breath before replying.

"Do not reach beyond your grasp, lieutenant. Objection remains overruled. Captain, please continue."

Walker Townsend smiled briefly. "I would think that the

tribunal might censure the lieutenant, sir, for impugning the integrity of a brother officer. . . ."

"Just continue, captain," MacNamara growled.

Townsend nodded, and turned back to Major Clark.

"Tell us, please, major, how you happened to arrive here."

Tommy sat back, listening closely, as Major Clark described the bombing raid that resulted in his plane crash-landing. Clark was neither boasting nor modest. What he was was accurate, disciplined, and precise. At one point, he declined to describe the B-17's ability to maneuver on one engine, because, he said, that information was technical and might serve the enemy. He said this and gestured toward Heinrich Visser. One thing did emerge that Tommy found intriguing, if not critical. It turned out that Visser was the major's first interrogator, before being released into the camp. Visser had been the man asking questions that Clark refused to answer, questions about the capabilities of the air-craft and strategies of the air corps. These had been standard questions, and all fliers knew to answer solely with their name, rank, and serial number. They also knew that the men who demanded these answers were security police, regard-less of how they identified themselves. But what Tommy found interesting was that Clark, and therefore the other high-ranking members of the American camp, were well aware of Visser's dual allegiances.

Tommy snuck a glance at the one-armed German. Visser was listening intently to Major Clark.

"So, major," Walker Townsend suddenly boomed, "did there come a time when, as part of your official duties, you were called to investigate the murder of Captain Vincent Bedford?"

Tommy swung his eyes over to the witness. Here it comes, he thought to himself.

"Yes. Correct."

"Tell us how that came about."

For a moment, Major Clark turned toward the defense table, fixing Tommy, then Lincoln Scott, with a harsh, unfor-giving glare. Then, slowly, he launched into his story, lifting his voice, so that it coursed past Captain Townsend, and reached out to every kriegie in the audience, and all those hanging by the windows and doors. Clark described being awakened in the predawn hours by the ferret's alarm—he did not identify Fritz Number One as the ferret who discovered the body—and how he had carefully entered the *Abort* and first seen Vincent Bedford's corpse. He told the assembly that the very first and only suspect had been Lincoln Scott, based on the prior bad blood, animosity, and fights between the two men. He also told how he had spotted the telltale crimson blood spatters on the toes of Scott's flight boots and on the left-hand shoulder and sleeve of his leather jacket, when the black airman had been confronted in Commandant Von Reiter's office. The other elements of the case, Clark said, fell into place rapidly. Trader Vic's roommates had told of Scott's construction of the murder weapon, and informed him about the hiding place beneath the floorboards where it had been concealed.

Clark stitched each element of the prosecution's case into a single tapestry. He spoke at length, steadily, persuasively, with bulldoglike determination, as he gave context to all the other witnesses. Tommy did not object to the major's words, nor to the damning portrait he created. He knew one thing: The major, for all his stiffness and military rigidity, was a fighter, much like Lincoln Scott. If Tommy battled him on every point, with a series of objections, he would respond like an athlete; each little struggle would only serve to make him stronger and more determined to reach the goal.

But cross-examination was a different matter.

As Major Clark finished his testimony, Tommy lay in wait, feeling for all the world like a cobra in the high grass. He knew what he was required to do. One single weakness in the steady, convincing story the major told. Just attack that one critical point and expose it for a lie, then the rest will crumble. At least that was what he hoped, and he knew where he was going to strike. Had known since the first minute he'd examined the evidence.

He stole a sideways glance over at Scott. The black airman was fingering the stub of the pencil again. Tommy watched as Scott suddenly took the pencil and wrote on one of the precious scrap pieces of paper the single word: *Why.*

It was a good question, Tommy thought. One that still eluded him.

"One last question, Major Clark," Walker Townsend was saying. "Do you have any personal animosity toward Lieutenant Scott, or toward members of the Negro race, in general?"

"Objection!"

Colonel MacNamara nodded toward Tommy Hart.

"The lieutenant is correct, captain," he admonished Townsend. "The question is self-serving and irrelevant."

Captain Townsend smiled. "Well, perhaps self-serving, colonel," he responded. "But hardly irrelevant, I would wager." He said this as he turned toward the audience, playing the moment for the assembled kriegies. It was not necessary for Major Clark to have answered the question. Merely by asking it, Townsend had answered it for him.

"Do you have other questions, captain?" MacNamara asked.

"No sir!" Townsend replied, snapping his words like a salute. "Your witness, lieutenant."

Tommy rose slowly, moving out from behind the defense's table with patience. He looked over at Major Clark and saw that the witness was sitting forward in his seat, eagerly anticipating the first question.

"Do you have, major, any particular expertise in criminal investigations?"

Major Clark paused, before responding.

"No, lieutenant. But every senior officer in the army is accustomed to investigating disputes and conflicts between men under our command. We are trained to determine the truth in these situations. A murder, while unusual, is merely an extension of a dispute. The process is the same."

"Quite an extension, I'd say."

Major Clark shrugged.

"So, you have no police training?" Tommy continued. "You've never been taught how to examine a crime scene, have you?"

"No. Correct."

"And you do not have any special expertise in the collection and interpretation of evidence, do you?"

Major Clark hesitated, then answered forcefully. "I have no

special expertise, no. But this case did not require any. It was cut and dried, right from the start."

"So you say."

"Correct, again, lieutenant. So I say."

Major Clark's face had reddened slightly, and his feet were no longer flat on the floor, but lifted slightly at the heels, almost as if he were about to spring up. Tommy took a moment to read the major's face and body, and he thought the man wary but confident. Tommy moved over to Scott and Renaday and whispered to the Canadian, "Let me have those drawings, now."

Hugh pulled out from beneath the table the three crime-scene sketches that Phillip Pryce's Irish artist friend had drawn. He handed them to Tommy. "Nail the pompous bastard," he whispered, perhaps just loud enough for any kriegie with keen hearing to understand.

"Major Clark," Tommy said loudly, "I am going to show you three drawings. The first shows the wounds in Captain Bedford's neck and hands. The second shows how his body was located in the *Abort* stall. The third is a diagram of the *Abort* itself. Please examine these, and tell me if you think they fairly represent what you yourself saw on the morning following the murder."

Walker Townsend was on his feet. "I'd like to see those," he demanded.

Tommy thrust the three drawings at Major Clark, then gestured toward the captain. "You can look over his shoulder, captain. But I do not recall your presence at the *Abort* crime scene, so I would question your ability to determine the accuracy of these pictures."

Townsend scowled and walked behind Major Clark. Both men examined each drawing carefully. Tommy saw Captain Townsend bend over slightly, and start to speak in the major's ear.

"Don't speak to the witness!" he shouted. His words creased the still air of the makeshift courtroom. Tommy stepped forward angrily, pointing a finger in Townsend's face. "You have had your opportunity with the witness, and now it is my turn for cross-examination. Don't try to advise him in the middle of my cross!"

Townsend's eyes were narrow, staring at Tommy Hart. Into this instant fury, Colonel MacNamara interjected himself, taking Tommy slightly by surprise by landing squarely on his side.

"The lieutenant is correct, captain. We need to maintain correct trial procedure as much as humanly possible. You will have a second opportunity under redirect. Now step back, and let the lieutenant continue, although, Mr. Hart, I'd like to see those drawings myself."

Tommy nodded, handing them up to MacNamara, who also took his time to inspect them.

"They fit with my recollection," he said. "Now, Major Clark, answer the question."

Clark shrugged. "I would concur, colonel. They seem accurate enough."

"Take your time," Tommy said. "I wouldn't want there to be some obvious error."

Clark glanced at the drawings again. "They appear quite skillfully drawn," he said. "My compliments to the artist."

Tommy took the three drawings, then held them up above his head, so that the audience could see what he was speaking about.

"That won't be necessary," MacNamara growled, speaking before Walker Townsend had a moment to object.

Tommy smiled. "Of course," he said to the colonel. Then he turned back to Major Clark. "Major, based on your examination of the crime scene in the *Abort*, based on your inspection of Trader Vic's body, and based on your collection of the evidence in this case, would you please tell the court precisely how you contend this particular murder took place?"

Tommy pivoted, leaning back against the defense table, half-sitting, crossing his arms and waiting for the major to tell his tale, trying to impose an attitude of disbelief in his stance. Internally, he was nervous about the question. Phillip Pryce had long before burned into him the credo that no one ever asks a question in a trial that they do not know the response to, and here, he was asking Scott's main accuser to take free rein and describe Trader Vic's death. This, he knew, was something of a gamble. But he counted on Major Clark's ego and pugnacity, and knew that the roosterlike officer would walk into the trap he'd set. He suspected the major didn't see the danger in the crime scene sketches. And, Tommy presumed, the major had no idea that waiting in the wings was Nicholas Fenelli, the mortuary man and doctor-in-training, who would contradict everything Clark was about to say when Tommy called him to the stand and showed him the same pictures just as he had already done in Fenelli's barebones infirmary. And in this conflict, Tommy thought, Scott's insistent denials would take force and suddenly gain the wind of truth.

Clark paused, then said, "You want me to describe the killing?"

"Exactly. Just tell us how it happened. Based on your investigation, of course."

Walker Townsend started to rise, then sat back down. He wore a small grin on his face.

"Very well," Major Clark responded. "This is what I believe took place—"

Tommy interrupted. "A belief based on your interpretation of the evidence, correct?"

Major Clark snorted. "Yes. Exactly. May I continue?"

"Of course."

"Well, Captain Bedford was, as everyone knows, a businessman. I contend that Lieutenant Scott saw Bedford arise from his bunk in the middle of the night in question. Bedford was clearly taking a risk going out after lights out, but he was a brave and determined man, especially when he saw a substantial reward. Moments later, using the light of a candle, Scott trailed after him, stalking him, his knife concealed beneath his coat, not knowing that he'd been spotted by others. I suppose if he'd known that, he might have changed his mind—"

"Well," Tommy interjected, "that would be a guess on your part. Right? Not part of what the evidence tells you?"

Major Clark nodded. "Of course. You are correct, lieutenant. I shall try to restrict myself from further suppositions."

"That would be helpful. Now," Tommy said, "he trails him outside . . ."

"Precisely, lieutenant. Scott trailed Bedford into the *Abort*, where they confronted each other. Because they were inside that building, no sound they made when they fought penetrated into the rooms in Huts 101 or 102."

"That would be a wonderfully convenient absence of noise," Tommy interjected again. He couldn't help himself. The major's pompous know-it-all tone of voice was too irritating to let pass. Major Clark scowled back at him.

"Lieutenant, whether it was convenient or not, I wouldn't know. I do know that questioning of men in the adjacent huts revealed no one who heard the noise from the fight. It was late. People were asleep."

"Yes," Tommy said. He wanted to say "thank you." "Please continue."

"Using the blade he'd fashioned, Scott stabbed Captain Bedford in the throat. Then he thrust the murdered man back into the sixth stall, where the body was subsequently discovered. Then, unaware his clothes were stained with blood, he made his way back to the bunk room. End of story, lieutenant. Cut and dried, like I said."

Major Clark smiled. "Next question," he added.

Tommy straightened up. "Show me," he said.

"Show you?"

"Show all of us how this fight happened, major. Take the knife. You be Scott. I'll be Bedford."

Major Clark rose eagerly. Captain Townsend thrust the knife toward him. The major gestured at Tommy. "Stand here," he said. Then he took a position a few feet away, holding the knife in his hand as one would hold a sword. Then, in slow motion, he made a fake slash at Tommy's throat. "Of course," the major said, "you are considerably taller than Captain Bedford, and I'm not as tall as Lieutenant Scott, so . . ."

"Maybe we should reverse positions?" Tommy said.

"Fine," Major Clark responded. He handed Tommy the knife.

"Like so?" Tommy asked, mimicking the mannerisms that the major had just displayed.

"Yes. That would be accurate," the major said. He wore a smile as he portrayed the victim. Tommy turned toward Captain Townsend.

"Okay by you, Mr. Prosecutor?"

"Looks fine," the Virginian said.

Tommy Hart gestured back toward the witness chair. "Okay," he said, as Major Clark resumed his seat. "And after slashing Trader Vic's throat, Scott pushed him back into the stall, correct? And then he departed the *Abort*? Is that how you see it?"

"Yes," the major said loudly. "Precisely."

"Then tell me, how does he get blood on the back of the left-hand side of his jacket?"

"I beg your pardon?"

"How does he get blood on the left-hand back side of his flight jacket?" Tommy walked over to the prosecution's table, picked up Scott's leather flight jacket, and held it up, displaying it for the court to see.

Major Clark hesitated. The redness had returned to his face. "I don't understand the question," he said.

Tommy pounced. "It would seem most simple, major," he said icily. "There's blood on the back of his coat. How does it get there? In your entire testimony, describing the crime, and now, in acting it out for this court, at no point do you ever suggest Lieutenant Scott turned his back on Bedford. How does that blood get there?"

Major Clark shifted about in his seat. "He may have had to lift the body up, before shoving it back in the stall. He would use his shoulder, and that might have put the blood there."

"You're not an expert at these things, right? You've never really been taught anything about crime scenes. Or blood patterns, correct?"

"I've already answered that."

Walker Townsend rose to his feet. "Your Honor," he said, "I think the defense is—"

Colonel MacNamara held up his hand. "If you have some problem, you can bring it out on redirect. For now, let the lieutenant continue."

"Thank you, colonel," Tommy said. He was surprised by MacNamara's decisiveness. "Okay, Major Clark. Let's suppose he did have to lift the body, although that's not what you said the first time through. Is the defendant right-handed or left-handed?"

Clark hesitated, then replied. "I don't know."

"Well, if he opted to use his left shoulder for this heavy labor, wouldn't that suggest to you he was left-handed?"

"Yes."

Tommy spun about, suddenly facing Lincoln Scott.

"Are you left-handed, lieutenant?" he abruptly, loudly, demanded.

Lincoln Scott, wearing a small smile of his own, reacted swiftly, before Walker Townsend had the opportunity to object. He thrust himself to his feet, and shouted out: "No sir! Right-handed, sir!" And then he made a fist with his right hand and held it up in front of him.

Tommy pivoted again, abruptly facing Major Clark.

"So," he demanded sharply. "Maybe the crime didn't happen that way. *Precisely.*" He mocked the major's own word with sarcasm in his tone of voice.

"Well," Clark responded, "perhaps not precisely—"

Tommy held up his hand, cutting him off.

"That's good enough," he said. "I wonder what else didn't happen *precisely* as you suggest. In fact, I wonder if *anything* happened *precisely* as you think it did!"

Tommy fairly shouted these last words. Then he shrugged his shoulders and raised his arms in a great questioning gesture, filling the courtroom with the elusive sense that it would be unfair to convict any man without precision.

"No further questions," he said with as much disgust as he could manage. "Not for this witness!"

He dramatically returned to his seat, making a clattering noise as he sat down. Out of the corner of his eye he saw Hauptmann Visser paying rapt attention to the cross-examination. The German wore the same nasty half-smile that Tommy recognized from other moments. Visser whispered something to the stenographer, who quickly scratched down the *Hauptmann*'s words on his sheet of paper.

From his seat next to Tommy, Lincoln Scott whispered, "Nicely done." On the other side, Hugh wrote on his own paper the single name *Fenelli*, followed by several dark exclamation points. The Canadian policeman knew what was coming, as well, and he wore a similar satisfied smile on his lips.

Behind them, voices were buzzing, as kriegies leaned together, like spectators at a closely played ball game, discussing the action on the field. Colonel MacNamara allowed the excited muttering to continue for a moment, then he banged his makeshift gavel down hard three times. His own face was rigidly set. Not angry, but clearly upset—although with the prosecution's flimsiness or Tommy's theatrics was impossible to tell.

"Redirect?" he coldly demanded of Walker Townsend.

The captain from Virginia rose slowly. There was something in the steady, patient way he moved that made Tommy suddenly nervous. He thought the captain should be flying erratically, trying to keep high and level even with one engine out.

Shaking his head, smiling wryly, Captain Townsend stepped forward. "No sir, we will have no further questions for the major. Thank you, sir."

This got Tommy's attention. The one thing he'd been certain of as he sat down was that Townsend would need to rehabilitate Major Clark's testimony. And he counted on the belief that every effort to make Clark look like he knew what he was talking about would only serve to make his inadequacies as a criminal investigator more obvious. Tommy felt an unexpected fear, not unlike a moment many months earlier inside the *Lovely Lydia*, making their way home to base one evening when the bomber had been jumped by an unseen fighter and the Focke-Wulf's tracer rounds creased the blue sky beside them. It had taken all the skill his old captain from West Texas possessed to climb into the nearby clouds and elude the threatening fighter.

Then Townsend turned, looking briefly at the defense, then out at the body of airmen crammed into the theater.

"Do you have another witness?" Colonel MacNamara asked.

"Yes, we do, colonel," Captain Townsend said carefully. "One last witness, and then we will be completed with our case, sir." Townsend's voice rose quickly, gaining momentum and strength with each word, so that when he finally spoke, it was close to a bellow. "At this point, sir, the prosecution would call Second Lieutenant Nicholas Fenelli to the witness stand!"

Hugh Renaday blurted out, "What the bloody hell?" Lincoln Scott dropped the pencil to the table, and Tommy Hart's head suddenly reeled, as if he'd stood up too quickly. He could feel the color drain from his cheeks.

"Lieutenant Nicholas Fenelli!" Colonel MacNamara called out.

There was commotion from the crowd of airmen in the audience, as they parted to allow the erstwhile physician to make his way forward. Tommy spun about in his seat, and saw Fenelli moving steadily down the center aisle of the theater, his eyes directly on the witness chair, scrupulously avoiding contact with Tommy's.

"What the hell's this?" Renaday whispered nearby. "A damn ambush!"

Tommy watched as Fenelli approached. He had obviously spiffed up his uniform as much as possible, shaved with a precious new blade, combed his stringy black hair, and trimmed his pencil-thin mustache. At the front of the theater, Fenelli saluted briskly, then reached out for the Bible, on which to swear to tell the whole truth. Tommy felt momentarily mesmerized by the medic's appearance, almost as if the scene in front of him were playing out in slow motion. But as Fenelli raised his hand to swear, Tommy managed to shake the surprise from his body, and he leapt up, slamming a fist down onto the table in front of him as he did so.

"Objection! Objection! Objection!"

The man being sworn in paused, still not looking in Tommy's direction. Walker Townsend moved to the front of the tribunal, and Colonel MacNamara leaned forward in his seat.

"State the basis for your objection, lieutenant," MacNamara said coldly.

Tommy took a deep breath. "This individual's name appears nowhere on the prosecution's list of witnesses, Your Honor! Therefore, he cannot be called to the stand without the defense having ample opportunity to discuss his testimony—"

Walker Townsend half-turned toward Tommy, as he interrupted. "But Lieutenant Hart, you are disingenuous! Why, you are completely familiar with Mr. Fenelli's connection to the case, and you have interviewed him at length! In fact, it is my belief you intended to call him to the stand yourself."

"Is that true, Mr. Hart?" Colonel MacNamara demanded.

Tommy scrambled inwardly. He felt adrift. He had no idea why the prosecution would call Fenelli, especially knowing what the medic would say about the nature of the wounds suffered by Trader Vic and the type of weapon that inflicted them. But something was deadly and wrong, and Tommy fought against the unknown.

"It is true that I interviewed Lieutenant Fenelli. It is true that I considered calling him . . ."

"Then I fail to see how you can object, lieutenant," MacNamara said stiffly.

"Sir, it remains true he is not on the prosecution's list! This fact alone should preclude him from taking the stand."

"We just went over this issue with Major Clark, lieutenant! Because of our unusual circumstances here, the court feels it critical to allow both sides some substantial leeway, while still maintaining the important integrity of the process."

"This is unfair, sir!"

"I think not, lieutenant. Mr. Fenelli, please take your seat! Captain Townsend, please continue!"

For an instant, Tommy swayed dizzily. Then he slumped back into his own chair. He didn't dare look to the side at Lincoln Scott or Hugh Renaday, though he could hear the Canadian muttering obscenities. Scott, however, sat stock-still, with both of his palms down on the table, the veins in the backs of his hands standing out rigidly.

Chapter Fourteen

THE SECOND LIE

Second Lieutenant Nicholas Fenelli sat uncomfortably on the witness chair, shifting once or twice as he searched for a more accommodating position, and finally leaning forward slightly, placing his hands on top of each of his thighs, as if to steady himself. He did not look over at Tommy Hart, Lincoln Scott, or Hugh Renaday, who wore a look on his face of distinctly murderous fury. Instead, he kept his eyes on Captain Townsend, who maneuvered his own body between Fenelli and the defense as best he could.

"Now, lieutenant," Townsend began slowly, his voice as soft yet cajoling as a teacher trying to prompt some brilliant but shy student, "please tell all of us assembled here how it is that you came to acquire some special expertise in the handling of murder victims."

Fenelli nodded and launched into the story he'd already told Tommy and Hugh, about working in his uncle's mortuary in Cleveland prior to attending medical school. He spoke without the brashness or the bravado that he'd displayed when Tommy first interviewed him. Now he was direct, modest, but complete, and certainly lacking any of the orneriness he'd shown before.

"Very good," Townsend said, calmly absorbing Fenelli's words. "Now, tell the court how it was that you came to examine the deceased man's remains."

Fenelli nodded. "It was my job to prepare Captain Bedford's body for burial, sir. I have performed this task on several other unhappy occasions. It was while doing my job that I took note of the wounds on his body."

Again, Townsend nodded slowly. Tommy sat quietly in his seat, noting that Townsend didn't ask anything about the order Clark gave Fenelli *not* to examine the body. But so far, Fenelli had not departed from anything Tommy had expected. That wasn't to last.

"Now, did there come a time when Mr. Hart approached you, with pictures of the crime scene, and questions about the manner in which Captain Bedford died?"

"Yes sir," Fenelli answered swiftly.

"And did you have some opinions about the murder that you expressed to him?"

"Yes sir. I did."

"And are those opinions the same today as they were during that interview?"

Fenelli paused, swallowing hard, then he smiled wanly.

"Well, not exactly," he said with a small hesitation.

Tommy was on his feet immediately. "Your Honor!" He stared directly at Colonel MacNamara. "I don't know precisely what's going on with this witness, but this sudden change of attitude stinks!"

Colonel MacNamara nodded. "It does, perhaps, lieutenant. But the man is now under oath in front of all of us. He's sworn to tell the truth. We need to hear what he's going to say before we can judge it."

"Sir, once a cat is out of the bag . . ."

MacNamara smiled, interrupting. "I see your point, lieutenant. But we're still going to listen to the man! Continue, please, Captain Townsend."

Tommy remained standing, his knuckles pressed hard and white against the defense table.

"Sit down, Mr. Hart!" MacNamara said sharply. "You may make your arguments at the appropriate time!"

Tommy slumped down.

Captain Townsend hesitated, then asked, "Well, let me back up a little, Lieutenant Fenelli. Did there come a time subsequent to your conversation with Mr. Hart that you spoke with myself and Major Clark?"

"Yes sir."

"And as part of that conversation, did you have the opportunity to examine the prosecution's evidence in this case? To wit, the homemade knife fashioned by Lieutenant Scott and the articles of clothing that we have here today?"

"Yes sir."

"Now, Mr. Hart didn't show you these things, did he?"

"No sir. He only showed me the drawings he had had prepared."

"Those drawings, did they seem accurate enough to you?"

"Yes sir. They did."

"They still seem that way?"

"Yes sir."

"Is there anything in those drawings that contradicts what you believe happened to Captain Bedford, based on your examination of the body?"

"No sir."

"Now, tell this court what you came to believe about the crime."

"Well, sir, my first impression, when I first laid out the captain's body, you see, was that Mr. Bedford had been killed by a stab from behind, which is just what I told Mr. Hart. I also believed right then that the murder weapon was something long and narrow. . . ."

"You told Mr. Hart this? That the murder weapon was thin?"

"Yes sir. I suggested the killing was performed by a man wielding some sort of narrow stiletto or switchblade-type knife."

"But he didn't show you this knife, did he?"

"No sir. He did not have it."

"In fact, you've never seen this weapon, have you?"

"Well, not here."

"Right. So, there is no evidence whatsoever that this second what did you call it . . ."

"Stiletto. Or switchblade, captain . . ."

"Right. This assassin's weapon. You've never seen it. There's no evidence at all that it even exists, is there?"

"Not that I know of."

"Right." Townsend paused, took a deep breath, then asked, "So, this killing that you first thought might have been performed with a knife that doesn't seem to exist . . . is that what you believe today?"

Tommy rose sharply. "Objection!" he blurted.

Colonel MacNamara shook his head. "Captain Townsend," he said stiffly, "try to ask your questions in an acceptable manner. Without all the unnecessary editorializing."

"Of course, Your Honor. Sorry," Townsend said. Then he looked over at Lieutenant Fenelli, and did not rephrase the question, but merely gestured, a small hand wave, as if encouraging his response.

"No sir. It's not exactly what I believe today. When I saw the blade in the prosecution's possession, the one you and the major showed me yesterday, well, then I was able to determine that the wounds inflicted upon Captain Bedford were possibly consistent with that weapon . . ."

Lincoln Scott muttered, "*Possibly* consistent . . . that's great." Tommy did not reply, instead focusing closely on each word that seemed to drag itself from Fenelli's lips.

"Was there another reason why you first thought the wounds Captain Bedford suffered were delivered with that special sort of knife?" Townsend questioned.

"Well, sir, yes. Those were the types of wounds that I saw in my mortuary experience back in Cleveland, sir. Because I was most familiar with those sorts of weapons and the damage they cause, that was sort of what I sort of automatically concluded. My fault. Sort of."

Townsend smiled at Fenelli's tortured grammar. "But upon further consideration . . ."

"Yes sir. Further consideration. A couple of further considerations, sir. I saw that there were also some contusions on the captain's face. I suspect what might have happened was that he was struck by a fist, hard, which slammed him sideways into the wall of the *Abort*, and exposing that portion of the neck where the primary wound was discovered. In this maybe semiconscious and vulnerable state, kinda twisted sideways, you know, the blade was used to kill, giving me the impression of a blow from behind. At least, giving me that impression at first. I musta been wrong. Or coulda been, maybe. It might have happened that way. I'm no expert."

Walker Townsend nodded. It was impossible for him to hide the look of pleased satisfaction on his face.

"That's right. You're not an expert."

"That's what I said. I'm not an expert," Fenelli repeated.

The medic from Cleveland shifted once or twice in his seat, then added, "I feel that I should have maybe gone to Mr. Hart and told him about my change of mind, sir. Shoulda gone, right after talking with you. I apologize for that. But I didn't have time, because—"

"Of course." Townsend sliced off Fenelli's words sharply. "Now I have just one more question, lieutenant," Townsend said loudly. "There has been much made of this right-hand, left-hand business. . . ."

"Yes sir."

"Did your examination of the body suggest to you anything in this regard?"

"Yes sir. Because of the contusions and the knife wound, and after talking with you, I kinda figured that whoever killed Captain Bedford was possibly pretty much ambidextrous, sir. Or real close to it."

Townsend nodded slowly. "Ambidextrous means someone who is equally capable of using either right or left hand, correct?"

"That is correct, sir."

"Like a particularly skilled boxer?"

"I suppose so."

"Objection!" Tommy again leapt to his feet.

Colonel MacNamara stared at him, and held up his hand for Tommy to halt before going further. "Yes, yes, I know what you're going to say, Lieutenant Hart. This is a conclusion that the witness is not capable of reaching. Absolutely correct. Unfortunately, Mr. Hart, it is a conclusion that is obvious to the entire tribunal." He waved Tommy back into his seat. "Do you have something further for Lieutenant Fenelli, captain?"

Townsend smiled, glanced over toward Major Clark, and shook his head.

"No sir. We have no more questions. He's your witness now, Lieutenant Hart."

Shaking with rage, his mind seared with every imaginable sensation of fury and betrayal, Tommy rose and, for a long second or two, simply stared across the room at the witness seated in front of him. His imagination was jumbled with confused emotions, all painted over in the red of anger. Tommy bit down on his lower lip, wanting to do nothing except savage Fenelli. He wanted to embarrass him and show him to the entire camp to be the back-stabbing dishonest gutless cowardly liar that Tommy believed him to be. He searched through the thicket of rage for the first question that would expose him to the assembly as the Judas Tommy considered him. Tommy was breathing hard and harsh, and he wanted his first query to be devastating.

He opened his mouth to fire this first salvo, but stopped, just as he caught, out of the corner of his eye, the look on Walker Townsend's face. The captain from Virginia was leaning slightly forward, not so much grinning as he was flush with eagerness. And Tommy, in that short moment, realized something he thought important—that what Captain Townsend, and Major Clark at his side, were anticipating was not what Fenelli had already said from the witness stand. But what he was *about* to say, when Tommy thrust his first infuriated question across the theater.

Tommy took a deep breath. He glanced down at both Hugh Renaday and Lincoln Scott, and he could tell the two men wanted him to verbally carve the lying medic into tiny pieces.

He let out air slowly.

Then he looked past Fenelli, up to Colonel MacNamara.

"Colonel," he said, plastering a small, fake smile onto his face. "Obviously Lieutenant Fenelli's change of tune takes the defense by complete surprise. We would request that you adjourn these proceedings until tomorrow, so that we can discuss strategy."

Captain Townsend rose. "Sir, there's almost an hour until the evening *Appell*. I think we should continue as late as possible. There's more than enough time for Mr. Hart to ask some questions, and then, if need be, continue in the morning."

Tommy coughed. He crossed his arms in front of him and realized that he had just avoided a trap. The problem was, he couldn't quite see what the trap was. He glanced sideways and noticed that Major Clark had curled his hands into fists.

MacNamara seemed oddly oblivious to what was going on. Instead, he started to shake his head back and forth. "Lieutenant Hart is correct," he said slowly. "There's less than an hour. Not really enough time, and these things are better when they're not cut in two. We'll recess now, and pick up again in the morning." He turned briefly toward Hauptmann Visser, sitting by the side of the room, and lectured him with an irritated, inconvenienced tone of voice: "We could be far more efficient here, *Herr Hauptmann,* and bring things to a much more rapid and orderly conclusion if we were not constantly having to interrupt ourselves for the regularly scheduled roll calls. Will you bring this up with Commandant Von Reiter?"

Visser nodded. "I will mention it to him, colonel," he replied dryly.

"Very good," MacNamara said. "Lieutenant Fenelli, please remember that just like the other witnesses, you are under oath and not to discuss your testimony or any other aspect of this case with any other person. Understand?"

"Of course, sir," Fenelli answered briskly.

"Then we are dismissed until tomorrow," MacNamara said, rising.

As before, Tommy, Scott, and Hugh Renaday waited for the theater to empty out, remaining at their table silently, until the last echo of flight boots faded from the cavernous room behind them. Lincoln Scott was staring straight ahead, his eyes fixed on the vacant witness chair.

Renaday pushed back from the table hard, and spoke first. "Blasted liar!" he said angrily. "Tommy, why didn't you go right after him? Tear his dishonest throat out!"

"Because that was what they wanted. Or, at the least, that was what they expected. And what Fenelli said was bad enough. But maybe what he was about to say was going to be worse."

"How do you know that?" Renaday sputtered.

"I don't," Tommy said flatly. "I'm just guessing."

"What could he say that was worse?"

Again, Tommy shrugged. "He was equivocating on all

those lies, lots of maybes and couldas and shouldas. Perhaps when I asked him about being paid a visit by Townsend and Clark, perhaps he wasn't going to be quite as unsteady. Maybe the next lie was going to sink us. But I'm guessing. Again."

"Bloody dangerous guesswork, my lad," Hugh said. "Just gives the deceitful bastard all night to ready himself for the onslaught."

"I don't know about that," Tommy said. "I think I'll pay Mr. Fenelli a little visit after dinner."

"But MacNamara said . . ."

"The hell with MacNamara," Tommy replied. "What the hell can he do to me? I'm already a prisoner of war."

This response tripped a slight, sad grin onto Lincoln Scott's face. He nodded. But he did not speak, seeming to prefer to keep all the terrifying thoughts that had to be burning within him contained. And one thing was obvious: Perhaps Colonel MacNamara couldn't really do anything worse to Tommy, but that wasn't the case for Lincoln Scott.

The evening sky was clearing, the irritating cold drizzle had ceased, and there was a little promise of milder weather ahead at the evening *Appell*. Tommy stood patiently beside Lincoln Scott as the mind-numbing process of being counted was repeated again. He wondered for a moment just exactly how many times the Germans had counted him during his years at Stalag Luft Thirteen, and he pledged that if he ever made it home to Vermont, he would never ever allow anyone to count his head out loud ever again.

He looked around, searching the rows of fliers for Fenelli, but was unable to spot him. Tommy figured he would be lurking in the back row of one of the formations, as distant from the men in Hut 101 as possible. This made no difference to Tommy. He intended to wait until the hour right before the lights were going out to make his real search. He was reviewing what he was going to say to the would-be medic, trying to find the right combination of anger and understanding that would get Fenelli to tell him why he'd changed his story. Clark and Townsend had reached him, Tommy knew. But just how he wasn't sure, and that was what he needed to

know. He also needed to know what it was that Fenelli was in-
tending to say in the morning.

Other than that pursuit, he recognized that he was more or
less out of tricks. He had no evidence to present. The only
witness for the defense was Scott himself. Scott and whatever
eloquence Tommy could muster. He shook his head. Not
much to offer. He expected Scott to be a terrible witness, and
he had great doubts over his own ability to sway anyone—
much less Colonel MacNamara and the other two members
of the court—with any sort of impassioned speech.

He heard the bellow of dismissal from the front of the formations and wordlessly he followed Scott and Hugh back
across the parade ground toward Hut 101. He paid no attention to the buzz of voices around them.

As they walked down the center corridor of the barracks,
Hugh spoke out. "We need to eat something. But there's not
much in the larder, I'll wager."

"You go ahead," Scott said. "I have almost a full parcel left.
Take whatever you need and fix something for yourselves.
I'm just not that hungry."

Hugh started to respond, then stopped. Both he and
Tommy knew this statement for the lie it was, because
everyone was always hungry at Stalag Luft Thirteen.

Scott stepped ahead of the two others and thrust open the
door to their room. He pushed inside, but stopped after traveling only a few feet. Behind him, both Tommy and Hugh
paused.

"What is it?" Tommy asked.

"We've had visitors again," Scott said flatly. "I'll be
damned."

Tommy slid past the black airman's broad shoulders. He
could see that Lincoln Scott was staring at something, and
Tommy fully expected another crude sign. But what he saw
stopped him in his tracks as well.

Stuck into the rough-hewn wooden frame of Tommy's
bunk, right above the threadbare pillow for his head, reflecting the harsh, bright light from the overhead bulb, was a
knife.

Not a knife. *The* knife. The death's head skull at the tip of
the handle seemed to grin directly at him.

Hugh had pressed forward as well. "Well, about bloody time someone here did the damn right thing," he muttered. "That's got to be it, Tommy, my boy. The murder weapon. And now, thank God, we've got it!"

The three men approached the knife carefully.

"Has anything else been disturbed?" Tommy asked.

"Doesn't look that way," Scott replied.

"Is there a note?"

"No. None that I can see."

Tommy shook his head. "There should be a note," he insisted.

"Why?" Hugh asked. "The damn thing pretty much speaks for itself. Maybe that fighter jock, the fellow from New York who first told you about it, maybe he's our anonymous benefactor."

"Maybe," Tommy said warily. He reached out and gingerly removed the blade from the wood. It glistened in his hand, almost as if it had a voice of its own, which, in a way, it did. He raised it and inspected the knife as closely as possible. It had been cleaned of any blood or other incriminating matter, so that it appeared almost brand new. He hefted it in his hand. It was light, yet solid. He ran a finger up and down the double edges. They were razor-sharp. The point had not been dulled, not by being thrust into Trader Vic's neck or by being stabbed into the wood of Tommy's bunk. The handle itself was onyx-black and polished to a reflective sheen and obviously carved by a craftsman. The death's head skull was a pearly white color, almost translucent. The dagger seemed to speak of ritual and terror, simultaneously. It was a cruel thing, Tommy thought, that combined an awful mixture of symbolism and murderous intent. It was, he realized suddenly, the most valuable thing he'd held in his own hand in months, and then, just as swiftly, he thought this untrue, that any single one of his law books was more important and, in their own way, more dangerous. He smiled, and realized that he was being sophomorically idealistic.

"Well, that's the first bit of luck we've had," Hugh exclaimed. "Something of a surprise for Lieutenant Fenelli tomorrow, I'd say." He took the blade from Tommy's hand, weighed it, and added, "A nasty bit of business, this."

Scott reached out and took his turn with the knife. He remained quiet until he handed it back to Tommy.

"I don't trust it," he said sharply.

"What do you mean?" Hugh asked. "That's the bloody murder weapon, all right."

"Yes. That's probably true. And it shows up here magically? Right at the darkest hour? At least that's what someone would say. A bad poet."

"Maybe. But maybe it's about time someone saw how damnably unfair this whole show has been!" Hugh blurted out. "Somebody finally thought to level the playing field a bit, and what right have we to complain?"

"You don't mean *we*, Hugh. You mean *me*," Scott replied softly.

Hugh snorted, but nodded in slow agreement.

Scott turned to face Tommy. "No one in the camp wants to help. Not a person."

"We've had this argument before," Tommy responded. "We don't know that what you say is true. At least, not for certain."

Scott rolled his eyes skyward. "Sure. If that's what you want to think." Then he looked down at the ceremonial dagger again. "Look at that knife, Tommy. It stands for evil and it's already served an evil cause. It has death all over it. Now, I know you may not be all that religious with your Vermont Yankee stubbornness and everything"—he was half-smiling as he spoke—"and after all, I like to think that I'm much more modern than my old preacher father, who gets up on the pulpit on Sunday mornings and likes to loudly and forthrightly proclaim that anything not directly connected to the Good Book has little or no value on this earth, but still, Tommy, Hugh, you look at that thing, and you realize no good and certainly no truth can come out of it."

"You're too bloody philosophical and not pragmatic enough," Hugh said.

"Perhaps," Scott replied. "We'll see, won't we?"

Tommy said nothing. He put the blade down on his bunk after stroking the handle a final time. Even cleaned, it wasn't hard to imagine how an expert handling such a weapon would find it easy to slip it into the throat of a man, commando-style, severing the larynx on the path to the brainpan. He shuddered. It was a type of killing that seemed hard and unfamiliar; though had he really considered it, he would have seen that in a war there was truly little difference between forcing the dagger into a man's neck and skipping a five-hundred-pound bomb across the waves toward him. But Tommy was trapped with the vision of Trader Vic's last seconds, and he wondered if the Mississippian had felt any pain, or if he was merely surprised and slightly confused as he felt the knife slide home.

Tommy shuddered. Scott was right, he thought. It was an evil thing. He realized right then that when he produced it at the trial in the morning, right before Hauptmann Visser's eyes, it would probably cost Fritz Number One his life, and perhaps demand a similar price of Commandant Von Reiter. At the least, the two men would soon be heading east to the Russian front, which was more or less the same thing. Tommy knew that Fritz had been telling the truth about that, at least. Visser also would know that there was only one way that knife came into the camp. Tommy had the odd thought that the blade resting on his thin gray blanket was capable of killing the two Germans without even piercing their skin.

He wondered whether the person who had delivered the blade to Tommy's bunk room knew the same. He was abruptly filled with suspicions. For a second, he glanced at Lincoln Scott, and thought to himself that the black airman was more right than wrong. The sudden appearance of the knife at this late hour might not be of help. He had the same sensation he'd experienced in the courtroom, when he'd stopped himself from launching questions like bombs at Fenelli. A trap? he wondered to himself.

But a trap for whom?

He shook his head. "Screw it," he said. "I think it's time that I go and have a little talk with our ex-witness," he said. "The one on whom we had so much riding. Maybe it's time to ask him, privately, why he changed his tale."

"I wonder what the hell they promised him," Lincoln Scott said. "What can you bribe a man with here?"

Tommy did not answer this, though he thought it an extremely good question. He reached over and took the knife and wrapped it in one of the few relatively intact pairs of woolen olive drab socks that he owned. Then he stuffed it into the interior pocket of his flight jacket.

"You're taking it?" Lincoln Scott asked. "Why?"

"Because," Tommy replied quietly, "it does occur to me that this is the real murder weapon we're holding, and what's to prevent Major Clark and Captain Townsend from sauntering in here in the next few minutes, just like they did before, and performing one of their little illegal searches and claiming in court tomorrow that we've had the damn thing in our possession for days? That maybe the only person who ever had possession of this knife was Lincoln Scott?"

Neither of the others had seen this possibility. Lincoln Scott smiled sadly. "You've become a suspicious type, Tommy," he said.

"With good reason," Tommy replied. He watched as Scott turned, his shoulders slumped by the weight of what was happening to him, and threw himself onto his bunk, where he rested immobile.

He seems resigned, Tommy thought. Perhaps for the first time, he thought he saw some defeat in the shadows beneath the black flier's eyes, and thought he'd heard failure in the tone of each word he spoke.

He tried not to think about this as he headed out into the early evening, searching for Fenelli, the lying medic, who, he thought, in his own way, might be every bit as dangerous as the knife concealed next to his breast.

The light was fading quickly as Tommy made his way across the camp to the medical services hut. It was that indistinct time of day when the sky only remembers the sunlight and insists on the promise of night. Most of the kriegies were inside already, many engaged in the elaborate and inadequate preparation of dinner. The more conscientious and deliberate a kriegie cook was in assembling the modest foodstuffs and organizing the evening meal, generally spoke to how little there was at that moment to eat. As he passed one hut, Tommy could smell the ubiquitous odor of processed meat being fried. It gnawed at his stomach in typical prisoner-of-war fashion. He desperately would have liked a slice, wet with greasy drippings, on top of a fresh hunk of *kriegsbrot*, yet at the same time he vowed that if he ever got home, he'd never touch a piece of processed meat again.

There was a single light shining in the dirty window of the medical services hut, which he spotted as he came around the corner of Hut 119. For a second, he looked past the buildings, out through the wire to the modest cemetery. He thought that it was a particular cruelty of the Germans that they had allowed the men who died to be buried outside the wire. It made a mockery of every kriegie's yearning for freedom and home. The only men no longer in prison were six feet beneath the ground.

Tommy scowled, took an angry deep breath of the cooling air surrounding him, and jogged up the wooden steps to the small clinic-hut, grabbing at the door, and surging inside.

There was a solitary kriegie sitting behind the desk, in the same position where Tommy had first met Nicholas Fenelli. The man looked up sharply.

"What's the problem, buddy?" he asked. "Gonna be dark soon, need to be in your hut."

Tommy stepped forward, out of the shadows by the door, into the light. He saw the captain's bars on the man's jacket, and so he threw a lazy salute in the officer's direction. He did not recognize the man. But the reverse wasn't true.

"You're Hart, ain't you?"

"Right. I'm looking for—"

"I know who you're looking for. But I was there today, and I heard Colonel MacNamara's orders—"

"You got a name, captain?" Tommy interrupted.

The officer hesitated, shrugged, then replied, "Sure. Carson. Like the scout." He held out a hand, and Tommy shook it.

"Okay, Captain Carson, let me try again. Where's Fenelli?"

"Not here. And he has orders not to speak with you or anyone else. And you have orders not to try to talk to him."

"You been in the bag long, captain? I don't recognize you."

"Couple of months. Came in right before Scott, actually."

"Okay then, captain, let me clue you on something. We may still be in the army, and we may still have uniforms and salute and call everybody by their rank and all, but you know what? It ain't the same thing. Now, where's Fenelli?"

Carson shook his head.

"He was moved out. They told me if you came looking not to tell you."

"I can go from hut to hut . . ."

"And maybe get shot by some goon in the towers for your troubles."

Tommy nodded. The captain was right. There was no way, without being told where to go, for Tommy to go from room to room, searching for Fenelli. Not in the short amount of evening left before the lights went out.

"You know where he is?"

The captain shook his head.

"This *they* who told you what to say if I came looking, this would be Major Clark and Captain Townsend, right?"

The man hesitated, which of course told Tommy the answer. Then Captain Carson shrugged. "Yeah," he said. "It was them. And they're the ones that helped Fenelli take his stuff. And they told me I was gonna have to help Fenelli in here, after the trial's over and things get back to normal. That's what they said. Back to normal."

"So you're going to be helping Fenelli? You got any experience? I mean, with medical problems."

"My old man was a country doctor. He ran a little clinic where I used to work, summers. And I was premed at the University of Wisconsin, so I guess I'm as qualified as anybody else. You know, I wonder why there aren't any real doctors here. I mean, you can find just about any other type of profession. . . ."

"Maybe the doctors are smart enough not to go up in a B-17. . . ."

"Or a Thunderbolt. Like I wasn't." Carson smiled. "You know, Hart, I don't want to come across like such a hard case. If I knew, I'd tell you. Hell, I don't even think they told Fenelli where they were moving him. And he knew you'd be coming around tonight, and so he told me to tell you he was goddamn sorry about today. . . ." Carson looked around for a moment, just double-checking to make sure the two men were alone. "And he left a note. You got to understand, Hart, those two guys were keeping a pretty close eye on Fenelli. Sitting on him pretty good. I didn't get the impression he was all that happy to be hustled off to some new hut. And he sure wasn't all that happy with the testimony today in court, but he wasn't talking about it one way or the other, especially with me. But he managed to scribble down something and slip it aside. . . ." Carson was reaching into his pocket, as he spoke. He removed a torn scrap of paper, folded twice. He handed it to Tommy. "I didn't read it," Carson said.

Tommy nodded, unfolded the scrap, and read:

Sorry, Hart. Trader Vic was right about one thing: Everything in this damn place is a deal. Good deal for some, maybe a bad deal for others. Hope you make it home in one piece. After all this is finished, you ever get to Cleveland, look me up so I can apologize properly.

He did not sign the note. It was written in a hasty, scribbled script, in thick dark pencil. Tommy read it through three times, memorizing it word for word.

"Fenelli said to tell you to burn that, after you got it," Carson said.

Tommy nodded. "What has Fenelli told you? About this place. The clinic, I mean."

The captain shrugged his shoulders in exaggerated fashion. "Since I got here, all he does is complain. He's damn fed up with never being able to really help no one, because the Krauts steal the medical supplies. He said the day he gets to retire from this job and get back to his reading and real studying would be the best day of his life. That's what he said you've been up to, right, Hart? Reading those law books. He told me to be smart and do the same. Get some medical texts and start studying. We got plenty of free time, right?"

"That's the only thing we do seem to have enough of," Tommy said.

Night's cold and dark had seized the camp as Tommy hurried beneath the encroaching gray-black skies. The last murky light streaked across the western horizon. There were only a few other stragglers making their way to their bunk rooms, and, like Tommy, they had their hats pulled down on their heads, their collars turned up against the few breaths of chilly wind that swirled in the alleyways between the huts. Everyone walked fast, eager to get inside before the grip of night tightened completely. His route from the medical services hut took him out to the main assembly area, now vacant, swept dry by the falling temperatures. To his left, he saw that the last of the moon, a single silver sliver, was just visible over the line of trees beyond the wire. He wished he could take a moment, wait for the stars to begin to blink and shine, injecting familiarity and the odd sense of companionship they gave him, into his troubled imagination.

But instead, as the few other men still abroad in the camp hurried past him, he kept his pace quick and his head down. As he approached the doorway to Hut 101, he tossed a single glance back over his shoulder, toward the main gate. What he saw made him hesitate.

There was a single electric light, beneath a tin shade, by the gate. In the weak inverted cone of light it shed, Tommy spotted the unmistakable form of Fritz Number One, lighting up a cigarette. He guessed the ferret was about to go off-duty.

Tommy stopped sharply.

Seeing the ferret, even that close to the end of the day, wasn't all that unusual. The ferrets were always alert to the final comings and goings of the camp, afraid that some clandestine meetings were taking place just beyond their sight under cover of darkness. In this, of course, they were absolutely correct. Unable to detect, of course, but correct nonetheless.

Tommy peered around for a moment, and saw that he was virtually alone, save for a distant figure or two, hurrying toward huts on the opposite side of the compound. And in that second, he made a sudden decision he knew was undoubtedly rash.

He abruptly turned away from the door to Hut 101, and quickly trotted across the compound assembly area, his boots making dull thudding noises against the packed dirt. When he was twenty yards away from the main gate, Fritz Number One spotted the movement coming toward him, and pivoted to face Tommy. In the growing dark, Tommy was anonymous, just a dark form moving rapidly, and he saw some mingled alarm and inquisitiveness on the ferret's face, almost as if he were frightened by the kriegie-apparition coming through the first gloom of night in his direction.

"Fritz!" Tommy said briskly, not hiding his voice. "Come here."

The German stepped out of the light, threw a fast glance around himself, determining that no one else was close by, and then paced forward quickly.

"Mr. Hart! What is it? You should be in your hut."

Tommy reached inside his flight jacket. "Got a present for you, Fritz," he said sharply.

The ferret stepped closer, still wary. "A present? I do not understand. . . ."

Tommy reached inside his jacket, and extracted the ceremonial dagger from his socks. "I need these," he said, holding up the socks. "But you need this."

With that, he tossed the knife into the dirt at the German's feet. Fritz Number One stared down at the knife for a second, a look of astonishment on his face. Then he reached down and grabbed for it.

"You can thank me some other time," Tommy said, turning as Fritz Number One rose up, grinning widely. "And you can be assured I'll ask for something, someday. Something big."

He did not wait for the German to reply; instead he jogged deliberately back across the yard, not turning even when he reached the entrance to Hut 101, and not hesitating until he'd slammed the door shut behind him, hoping that he had just done the right thing, but not at all sure that he had.

None of the trio of men in the bunk room in Hut 101 slept well that night, all of them suffering from nightmares that pitched them sweatily from their reveries, waking them to the deep midnights of imprisonment more than once. No steady breathing, no light snoring, no real rest throughout the long Bavarian night. None of the three spoke. Instead, each man awakened sharply, and lay alone with his thoughts and terrors, fears and angers, unable to calm himself with the usual soft, safe, and familiar visions of home. Tommy believed, as he lay awake, that it was probably worst for Scott. Hugh, like Tommy, only faced failure and frustration. Defeat for them was psychological. For Lincoln Scott it was all the same, and one step more. Perhaps a fatal step.

Tommy twitched and shivered beneath his blanket. For a moment or two, he wondered if he could ever continue with the law if, on the first occasion he stepped to the bar, he lost an innocent man to a firing squad. He breathed in slowly. He understood in the darkness of the bunk room that all the odds stacked against them, the cheating and lies that had been arrayed against the black flier, every aspect of the case that was so infuriating, that if he allowed all those evils to win and take Scott's life, that he would never be able to stand up in any other courtroom and defend a man or an idea again.

He hated this thought, and tossed about in the bunk, trying to persuade himself that he was simply being naive and juvenile, and that a more experienced attorney, like Phillip Pryce, would be able to accept defeats with the same equanimity as victories. But he also understood, deep within the same difficult crevasses of his heart, that he wasn't like his friend and mentor, and that a loss in this trial would be his first and only loss.

He thought it a terrible thing to be trapped, imprisoned behind the rows of barbed wire, and still be standing at a crossroads. He abruptly found his imagination crowded by the ghosts of his old bomber crew. The men of the *Lovely Lydia* were in the room with him, silent, almost reproachful. He understood that he was on that flight with really a single task that they all counted on him for: to find them the safe route home. He had not done it for them.

In a funny way, he thought the odds of success about the same for the *Lovely Lydia*, when it had turned and started its bombing run directly into every gun in the convoy, and Lincoln Scott, imprisoned by his country's enemies, only to find that arrayed against him were the men who should have been his friends.

Tommy put his head back, his eyes open and staring up at the ceiling, almost as if he could look straight through the wooden planks and tin roof, to the sky and the stars.

Who knows the truth about the murder of Trader Vic? he asked himself. Someone does, but who? He took another deep breath and continued to argue in his mind all the issues, over and over again, back and forth. He thought of what Lincoln Scott had said earlier and repeatedly: No one in the camp was really willing to help.

Tommy took a sharp breath, as an idea grabbed hold of him. It was something so obvious, he wondered why he hadn't thought of it earlier. And for perhaps the first time that night, he managed a small grin.

The men of Hut 101 awakened to the harsh noise of whistles and German shouts of *"Raus! Raus!"* punctuated by pounding against the wooden doors. They lurched from their beds as they had on so many mornings, pulling on their clothing and double-timing through the central corridor of the hut, heading to the morning *Appell*. But as they exited the doors to the barracks, they were greeted with the unusual sight of a squad of gray-clad German soldiers standing in formation in front of the hut, perhaps twenty men, armed with rifles. A thick-chested *Feldwebel* was at the foot of the stairs, a scowl across his face, directing traffic like a surly cop.

"You men, in Hut 101, assemble here! *Raus!* Be quick! No one to go to *Appell*!" The *Feldwebel* motioned to a pair of *Hundführers* who snatched back the chains of their snarling dogs, making the animals leap in excitement, growling and barking.

"What the hell's going on?" Scott asked beneath his breath, as he stood beside Tommy in the midst of the gathered men from Hut 101.

"I know," Hugh answered for him. "It's a bloody hut search. What the hell do the Krauts think they're going to find? Another damn waste of all our time!" Hugh blurted out this last sentiment loudly, directing it at the German sergeant, who was struggling to get the kriegies into well-dressed lines. "Hey, Adolf! Better make sure you check the privy! Someone might be swimming to freedom!" The other men from Hut 101 burst into laughter and a couple of fliers applauded the Canadian's sense of humor.

"Quiet!" the *Feldwebel* shouted. "No talking! At attention!"

Tommy pivoted about as best he could, and as he looked, he saw Hauptmann Visser, accompanied by an ashen-faced

Fritz Number One, emerge from the rear of the formation of German soldiers.

The *Feldwebel* spoke in German, and one of the kriegies softly translated, the words being passed down the rows of men.

"Prisoners of Hut 101 all present and accounted for, *Hauptmann!*"

"Good," Visser said. He gestured to Fritz Number One. "Begin the search."

Fritz barked out an order, and half the squad of goons peeled off and tramped into the hut. After a moment, both Fritz and Visser followed them.

"What're they really searching for?" Scott whispered.

"Tunnels. Dirt. Radios. Contraband. Anything out of the ordinary."

From inside the hut, there was the sound of tramping feet and deep thuds and cracks, as men went from room to room.

"They ever find anything?"

"Not usually," Hugh replied. He smiled. "Krauts don't really know how to perform a proper search," he said. "Not like a policeman. Usually they just tear up stuff, make a damn mess of things, and come away angry. Happens all the time."

"Why did they pick this hut? This morning?"

"Real good questions," Hugh replied.

Real good questions, Tommy repeated to himself.

After a few minutes, as the kriegies remained in their almost orderly rows, they saw German soldiers begin to exit the hut. The goons came out singly or in pairs, and almost all were empty-handed, grinning sheepishly, shrugging, and shaking their heads. Tommy noticed that most of the squad of goons were old, many of them nearly as old as Phillip Pryce had been. The others, of course, were impossibly young, barely into their teens, with uniforms they didn't quite fit into hanging poorly from their young limbs. After a few more seconds, there was a shout of excitement from deep within the hut. A moment passed, and then one man emerged, grinning, holding a makeshift radio that had been concealed in an empty coffee tin. The German held this up high, a look of delight on his wrinkled, old man's face. Right behind him was another goon, barely a third the older man's age. He, too, was smiling and excited. From several rows behind him, Tommy heard an airman mutter, "Ahh, goddamn it! They got my radio! Son of a gun! I traded three cartons of smokes for that!"

Perhaps the last to emerge from the hut were Fritz Number One and Heinrich Visser. The one-armed German officer scowled at Tommy. With his only hand, he gestured at Tommy, Hugh, and Lincoln Scott, pointing a sharp index finger at each man. Visser did not see Fritz Number One, standing just to his side and behind him, just shake his head slightly back and forth.

"You three!" he said loudly. "Step forward!"

Wordlessly, the three men stepped away from the formation.

"Search these three! Immediately!" Visser ordered.

Tommy raised his hands above his head, and one of the German goons started to pat him down. The same was being done to Lincoln Scott and Hugh Renaday, who laughed when he was touched.

"Hey!" Hugh said, eye to eye with Visser, "*Hauptmann,* tell your goons not to be quite so friendly and a little less familiar. They tickle!"

Visser locked eyes with the Canadian humorlessly. He said nothing. Then, after a second, he turned to the soldier who had patted Tommy down.

"*Nein, Herr Hauptmann,*" the goon said, rising and saluting.

Visser nodded. He stepped closer to Tommy, staring at him. "Where is your evidence, lieutenant?"

Tommy did not reply.

"You have something that belongs to me," he said. "I want it returned."

"You're mistaken, *Hauptmann.*"

"Something you perhaps intended to use this morning at the trial."

"You're still mistaken, *Hauptmann.*"

The German stepped back. He seemed to consider what he was about to say, then opened his mouth slowly, only to be interrupted by a shout from the rear.

"What is going on!"

All the men turned, and saw that Commandant Von Reiter, with both Colonel MacNamara and Major Clark at his side, trailed by his usual coterie of bustling adjutants, was hurrying forward, quick-marching past the squad of soldiers, who instantly snapped to rigid attention.

Von Reiter stopped in front of the gathered men. His face was slightly flushed and the riding crop he liked to carry danced nervously in his hand.

"I ordered no search of this hut!" he said loudly. "What is going on!"

Heinrich Visser snapped his heels together, the clicking of his boots resounding through the morning damp. "I ordered the search, *Herr Oberst*. I most recently came into information to believe that contraband was present here! And so I ordered the immediate search, upon my own initiative!"

Von Reiter looked coldly at Visser.

"Ah," he said slowly. "This was your idea. And you did not think I should be informed?"

"I thought it necessary to move quickly, *Herr Oberst*. I fully intended to keep you abreast of developments."

Von Reiter narrowed his look. "I'm sure. And did you find contraband? Or any other signs of forbidden activities?"

"Yes, *Herr Oberst*!" Visser answered sharply. "An illegal radio. Concealed in an empty coffee tin! Expressly against all regulations and your direct orders!"

The elderly goon holding the radio stepped forward at a nod from Visser, holding the radio out toward the camp commandant.

Von Reiter smiled nastily. "Very good, *Hauptmann*." He turned to MacNamara and Clark. "Radios are *verboten*! You know this. You must control your men!"

MacNamara didn't reply, and Von Reiter turned back to Visser.

"And what other critical items have you uncovered in your search, *Hauptmann*? What else has been found to justify this disruption in the camp routine?"

"That is all, *Herr Oberst*."

Von Reiter nodded.

"This is a most fortunate radio for you, *Hauptmann*," he said, much more quietly than before. Von Reiter smiled, with all the affection that an alligator musters when confronting an animal that has strayed a little too close to the water's edge, but still remains just beyond the beast's lunge and snapping jaws. Then he turned to Tommy.

"Ah, Mr. Hart. The young defender. Is it not your opportunity this morning? Or so I am reliably informed."

"It is, *Herr Oberst*."

"Excellent. Duties permitting, I will attempt to enjoy some of your performance."

"We are already delayed," Colonel MacNamara interrupted. "Can we please get on with the trial? I've warned you, commandant, that passions are running high in the camp, and the men are eager for answers! They demand this matter be brought to a satisfactory conclusion!"

Von Reiter nodded. "Americans are always in a hurry for answers to all their questions, colonel. We Germans are much more accustomed to accepting merely what we are told."

"That's your problem," MacNamara said crisply. "Now, can we please get on with business?"

"Of course," Von Reiter replied. "I believe the *Hauptmann* has finished here. Yes?"

Visser shrugged. He did little to conceal the frustration within him. Tommy knew right then that he'd been searching for the murder weapon. Someone had told him what hut to look inside, and probably told him which of the barracks rooms to search personally. Tommy thought all this most intriguing, and a little amusing, as he saw the one-armed German unable to hide his disappointment and anger, because what he wanted to find remained hidden from him. Tommy threw quick glances at Clark and MacNamara, wondering if they, too, were surprised by the search's lack of success, but he could read nothing from their faces, so he was unsure what to conclude. But he did know that someone in the camp was surprised that Heinrich Visser did not have the murder weapon in his hand right at this moment, and that the German hadn't already begun to compose the memo for his Gestapo supervisors in Berlin that very well might have translated into the arrests of both the commandant and the ferret. Tommy took note that these two men had marched off toward the assembly area together, seemingly engaged in close conversation.

* * *

Once again, Lieutenant Nicholas Fenelli made his way to the witness chair through the overcrowded aisles and makeshift pews crammed with kriegies. As he passed by, Tommy could hear voices trailing after him, so that the courtroom bubbled with soft conversation, causing the Senior American Officer at the head of the theater to bang his gavel hard. Fenelli had not shaved that morning; his chin was stained with dark stubble. His uniform seemed rumpled and haphazardly collected. There were some circles under his eyes from lack of sleep, and he looked to Tommy like a man unfamiliar with lying, but oddly committed to it all the same.

MacNamara launched into the usual speech, reminding Fenelli he remained under oath, and then gestured to Tommy to get started.

Tommy rose at the defense table. He could see the medic twisting in his seat momentarily, then finally squaring his shoulders, awaiting the onslaught.

"Lieutenant . . ." Tommy began slowly, his voice steady, "do you recall our conversation shortly after Mr. Scott's arrest in this matter?"

"Yes sir."

"And do you recall telling me, on that occasion, that you believed the murder was performed by a man situated behind Captain Bedford, wielding a narrow, extremely sharp knife? The type of knife one would not usually find in this camp?"

"Yes sir."

"I didn't offer you anything for that opinion, did I?"

"No. You didn't."

"And I was not able to show you that knife, was I?"

"No."

Tommy turned away, back toward the defense table. He reached down to his law books and papers, exaggerating every movement as theatrically as possible. To his side, he was aware that both Townsend and Clark had leaned forward expectantly, and he knew right then that this was a moment that they'd anticipated. He suspected that Visser, too, in his observer's seat across the room, and all the members of the tribunal, as well, were eagerly awaiting his next motion. He spun about, quickly, holding both empty hands out wide.

"But now, you are unsure of those opinions, would that be correct to say?"

Fenelli stopped, looked at both of Tommy's hands, knit his brows for an instant, then nodded. "No. That would be right. I guess."

Tommy let a pause fill the courtroom air, before continuing.

"You're not a murder expert, are you, lieutenant?"

"No. I am not. That's what I told them." He pointed over at the prosecution.

"Back in the States, this murder would have been investigated by professional homicide detectives, correct? Who would have been assisted in collecting evidence by specially trained crime scene analysts, true? And the autopsy on Trader Vic would have been performed by a competent, experienced forensic pathologist, isn't that true, as well?"

Fenelli hesitated, a look of uncertainty on his face, almost as if he'd been told to expect one thing from Tommy and was getting something different. In this hesitation, Captain Townsend rose, pushing back from the prosecution table slowly. Colonel MacNamara looked in his direction.

"Do you have an objection, captain?" he asked.

"Well, perhaps, sir," Townsend said slowly, hiding the hesitation in his voice unsuccessfully. "I simply wonder where the lieutenant is going with this line of questions. What might have been done in this case, back in the States, is not wholly relevant to the issues here today. This is a war, and our circumstances are totally extraordinary. . . ."

MacNamara nodded, and looked over at Tommy.

"These questions, Mr. Hart . . ."

"If I might have some small leeway, Your Honor. It will become clear in a moment."

"Rapidly, I trust."

Tommy smiled, looked over at Fenelli, and said, "So, your answer would be . . ."

Fenelli shrugged. "You're correct, Lieutenant Hart. Things would be different back in the States. Real experts would have been all over this case."

"Thank you," Tommy said quickly, giving a small nod to

the mortuary man. "No further questions of this witness, Your Honor."

Fenelli's face instantly creased into a surprised grin. With a quizzical look, MacNamara gazed down at Tommy. "Nothing further?" he asked.

"Nope." Tommy made a sweeping gesture toward Fenelli. "The witness can be excused."

As Fenelli rose to his feet, he scrutinized the Senior American Officer and the two other members of the tribunal. MacNamara spoke out: "Just a second, lieutenant. Anything else from the prosecution?"

Townsend hesitated, then shook his head. He, too, wore a look of some confusion.

"No sir. At this point, the prosecution rests."

"The witness is excused."

"Yes sir!" Fenelli said, grinning. "I'm outta here!"

This comment brought a smattering of laughter from the kriegies in the audience, and once again MacNamara resorted to the gavel. Fenelli crossed the room swiftly, tossing a single glance at Tommy that he took to be gratitude. Behind him, the room quieted.

MacNamara spoke first. "That's it from the prosecution?" he demanded of Townsend.

"Yes sir. As I said, at this point we rest our case."

The Senior American Officer turned to Tommy Hart. "You did not make an opening statement. Did you wish to do so now?"

Tommy smiled. "Yes sir. Briefly, sir . . ."

"That would be good."

Tommy coughed, and spoke loudly. "I would take this opportunity to remind the members of the tribunal, the prosecution, and all the men of Stalag Luft Thirteen that Lincoln Scott stands here today only accused of this murder. Our Constitution guarantees that until the prosecution proves beyond and to the exclusion of all reasonable doubts, he is cloaked in innocence. . . ."

Walker Townsend rose, interrupting Tommy.

"Sir, isn't it a little late for a lesson in civics?"

MacNamara nodded. "Your statement, lieutenant—"

Tommy cut him off. "But that is it, Your Honor. The defense is ready to proceed."

MacNamara's left eyebrow shot up in modest surprise and he let out a small sigh of relief. "Very good," he said. "We can continue on schedule. Do you intend to call Lieutenant Scott to the stand now?"

Tommy paused and shook his head.

"No sir."

There was a moment's quiet, and MacNamara stared at Tommy.

"You do not?"

"Correct, sir. Not at this point."

Both Townsend and Clark had risen again, but they did not speak.

"Well," Colonel MacNamara asked sharply, "do you have some other witness? We were all expecting Lieutenant Scott on the stand at this juncture."

"That's what I thought, colonel," Tommy replied with a smile. His eyes lit up, as if amused, which, in a superficial way, he was. But deep within his heart he felt nothing except a cold and single-minded, murderous savagery of his own, because, for the very first time in the trial, he felt he was about to deliver a stroke that had not been anticipated, either by the prosecution or the judges, and this was to him both raw and delicious. He knew that everyone in the courtroom believed that the prosecution had left him with nothing to present except an angry, accused man's shaky protests of innocence.

"Well then, who?" MacNamara demanded.

"No sir. The defense will not be calling Lieutenant Scott. Not at this point."

Tommy pivoted sharply, and pointed to the corner of the courtroom-theater. He shouted out his words.

"At this point, the defense calls Luftwaffe Hauptmann Heinrich Visser to the witness stand!"

Then Tommy folded his arms across his chest, satisfaction beating in his chest, appearing to be an island of calm in a courtroom suddenly buffeted by the winds of wildly excited voices.

Chapter Fifteen

AN OFFICER AND
A MAN OF HONOR

Tommy took some little satisfaction in the uproar that erupted in the courtroom behind where he stood. Everyone seemed to have an opinion, and the immediate need to blurt it out loudly. Voices cascaded around him, mingling curiosity, anger, and excitement. It took some determined gaveling by Colonel MacNamara to get the overflow theater crowd of kriegies to quiet down. Behind him, arcing through the jammed throngs of airmen, was a fascination like electricity. If the trial of Lincoln Scott for the murder of Vincent Bedford was already the best show in town, in one single stroke, Tommy had made it even more compelling, especially to the hundreds of men crippled by the boredom and anxiety of their imprisonment.

By the tenth time MacNamara had shouted "Order!" the men quieted enough for the proceedings to continue. Walker Townsend was already on his feet, gesturing widely with his arms. So was Major Clark, whose usually red face was now nearly crimson, and Tommy thought he looked like a man on the verge of exploding.

"Your Honor!" Townsend shouted. "This is highly irregular!"

MacNamara crashed the gavel down again, even though the room had grown silent enough to continue.

"We would most strenuously protest!" the captain from Virginia persisted. "To call a member of an enemy force to the stand in the midst of an American trial is outrageous!"

Tommy remained quiet for a moment, waiting for MacNamara to bang his gavel once again, which is what the SAO did, finally turning toward the defense. Tommy took a single step forward, this motion alone doing more to quiet the room behind him than all the hammering from the head of the tribunal. Kriegies hushed each other and craned forward.

"Colonel," Tommy began slowly, "the argument that this request is irregular is silly. This entire proceeding is irregular! Captain Townsend knows that, and the prosecution has already benefited from the loosening of the ordinary rules governing a military court of justice. He protests simply because he has been caught unprepared. At the beginning of this trial, you promised both defense and prosecution that there would be considerable leeway given both sides in order to find the truth! It was also promised that the defense could call *anyone* who might assist in establishing innocence. I would merely remind the court of those promises. And remind the court as well, that we are here under unique and special circumstances, and that it is important for all to see the elemental fairness of our democratically applied system of justice. Especially the enemy."

He crossed his arms again, with the thought that his little speech would have been better had a brass band been playing "America the Beautiful" in the background, and would have the dual effect of infuriating MacNamara and instantly cementing him into a position where Tommy could not be turned down. He stared directly at the Senior American Officer, doing little to hide the satisfied smirk that he wore.

"Lieutenant," MacNamara responded coldly, "you do not have to remind the tribunal of their wartime duties and responsibilities."

"I'm glad to hear that, Your Honor. Delighted to hear that." Tommy knew he was dancing dangerously close to censure.

"Your Honor," Walker Townsend said angrily, "I still do not see how this court can permit an officer of an enemy army to testify! I would argue that you could never be sure anything he might say would be truthful!"

As soon as he spoke, Townsend appeared stricken by the words that had tumbled from his mouth. Too late he saw the mistake in the claim he made. In one sentence, he'd insulted two men.

"The court is more than capable of determining the truth-fulness of any witness, captain, regardless of where they come from, and where their allegiances might rest," MacNa-mara replied dryly, far more caustically than he had before when making the same comment.

Tommy snuck a glance over at Heinrich Visser. The German was standing. His own face was pale, and his jaw tight. His eyes had narrowed, but he was glaring at Walker Townsend, not at Tommy. He looked like a man who had just been slapped across the cheek by a rival.

This, Tommy had half-expected. Visser was probably infu-riated at being called to the stand. But, Tommy suspected, he was undoubtedly far more outraged at having his pristine Nazi integrity challenged. Nothing was more irritating than hearing oneself called a liar before one has a chance to utter a single word.

MacNamara rubbed his chin and nose once, then turned toward the one-armed German. *"Hauptmann,"* he said slowly, "I am inclined to allow this. Are you willing to take the stand?"

Visser hesitated. Tommy could see him measuring as many factors as possible in those seconds. He began to open his mouth to reply, when there was a sudden, booming voice from the rear of the theater.

"The *Hauptmann* will certainly testify, colonel!"

Heads pivoted in unison to see Commandant Von Reiter standing in the doorway. He stepped forward, his polished black riding boots striking against the wooden plank flooring like so many pistol reports.

Von Reiter arrived in the front of the courtroom, clicked his heels together and made a small salute and bow, simulta-neously. "Of course, colonel," he said briskly, "the *Haupt-mann* will be restricted from dispensing any critical military information, you understand? And he will not be able to an-swer questions that might compromise war secrets. But, as to his understanding of this crime, why, I would think his exper-tise would be most helpful for the court in determining the truth of this most unfortunate event!"

Von Reiter half-turned, nodding toward Visser, before he added: "And, colonel, I can personally attest to his integrity!

Hauptmann Visser is a highly decorated officer! He is a man of complete honor and commands utter respect from his subordinates! Please, be so kind as to swear him in promptly."

Visser kept a flat, poker face, and stepped forward slowly and clearly reluctantly, even more so, Tommy imagined, because he now had Von Reiter's blessing and he was undoubtedly assessing how the commandant might seize some political advantage from his testifying. He sharply saluted his commanding officer, turned to Colonel MacNamara, and said, "I am prepared, colonel." The Senior American Officer shoved the Bible toward him, and motioned toward the witness chair.

"Sir," Captain Townsend tried one last time, "again, I protest . . ."

MacNamara scowled and shook his head. "Here is your witness, Lieutenant Hart. Let's see what you make of him."

Tommy nodded in response to that particular challenge. He noticed a small malevolent grin on Von Reiter's face as the camp commandant took up a position in a seat by a window, sitting on the edge of the chair and leaning forward, just like the prisoners in the camp, eager to hear every word. Then Tommy turned, and faced Visser. For a moment, he tried to reconnoiter the German's unspoken language, trying to read the man in the tilt of his head, the lingering narrowing of his eyes, the set of his jaw, and the way he crossed his legs. Visser was a man of deep hatreds and angers, Tommy thought. The problem Tommy faced was sorting through them all and finding the right ones to help Lincoln Scott—although he understood, simply from the way Visser tossed a single furious glance over at Townsend, that the prosecution, by questioning his integrity, had already helped Tommy on the path to Visser's core.

Tommy cleared his throat. "Just for the official record, *Hauptmann,* would you give us your full name and rank."

"Hauptmann Heinrich Albert Visser. I am currently a captain in the Luftwaffe, recently assigned to Allied prisoner-of-war airman's camp thirteen."

"Your duties here would include administration?"

"Yes."

"And security?"

Visser hesitated, then he nodded. "Of course. We are all charged with that duty, lieutenant."

Yes, Tommy thought, but you more than the others. He did not follow this thought out loud.

Visser kept his voice even, steady, and loud enough to carry through the now-hushed crowd.

"And where did you acquire your command of English?"

Visser paused again, shrugged slightly, and replied, "From the age of six until the age of fifteen I lived in Milwaukee, Wisconsin, in the home of my uncle. He was a shopkeeper. When his business failed during the Depression, the entire family returned to Germany, where I completed my studies, continuing to polish my English."

"So you left America when?"

"In 1932. There was nothing there for my family and myself. And great events were taking place in our own nation, of which we were eager to become part."

Tommy nodded. He could easily imagine what those events were—brownshirts, book burnings, and thuggery. For a moment, he eyed Visser carefully. He knew from Fritz Number One that Visser's father was already a Nazi party member when the teenager returned to Germany. School and the Hitler Youth had probably been his immediate legacy. Tommy warned himself to tread lightly until he'd managed to extract from Visser what he needed. But his next question was neither light nor careful.

"How did you lose your arm, *Hauptmann*?"

Visser's face seemed immobile, frozen, as if the ice he wore in his eyes was the best way to conceal the fury that smoked beneath the surface.

"Near the coast of France in 1939," he said stiffly.

"A Spitfire?"

Visser cracked a small, cruel smile.

"The British Spitfire is a single-engine fighter powered by a Rolls-Royce Merlin engine capable of speeds in excess of three hundred miles per hour. It is armed with eight sequentially firing fifty-caliber machine guns, four mounted in each wing. One of these formidable planes managed to surprise me while I was flying routine escort duty. A most unfortunate encounter, although I did manage to parachute to safety. My arm, however, was shredded by a bullet and removed at a nearby hospital."

"And so, flying was no longer an option."

Visser laughed although there was no joke. "It would seem that way, lieutenant."

"But then, in 1939, you were unwilling to give up your career in the military. Certainly not at that point, when Germany's successes were substantial."

"Our successes, as you call them, were the envy of the world."

"And you did not want to retire, despite your wound, true? You were young, you were ambitious, and you wanted to continue to be a part of this greatness."

The German took a moment to reply, considering his words first. "This is true," he said after a second or two passed. "I did not want to be passed over. I was young, and despite my wound, still strong. Strong both physically and in my heart, lieutenant. There was much I believed I could contribute."

"And so, you were retrained, were you not?"

Again, Visser hesitated. "I suppose there is no harm in saying yes. I was given new training and new duties."

"This new training, it didn't have anything to do with flying a fighter, did it?"

Visser smiled. He shook his head. "No. It did not, lieutenant."

"You were trained in counterintelligence operations, true?"

"No, this I will not answer."

"Well," Tommy said carefully, "did you have the opportunity to study modern police techniques and tactics?"

Again Visser paused, thinking before replying. "I had this opportunity."

"And you gained this expertise?"

"I have been well-educated, lieutenant. I have always finished any schooling—whether it was flight school, studying languages, or forensic techniques—at the top of my class. I now take on whatever new responsibilities are defined by my superior officers, to the best of my abilities."

"And one of those responsibilities was the investigation

of this matter that brings us here. The murder of Captain Bedford."

"That is obvious, lieutenant."

"Why was the murder of an Allied officer in a prisoner-of-war camp of any importance to the German authorities whatsoever? Why did your superiors care in the slightest?"

Visser hesitated a moment. "I will not answer this question," he replied.

A murmur of voices raced through the courtroom.

"Why won't you answer?" Tommy demanded.

"This would be a matter of security, lieutenant. I will say no more."

Tommy crossed his arms, trying to think of another route to the answer, but was unable to think of one rapidly. Inwardly he took note of a single, pulsating concept: If the murder of Trader Vic weren't somehow important to the Germans, they would never have sent a man such as Visser to the camp.

"Lieutenant," Colonel MacNamara said harshly, "please get on with your questioning of this witness!"

Tommy nodded, wondering also what the big hurry was, and asked: "So, of all the men you've heard from the witness stand, and all the men involved in this case to this point, isn't it fair to say that you are the only one who has actually been trained in criminal investigations and procedures? The only one so trained who actually examined Trader Vic's body and the crime scene surrounding it? You are the only true expert to investigate this crime?"

"Objection!" Walker Townsend cried out.

"Overruled!" MacNamara answered, just as swiftly. "You may answer, *Hauptmann*!"

"Well, lieutenant," Visser replied slowly, "your compatriot, Flying Officer Renaday, has some limited understanding and skills based on his primitive experiences in a rural police force. Wing Commander Pryce, who is no longer with us, had considerable knowledge on these subjects. It would appear that Captain Townsend, as well, is well educated on these procedures." The German could not hide his grin, as he sent a singular thrust toward the prosecution: "Which only makes me very suspicious as to why he would try to devise such a ludicrous and ridiculous scenario for this murder, as he has. . . ."

Townsend slammed both hands down on the prosecution table as he threw himself to his feet, shouting, "Objection! Objection! Objection!" as he rose. Visser stopped speaking, wearing a mocking smile of false politeness on his face, as Townsend furiously responded. Behind Tommy, the kriegies once again burst into babbling discussions, dozens of voices competing at once.

Banging away, Colonel MacNamara managed to regain order in the courtroom. He turned to Hauptmann Visser and coldly said, "*Hauptmann,* it would help matters considerably were you to merely answer the questions you are asked without any further characterizations."

"Of course, *Herr* Colonel," the German responded. "Let me rephrase my statement: My examination of the crime scene and the evidence collected to this point suggest a different series of events from those claimed here. Is that preferable, Your Honor? I should, perhaps, eliminate the words *ludicrous* and *ridiculous*?" Visser managed to infect his words with distaste.

"Yes," MacNamara answered. "Precisely." It seemed to Tommy that the hatred in the courtroom was almost palpable. Best deal with that right away, he thought to himself.

He cleared his throat harshly. "Let me get something straight, let's everybody get something straight, before we go on about this case, *Hauptmann.* You hate us, correct?"

Visser smiled. "I beg your pardon?"

"Us," Tommy said, sweeping his arm to indicate the assembled kriegies. "You hate us, without knowing us. Merely because we're American. Or English. Or any Allied airman. You hate me. You hate Captain Townsend and Flying Officer Renaday and Colonel MacNamara and every last one of us sitting in the audience. Is this not true, *Hauptmann*?"

Visser hesitated, shrugged, then nodded.

"You are the enemy. One should always hate the enemies of the fatherland."

Tommy took a deep breath.

"That's too easy an answer, *Hauptmann.* That sounds like a

schoolboy's memorized response. Your hatred seems somewhat greater."

Again Visser paused, measuring his words carefully, doling them out in an even, hard-edged, and cold voice.

"No one who has been wounded, as I have, who has seen his family—mother, father, sisters—killed by terror-bombing, as I have, who has seen his friends die, as I have, and who can remember all the hypocrisy and lies spoken by your nation, can avoid feelings of anger and hatred, lieutenant. Does that answer your question perhaps better?"

Visser's response was as frozen as winter rain. Each word pelted the men in the audience, because there were aspects of everything he said that they, too, felt. In that second, Visser managed to remind everyone that outside the wire the world was gathered in homicidal rage, and they all felt stricken that they were no longer taking part in it.

"It must be hard for you," Tommy asked slowly, "to be stuck here in charge of keeping men alive whom you would rather see killed."

Visser's lip curled in a small, nasty smile.

"This is an oversimplification, Lieutenant Hart. But true."

"So if I were to die tomorrow, or Captain Townsend or Colonel MacNamara or any of the men here at Stalag Luft Thirteen, this would please you?"

Visser's smile did not so much as budge a millimeter, as he replied, "That is almost entirely true, Mr. Hart."

Tommy stopped, paused, then asked, "Almost entirely?"

Visser nodded. "The sole exception, Mr. Hart, of course, would be your client. The *Schwarze* airman, Scott. Of him, I do not care one way or the other."

This comment took Tommy slightly off-guard. He asked his next question rather foolishly, before first considering it.

"Why is that?"

Visser lifted his shoulders slightly, almost as if with that gesture he was taking the time to install the mocking tone into his voice: "We do not consider the Negro to be human," he said calmly, staring directly at Lincoln Scott as he spoke. "The rest of you, yes, you are the enemy. He, on the other hand, is merely a mercenary beast employed by your air corps, lieutenant. No different from a *Hundführer*'s dog patrolling the camp wire. One may fear that dog, lieutenant, perhaps even respect it for its teeth and claws and devotion to its master. But it remains little more than a trained beast."

Tommy did not have to turn around to see Lincoln Scott stiffen his back and clench his fists. He hoped the black airman would manage to keep his own fury in check. From the crowded kriegie audience, Tommy heard a ripple of conversation, like a wind racing through treetops, and he knew Visser had just helped him to take the trial of Lincoln Scott across an important line.

For a moment, he rubbed his chin.

"What makes a man a man, *Hauptmann*?"

Visser did not reply immediately, letting a smile curl across his face. The scars he wore on his cheeks from his encounter with the Spitfire seemed to glisten, and finally, he shrugged.

"A complex question, lieutenant. One that has bedeviled philosophers, clerics, and scientists for centuries. Surely you do not expect me to be able to answer it here, today, in this military court?"

"No, *Hauptmann*. But I would expect you to be able to give all of us your own definition. Personal definition."

Visser paused, thinking, then replied, "There are many factors, Lieutenant Hart. Sense of honor. Bravery. Dedication. These would be combined with intelligence. The ability to reason."

"Qualities Lieutenant Scott does not possess?"

"Not to the degree sufficient."

"You consider yourself to be an intelligent, educated man, *Hauptmann*? A sophisticated man?"

"Of course."

Tommy decided to take a chance. He could feel his own fury at the fanatic German's smug responses fighting to take over his emotions, and he had to struggle to keep a certain coldness in his voice and in his questions. At the same moment, he hoped that all his prep school training from a decade earlier had stuck with him. The faculty back at his old school had always said there was a reason for memorizing certain great works, and that someday a recitation might prove important. He trusted this to be one of those times.

"Ah, an educated, intelligent man would understand the classics, I suppose. Tell me, *Hauptmann,* are you familiar with the following: *Arma virumque cano, Troiae qui primus ab oris Italiam fato profugus . . .*"

Visser stared harshly at Tommy Hart. "Latin is a dead language, from a corrupt and decadent culture, and not among my skills."

"So you do not recognize . . ." and Tommy stopped. "Well, don't let me tell you . . ." He spun sharply about, taking a gamble. "Lieutenant Scott?" he demanded in a loud voice.

Scott sprang to his feet. He stared across at the German, a small, cruel smile of his own on his face.

"It would seem to me that any truly educated *man* would recognize the opening lines to Virgil's *Aeneid,*" Scott said sharply. " 'I sing of arms and the man who first from the shores of Troy came destined an exile in Italy . . .' Would you like me to continue, *Hauptmann*? '. . . *multum ille et terris iactatus at alto Vi superam, saevae memorem Iunonis ob iram . . .*' That would be: '. . . Much buffeted he on land and on the deep by force of the gods because of fierce Juno's never forgetting anger. . . .' "

Lincoln Scott stood stock-still as he recited the poet's words. The courtroom remained silent, a long, electric moment, and then Scott, still wearing a look of barely constrained fury, spoke out loudly, but evenly, not removing his eyes from the German. "A dead language, for sure. But the verses can speak as loudly today as they did centuries ago." Scott hesitated, then added, "But Mr. Hart, it is perhaps unfair to ask this highly educated man a question about a language he doesn't know. So, *Hauptmann,* perhaps you could use your knowledge to identify, *'Es irr der Mensch, so lang er strebt. . . .'* "

Visser smiled nastily at Lincoln Scott. "I am pleased that the lieutenant has read the German masters as well. Goethe's *Faust* is a standard work in our colleges and universities."

Scott seemed coolly pleased. "But not so much in ours, in America. Would the *Hauptmann* be so kind as to translate for the audience?"

Visser's smile faded just a touch. He nodded.

" 'Man is in error, throughout his strife . . .' " the German said sharply.

"I'm sure you can understand what the poet meant by that, *Hauptmann*," Scott said.

Then the black flier sat down, with a small nod in Tommy's direction. Tommy noticed that even Walker Townsend was hypnotized by the exchange. Tommy looked over at the German. Visser seemed outwardly unruffled, unaffected by the give-and-take. He doubted that was true deep within the German. Tommy thought Visser was as much a performer as he was a policeman, and he suspected that some of Visser's strength came in his ability to shield his real feelings. Tommy took a deep breath and reminded himself that Visser remained coiled, alert, and extremely poisonous.

"And so, *Hauptmann*, there came a time when you were summoned to the *Abort* where Captain Bedford's body was discovered. . . ."

Visser shifted in his chair and nodded. "Ah," he said, "we have finished with the philosophical inquiries, and returned to the real world?"

"For the moment, *Hauptmann*, yes. Please explain to all assembled what you were able to deduce from the crime scene in the *Abort*."

Visser settled back.

"To begin with, lieutenant, the crime scene was not the *Abort*. Captain Bedford was murdered in a different location and then transported to the *Abort* where his body was abandoned."

"How can you tell this?"

"There was a bloody footprint of a shoe on the floor of the *Abort*. It was pointing toward the stall where the body was located. Had the murder taken place in that location, then the blood would have been on the shoe, exiting the *Abort*. In addition, the bloodstains on the body, and the adjacent privy area, suggested that most of the victim's bleeding was done elsewhere."

Walker Townsend rose, opened his mouth, seemed to think better of it, then returned to his seat.

"Do you know where Trader Vic was actually killed?"

"No. I have not uncovered that location. I suspect steps have been taken to conceal it."

"What else did you learn from examining the body?"

Visser smiled again, continuing to speak in a self-satisfied and self-assured voice. "As you previously suggested, lieutenant, it appeared that the blow which took the captain's life was delivered from behind, by someone wielding a narrow, double-edged blade. A dagger, I suspect. And this weapon was in the assailant's left hand, as you surmised. This is the only possible explanation for the type of wound on the victim's neck."

"The weapon the prosecution claims was used to commit the murder?"

"It would have produced a large, ragged, bloody slash-like wound. Not the more precise stab that Captain Bedford suffered."

"Now, you have not seen this other weapon, have you?"

"I have searched. Unsuccessfully," Visser said coldly. "A weapon such as that would be *verboten*. Prisoners of war are not permitted to have such a weapon in their possession."

"And so, *Hauptmann*. The murder did not occur where the prosecution says it did, did not happen as the prosecution claims it happened, was not performed by the weapon the prosecution contends is the murder weapon, and left clear-cut evidence suggesting a completely different series of events. Is that not the sum of your testimony?"

"Yes. An accurate recitation, Mr. Hart."

Tommy left unsaid the obvious. But he left his own words hanging long enough in the air so that every kriegie in the jam-packed room—those hanging from each window, and those gathered outside, having every element of the testimony relayed to them—could find the same conclusion.

"Thank you, *Hauptmann*. Most instructive. Your witness, captain."

Tommy went and sat down, as Walker Townsend rose from his seat. The captain from Virginia seemed patient, and he, too, wore a small smile.

"Let me get this straight, *Hauptmann*. You hate Americans, although you lived as one for nearly a decade. . . ."

"I hate the enemy, yes, captain. And you are the enemy of my country."

"But you had two countries . . ."

"I did, captain. But my heart only belonged to one."

Captain Townsend shook his head. "That seems most obvious, *Hauptmann.* Now, you also believe Lieutenant Scott is an animal?"

Visser nodded. "He is fast. He is strong. And he has clearly been well-trained to be able to quote such great writers. But he occupies a position somewhat less than human. A cheetah is fast, captain, and a seal can be trained by the zookeeper to perform most wonderful tricks. I would remind you, *Herr Kapitän,* that less than a century ago, the slaveowners of your own state would have been likely to say much the same thing about their property working in their tobacco fields from dawn to dusk."

Townsend seemed abruptly trapped by this last statement. The Nazi was infuriating. Arrogant and unshaken, absolutely persuaded by his beliefs and undaunted by any evidence to the contrary. Tommy could sense a sort of fury on the prosecutor's part, angered by the obstinate and self-important tones Visser used, but unsure just how greatly they were damaging his case. Tommy hoped Townsend would slide into the mire created by the Nazi's conceit.

But Townsend did not.

Instead, the prosecutor asked, "Why should we believe what you say about anything?"

Visser twitched his shoulders. "I do not care in the slightest what you do or do not believe, captain. It makes absolutely no difference to me personally whether we shoot Lieutenant Scott, or not, although I would prefer we do, because he himself is so untrustworthy. This, of course, is not truly his fault. It is a function of his race."

Townsend gritted his teeth.

"It makes no difference to you, *Hauptmann,* but still you take the stand, swear to tell the truth, and then say that Scott did not commit this crime—"

Visser raised his only hand, cutting Townsend off.

"But, captain, that is not what I said," he replied, slight amusement creeping into his voice. "Nor is that what I even suggested."

Townsend stopped. He lifted a single eyebrow and stared at the unrepentant Nazi.

"You said—"

"What I said, captain, was that to trained eyes it was clear that the crime did not occur as you claim it did. I said nothing about Scott. In fact, he remains to me the chief suspect, and the man most likely to have committed the crime, however it was actually committed."

Townsend broke into a grin. "Tell us how you reach that conclusion, *Hauptmann*—"

Tommy rose sharply. "Objection, Your Honor!"

But MacNamara shook his head. "You opened this can of worms, lieutenant. And now you must live with it. Sit down. Let the *Hauptmann* testify. You will have a chance to redirect some questions when Captain Townsend has completed his cross-examination."

"Using your unique expertise, of course, *Hauptmann*," Townsend added swiftly.

The German shifted in his seat, thinking before he answered.

"The evidence of the bloodstains on Lieutenant Scott's clothing is compelling. Particularly the stains on the jacket, which are located in a fashion suggesting someone carried the body over his shoulder. This has already been discussed here. And, despite Lieutenant Hart's quite entertaining theatrics with the homemade blade belonging to Scott, it was clear that the weapon was used in the crime—"

Townsend cut off Visser. "But you said . . ."

"Ah, I said that the killing blow was struck by this other blade. The one that cannot be uncovered. But Captain Bedford also suffered what are called defensive wounds on his hands and chest. These are suggestive of him fighting back, even if briefly, against a man in front of him. A man, in all likelihood, wielding this homemade blade."

Townsend looked confused for an instant. "But why would someone carry two—"

Visser interrupted the question. "One person did not carry both blades, captain. The evidence clearly suggests that two men were involved in this murder. Or should I say: one man accompanied by his murderous lackey, the Negro Scott. One who stood in front, occupying Captain Bedford's attention while this second man, who struck silently, came up from behind."

The courtroom surged with noise, pent-up kriegies again unable to keep from turning to their neighbors and whispering shock, surprise, and wonderment at the testimony. The voices of the Allied airmen burst forth, an excited, confused wave, which carried up and over the men at the front of the theater. Tommy did not turn toward either of the two men sitting beside him, but instead took note of several intriguing reactions. Townsend seemed to be momentarily nonplussed, his mouth slightly open. Visser had regained a totality of smugness, leaning back, relaxed and exuding superiority. Off to the side, Von Reiter's eyes had narrowed and he wore a look of deep concentration. And in the center of the tribunal, Colonel MacNamara had paled, a stricken, worried, and anxious frown firmly scoring his face.

In that second, Tommy thought the Nazi's arrogant opinion had meant something different to each man.

The babbling, tangled sounds of vying voices from the audience finally seemed to shake Colonel MacNamara from his shock, and he energetically once again began banging away with the gavel, and crying out for order. The noise subsided rapidly.

Into the abrupt silence, Walker Townsend stepped. He wore a cobra's smile of his own.

"I see, *Hauptmann*. I see. One man owned a weapon. One man alone was seen abroad on the night of the murder. One man wore bloodstained shoes and jacket the following day. One man hated enough to kill. Motive. Opportunity. Means. But you think two men committed the crime. And you base this fantastic supposition on the most excellent training you have received from the German military. . . ." Townsend slid a long pause into his words, and then spoke in tones colored with the slick southernisms of his home state. "Well, hell's bells, *Hauptmann*. It ain't no wonder why y'all Krauts are losin' the damn war so bad!"

Visser instantly stiffened in his seat. His own smile evaporated.

Townsend waved his arm wildly at the German. "No more questions of this *expert*," he said sarcastically. "You can have 'im back, Tommy. For whatever the hell he's worth!"

Townsend took a pair of quick paces back to his seat and threw himself down.

Tommy stood, but did not move out from behind the defense table.

"Briefly, Your Honor," he said, with a quick glance to Mac-Namara. "*Hauptmann,* once again, why are you here?"

Visser said sharply: "I am here because you called me, lieutenant."

"No, *Hauptmann.* Why are you here? At this camp. Now. Why?"

Visser kept his mouth shut.

"Why do the Germans regard the murder of Captain Bedford as an event requiring an investigation? And why would they send to this camp someone seemingly as important as yourself?"

Visser again remained silent, but Colonel MacNamara did not. His voice boomed forth: "Lieutenant! You attempted to ask these questions earlier and were refused. And they go far beyond the scope of Captain Townsend's cross-examination! I will not allow them!"

Colonel MacNamara took a deep breath. "Hauptmann Visser, you are excused! We thank you for your testimony."

The German rose, and came to attention, saluting the court briskly and glaring toward his own commanding officer. Visser returned to his seat and immediately resumed his observer's role. He removed one of his thin, brown cigarettes from a silver case, and then bent toward the stenographer at his side, who fumbled for a moment and then produced a match.

Colonel MacNamara waited, then turned to Tommy. "What else do you have for us, lieutenant?"

"One last witness, colonel. We would call at this point Lieutenant Lincoln Scott," Tommy said firmly.

MacNamara nodded, but then the nod changed into a shake, and he glanced over at Commandant Von Reiter, before returning his eyes to Tommy.

"The defendant will be your final witness, lieutenant?"

"Yes sir."

"In that case we will hear from him in the morning. That way we will have time for the direct, the cross, and final arguments. Then the tribunal will begin deliberations." He smiled, but not humorously. "This will give both sides a little extra time to prepare."

Then he banged his gavel hard, ending the day's session.

Chapter Sixteen

A SURPRISING ORDER

The morning count seemed interminable. Every mistake, every delay, every time a ferret retraced his steps down the lines of Allied airmen mumbling numbers, the men cursed and raged and held their positions, as if by standing even more still they could somehow hurry the process. The ever-erratic weather had changed once again; as the filmy gray of the early morning burned away around them, the sun rose eagerly into a deepening blue sky, throwing warmth over the impatient kriegies. When the dismissal finally came, the formations broke apart rapidly and crowds of men streamed toward the theater, vying for the best seats in the courtroom. Tommy watched the flow of men and realized that the entire camp would be gathered at the trial that day. The excited kriegies would shoehorn themselves into every available space in the theater building. They would hang from the windows and crowd forward to the doors, trying to find a spot where they could both see and hear. He stood for a moment, probably the only man in the entire camp feeling no hurry, no urgency. He was a little unsettled and perhaps more than a little nervous about what he would do and say that day and wondering whether any of it would have the single necessary effect of saving Lincoln Scott's life. The black flier stood at his side, also watching the camp disperse in the direction of the trial, his face impassive, wearing the iron look that he almost always adopted in public, but with his eyes darting about, taking in the same things that Tommy saw.

414

"Well, Tommy," Scott said slowly. "I suppose the show must go on."

Hugh Renaday also stood nearby. But the Canadian had his head turned skyward, his gaze sweeping the wide blue horizon. After a moment, he spoke softly. "On a day like this, visibility unlimited, you know, if you just look up for a long enough time, you can almost forget where you are."

Both Tommy's and Lincoln Scott's eyes turned up, following the Canadian's. After a second's silence, Scott laughed out loud. "Damn it, I think you're almost right." He paused, then added, "It's almost like for just a couple of heartbeats you can kid yourself that you're free again."

"It would be nice," Tommy said. "Even the illusion of freedom."

"It *would* be nice," Scott repeated softly. "It's one of those rare things in life where the lie is far more encouraging than the truth."

Then all three men lowered their eyes, back to the earth and the wire and the guard towers and the dogs—the constant reminders of how fragile their lives were. "It's time to go," Tommy said. "But we're not in a hurry. In fact, let's show up a minute late. Exactly one minute. Just to piss off that tightass MacNamara. Hell, let 'em start without us. . . ."

This made the other two laugh, even if admittedly not a particularly sound strategy. As they crossed the assembly yard, all three men suddenly heard the start-up of construction noise, coming from the nearby thick forest, on the far side of the wire. A distant whistle, some shouts, and the rat-a-tat of hammers and the ripping sound of handsaws. "They start those poor bastards early, don't they?" Scott asked rhetorically. "And then they work them late. Makes you glad you weren't born a Russian," he said. Then he smiled wryly. "You know, there's probably a joke in that somewhere. Do you suppose right now one of those poor s.o.b.'s is saying he's glad he wasn't born black in America? After all, the damn Germans are just working them to death. Me? I've got to worry about my own countrymen shooting me."

He shook his head and continued to stride forward, at a determined pace. As they marched across the yard, at one point the black flier glanced over toward the two white men and grinned as he said, "Don't look so glum, Tommy, Hugh. I've been looking forward to this day since I was first accused of this crime. Usually lynchings don't work this way for black folks. Usually we don't get the chance to stand up in front of everyone and tell them how goddamn wrong they are. Usually we're just beaten down in silence and strung up real quiet and with hardly a mouse squeak of any protest. Well, that's not what's going to happen today. Not in this lynching."

Tommy knew this was true.

The night before, after the completion of Visser's testimony, the three men had returned to Hut 101 and sat around the bunk room. Hugh had fixed a modest meal, more of the processed meat fried alongside a canned vegetable paste from a Red Cross parcel, creating a taste that was somewhere between grease and stew and like nothing they had ever experienced before, which was, on the whole, a positive thing. It was the sort of concoction that would have been revolting back in the States, but there, inside Stalag Luft Thirteen, bordered on the gourmet.

Between bites, Tommy had said, "Scott, we need to be sure you're prepared for tomorrow. Especially for cross-examination . . ."

And Scott had replied, as he mouthed some of Hugh's invention, his hunger apparently restored by the prospect of testifying, "Tommy, I've been preparing for tomorrow for the entirety of my life."

So instead of talking about the two knives, the bloodstains, and Trader Vic's racist baiting, Tommy had suddenly asked Lincoln Scott: "Lincoln, tell me something. Back home, when you were growing up, and it was a Saturday afternoon, the sun was shining and it was warm and you didn't have anything that anyone was making you do—you know, chores finished, homework finished—what would you do with yourself?"

Lincoln Scott had stopped eating, slightly taken aback. "You mean, free time? When I was a kid?"

"That's right. Time to yourself."

"My preacher-daddy and my schoolteacher-mother didn't really believe in free time," he said, smiling. " 'Idle hands are the Devil's playground!' I heard that more than once. There was always time to work at something that was going to make me smarter or stronger or—"

"But . . ." Tommy had interrupted.

Scott had nodded. "There's always a 'but.' That's the one thing in life you can count on." He had burst into a small laugh. "You know what I liked to do? I'd sneak down to the freight yards. There was a big water tower down there, and I knew just how to climb up on it, so that I could get a view of the whole place. You see what I'm saying? From where I would perch, I could see the whole switching system. It's called a roundhouse. Train after train, rattling through the yard, tons of iron being moved about by someone throwing those electric switches, moving cattle one way to the stock-yards, and shifting corn and potatoes onto a track heading east, just moving out in time to miss the steel carriers coming in from the mountains. It was like a great elaborate dance, and I thought the men who ran the yards were like God's angels, moving everything through the universe according to a great, unwritten plan. All that speed and weight and commerce coming together and being sent out, never ending, never stopping, never even pausing for a breath of air. Man's greatest works on constant display. The modern world. Progress at my feet."

The men had remained silent for a moment, before Hugh had shaken his head. "It was sports for me," he had said. "Hockey with the other lads on a frozen pond. What about you, Tommy? It was your question. What did you do when you had the time?"

Tommy had smiled. "What I liked to do is what landed me here," he had said softly. "I liked to chart the stars in the heavens. They're different, you know. They make the smallest adjustments for the time of night and the time of the year. Positions change. Some shine more brightly. Others dim, then reemerge. I liked to look up at the constellations and see the endlessness of the night. . . ."

The others had remained quiet, and Tommy had shrugged. "But I should have had another hobby. Like tying flies or playing hockey, like you, Hugh. Because when the air corps found out I could perform celestial navigation, well, next thing I knew I was in a bomber, flying hell for leather above the Mediterranean. Of course, most all our sorties were in the daylight, so the usefulness of my ability to chart a course using the stars was, ah, limited. But that's the air corps way of thinking and that's what landed me here."

Both men had laughed. To make a joke about the army was always worth a laugh. But after a few seconds, the smiles had seeped away and they grew silent until Lincoln Scott had said, "Well, maybe you'll be able to navigate us out of here one day."

Hugh had nodded.

"That would be a happy day," he had said, which was the last time they talked of that most difficult of subjects, though throughout the long night in the bunk room that thought had never strayed far from Tommy Hart's imagination, as sleep eluded him and his mind increasingly centered on the courtroom and the drama that awaited them in the morning.

The Senior American Officer was drumming his fingers against the table, doing little to conceal his irritation as Tommy, Hugh, and the defendant picked their way through the audience. The center aisle was so congested with kriegies that any attempt to enter in formation, as they had before, would have been thwarted by the overflow crowd, which barely had enough room to squeeze tightly together and let the three men pass. Murmurs, whispers, and a few softly spoken comments flowed behind them like the modest white frothy wake behind a sailboat. Tommy did not listen to the words, but took note of the different tones, some angry, some encouraging, some merely confused.

He took a quick glance at Commandant Von Reiter, who now occupied a seat just to the left of Heinrich Visser. The German commander was rocking slightly in his seat, grinning faintly. Visser, however, was stone-faced, impassive. Tommy was still unsure whether Visser had helped or hurt the case, but he had done one important service, which was to remind all the kriegies who the real enemy was, which, on balance, Tommy thought, was better than anything else he could have wished for. The problem that remained was to make the men of Stalag Luft Thirteen remember that Scott was on their side. One of them. And that, Tommy thought, would be diffi-cult enough and maybe impossible.

"You are supposed to be in position, ready for trial, along with the rest of us, Mr. Hart," Colonel MacNamara said stiffly.

Tommy did not reply to this statement, but merely said, "We are ready now to proceed, colonel."

"Then please do so," MacNamara said. His words were singularly cool.

"The defense at this time would call First Lieutenant Lin-coln Scott of the 332nd Fighter Group to the witness stand!" Tommy said as forcefully as he could, his own voice lifted up over the heads of all the gathered men.

Scott pushed himself out of his seat at the defense table and crossed the space to the witness chair in three great strides. He rapidly seized the Bible offered to him, swore under oath to tell the truth, and thrust himself into the seat. He looked up toward Tommy with the eagerness of the boxer he was, awaiting the sound of the bell.

"Lieutenant Scott, tell us how you arrived at Stalag Luft Thirteen."

"I was shot down. Like everyone else."

"Then how was it that you were shot down?"

"A Focke-Wulf got on my tail and I couldn't shake him be-fore he got off a lucky shot. End of story."

"Not exactly," Tommy said. "Let's try this differently: Did there come a time when, having completed your regular patrol and en route to your base, you heard a stricken and crippled B-17 broadcast a call for help across an open air channel?"

Scott paused, and nodded. "Yes."

"A desperate call?"

"I suppose so, Mr. Hart. He was all alone and had two en-gines out and half his tail stabilizer shot away and was in trouble. Big trouble."

"Two engines out and he was under attack?"

"Yes."

"By a half-dozen enemy fighters?"

"Yes."

Tommy paused. He understood that every man in the audience knew exactly what the men in that bomber's chances had been at the moment they pleaded for help from anyone who might hear them. As close to zero as a flier could get. Death for them was only seconds away.

"And you and your wing man, the two of you, you went to this crippled plane's aid?"

"That is what we did."

"You didn't have to?"

"No," Scott replied. "I suppose not technically, Mr. Hart. The plane belonged to a group that was not one we were assigned to protect. But you and I know that that is only a technical consideration. Of course we had to help. So, to suggest that we didn't have to, well, that's a foolish statement, Mr. Hart. We did not think we had a choice in the matter. We simply attacked."

"I see. You didn't think you had a choice. Two against six. And how much ammunition did you have remaining when you dove into the attack?"

"A few seconds. Just enough for a couple of bursts." Scott paused, then added, "I don't see why I need to go through this, Mr. Hart. It hasn't got anything to do with the charges here."

"We'll get to those, lieutenant. But everyone else who's taken the stand has explained how they managed to land here in this camp, and so will you. So, you attacked a vastly superior enemy force all the time knowing you did not have enough ammunition to make more than one or two passes?"

"That is correct. We both managed to down a Focke-Wulf on the first attack, and we hoped that would draw them off. It didn't work out that way."

"What happened?"

"Two fighters tangled with us, two pursued the bomber."

"And what happened next?"

"We managed to scare off the two, by getting around behind them. With the last of my ammunition I shot down another. Then we went after the remaining fighters."

"Without ammunition?"

"Well, it had worked before."

"What happened this time?"

"I got shot down."

"Your wing man?"

"He died."

Tommy paused, letting this sink in to the audience.

"The B-17?"

"He made it home. Safe and sound."

"Who flies in the 332nd?"

"Men from all over the States."

"And what distinguishes you?"

"We are volunteers. No draftees."

"What else?"

"We are all Negroes. Trained at Tuskegee, Alabama."

"Has any bomber being protected by the 332nd Fighter Group been lost to enemy fighter action?"

"Not yet."

"Why is that?"

Scott hesitated. He had kept his eyes directly on Tommy throughout the exchange, and they did not waver now, save for one wide look, where Scott took in the expanse of the audience, before returning to fix Tommy with his singular, rigid stare.

"We had all agreed, when we first got our wings. Made a rule. A credo, you might say. No white boy *we* were assigned to protect was going to die."

Tommy paused, letting this statement reverberate above the silent crowd in the courtroom.

"Now, when you arrived here," Tommy continued, "did you make friends with any other kriegie?"

"No."

"None?"

"That's right."

"Why is that?"

"I had never had a white friend, Lieutenant Hart. I did not think I needed to start here."

"And now? Do you have any friends now, Lieutenant Scott?"

He hesitated again, shrugged slightly, and said, "Well, Mr. Hart, I suppose that I would now consider yourself and Flying Officer Renaday to be somewhat closer to that category."

"And that would be it?"

"Yes."

"Now, Captain Vincent Bedford . . ."

"I hated him. He hated me. The color of my skin seemed to be the basis for that hatred, Mr. Hart, but I suspect it went further. When he looked at me, he did not see a single man thrust into the same circumstances as he was. He saw an enemy that went back centuries. A far greater enemy than any German we might be at war with. And I, I must admit, unfortunately, saw much the same in him. He was the man who enslaved, tortured, and worked my ancestors to death. It was like being confronted by a nightmare that has not only afflicted yourself, but your father and your grandfather and every generation that went before you."

"Did you kill Vincent Bedford?"

"No. I did not! I would have gladly fought Vincent Bedford, and if, in that fight, he should have died, then I would not have been saddened. But would I have stalked him through the night, as these men suggest, and crept up and attacked him from behind like some sort of weak and reprehensible coward? No sir! I would not now, not ever, do such a thing!"

"You would not?"

Scott was sitting forward, his voice ringing through the courtroom. "No. But did I rejoice when I heard that someone had? Yes. Yes, I did! Even when they falsely accused me, I still, within myself, was thankful for what had happened, because I believed Vincent Bedford to be evil!"

"Evil?"

"Yes. A man who lives a lie, as he did, is evil."

Tommy stopped then. What he heard in Scott's words went in a direction different from what he thought the black flier meant. But he felt a rush straight through the core of his body, for he had just seen something about Vincent Bedford that he doubted anyone else saw, with the possible exception of the man who murdered him. For a second, Tommy paused, almost swaying as he was buffeted by thoughts. Then he scrambled, turning back to face Scott, who eagerly awaited the next question.

"You heard Hauptmann Visser suggest that you assisted someone else in the commission of this crime. . . ."

Scott smiled. "I think everyone here knows how crazy that

suggestion was, Mr. Hart. What were the *Hauptmann*'s own words? *Ridiculous* and *ludicrous*. No one in this camp trusts me. There's no one in this camp I trust. Not with some wild conspiracy to murder another officer."

Tommy stole a look toward Visser, whose face had reddened, and who shifted in his seat uncomfortably. Then he turned back to his client.

"Who killed Vincent Bedford?"

"I do not know. I know only who they want to blame."

"And that would be?"

"That would be me."

Scott hesitated one more time, then loudly added, with all the intensity of the preacher calling up to the heavens, "This war is filled with innocent people dying every minute, every second, Mr. Hart. If this is my time, innocent though I am, then so be it! But I am innocent of these charges and will remain that way until the day I die!"

Tommy let these words fill the courtroom, echoing above the crowd of kriegies. Then he turned to Walker Townsend.

"Your witness," he said quietly.

The captain from Virginia rose, and moved slowly to the center of the courtroom. He had one hand upon his chin, stroking the stubble gathered there, in the almost-universal aspect of a man considering his words very carefully. Across from him, Tommy could see that Scott was poised in his seat, a portrait of both electricity and energy, anticipating the first question from the prosecutor. There was no nervousness in Scott's eyes, only an alertness and a fighter's concentration. Tommy recognized in that second why Scott must have been such a force behind the stick of his Mustang; the black airman had the unique capacity to focus solely on the fight in front of him. He was a true warrior, Tommy thought, and in his own way far more professional than even the career officers hanging on his every word. The only man in the courtroom who Tommy believed could approach the intensity in which Scott cloaked himself was Heinrich Visser. The difference was that Scott's singleness of purpose came from a righteousness, whereas Visser's was the dedication of the devoted fanatic. In a fair fight, Tommy thought, Scott would be more than a match for Visser and far more capable than Walker Townsend. The problem was, the fight wasn't fair.

"Let us take this slowly and carefully, lieutenant," Townsend started, his words almost caressing. "Let's talk first about the means . . ."

"As you wish, captain," Scott replied.

"You do not deny, do you, lieutenant, that the weapon produced by the prosecution was manufactured by yourself?"

"I do not. I did indeed build that knife."

"And you do not deny making the threatening statements, do you?"

"No sir. I do not. I made those statements in an effort to create some space between myself and Captain Bedford. Perhaps by threatening him, he would keep his distance."

"Did this happen?"

"No."

"So we have only your word that these statements were not actual threats, but an effort to . . . what did you say, 'create distance'?"

"That is correct," Scott answered sharply.

Walker Townsend nodded, but the motion clearly implied that he understood something the opposite of what Scott had said. "And on the night of Captain Bedford's murder, lieutenant, you do not deny rising from your bunk and being abroad in the corridor of Hut 101, do you?"

"No. That, too, is true."

"All right. Now sir, you do not deny that you have the strength to have lifted the body of Captain Bedford and carried him some distance—"

"I did not do this. . . ." Scott interrupted.

"But do you have the strength, lieutenant?"

Lincoln Scott paused, thought for a second, then replied, "Yes. I do have the strength. And with either arm, captain, and over either shoulder, as well, if I may anticipate your next question."

Walker Townsend smiled slightly, nodding. "Thank you, lieutenant. You most certainly did. Now, let's discuss motive for a moment. You do not hide your contempt for Captain Bedford, even in death, do you, sir?"

"No. That is correct."

"You would say your life has improved by his death, true?"

It was Scott's turn to smile faintly. "Well, you probably want to rephrase that question, captain. Is my life better because I no longer have to confront the cracker bastard every day . . . well, yes. But this is an illusory advantage, captain, when one's days may very well be limited by a firing squad."

Walker Townsend nodded. "I concede your point, lieutenant. But you do not deny that every day the two of you existed in this camp together, that Vincent Bedford provided you with a motive to kill him, do you?"

Scott shook his head. "No, captain, that is not correct. Captain Bedford's actions provided me with a motive to hate him and what he stood for. They provided me with a motive to confront him, to show him that I would not be cowed or intimidated by his racist statements. Even when he tried to get me to cross the deadline to retrieve that softball, which could have cost me my life were it not for Lieutenant Hart's shout of warning, still, that act and the others provided me with a motive to fight Captain Bedford. Fighting and confrontation and a refusal to shuck and shuffle and accept his behavior passively do not constitute a motive to murder, captain, despite your need to twist it into one."

"But you did hate him . . ."

"We do not always kill what we hate, captain. Nor do we always hate what we kill."

Townsend did not follow up immediately with another question, and a momentary silence shifted onto the courtroom. Tommy had just enough time to think that Scott was doing quite well, when a strident voice burst from the crowd at his back, searing across the room.

"Liar! Lying black bastard!" There was an unmistakable southern accent marring each of the words.

"Killer! Goddamn lying murderer!" a second voice shouted out from a different section of the audience.

And then, just as rapidly, a third cry, only this time the words seemed directed at the men who'd first shouted. "It's the truth!" someone yelled. "Can't you tell the truth when you hear it?" These words had a Boston flat *A* tone that Tommy recognized from his days at Harvard.

In a corner of the theater, there was a scuffling sound, and pushing and shoving. As Tommy pivoted, staring back into the mix of kriegies, he saw a couple of fliers suddenly chest to chest. Within seconds the noise of anger and confrontation erupted in more than one spot in the large room, and jam-packed men started to push and gesture. It seemed almost as if three or four fights were about to break out before Colonel MacNamara started to crash his gavel down furiously, the hammering noise punctuating the cascade of angry voices.

"Damn it! Order!" MacNamara cried out. "I will clear this court if you cannot maintain discipline!"

The room seemed to glow red for an instant, continuing to throb before settling into an uneasy quiet.

Colonel MacNamara allowed the tense silence to continue, before he threatened the crowd of kriegies again. "I recognize that there are differences of opinion, and that feelings are strong," he said flatly. "But we must remain orderly! A military trial must be a public event, for all to witness! I warn you men, do not make me take steps to control any further outbursts before they should happen!"

Then MacNamara did something that, to Tommy's eyes, seemed unusual. The SAO briefly turned toward Commandant Von Reiter, and said, "This is exactly what I have repeatedly warned you about, *Herr Oberst*!"

Von Reiter nodded his head in acknowledgment of what MacNamara said. Then the SAO turned back to Walker Townsend, and made a small gesture for the prosecutor to continue.

Something else struck Tommy in that second. Every other time there had been even the slightest disruption in the proceedings, MacNamara had been furiously quick with his gavel. In fact, Tommy thought, the one thing that MacNamara seemed most capable of doing was slamming that gavel onto the table, because he certainly wasn't astute about the law or criminal procedures. This time, however, it almost seemed to Tommy as if the SAO had waited until after the first outburst, and that MacNamara had allowed the tensions to bubble close to the boil-over point, before demanding order. It was, to Tommy's mind, almost as if MacNamara had *expected* the outburst.

He considered this most curious, but did not have the time

to reflect further, as Walker Townsend immediately launched into another question.

"What you want, Lieutenant Scott, is for this tribunal, and for all the men gathered here listening to you, what you want all of us to believe is that on the night of Captain Bedford's death, at some point after you went out to the corridor, and were seen skulking around in the dark, that you returned to your bunk and did not notice that some unknown person had removed your flight jacket and boots from their customary locations, and had stolen this sword you constructed from your kit, taken these items and utilized them in the murder of Captain Bedford and then returned them to your room, and that subsequently you did not observe the blood staining them? This is what you want us all to believe, is it not, lieutenant?"

Scott paused, then responded firmly.

"Yes. Precisely."

"Lies!" shouted out a voice from the back, ignoring Mac-Namara's warning.

"Let him talk!" came the almost instant reply.

The SAO reached for the gavel again, but a grudging silence crept back into the courtroom.

"You don't think that's far-fetched, lieutenant?"

"I don't know, captain. I have not now, nor have I ever committed a murder! So I have no experience. You, sir, on the other hand, have prosecuted numerous murder cases. Perhaps you should provide us with the answer. Have none of the cases you've prosecuted ever been unusual? Surprising? Have events never been mysterious and answers hard to come by? You're far more expert than I, captain, so perhaps you should be answering these questions."

"It's not my job to answer questions here, lieutenant!" Townsend replied, anger creeping into his own voice for perhaps the first time. "You're on the witness stand."

"Well, captain," Scott responded coldly, infuriatingly, and Tommy thought, nearly perfectly, "it is my belief that that is what we are put on this earth to do. Answer questions. Every time any one of us stepped up into a plane to go into battle, we were answering a question. Every time we face the real enemies in our lives, whether they are Germans or southern cracker racists, we are answering questions. That's pretty much all that life is, captain. But maybe here, in the bag, stuck behind the wire, you've forgotten all that. Well, I, for damn certain, haven't!"

Townsend paused again. He shook his head slowly back and forth, and then started to walk back toward the prosecution's table. He was halfway there, when he stopped, and looked up at Scott, as if something had just occurred to him, a question that was more an afterthought. Tommy instantly recognized this for what it was, which was a trap, but there was nothing he could do. He hoped that Scott would see through the histrionics, as well.

"Ah, lieutenant, just one final inquiry, then, if you don't mind."

Tommy abruptly reached out and pushed one of his law books to the floor, where it fell with a thudding sound that distracted Scott and Townsend. "Sorry," Tommy said, reaching down and making as much disturbance collecting the law book as he could possibly manage. "Didn't mean to interrupt you, captain. Please continue."

Townsend glared, then repeated, "One more question, then . . ."

Lincoln Scott's eyes caught Tommy's for a split second as he read the warning in Tommy's small accident, then he nodded toward the prosecutor. "What would that be, captain?"

"Would you be willing to lie to save your own life?"

Tommy pushed back, rising from his seat, but Colonel MacNamara had anticipated the objection, and he waved his hand sharply in front of himself, making a slicing motion to cut Tommy off. "The defendant shall answer the question," he said swiftly. Tommy grimaced, and felt his insides constrict. He thought this the worst question, an old-fashioned trick of the prosecutor's trade, one Townsend could never get away with in a real court, but there, inside the shadow trial of Stalag Luft Thirteen, it was allowed in ultimate unfairness. There was no way to answer the question, Tommy knew. If Scott said *yes* he made everything else he'd said appear to be a lie. If Scott said *no*, then every kriegie in the audience, every man who'd felt the cold breath of death on their neck and knew they were wildly lucky to still be alive, would be-

lieve that he was lying right then, because it was worth anything to stay alive.

Tommy locked eyes for a moment with Lincoln Scott, and
he thought the black flier saw the same danger. It was like
passing between the twin terrors of Scylla and Charybdis.
One couldn't extract oneself without suffering a loss.

"I don't know," Scott replied slowly but firmly. "I do know
that I've told the truth here today."

"So you say," Townsend said with a snort and a shake of
his head.

"That's right," Scott boomed. "So I say!"

"Then," Townsend said, trying successfully to infect his
words with a deadly combination of frustration and utter disbelief, "I have nothing else at this time for this witness." He
resumed his seat.

Colonel MacNamara eyed Tommy. "Do you wish to redirect, counselor?" he asked.

Tommy thought for a moment, then shook his head. "No
sir."

The SAO glanced down at Lincoln Scott. "You are dismissed, then, lieutenant."

Scott rose, pivoted, and saluted the tribunal sharply, then,
shoulders straight, marched back to his seat.

"Anything else, Mr. Hart?" MacNamara asked.

"The defense rests, colonel," Tommy said loudly.

"All right, then," MacNamara said. "We will reconvene
this afternoon for final arguments from both sides. Gentlemen, these should be brief and to the point!" He banged his
gavel down hard. "Dismissed!" MacNamara said.

There was a rustling as men started to rise, and in that moment of confusion, a voice rang out: "Let's shoot him now!"
Only to be met by a second voice, equally outraged, crying,
"You southern bastards!" Immediately there was a tangle of
men, pushing, shoving, their voices all blending together in a
cacophony of angers and opinions. Tommy could see kriegies
restraining kriegies, and men looking to take a swing at each
other. He wasn't sure how the camp divided on the question
of Lincoln Scott's guilt or innocence, only that it was filling
the men with tension.

MacNamara banged away. In a second, silence slipped

over the angry men. "I said 'Dismissed!' " MacNamara bellowed. "And that's what I meant!" He eyed the tangled crowd of kriegies furiously, waiting in the edgy silence in the theater for a moment, then rising, and striding purposefully, he moved from behind the tribunal's table and stepped through the mass of men, eyeing each carefully, in that way he had which made it seem as if he were taking names and putting them to faces. Behind him, there was some grumbling, and a few more sharp words, but these faded as the men slowly began to file out of the courtroom, out into the sunshine of midday.

Alone with his thoughts and troubles, Tommy walked the deadline. He knew he should have been back inside the barracks room, pencil and paper in hand, scribbling down the words he would use that afternoon to try to save Lincoln Scott's life, but the wildly tossing seas within his own heart had driven him out into the liar's sun, and he marched along, his pace dictated by the sums and subtractions he was making within himself. He could feel the warmth on his neck, and knew it to be dishonest, for the weather would change again, and gray rain would overcome the camp soon enough.

The other kriegies out in the assembly yards, or walking the same route as Tommy, gave him a wide berth. No one stopped, not to curse him out or to wish him luck or even to admire the afternoon that surrounded them as tenaciously as did the barbed wire. Tommy walked in solitude.

A man who lives a lie . . . Tommy considered Scott's words describing Vincent Bedford. He understood one thing about the murdered man: There had never been a bargain that Trader Vic struck where he did not come out ahead, except for the last, and that was the one that had cost him his life. High price, Tommy thought with a cynical fervor. If Trader Vic had cheated someone on a deal, would that have been enough reason to kill him? Tommy walked on, asking himself: What did Vic deal in? And then he provided the answer: Vic dealt in food and chocolate and warm clothes, cigarettes and coffee and occasionally in an illegal radio and maybe a camera. What else?

Tommy almost stopped. Trader Vic dealt in information.

Tommy glanced over at the woods. He was passing behind the rear of Hut 105, near the slightly hidden spot that he believed was the actual murder location. Killed and then moved. He measured the distance to the wire from the rear of the hut, then looked farther, into the trees.

For a moment, he reeled under the pressures of the moment. He thought of Visser and men moving around late at night and men threatening Scott against orders and all the evidence that pointed one way abruptly disappearing, and Phillip Pryce being summarily removed from the scene. Everything came pouring at him, and he felt as if he were standing up in the face of a strong ocean wind, one that slung froth off the tops of wildly tossing whitecaps, and turned the water to a deep, murky gray color, promising a great storm that was moving steadily on the horizon. He shook his head, and berated himself: *You have spent too much time staring at the currents at your feet, instead of looking to the distance.* He believed that this was the sort of observation Phillip Pryce would have made. But again, he felt trapped by all the events.

In his reverie, he heard his name being called, and for a moment, it seemed to him almost as if it were Lydia, calling him from the front yard, urging him to come out from indoors, because there was a scent of Vermont spring in the air, and it would be criminal not to snatch at it. But as he pivoted about, he saw that it was Hugh Renaday calling his name. Scott stood nearby, and was gesturing toward him. Tommy glanced down at the watch he wore and saw that it was closing on the time for the final arguments to begin.

Even Tommy was forced to concede that Walker Townsend was eloquent and persuasive. He spoke in a low-key, almost hypnotic tone, steady, determined, the slight southern lilt in his voice giving his words an illusory credence. He pointed out that of all the elements of the crime, the only one truly denied by Lincoln Scott was the actual murder. He seemed to take delight in pointing out that the black airman had admitted to virtually everything else that constituted the killing.

As the entire camp, jammed into every inch of space in the theater, listened to Townsend's words, it seemed to Tommy that innocence was slowly, but certainly, being stripped away from Lincoln Scott. In his own quiet yet sturdy manner, Captain Townsend made it clear that there was only one suspect in the case, and only one man to be assigned guilt.

He called Tommy's efforts mere smoke screens, designed to deflect attention from Scott. He argued that the limited forensic capabilities within the camp made it all the more critical that the circumstantial evidence be given even more weight. He had nothing but contempt for Visser's testimony, though he was careful not to examine what the German had said, but instead to emphasize how he'd said it, which, Tommy recognized, was the best way of diminishing it.

And finally, in what Tommy was forced to swallow bitterly when he saw its brilliance, Walker Townsend suggested that he did not truly blame Lincoln Scott for killing Trader Vic. The captain from Virginia had lifted his own voice, making certain that not only the tribunal but every kriegie craning to hear actually did hear.

"Who among us, Your Honors, would really have behaved differently? Captain Bedford did much to bring his own death upon himself. He underestimated Lieutenant Scott from the outset," Townsend said, firmly. "He did this because he was, as we have heard here, a racist. And he thought, in the cowardly way that racists have, that his target would not fight back. Well, sirs, we have all seen, if nothing else, that Lincoln Scott is a fighter. He has told us himself how the odds did not affect him when he went into battle. And so, he took on Vincent Bedford, just as he took on those FWs arrayed against him. That death ensued is understandable. But, gentlemen, just because we can now understand the causes of his actions, that does not make him less accountable, nor does it make them any less despicable! In a way, Your Honors, this is the simplest of situations: Trader Vic got what he deserved for the way he behaved. And now, we must hold Lieutenant Scott to no less a standard! He found Vincent Bedford guilty and executed him! Now we, as civilized, democratic, and free men, must do the same!"

With a nod to Colonel MacNamara, Walker Townsend sat down.

"Your turn, Mr. Hart," the SAO said. "Be brief."

Tommy rose. "I will, Your Honor."

He stepped to the front of the auditorium and raised his voice just loud enough so that everyone could hear.

"There is one thing that we all, every man here in Stalag Luft Thirteen, understands, Your Honors, and that is uncertainty. It is the most elemental province of war. Nothing truly is certain until it is past, and even then, many times, it remains shrouded by confusion and conflict.

"That is the case with the death of Captain Vincent Bedford. We know from the only real expert who examined the crime scene—Nazi though he is—that the prosecution's case does not fit the evidence. And we know that Lieutenant Scott's denial remains uncontroverted by the prosecution, and unshaken by cross-examination. And so, members of the court, you are being asked to make a decision from which there is no appeal, and which is utterly final in its certainty on the most subjective of details. Details cloaked in doubt. But there is no doubt about a German firing squad. I do not think you can order this without an absolute belief in Lincoln Scott's guilt! You cannot order it because you do not like him, or because he is the wrong color, or because he can quote from the classics and others cannot. You cannot order it, because a death penalty cannot be based on anything except the most clear-cut and uncompromising set of undeniable facts. The death of Trader Vic doesn't come close to meeting that standard."

Tommy paused, trying hard to think of something else to say, and believing that he had fallen short of Townsend's professional eloquence. And so, he added one last thought:

"We are all prisoners here, Your Honors, and unsure as to whether we will live to see tomorrow, or the day after, or the day after that. But I would suggest to you that taking Lincoln Scott's life under these circumstances will kill a little bit of each of us, just as surely as a bullet or bomb would."

And with that, he sat down.

Behind him, voices suddenly babbled together, breaking first into murmurs, followed by cries and shouts, re forming as arguments and closing in on fights. Kriegies in pockets throughout the theater pushed and shoved, confronting each other angrily. Tommy's first thought was that it was abundantly clear that the two final statements from Walker Townsend and himself had done nothing to defuse the tension among the men, and, probably, had done more to cement already held beliefs.

Again the gavel pounded from the front of the theater.

"I will not have a riot!" Colonel MacNamara was shouting. "And we will not have a lynching!"

"Hope not," Scott whispered under his breath. He wore a wry smile.

"You will come to order!" MacNamara cried out. But it took the kriegies almost a minute to settle down and regain some composure.

"All right," MacNamara said, when silence finally gripped the room again. "That's better." He cleared his throat with a long, protracted cough. "The obvious tension and conflict of opinions surrounding this case has created special circumstances," MacNamara blared out, as if he were on the parade ground. "Consequently, in consultation with the Luftwaffe authorities"—MacNamara nodded toward Commandant Von Reiter, who touched the shiny black patent leather brim of his cap in a salute of acknowledgment—"we have decided upon the following. Please understand. These are direct orders from your commanding officer, and they will be obeyed! Anyone not following orders precisely will find themselves in the cooler for the next month!"

Again, MacNamara paused, letting the threat sink in.

"We will reconvene here at exactly zero eight hundred tomorrow morning! The tribunal will render the verdict at that point! That will give us the remainder of this night to deliberate. Following that verdict, the entire contingent of prisoners will proceed directly to the assembly ground for the morning *Appell*! Directly! There will be no exceptions to this! The Germans have graciously agreed to delay the morning count to accommodate the conclusion of this case! There will be no uproar, no fights, no discussion whatsoever about the verdict, until after the count is completed. You will remain in formation until dismissal! The Germans will provide added security to prevent the outbreak of any unauthorized action! You men are warned. You will behave as officers and gentlemen, regardless of what our verdict is! Am I completely clear about this?"

This was a question that didn't need answering.

"Zero eight hundred. Right here. Everyone. That's an order. Now you are dismissed."

The three members of the tribunal rose, as did the German officers. The kriegies struggled up as well, and began to file out.

Walker Townsend bent down toward Tommy, offering his hand.

"You did a fine job, lieutenant," he said. "Far better than anyone had the right to expect from a fella standing up for the first time in a capital case. They must have taught you well at Harvard."

Silently, Tommy shook the prosecutor's hand. Townsend didn't even acknowledge Scott, turning instead to catch up with Major Clark.

"He's right, Tommy," Scott said. "And I appreciate it, no matter what they decide."

But Tommy did not reply to him, either.

Instead, he felt an utter coldness inside, for finally, in those last few seconds, he believed he'd seen a glimpse of the real reason Trader Vic had been killed. It was almost as if the truth were floating just in front of him, vaporous, elusive as always, almost invisible and ever slippery. Tommy reached out inadvertently, grasping at the air in front of him, hoping that what he'd finally seen was, if not the complete answer, at least the greatest part of it.

Chapter Seventeen

A NIGHT FOR
SETTLING DEBTS

Scott was the first to speak when they finally arrived back at their barracks room inside Hut 101. The black flier seemed alternately both depressed and excited, reflective yet energized, as if filled with conflict and compromise and unsure exactly how to react to the long night that stretched in front of them. He paced fast across the room, pounding his fists against imaginary opponents dancing in the emptiness before him, then he turned, and slumped against the wall, like a man in the tenth round finding the ropes and hoping for a second or two's respite from the onslaught. He looked at Hugh, reclining on his bunk like a workingman fatigued from a long hard day's labor, then over to Tommy, who of the three of them seemed the most impassive and yet, oddly, the most volatile.

"I suppose," Scott said almost wistfully, "that we should celebrate because this is my last night of . . ."

He hesitated, smiled a little sadly, then finished his sentence: ". . . my last night of something. Innocence? Freedom? Being accused? No, that is unlikely. And I suppose it's not exactly right to say *freedom*, because we're all stuck here and none of us are free. But it's the last night of something, and I guess that's notable enough. So, what do you think? Break out the champagne or the hundred-year-old Napoleon brandy? Grill up some sirloin steaks? Bake a chocolate cake and decorate it with candles? Whatever will get us through the night."

Scott pushed off the wall and walked over to Tommy Hart. He touched him on the shoulder in what, had Tommy been paying close attention, he would have recognized was perhaps the first spontaneous display of some sort of affection that the black airman had managed since his arrival at Stalag Luft Thirteen.

"Come on, Tommy," he said softly, "the case is over. You did what you were supposed to do. In any civilized world, you would have succeeded in creating a reasonable doubt, which is all that the law is supposed to require. The trouble is, we just don't currently live in a civilized world."

Scott paused, breathing in deeply, before continuing. "I guess now all we have to do is wait for the verdict that we've known was coming straight at me since the morning Vic's body was found."

This statement finally shook Tommy loose from the near-trance he'd been in, since the end of the court session that day. He looked over at Lincoln Scott and slowly shook his head.

"Over?" Tommy said. "Lincoln, the case has just begun."

Scott looked at him quizzically.

From the bunk, Hugh said, almost exhausted, "Now, Tommy, you've managed to lose me on that one. Begun? How?"

Tommy abruptly pounded one fist into an open palm, and then, just like Scott, he suddenly punched out at the emptiness in the room, whirling about, snapping off a couple of jabs, then throwing a wild left hook at the air in front of them. The single harsh overhead bulb burning above him threw exaggerated streaks of light across his face.

"What am I doing?" he demanded suddenly, stopping in his tracks in the center of the room, grinning maniacally at the other two men.

"Acting like a crazy fool," Hugh said, managing a smile.

"Shadow-boxing," Scott replied.

"That's right. Exactly right! And that's what's been going on over the past few days." Tommy put a hand to his head, pushed his shock of hair away from his eyes, then lowered his index finger to his lips. He tiptoed over to the door, opened it gingerly, and looked out into the corridor, checking to see if anyone was watching them or listening in. But the corridor was empty. He closed the door and turned back to the two other men, an exaggerated look of excitement on his face.

"I have been a fool not to have seen it earlier," he said quietly, though each word seemed to glow incandescently.

"See what?" Scott asked. Hugh nodded in agreement.

Tommy stepped toward the two others, and began to whisper. "What do we know Trader Vic traded for, right before his death?"

"The knife that killed him."

"Right. Right. The knife. The knife we needed. The knife we had, then gave up, and which Visser seems so intent on finding. The damn knife. The all-important damn knife. Okay. But what *else*?"

The other two looked at each other. "What do you mean," Scott started. "It was the knife that was critical. . . ."

"No." Tommy shook his head. "The knife had everybody's attention, right. It killed Vic. No doubt. But what Bedford also managed to acquire for some unknown men in this camp was just as important. That fighter pilot, the guy from New York, he told us he saw Vic with some German currency and official papers and also with a train schedule. . . ."

"Yes, but . . ."

"A *schedule*!"

Lincoln and Hugh remained silent.

"I just didn't think about it, because I was, like everybody else, thinking about the goddamn knife! Now, why would any kriegie need a schedule, unless someone thought he could catch a train? But that's impossible, right? No one has ever escaped from this camp! Because even if you could somehow get past the wire and then through the woods into town without being spotted, and managed to get to the station platform, why, by the time the seven-fifteen or whatever train that's heading to Switzerland and safety came chugging in, the place would be crawling with Krauts and Gestapo goons looking for your sorry butt, because the alarm would already have sounded right here at dear old Stalag Luft Thirteen! Right. We all know that! And we all know that the fact that no one has ever gotten out of here has been eating away at Colonel MacNamara and his slimy little sidekick Clark for months." Then Tommy lowered his voice yet another octave, so that his words were spoken in little more than a whisper.

"But what is different about tomorrow that has never once been different?"

Again the others simply stared at him.

"Tomorrow is different because of one thing, and it's the one thing that this trial has required the Germans to do. Different from any other day that we've been here. Think about it! What never changes? Not on Christmas or New Year's. Not on the nicest day of summer. Not on goddamn Adolf Hitler's official birthday! What is the one thing that never changes? The morning count! Same time. Same place. Same thing every day! Day in. Day out. Three hundred and sixty-five days a year and leap year, too. Like clockwork, the sun comes up and then the damn Krauts count us every morning. Except for tomorrow. Because the Germans have *graciously* agreed to postpone the *Appell* because everyone is concerned that the rendering of the verdict in this case will cause a riot! The Krauts, who never, ever change their damn routines, are changing theirs tomorrow! So, tomorrow, and tomorrow only, the count will be delayed. What? An hour? Two hours? All those damn nice convenient formations five-deep to make it easier for the Krauts to count us! Well, tomorrow the formations won't happen until far past their usual time."

Scott and Hugh looked at each other. There was a wildness in Tommy's eyes that seemed infectious, and passed quickly to the others.

"You're saying . . ." Scott started.

But Tommy finished for him. "Tomorrow those formations will be short some men."

Scott said, "Keep going, Tommy," as he listened.

"You see, if only one man, or two, maybe as many as three or four were blitzing out, well, you could probably cover up for them when the ferrets make their way up and down the rows—although that's never happened. I suppose it's conceivable that you could find a way to give them the couple of hours' head start they would need. But more? How about twenty men? Thirty? Fifty? That number missing would be obvious from the first minute at *Appell*, and the alarm would sound. So, how do you give them enough time, especially when you can't have all fifty jump on the first train that comes

rolling into the station? When you need to spread out the numbers and catch trains over the course of the entire morning?"

Hugh pointed a finger at Tommy, as he nodded his head.
"Makes bloody sense," he said. "Makes absolutely bloody
sense. You've got to delay that morning count! Except I still
don't see what Vic's death has to do with an escape."

"I don't know, either," Tommy said. "Not quite yet. But
I'm damn certain it has something to do with it, and I'm
going to find out what tonight!"

"Okay, I'll go along with that. But how does Scott facing a
firing squad fit into this?" Hugh asked.

Tommy shook his head. "Another good question," he said.
"And another answer I'm going to get tonight. But I'd be
willing to wager my last pack of smokes that someone ready
and willing to kill Trader Vic in order to get out of this damn
place sure as hell wouldn't think twice about leaving Lincoln
behind to face a German firing squad, either. A very angry
German firing squad."

This statement drew no response from the others because
its truth was so glaringly obvious.

It was a few minutes before one A.M. on the luminescent dial
of the watch that Lydia had given him when Tommy Hart
heard the first faint sounds of movement in the corridor outside their barracks room. Since the moment the Germans had
extinguished the electricity throughout the camp, the three
men had taken turns perched beside the door, craning to pick
up the telltale noises of men moving as silently as possible
toward the exit. Waiting had been a gamble. More than once
Tommy had to overcome the urge to simply gather the others
and head out into the night. But he had remembered that on
another night he'd awakened to hear men heading out, and he
guessed that the same trio as before were on the list of men
taking their chance for freedom that morning. Following was
a better idea than simply launching himself and the others out
into all the dangers of the searchlights and trigger-quick
goons, not really knowing where they were heading. Tommy
had a good idea that he knew which of the huts were strong
possibilities as the gathering place for the escapees: either
105, where the murder had taken place, or 107, the next hut

over, and although not the closest to the wire and the forest beyond, not the farthest, either.

His companions sat behind him, waiting on the edge of a bunk, wordlessly. Tommy could see their faces in the glow of Hugh's cigarette.

"There!" Tommy whispered. He held a hand up in the air and bent even closer to the thick wooden door. He could hear the slightest vibration of footsteps padding against the floor planks. He envisioned what was taking place in the corridor a few feet away. The kriegies would have been briefed, and they would have already prepared their escape kits. They would be wearing clothes tailored to make them appear to be civilians. They might carry a suitcase or a valise. They would have collected some extra rations. Their forged identity papers, work and travel permits, maybe even tickets for the train, would be sewn inside their jacket pockets. There would be no need for words, but each man, inwardly, silently, would be practicing the few phrases of memorized German that they hoped would be enough to carry them to the Swiss border. Following a precise order, they would stop at the door, wait for the lights to swing past, then exit rapidly. They wouldn't chance even a candle on this night, Tommy thought. Instead, each man would have counted the number of paces from his bunk to the door.

Tommy wheeled toward the others. "Not a sound," he said. "Not one sound. Get ready . . ."

But Scott, curiously, put his hand out, grasping the other two men on their shoulders and pulling them close, so that their faces were only inches apart, and so that he could whisper with a sudden, almost fierce intensity.

"I've been thinking, Tommy, Hugh . . ." he started slowly, making sure his soft words were crisp and clear, "there's something we need to keep in mind about tonight."

His words made Tommy pause, almost chilling him.

"What?" Hugh asked.

Tommy could hear Scott inhale deeply, as if the weight of what he was about to say bore down on him, creating a burden none of them had foreseen. "Men have *died* to bring about tonight," he whispered. "Men have worked hard and then died hard to give others a chance at freedom. There were two men trapped, digging in a collapsed tunnel, right before I arrived here. . . ."

"That's right," Hugh chimed in quietly. "We even heard about it over in the other camp."

Scott hesitated, catching more wind before he said as softly yet forcefully as he could: "We *have* to remember those men! We cannot screw this up for everyone heading out tonight! We have to be careful. . . . Very careful!"

"We have to find the truth," Tommy bluntly replied.

He could just see Scott's head nodding in agreement. "That's right," he said. "We have to find the truth. But we have to remember the cost. Others have died. There are some debts being paid tonight, and we have to keep that in mind, Tommy. Remember, when all is said and done, we are still officers in the air corps. We took oaths to defend our country. Not to defend me. That's all I'm saying."

Tommy swallowed hard. "I'll remember," he said. He felt as if everything he had to do that night had just been made far more difficult. The stakes are high, he told himself.

Hugh was silent for a second, before he whispered, "You know, Scott, you're a bloody good soldier and a patriot, and you're absolutely right, and all these bastards who've been lying and cheating probably don't deserve what you're saying even though you're right. Now Tommy, you're the navigator. . . ."

Tommy could see Scott's abrupt wide grin.

"That's right, Tommy. You chart the course. We'll follow."

There was nothing he could say. Unsure about anything except that all the answers lay somewhere in the darkness ahead of him, Tommy gently slid the bunk room door open, and stealthily began to move down the corridor, aware that his two companions were trailing a few steps behind. There was nothing in the air around them except black night and the crippling harsh fear of uncertainty.

They had maneuvered halfway down the barracks when a small shaft of light filtered through the cracks in the front door as the searchlight swept past, and for the smallest of seconds, Tommy caught sight of three figures huddled together. Then, just as quickly as the light was there, it exited, plunging the barracks into darkness again. But Tommy saw through the blackness what he expected; three men silently diving out into the ocean of night. He could not tell who they were, nor could he see how they were dressed, or what they carried. All he saw was the shape of movement, and he pushed ahead rapidly.

There was no need to say anything when they reached the end of the corridor and hunched down, waiting for the same moment when the light would slide past. Save for the sharpened breaths from the two men beside him, Tommy could hear nothing.

They did not have to wait long. The searchlight glow smacked the door, seemed to hesitate, then pushed on, carving away slices of darkness from the other huts. In that moment, Tommy reached up, grabbed the door handle, and pushed it open, diving out into the night as he had before, making fast for the lee of the hut and the shadows that lurked there. The two others were directly behind him, and when they all thrust themselves up against the wall of Hut 103, they were breathing much harder than they would have expected, given the modest distance they'd covered.

Tommy peered around, trying to find the three men who had exited before them, but he could not pick them out of the night. "Damn," he whispered.

Hugh wiped his forehead. "I'm not sure I like being ass-end Charlie here tonight," he spat, but his words were punctuated by a smile.

Tommy nodded, feeling a little lighter at hearing the Canadian's brusque voice. "Ass-end Charlie" was the British fighter pilots' inelegant description for the last man in a six-plane wing attack formation—the most dangerous and deadly position. The war had been almost a year old before fighter command ordered an alteration in the basic flying formation, switching to a V similar to the way the Germans flew into combat, instead of the elongated wing, which left the last man uncovered. No one ever watched the tail of ass-end Charlie, and dozens of Spitfire pilots had died in 1939, because the Germans flying Messerschmidts would simply sidle up behind, unseen, fire a burst, and then flee, before the wing could get turned to meet the threat.

"Ah, never mind," Hugh added. "Where to now?"

Tommy strained his eyes to penetrate the night. It was

clear, cold. The sky was lit with stars and a partial moon glowed above the distant line of trees, outlining the forms of the goons manning the machine-gun towers. The three men traveling ahead of them had disappeared.

"Maybe under the hut, like before, Tommy?" Scott whispered. "Maybe they went that way."

Tommy shook his head and shivered at the thought. "No," he said, welcoming the pitch black around them. "Around the front, then over to the side of 105. Follow me."

Without waiting for a response, the three men bent over and raced forward, dodging the stairs into 103, passing along the edge of the open space and danger, then letting the narrow alley between the huts close in on them.

Just as they passed from the danger of the exposed front into the safety of the alley, Tommy heard a small thudding sound, followed by a whispered, but frantic curse. Without breaking his stride, as he dodged into the darkness, he saw the shape of a man a few dozen yards away, directly in front of Hut 105.

The man was scrambling, picking up a valise dropped in the dirt. He was bent over, moving frantically, grabbing at the small suitcase and a few indistinct items that had fallen out, then immediately sprinting ahead, disappearing from Tommy's sight. Tommy realized instantly that this was the third man in the trio moving ahead of them. The third man, who faced most of the danger.

As if to punctuate this threat, a searchlight swung over the spot where the man had dropped his suitcase only seconds before. The light seemed to dance about, swaying back and forth, almost as if it were only mildly curious. Then, after a few seconds, it shrugged and skipped on, moving ahead.

"You see that?" Lincoln Scott hissed.

Tommy nodded.

"You got an idea where they're going?" Renaday asked.

"My guess is Hut 107," Tommy said. "But we won't know for sure until we get there."

Dodging across the alley, covered by the blackness, the three men maneuvered to the front of the next hut. The air was still, soundless. It was so quiet that Tommy thought that every infinitesimal noise they made was magnified, trumpet-like, a klaxon noise of alarm. To move silently in a world absent all external noises is very difficult. There were no nearby city sounds of cars and buses or even the deep whomp-whomp-whomp of a distant bombing raid. Not even the joking voices of the goons in the towers or a bark from a *Hundführer*'s dog creased the night to distract or help conceal every footstep they made. For a moment, he wished the British would break into some rowdy song over in the northern compound. Anything to cover over the top of the modest noises they made.

"Okay," Tommy whispered, "same drill as before, except this time, we're going one at a time. Around the front and then into the shadow on the far side. I'm first, then Lincoln, and then you, Hugh. Nobody rush anything. Be careful. We're a lot closer to the tower across the yard. It was their light that almost caught the other guy. They might have heard something and they may be looking this way. And there's usually one of those damn dogs over by the front gate. Take your time and wait until you're sure it's safe."

"Right," Scott said.

"Those damn dogs," Hugh muttered. "You think he can smell how scared I am?" The Canadian cracked a small, joyless laugh. "Shouldn't be too bloody hard to pick up my scent right about now. And if those damnable lights come any closer, you'll be able to smell my drawers from a mile away."

This made both Tommy and Lincoln smile, despite themselves.

The Canadian grasped Tommy on the forearm. "You lead on, Tommy," he said. "Scott'll be right behind you, and I'll be along in a minute or two."

"Wait until you're sure," Tommy repeated. Then, hunched over, he crab-walked up to the front of the hut, right to the last shadow on the lip of the exposed area. He paused there, reaching down and double-checking his shoes to make sure they were fastened tightly and that his jacket was zipped tight, and pulling his cap down hard on his head. He wore nothing that would jangle, nothing that might catch on the steps as he slipped past. He performed a small inventory of his person, checking for anything that might betray him, and could find nothing. He thought, in that second of hesitation, that he had traveled far without reaching his destination, but that some things that had been hidden from him were much closer to coming into focus. Every rational bone in his body argued against exposing himself to the chances of the search-light, the dogs, and the goons, but Tommy knew these voices of caution were cowards, and realized, too, that there was the chance that dodging the Germans right at that moment might be the least dangerous thing he had to do that night.

Tommy took a deep breath, and balanced forward on the balls of his feet. He looked up, gritted his teeth, and then, without any warning to the others, launched himself around the front of Hut 105.

His feet kicked up small puffs of slippery dust, and he almost stumbled when his boot caught the lip of a small ridge in the dirt. He had the momentary realization that it must have been that same lip that tripped the man before him, but like a skater momentarily thrown off stride, he regained his balance and sprang forward.

Breathing hard, he ducked around the corner, tossing himself against the wall and the welcome darkness. It took him a second or two to calm himself. The beating in his ears was drumlike, perhaps even like the sound of an airplane's engine, and it faded slowly.

Tommy waited for Scott to traverse the same distance, letting the silence flow around him. He sharpened his eyes and ears, and then turned his eyes to the front door of Hut 107. As he watched and listened, he heard the unmistakable sound of an American voice. He bent toward the sound and what he heard didn't surprise him. Penetrating the darkness, even though it was whispered, a man said, "Number thirty-eight . . ." And then there was a small, distant noise as someone rapped twice on the wooden barracks door. Tommy strained to see through the night, and caught a glimpse of the door swinging open, and a bent-over form taking the front steps two at a time and leaping inside.

He immediately could see why Hut 107 was selected. The front door was in a lee, seemingly shielded from the direct glare of the searchlights, almost a blind spot, because of the odd angles of the assembly yard and the way the other huts were placed. It was not as close to the back wire as Hut 109, but the additional distance was surmountable. Escape planners never chose the huts closest to freedom, anyway, because they were the barracks most frequently searched by the ferrets. Tommy could see that the forest was a mere seventy-five yards on the far side of the wire. Other tunnels had almost made it that distance, he knew. And, Tommy realized, Hut 107 had the further advantage of being on the town side of the camp. If an escaping kriegie actually made it into the trees, he could keep going straight, instead of trying to navigate with a homemade compass in the deep black of the Bavarian forest.

Tommy pressed himself against the wall, waiting for Scott. He could tell what the delay was: a searchlight was probing the area they had just traveled, moving behind them, trying to scour the alleyways between the huts.

As Tommy waited, he heard another whisper and double-knock. The door to 107 briefly swung open again. He guessed two men, arriving from the other side of the compound.

The searchlight swept back, toward Hut 101, and Tommy heard the heavy tread of Scott's boots, swinging around the front of the building, as he seized the opportunity. The black flier nearly stumbled as well, and when he threw himself next to Tommy, he was muttering, "Jesus Christ!"

"You okay?"

Scott breathed in deeply. "Still alive and kicking," he said. "But that's too damn close. The searchlight is all over the front of 101 and 103. Bastards. I don't think they saw anything, though. Just typical Kraut behavior. Hugh will be along in a minute, or whenever those goons with that light swing it around somewhere else. You see anything?"

"Yes," Tommy said quietly. "Men going into 107. Whisper a number and knock twice and the door opens."

"A number?"

"Yeah. You be forty-two. I'm forty-one. A little lie, but it'll get us through the door. And Hugh, if he ever manages to get here, he can be forty-three."

"May take him a minute. The lights were close. And there's something in the way. . . ."

"I almost tripped, too."

"Hope he saw that."

The two men waited. They could just make out the shaft of light moving relentlessly over the territory they'd passed through, hunting the darkness. They knew that Hugh was hunched over, hugging the wall, waiting for his chance. It seemed far longer than it probably was, but finally the light snapped off.

"Now, Hugh!" Tommy whispered.

He could hear the pounding of Hugh's boots, as the hulking Canadian leapt forward into the darkness. And then, almost instantly, a deep thud, a muffled curse, and silence, as the same indentation that had tripped each of them did the same to Renaday.

But the Canadian did not immediately leap up.

Instead, Tommy heard a low, harsh moan.

"Hugh?" he whispered as sharply as possible.

There was a moment of quiet, and then both men heard the Canadian's distinctive accent.

"It's my bleeding knee," he groaned.

Tommy crept to the edge of the hut. He could see Hugh still sprawled in the dirt perhaps fifteen feet away, clutching his left knee in agony.

"Wait there," Tommy hissed. "We'll come get you!"

Scott was at Tommy's side, ready to leap into the darkness, when a sudden shaft of light smashed the air above their heads, forcing them to throw themselves down to the ground. The searchlight slammed into the roof of Hut 105, and then crawled lizardlike down the wall toward them.

"Don't move," Hugh whispered.

The light seemed to step away from Tommy and Scott and then hover just beyond where Hugh lay, still grabbing his knee, but motionless, his face buried down in the cold dirt. It seemed as if the edge of the light were only inches away from his boot and discovery. The Canadian seemed to reach out for the darkness, as if it were some sort of protective blanket he could pull over him.

For an instant, the light poised, blurrily licking at the prone form of Tommy's friend. Then, languidly, almost as if it were teasing them, it swung a few feet away, back toward Hut 103.

Hugh remained frozen. Slowly, he twisted his face out of

the dirt and toward the darkness a few feet away, where Tommy and Lincoln Scott remained frozen in position.

"Leave me!" he said quietly, firmly. "I can't bloody well move anyway. You go on!"

"No," Tommy replied, keeping his voice as soft as possible, but stricken with urgency. "We'll get you when the light goes off."

The searchlight stopped again, illuminating the ground perhaps twenty feet away from Hugh.

"Leave me, goddamn it, Tommy! I'm finished for tonight! Kaput!" Scott reached out and touched Tommy on the arm.

"He's right," Scott said. "We've got to go on."

Tommy spun toward the black flier. "If that light catches him they'll shoot him! I'm not leaving him out there!"

"If that light catches him, this place'll be crawling with Krauts in thirty seconds! And all hell will break loose."

"I won't leave him! I left someone behind once before, and I won't do it again!"

"You go out there," Scott hissed, "and you'll end up killing him and yourself and God knows who else tonight."

Tommy turned, in agony, toward Hugh. "He's my friend!" Tommy whispered painfully.

"Then act like one!" Scott replied. "Do what he says!"

Tommy turned, searching the shadows for Hugh. The searchlight continued to bounce around, firing light a few feet away from the Canadian. But what Tommy saw astonished him, and must have done the same for Scott, because Tommy could feel the black flier's grip tighten on his arm.

Hugh had rolled over onto his stomach, and moving with a deliberate and utterly agonizing slowness, was crawling forward, away from the front of the hut, heading steadily, painstakingly, and inexorably toward the assembly yard, pointing himself away from his friends who might have tried to help him, and directly away from the men making their way to Hut 107. He was moving away, as well, from the searchlight's beam, which was only a momentary relief because he was steadily proceeding into the vast central open area of Stalag Luft Thirteen. It was the neutral area, a black expanse without any place to conceal himself, but Tommy knew that Hugh had realized that if he were spotted there, it would not immediately alert the Germans to anything happening in the darkened row of huts. The problem was, there was no way to immediately return to safety from the center of the exercise area. Over the course of the night's remaining hours, he might be able to loop around, crawling all the way, back to Hut 101. But far more likely Hugh would have to wait out in the yard until morning or discovery, and either one might mean his death.

Tommy could just make out the Canadian's faint shape working against the cold earth, as Hugh snaked his way into the yard. Then Tommy turned to Scott and pointed to the entrance to Hut 107. "All right," he said. "Now it's just us."

"Yeah," Scott replied. "Us and whoever's inside waiting."

Silently, the two men made their way over to the deep shadow at the side of the stairs leading into Hut 107. They paused there for just an instant, both Tommy Hart and Lincoln Scott filled with renegade thoughts. Tommy tossed one glance back in the direction where Hugh had crawled off, but he could no longer make out the shape of his friend, who'd been, for better or worse, swallowed up by the darkness.

Tommy reached up, knocked twice, and whispered: "Forty-one and forty-two . . ."

There was a momentary hesitation, then the door creaked slightly as someone inside the hut cracked it open.

They jumped forward, grabbing at the opening, and pushing into the hut.

Tommy heard a voice, alarmed, but still whispering, say, "Hey! You're not . . ." and then fade away. He and Lincoln Scott stood, inside the door, staring down the corridor.

There was an overwhelming eeriness to the scene that greeted them. A half-dozen candles flickered weakly, spaced out perhaps every ten feet or so. Kriegies lined the corridor, all seated on the floor, their legs pulled up beneath them so as to use less space. Perhaps two dozen of the men were dressed in what they hoped would pass for civilian clothing, their uniforms retailored by the camp's sewing services, dyed by ingenious combinations of ink and paints, so that they no longer were colored in the familiar khaki and olive drab of the U.S. Army. Many men, like the man Tommy had spotted leaving Hut 101, carried makeshift suitcases or portfolios. Some wore workmen's hats and carried mock toolboxes. Anything extra that might make them appear to be other than what they truly were.

The man who'd opened the door was still in uniform. Not heading out that night, Tommy realized. He could see, as well, that every few feet there were support staff, still in their uniforms. In all, there had to be close to sixty men silently stretched down the length of the hut's center corridor. Of these, probably only two dozen were on the escape plan and patiently waiting their turn.

"Goddamn it, Hart!" the man at the door hissed. "You're not on the list! What are you doing here?"

"You could call this a truth-seeking mission," Tommy replied briskly.

He said no more, but stepped over the feet of the last man waiting, and started down the corridor. Lincoln Scott picked his own way, directly behind Tommy. The weak candlelight threw odd, elongated shadows against the walls. As they passed, the kriegies remained silent, saying nothing, but watching the two men as they stepped forward. It was as if Tommy and Lincoln were penetrating the secret midnight ritual of some unusual order of monks.

Ahead of them they could see a small cone of light coming from the single-toilet privy at the far end of the hut. A kriegie emerged, holding a makeshift bucket filled with dirt, which he passed to one of the uniformed men standing nearby. The bucket was handed on, and finally disappeared into one of the bunk rooms, like an old-fashioned fire brigade passing water to the base of some flames. Tommy peered into the room as he stepped past, and saw that the bucket was being lifted up into a hole in the ceiling, where another pair of hands grabbed for it. He knew that above, in the crawl space below the ceiling, the dirt was spread about, and then the empty bucket passed down, making its way through pairs of eager hands, back toward the privy.

Tommy stepped up to the door. The men's faces seemed streaked with anxiety, marked by the tension of the night and the flickering light from the candles, as another bucket filled with dirt was lifted from a hole in the floor of the hut's sole bathroom.

The tunnel went down beneath the toilet. Kriegie engineers had managed to lift the entire commode and move it several feet to the side, making an opening perhaps four feet square. The waste pipe descended in the midst of the opening, but had been blocked off at the top. The men in Hut 107 had clearly disabled the toilet in order to dig the tunnel. Tommy was struck with a momentary admiration for the scheme. Then he heard a sharp, angry voice coming from his side.

"Hart! You son of a bitch! What the hell are you doing here?"

Tommy turned and faced Major Clark.

"Well, major," he replied coldly, "I'm looking for some explanations."

"I'm going to see you brought up on charges, lieutenant!" Clark blustered, still keeping his voice low, but unable to conceal his anger. "Now, get the hell back into that corridor and wait there until we're finished here! That's an order!"

Tommy shook his head. "Not tonight it isn't, major. Not yet."

Clark stepped across the small space, thrusting his face into Tommy's. "I'll have you . . ." he started, only to be interrupted by Lincoln Scott, who pushed his broad shoulders forward, and jabbed a finger in the diminutive major's chest, stopping him in his tracks.

"You'll have us what, major? Shot?"

"Yes! You're interfering with a military operation! Disobeying an order in combat! That's a capital offense."

"Well," Scott said, with an angry smile on his lips, "I seem to be accumulating those sorts of charges with some frequency."

To the side, they heard a muffled laugh from several of the other men, a burst probably caused as much by the tension of the night as by what Scott had said.

"We're not going anywhere until we have the truth!" Tommy said, pushing his own face down at the major's.

Clark's face twisted, contorted with rage. He turned to several kriegies standing nearby, just beyond the tunnel entrance. "Seize these men!" Clark hissed.

The kriegies seemed to hesitate, and in that taut second, a different voice rose, filled with a surprising humor, and accompanied by a truculent laugh.

"Hell, major, you can't do that! And we all know it. Because those two guys are just as important as anyone else here tonight. Only difference is, they didn't know it. So I guess they ain't as stupid as you thought, huh, major?"

Tommy looked down and saw that the man who had spoken was hunched over by the side of the tunnel. He was wearing a dark blue suit, and looking like a somewhat bedraggled businessman. But his grin was unmistakable Cleveland.

"Hey, Hart," Lieutenant Nicholas Fenelli said lightly. "I really didn't think I'd see you again until we made it home to the States. So, what do you think of the new threads? Pretty sharp, huh? Think the girls back home will be lining up for me?"

Fenelli, still smiling, gestured to his suit jacket.

Major Clark turned angrily to the camp medic. "Lieutenant Fenelli, you're not a part of this!"

Fenelli shook his head. "That's where you're wrong, major. And every flier here knows it. We're all a part of the same thing."

Just then another bucket of dirt rose from the tunnel entrance, seemingly pinning Major Clark between the need to distribute the dirt and to deal with Tommy Hart and Lincoln Scott. Clark glared at the two lieutenants, and down at Fenelli, who just grinned insouciantly back at him. He pointed at the bucket brigade to move the dirt along, which it did, swinging past Tommy and Lincoln. Then Clark bent down and whispered to the men in the tunnel: "How much farther?"

It took almost a minute of silence for the question to be relayed up the tunnel and another minute for the answer to come boomeranging back.

"Six feet," a disembodied voice said, rising from the hole in the floor. "Just like digging a grave."

"Keep at it," the major said, frowning. "Stick to the schedule!" Then he turned back to Tommy and Lincoln. "You two are not welcome here," he said coldly and calmly, apparently having regained his composure in the time it took for the message to be sent up the tunnel and returned.

"Where's Colonel MacNamara?" Tommy asked.

"Where do you think?" Clark asked. Then he answered his own question sourly. "In his bunk room, deliberating with the other two members of the tribunal."

Tommy paused, then asked, "And he's writing a speech, too, isn't he? Something that will keep that morning *Appell* delayed even further, right?"

Clark grimaced and didn't reply. But Fenelli did.

"I knew you were smart enough to figure that out, Hart," he said with his small laugh. "I told the major that, when he first approached me about making some small alterations in my testimony. But he didn't think you could."

"Shut up, Fenelli," Clark said.

"Alterations?" Tommy demanded.

Clark did not reply to this. He turned to Hart, his face set, illuminated by candles that exaggerated the red rage coloring on his cheeks. "You are correct that the ending of the trial provided us with a crucial opportunity that we elected to seize. Take advantage of. But that's all it provided. An opportunity. There. Now you've had your damn question answered. Get out of the way. We don't have any time to waste, especially on you, Hart, and you, too, Scott."

"I don't believe you," Tommy said. "Who killed Trader Vic?" he asked insistently.

Major Clark pointed a finger directly at Lincoln Scott. "He did," he replied harshly. "All the evidence points to him. It has from the start. And that's what the tribunal will conclude tomorrow morning. You can take that to the bank, lieutenant. Now get the hell out of the way."

Another bucket rose from the hole in the floor and was seized by a kriegie, who silently moved it into the corridor. Tommy was only peripherally aware that many of the men behind him had pushed forward, trying to hear the words being spoken above the tunnel entrance.

"Why was Vic killed?" Tommy asked. "I want the damn answers, major!"

For a moment, the entire corridor jammed with men, and the men working in the tunnel entrance all seemed to hesitate, letting this question echo about the tiny space, painting each kriegie with the same doubt.

Clark folded his arms in front of his chest. "You won't be getting any more answers from me, lieutenant," he said. "All the answers you need have already come out at trial. Everyone here knows that. Now stand aside and let us get finished!"

The major seemed rocklike. Uncompromising. Tommy was suddenly at a loss as to what to do. It seemed to him that somewhere close by everything that had happened in the camp over the past weeks could be explained, but he had no idea where to turn. The major was turning obstinacy into a rock-solid lie, and Tommy did not know how to break that barrier. He could sense Lincoln Scott wavering at his side, almost defeated by this final obstacle before them. Tommy searched about, trying to find his next step, next maneuver, but was greeted with a confused emptiness within himself. He knew he couldn't compromise the escape effort. He did not know what threat he could make, what lever he could pull, what invention he could come up with that would break the sudden stalemate in the privy. He thought right at that second that on the other end of the tunnel men were going to break free, and the truth was going to leave with them.

And just as this thought crept into his heart, Nicholas Fenelli abruptly piped up again. "You know, Hart, the major isn't going to help you. He hates Lieutenant Scott as much as Trader Vic did, and probably for the same damn reasons. He probably wants to be there to see that Kraut firing squad take aim. Hell, sounds to me like he'd be willing to give the damn order to fire. . . ."

"Shut up, Fenelli!" Clark said. "That's a direct order!"

Tommy looked down at the man who wanted to be a doctor, who shrugged, again ignoring the major.

"You want some answers, Tommy? Well, it seems to me you're going to have to dig hard for them tonight."

Tommy felt a sudden chill in the room, as if he'd stepped into a pocket of cold air. "I don't follow," he said, hesitating.

"Sure you do," Fenelli answered, with another small, braying laugh, and a mocking sneer directed toward Major Clark. "Let me put it to you this way, Tommy. . . ."

The medic held out a small piece of white paper. Tommy saw the number twenty-eight written in black pencil in the middle of the sheet. He looked at Fenelli.

"I'm twenty-eight," Fenelli said slowly. "In order to get that number, all I had to do was maybe change my trial testimony a bit. Maybe lie a little. Just take away your defense. Of course, they didn't expect your little maneuver with Visser. Didn't expect that at all. That was pretty neat. Anyway, Tommy, the guys right in front of me, well, they're not rotten bastards like I am, who paid a price for their spot in this line. Most of those guys are the good guys, Hart. There are some forgers and some engineers and some tunnel rats. They get the higher numbers, right? They're the guys who designed this thing, and did all the really hard work and just about everything else. Just about everything. But not quite everything. So, let me ask you a question, Tommy. . . ."

Fenelli's smile faded instantly, replaced with a harsh, hard look that said almost as much as the words that followed. "I'm just a liar, and I got number twenty-eight. So, where do you suppose the men willing to kill a man in order to keep this tunnel a secret would be? Do you think maybe they might be at the very top of the list?"

Tommy was about to blurt out *But how?* when he saw the answer.

A deep, almost painful, cold shaft of fear sliced through his heart and lodged deep in his stomach. He could feel sweat burst forth on his temples, beneath his arms, and his throat went abruptly dry. He knew his hands were starting to shake, and the muscles in his thighs twitched in sudden terror.

At his side, Scott must have understood the panic that settled within Tommy, because he said quietly, "I'll go. You can't go down there. I know that. You wait here."

But Tommy shook his head back and forth hard.

"They won't believe you, even if you did manage to come back with the truth. But they'll have to believe me."

From his position near the tunnel entrance, Fenelli chimed in: "He's right, Scott. You're the one facing the firing squad. Got nothing to lose by lying. But there's a good chance that all these guys here, the ones not going out tonight, well, they're likely to believe what Tommy says. Because he's one of them. Been in the bag for goddamn nearly forever, and he's as white as they are. Sorry, but that's the truth."

Scott seemed to grow tense, his arms rigid. Then he

nodded, although it clearly took a great effort for him to do this.

Tommy stepped forward.

Major Clark stepped into his path. "I won't allow . . ." he began.

"Yes, you will," Scott said coldly. He did not need to say anything else. The major eyed the black flier, then stepped back quickly.

"You watch my back, Lincoln," Tommy said. "I won't be long. I hope."

He did not wait to hear the black airman's acknowledgment. Knowing that if he hesitated in the slightest, he wouldn't be able to force himself to do what he now knew he had to do, Tommy stepped to the edge of the tunnel. There were candles spaced out, on handcarved ledges, leading down into the narrow pit. A single strand of half-inch-thick black German telephone cable probably stolen from the back of a truck and strong enough to hold a man's weight was fastened to the edge of the toilet, anchored there. Tommy sat down on the lip of the tunnel hole. The man beneath him passed up a bucket filled with dirt, and then squeezed back, pressing himself into the dirt of the tunnel wall. Tommy seized hold of the cable and, filled with utter terror remembered from his childhood and many hard nightmares, slowly lowered himself down into the cold emptiness waiting below him.

Chapter Eighteen

THE END OF
THE TUNNEL

By the time he reached the bottom of the shaft, Tommy thought he could no longer breathe. Every foot he dropped himself into the earth seemed to rob him of air, so that when finally his toes touched the hard, packed dirt twenty feet down, his breath was already coming in short, spasmodic bursts, wheezy and harsh, his chest feeling as if a giant rock were pressing down upon it.

There were two men working in a small space, almost an anteroom at the head of the actual tunnel, perhaps six feet in width and barely four feet high. Their faces were illuminated by a pair of candles mounted in emptied meat tins; the faint light seemed to struggle against the shadows that threatened to overcome the entire space. Both men wore rings of sweat around their foreheads; their cheeks were streaked with dirt and exhaustion. One man was dressed in a suit not that different from the one Fenelli wore, and he was seated behind a makeshift bellows, operating the pump furiously. The bellows made a small whooshing sound, as it pumped air up the tunnel; Tommy guessed this kriegie must be number twenty-seven. The other man wore only skivvies. He was small, compact, and heavily muscled. It was his job to take each bucket of dirt that was passed back and climb it up the shaft for distribution.

The man in the suit spoke first. He didn't stop his pumping at the bellows, but astonishment marked each of his words. "Hart! Jesus, buddy, what the hell are you doing here?" Tommy peered through the flickering light and saw that the man doing the pumping was the fighter pilot from New York, the man who had helped him in the assembly yard.

"Answers," Tommy wheezed. He pointed up the tunnel. "In there."

"You're going up the tunnel?" the New Yorker asked.

Tommy nodded. "Need the truth." He choked out each word harshly.

"The truth is up there? About Trader Vic?"

Tommy nodded again.

The man continued to work, but looked surprised. "You sure? I don't get it. The tunnel and Vic's death? Major Clark never said anything to anybody working this dig that Vic had something to do with this."

"All hidden," Tommy coughed out. "All connected." It took an incredible effort for him to drag enough air past all his fear to find enough wind to speak. "Got to go up there and get the truth."

"Well, I'll be damned," the pilot said, shaking his head back and forth. His face glistened with the effort from pumping the bellows. "I'll say this for you, buddy. You may not find that whoever it is you're looking for is all that eager to talk. Especially with freedom only a coupla feet away."

"Got to go," Tommy repeated, "got no choice anymore." Each word he spoke seemed to sear his chest like a burst of superheated air exploding from a fireball.

The New Yorker continued his hard work without hesitation. He shrugged.

"All right," he said, "here's the deal. There are twenty-six guys spaced out down the length of the tunnel. A kriegie every ten feet or so. Each bucket gets passed forward to the front, filled up, then passed back. Each guy scoots forward like a crab, then backs up, sorta like some crazy turtle in reverse. We're on a pretty tight schedule here, so you better keep moving and get whatever it is you're gonna do, done. And you're gonna hafta squeeze by every guy in the tunnel. There's a rope to help you pull yourself along. But for Christ's sake don't hit the goddamn ceiling! Try not to lift your head at all. We used wood from the Red Cross parcels to shore up the roof, but it's unstable as hell, and if you bang into it, it's likely to come down on your head. Maybe on everybody's heads. Try not to scrape the walls, either. They ain't much better."

Tommy took in everything the man said. He turned his eyes toward the tunnel shaft. It was narrow, terrifying. No more than two feet by three feet. Each kriegie waiting in the tunnel had a single fat candle creating little islands of light around them; those were the only sources of illumination along the entire length.

The New Yorker smiled. "Hey, Tommy," he said, grinning through the exertion, "when I get home and make my first million and I need some damn sharp polished-shoes Ivy League lawyer to watch out for my money and my butt, you're gonna be the guy I'm gonna call. You can count on it. Anyway, hope you find what you're looking for," he said. Then he bent forward, peering up into the tunnel, and he half-whispered, half-shouted a sort of warning: "Man coming up. Make way!"

"Hope you make it home okay," Tommy managed to say, his throat already parched with dust and fear.

"Gotta try," the New Yorker said. "Better than spending another minute wasting away in this damn place."

Then he bent down and renewed his pumping with increased vigor, forcing blast after blast of air up the length of the tunnel.

Tommy ducked down, on his hands and knees. He hesitated for just an instant, finding the rope with his fingers and grasping hold of it, then he thrust himself forward, on his belly, crawling forward like some eager newborn, but with none of a child's sense of adventure. Instead, all he could discern was a deep, cavernous terror echoing within him, and all he knew was that the answers he needed that night lay some seventy-five yards ahead, at the very end of what any reasonable person would take one single glance at and recognize was little more than a long, dark, and dangerously narrow grave.

Hugh Renaday was also crawling.

Moving slowly, with painstaking deliberateness, he'd managed to cover almost a hundred yards, so that he was now well into the center of the open exercise and assembly area, and he deemed it reasonable now to turn and try to maneuver back close enough to the front of Hut 101 where he could burst up and sprint for the doorway when the final shadows of the night aligned themselves conveniently. Of course, he realized, sprinting was going to be an experience. The pain in his knee was excruciating, a flower of agony dropping throbbing petals of hurt throughout his entire leg.

For a moment, the Canadian lowered his face into the dirt, tasting the dry, bitter grime on his tongue. The exertion of crawling had forced him into a sweat, and now, taking a second to rest, he felt a hard chill move through the core of his body. He remembered a time when he was younger and he'd had the wind knocked out of him during a game, and he'd lain on the ice, gasping, feeling the deep cold seep through his jersey and socks, as if to remind him who was really the stronger. He kept his face buried down, thinking that this night was trying to teach him much the same lesson.

A part of him had already accepted that he would be shot and killed that night. Maybe in the next few minutes. Maybe he had an hour or two left. This gloomy sense of despair fought hard against a wild and almost uncontrollable urge to live. The fight between these two conflicting desires was clouded by all that had happened, and the more pure need that Hugh inwardly seized on that regardless of what happened to him, he would do nothing to compromise his friends' lives. And he supposed not compromising them meant not compromising the escape that was being mounted that night.

A great quiet surrounded him, and he listened to his raspy breathing. For a moment, silently, he spoke to his own knee, berating it: How could you do this to me? It wasn't that hard a cut. I've asked you to do much more difficult things, turns and spins, and drives on the ice, and you've never complained before, and certainly never betrayed me. Why this bloody night? The knee did not answer back directly, but continued to throb, as if settling into a comfortable pain that it could deliver steadily. He wondered what he had done. Torn ligaments? Dislocation? Then, still face down in the dirt, he shrugged, as if to say that it made no difference.

Slowly he lifted his eyes, carefully surveying the area around him. The guards in the towers, the *Hundführers* leading their dogs around the perimeter, were nowhere to be seen, but, he told himself, that didn't mean they were not there. All it meant was that he could not see them. Still, he was encouraged. If he could not see them, then perhaps they could not see him.

Carefully, still hugging the earth, Hugh Renaday turned slightly, snaking himself forward again, but now angling back on a diagonal path toward Hut 101. He made a plan, which also reinvigorated him: crawl another fifty yards, then wait. Wait at least an hour, maybe two. Wait for the last and deepest part of the night to arrive, and then make an attempt for the hut. That would give Tommy and Scott enough time to do whatever it was that they had figured out they had to do. And, he hoped, it would give the escapees enough time as well.

Hugh sighed sharply, as he pushed forward with slow, yet steady determination. It seemed to him that there were many needs being filled that night, and he was damned if he knew which was the most important. He knew only that he was crawling along a razor-thin edge himself. He had an odd, almost funny memory strike him right then. He recalled a science class in high school, where the teacher had boastfully told a disbelieving bunch of students that a slug could actually crawl across the straight edge of a razor without slicing itself in two. And the teacher had backed this up, producing a brown, slimy slug and the obligatory shiny razor, and the students had lined up and watched in astonishment as the snail did precisely as advertised. He thought that this night he had to be no different from that snail. At least, that was what he believed.

Thirty yards to his right, the barbed-wire barricade loomed up. He kept himself pressed down, told himself to measure progress in inches, maybe even centimeters. He told himself: Let the night work for you.

At that moment, though, he heard a single, sharp bark, from just beyond the wire fence, followed by a clear, harsh, low growl. He froze, pushing himself down as far as he could into the embrace of cold dirt.

There was a metal jangle as a *Hundführer* pulled back hard on his dog's chain. He heard the goon talk to his animal, calling it by name. *"Prinz! Vas ist das? Bei Fuss! Heel!"* The dog's growl had changed into a constant teeth-bared guttural sound, as it struggled to pull ahead.

Hugh shuddered, barely with enough time to be afraid.

Each *Hundführer* carried a small, battery-driven flashlight. The Canadian heard a click, and then saw a weak cone of light sweep back and forth a few feet away. He dug himself even deeper, still frozen in position. The dog barked again, and Hugh saw the edge of the torch's beam trickle across the back of his outstretched hands. He did not dare move them.

Then he heard a voice cry out in the darkness: "Halt! Halt!"

The dog began to bark over and over, frantically, its voice shattering the night as it strained to get forward. He heard the *Hundführer* chamber a round in his rifle, and, in the same second, a searchlight from the closest tower switched on with an electric thud. It creased the darkness, blistering him with sudden brightness.

He struggled quickly to his feet, his leg pulsating in objection, immediately lifting his hands far above his head. Hugh cried out desperately, *"Nicht schiessen! Nicht schiessen!"* as he stood alone in the glare of exposure. He took a deep breath, and whispered to himself, "Don't shoot . . ." Then he closed his eyes, and thought of home and how, in the early days of summer, dawn always seemed to sweep across the Canadian plains with a purple-red clear intensity, as if overwhelmed, excited, and undeniably joyous at the idea of another day. For a single microsecond he felt a complete and ineffable sadness that he would never be awake to see those moments again. Then, crowded into this final thought, he managed to wish Tommy and Lincoln good luck.

Hugh squeezed his eyes tight against the last second about to arrive for him and heard his own voice, strangely distant and oddly unafraid, try one more time: *"Nicht schiessen!"* he shouted. He wished, in that moment, that he could have found a braver, more glorious, and less lonely place to die. Then he quieted, hands raised high in the air, and simply waited with surprising patience to be murdered.

In the undiluted terror that had overtaken him, twenty feet beneath the surface, Tommy could no longer tell whether it was stifling hot or bone-chilling cold. He shivered with every inch forward, and salty sweat clogged his eyes. Every foot he traveled seemed to take the last of his ebbing strength, rob the final breath he could pry, wheezing, from the air of the tunnel that threatened to entomb him. More than once he'd heard an ominous creak of flimsy wood shoring up the walls and ceiling, and more than once dusty rivulets of dirt had streamed down onto his head and neck.

The darkness that surrounded him was marred only by the candles held by each man he worked his way past. The kriegies in the tunnel were astonished at his presence, but still they moved aside as best they could, pushing themselves dangerously against the wall of the tunnel, giving him precious inches of empty space to squeeze past. Every man he met held their breath as he scraped by, knowing that even taking a single extra breath might bring the roof down on all of them. There were a few curses, but no objections. The entire tunnel was filled with fear, apprehension, and danger, and to the men waiting in the darkness, Tommy's steady trip to the front was merely another awful anxiety on what they dreamed would be the road to freedom.

He recognized several of the men—two from his own hut, who grunted an acknowledgment as he crept past, and a third who'd once borrowed one of his law texts, desperate for anything to read to break the monotony of a snowy winter week. There was a man with whom he'd once had a funny conversation in the yard, sharing cigarettes and ersatz coffee, a wiry, grinning fellow from Princeton who had insulted Harvard most wildly and hilariously, but who had readily agreed that any Yale man was probably not only a shirker and a coward but likely to be fighting for the Germans or the Japanese, anyway. The Princeton man had pushed back against the wall, and gasped when some dirt from the roof streamed onto both their heads. Then he'd urged Tommy on with a whispered, "Get what you need, Tommy." This alone had encouraged Tommy to travel another half-dozen feet forward, stopping only to seize the dirt-filled bucket from the man ahead, and pass it back to Princeton, behind him.

The muscles in his arms and legs screamed pain and fatigue at him. His neck and back felt as if they were being hammered by the red-hot tongs of a blacksmith. For an instant, he lowered his head, listening to the yawing sound of the wooden supports, and thought that nothing in the world was more exhausting than fear. No race. No fight. No battle. Fear always ran faster, hit harder, and fought longer.

He dragged himself forward, struggling past each of the designated escapees. He was no longer able to tell whether he'd been crawling for minutes or hours. He thought he would never get out of the tunnel, and then imagined that it was like some particularly terrifying dream from which he was destined never to awaken.

He pushed on, gasping for air.

Tommy had counted the men in the tunnel, and knew that he was squeezing past Number Three, a bankerly type wearing wire-rim glasses streaked with moisture, whom Tommy presumed was the chief camp document forger. The man twisted aside, grunting, wordless, as Tommy maneuvered past him. For the first time, Tommy could hear the sounds of digging coming from up ahead. He guessed there were two men, working in a small space not unlike the anteroom where he'd found the pilot from New York. The difference would be that they would have no abundance of crate boards to shore things up. Instead, they would be scraping the dirt from above their heads, packing it in the empty buckets and passing it back. There would be no need for an elaborate, concealed exit, the way the entrance was so cleverly hidden back in the privy in Hut 107. The exit would be the smallest possible hole a kriegie could worm through.

Tommy thrust himself toward the sound of the digging. There must have been two candles in that space, because he could just make out a flickering, indistinct shape. He crept forward, still without a concrete plan beyond confrontation, thinking hard to himself that what he needed to know was just at the edge of his reach.

He knew only that he wanted to reach the end. The end of the tunnel. The end of the case. The end of everything that had happened. He could feel panic surging through him, mingling freely with confusion and desire. Driven by the difficult twins of fear and fury, he pushed himself the final few feet, almost popping into the anteroom to the escape's exit.

Above him, the tunnel rose sharply toward the surface.

A makeshift ladder built from scraps of wood was thrust against the side of the shaft. Near the top of the ladder, one man hacked at the remaining clods of dirt. Midway down, a second man caught the earth as it fell from beneath the pickax, collecting it in the ubiquitous bucket. Both men were nearly naked, their bodies glistening in the candlelight with sweat and streaks of dirt that made them seem prehistoric, terrifying. Thrust to the side of the anteroom were two small valises and a pile of clothes they would change into as soon as they burst through to the air. Their escape kit.

From above him, the two men hesitated, looking down in surprise.

Tommy could not make out the face of Number One, the man with the pickax. But his eyes met Number Two.

"Hart!" the man whispered sharply.

Tommy struggled halfway to his feet in the tight, narrow space, ending on his knees like some supplicant in a church looking up at the figure on the Cross. He peered through the flickering light, and after a single, long silent moment, recognized Number Two. "You killed him, didn't you, Murphy?" Tommy said harshly. "He was your friend and your roommate and you killed him, didn't you?"

At first, the lieutenant from Springfield didn't reply. His face wore an eerie look of astonishment and surprise, and then slowly dissolved into recognition, followed by rage.

But what he said was, "No, I didn't. I didn't kill him."

Then he hesitated for a half-second, just long enough for the denial to toss Tommy wildly into confusion, and then he threw himself down on Tommy, grunting savagely, his dirty, strong hands reaching inexorably for Tommy's throat.

At the tail of the tunnel in Hut 107, Major Clark glanced down at his wristwatch, shook his head, then turned his stare toward Lincoln Scott. "Now we're behind," he said bitterly. "Every minute is critical, lieutenant. In another couple of minutes, the entire escape will be in jeopardy."

Scott stood by the entrance to the tunnel, almost straddling it, like a policeman guarding a door. He returned the major's glare with a singularly cold gaze of his own.

"I do not understand you, major," he said. "You would allow Vic's killers to go free and the Germans to shoot me. What sort of man are you?"

Clark stared, coldly, harshly, at the black airman.

"You're the killer, Scott," he said. "The evidence has always been clear-cut and unequivocal. It has nothing to do with this escape tonight."

"You lie," Scott replied.

Clark shook his head, answering in a low, awful voice, with a small and terrible smile. "Do I, now? No, that's where you're wrong. I know nothing of any conspiracy to set you up as the killer. I know nothing of any other man's participation in the crime. I know nothing that would support your ridiculous story. I know only that an officer was killed, an officer you made no secret of hating. I know that this officer had previously provided valuable assistance to prior tunnel escape efforts, to wit, acquiring documents for forgers to work on, German cash, and other items of importance. And I know that the German authorities were very interested in this murder. More interested than they had a right to be. And because of this interest, I know that this particular tunnel, our best chance to get some men out, was severely threatened because had they decided to hunt for the killer and the evidence to support charges, they would have torn the camp completely apart, probably exposing this escape attempt in the process. So the only thing you are possibly correct about, lieutenant, is that as chief of escape security, I was genuinely pleased that you presented yourself covered with blood and guilt at a critical moment. And I have been pleased that your little trial and your little conviction and your little execution, which I'm certain is to follow quite quickly, has proven to be such a wonderful distraction for the Krauts."

"You don't know about those men at the front of the tunnel?" Scott asked, almost incredulous at the venom served in his direction.

Major Clark shook his head. "Not only do I not know, I don't want to know. The obviousness of your guilt has been very helpful."

"You would shoot an innocent man to protect your tunnel?"

The major grinned again. "Of course. And so would you, if

you were in my position. So would any officer in charge. Men are sacrificed in war all the time, Scott. So you die and we protect a larger good. Why is that so strange for you to understand?"

Scott did not reply. He wondered, in that second, why he was not filled with outrage, filled with fury. Instead, he looked over at the major and felt nothing but contempt, but it was the most curious sort of contempt, for a part of him understood the precise truth in what the man had said. It was an evil truth and a terrible one, but a truth of war nonetheless. He hated that, but oddly, accepted it.

Scott looked back into the tunnel shaft.

Fenelli spoke then. "Man, I wonder what's taking him so long?" The would-be doctor was perched by the tunnel entrance, balancing, craning forward to hear something other than the steady whoosh-whoosh of the homemade bellows.

The black flier swallowed hard. His own throat was dry. In that moment he realized that he'd allowed a terrified man, the only man who'd really befriended him, to struggle into the darkness alone only because he was so eager to live. He thought that all his own proud words about willingness to die and sacrifice and taking a stand and dignity had abruptly been proven hollow by the simple act of letting Tommy crawl into that tunnel searching for the truth necessary to set him free. Tommy had not made any of the same fine and brave speeches that he had made, but had quietly faced down his own terrors and was sacrificing himself. Too dangerous. Too uncertain, Scott thought suddenly. It was a trip that Scott suddenly realized he should never have allowed Tommy to take on his behalf.

But he had no idea what to do, other than stand guard and wait. And hope.

He looked back at Major Clark. Then he spoke to the smug and pretentious officer with an unbridled cold hatred: "Tommy Hart doesn't deserve to die, major. And if he doesn't come back out of that tunnel, well, I'm going to hold you personally responsible, and then trust me: There won't be any goddamn uncertainty at all about the next murder charge I face."

Clark took a short step back, as if he'd been slapped across the cheek. His own face was set in an unruly combination of fear and fury. Neither emotion was particularly well hidden. He glanced over at Fenelli and choked out a few words.

"You heard that threat, didn't you, lieutenant?"

Fenelli grinned. "I didn't hear a threat, major. What I heard was a promise. Or maybe just a statement of fact. Kinda like saying the sun's gonna come up tomorrow. Count on it. And I don't think you've got even the slightest understanding why they're different. And you know what else occurs to me, right now? I'm thinking it might be a real good thing for you and your immediate future if Tommy gets back here safe and sound pretty damn fast."

Major Clark did not reply to this. Nervously, he, too, stared toward the tunnel entrance, which yawned silently in front of them. After a moment, he said to everyone and no one, "We're running out of time."

To his astonishment, the *Hundführer* did not immediately shoot him. Nor did the tower guards who put his chest in the crosshairs of the thirty-caliber machine gun they manned.

Hugh Renaday stood motionless, arms lifted high, almost suspended in a single shaft of light. He was blinded by the searchlight's glare, and he blinked hard, trying to peer past the cone of brightness into the night beyond and the German soldiers he could hear calling to one another. He allowed himself a small measure of relief: No general alarm had been sounded. And, so far, he had not been shot, which also would have triggered a campwide alert.

Behind him, he heard the creaking sound of the compound's main gate swinging open, followed by two pairs of footsteps pounding across the assembly yard toward where he remained standing. Within a few seconds, two helmeted goons, their rifles at the ready, lurched into the spotlight, like actors joining a play in progress on the stage. *"Raus! Raus!"* one of the goons blurted out. "Follow! *Schnell!*" The second goon quickly patted Hugh down, then stepped back, prodding him in the center of the back with the barrel of his rifle.

"Just out taking in a little of the fine spring German air," Hugh said. "Can't exactly see what you chaps believe is the problem. . . ."

The goons did not reply, but one man thrust his gun barrel into the small of his back with a little more vigor. Hugh limped forward, the pain renewed in his knee, deep core-striking bolts of agony. He bit down hard on his lip and tried to hide the limp as best he could, swinging the bad leg forward.

"Really," he said briskly, "can't see precisely what all the fuss is about. . . ."

"*Raus,*" the goon answered glumly, now pushing the limping man forward with his rifle butt.

Hugh gritted his teeth and, dragging his leg, followed close. Behind him, the searchlight shut off with a thud, and it took several seconds for the Canadian's eyes to adjust again to the darkness. Each of those seconds was punctuated with another shove from the guard. For a moment, he wondered whether the Krauts meant to shoot him in privacy, somewhere where his body wouldn't be on display for all the other kriegies. He thought this very possible, given the sensitivity to the trial and the high-running emotions in the camp. But the pain that was racing through his leg prevented him from much further speculation. Whatever was going to happen would happen, he told himself, although it was with some relief that he realized the two guards were heading toward the primary administration building. He could see a single light flick on inside the low, flat house, almost as if in greeting.

They reached the bottom of the stairs and the goon shoved Hugh again, a little harder, and Hugh stumbled forward, almost falling on the front steps. "Curb your enthusiasm, you bastard," he muttered as he regained his balance. The German gestured, and Hugh mounted the stairs as rapidly as his leg would permit.

The front door swung open for him, and in the weak light emanating from the interior, Hugh made out the unmistakable form of Fritz Number One, holding the door. The ferret seemed surprised when he recognized the Canadian.

"Mr. Renaday," Fritz whispered. "Whatever are you doing? You are most fortunate you were not shot!" The ferret kept his voice low, concealed.

"Thank you, Fritz," Hugh answered quietly, but with a half-smile, as he stepped inside the administration building. "I hope to bloody well stay that way. Unshot."

"This could prove to be difficult," Fritz Number One said in reply. And in the same second, Hugh saw a disheveled and clearly dangerously angry Hauptmann Heinrich Visser sitting at the side of a single desk, reaching for one of his ever-present brown cigarettes.

Tommy blocked the first assault with his forearm, slamming Murphy across the face. The lieutenant from Springfield grunted, and pushed Tommy back savagely against the dirt wall of the anteroom. Tommy could feel sandy grit tumbling down his shirt collar as Murphy's fingers clawed at him. He was able to wedge his left arm up under his attacker's neck, forcing the man's head back, and then he rocked him hard against the opposite wall.

Murphy replied, getting his right hand free and landing a punch to Tommy's cheek, cutting it, so that blood immediately started to trickle down, mingling with dirt and sweat. The two men twisted together in the narrow confines of the tunnel, kicking, pushing, trying to gain some sort of advantage, fighting in a ring that provided none to either man.

Tommy was only vaguely aware of the third man, higher on the ladder, Number One on the escape list, who still held a pickax in his hands. Murphy threw Tommy back, snarling, and Tommy managed to throw a short uppercut into his jaw, hard enough so that Murphy shot backward momentarily. It was a fight without room, as if a dog and cat had been dropped into a single burlap bag together, and tore at each other in that impossible place, neither able to use whatever advantages or cunning Nature had designed for them. Tommy and Murphy ricocheted back and forth, slamming the wall, muscle against muscle, scratching, clawing, throwing wild fists, kicking, punching, trying to find some means of gaining the upper hand. Shadows and darkness slithered like snakes around them.

An elbow caught him in the forehead, and he was almost stunned. In dizzy fury and complete rage, Tommy kicked out, striking Murphy in the shin with a nasty crack. Then, in almost the same motion, he lifted his knee hard, and drove it into Murphy's groin and stomach. The lieutenant from

Springfield moaned deeply, and fell back, clutching his mid-section. At the very same second, out of the corner of his eye, Tommy caught the sensation of something moving his way, and he ducked down, just as the point of the pickax whizzed past his ear. But the force of the miss drove the blade deep into the dirt, and Tommy was able to swing around, smashing upward with his right hand. He felt his fist slam into the other man's face. There was a creaking sound and a snapping noise as a rung on the ladder broke. Tommy realized that by trying the one deadly swing with the ax from above, the man had risked everything, and in the same motion, Tommy grabbed at the short handle, finding it and wrenching it loose, and pulling the attacker off balance, so that he tumbled down wildly, smashing his face into the wall of dirt.

Tommy threw himself back against the opposite wall, brandishing the ax in front of him, breathing harshly. He lifted the ax above his shoulder, ready to crash it down into the back of the third man's neck. Murphy started to reach for him, then stopped, crying out sharply "Don't!" The eerie candlelight threw alternating shadows and streaks of light across his terrified face.

Tommy hesitated, wrenching control past rage. He lifted the ax a second time, as the third man started to roll over, lifting his own forearm to try to deflect the thrust heading his way.

"Don't move!" Tommy hissed. "Nobody goddamn move!" He held the ax in a ready position.

Murphy seemed taut, about to spring, then stopped. He slumped back.

"Killer!" Tommy started to shout, but before he was able to speak another word, the third man said quietly, in a voice held low, that defied the murderous fight they'd just engaged in, "Hart, don't say another word!"

Tommy half-turned toward the voice. It took him a half-second to recognize the slightly tinged, soft southern tones, and to remember where he'd heard them before.

The leader of the Stalag Luft Thirteen Prisoner Jazz Band stared across at Tommy. He smiled wickedly, as if amused.

"You are a right tenacious fellow, Hart," the bandleader said. He shook his head back and forth. "Like some damn half-crazed Yankee bulldog, I must admit. But you're wrong about one thing. Murphy didn't kill our mutual friend, Vic. I did."

"You!" Tommy whispered sharply.

The man grinned. "That's right. I did. And pretty much the way you and that goddamn Kraut Visser had it all figured, too. Imagine that. You kill a man in old-fashioned New Orleans style"—the bandleader mimicked sticking a knife in the throat as he spoke—"and some Kraut Gestapo-type goon figures it out. Damn. And you know what else, Hart? I'd do it again tomorrow, if I had to. So, there you have it. Are you gonna fight us some more, now?"

Tommy brandished the ax. He did not know how to reply.

The bandleader continued to smile. "We got a little bit of a problem here, Tommy," he said. He kept his voice low. "I need that ax. I'm one swipe, maybe two, from breaking through. And we're on a little bit of a tight deadline here. We gotta get going if we're like to have any chance. There are three trains heading to Switzerland this morning. Men that catch the first, likely to have the best chance of making it close enough to the border so that they can find their way across. So I need that ax, and I need it right now. Sorry I tried to kill you with it. You sure did duck at the right moment. But, hell, now you gonna have to give it up."

The bandleader held out his hand. Tommy did not budge.

"The truth, first," he said.

"Gotta keep your voice down, Hart," the bandleader said. "If there are any goons in the trees, they might hear us. Even down here. Voices carry. Of course, it likely would seem to one of them like it was somebody whispering from the grave, but that ain't so far from the truth, now is it?"

"I want to know," Tommy replied.

The bandleader smiled again. He motioned toward Murphy, who started to dust some of the dirt from his body. "Get dressed," he said. "We're going to move soon."

"Why?" Tommy demanded softly.

"Why? You mean why are we trying to get out?"

Tommy shook his head. "No. Why Vic?"

The bandleader shrugged. "Two reasons, Tommy. The best of reasons, too, when you think about 'em. First, Trader Vic was trading information with the damn Krauts. Sometimes, when he needed something special, like a radio or a camera or something, he would whisper a number to some ferret. Usually Fritz Number One, you know. That would be the number of the hut where a tunnel was getting started. Coupla days later, Krauts would show up. Pretend it was a routine search. Bust it up. We'd start digging someplace different. Run through the whole charade again. Vic, I think, he never figured he was doing all that much harm, you see. The Krauts would ruin the tunnel, maybe toss somebody in the cooler for a week or so. Mostly, what Vic figured, was that nobody was getting hurt and everybody was getting ahead. Especially him. Only thing that wasn't happening was nobody was getting out. Which might be a good thing, we'll see. Anyway, it like to kill old MacNamara and Clark. They started digging deeper tunnels. Longer tunnels. Harder tunnels. Those two figured that if they didn't manage to get at least one of us out of here, they would be failures as commanding officers. Wouldn't never be able to face one of their old West Point buddies after the war. Why, Tommy, you can see that. And they didn't know for sure what Vic was doing. No one did, because Vic, he kept these things pretty close to his vest. He thought he had it all figured out. Playing everybody against everybody. Weren't that just like Vic? Anyway, he figured he had it all doped out. And he did. He was some sort of operator, Vic. Until those two guys died in that tunnel. . . ."

The bandleader stopped, took a deep breath of the thin harsh air surrounding them, then continued.

"They was my friends, those two. That one boy was the sweetest clarinet I ever heard. Back home in New Orleans, people like to sell their souls to be able to play one note half as good as him. And they wasn't supposed to be down there, not at night, you see. Vic hadn't figured on anyone digging that late. But MacNamara and Clark, they ordered round-the-clock digging. Two tunnels. That one and this one. Only that one caved in with my friends inside when the goddamn Krauts drove one of their trucks right over the top. They wouldn't have known where to do that if it weren't for Vic."

Tommy nodded. "Revenge," he said. "There's one reason. And betrayal, too, I guess."

Murphy looked over at Tommy. "Best reasons of all," he said. "The sorry bastard. All he did was make one mistake. You shouldn't go around making deals with the devil, because he might just come back and ask a higher price than you want to pay. That's what happened. Funny thing, you know, Vic was a fine flier. Better than fine. A real hotshot. A brave man in the air. Deserved every medal he got. It was on the ground that he couldn't be trusted none."

Tommy slumped back, trying to sort through everything the bandleader said. Like a deck of cards being shuffled, details started to fit together, stacking one after the other neatly.

"So," the bandleader continued, "there you have it. Vic got me the knife, just as I asked him, and then I turned around and I used it on him, while Murphy here kept him occupied from the front. At first we figured to pin the whole thing on one of the ferrets, you see, make it look like Vic got killed when some big old trade went wrong, but your boy Scott made it so damn easy. Weren't no special hardship framing him up for the killing. And it sure as hell kept the Krauts from poking around none, too. You think old Lincoln Scott realizes what a service he's provided? I don't suppose he'll take much comfort in that."

"Why didn't you tell the truth? Why didn't . . ."

The bandleader held up his hand. "Why, Tommy, you ain't thinking this through. What the hell good would it do me, and my Yankee helpmate here, if anyone knew the truth? I mean, we'd just be facing charges back home, wouldn't we? All this trouble to escape, only to get back to the States and be charged with Vic's murder? Not very likely, I think. Not after all this trouble."

Tommy nodded. He knew instantly that unsaid in what the bandleader implied was a single necessity: Lincoln Scott would have to be blamed, tried, convicted, and shot. It was the only way the men in the tunnel escaping could actually be free.

"MacNamara and Clark," Tommy said slowly, "they didn't want the truth, did they?"

The bandleader grinned. "No sir, they did not. I doubt they'd have wanted to hear it, even if it'd come up and smacked them in the face. They wanted Vic taken care of. They didn't want nothing to do with it. The truth, Tommy, as you can hear, is right messy for all involved. Trader Vic was a hero, and the army don't like its heroes tarnished none. And blaming Scott, well, that particular lie, well, it was working real fine for just about everybody. Everybody save Scott, that is. And I don't know this for sure, but I'm guessing right about now Clark and MacNamara didn't count on this quiet boy from Harvard making such a mess and all, either."

"No," Tommy replied. "I guess they didn't."

"Well, you sure have. There you have it. Now, I need that ax," the man said. His voice was barely above a whisper, but it carried both threat and urgency. "Either you let me dig us out of here, or go ahead and kill me, 'cause one way or the other, I will be free by the time the sun comes up!"

Tommy smiled. It was a great word, he thought, the word *free*. Four letters that meant much more. It really should have been a great, long, exultant word, a word with power and strength and pride. He paused and realized that he had to find a way to accommodate everyone that night. "Stalemate," he said abruptly.

The bandleader looked surprised.

"What you mean by that?"

"I mean, no ax. I mean, maybe I'll raise my voice. I don't know what the hell I'll do. Maybe kill you, like you tried to kill me. And then dig these other men out." This was a bluff, Tommy knew. But he said it nonetheless.

"Hart," the bandleader said sharply, "it ain't just us. There's seventy-five men heading out tonight. And ain't none of them waiting behind us done anything to deserve losing their chance at freedom. They worked long and hard and dangerous for this chance tonight. You can't be taking that away. And maybe what I've done ain't perfect by all accounts, but I ain't sure it's altogether wrong, either."

Tommy eyed the man carefully. "You killed a man."

"I did. That's what happens in war. Maybe he deserved to die. Maybe not. Only I don't want to be blamed for it. I don't want to dig my way out of this Kraut hellhole to face an American firing squad."

"True," Tommy said softly. "So, how do you want to solve this, because I'm not leaving here until I know that Lincoln Scott isn't going to face the damn firing squad!"

"I want you to hand me that ax."

"And I want Lincoln Scott to go free."

"There's no time," Murphy piped up. "We gotta get going!"

Silence filled the tiny space, closing in on the three men jammed into the area, covering them like a dark wave closing over their heads.

The bandleader seemed to think hard for a moment. Then he smiled.

"I guess what we'll all have to take is some chances here," he said slowly. "What do you think, Tommy? This is a good night for taking chances. You ready to take some risks?"

"Yes, I am."

Again the bandleader laughed. "Then I guess we got a deal," he said. He stuck out his hand to shake Tommy's, but Tommy continued to wield the pickax. The bandleader shrugged.

"Hart, I gotta say this: You are some sort of hard man."

Then he scrambled to the wall where the tunnel opened into the small anteroom. The bandleader took one of the candles and waved it back and forth. Then he hissed as loudly as he dared: "Number Three? Can y'all hear me?"

There was a momentary silence, then a voice crept up the dark tunnel. "What the hell's going on up there?"

Even Murphy smiled at that most obvious question.

"We're having a little conversation about the truth," the bandleader whispered back. "Now, Number Three, you listen real carefully and you make damn sure you get this right. Lincoln Scott, the Nigra flier, he didn't kill nobody! Especially not Trader Vic! You have my absolute swear to God word on that. You got that?"

There was another small hesitation, then Tommy heard the voice rise up the tunnel, asking, "Scott is innocent?"

"That's one hundred percent right," the bandleader said. "Now, you pass that back in line. And keep right on passing it back, got it? So that everybody knows the real truth. Including that sorry bastard Clark, waiting back there at the start of the tunnel!"

There was another hesitation from Number Three, and then the most critical question. "Well, if Scott is innocent, then who killed Trader Vic?"

The bandleader grinned again, turning to Tommy for an instant, before whispering his response up the tunnel. "The war killed Vic," he said. "Now, you pass that word back just like a bucket of dirt, because we are going to start moving outta here in the next ten minutes!"

"Okay. Scott is innocent. Got it."

Tommy craned forward into the tunnel and heard Number Three scramble backward and then say to Number Four, "Scott is innocent! Pass it back!"

He listened for a moment, as the message was relayed down the length of the tunnel. "Scott is innocent! Pass it back!" He heard it over and over, echoing in the small space, "Scott is innocent! Pass it back! Scott is innocent! Pass it back!" until the words faded totally into the great blackness behind him. Then Tommy slumped over, suddenly exhausted. He did not know for certain whether those three words broadcast to all the men in line in the tunnel and waiting up in Hut 107 would be sufficient to free Scott. *Scott is innocent!* But in the sudden total fatigue that overcame him, he understood they were the three best he could pry out of this night. He held out the pickax to the bandleader, who took it from him.

"I don't even know your name," Tommy said.

For a moment, the bandleader brandished the ax, as if he were going to strike Tommy. "I don't want you to know my name," he said. Then he smiled. "You got lots of faith, Hart. I'll give you that. Not precisely a religious faith, but faith anyhow. Now, as to the rest of our little discussion here tonight . . ."

Tommy shrugged. "I would say that somehow comes under the attorney-client privilege. I'm not exactly sure how, but if anyone ever asked me, that's what I'd say."

The bandleader nodded. "Tommy, I think you maybe shoulda been a musician. You sure know how to carry a tune."

Tommy took this as a compliment. Then he pointed toward the roof. "Now's your chance," he said.

The bandleader grinned again. "Ain't gonna be all that simple for you now, Tommy boy. This little misunderstanding has caused us a significant delay. First, Tommy, I done something for you. That's the chance I took. Now, you're gonna do something for me. Take a chance for me. Not only for me; for all the other kriegies waiting in this damn tunnel and dreaming about getting home. You're gonna help us get outta here."

Chapter Nineteen

THE ESCAPE

Visser motioned Hugh across the administration room to a stiff-backed wooden chair next to his desk. The German's eyes followed the Canadian's progress closely, measuring the difficulty that Hugh had with each step. Hugh slumped down into the seat hard, his face tinged red with exertion, a line of sweat on his forehead and dampening the blouse beneath his armpits. He kept his mouth shut while the German officer slowly lit his cigarette, then leaned back, letting the gray smoke curl around them both.

"I am impolite," Visser finally said softly. "Please, Mr. Renaday, indulge yourself if you so desire." Visser motioned with his only hand to the case of cigarettes lying on the flat table between the two men.

"Thank you," Hugh answered. "But I prefer my own." He reached into his breast pocket and removed a crumpled package of Players. The German remained silent while Hugh carefully removed a cigarette and lit it. When he inhaled the harsh smoke, he leaned back slightly in the chair. Visser smiled.

"Good," he said, "now we are behaving as civilized men, despite the lateness of the hour."

Hugh did not respond.

"So," Visser continued, maintaining an even, almost jocular tone, "perhaps, as a civilized man, you will tell me what it is you were doing out of your assigned quarters, Mr. Renaday? Crawling flat on your belly at the edge of the assembly yard. Most undignified. But why would you be doing this, flying officer?"

Hugh took another long drag on the end of the smoke. "Well," he said carefully, "just as I told your goon who arrested me, I was simply out, taking a breath of fine German night air."

Visser grinned, as if he appreciated the joke. It was not the sort of grin that meant he was actually amused, and Hugh was filled with the first sensations of dread.

"Ah, Mr. Renaday, like so many of your countrymen, and the men they fight alongside, you seek to make sport of what I assure you is a most dangerous situation. I ask you again, why were you out of your assigned quarters after lights out?"

"No reason that concerns you," he said coldly.

Visser continued to smile, although it seemed that the grin was using up more energy than the *Hauptmann* thought necessary.

"But, flying officer, everything that occurs in our camp concerns me. You know this, and still you evade my most simple question: What were you doing out of your assigned quarters?"

This time, Visser punctuated each word of the question with a small thump on the tabletop with his index finger. "Please answer my question with no further delay, flying officer!"

Hugh shook his head.

Visser hesitated, eyeing Renaday closely.

"You think it is unreasonable for me to ask? Flying officer, I do not believe you entirely appreciate the jeopardy of your current position."

Hugh remained silent.

The German's grin had dissolved now. He wore a singular flat, angry appearance in the set of his jaw, the hardness at the corners of his eyes and the edges of his mouth. The scars on Visser's cheeks seemed to grow pale. He shook his head back and forth one time, then slowly, without moving from his seat, Visser reached down to his waist and with a frightening deliberateness, unstrapped the holster flap he wore, and removed a large black steel handgun. He held this up momentarily, then set it down on the desktop in front of Renaday.

"Are you familiar with this weapon, flying officer?"

Hugh shook his head in reply.

"It is a Mauser thirty-eight-caliber revolver. It is a very powerful weapon, Mr. Renaday. Every bit as powerful as the Smith and Wesson revolvers policemen in the States are armed with. It is significantly more powerful than the Webbly-Vickers revolvers that British pilots carry in their bail-out gear. It is not the standard issue for an officer of the Reich, flying officer. Ordinarily men such as myself carry a Luger semiautomatic pistol. A very effective weapon. But it requires two hands to cock and fire, and I, alas, have but the one. So I must use the Mauser, which, admittedly, is far heavier and much more cumbersome, but can be operated with a single hand, and thus it accommodates me far better. You do understand, flying officer, do you not, that a single shot from this weapon will remove a good portion of your face, much of your head, and certainly the majority of your brains?"

Hugh took a long look at the black barrel. The gun remained on the tabletop, but Visser had swung it around so that it pointed at the Canadian. Hugh nodded.

"Good," Visser said. "Perhaps we make some progress. Now, I ask again, what were you doing out of your quarters?"

"Sightseeing," Hugh said coldly.

The German burst into a humorless laugh. Visser looked over at Fritz Number One, who hovered in a corner of the room, remaining in the shadow.

"Mr. Renaday seeks to play the fool, corporal. And yet perhaps the joke will be on him. He does not seem to understand that I am well within my rights to shoot him right here. Or if I were to prefer not to make a mess in our office, to have him removed and shot directly outside. He is in violation of a clear camp rule, and the punishment is death! He hangs by the thinnest of threads, corporal, and still he plays games with us."

Fritz Number One did not reply, other than to nod and stand at attention. Visser turned back to Hugh.

"If I were to send a squad to roust the entire contingent of prisoners in Hut 101, would I find your friend Mr. Hart? Or perhaps Lieutenant Scott? Was your sortie out this night connected to the murder trial?"

Visser held up a hand.

"You do not have to answer that, flying officer, for, of course, I already know that answer. Yes. It must be. But what?"

Hugh shook his head again.

"My name is Hugh Renaday. Flying Officer. My serial number is 472 hyphen 6712. My religion is Protestant. I believe that is all the information I am required to provide at this or any other time, *Herr Hauptmann*."

Visser leaned back in his own seat, anger flashing from his eyes. But the words he spoke in reply were slow, icy, and filled with a patient and awful menace.

"I could not help but notice your limp, as you entered, flying officer. You have an injury?"

Hugh shook his head. "I'm fine."

"But then, why the so-apparent difficulty?"

"An old sports injury. Aggravated this morning."

Visser smiled again. "Please, flying officer, place your foot up here on the desktop, so that your leg is straight."

Hugh didn't move.

"Raise your leg, flying officer. This simple act will delay my shooting you, and give you perhaps a few more seconds to consider precisely how close you are to dying."

Hugh pushed his chair back slightly, and with a great force of will raised his right leg, slapping the heel down onto the center of the table. The awkwardness of his position sent rays of pain radiating up through his hip, and for a moment, he closed his eyes to the collection of hurt that gathered in his leg.

Visser hesitated, then reached over, seizing Hugh at the knee, pressing his fingers hard into the joint, twisting them savagely.

The Canadian nearly tumbled. A bolt of agony surged through his body.

"This is painful, no?" Visser said, continuing to tear at the leg.

Hugh did not reply. Every muscle in his body was taut, fighting against the red-hot lightning of hurt that exploded within him. He was dizzy, almost unconscious, and he fought to maintain some control.

Visser released the leg.

"I can have you hurt, before I have you shot, flying officer. I can have it so that the pain will be so intense that you will welcome the bullet that ends it. Now, I ask one last time: What were you doing out of your quarters?"

Hugh breathed in sharply, trying to calm the waves of agony that ebbed and flowed within him.

"Your answer, please, flying officer. Please keep in mind that your life depends upon it," Visser demanded sharply.

For the second time that night, Hugh Renaday realized that the string of his own life had reached its end. He took another deep breath, and finally said, "I was looking for you, *Herr Hauptmann.*"

Visser looked slightly surprised. "Me? But why would you want to see me, flying officer?"

"To spit in your face," Hugh replied. As he finished, he spat hard at the German. But his parched, dry mouth could not summon any saliva, and he merely sprayed futilely in Visser's direction.

The *Hauptmann* recoiled slightly. Then he shook his head, and wiped at the desktop with the sleeve of his one arm. He raised his pistol and pointed it in Hugh's face. He held it there for several seconds, aiming straight at Hugh's forehead. The German thumbed back the pistol hammer and then pressed the barrel directly against the Canadian's flesh. A cold that went far beyond all the pulsating pain in his body filled Hugh. He closed his eyes and tried to think of anything except the moment about to arrive. Seconds passed. Almost a minute. He did not dare open his eyes.

Then Visser smiled again.

He pulled the weapon back.

Hugh felt the pressure of the barrel slide away, and after a pause, opened his eyes. He saw Visser slowly lower the huge Mauser and, with an exaggerated motion, return it to his holster, snapping the leather flap shut tightly.

Hugh's breath came in raspy bursts. His eyes were fixed on the revolver. He wanted to feel relief, but felt nothing but fear.

"You think yourself fortunate, flying officer, to still be alive?"

Hugh nodded.

"This is sad," Visser said harshly. He turned to Fritz Number One. "Corporal, please summon a *Feldwebel*, and have him collect an appropriate squad of men. I want this prisoner taken out immediately and shot."

"Scott is innocent."

"Scott is innocent."

From man to man down the length of the tunnel, the single message echoed. That the three words dragged along with them dozens of other questions was ignored in the close, hot, dirty, and dangerous world of the escape. Each kriegie knew only that the message was as important as the final two or three strokes with the pickax, and each kriegie knew that there was a sort of freedom contained within the three words, a freedom nearly as powerful as that they were crawling toward, so the message was passed along with a ferocity that nearly matched the intensity of the battle that Tommy had fought to acquire them. None of the men knew what had taken place at the front of the tunnel. But they all knew that with the twin extremes of death and escape so close, no one would lie. So by the time the message reached back to the anteroom at the base of the shaft leading down from the privy in Hut 107, the words carried a sort of intoxicating religious fervor.

The fighter pilot from New York leaned forward, over the top of the bellows, craning to hear the message being passed back from the next man in line. He listened carefully, as did the man working beside him, who used the moment to seize a second's rest from the backbreaking work of lifting the buckets of sandy earth.

"Repeat that," the fighter pilot whispered.

"Scott is innocent!" he heard. "Got it?"

"I got it."

The fighter pilot and the kriegie lifting buckets looked at each other momentarily. Then both grinned.

The fighter pilot turned and peered up the shaft of the tunnel. "Hey, up there! Message from the front. . . ."

Major Clark stepped forward, almost elbowing Lincoln Scott aside in his eagerness. He knelt at the side of the entranceway, bending over into the pit. "What is it? Have they reached the surface?"

The weak candlelight flickered off the upturned faces of the two men in the tunnel anteroom. The pilot from New York shrugged. "Well, kinda," he said.

"What's the message?" Clark demanded sharply.

"Scott is innocent!" the fighter pilot said. The bucket man nodded hard.

Clark did not reply. He straightened up.

Lincoln Scott heard the words, but for a moment, the impact of them did not occur to him. He was watching the major, who was shaking his head back and forth, as if fighting off the explosion of the words spoken in such a small space.

Fenelli, however, caught the importance immediately. Not merely in the message, but how it was passed along. He, too, leaned over into the shaft and whispered down to the men below: "That come all the way from the front? From Hart and Numbers One and Two?"

"Yes. All the way. Pass it back!" the fighter pilot urged.

Fenelli sat up, smiling.

Major Clark's face was rigid. "You'll do nothing of the sort, lieutenant! That message stops right here."

Fenelli's mouth opened slightly in astonishment.

"What?" he said.

Major Clark looked at the doctor-in-training and spoke, almost as if Lincoln Scott abruptly had disappeared from the room, ignoring the black flier. "We don't know for sure how or why or where that message came from and we don't know, I mean, Hart could have forced it out or something. We don't have any answers, and I won't allow it to be spread."

Fenelli shook his head. He looked over at Scott.

Scott stepped forward, thrusting his chest in front of Major Clark. For a moment his outrage seemed to take him over, and the black flier quivered with the desire to simply lay a right uppercut into the chin of the major. But he fought off this urge, and replaced it with the hardest, coldest stare he could manage.

"What is it about the truth that bothers you so much, major?"

Clark recoiled. He did not reply.

Scott moved to the edge of the tunnel entrance. "Either the truth comes out, or no one goes in," he said quietly.

Major Clark coughed, eyeing the black flier, trying to measure the determination in his face. "There's no time left," Clark said.

"That's right," Fenelli said briskly. "No damn time left."

Then the medic from Cleveland looked past the major, and made a small wave toward one of the dirt bucket men, hovering in the doorway to the privy. "Hey!" Fenelli said loudly. "You got the word from the front?"

The man shook his head.

"Well," Fenelli said, breaking into a grin. "Scott is innocent. It's the real dope and it came from the head of the tunnel. Now, you pass that on. Everybody in this hut is to know. Scott is innocent! And you tell everybody the line is gonna move any second now, so to get ready."

The man hesitated, looked once over at Scott, and then smiled. He turned and whispered to the next man in the corridor, and that man nodded, once he heard the message. It went down the center of the hut, to all the men waiting to escape, and all the men standing by in the support roles, and all the fliers gathered in the doorway of each barracks room, creating a buzz of excitement that seemed to reverberate in the enclosed tight spaces.

Scott stepped away from the tunnel entrance, pushing to the side of the small privy. He understood what the weight of the single phrase was, spread through the men in Hut 107. He knew it would sweep rapidly far beyond the confines of the hut, as soon as the sun rose. It would certainly be all over the camp within hours, and might possibly, if the men escaping were lucky, be the words they carried with them to freedom. It was a weight that Major Clark and Colonel Mac-Namara and Captain Walker Townsend and all the men trying to put his back against a wall and make him face a firing squad would not be able to lift. The weight of innocence.

He took a deep breath and looked toward the hole in the floor. Now, Lincoln Scott thought quietly, that the truth has come out from underground, it is time for Tommy Hart to emerge.

But instead of the lanky form of the law student from Vermont, another message came ricocheting down the tunnel. Nicholas Fenelli, eyes brightening, voice husky with sudden excitement, looked over toward Scott and whispered: "They're through! We're moving out!"

Tommy Hart stood, balancing precariously near the top rung of the ladder, his face lifted toward a six-inch hole in the roof of dirt, drinking in the heady wine of the fresh night air that poured into the tunnel. In his right hand, he held the pickax. Below him, Murphy and the bandleader were feverishly wiping dirt from their faces with a thin piece of cloth, and scrambling into their escape clothing.

The bandleader—musician, murderer, tunnel king—could not resist a single hushed question: "Hart? How does it smell?"

Tommy hesitated, then whispered his reply: "Sweet."

He, too, was covered with the sweaty grime of digging. For the past ten minutes he had taken over from the two other men, who had fallen back, exhausted with the effort that digging the last few feet required. Tommy, though, felt a surge of energy. He had flailed away at the dirt with a furious vigor, tearing at the clods of earth with the pickax until one clod came free covered with grass.

He continued to breathe in deeply. The air was so rich he thought it might make him dizzy.

"Hart! Come on down," the bandleader hissed.

Tommy took one long swig of night, and reluctantly lowered himself back into the pit. He faced the two men. Even in the light of a single candle, Tommy could see both their faces flushed with excitement. It was as if, in that moment, the lure of freedom were so powerful that it managed to overcome all the doubts and fears about what the next hours would hold.

"Okay, Hart, here's the drill. I'm going to fix a rope from the top rung and lead it out to a nearby tree. You're gonna be the watchdog by the tree, Hart. Each kriegie's gonna come to the top of that ladder and wait there for a signal—two quick tugs—that will let him know the coast is clear. Try to move a man along every two to three minutes. No faster, but no slower, either. That'll avoid attention and maybe get us back on our timetable. Once they get out, they know what to do. When everybody's out, you can head back down the tunnel and get back inside the compound."

"Why can't I wait here?"

"No time, Hart. Those men deserve their chance and you can't get in the way. Literally."

Tommy nodded. He could see the sense in what the bandleader was saying. The musician stuck out his hand. "Look me up in the French Quarter sometime, Hart."

Tommy looked down at the man's hand. He imagined it reaching up around Trader Vic's throat. He understood, too, that only a few minutes earlier, that same hand was trying to kill him. Amid the heat, the dirt, and the fear that closed in on all of them waiting inside the tunnel, everything had abruptly changed. He reached out and took the man's hand. The bandleader smiled, his wide grin flashing white in the darkness. "You were right about another thing, too, Hart. I am indeed left-handed."

"You're a killer," Tommy said quietly.

"We're all killers," the man replied.

Tommy shook his head slowly, but the musician laughed.

"Yes, we are, no matter what you say. We may not be again, when all this is said and done and we're home sitting around the fireplace growing old and telling war stories. But right now, right here, we all are. You. Me. Murphy, there, and Scott, too. MacNamara, Clark, hell, everybody. Including Trader Vic. He just might have been the worst of all of us, 'cause he ended up killing even if by mistake for no reason other than to make his own sorry life a little easier."

The musician shook his head. "Not much of a reason for dying, is it?" Then he looked over at Tommy, still holding onto his hand. "You think, Tommy boy, that the truth about all this is ever gonna see the light of day?" Before Tommy could reply, the musician shook his head. "I'm not thinking so, Tommy Hart. I'm not thinking that the army is all too fine on the idea of telling the world that some of its finest heroes are also some of its very best killers. No sir. I don't think this is a story they'll be particularly eager to tell."

Tommy swallowed hard. "Good luck," he said. "New Orleans. I'll make a point of it, someday."

"Buy you a drink," the bandleader said. "Hell, Tommy, we make it home in one piece, I'll buy you a dozen drinks. We can drink to the truth and how it don't never do nobody no good."

"I don't know that's right," Tommy replied.

The musician laughed, shrugged, and climbed the ladder. In his hand, the bandleader carried a long coil of thin rope. Tommy could see him fix the rope to the top rung, and then tear a few more clods of dirt free. They tumbled down onto Tommy, and he blinked, and ducked his head away. The musician paused, and suddenly blew out the last candle. In the split-second that followed, the bandleader wiggled through the hole in the earth, suddenly bathed in a wan half-light from the moon, and disappeared.

Murphy grunted. He had no similar pleasantries for Tommy. He rose up, following. Behind him, Tommy could hear Number Three moving down the tunnel like some excited crab scrambling through the sand. Tommy saw Murphy's legs kick for a moment, trying to gain some purchase in the crumbling dirt of the tunnel exit. Then Tommy lifted himself up the ladder.

At the top, he seized the rope. There were two sharp tugs, and then Tommy, without thinking, thrust himself out of the hole, climbing as quickly as he could. He was barely aware that, suddenly, he had climbed out and was scrambling across the moss and pine-needle floor of the forest. He felt a wave of cold air encapsulate him, washing over him like a shower on a hot day. He threw himself forward, keeping the rope in his hands, until he reached the base of a large pine tree. The rope was tied there, perhaps forty feet away from the hole in the ground. Tommy slumped back against the tree. He could hear scratching noises coming from the underbrush, and he guessed that was the noise of Murphy and the bandleader making their way through the tangled forest foliage, heading for the road to town. For a second he thought it was immense, a thunderous noise, destined to draw every light, every guard, and every gun, right in his direction. He shrank back against the tree, and listened, letting the world fill with silence.

Tommy took a deep breath and pivoted about.

The tunnel had emerged just inside the dark edge of the forest. The barbed-wire walls glinted perhaps fifty yards distant. The nearest machine-gun tower was at least another thirty yards beyond that, and facing in, toward the center of the camp. The goons inside would have their backs to the escape. And any *Hundführer* walking the outside perimeter would also be looking in the opposite direction. The tunnel engineers had painstakingly surveyed their distances, and had done an excellent job.

For a moment, his head reeled, as he understood suddenly where he was. Beyond the wire. Beyond the searchlights. Behind the machine-gun sights. He looked up, and through the covering canopy of tree branches he could see the last stars of the night blinking in the great expanse of the heavens. For a second, he felt as if he were one with all that distance, all those millions of black miles of space.

Tommy thought: I'm free.

He almost burst out in laughter. He rolled back against the tree trunk, squeezing his arms tight around his body, as if he could contain within himself the burst of excitement.

Then he turned his attention to the task before him. A quick glance at the watch Lydia had placed on his wrist so many years earlier told him that dawn's light would begin to creep out of the east in not nearly enough time for all seventy-five men to get out. Not at a rate of one every three minutes. Tommy took a fast look around, inspecting the darkness, and saw that he was completely alone. He gave the rope two quick tugs. Seconds later he saw the shaky outline of Number Three kicking his way free of the tunnel.

The two guards who had accompanied Hugh from the assembly yard to the command barracks were sitting on the wooden front steps, smoking the bitter German ration of cigarettes and complaining to each other that they should have searched the Canadian and seized his Players before leading him into the offices. Both men leapt up when Fritz Number One walked out of the front door, snapping quickly to attention, tossing their smokes into the darkness, where they made red ellipses of burning coal for an instant, before dying out.

Fritz threw a single look back over his shoulder, making certain that Hauptmann Visser had not followed him outside. Then he spoke rapidly and sharply to the two privates. "You," he pointed at the man on the right. "You are to go inside directly and keep the prisoner under guard. Hauptmann Visser has ordered the prisoner's execution, and you are to make certain that he does not attempt to escape!"

The guard snapped his boots together and saluted. *"Ja wohl!"* he said briskly. The guard grabbed his weapon and headed toward the office entrance.

"Now you," Fritz said, speaking softly and with caution. "You are to follow these orders precisely."

The second guard nodded, listening closely.

"Hauptmann Visser has ordered the execution of the Canadian officer. You are to go directly to the guards' barracks and find Feldwebel Voeller. He is on duty this night. You are to inform him of the *Hauptmann*'s order, and request that he immediately assemble a firing squad and bring it here double-time. . . ."

The man nodded a second time. Fritz took a deep breath. His own throat was parched and dry, and he realized that he was walking a line every bit as dangerous as the one walked that night by Hugh Renaday.

"There is a field telephone in the guards' barracks. Tell Voeller that it is imperative that he receive confirmation of this order from Commandant Von Reiter. Imperative! He is to do this without delay! In that way, he will arrive back here with the firing squad before the prisoners have awakened! This must all be accomplished quickly, do you understand?"

The man threw his shoulders back. "Confirmation from the commandant—"

"Even though it means awakening him at his home . . ." Fritz interrupted.

"And returning with the firing squad. As ordered, corporal!"

Fritz Number One nodded slowly himself, then dismissed the guard with a wave. The man pivoted and took off at a run, pounding up the dusty camp road toward the guards' barracks. Fritz hoped the telephone in the hut was operating.

It had a nasty habit of failing three out of four times. He swallowed hard and dry. He did not know whether Commandant Von Reiter would confirm Hauptmann Visser's order or not. He knew only one thing: Someone was going to die that night.

Behind him, Fritz Number One heard the door open and bootsteps on the wooden planks. He turned about and saw Hauptmann Visser exiting from the offices. He, too, snapped to attention.

"I have given your orders, *Herr Hauptmann*! A man has gone to bring Feldwebel Voeller and a firing squad."

Visser grunted and returned the salute. He stepped down from the stairs and looked up into the sky. Visser smiled.

"The Canadian officer was correct. It is a fine night, do you not think, corporal?"

Fritz Number One nodded. "Yes sir."

"It would be a fine night for many things." Visser paused. "Do you have an electric torch, corporal? A flashlight?"

"Yes sir."

"Then give it to me."

Fritz Number One handed over the flashlight.

"I think," Visser said, still peering up into the dark heavens, before lowering his eyes and sweeping them across the expanse of the camp, and the wire that glinted in distant lights, "that I shall take a bit of a walk myself. Just to take in a little of the fine night air, as the flying officer so helpfully suggested." Visser clicked on the flashlight. Its weak spray of light illuminated the dusty ground a few feet in front of him. "Make certain that my orders are followed without delay," he said.

Then, without another look, Visser started off, marching quickly, with determination, heading toward the line of trees on the far side of the compound.

Fritz Number One watched for several minutes, alone in the darkness outside the administration building. He was torn between the conflicts of orders and duties. He understood, however, that the commandant, who was his great benefactor, did not approve of Visser operating unseen. Fritz thought it ironic that his job at the camp required him to spy on both types of enemies.

He gave the *Hauptmann* a head start of another couple of minutes. Just to the point where the weak light the officer held in his only hand had almost disappeared in the faraway darkness. Then Fritz Number One stepped out from the front of the building and moving steadily through the last of the night, followed after him.

Tommy kept moving the escaping kriegies through the tunnel in sturdy, slow fashion, patiently sticking to the timetable that the bandleader had told him, tugging on the rope every two to three minutes. Flier after flier launched himself through the ragged hole in the earth and crawled to the base of the tree, where Tommy remained poorly hidden. A couple of the men seemed surprised to see him alive. Others merely grunted before disappearing into the woods that stretched out behind him. But most of the kriegies had a quick, reassuring word for Tommy. A pat on the back. A whispered, "Good luck," or "See yah in Times Square!" The man from Princeton had added a "Well done, Harvard. They must have taught you something worthwhile at that second-rate institution. . . ." before he, too, slipped silently into the cover of trees and bushes.

It was frustrating going. More than once Tommy had held his breath when he'd detected the figure of a *Hundführer* and his dog moving along the far edge of the wire. Once a searchlight had clicked on in the tower closest to the escape, but had swung its probing beam in the opposite direction. Tommy remained huddled by the tree, trying to be alert to every sound around him, thinking that any single noise could be the noise of betrayal. And any sound could signal death. Either for himself or for one of the men setting off toward town, the station, and the series of morning trains that would carry them away from Stalag Luft Thirteen.

Every few seconds, Tommy glanced down at the dial of his watch and thought that the escape was moving along too slowly. The steady creep of morning would bring the escape to a halt as rapidly as discovery. But he knew also that hurrying would just as swiftly defeat the escape. He gritted his teeth and stuck to the plan.

Some seventeen of the men spread down the length of the tunnel had made it up and out when Tommy first spotted the weak flashlight beam bouncing erratically toward him, probably no more than thirty yards away. The light was moving right at the edge of the forest, not along the wire in the hands of a *Hundführer*, on a collision path with the tunnel exit.

He froze in position, watching the light.

It probed and penetrated, swinging first one way, then another, like a dog just picking up an unusual scent on a wayward wind. He could tell that whoever was behind the light was hunting, but not searching in a systemized, deliberate fashion. More curious, almost questioning, with a slight element of uncertainty in each movement. Tommy pushed himself back, trying to blend against the tree, gingerly swinging around behind, so that he was completely concealed. And then, he understood, hiding did him no good.

The light moved forward, closing the distance.

He could feel his heart accelerating within his chest.

There is a spot far beyond fear that soldiers find, where all the children of terror and death are arrayed against them. It is a terrible and deadly location where some men find paralysis and others are trapped within a miasma of loss and agony. Tommy was perilously close to that spot, as his muscles twitched and his breath came in short raspy bursts, watching the slow progress of the light inexorably closing in on the escape hole. He could see that there was no chance that the German on the other end of the light would miss the exit, and certainly no chance he would miss the rope stretched across the ground. And Tommy could see, as well, that there was no way he could race forward and throw himself down the tunnel without instantly being seen and an alarm sounded. In that second, he understood: He was as good as captured. Perhaps as good as shot.

He caught his breath.

Tommy knew, as well, that waiting on the top rung of the ladder, eagerly anticipating the two tugs on the rope that would signal his chance had arrived, was Number Eighteen. He tried, in that moment, to remember who Eighteen was. He had pushed past him, in the narrowness of the tunnel, it seemed hours earlier, been close enough to smell the man's anxious sweat, feel his breath, but still Tommy couldn't put a face to the number. Number Eighteen was a flier, just as he was, and Tommy knew he was poised, inches below the surface of the earth, eager, nervous, excited, and expectant, perhaps a little impatient, the rope tight in his hands, praying for his opportunity and praying, probably, for the same thing that all men who know that death is lurking close by, with all its capriciousness, pray for.

The light swung a few yards closer.

In that second, Tommy realized it was completely up to him.

With every foot that brought the light closer, the choice became clearer. More defined. It was not that he was being called upon to risk everything as much as it was that everyone else had risked so much and he was the only man available to protect the chances and hopes taken that night. He had foolishly believed that descending into that tunnel and fighting for the truth about Lincoln Scott and Trader Vic had been the only test he would undergo that night. But he was wrong, for the real battle lay directly in front of him, moving slowly yet steadily toward the tunnel exit. He had been young when he enlisted in the air corps, and filled with a patriotic fervor when he entered his first battle, only to come quickly to understand that there is much in war that is brave, little that is truly noble. It is only in the distant outcome that historians debate where some sense of nobility reigns. Instead, what is delivered in the most hellish of fashions are the most elemental of hard and dirty choices, where all that Tommy had once been and all he hoped he might be paled harshly when measured against the urgent needs of so many men that night.

Bookish Tommy Hart—a student of laws and a most unlikely warrior, who in truth wanted nothing more than to return home to the girl he loved and the life he'd lived, and the life he'd promised himself with all his hard work and studies—swallowed hard, clenched his hands into fists, and slowly started to move, angling toward the approaching light. He moved stealthily, commandolike, his eyes focused on the threat, his throat parched, his heart pounding, his task suddenly and terribly crystalline.

He remembered what the bandleader had said in the tunnel: We're all killers.

He hoped the musician was right.

Tommy closed on the target, barely daring to breathe.

The hole in the ground that he was maneuvering to protect was behind him, obliquely. The light beam in front still swung haphazardly back and forth. He could not see who wielded the light, but he was relieved when he craned his head forward, and couldn't detect the accompanying sound of a dog's sniffing and shuffling.

The light moved a few steps closer, and Tommy tensed each muscle, poised in ambush.

A few feet behind him, hidden just beneath the surface of the ground, Number Eighteen could no longer stand the tension of waiting for a signal. He had raced through all the possibilities for delay in his head, measuring each of the dangers against the overwhelming need to get up and get moving. He knew how tight the schedule was, and knew, as well, that the only men who truly stood a chance at successfully escaping were the men who made it to the train station before any sort of alarm was given. Number Eighteen had worked many hours digging the tunnel, and more than once had been pulled choking from dusty cave-ins, and with an impulsiveness born of youth, had rashly decided within himself that breaking free was more important even than life. He could not stand the idea of coming so close to the outside of the wire and not making a run for it. And so his impatience overcame whatever bonds of reason he had remaining after spending so many hours flat on his stomach in the tunnel, and he decided in that second to make his move, signal or not.

He reached both hands up, thrusting himself through the hole, up into the clear air, pushing himself like a man vaulting out of a pool of water.

The noise froze Tommy.

The light beam swung in the direction of the scrambling sound, and Tommy heard a surprised and whispered German, *"Mein Gott!"*

Visser could just see, at the edge of the faint beam, the dark shape of Number Eighteen, bursting forward out of the exit hole and hightailing it into the woods. The shocked *Hauptmann* took several quick steps forward and then stopped. As quickly as he could, he lifted the flashlight to his mouth, to hold it there, the only way that he could get his hand free to seize his pistol. It was, of course, the luckiest thing for the escapees, for the pressure of the light between his teeth kept Visser from immediately shouting out an alarm. The German pulled furiously at the holster flap and grabbed at the Mauser strapped at his waist.

He had nearly tugged the weapon free when Tommy smashed into him, aiming high on his chest, like a fullback protecting a ball carrier.

The impact nearly knocked the wind from both men. The flashlight was thrown into a bush, its deadly beam smothered by leaves and branches. Tommy did not see this. He thrust himself at the German, grabbing for the man's throat.

The two men tangled together, falling backward, the force of Tommy's assault carrying them just within the line of trees at the forest's edge, pushing them out of sight of the towers and the guards walking the far perimeter. They were locked together, anonymously, in the pitch black.

At first, Tommy did not know who he was fighting. He knew only that the man was the enemy, and that he had with him a light, a gun, and perhaps the most dangerous weapon of all, his voice. Each of these three things could kill him with ease, and Tommy knew that he had to fight against each. He tried to find the light, but it had disappeared, and so he punched out, flailing fists desperately, trying to neutralize the other two dangers.

Visser rolled sideways against the force of the assault, fighting back. He was a cold, highly trained, and experienced soldier, and he knew instantly what the stakes were. He absorbed the blows from Tommy's fists raining down on him, and concentrated on finding the Mauser. He kicked back with both legs, landing one shot to Tommy's midsection, hearing a sharp exhale of breath.

Although it was not in Visser's nature to call for help, he tried to do this. "Help!" he managed to squeeze out weakly, his own lungs still raging with the loss of air from Tommy's initial attack. The word seemed to linger around the two struggling men, then dissipate in the darkness surrounding them. Visser seized at the night air, filling his chest to bellow a cry for assistance, but, in that second, Tommy's hand found his mouth.

Tommy had landed nearly behind the German. He was able to wrap one leg around the German's midsection, pulling him back on top of him, deeper into the shadows of the forest. At the same time, Tommy thrust his left hand deep into the German's mouth, stuffing Visser's throat with his own fingers, trying to choke the German. He was still only obliquely aware that there was a weapon, and it took him another half-second to realize that the man he fought had but one arm.

"Visser!" he whispered sharply.

The German didn't reply, although Tommy could sense that he had recognized Tommy's voice. Instead, he kicked and struggled and grasped at his pistol. He also brought all his teeth crunching down into the soft flesh of Tommy's left hand, biting deeply into the skin.

The pain shot through Tommy as teeth tore through muscle and tendon, searching for bone. He groaned as a sheet of red agony nearly blinded him.

But he fought on, pushing his now ravaged hand deeper into the German's throat. With his free hand, he found Visser's wrist. He could sense from the weight that the German had almost managed to free the pistol, and was directing all his strength to withdrawing it and firing a shot.

Tommy understood, even though his head was filled with nothing but hurt and he could feel blood pulsing from his hand, that merely firing a shot into the air could kill him as effectively as putting the barrel to his chest and firing a shot into his heart. So he ignored the growing fury of the pain in his left hand, and concentrated on the German's only arm, and the effort it was making to reach the pistol butt and trigger. In the oddest of ways, the entire war, years long, millions of deaths, a struggle between cultures and nations, came down, for Tommy, to the single fight to control that pistol. He ignored the savagery Visser's teeth were wreaking on his left hand and fought only for the smallest victory, over that pistol. He could sense Visser's fingers straining to reach the trigger guard, and he furiously pulled back. The Mauser seemed balanced, partway free of the stiff and shiny black leather holster. Its cumbersome shape and heavy weight were the smallest of advantages in Tommy's favor, but Visser's strength was considerable. The German was a powerfully built man, and much of his strength was concentrated in that sole remaining arm, and Tommy could sense that the balance of this fight within the fight was shifting in Visser's favor.

And so he took a chance. Instead of pulling back, he suddenly thrust forward, twisting with his hand. Visser's fingers jammed against the trigger guard, and one of them abruptly snapped. The German moaned in pain, pushing the guttural sound past Tommy's bloody left hand that still threatened to choke him.

The Mauser seemed to teeter on the edge of possession, and then tumbled away, falling into the moss and dirt of the forest, its black metal body immediately swallowed up by the surrounding darkness.

Visser knew the gun was lost, and so he redoubled his fight, crunching down again with his teeth, destroying much of Tommy's left hand, and flailing away with his right. The German tried to struggle up, but Tommy's legs wrapped around him, so that they fought almost as close as lovers, but with murder their only kiss.

Tommy ignored the punches that crashed painfully against him, ignored the agony that shot from his hand, and pulled Visser back. He had never been trained in how to kill a man with his hands, had never even considered it. The only fights he'd had growing up were shoving and pushing matches that relied mostly on angry words and insults and usually ended with one or both boys in tears. No fight he had ever experienced, not even the battle in the tunnel earlier that night, when he'd fought for the truth, seemed as concentrated as this one. None were even as deadly as the battles that Lincoln Scott fought, gloved and refereed, in a boxing ring.

This, he knew, was something far different. It was a fight that had only one answer. The German punched and kicked and crushed down with his teeth, tearing away at the flesh of Tommy's hand, but Tommy suddenly felt no more pain at all. It was as if a total coldness of instinct and desire overwhelmed him in those few seconds and he gritted his teeth and started to pull back as hard as he could on the German's neck, working his right knee into the small of Visser's back for leverage.

Visser instantly felt the threat, felt the strain filling his neck, and struggled to break free. He clawed with every ounce of hatred he could muster to overcome the fierce grip that Tommy held on him. If he'd had two arms, the fight would have ended swiftly in the German's favor, but the Spitfire bullet that took Visser's arm had crippled him in other ways, too. For an instant, they teetered on the edge of indecision, one man's strength against the other, each man's body twisted as taut and stiff as dried leather.

Visser mounted one great surge, biting, kicking, pounding with his free hand. The blows crashed down on Tommy, who closed his eyes and pulled harder, realizing that to slip even the smallest measure would cost him the fight and his life.

And then Tommy heard a sickening crack.

The sound of Visser's back snapping was perhaps the ugliest, most urgent sound he'd heard in his entire life. The German gasped once in the astonishment of death before going limp in Tommy's arms, and it was another few seconds before Tommy let slide the unconscious man's body.

He pulled his left hand free from Visser's mouth. The pain redoubled, almost unbearably, and for a second he felt his own head swimming, on the edge of blackness himself. He leaned back, clutching his torn and bloody hand to his chest. The night around them seemed suddenly pristine, utterly quiet. He put his head back and took in a deep breath of air, trying to regain his own senses, struggling to impose order and reason on the world around him.

He became aware slowly of the other sounds nearby. The first was that Visser was still breathing. Tommy realized then that he had to finish the job. And for perhaps the first time in his life, he prayed that the German would die before he was forced to steal the unconscious and dying man's last breath. "Please die," he whispered.

And this the German did, rattling once softly.

Relief flooded Tommy, and he almost burst out in a laugh. He looked up into the stars and sky, and saw that there was the smallest suggestion of light beginning to streak across the eastern horizon. It is an astonishing thing, he thought, to be alive when you have no right to be.

His hand was throbbing with pain. He could sense that Visser's teeth had nearly severed one, maybe more, of his fingers, which flopped uselessly against his chest. The flesh of his fist was torn and ripped. Blood pulsed over his shirt and surges of pain raced up his forearm and clouded his head.

He knew he had to bind the wound, and he bent over to Visser's inert body. He quickly found a silken handkerchief in the dead German's tunic pocket. Tommy wrapped this as tightly as he could around his hand to try to stem the bleeding.

Tommy tried to sort through the situation. He knew only that much was at risk, but his exhaustion and pain prevented him from thinking altogether clearly. He could remember only that there were men still waiting in the tunnel, and that now the escape was even more behind schedule, so he determined that the only thing he could do was get it back up and moving, and although fatigue and hurt filled every fiber of his body, that was what he decided to do.

But although he made this decision deep within himself, he was at first unable to get his ravaged muscles to respond. He stole one more breath of air, trying to push himself to his feet, only to slump back against a nearby tree. He told himself that it would be all right to rest for just a second and he started to close his eyes, only to feel a sudden shaft of fear crash through him. His eyes went almost blind with cold terror.

The flashlight's beam, which had been swallowed up by the forest, suddenly rose, ghostlike, a few feet away, swung around once, as it renewed its awful search, and then, before he could gather any of whatever remaining strength he possessed to scramble for cover, landed directly on his face.

Death is a trickster, Tommy thought. Just when you think you have it fooled, it turns the tables on you. He leaned back and lifted his good hand in front of his eyes to deflect the light and the shot he expected to hear within seconds.

But what he heard, instead, was a familiar voice.

"Mr. Hart! My God! What are you doing here?"

Tommy smiled and shook his head, unable to answer Fritz

Number One's most sensible question. He made a small gesture with his good hand, and in the same second the ferret's light captured the twisted form of the German officer, lying prone a few feet away.

"My God!" the ferret whispered.

Tommy leaned back, closing his eyes. He did not think he had the strength to fight again. He could hear Fritz Number One gasping, repeating, now in German, *"Mein Gott! Mein Gott!"* and then adding, "Escape!" as the ferret sorted through what was happening. Tommy was only slightly aware that Fritz Number One was tearing at his own holstered sidearm, and reaching for the ubiquitous whistle that all the ferrets carried in their tunic pockets. He wanted to shout a warning to Number Nineteen, waiting at the top rung of the ladder inside the tunnel, but he didn't even have the strength for that.

He waited for the sound of the alarm.

It did not come.

Tommy slowly opened his eyes, and saw Fritz Number One standing beside Visser's body. The ferret had the whistle at his lips, and his own weapon in his hand. Then Fritz slowly turned and stared at Tommy, the whistle still pointed at his mouth.

"They will shoot you, Mr. Hart," he whispered. "To kill a German officer while attempting to escape . . ."

"I know," Tommy said. "Didn't have a choice."

Fritz raised the whistle to his lips, then stopped, slowly lowering it. He swung the flashlight beam toward the hole in the earth that Tommy had protected, and let it linger on the rope tied to the tree. "My God," he said again, softly.

Tommy remained silent. He did not understand why the ferret had not summoned assistance and sounded the alarm.

Fritz Number One seemed to be trapped in thought, assessing, measuring, weighing details and debts. Then, suddenly, he bent down toward Tommy and whispered sharply: "Tell the men in the tunnel the escape is finished! *Kaput!* Over! Go back to their barracks immediately! The alarm is about to sound. Tell them this now, Mr. Hart. It is your only chance!"

Tommy caught his breath. He wasn't certain what the

German was doing, but he recognized he was being given some sort of an opportunity, and he seized at it. Not certain from where he managed to summon the energy, he scrambled across the mossy forest grass to the edge of the tunnel. He leaned over and saw the upturned face of Number Nineteen, waiting.

"Krauts!" Tommy whispered urgently. "Everywhere! Everybody back up fast! The jig is up for tonight!"

"Shit!" Number Nineteen swore under his breath. "Goddamn it to hell!" he added, but he didn't hesitate. Number Nineteen dropped swiftly through the narrow tunnel shaft and started to crawl back down the tunnel. Tommy could hear the muffled sound of conversation when Nineteen met Twenty, but could not make out the words, though he knew what they had to be.

He rolled over, and saw that Fritz Number One stood a few feet away. He had extinguished the flashlight, but there was just enough of the first light of morning beginning to creep through the tops of the trees to give his form a dark and ghostly outline. The ferret was waving toward Tommy urgently.

Tommy half-crawled, half-ran, back to where the ferret stood.

"There is only one chance for you, Mr. Hart. Bring the body and follow me, now. Do not ask any questions, but hurry!"

Tommy shook his head. "My hand," he said. "I don't think I have the strength . . ."

"Then you will die here," Fritz Number One replied flatly. "The choice is yours, Mr. Hart. But you must make it now. I cannot touch the *Hauptmann*'s body. Either lift it now, or die beside him. But, I think, it would be wrong to let a man such as he kill you, Mr. Hart."

Tommy inhaled deeply. His imagination flooded with images of home, of school, of Lydia. He remembered his captain from Texas with his flat, dry laughter: *Find us the way home, Tommy, willya?* And Phillip Pryce, with his own sniffling sort of joy in the smallest and smartest of things. He thought right then that only a true coward turns his back on a chance at life, no matter how hard and slender that chance might be. And so, knowing that his reserves were well past exhaustion, with only the strength of desire remaining to him, Tommy bent down and with a great grunt, managed to sling the German officer's body over his shoulder in a fireman's carry. The body crunched sickeningly, and for a moment Tommy thought he might throw up. Then, staggering, he lifted himself to his feet, struggling to maintain his balance.

"Now, quickly," Fritz Number One urged. "You must beat the morning light or all will be lost!"

Tommy smiled at the German's archaic turn of phrase, but saw as well that the gray streaks of dawn flitting on the horizon were taking root, growing stronger with each second. He took a single step forward, half-stumbled, righted himself, and with what little voice he had, said, "Go ahead. I'm ready now."

Fritz Number One nodded, then pushed forward, deeper into the forest.

Tommy struggled after the German. Visser's weight was crushing, almost as if, even in death, the German was fighting to kill him.

Branches tore at his face. Tree roots threatened to trip him. The forest ripped and grabbed at his every step, slowing him, trying to knock him to the ground. Tommy pushed through, slogging beneath the dead weight, fighting with every stride to maintain his balance, searching with every foot forward for the strength to go another.

His breathing was coming in exhausted short bursts. Sweat clogged his eyes. The pain in his left hand was nearly unbearable. It throbbed and surged and sent fierce reminders searing through the rest of his body. It seemed to Tommy that he had no more strength, and then he would refuse to admit this and he would find just a little more, enough to stumble forward a few more feet.

He had no idea how far they traveled. Fritz Number One turned and urged him, "Quickly, Mr. Hart! Quickly. Not much farther!" and with those words, Tommy battled ahead. Visser on his shoulder no longer seemed like something of this world; instead, he was like some great black crushing evil, trying to defeat him.

Just when he reached the point where he did not think he

could travel another foot, he saw Fritz Number One abruptly stop, and kneel down. The German gestured for Tommy to come forward next to him. Tommy staggered these few yards, and then dropped to the earth.

"Where . . ." he managed, but Fritz hushed him.

"Quiet. There are guards nearby. Can you not smell where you are?"

Tommy wiped his face with his good hand and breathed in through his nose. Only then did he become aware of the mingled smells of human waste and death that clogged the forest air around them. He looked at Fritz Number One quizzically.

"The Russian work camp!" Fritz whispered.

Then the German pointed.

"Take the body as close as you dare and leave it. Be quiet, Mr. Hart. The guards here will not hesitate to shoot at any noise. And put this in the *Hauptmann*'s hand."

Fritz Number One reached into his own tunic pocket and removed the Russian belt buckle that he had tried to trade to Tommy days earlier. Tommy nodded. He took the buckle, turned, and dragged Visser's body onto his shoulder. He fought forward, only to have Fritz Number One hold out his hand. The ferret stared at Visser's dead eyes.

"Gestapo!" he muttered. Then he spat once into the murdered man's face. "Now, go, and be quick!"

Tommy battled through the trees. The smell was nearly overwhelming. He could just make out a small opening, almost a glade, perhaps two dozen yards from the makeshift barbed wire and sharpened stakes of the Russian work encampment. There was nothing of permanence in the Russian area; after all, the men it was designed to hold were not expected to survive the war, and there was no Red Cross organization in Geneva ostensibly monitoring their conditions.

To his right, he heard a dog bark. A pair of voices tripped the air around him.

He thought: This is as far as I dare.

With a great shrug, he tossed Visser's body to the earth. It thudded, then lay still. He bent over, thrust the Russian belt buckle into the German's dead fingers, then stepped back and wondered for a moment if he had truly hated Visser enough to kill him, and then understood that that wasn't really what counted. What counted was that Visser was dead and he was still clinging precariously to life. Then, without another look at the dead man's face, he turned, and moving as quietly, yet as swiftly, as he could, returned to the spot where Fritz Number One remained.

The German nodded when he arrived.

"You may have a chance, now, Mr. Hart," he said. "But still, we must hurry."

The return through the forest was faster, but Tommy thought he was closing in on delirium. A breeze sliding through the treetops whispered at him, almost mocking his exhaustion. Shadows were lengthening around him, like dozens of searchlights trying to seize hold of his face, expose him. Kill him. His hand screamed obscenities of hurt, trying to blind him with pain.

It was the moment of the morning when dawn seems to decide to insist on taking hold of the day. Black fades to gray, and the first streaks of blue were soaring through the sky, chasing away all the stars that had been so comforting to him earlier. From a few feet distant, Tommy could easily make out the black hole of the tunnel exit.

Fritz Number One stopped, hiding behind a tree. He pointed at the tunnel. He took Tommy by the arm.

"Mr. Hart," he whispered sharply, "Hauptmann Visser would have had me shot when he learned that it was I who traded the weapon that killed Trader Vic. The weapon that you returned to me. I was in your debt, but now, tonight, that debt is paid. Understand?"

Tommy nodded.

"Now we are, how you say, equal?" the ferret added.

"Even Steven," Tommy replied.

The German looked slightly surprised.

"Who is Steven?"

"It's another figure of speech, Fritz. When things are all equal, we say they're 'Even Steven'. . . ." Tommy smiled, thinking that he had finally gone completely crazy with exhaustion, for now he was giving an English lesson.

The ferret grinned. "Even Steven. I will remember this, too. There is much this night to remember."

He pointed at the hole.

"Now, Mr. Hart, I will count to sixty, and then I will blow the alarm."

Tommy nodded. He pushed himself up and raced to the hole. He did not look back, but instead, almost threw himself back into the darkness, his feet finding the rungs of the home-made ladder, and climbing down into the pit. He fell to the dirt at the bottom, the pain in his hand screaming insults at him. Without thinking of all the terrors he remembered from childhood, or any of the terrors that night had held, Tommy thrust himself down the tunnel. There were no lights, not even a stray candle left behind to guide him. It was all a great and infinite blackness, mocking the dawn that was lighting the world beyond his reach.

Tommy crawled back to prison, alone, exhausted, blind, and deeply hurt, chased by the faraway sound of Fritz Number One's whistle shattering the orderly world above him.

Chapter Twenty

A FIELD DRESSING

It was near chaos in Hut 107.

The would-be escapees gathered in the central corridor were frantically changing out of their retailored suits, back into their frayed and worn uniforms. Many men had collected extra rations for the escape, food to eat while on the lam, and they were now stuffing their mouths with chocolate or processed meat, fearful that any second the Germans were going to arrive and confiscate everything they'd hoarded so diligently over the past weeks. The support personnel were seizing the clothing, forged documents, tickets, passports, work orders, anything the kriegies had constructed to give false legitimacy to their anticipated existence beyond the wire, and stuffing these into hollowed-out books, or behind walls in concealed hiding spots. The men who'd been part of the bucket brigade of dirt dropped down from the hole in the ceiling, furiously wiping sweat and grime from their faces while one flier carefully fixed the access panel back in place on the off chance that the Germans would not discover it. An officer stood by the front door of the hut, peering through a crack in the wood, shuffling men out of the hut singly and in pairs, as long as the coast stayed clear.

There had been twenty-nine men stretched out in the tunnel when Tommy had given the word of warning to Number Nineteen. The alarm moved more rapidly than the men, passed back in a series of shouts, just as the message about Scott's innocence had been. But as the warning streamed

back, the men in the tunnel had fought to start their own retreat, which was far more difficult in the cramped and dark
quarters. The men had moved desperately, almost frantically,
some crawling backward, some struggling to get turned
around. Even with the urgency passed back, it still took some
time for each man to retrace his steps, filled with disappointment, some fear, plenty of anxiety, and a furiousness at the
harshness of life that had stolen this chance from them.
Curses resounded in the tight spaces, obscenities rebounding
off the walls.

When the men first started to emerge from the tunnel, Lincoln Scott had been poised near the edge of the entrance, adjacent to the privy. Major Clark was giving sharp orders a few
feet away, trying to keep discipline among the frenzied men.
Scott had turned and absorbed the disintegration of the scene
around him. He reached down and helped to lift Number
Forty-seven from the entrance.

"Where's Hart?" Scott demanded. "Did you see Tommy
Hart?"

The flier shook his head. "He must still be up at the front,"
the man replied.

Scott helped push the kriegie back toward the corridor,
where the man began to tear at his escape clothes. Scott
looked down into the pit of the tunnel. The candlelight
seemed to throw scars across the faces of the disappointed
men as they struggled to crawl from the tunnel entrance. He
reached down and grasped Number Forty-six's hand, and
with an immense jerk, lifted the next in line to the surface,
asking the same question: "Did you see Hart? Did you hear
him? Is he okay?"

But Number Forty-six shook his head.

"It's a damn mess in there, Scott. You can't see a damn
thing. I don't know where Hart is."

Scott nodded. He guided the flier out of the privy toward
the corridor, then reached down and seized the black cable
leading into the hole.

"What are you doing, Scott?" Major Clark demanded.

"Helping," Scott replied. He twisted about, almost like a
mountaineer preparing to rappel down a cliff, and without
saying another word to the major, lowered himself down to

the anteroom. He could sense a fierce tautness in the cheap air of the tunnel, almost like entering a medical ward where disease lingers in the corners and no one has ever opened a window to bring in fresh air. In the rush to retreat, the bellows had been abandoned, kicked to the side of the space by one of the first kriegies to emerge from the tunnel. Scott saw that Number Forty-five was struggling with a suitcase, and he reached into the gray semidarkness and tore it from the grateful man's hands. "Jesus," the kriegie whispered. "That damn thing almost brought the roof down on my head. Thanks." The man leaned up against the wall of the anteroom. "There's no air," he whispered. "No damn air up there at all. I hope nobody passes out."

Scott helped to steady the gasping man against the side of the pit, and put the access cable in his hands. The kriegie nodded thanks and started to pull himself up, hand over hand. As soon as he'd managed to lift himself over Scott's head, the black flier turned and grabbed the bellows.

He set it upright, and then plunked himself down, straddling it as had the captain from New York earlier that long night. With a strength born of urgency, he started to pump away furiously, sending blasts of air down the tunnel.

Nearly a full minute passed before the next kriegie slid through the tunnel entrance. This flier seemed exhausted by the tension of the failed escape. He coughed and tore at the air in the anteroom gratefully with wheezing breath and pointed at the bellows. "Good," he whispered dryly. "You can't breathe up there. Not at all."

"Where's Hart?" Scott demanded, between grunts. His face glistened with the sweat of exertion.

The man shook his head. "I don't know. Coming, maybe? I don't know. You can't see. Can barely breathe. There's goddamn sand and dirt everywhere and all you can hear are the other guys yelling to back up, get out, get out, get out. That and you can hear the damn boards in the roof creaking and snapping. I hope the whole thing doesn't come caving in. Are the Krauts here yet?"

Scott gritted his teeth. He shook his head.

"Not yet. You've got a chance to get out, quick."

Number Forty-five nodded. He sighed, gathering strength.

Then he, too, struggled up the cable, reaching toward the hands at the privy entrance that were extended to him.

Below, Scott continued to pump air with deadly speed. The bellows creaked and whooshed, and the black flier grunted hard at the effort.

Slowly, one after another, the men crawled out of the tunnel. All were filthy, all were scared, all were relieved to be able to see the surface. One man said, "That's what dying must be like." Another said, "It's like a damn grave in there." Every kriegie filled his lungs with air, and more than one took one look at Scott behind the bellows and whispered grateful thanks.

Time seemed to stretch around them dangerously, tugging at each man like the undertow on the beach, threatening to pull them into the shifting currents of deep waters. The tunnel itself, Scott thought, must be a little like drowning. Then he shoved this thought away, and demanded of the next man the only question that seemed to matter to him any longer, "Have you seen Hart? Where's Hart?"

No one could answer.

Fenelli, who was Number Twenty-eight, pulled himself forward, landing in a heap by Scott's legs. He gestured at the bellows. "Damn good thing you started to do that," he hissed. "Otherwise we'da had unconscious men stuck all over the damn tunnel. It's almost toxic in there."

"Where's Hart?" Scott demanded for the hundredth time.

Fenelli shook his head. "He was at the very front. Outside the wire. Giving the men the go ahead. I don't know where he is, now."

Scott was filled with the anger of impotence. He didn't know what the hell else he could do, except continue to shoot the lifesaving air down the tunnel.

"You better get out of here," he grunted. "They'll help you up topside."

Fenelli started to rise, then slumped back down. He smiled. "You know, I have a cousin in the navy. Goddamn submarines. He wanted me to join up with him, but I told him only a fool would try to swim around under the damn ocean, holding their breath and looking for Japs. You'd never catch me doing anything so stupid, I told him. Hah! Now, look at me. Twenty feet under the ground, still stuck in a damn prison. It sure is a long way from flying."

Scott nodded, still working hard. He managed a small smile.

"I think," Fenelli said, "I'll stick here with you for a couple of minutes."

The medic from Cleveland bent over, peering back into the pitch black tunnel. Perhaps sixty seconds passed, and then he reached forward, helping Number Twenty-seven through the last few feet. This was the captain from New York. He, too, dropped immediately to the floor, gasping like a fish out of water. "Jesus," he said. "Jesus, Mary, and Joseph. What a fucking mess. I had to dig through a pile of sand more than once. Things are getting pretty shaky in there."

"Where's Tommy?"

The man shook his head. "There's still men coming down the tunnel behind me," he said. He seized a breath of air and struggled to his feet. "Jesus. Feels good to stand up. Now, I'm out of here. Kee-rist!" He grabbed at the cable and with Fenelli steadying him, began to lift himself toward the safety of the surface.

It was right when Number Nineteen finally pushed through the tunnel entrance, that Major Clark leaned over the edge of the pit and shouted down, "That's it! They just sounded the damn alarm!"

The howl of a distant air-raid siren managed to penetrate even to the depth where they were gathered.

"Where's Hart?" Scott cried.

Number Nineteen shook his head. "He shoulda been right behind me," he said. "But I don't know where he went."

"What happened?" Fenelli demanded, kneeling down and staring into the tunnel darkness. He craned his head into the hole, trying to hear sounds of crawling.

"Come on, you men, hurry up!" Major Clark cried out from above. "Let's move!"

Number Nineteen continued to shake his head. "I don't know," he said. "I was at the top of the ladder, waiting for the signal to run, you know, just like we'd been briefed, 'cept it was Hart on the other end of the rope, giving the signals, not the guy in front of you, like we expected. Anyways, I'm waiting and waiting and wondering what the hell, 'cause it's been more than a coupla minutes and we're supposed to be going every two, three minutes, and all of a sudden, all I can hear is the sound of two men fighting. And some kinda fight, too. No voices, not at first. Just grunts and hard breathing and punches being thrown and landing, too. Then there's silence and then like from nowheres, I can just hear some voices finally. Can't hear what the hell anyone's saying, but that don't matter, 'cause next thing I know, there's Hart, right in the entrance, saying there's Krauts everywhere and to get my tail back up the tunnel fast, get everybody out, 'cause the alarm's gonna go off any second. So I drop back down and start back, but it takes damn near forever, 'cause guys are panicking, and fighting to get turned around and you can't barely breathe and there's dirt everywhere and you can't see a damn thing 'cause every candle is out. And then, here I am."

"Where's Hart?" Scott shouted.

Number Nineteen shrugged, still catching his breath.

"I can't tell you. I thought he'd be right behind me. But he ain't."

From above, Major Clark's voice bellowed down.

"Hurry up! Germans will be here any second! We have to close up!"

Scott turned his face up. "Hart's not back!" he answered sharply.

Major Clark seemed to hesitate.

"He should be behind the last man!"

"He's not back!"

"We have to close up before they get here!"

"He's not back!" Lincoln Scott roared. Insistent.

"Well, where the hell is he?" the major demanded.

Tommy Hart could no longer separate the different pains that swept through his body. His mangled hand seemed to have distributed agony throughout every inch of his being. Every surge of blinding hurt was fueled by an exhaustion so total and utterly complete that he no longer really believed that he had the strength to pull himself down the entire length of the tunnel. He had traversed past the point where fear and terror held sway, deep into death's arena. That he was able to crawl forward almost surprised him; he had no real understanding where the energy came from. His muscles screamed threats of fatigue. His imagination was a fevered blank fire of pain. Still he dragged himself ahead.

It was darker than any night he'd known and he was terribly alone.

Sand rivulets leaked onto his head. Dust clogged his nostrils. It seemed that there was no air left inside the narrow tunnel confines. The only sound he could make out was the creak of support boards seemingly ready to give way. He pulled himself along, using a swimming motion, thrusting aside dirt that clogged his route, fighting every centimeter of the way.

He held out no real hope of being able to crawl the entire seventy-five yards. And he certainly no longer held any belief that he could cover the distance before the Germans descended upon Hut 107. In an odd way, though, the exhaustion, coupled with pain, and the immense effort it took to work his way ahead, all conspired to prevent him from being crippled by fear. It was almost as if all the other competing agonies that screamed inside his body didn't leave enough room for the most obvious and the most dangerous. And so defeat in this final fight didn't really dare enter his thinking.

Tommy grabbed at each inch of darkness and hauled himself forward.

He did not stop. Nor did he even hesitate, despite his exhaustion. Even when he found his way partially blocked, and the narrow space made even smaller, he still snaked ahead, his lanky form slithering through the tightest of gaps. His head spun dizzily with exertion. Each breath of air he squeezed from the blackness around him seemed thinner, more fetid, filled with evil.

How long he had traveled, or how far, was unknown to him. In a way, it seemed to him as if he'd always been in the tunnel. That there never was an outside, never was a clear sky filled with fresh air and a great expanse of stars above. For a moment, he almost laughed, thinking that everything else must have been a dream; his home, his school, his love, the war, his friends, the camp, the wire—all of it. None of it really ever took place. He had died, right there in the Mediterranean Sea, right alongside the captain from Texas, and everything else was merely some odd fantasy of the future that he was carrying with him into oblivion. He gritted his teeth and dragged himself another yard forward, thinking perhaps nothing was real, and this tunnel was hell, and that he had always been there and would always remain inside. There was no exit. There was no air. There was no light. Not ever.

And into this delirium that overcame him, he heard a voice.

It seemed familiar. He thought at first it was Phillip Pryce's, and then no, it was his old captain calling for him. He struggled forward a little more, and broke into a smile, because he realized it had to be Lydia summoning him. It was home in Vermont, and it was summer, and she wanted him to sneak from his house into the warm midnight and give her just a single, deep kiss goodnight. He whispered a reply, just like any delighted lover reaching across a bed late at night in response to the merest of suggestive touches, a beckoning.

"I'm here," he said.

The voice called out again, and he stretched forward.

"I'm here," he said, louder. He did not have the energy to speak any harder, and what he managed was really barely approaching a normal tone. Again, he pulled himself ahead, half-expecting to see Lydia's hand reaching for his, her voice coaxing him toward her.

But what he heard instead was a terrible crack.

He did not even have time to panic when the roof above him shattered, and he was abruptly enveloped in a cascade of sandy dirt.

"I heard him!" Lincoln Scott shouted. "He's there!"

"Jesus!" Fenelli cried out, recoiling from the tunnel entrance as a blast of dirt like an explosion billowed through. "Goddamn it!"

From above in the privy, Major Clark yelled down: "What is it? Where's Hart?"

"He's there!" Scott answered. "I heard him!"

"It's a goddamn cave-in!" Fenelli screamed.

"Where's Hart?" the major yelled again. "We have to close up! The Krauts are rousting everyone out of the huts. If we don't close this up now, they'll find it!"

"I heard him," Scott screamed. "He's trapped!"

Both Scott and Fenelli looked up at Major Clark in that second. The major seemed to sway, like heat vapors above a black macadam highway on a hot August afternoon, before he made a decision.

"Get the buckets moving," he shouted, turning toward the other men in the corridor. "No one leaves until we dig Hart out!" He bent toward the tunnel anteroom. "Coming down," he yelled out. And then he grabbed a makeshift pickax and spade and launched them down into the hole in the earth.

They thudded to the ground. But Lincoln Scott had already thrust himself into the tunnel, burrowing forward, where he was tearing at the loose sand and dirt frantically, digging like some crazed subterranean beast. Scott ripped at the cave-in, kicking the dirt back behind him, where Fenelli shoveled it to the back of the anteroom.

Nothing Lincoln Scott had ever done in his life seemed as urgent. No moment of confrontation, no anger, no rage, nothing equaled his assault on the intractable loose sand. It was like trying to do battle with a ghost, with a vapor. He had no idea whether he had to dig through one foot or a hundred. But distance made utterly no difference to him. He snatched at the dirt, throwing handfuls behind him, and he began to whisper a mantra, "You're not dying! You're not dying . . ." as he dug toward the spot where he believed he'd heard the last faint sound of Tommy Hart's voice.

A few feet behind him, Fenelli cried out, "Keep going! Keep going! He's only got a few minutes before he chokes! Dig, goddamn it! Dig!"

Major Clark remained poised on his hands and knees at the edge of the tunnel entrance, next to the privy, peering down. "Hurry," he cried. "Goddamn it! Get a move on!"

At the end of the central corridor of Hut 107, the officer keeping watch at the front door abruptly turned and shouted back toward the privy: "Krauts! Coming this way!"

Major Clark stood up. He turned to the bucket brigade standing in the corridor. "Everybody out!" he ordered. "Out to the assembly yard! Now!"

Somebody asked, "What about the tunnel?"

And Clark replied, "Ah, screw it!" But then he held up his

right hand, as if holding the men back from following his first order. The major slid a wry, tension-riddled smile across his face. He looked at the gathered kriegies. "Okay," he said briskly. "We need a few more minutes! Delay, delay, that's what we need. This is what I want: I want you men to disrupt the goddamn squad of Krauts heading this way. Like fourth and goal on the one-foot line! Just barrel-ass right into them, give 'em a real shot or two. Knock their butts flying! But keep on going, don't stop to throw more than one punch or two! Keep going straight out into the yard and get into formation. You understand what I'm saying? The old flying wedge, right through the enemy! But keep on going! Nobody gets himself shot. Nobody gets arrested! Just delay them as long as you can. Got it?"

Men up and down the corridor nodded. A few smiles broke out.

"Then get going! Give 'em hell!" Major Clark shouted. "And when you hit that door, let's hear your voices."

Some of the men grinned. A couple pounded fists into palms, stretched their knuckles. Muscles tensed. The officer watching at the door suddenly shouted, "Get ready!"

Then: "Go!"

"Go you kriegies!" Clark bellowed.

With three dozen furious bansheelike shouts of angry defiance, the phalanx of American airmen poured down the corridor shoulder to shoulder, bursting through the front door.

"Go! Go! Go!" Major Clark cried out.

He could not see the entire impact of the assault, but he could hear a sudden tangle of voices as the men slammed into the approaching squad of Germans, instantly creating a melee in the dust of the assembly yard. He could hear cries of alarm and the thud of bodies coming together savagely. It was, Major Clark thought, a very satisfying sound.

Then he turned and yelled down into the tunnel. "Germans! Any minute now! Keep digging!"

Lincoln Scott heard the major's words, but they no longer meant much to him. It seemed the threat created by the cave-in was far greater than the squad of goons racing toward Hut 107. He battled against the darkness that threatened to

envelop him, as well. He savaged the dirt in front of him with
a fury born of years of unremitting rage.

Tommy Hart was surprised. Death seemed to be coming
softly for him.

He had managed to curl up slightly as the cave-in dropped
onto his head, giving him the smallest of air pockets, one with
only a few precious breaths of stale and used air. He had not
thought that the world could be any darker than it had been,
but it was now.

For the first time that night, perhaps even in days and
weeks, he felt calm. Completely relaxed. All the tension in
every fiber of his body seemed to suddenly dissipate, sliding
swiftly away from him. He smiled inwardly, realizing that
even the great pain in his hand, which had managed to enflame his entire body, seemed to be extinguished in that moment, as surely as if it had been doused with water. He
thought this was an odd, but welcome, gift that death brought
to his last moments.

Tommy took a deep breath. He almost laughed out loud. It
was the most curious thing, he wondered to himself. One
takes breathing so much for granted. Each pull of air, tens of
thousands of times every day. It is only when one has only a
few breaths left, he thought, that one realizes how special
each was, how sweet and delicious they each tasted.

He took another breath and coughed. The cave-in had
pinned his head and shoulders, but not his feet, and he pushed
a little, almost involuntarily struggling forward, still fighting
in those last seconds. He thought of all the people in his life,
seeing each as if they stood directly in front of him, and was
saddened that he was about to slip into memory for each of
them. He wondered if that was what death truly was, simply
passing from flesh to memory.

And in this last reverie, Tommy was surprised again, this
time by an unmistakable scratching noise. He was perplexed.
He thought he was completely alone, and he didn't understand how any ghost could make this particular earthly noise.
It was a noise born of life, not death, and this confused him
and astonished him greatly.

But it was not a ghost that suddenly seized his torn hand.

In the utter blackness of the tunnel, he was suddenly aware that a space had opened up in front of him. In that hole before him he heard words, grunted, spoken between teeth gritted in the totality of exertion. "Hart? Damn it! Talk to me! You are not going to die! I will not allow you to die!"

He could feel a great strength pulling him forward, sliding him through the dirt that he'd thought would form his grave.

In the same moment, all the hurts and agonies that had fled, returned, almost blinding him as pain surged once again through his body. But curiously, he welcomed this, for he thought that it meant that Death had decided to loosen its grip upon him.

He heard again, "You're not going to die, damn it! I will not permit it!"

And so he whispered back, hoarsely, "Thank you." It was all he had the energy to say.

Lincoln Scott put both hands on Tommy's shoulders, dug his powerful fingers deep into shirt and flesh, and with a great and violent grunt, tugged him from the cave-in. Then, without hesitation, Scott pulled Tommy ahead, dragging him down the tunnel. Tommy tried to help by crawling, but he could not. He had no more strength. Not even a child's. Instead, he let Scott swim him forward with jerks and twitches, hauling him toward the questionable safety of the tunnel entrance.

At the privy entrance, Major Clark stood, arms folded in front of his chest, blocking the approach of a German lieutenant and a squad of helmeted goons carrying rifles.

"*Raus!*" the German officer cried. "Get out of the way!" he added in acceptable but accented English. The officer's uniform was torn at the knee and frayed at the shoulder, and a thin trickle of blood marred his jaw, dripping from the corner of his mouth. The men in the squad had many similar injuries and their uniforms were also ripped and dirtied from the mix-up with the kriegies that had come charging out of Hut 107.

"Not a chance," Major Clark said briskly. "Not until my men are out."

The German officer fumed. "Out of the way! To escape is *verboten*!"

"To escape is our duty!" Clark blustered. "And anyway, no one's escaping, you damn idiot," Major Clark sneered, still not budging. "Not any more! They're coming back. And when they come out, you can have the damn tunnel. For what it's worth."

The German officer reached into his holster and removed his Luger semiautomatic pistol.

"Out of the way, *Herr* major, or I will shoot you here!"

To emphasize his words, he chambered a round in the weapon.

Clark shook his head. "Not moving. Shoot me here, and you will face a hangman's noose, lieutenant. It's your own damn stupid choice."

The German officer hesitated, then raised his weapon to Clark's face. Clark eyed him with unrelenting hatred.

"Halt!"

The officer hesitated, then turned. The men in the squad all came abruptly to attention as Commandant Von Reiter strode down the corridor. Von Reiter's face was flushed. His own fury was evident, as prominent as the red silk lining of his dress coat. He stamped his feet hard against the wooden floor.

"Major Clark," he demanded sharply. "What is the meaning of this? You are to take your place in the formations immediately!"

Major Clark shook his head again. "There are men down below. When they come up, I'll accompany them to the *Appell*."

Von Reiter seemed to hesitate, only to have whatever his next command was to be interrupted by Fenelli's excited voice, rising from the tunnel pit entrance. "He's got 'im! Goddamn it, major! Scott dug him loose! They're coming out!"

Clark turned to the medic.

"Is he okay?"

"Still alive!"

Then Fenelli turned and reached back into the tunnel, helping Lincoln Scott pull Tommy Hart the final few feet. The two men tumbled into the anteroom, falling exhausted to the litter of dirt. Fenelli dropped down beside Tommy, cradling his head, while Lincoln Scott, breathing hard, tearing gasps of air from the tunnel shaft, slumped to the side. Fenelli produced a canteen with water, which he dripped onto Tommy's face.

"Jesus, Hart," Fenelli whispered. "You must be the luckiest son of a bitch I know."

Then he looked down at Tommy's mangled hand and gasped.

"Or maybe the unluckiest. Jesus, that's a mess. How the hell did that happen?"

"A dog bit me," Tommy answered weakly.

"Some dog," Fenelli said. Then he whispered another question. "What the hell happened out there?"

Tommy shook his head and replied softly, "I got out. Not for long. But I got out."

"Well," the medic from Cleveland replied, through his wide, dirt-smeared grin, "you made it farther than I did, and at least that's something."

He reached down, passed an arm under Tommy's shoulder, and helped Tommy rise to his feet. Scott grunted, and scrambled up as well. It took a minute or two for the two of them to lift Tommy through the pit, to the surface, where German hands seized him and angrily thrust him to the floor of the corridor. Tommy had no idea what was next, only that he felt drunk with the heady taste of air. He did not think he had the strength to rise on his own, nor was he at all sure he could walk, if the Germans demanded it. All he could feel was immense pain and a similar store of gratitude, as if the two conflicting sensations were more than happy to share space deep within him.

He was aware that Lincoln Scott stood nearby, at Major Clark's side, as if standing guard. Fenelli, however, bent toward him again, lifting Tommy's hand up.

"This is a mess," the medic said again. Fenelli turned toward Commandant Von Reiter. "He needs medical attention for these wounds immediately."

Von Reiter bent down, inspecting the hand. He staggered back slightly, as if shocked at the sight. The German seemed to hesitate, but then he reached forward and slowly and gingerly unwrapped the handkerchief from around the torn flesh. Von Reiter took the handkerchief and placed it in his tunic pocket, ignoring the deep wet crimson blood that stained the white silk. He frowned at the extent of Tommy's injury. He could see that the index finger was almost entirely severed and deep gouges and gashes marred the palm and the other fingers. Then he looked up and abruptly turned to the German lieutenant.

"A field dressing, lieutenant! Immediately."

The German officer saluted, and gestured toward one of the goons, still standing nearby at attention. The German soldier pulled a paper-covered pad of gauze impregnated with sulfa from a leather compartment on his campaign belt and handed it to Commandant Von Reiter, who, in turn, passed it to Fenelli.

"Do what you are able, lieutenant," Von Reiter said gruffly.

"This won't be adequate, commandant," Fenelli replied. "He'll need real medicines and a real doctor."

Von Reiter shrugged. "Bind it tightly," he said.

Then the German commandant rose stiffly and turned to Major Clark.

"These men," he said, gesturing toward Fenelli, Scott, and Hart. "Cooler."

"Hart needs prompt medical attention, commandant," Major Clark objected.

But Von Reiter merely shook his head and said, "I can see that, major. I am sorry. Cooler." This time he repeated the order to the German officer standing nearby. "Cooler! *Schnell!*" he said loudly. And then, without another word, or even a glance toward the Americans or their tunnel, Von Reiter abruptly turned on his heel and marched quickly from the hut.

Tommy tried to stand, but fell back dizzily.

The German lieutenant prodded him with a boot. *"Raus!"* he said.

"Don't worry, Tommy, I've got you," Lincoln Scott said, pushing the German to the side with a shoulder. He reached down and helped Tommy to his feet. Tommy rocked unsteadily. "Can you walk?" Scott asked beneath his breath.

"I will damn well try," Tommy replied, gritting his teeth together.

"I'll help you," Scott said. "Put your weight on me." He

kept his arm under Tommy's shoulder, snaking around his back, holding him steady. The black airman grinned. "You remember what I told you, Tommy?" he said quietly. "No white boy's gonna die when a Tuskegee flier's watching over you."

They took a tentative step forward, then a second. Fenelli slid ahead of them and held open the front door to Hut 107.

Surrounded by helmeted, unsmiling German guards, watched by every man in the entire compound, Lincoln Scott slowly supported Tommy Hart across the width of the exercise yard. Without saying a word, not even when prodded by the occasional shove from a goon's rifle, the two men traveled arm in arm directly through the gathered formations of American airmen, who silently moved aside to let them pass.

They marched out of the barbed-wire enclosure, the front gate swinging shut behind them with a crash, moving steadily toward the cooler block. It was only when they finally walked through the door to the punishment cells that they heard a great swelling sound of cheers suddenly rising up from the rows and rows of assembled men behind them. The cheers soared, filling the sunlit morning air, following them into the dank cement world of the cooler, penetrating the thick concrete building, tumbling through the open barred windows, resounding and echoing throughout the small space, overwhelming the sound of the doors locking behind them, making a wondrous music not unlike that of ancient Joshua's great horn when he stood defiant before the mighty walls of Jericho.

Chapter Twenty-one

EIGHTY-FOUR HATS

Tommy Hart shivered alone in the barren cement cooler cell for nearly a fortnight, the wounds in his hand worsening with every hour. His fingers swelled sausagelike with a fierce infection. The skin of his forearm was streaked with yellow-green marks, and he spent most of his hours leaning beside the cold wooden door, clutching his clublike hand to his chest. Searing pain was nearly constant and he weakened with every passing minute, frequently tumbling into a near-delirium that seemed to come and go as it pleased. The other men, in the adjacent cells, could hear him deep in the night-time talking erratically to people long dead or far distant, and they would shout out, trying to seize Tommy's attention, drag him back to some sort of reality, as if stealing him away from hallucination was medicinal.

He was only vaguely aware that every day the other men screamed imprecations at any German guard who ventured into the cooler building, carrying black *kriegsbrot* and water for the prisoners, demanding that Tommy be taken to a hospital. The Germans who were in charge of delivering the meager rations, or emptying the waste buckets from the cells, ignored these demands, wearing only stoic refusals to comprehend on their faces.

Only one of their captors, in the midst of the second week, showed any concern. That, of course, was Fritz Number One, who showed up shortly after the morning *Appell*, took a single look at Tommy's horrendous fist, and had Fenelli brought over from his nearby cell.

The medic from Cleveland had pulled back Tommy's fingers gently, shaking his head. He cleaned Tommy's face and wounds as best he could with a dry rag and clear water.

"It will be gangrenous within days," he told Fritz Number One, whispering furiously, when they returned to the hallway beyond Tommy's earshot. "Sulfonamide. Penicillin. And surgery, to clean out the infected tissue. For Christ's sake, Fritz, tell the commandant that Tommy will die without help. And soon."

"I will speak with the commandant," the ferret had promised.

"It's on your head," Fenelli had said. "And on Von Reiter's too, and trust me, there are folks here who won't forget what happens to Tommy Hart!"

"I will tell the commandant," Fritz Number One had repeated.

"Tell him! Don't wait. Tell him right now," Fenelli had half-demanded, half-begged.

But nothing happened for several more days.

Trapped in pain, fantasy, delirium, and cold, Tommy seemed to be entering some sort of odd netherworld. Sometimes he dreamed that he was still in the tunnel, and then he would awaken, crying out in fear. Other times, the pain grew so great that it seemed to rocket him to a different plane of existence, where all he could see and feel were the memories of home that had served him so well in the months he'd been a prisoner in Stalag Luft Thirteen. It was this state that Tommy longed for, because as he envisioned the sky above the Green Mountains beyond the door to his Vermont home, the pain fled, if only briefly, and he was able to rest.

On the sixteenth day in the cooler, he could no longer eat. His throat was too dry. Almost the entirety of his strength had evaporated. He was able to manage a few sips of water, but that was all.

The others called to him, tried to get him to join them in song, or conversation, anything to keep him alert, but he was unable. Whatever resources he had left, he used to battle the hurt emanating in red-hot surges up into his body. He was filthy, sweat and dirt covered him, and he was afraid he was going to lose control over his bowels. He thought, in one of the few rational moments that managed to overcome the delirium threatening to surround him completely, that it seemed a particularly stupid and silly way to finally die, bitten by a Gestapo officer, when he'd been through so much, and already been saved so many times.

Into this reverie came voices, which he ignored, because by this time he was forever hearing voices, and most of these belonged to people long dead. Even Visser had spoken to him angrily once, but Tommy had arrogantly sneered at this ghost.

It was, however, not a fantasy when the cell door was thrust open. Tommy looked up through cloudy, bleary eyes, and saw the unmistakable form of Hugh Renaday lurching through the entranceway.

"Bloody hell!" Hugh blurted, as he bent toward Tommy, who was unable to rise from his spot on the floor.

Tommy smiled through the hurt. "Hugh. I thought you'd . . ."

"Bought it? Damn close. That bastard Visser ordered me shot. Lucky thing Von Reiter wouldn't go along with it. So I'm still alive and kicking, my friend."

"What about the others?"

"What others?"

"The men who got out. . . ."

Hugh grinned. "The bloody Krauts caught ten guys wandering around in the forest lost as newborn babes that morning. Another five men were arrested at the station, waiting for the second train through. Seems like there was some problem with the tickets that got forged and the Gestapo didn't have any trouble picking them out of the crowds. But three guys, the first three up and out of the tunnel, are still missing and unaccounted for. Their tickets must have been acceptable and their train pulled in and took off before the alarm was sounded. Lots of rumors around, but nothing definite."

Tommy nodded. "That's good," he said. "They were lucky."

"Luck? Hell, who knows? Oh, and our boy Fritz Number One, he got a medal and a raise. He's now a sergeant, and he gets to wear one of those shiny black crosses around his neck. He's been strutting around the camp like the cock o' the roost, as you can imagine."

Hugh reached down and thrust his hands around Tommy,

lifting him as he spoke. "Come on now, counselor. We're getting you out of here," he said.

"Scott and Fenelli?"

"They're getting out, too."

Tommy smiled. "Good, good," he said weakly. "Hugh, my hand . . ."

The Canadian clenched his teeth. "Hang in there, lad. We're going to get you some help."

The cooler corridor was crowded with rifle-bearing German guards. Hugh half-carried Tommy from the cell, where Lincoln Scott reached over and wordlessly took half the burden of Tommy's weight. Tommy felt skeletal, almost rubber-legged, when he tried to walk, as if each joint in his body had somehow worked itself loose and no longer held him together.

Fenelli was cursing under his breath, leading them out of the cooler block into the sunlight outside. All the men blinked at the sudden blast of brightness, and inhaled the warm air greedily. There were more Germans waiting for them, as well as Colonel MacNamara and Major Clark, who paced back and forth in front of the cooler building, impatiently.

"How is he?" Colonel MacNamara instantly demanded of Fenelli.

"He's hurting bad," the medic replied.

MacNamara nodded, then pointed toward the camp administration building. "Right in there," he said. "Von Reiter is waiting."

With Tommy at the center of the odd procession, the men were ushered directly into Commandant Von Reiter's office. The German officer was seated behind his immaculate desk as usual, but he rose when they entered. He straightened his uniform self-consciously and clicked his heels together, bowing slightly at the waist. A studied, tight performance.

The kriegies, with the exception of Tommy, all saluted.

Von Reiter gestured toward a chair, and Tommy was helped into it by Fenelli and Lincoln Scott, who stood directly behind him.

The German cleared his throat and stared again at

Tommy's disfigured hand. "You do poorly, Lieutenant Hart?" he asked.

Tommy laughed through all the hurt. "Had better days," he whispered hoarsely.

Colonel MacNamara stepped forward, speaking sharply, his back rigid, his face set with furious demand. "I want this man attended to immediately! His wounds are serious, as you can easily see. Under the Geneva Convention, he is entitled to proper medical care! I warn you, commandant, this situation is of critical importance. We will tolerate no further delays—"

Von Reiter held up his palm.

"Lieutenant Hart will receive the best of care. I have made the necessary arrangements. I apologize for the delay, but these are delicate matters."

"Well, every minute we delay further endangers this officer!"

Von Reiter nodded. "Yes, yes, colonel, this I can see. But much has happened and while we are eager to be efficient, there are some questions that remain. Mr. Hart? You are perhaps capable of answering a few questions? So that the paperwork I send to my superiors will be complete."

Tommy tried to shrug.

"He doesn't have to answer anything," Major Clark blurted.

Von Reiter sighed. "Major, please, indulge me. You have not heard the questions yet."

The commandant allowed a second or two of silence to penetrate the room. Then he turned back to Tommy Hart.

"Lieutenant, do you know who murdered Captain Vincent Bedford of the United States Army Air Corps?"

Tommy smiled. He nodded and replied weakly, "Yes, I do."

"It was not Lieutenant Scott?"

Before Tommy could reply to this, Colonel MacNamara interrupted. "Commandant Von Reiter! As you are well aware, Lieutenant Scott was acquitted of this crime by the unanimous verdict of a military tribunal sitting in court-martial! While Lieutenant Scott was imprisoned in your cooler, the tribunal concluded that there was not evidence beyond and to the exclusion of a reasonable doubt concerning this killing, and Lieutenant Scott was declared not guilty! I fail to see why—"

"Please, colonel, I have not completed my examination."

"Acquitted?" Scott asked, with a short laugh. "It might have been nice if someone had told me."

"The camp knows," MacNamara said. "We made an announcement at *Appell* the morning after the escape."

Scott smiled. He placed a hand on Tommy's shoulder and gave him a congratulatory squeeze.

MacNamara quieted. Von Reiter paused, looked from face to face, then continued to ask questions.

"Lieutenant Hart, let me put this another way. Your investigation determined the identity of the real killer, did it not?"

"It did," Tommy answered as strongly as possible.

Von Reiter smiled. "I thought it would." The German shook his head slightly. "I thought some people might have underestimated you, Mr. Hart. But that, of course, concerns us little now. To continue, lieutenant, this murderer . . . he was not a member of the Luftwaffe, was he?"

"No sir."

"Nor was he a member of any other German armed force, correct?"

"That is correct, commandant," Tommy replied.

"In other words, Captain Bedford's assassin was a member of the Allied forces imprisoned here at Stalag Luft Thirteen?"

"Yes."

"You will be willing to sign a statement confirming this fact?"

"As long as I am not required to identify the actual murderer."

Von Reiter laughed briefly. "That, of course, lieutenant, is a matter for your own authorities to discuss with you at some later, more convenient point. My superiors have declared that the purposes of the Luftwaffe will be served by merely swearing that the killer does not belong to our service, thereby relieving us from any lingering culpability in this unfortunate matter. You can do that?"

"Yes, commandant."

Von Reiter seemed pleased. "I have taken the liberty of having this document prepared. You will have to have trust that the German language reflects what I have just stated and you have confirmed. Unless your own officers would like to supply a translator . . ."

Von Reiter grinned wickedly at MacNamara, before adding, "But I suspect they would not wish to do that, for they prefer that we do not know the names of the American officers fluent in German."

"I'll take your word for it," Tommy whispered.

"I thought as much," Von Reiter said. He retreated behind his desk, opened the center drawer, and removed a piece of paper with typing on it. There was a large embossed black eagle at the head of the page. The German gestured at the spot where Tommy's name was already written in. He offered Tommy a fountain pen. Struggling with the pain that constantly sent rivets of hot agony through his arm and into his chest, Tommy bent forward and signed the paper. It was exhausting.

Von Reiter took the paper, held it up, examined it, blew once on the ink to dry it, then returned the paper to his desk drawer. Then he barked out a quick command in German and a side door immediately opened. Fritz Number One entered and saluted.

"Sergeant! Bring Herr Blucher, please. And that other item that we discussed."

Von Reiter turned to Tommy as the molelike Swiss entered the office. He wore the same black homburg and carried the same worn black briefcase that he'd had with him on the day Phillip Pryce had been turned over to his care. Von Reiter smiled again. "This, Mr. Hart, is Herr Blucher of the Swiss Red Cross. He will accompany you to a hospital in his country. Alas, German facilities are inadequate, I believe, for your needs at this time." The German commandant lifted an eyebrow. "You have met Herr Blucher, I understand? And mistakenly assumed him to be a member of our esteemed state police? Gestapo? I assure you, he is not."

Von Reiter hesitated again, before adding, "And he carries with him a small gift from a friend of yours, Mr. Hart. Wing Commander Pryce managed to send these items through diplomatic courier. I believe he obtained them at the hospital in Geneva where he currently resides. Lieutenant Fenelli, perhaps your assistance at this point?"

"Phillip!" Hugh Renaday burst out. "How did he learn . . ."

Von Reiter shrugged. "We are not beasts, flying officer. At least not all of us. Lieutenant Fenelli, if you would be so kind . . ."

Fenelli stepped forward, and Herr Blucher handed him a small parcel wrapped in string and brown paper. The medic from Cleveland swiftly tore it open and gasped out a sudden, heartfelt, "Jesus Christ! Thank God, thank God . . ."

He turned and the others could see that inside the parcel was sulfa, disinfectant, sterile wraps, several syringes, and a half-dozen precious vials of penicillin and a similar amount of morphine.

"Penicillin, first!" Fenelli said. Without hesitating, he was filling a syringe. "As much as possible, as fast as possible." He rolled Tommy's sleeve up and cleared a spot near the shoulder. He plunged the needle in, whispering, "Fight hard, Tommy Hart. Now you got a real chance."

Tommy leaned his head back. For the barest of moments, he started to allow himself to believe he might live.

Fenelli continued to talk, seemingly to himself, but to all the others in the room, as well. ". . . Now some morphine for the trip. Kill that pain for a bit. That sounds pretty good, huh, Hart?"

Von Reiter held up his hand again. "Ah, lieutenant, before you administer the morphine, please, one more moment."

Fenelli stopped in the midst of filling the syringe.

Von Reiter looked over toward Fritz Number One, who had come through the door and was carrying a makeshift box. The German commandant smiled one more time. But it was the coldest of smiles, one that spoke of many hard years spent in the harsh service of war.

"I have two gifts for you, Mr. Hart," he said quietly. "So that you may remember these days."

He reached inside his tunic pocket and carefully removed a handkerchief. It was the bloodstained silk handkerchief with which Tommy had first bound his hand in the moments after his battle with Visser.

"This is yours, I believe, Mr. Hart. Undoubtedly an important gift from a woman friend back in the States, and I suspect of some sentimental value . . ."

The German smoothed the brilliant white handkerchief out flat on the desktop in front of him. The crimson stains had dried into deep maroon colors.

"And so, I return what is yours, lieutenant. But I do note the odd coincidence that your lady friend back home seems to possess the precise identical initials as my former second-in-command, Hauptmann Heinrich Albert Visser, who died so bravely in service of his country."

Tommy could see the HAV embossed in flowing script in a corner of the handkerchief. He looked up at Von Reiter, who shook his head.

"War, of course, is a series of the most perplexing coincidences."

Von Reiter sighed and picked up the silk square, folding it carefully three times, and handing it across the desktop to Tommy Hart.

"I have one other gift for you, Mr. Hart, and then Mr. Fenelli can feel free to administer the morphia, which I know will provide you with great relief on your journey to Switzerland."

Von Reiter gestured sharply toward Fritz Number One, who stepped forward and placed the box he held at his waist at Tommy's feet.

"What the hell are those?" Colonel MacNamara burst out. "Looks like a bunch of damn hats!"

Von Reiter let his awful smile curl around the corners of his mouth before replying. "You are indeed correct, colonel. They are hats. Some wool caps, some fur hats, some are mere cloth head coverings. There are many different shapes and sizes and styles. They have but one detail in common. Like the handkerchief that I have already returned, they are marked with blood, and thus will need to be cleaned before they can ever hope to be used again."

"Hats?" the Senior American Officer asked. "What is Hart to do with a bunch of hats? Especially bloody ones."

"They are Russian hats, colonel."

"Well," MacNamara continued, "I don't see why—"

But Von Reiter coolly interrupted him.

"Eighty-four hats, colonel. Eighty-four Russian hats."

The commandant turned to Tommy Hart.

"Sixteen men went to the firing squad bareheaded, Lieutenant Hart."

Then Von Reiter shrugged.

"This surprised me immensely," he added. "I thought that for the cold-blooded murder of a highly decorated German officer, the Gestapo would shoot the entire work camp. Each and every Russian. But to my astonishment, they selected only one hundred men to kill in retaliation."

Von Reiter walked back around the desk, and seated himself. He allowed a moment of quiet to fill the room before he nodded and gestured to Fenelli, who held the morphine needle ready.

"Go with Herr Blucher, Mr. Hart. Leave here and take all your secrets with you. His car will take you to the train. The train will carry you to Switzerland, where your friend Wing Commander Pryce, a hospital, and surgeons all await your arrival. Do not think about those one hundred men. Not for another moment. Wipe them from your memory. Instead, you should endeavor to survive. Return home to Vermont. Live to be old and rich and happy, Lieutenant Hart. And when your grandchildren come to your side one day to ask you about the war, you can say that you passed it most uneventfully, reading legal textbooks, inside a German prisoner-of-war camp named Stalag Luft Thirteen."

Tommy had no words left to reply with. He was only peripherally aware of the needle penetrating his flesh. But the sweet dulling sensation of morphine sweeping through him was like drinking from the greatest and freshest clear, cold mountain stream of home.

Epilogue

A CHURCH NOT TOO FAR FROM
LAKE MICHIGAN

Lydia Hart was in the bathroom, putting the finishing touches to her hair, when she called out, "Tommy? Do you need help with your tie?" She paused, waiting for a response, which came merely as a grunted negative, which was precisely what she'd expected and made her smile as she ran the brush through the silver cascade she still wore down around her shoulders. Then she added, "How are we doing on time?"

"We have all the time in the world," Tommy replied softly.

He was seated by the large window of their hotel suite, and from where he was positioned, he could see both his wife's reflection in the mirror and, when he pivoted and looked through the windowpane, all the way to Lake Michigan. It was a summer mid-morning, and streaky sunlight flitted off the dark blue surface of the water. He had spent the past quarter hour studiously watching sailboats pirouette across the slight roll of the waves, cutting back and forth in seemingly aimless patterns. The grace and speed of each sleek hull, circling beneath a billowing white sail, was hypnotic. He wondered a bit why he'd always gravitated to fishing boats and noisy motors, guessing this preference had something to do with his inclination for destinations, but then decided also that he would have had too much trouble handling both the tiller and the mainsheet of a sailboat driven fast before the wind.

Tommy looked down and stole a glance at his left hand. He was missing his index finger and half of the little finger. Purplish scar tissue had built up in the deep gouges ripped from

535

his palm. But, he thought, the hand appeared to be far more crippled than it truly was. For more than fifty years his wife had been asking him if he needed help tying his tie, and for all that time he'd always replied that he did not. He had learned how to tie knots in both the ties he wore to his office and the fishing lines he used on his boat. And every month when the government had dutifully sent him a modest disability check, he'd just as dutifully signed it over to the general scholarship fund at Harvard. Still, his war-damaged hand had lately developed a tendency to the stiffness of arthritis, and on more than one recent occasion had frozen painfully on him. He had not told his wife about these small betrayals.

"Do you think there will be anyone there we know?" his wife asked.

Tommy reluctantly turned away from the vision of sailboats, and fixed his eyes on his wife's reflection. For a single heady moment he thought she had not changed one bit since the day they were married in 1945.

"No," he said. "Probably just a lot of dignitaries. He was pretty famous. Maybe there will be some lawyers I met over the years. But not really anyone we know."

"Not even someone from the prisoner-of-war camp?"

Tommy smiled and shook his head. "No. I don't think so."

Lydia put the hairbrush down, replacing it in her hand with an eyebrow pencil. She worked on her face for a moment, then said, "I wish Hugh were still alive so he could keep you company."

Tommy felt a sudden twinge of sadness. "I do, too," he said.

Hugh Renaday had died a decade earlier. A week after being diagnosed with terminal cancer and well before the inevitable progression of the disease could rob his limbs and heart of strength, the hulking hockey player had taken down a favorite hunting rifle, gathered up snowshoes, tent, sleeping bag, and a portable backpacker's stove, and after writing a series of unequivocal farewell notes to his wife, his children, his grandchildren, and one to Tommy, he had loaded everything into the back of his four-wheel-drive truck and driven deep into the cold wilderness of the Canadian Rockies. It was January, the dead of winter, and when his car would go no farther through the piled snow of an old, abandoned logging trail, Hugh Renaday had started to hike in. When his legs tired of fighting through the northern Alberta drifts, he had stopped, made a modest camp, cooked himself one last meal, then patiently waited for nighttime's falling temperatures, plummeting far below the freezing point, to kill him.

Tommy understood later from one of Hugh's fellow Mounties that freezing to death was not considered a terrible way to die in the North country. One shivered a few times, then eventually slipped into an unconsciousness that mimicked a deep and restful sleep, the years' memories sliding away slowly along with the final breaths of life. It was a sturdy and efficient way to die, Tommy had always thought, as organized and steady and dependable as the longtime policeman had been every second of his life.

He did not like to think of Hugh's death much, though once, when he and Lydia had taken a cruise ship to Alaska and he'd stayed up late into the night mesmerized by the aurora borealis, he'd hoped that the great sheet of colorful lights startling the black sky had been the last thing that Hugh Renaday had seen of this world.

Instead, when he remembered his friend, he preferred to think of a moment the two men had shared, fishing not far from Tommy's retirement home in the Florida Keys. Tommy had spotted a huge barracuda, a torpedolike brute, lurking on the edge of a flat, just hanging in a few clear feet of water waiting in ambush for some unsuspecting jack crevalle or needlefish to wander by. Tommy had rigged up a spinning rod with a fluorescent red tube lure and a wire leader. Hugh had thrown the lure just a few feet from the 'cuda's gaping mouth. The fish had surged forward without hesitation, and then, once hooked, had cartwheeled and exploded, its long silver sides tearing free from the water's surface, blasting immense white sheets across the waves. Hugh had landed the fish, and while posing for the obligatory photographs to send home, had taken a moment to stare at the great rows of almost translucent razor-sharp canine teeth in the massive jaws of the fish.

"The business end of a barracuda," Tommy had said. "Reminds me of some of my honorable fellow members of the bar."

But Hugh Renaday had shaken his head.

"Visser," the Canadian had replied. "Hauptmann Heinrich Visser. And this is a Visser-fish."

Tommy glanced down at his hand again. Visserfish, he thought.

He must have mumbled the word out loud, because Lydia asked from the bathroom, "What was that?"

"Nothing," Tommy replied. "Just wondering. Do you think the red tie is too bright for a funeral?"

"No," his wife said. "It's just right."

He guessed that the morning's gathering would be a little like Phillip Pryce's funeral, which had been held in one of London's finer cathedrals a dozen years after the war had ended. Phillip had had many prominent friends from both the military and the legal profession, and they had crowded into the pews while a boys' choir sang in high-pitched and pristine Latin. Tommy and Hugh often later joked that undoubtedly many of the barristers who'd occupied the opposite side of some issue had attended only to make absolutely certain that Phillip was indeed dead.

Phillip Pryce had died, both Tommy and Hugh had agreed, most wondrously.

On the night he'd managed to extricate a conservative member of Parliament from a messy entanglement with a woman half his age plying the most ancient of traditions, Pryce had allowed the junior members of his firm to take him out for a lengthy, elegant dinner in celebration. Afterward, he'd stopped off at his private club for a late-night brandy. Napoleon. Over a hundred years old. One of the butlers had assumed that Phillip had fallen asleep, resting deep in the overstuffed leather of a wing chair, snifter in his hand, only to discover that Pryce had actually died quite quietly of sudden heart failure. The old barrister was smiling ear-to-ear, as if someone familiar and beloved had been at Death's side when he came beckoning. At Phillip's funeral, his entire law firm, from most senior to most junior, had marched into the cathedral, shoulder to shoulder, like a Roman cohort, tears filling their eyes.

Phillip Pryce had left a will that asked Tommy to read something at the service. Tommy had spent a restless night in the Strand Hotel, frantically flipping through passage after passage of both the Old and New Testaments, unable to find words large enough to honor his friend. Anxious, he'd risen shortly after dawn and taken a cab over to Phillip's Grosvenor Square town house, where the manservant had let him inside.

At the table beside Phillip's modest bed, Tommy had noticed an old, dog-eared, much-read, first edition of Kenneth Grahame's *The Wind in the Willows*. On the flyleaf Phillip had written an inscription, and Tommy had understood instantly that the book had been a gift for Phillip Junior. The message read simply: *My darling boy, no matter how old and wise one struggles to become, it is always important to remember the joys of youth. Here is a book that should help you to remember in years to come. With greatest love on the wondrous occasion of your ninth birthday from your devoted father . . .*

Tommy discovered two sections of the book that were both underlined and faded, as if worn thin by the repeated passing of a child's eyes over the words. The first was in the chapter "The Piper at the Gates of Dawn" and read: "For this is the last best gift that the kindly demigod is careful to bestow on those to whom he has revealed himself in their helping: the gift of forgetfulness. Lest the awful rememberance should remain and grow, and overshadow mirth and pleasure, and the great haunting memory should spoil all the after-lives of little animals helped out of difficulties, in order that they should be happy and light-hearted as before. . . ."

The second of the underlined passages was almost the entirety of the final chapter, where the faithful Mole, Rat, Badger, and the irrepressible Mr. Toad arm themselves and attack the vastly superior force of weasels occupying Toad Hall, overwhelming the interlopers through their righteousness and daring.

And so, later that afternoon, disdaining the Bible and Shakespeare and Sir Thomas More and Keats, Shelley, Byron, and all the other famous poets who so frequently lend their words to solemn occasions, Tommy had risen and read to the distinguished assembly the passages from the children's book. This, he thought afterward, and Hugh Renaday had mightily agreed, was a little unexpected and more than a touch outrageous and also precisely what Phillip would have most enjoyed.

"I'm ready," Lydia said, finally emerging from the bathroom.

"You look quite exquisite," Tommy said admiringly.

"I would rather we were going to a wedding," Lydia replied,
shaking her head a little bit disarmingly. "Or a christening."

Tommy stood up and his wife straightened the tie at his
neck that did not need straightening. The gift of forgetfulness, he thought. So we can all be as happy and lighthearted
as before.

It was the finest of days, bright, warm. The sort of day that
seems misplaced at a funeral. Shafts of vibrant summer light
eagerly pierced the stained-glass windows of the cathedral,
delivering odd sheets of reds, greens, and golds in wide
splashes onto the gray stone floor.

The rows of pews were packed with mourners. The vice
president and his wife were there, representing the administration. They were joined by both senators from Illinois, a
gaggle of congressmen, dozens of state officials, and at least
one Supreme Court Justice that Tommy had once argued a
case before. Eulogies were delivered by prominent men in the
field of education, and there was a lengthy, excited, and almost musical reading from the Scriptures by a very young
and probably slightly nervous Baptist preacher from Lincoln
Scott's father's old church.

A flag draped the casket at the front of the church. In front
of the casket were three enlarged photographs. On the right
was a picture of Lincoln Scott as an old man, in his flowing
academic robes, giving a rousing speech to university graduates. On the left was a newspaper photo from the 1960s of
Scott, arm in arm with Dr. Martin Luther King Jr. and Ralph
Abernathy, leading a march down some unidentifiable southern
street. But in the center, the largest picture of the three, was a
young Lincoln Scott, eyes turned skyward, mounting the
wing of his Mustang before flying a mission in German skies.
Tommy stared at the portrait and thought that whoever took
the snapshot had probably mainly by luck managed to capture much about Lincoln Scott, just in the eagerness of his
step and the ferocity in his eyes.

Tommy sat in the middle of the church, his wife at his side.

He was unable to listen to all the fine words of praise ringing out above his head from speaker after speaker who rose to the pulpit.

What he heard, instead, was the long-forgotten sound of engines howling in attack, the staccato racheting noise of machine guns mingling with the thuds of flak exploding outside, raining metal against the exterior of the bomber. For the longest of moments, he felt his throat growing dry, and sweat starting to form beneath his arms. He could hear the cries and calls of men racing into battle and the screams of men embraced by death. The noise threatened to overcome the cool interior of the cathedral where he sat. Tommy breathed out sharply, and then shook his head slightly, as if he could shake away all the memories like a dog shaking water from his fur. *Three hundred miles per hour, twenty feet above the water, and the whole world shooting at you. How did you ever live?* He couldn't answer his own question, but he could the one that followed: *Twenty feet beneath the ground, bleeding and trapped, and no way out. How did you ever live?* He took another deep breath. *I lived because of the man in the casket.*

At a signal from the priest, the mourners all rose and sang the first and third verses of "Onward Christian Soldiers." The strongest voices, Tommy thought, thundered from his left, from the first two pews of the cathedral, where Lincoln Scott's extended family was gathered, surrounding a small, coffee-colored elderly black woman.

The priest at the pulpit shut his hymnal with a snap and launched into another reading from the Bible. How David fought great Goliath armed with nothing save his shepherd's sling and came away victorious.

Tommy leaned back, feeling the unforgiving wood of the bench against his bones. In a way, he thought, they were all in that cavernous room, listening to the priest. MacNamara and Clark, who'd both received medals and promotions for their command of the escape from Stalag Luft Thirteen, although Tommy had always thought that it was only that true rat-bastard Clark, who had contradicted everything Tommy had believed about him by ordering the unarmed kriegies of Hut 107 to attack the approaching Germans and buy Scott some extra time in the collapsed tunnel, who deserved the honors. Fenelli, who'd gone on to become a cardiovascular surgeon in Cleveland. Tommy had run into him once, when he was staying at a hotel that was also hosting a medical convention, and he'd spotted the onetime medic's name on a list of speakers. They'd had drinks in the lounge and some moments of alcohol-aided laughter. Fenelli had admired the work of the Swiss surgeons who'd cut up his hand, but Tommy had told him that Phillip Pryce had threatened to shoot any doctor who dared to mess up, which, Fenelli had agreed, had probably encouraged attentiveness.

Fenelli had asked him if he'd stayed friends with Scott after the war, but Tommy had told him no, which surprised the doctor.

It was the only time he'd seen Fenelli, and he halfway hoped that when he scanned the faces of the mourners at the church he would spot the medic from Cleveland. But he did not. He'd partially expected, as well, that Fritz Number One might have flown in for the services from Stuttgart, because the former ferret owed a significant debt to Lincoln Scott. Eight months after Tommy's repatriation, when elements of General Omar Bradley's Fifth Army had liberated the airmen of Stalag Luft Thirteen, it had been Scott who told army debriefers of Fritz's language skills and helpfulness. This had led to a position helping U.S. military police interrogate captured German soldiers, as they searched for Gestapo trying to hide among the rank and file. And Fritz later used these same skills to rise to an executive position with Porsche-Audi A.G. in postwar Germany.

Tommy knew all this from the letters Fritz sent at Christmas time. The first of these had been sent to: T. Hart, Famous Lawyer, Harvard University, Harvard, Massachusetts. How the postal service managed to get it to the law school in Cambridge, which subsequently sent it to Tommy at his firm's Boston office, had always been something of a mystery to him. Other letters over the years, always containing photographs, had shown the lean ferret growing considerably thicker around the middle, with wife and then children and grandchildren and a selection of different dogs at his side. Fritz had only sent Tommy one unhappy letter in all the years after the war, a short note that arrived not long after the reunification of Germany, when the automobile executive had finally learned from declassified East German documents that Commandant Von Reiter had been shot in early 1945. In the confused days following the fall of the German Reich, Von Reiter had been captured by the Russians. He did not survive his first interrogation.

Lydia nudged Tommy, holding open the printed funeral program. Belatedly, Tommy joined in as the gathered mourners recited a Psalm in unison. "For they that carried us away captive required of us a song . . ."

Of the three men who made it through the tunnel and onto the first train that morning, two managed to return home. Murphy, the meatpacker from Springfield, had disappeared, presumed dead.

In New Orleans once, fifteen years after the war ended, Tommy had won a death penalty case. It was something that he insisted his firm let him do. The bulk of their business was moneymaking corporate law, but every so often he very quietly took on some seemingly hopeless criminal case in some distant part of the nation, charging no fee and working late hours. It was a task he did not require of the associates he hired, or the partners he formed, though more than one of them did precisely the same. Winning these cases was hard, and when he did, there was always a celebratory air.

On this occasion, long after midnight, he'd found himself in a small jazz club, listening to a particularly good trumpet player. The musician had spotted Tommy, sitting near the front, and almost stumbled on a note. But he'd recovered, smiled, faced the audience, and told them all that sometimes on some nights, he found himself remembering the war, and that this caused him to play something more reflective. He'd then launched into a solo version of "Amazing Grace," turning the hymn into rhythm and blues, striking long trilling notes that filled the entire room with a plaintive urgency. Tommy had been sure that the musician would come over to speak with him, but instead the bandleader had sent over a bottle of the club's best champagne, and the note: *Better to leave some things unsaid. Here's that drink I promised you. Glad you made it home, too.* When Tommy asked the club manager if he could thank the musician in person, he was told that the trumpet player had already left.

As best as Tommy could figure, the truth about the murder of Captain Vincent Bedford and Lincoln Scott's trial and the escape from Stalag Luft Thirteen never really was written, which, he thought, was probably an acceptable thing. He had spent many hours, after he finally returned home to Vermont, thinking about Trader Vic, trying to discover for himself some sort of reconciliation with Bedford's death. He was not convinced that Vic deserved to die, not even for the mistake of trading information that inadvertently caused the deaths of men and turned him into a threat to the escape plans of others. But then again, he sometimes also thought that Vic's murder was the only just thing that had happened in the camp. As the years had passed, Tommy came to understand that, ultimately, the most complicated man, and the hardest of them all to fathom, had been the used-car salesman from Mississippi. He might have been the bravest of them all, the stupidest, the most evil, and the most clever, because, for every single aspect of Vic's personality, Tommy could find a contradiction. And, finally, he supposed it was all those contradictions that had killed Trader Vic just as surely as that ceremonial SS dagger did.

Tommy glanced down at the watch he still wore on his wrist, not because he was curious about the time, but more about the memories it held, deep within its mechanical gears and levers. He followed the second hand creeping around the watch face and he thought: We were all heroes once, even the worst of us. The watch no longer kept good time, and more than one repairman had examined it with dismay, suggesting that keeping it running was far more expensive than the watch was worth. But Tommy always paid the bill, because none of the repairmen had even the vaguest idea what its true value was.

Lydia nudged Tommy again, and they rose.

Lincoln Scott's casket was being wheeled down the center of the cathedral while the organ resounded with "Jesu, Joy of Man's Desiring." The most prominent of the dignitaries formed an honorary squad of pallbearers directly behind the vibrant colors of the American flag. And just behind them followed Lincoln Scott's family. They moved slowly, their pace set by the small, silver-haired, delicate form of the black airman's widow. Her step had the patience of age.

The pews emptied out behind the procession. Tommy waited his turn, then stepped out into the aisle. He found Lydia's arm, and the two of them walked out of the cathedral together.

Tommy blinked for a moment, when the warm sun hit his face. He heard a familiar twangy voice speaking in his own ear say, *Find us the way home, Tommy, willya?* and he answered to his own heart, I suppose I did find the way home. For as many of us as I could.

Next to him, he felt Lydia squeeze his arm tight to her side for just a second. Tommy looked up and saw that Lincoln Scott's family had gathered on the right, spread out over the first few steps of the cathedral, surrounding the widow. She was receiving condolences from the many mourners, who lined up to pay their respects. Tommy nodded to his wife and maneuvered to the end of the line.

They moved forward steadily, approaching the widow. Tommy tried to form some words in his head, but was surprised to realize that he could not. He'd made many elaborate and dramatic speeches in hundreds of courtrooms, often extemporaneously finding the right words, just as he had in 1944 at Stalag Luft Thirteen. But in these few moments, as he shuffled toward Lincoln Scott's bride, he was at a loss.

And so, he had nothing prepared when he finally reached the widow's side.

"Mrs. Scott," he said hesitatingly, clearing his throat with a cough. "I am very sorry for your loss."

The widow looked up at Tommy, measuring him, an almost quizzical look flitting behind her eyes, as if he were someone she thought she should know, but couldn't quite place. She took Tommy's hand in hers, and then, in that way people have at funerals, lifted her left hand to cover his right, as if further solidifying the handshake. And then, just as inadvertently, Tommy lifted his own left hand and covered hers.

"I knew your husband years ago. . . ." he said.

But the widow suddenly looked down and, for a moment, stared at Tommy's damaged hand, resting on top of her own.

Then she lifted her eyes to his and broke into a great, wide smile of utter recognition.

"Mr. Hart," she said melodically, a singer's vibrant voice, "I am so honored that you came. Lincoln would have been ever so pleased."

"I wish," Tommy started, stopped, then started again, "I wish that he and I . . ."

But he was interrupted by the widow's eyes, which glistened with an unabashed joy.

"Do you know what he used to tell his family, Mr. Hart?"

"No," Tommy replied softly.

"He used to say that you were the single greatest friend he had ever had. Not really the best, you see. Perhaps I fit that category. But the greatest, Mr. Hart."

Lincoln Scott's widow would not release Tommy's hand. But she turned to the gathered children, grandchildren, and great-grandchildren, that were arrayed on the steps beside and behind her. Tommy looked over at the faces, all of whom were turned toward him, all wearing some curiosity, some solemnity, and perhaps, among the very young, just a little eagerness to have things move along. But even the little ones who were fidgety quieted rapidly when the widow spoke.

"Gather round," she told them all, her voice suddenly carrying an authority that went far beyond her tiny figure. "Because this is someone you must all meet. Everyone: This is Mr. Tommy Hart. Children, he was the man who stepped up to help your grandfather when he was all alone in the German prisoner-of-war camp. You've all heard him tell the story many times, but here is the very man that Grandfather spoke of so often."

Tommy could feel words choking in his throat. "In the war," he said quietly, "it was your husband who saved my life."

But the widow shook her head back and forth like the schoolteacher she once was, as if she were correcting a favorite but mischievous student.

"No, Mr. Hart. You are mistaken. Lincoln always said it was you who saved him." She smiled. "Now children," she added briskly, "come up quickly." And with that, the first of Lincoln Scott's sons stepped forward, took Tommy's hand out from his mother's strong grip and pumped it firmly as he murmured, "Thank you, Mr. Hart." Then, one after the other, from the tallest and oldest right down to a tiny baby held in his young mother's arms, Lincoln Scott's family moved to the front of the cathedral steps and Tommy Hart shook hands with each and every one.

Author's Note

My father was three months into his junior year at Princeton University when Pearl Harbor was bombed. Like so many other men of his generation, he promptly enlisted, and slightly over one year later was navigating a B-25 Mitchell bomber above the waters near Sicily. *Green Eyes* was shot down in February 1943 after skip-bombing a German convoy seeking to reinforce Rommel's Afrika Korps. My father, and the other men in *Green Eyes*, were plucked from the ocean by the Germans. They initially spent some weeks at an Italian POW camp in Chieti, before being shipped on boxcars to Stalag Luft Three, near the Polish border in Sagan, Germany. That was where he spent almost the entirety of the war. On a prominent bookshelf in his home, occupying a spot of some respect, is a first edition copy of David Westheimer's classic adventure novel of escaping prisoners, *Von Ryan's Express*. It is simply and affectionately inscribed by the onetime kriegie author: "Dear Nick . . . If only it had been like this . . ."

When I was growing up, my father's experiences in the POW camp were not often discussed in our household. No talk about starvation rations, deprivation, freezing cold, crippling fear, and ever-present tedium. The only real detail of his imprisonment and the hardships he underwent that we were told about as children was how he had managed to obtain all the books he would need for his junior and senior years at Princeton from the YMCA organization. He studied these, replicating the courses he would have taken were he still a student, and upon his return to the States, persuaded the university to allow him to take two years' worth of exams in six weeks, so that he could graduate on time, with his class. What my father did, remarkable as it was, took on a sort of mythic value in our household. The lesson was simple: An opportunity could be created out of any situation, no matter how harsh.

It was that opportunity that he seized back in 1943 that

549

eventually became the inspiration for *Hart's War*. But, that acknowledgment aside, it is important to note that the characters, the situation, and the plot of the novel are mine alone. While I have spent considerable time over the past eighteen months peppering my father with questions about his experiences, seeking accuracy and verisimilitude, the ultimate responsibility for what is described on the pages of the novel is mine. The world of my fictional Stalag Luft Thirteen is a composite of several camps. The events that form the novel, while grounded in the realities of the POW experience, are inventions. The officers, both German and Allied, that are collected on these pages are not directly based on any real men, living or dead. Any resemblances to actual persons is unintended.

Some thirty-two Tuskegee airmen were shot down and captured by the Germans during the war. As best as I can determine, none experienced the sort of ostracism and racism that Lincoln Scott does. The worst of the prejudice they faced was back in the States. There is an excellent book, *Black Wings*, which describes how these exceptional men broke the color barrier in the army air corps. There is also a small, but deserved, exhibit about them at the Air and Space Museum in Washington, D.C. It is one of the ironies of racism that by the time the Tuskegee men managed to overcome the exceedingly rigid standards demanded of them, they had become some of the finest pilots and fighters in the entire air corps. The Tuskegee men ended up flying more than fifteen hundred combat sorties over Europe. And it is one of the more delicious facts of war that they, indeed, never lost a bomber they were escorting to enemy action. Not a one. But not without cost. To maintain this pristine record, more than sixty of these young men sacrificed their lives.

There are a number of fine works about the kriegie experience. Lewis Carlson's *We Were Each Other's Prisoners* is a fascinating collection of oral histories. Arthur Durand's history of Stalag Luft Three is complete. David Westheimer's *Sitting It Out* is a detailed and elegant memoir of his time in the camps. (I borrowed the slightly risqué words to "Cats on the Roof " from this estimable book.)

Once, while talking with my father—I think we were discussing fear and food, two subjects that had more in common than one might initially believe—he suddenly mused, "You know, being in that camp was probably one of the most important things that ever happened to me. It probably changed my life." Given what he has accomplished over the arc of his years, I suppose one could argue that whatever changes came about within him because of his war experience, they were for the best. But that is an observation that might well be true for an entire generation of men and women.

Sometimes I think we live in a world so obsessively devoted to looking forward that it frequently forgets to take the time to look back. But some of our best stories reside in our wake, and, I suspect, no matter how harsh these stories are, they help tell us much about where we are heading.

JOHN KATZENBACH

Look for these other novels
by the author of *HART'S WAR*:

IN THE HEAT OF THE SUMMER

THE TRAVELER

DAY OF RECKONING

JUST CAUSE

THE SHADOW MAN

STATE OF MIND